FIC WOOD
Wood, Barbara

The far river

THE FAR RIVER

OTHER BOOKS *by* BARBARA WOOD

Land of the Afternoon Sun

Rainbows on the Moon

The Serpent and the Staff

The Divining

Virgins of Paradise

The Dreaming

Green City in the Sun

This Golden Land

Soul Flame

Vital Signs

Domina

The Watch Gods

Childsong

Night Trains

Yesterday's Child

Curse This House

Hounds and Jackals

BOOKS *by* KATHRYN HARVEY

Butterfly

Stars

Private Entrance

The

FAR
RIVER

A NOVEL

Barbara Wood

TURNER

Turner Publishing Company
Nashville, Tennessee
New York, New York

www.turnerpublishing.com

The Far River: A Novel

Cover design: Maddie Cothren
Book design: Glen Edelstein

Library of Congress Cataloging-in-Publication Data

Names: Wood, Barbara, 1947- author.
Title: The far river / Barbara Wood.
Description: Nashville, Tennessee : Turner Publishing Company, [2018]
Identifiers: LCCN 2017055077| ISBN 9781683367659 (hardcover : acid-free
  paper) | ISBN 9781683367673 (e-book)
Subjects: LCSH: Family secrets--Fiction. | Vendetta--Fiction.
Classification: LCC PS3573.O5877 F37 2018 | DDC 813/.54--dc23
LC record available at https://lccn.loc.gov/2017055077

[9781683367659]

Printed in the United States of America
18 19 20 21 10 9 8 7 6 5 4 3 2 1

This is for my husband Walt, with love.

THE FAR RIVER

PROLOGUE

Largo Valley, California

The Present Day

"I'M SORRY, DADDY," NICOLE said as she lovingly touched the tender grapes clustered on the vines. "But I have to do this. I can't stay here anymore. I have to go. But I promise to sell the farm to good people who will be the wonderful caretakers that our family always were."

She didn't know if Big Jack could hear her. He'd died last year. But she liked to think that his spirit was out here under this blue sky and among these green vines heavy with fruit. "It wasn't an easy decision to make," she said, the wind stirring her shoulder-length hair. "It still isn't. But it's something I must do if I am ever to make my own way through life. I have to find myself, Daddy. I know it sounds trite. But it's true. And it tears me up to have to go, but I have to do something in this life that's all my own and not something that was handed to me. I've been thinking about it a long time, Daddy. Don't get me wrong. I love this farm and I love this valley. But my pride and my need to be my own person are greater."

She paused among the fat green grapes to lift her face to the sky, her heart heavy. A red-tailed hawk circled against the blue. She wished her heart could be soaring up there with him. A memory: when Nicole was little, her father had let her spread shaving cream on his cheeks and jaw, and he'd told her she did it better than the most expert barber. She liked sitting on the edge of the sink, swinging her legs as she watched him shave.

Gone a year, but it seemed like only yesterday she had walked among the vines with him, discussing the harvest.

Most of the Schaller vineyards went into wine-making, but this particular vineyard produced table grapes, the fruit bagged in clusters and sent to grocery stores. Schaller's brand was popular because they were known for the sweetness of their grapes. Shoppers didn't like it when they picked out what looked like a scrumptious bunch and then brought them home to discover that they were sour. How could the grocery store allow that? That was because the poor quality did not begin in the store, but out in the field before the grapes even left the vineyard.

Nicole knew that a lot of the small local farms harvested grapes when they *appeared* ready, not when they had reached their peak levels of sugar and flavor. The business sense was: the sooner the grapes were harvested, the sooner a profit could be made. So a lot of growers removed all their grapes at once, whether or not all the bunches had reached the same ripeness. After all, it took skill to determine which grapes were perfect and which needed more time. And then that required more cash outlay on the part of the grower to hire on more skilled workers and to spend time going back over the same vines. It was cheaper to pay someone to pick them all at once and move on.

But not Schaller grapes: that was their promise to the consumer. As reckless as Big Jack was, as obsessed with gambling and women as he had been, Jack Schaller still knew the value of his family name. He would want Nicole to make sure the new owners knew when to harvest, when to leave the grapes a while longer, when to come back, no matter the time and cost overall. The Canadian couple seemed very keen on buying the farm and winery; Nicole was going to make sure they understood that they couldn't pass sour grapes along to supermarkets and dupe unsuspecting grocery shoppers into buying them. Schaller was a name the consumer could trust, whether it was wine, raisins, jams, or table grapes.

She plucked a fat purple grape and bit into it.

This was the part Nicole liked the most—testing the grape for harvest. Rolling the firm grape between thumb and forefinger the way Big Jack had taught her. Holding it up to the light to see through the delightful colors of crimson, black, dark blue, yellow, green, orange, and pink. And then that first bite, to test for sweetness. Too soon, and the fruit was sour. Nicole never minded that. Her father would stand with his hand on her shoulder and say "Is it ready?" She would make a face. "Not yet. Too sour." "There's my girl; you're a natural," he would say, and Nicole would have eaten a thousand sour grapes just to hear those words.

She paused and looked up and down the green paradise. Nothing ever stops growing, she thought as she squinted through the bees and the sunshine. That is the miracle of nature, of life. Nothing ever really dies, it all just keeps going.

She looked at her watch. Time to get ready to meet with the potential buyers. As she walked back to the main house, she passed the barrel room where repairs were being done. As she heard the pounding of sledgehammers and the calls of workmen, she reminded herself that she must assure the buyers that the work would be finished by the closing of escrow.

*   *   *

JOSÉ RODRIGUEZ WAS THINKING of three things as he took a sledgehammer to the old stone wall: his fat wife's spicy enchiladas that he would be enjoying that evening, the bottle of wine he was going to be given as a bonus for this extra work at the winery, and making love to his fat and welcoming Maria—not necessarily in that order—when the head of his sledgehammer suddenly went through a soft spot in the wall, falling free into empty space and causing the daydreaming José to lose his balance and tumble forward nearly flat on his face.

"Aii!" he cried, and the men who were working with him burst into laughter.

A minor earthquake had caused some weakening of the outer wall of the winery's barrel room, resulting in a sudden sagging in the roof and the threat of destabilizing the temperature and humidity of the storage room. Miss Schaller had ordered an immediate inspection of the wall to see what had caused it to weaken so, and to find a way to shore it back up before damage was done to the fine wines stored there.

With José's mind still on the luscious flesh of his Maria, and the promise of spicy enchiladas and rich red wine, he brushed himself off and, laughing with his amigos, did not at first realize that he had exposed a hole within the solid rock and adobe wall.

"*Qué es esto?*" said Tomás, his cousin, who pointed at the gaping hole.

José used his dusty knuckles to rub the sweat from his eyes and leaned forward to blink at the dark space in the wall. A queer odor wafted out, and he wasn't sure he liked it. In fact, it made his flesh crawl, and all thoughts of food, wine, and sex left him. He bent closer. The men behind him bent closer—Mexican laborers who roamed the valley in search of work. They stared, and then their eyes widened—and then, registering what they had found, they all jumped back. "*Madre de Dios!*" cried Tomás and José at the same time, and they all crossed themselves and silently called upon as many saints as they could think of.

"Go for Miss Schaller," José Rodriguez hissed at them. When none of the men moved, he whirled on them and shouted, "*La Señorita! Pronto!*"

And they *all* went running, every single one of them, to get away from the thing in the wall and the curse it was certain to bring down on their heads, each man trying to remember the next time Father Ramon, the valley's traveling priest, was bringing the mass and the Holy Sacrament to the farms.

* * *

"OUR FAMILY WERE THE first Germans to come to this valley," Nicole explained to her visitors as she escorted them from the car park to the house. "We were the first to bring Rieslings to California, wines for which we are known today," she added with a smile to hide her nervousness.

She was more than nervous, she was anxiety-ridden about leaving her home and tried very hard not to let it show during this vital presentation to her visitors. Nicole had spent an hour getting dressed, changing outfit after outfit, minimizing her makeup and then applying extra, worrying over her hair, making sure she looked smart, amiable, chipper, and above all someone you would buy a winery from.

Nicole *had* to sell. She *had* to get away.

How could she possibly stay? Sure, she lived in a big white three-story house with a swimming pool and tennis courts and an enormous barbecue patio for big parties. But this valley and nearby Lynnville were the back of beyond, the sticks, the tules, a one-horse town. In school, all her friends had talked of little else than getting out of "Sleepy Hollow," as they called it. To San Francisco, Los Angeles, maybe even as madcap far away as New York. No one, except your grandma, *stayed* in Lynnville. And how were you to meet a man? they all asked one another. This valley was filled with farmers, rednecks, yokels, and hicks. They wore cowboy hats and high-heeled boots and said, "ain't" and "shit howdy." Now, big cities like Chicago and St. Louis, Seattle, Boston—those were places you met men who worked high up in corporate offices and carried briefcases and smelled so nice and wore three-piece suits and showered more often than just on Saturday nights.

Those had been *their* excuses, the girls who had all fled the valley. Those were not the reasons Nicole was leaving. She loved this valley and did not think of it as the back of beyond. She was twenty-seven, had been born here and had barely ever been out of the valley, and she saw nothing at all wrong with farmhands and growers and men who drove pickup trucks. What was wrong with a man who had honest, callused hands and rode a horse? No, Nicole's reasons for selling the winery and moving far away had to do with a house full of negative memories, the stifling life she had lived with a domineering father (whom she had loved nonetheless), and the weight of family baggage that could only be gotten rid of by selling up and leaving.

"You can't escape the past in this place," she had told her best friend. "I feel like I'm stuck in a time warp. There is no forward momentum."

When had it suddenly hit her, the *knowing* that she had to go away, that if she was ever to be an individual human being and acknowledged in her own right, she was going to have to break away from Big Jack and the farm and sever the vines that bound her to them? She was twelve and home with the flu and watching an afternoon talk show, and the guest was a woman who had started her own business and was now famous. She was thirteen and it was Career Day at school, and a doctor talked about clinics she had founded in Africa. She was fourteen and reading the biographies of courageous women like Marie Curie and Florence Nightingale.

It hadn't been just one thing but a gradual process that opened her eyes to life's possibilities. Upon the passing of her father, Big Jack, Nicole had seen the chance suddenly open to her.

New York had been her first choice. A connection through a friend, who knew a friend who had heard of a job opening. The trip east had been a resounding success. Nicole had secured a job with a cosmetics firm to which she was bringing experience in marketing and distribution, plus a knowledge of supply and demand, and how to build brand name loyalty. Her MBA from a prestigious business school was icing on the cake. During her interview she had shown energy, creativity, and spark, and a willingness to listen to and work with clients rather than rigidly dictate to them. She had demonstrated open-mindedness and enthusiasm to run with other people's ideas. A team player. It was entry level to be sure, but with plenty of upward mobility. Her prospects were exciting and bright.

She was already working on some ideas for the company. The man who had interviewed her was familiar with Schaller wines and said that her winery was known for its innovations in the wine industry, especially in the 1950s and, '60s when the California wine industry literally burst onto the world scene with new, modern, and hip products and marketing concepts. He had assured Nicole that they had every confidence that she would draw upon her family's business history and bring that same verve and acumen to his firm.

It was at that interview and with those very words about her family that everything had suddenly snapped into sharp focus: yes, that was it precisely, what had filled her restless soul these past few years. Nicole didn't want to follow in the footsteps of others. She wanted to blaze her own trails—not to inherit something but to *create* something.

Now all she had to do was sell the vineyards and winery and be at her New York desk in six weeks.

She normally preferred blue jeans and T-shirts when she went about the property, overseeing the work. But in the tasting room where she played hostess to tourists who arrived in limousines that hopped from winery to winery with their giddy-drunk clientele, Nicole always wore tasteful pleated slacks and silk blouses. Not too elegant as to be snobbish, but stylish enough to send the message that Schaller Winery was one of the "better" establishments. She believed, as her mother had believed, and her grandmother before her, that the family's image reflected the quality of the winery and their label.

And in her desperation to sell the family business, Nicole did her best to present herself well. She had even abandoned her usual ponytail in a plain rubber band for a bit of teasing of her brown hair, drawn back in trendy gold clips. She was slim and she thanked her propensity for taking long walks for that.

"A property this old must have a colorful history," said the polite lady from Canada as they went up the front steps and entered the house. Nicole suspected the small, bunlike woman was digging for gossip and scandal and skeletons in closets. But Nicole knew better than to disclose family secrets. If she did, not only would these nice polite people not buy the place, they would run for the hills. It wasn't just the outside walls of the house and winery that had been whitewashed but the family history was well.

"Schaller farm used to be big at one time, didn't it?" said the husband, a tall bow-legged man who walked through the main house with his thumbs hooked in his belt. Nicole knew that his question was simply another tack to finding out what had caused the downfall of what had once been a financial and agricultural empire.

"Yes, my family used to be one of the biggest wine producers in the country," she said airily, refusing to be drawn into the drama of her past. These people were looking to purchase a small, boutique vineyard and winery for themselves and that was exactly what Nicole Schaller was selling. The acres, the main house, the outbuildings, and the hundred-year-old winery famous for its Rieslings grown from vines brought over from Germany long ago. The purchase price did not entitle them to her family's dirty laundry.

"But in the past few years, my father decided to downsize and sell off acres to people such as yourselves, looking to own small wineries." The causes for the downsizing—the gambling debts and drinking and expensive women and opening his wallet for anyone with a sob story—need not be disclosed. It was all in the past now anyway, dead and buried with her father. "And of course, I'm on my own now," she added unnecessarily. *On my own* ... it sounded so sad and lonely that she gave a little laugh, as if needing to convince these strangers that she didn't mind in the least being on her own.

"Does all this come with the sale?" They had arrived at the enormous living room filled with antiques, mementoes, souvenirs, all the stuff that was brought over from the Old Country a century ago, and things collected since.

"Yes," Nicole said, feeling sad to be saying good-bye to familiar things.

"Including that?" The woman from Alberta, Canada, pointed to a portrait over the fireplace.

Nicole looked up. "Yes."

"She's lovely. Who was she?"

"My great-grandmother, Clara Schaller."

"Oh yes, I see the resemblance."

You couldn't possibly, Nicole thought. After three generations of marriages any genetic inheritance would have gotten all co-mingled and watered down. If Clara handed anything down to me it would be the striking widow's peak on our foreheads and nothing else.

Having never known her great-grandmother, Nicole felt no great attachment or affection toward her legendary ancestress, Clara Schaller, who was famous in the Largo Valley. But as she stared up at the gray eyes surrounded by black lashes, a well-formed brow that made one think Clara was all business and no-nonsense, as she remembered the stories she had heard about the formidable family matriarch—some of them a bit far fetched, Nicole thought, suspecting they must have been embellished over the years—she suddenly said, "On second thought, the portrait is not for sale. It's personal. It belongs in the family."

But what family? Who was there to save this portrait for? Nicole was an only child, and she didn't have a current boyfriend so there were no marital prospects on her immediate horizon. She was headed for a career in a new town. Would there even be time for men and babies? Who would she hand the portrait down to? But if she sold it to these people, she thought now, it might end up forgotten and dusty and unidentified in some future antique shop.

Nicole shuddered. She couldn't let Great-Grandmother Clara end up like that.

The Canadians walked slowly around admiring the antiques in the living room: a Gustav Becker wall clock made in 1890; pieces of Dresden porcelain and china; a bisque boy-doll wearing lederhosen; a wooden rocking horse, hand carved and gaily painted; 19th-century German Christmas ornaments in a glass cabinet; an original 1890 map of the German Empire in a gilt frame; a collection of Nymphenburg cup and saucer sets dating back to the 1800's; a pair of Philipp Rosenthal hand-painted, gilded jugs, dating back to 1890; a stand holding carved Meerschaum pipes; and in one corner, the jewel of the collection, a Carl Ludwig Bachmann violin from 1765. The large, high-ceilinged living room was a veritable museum of arts and antiques that had been carefully brought over from the Old Country a century ago and lovingly preserved and added to ever since.

A startling new thought suddenly occurred to Nicole, that these things should have survived all this time when so little else had. *I am the last Schaller ....*

As Nicole stood in a column of lazy September sunlight that streamed through the high window, a wave of sadness washed over her. From the day she was born she had celebrated every Christmas in this grand living room. Big Jack would strike off into the nearby woods, select a tree, cut it down, and install it in the corner of the room where the Bachmann violin now perched. An enormous pine that the family would lovingly and joyously decorate while drinking Schaller wine and getting merry. Nicole was not only selling her home and these antiques to strangers, she was selling them her twenty-seven Christmases.

She decided she liked this polite couple from Canada. Other potential buyers had come through but the chemistry hadn't been there. This pair, in their forties and looking to make an investment and a new life away from the Alberta winters, gave off a good vibe. They would take care of Nicole's home, she knew, they would be good to the vines. She could go away with peace of mind. Yes, these were the ones, and she prayed they wanted to buy it.

She opened the portfolio she had been carrying and produced a detailed map of the property, indicating the planted acres, the buildings, main house, parking areas. "What's this over here?" Mr. Macintosh asked, pointing with a stubby finger to a blank spot at the western edge of the farm.

When Nicole's father, Big Jack, was selling off pieces of the farm to cover his gambling debts, this was one swath of land he couldn't even *give* away. "It's a patch of barren land," Nicole said. "The soil is poor and it isn't cost effective to divert water to irrigate it. My great-grand-father decided to let it lie fallow and it has basically stood neglected ever since. Ironically, the land abuts a picturesque hill called Colina Sagrada. Sacred Hill."

"It sounds romantic," Mrs. Macintosh said. "May we see it?"

"I'll be happy to drive you over there."

"Miss Nicole!" a sharp voice sounded in the distance. "Miss Nicole!" She looked through the window and saw a mob of workmen running toward the house. Dear God, she thought as she rushed to the front door. Was there a fire?

The husband and wife from Alberta exchanged looks while a hurried dialogue was conducted in the front entry.

"What!" Nicole said to the Mexican workman. "Are you *sure*?" The man nodded vigorously. She turned to her visitors. "I'm sorry," she said, suddenly pale and flustered. "Something has come up. I'll be right back."

They were startled to see her drop the portfolio and break into a run to follow the workmen across the lawns to the collection of brick and adobe buildings that made up the winery. She ran through the vat room and the press room, through the tasting room until she arrived where the barrels of Riesling were stacked and stored. She went straight to the hole in the wall, with brick and stone and dust littering the floor.

She stopped. Her mouth dropped open. "My God," she whispered, and the Mexicans crossed themselves again and mentally recited a few Ave Marias.

Nicole bent close, slowly, gingerly, as if the thing in the wall might suddenly strike out. But she knew it couldn't. It was dead—beyond dead: the skeleton hadn't a shred of flesh or skin on it. Decomposition was complete. Clothing remnants were rotten tatters. She stared in fascination at the bony face, the big cavernous eye sockets with no eyes in them, the gaping mouth with sagging mandible and hideous broken teeth.

"Pardon me, Miss Nicole," said José, who spoke decent English. He pointed with a shaking hand to the small round hole just above the brow ridge. "Is that . . . is that. . . ?"

She nodded. "It appears to be a bullet hole." She looked up at him. "Call the police, José. Please," Nicole said as calmly as she could, fearing to look at the Canadians who had joined everyone in the barrel room and who she knew must be looking at the skeleton in horror—and perhaps rethinking their plan to buy a winery where a murder and grisly burial had taken place.

As the world slowed around her and people moved at a snail's pace and spoke in long, stretched-out syllables as if a movie reel were slowing down, she stared at the skull with the homicidal bullet in its center and found herself suddenly asking the most important question she had ever asked, silently, but forcefully, and angrily even, blaming the victim for the calamity he or she had suddenly brought to Schaller Winery: "Who *are* you. . . ?"

And then her thoughts flew to the main house where she pictured the elegant woman in the portrait over the fireplace, Clara Heinze Schaller, who had come to this valley over a hundred years ago as a new bride. And Nicole wondered what that nineteen-year-old girl, fresh from Germany's Rhineland with dreams in her eyes and vine cuttings in her baskets, would think of where that dream had ended up . . . with Canadians wanting to turn her winery into a yuppie boutique and the discovery of a homicide victim inside the walls.

PART ONE

1912 .

THE YOUNG IMMIGRANTS ARRIVED on a beautiful spring day in California, twelve of them—five married couples and two eager bachelors, all of strong and optimistic German stock. They arrived weary, excited, hopeful, and afraid. They had come in a convoy of cars and wagons, ready to make new homes for themselves.

In the first car rode the two Schaller brothers, Wilhelm and Johann, and the bride of one of them, Clara. They had come up from Santa Barbara on the coast to make the forty-mile trek through hills and forests, along dirt tracks and lanes to reach the new, green valley that was to be their home. The convoy came to a halt on the rise of the rural road. Clara Schaller, in the front seat, next to the man hired to drive them out here, looked out at the vista. She was silent and overwhelmed, having not fully recovered from a recent ordeal with influenza and still very weak.

Without a word, one of the Schaller brothers jumped out of the car and bounded ahead to embrace his new world. The other brother waited a moment; then he got out, came around, and, gently lifting Clara in his arms, carried her to join the others. As she lay cradled in his arms, she took in the breathless landscape that swept away before her, with green pastures and neat little farms and tidy little houses and spreading willows and oaks. "We'll be happy here," she whispered, leaning her head on his strong shoulder. Suddenly, a single tear wet her cheek.

As she curled her arm around his neck and held tightly to him, she closed her eyes and let her mind slip back over the many miles they had traveled, over the months they had prepared for this day, the weeks of hardship and heart break, back to the morning when it had all begun. . . .

*   *   *

THE LITTLE BELL OVER the door tinkled, and Clara, behind the counter, looked up to see who had entered the shop.

She had been giggling over a remembered story, something amusing her father had read out of the newspaper at breakfast, and it had been keeping her light and buoyant all morning. And then the bulky stranger came into the shop, and she was suddenly filled with sobering shyness.

"Hello," he said, coming down the center aisle and straight up to the counter. "I am looking for something for seasickness."

Clara couldn't help staring. He filled her eyes with his height and breadth, a young man with a sweep of blond hair that went this way and that when he removed his cap and politely requested a medicine. But mostly it was his flaming beard—it made him look like a figure out of myth. Clara was eighteen years old and believed in the existence of heroes.

Because her father was the local chemist, Clara was familiar with everyone in the village and the nearby farms. This young man with the fiery beard and blue eyes was a stranger.

He seemed nervous. Or perhaps her stare was making him nervous, because he added "I am not from here. I am staying with cousins." He waved a large hand in a vague direction, as if trying to explain his existence, and she saw an endearing blush above the red-gold beard. She thought he was in his early twenties, and he had the look of the farmer about him—the rumpled work pants and jacket, the shirt that was clean but not pressed, and he hadn't bothered to attach a collar. But it was the wide-brimmed straw hat that gave him the look of outdoors. And there was dirt under his fingernails. *Honest* dirt, she told herself.

Young Clara Heinze didn't have a real beau yet, but there were expectations. Her parents encouraged her to be nice to Hans Zimmerman, the doctor's son. What a brilliant match, everyone said—the village doctor's son married to the village chemist's daughter. Hans was nice and all that, if a bit gangly and awkward, and he still had pimples at age twenty.

But *this* young man. . . .

She shook herself out of her trance, turned and opened a drawer in the cabinet behind her, and brought out a packet, to place it before him on the counter. He looked at it and said, "I wonder if this will be enough."

"How long will you be on the boat?"

"Well, it's a ship, really. And the voyage takes seven days, depending on the weather."

"Goodness. Where are you going?"

"To America," he said as casually as if he were talking about the weather. He looked around to see if there were other things he should pick up for the journey. When he came back to the girl behind the counter, he found her staring at him, her lips parted. "America?" she whispered.

"My father has bought some land in a place called California. He and my brother and I are going to start a vineyard there, and a winery."

"Really!" she said, her eyes wide and bright. America, she thought. So far away. . . .

Clara was a reader. When not working in her father's shop or helping her mother upstairs in their living quarters, Clara read books. She especially liked adventure stories in faraway places, tales about ordinary people finding themselves in extraordinary circumstances and dealing with challenges, finding strengths and courage within themselves that they hadn't known they had.

"That is so brave of you," she said with a sincere smile.

He blinked at her. Brave? He was simply joining his father to start a vineyard.

"And so courageous," she added, and he saw how her hand fluttered to her throat.

It made him suddenly uncomfortable. No one had ever called him brave and courageous before. Certainly no girl had ever said that to him— and certainly not a *pretty* girl. He didn't know what to say. He was just one of thousands of men emigrating to another country. *Was* it brave? He had only thought of it as something that could be done, with hardships to be endured in the doing of it.

He looked around the shop again, like a man suddenly lost. Twenty-four-year-old Wilhelm Schaller came from a very masculine world where there was no mother or sisters, just himself, his father, and his brother. Their housekeeper was fat, middle-aged, and fussy like a hen. Wilhelm was struck mute in the presence of this girl's demure femininity. And now she thought he was *brave*?

He mumbled that he might have a look around, to see if he would need something more for the long voyage, something he had overlooked— because, for some reason he could not understand, he suddenly didn't want to leave the chemist's shop. Not just yet. Not while the pretty girl behind the counter thought he was brave and courageous.

She watched him, tall and brawny and so very masculine, and thought he must be the most exotic man in the world. Clara had grown up in this small village on the Rhine River, located between the more significant towns of Koblenz and Mainz, in the region where the mountains of the Hunsrück on the west and the Taunus on the east come straight down to the river forming a narrow valley. The town was centuries old, with cobblestoned streets and quaint houses and shops that had been built generations ago. Clara's town was known for the surrounding vineyards that lifted up from the waters of the cold Rhine into sunny terraces and hillsides so green they blinded the eye. "Picturesque," tourists called Clara's town, like stepping back in time, with its castles and Roman ruins and claims that Neanderthals had lived here fifty thousand years ago. But they were in the modern age as well, with gas lighting and the promise of electricity to come and a telephone or two. After all, this was Germany, the most technologically progressive country in the world—a heavily industrialized nation unsurpassed in science, medicine, and mathematics, and the leading exporter of steel.

Clara's father prided himself on offering the latest in modern German pharmaceuticals, including Bayer's Aspirin and Bayer's Heroin. The Heinzes were prosperous and lived in a well-appointed apartment over the chemist's shop. They could afford nice clothes and food on the table, and a cook and a maid. Clara Heinze lived in a clean, comfortable, respectable world governed by honest traditions, home values, and Christian morals.

It was a nice town, Clara thought now, but it wasn't faraway and exotic. It wasn't an adventure to live here. Not like plunging into the unknown and sailing dark seas to cross a frightening, barely tamed continent. . . .

When the young man with the flaming beard came back to the counter empty-handed, he reached into his pocket to pay for the seasickness powder. Even though he was only passing through town, he suddenly felt the need to tell her his name, the town he was from, and the cousins he was currently staying with nearby. Clara had never been so enthralled. He had come from so far away. Even though he was German, Wilhelm Schaller was practically a foreigner, and Clara was one of those girls who were always intrigued by foreign men. Weren't they so much more intriguing than the boring boys in her own small town? And now he was talking about America, on the other side of the world. . . .

He handed her his money, his coarse fingertips brushing her smooth palm. As she opened the till, she asked: "And your mother? What does she think of this great move?"

"My mother died of a tonsil infection when I was ten."

"I'm so sorry," she said.

She was very pretty, Wilhelm thought. Around eighteen years old with long chestnut hair hanging in shiny ringlets. She wore a white blouse with a high neck and long sleeves, a long black skirt cinched at her narrow waist. Her face was oval with a delicate, pointed chin that emphasized her big eyes and high forehead. And the widow's peak in the center of her hairline lent a heart shape to her face. Very pretty indeed, he thought.

He spoke haltingly and shyly, but gradually the picture emerged: his father, Jakob Schaller, unsatisfied with working a small ancestral vineyard that had no hope of ever expanding, working with a cooperative of vintners so that there was no chance of getting ahead in the future, had come across one of those pamphlets that were always floating around Europe about the opportunities in America that awaited men of strength and vision. Jakob had sold their small holding of vines and vats and had gone ahead to a place called California to claim their land and get it started. His son had come to Clara's village to stay with cousins while he awaited the summons from his father.

Yes, Clara knew Siegfried and Dagmar Schmidt, a young tailor and his new wife, a seamstress. No, she had not heard that they were going to America with their cousins the Schallers. What a wonderful and exciting thing, Clara said as she counted out his change, and found that she meant her words. It *was* wonderful and exciting, and she found herself envying Siegfried and Dagmar.

As Wilhelm Schaller took his purchase and started to leave the shop, Clara called out impulsively, "When will you and your cousins be leaving for America?"

He paused at the door to say, "We are waiting for the passports and papers and tickets for passage, and my brother will be finishing his studies at university and come to join me, and my father will send for us when the fields are ready—we don't know precisely the date of departure."

He had blurted it all in a flustered way that made Clara think that Wilhelm Schaller wasn't used to talking about himself to strangers. And she thought it was terribly endearing. She also thought: I will ask Mama to invite him for afternoon coffee and cake. Clara wanted to hear more about America.

She didn't have to wait long to extend the invitation, which her mother had agreed to, as she knew Siegfried and Dagmar and wanted to extend hospitality to their cousin who had come all alone to their town.

Wilhelm was in the shop the very next day, saying that he thought one packet of seasickness powder wouldn't be enough after all.

The truth was, after leaving the shop yesterday, he hadn't been able to put the chemist's daughter out of his mind. Clara Heinze was so delicate and refined. A true lady, such as you see riding in a handsome carriage. He was not of her class. There were boundaries here. Nonetheless, there she was in his mind, laughing, giving off a delicate lavender fragrance. He couldn't stop thinking of the bit of lace at her cuffs and collar, dainty little feminine touches that you didn't see in the countryside.

He couldn't stay away. So he made up an excuse and came back to Heinze's shop, hoping she would be at the counter and not her father. He was in luck. And the way her face lit up when he came in. Not just the pleasant, fixed-in-place smile one saw on the faces of shop clerks. But genuine happiness to see him. And it elevated him. Clara's radiant smile and obvious pleasure to see him actually made Wilhelm feel ten feet tall. Imagine, a girl like *her* noticing a humble fellow like himself. It made him feel like a king. He had always seen himself as somewhat ordinary. But this young woman seemed to find something special about him. She almost made him feel heroic and not ordinary at all. It was a new feeling and he had to think about it.

"I got our atlas out last night," she said as she retrieved another packet of the powder. "And I looked at California. My, it's so far away! And it's big! Where in California is your land?"

Wilhelm didn't know what to say. All thoughts fled his mind in the face of such enthusiasm. What *was* the name of the valley with so much farm land? He was suddenly tongue-tied, and he worried it made him look like a simpleton.

He tried to stretch the moment. He couldn't think of anything to bring up and yet he couldn't just stand there. But he had already browsed around the shop yesterday. Luckily, Clara came to his rescue and banished the awkward moment by saying "My mother knows your cousins and would like to invite you and them to our home for afternoon coffee and cake. Would tomorrow be convenient?"

He had no idea if tomorrow was convenient or not, but he stumbled out a "grateful to be invited and happy to be here and what time?" And then he paid for the seasickness powder and left the shop without having picked up the packet.

It had turned out to be inconvenient for his cousins, who had suits to make and dresses to sew for impatient customers, so Wilhelm had come alone in what was clearly his best suit, his hat in his hands, and smelling of soap. He beard looked as if it had been brushed a hundred times.

Clara wore a white cotton afternoon dress and her mother had appointed the parlor with newly bloomed spring flowers. Gerda, the housemaid, brought in coffee and Black Forest cake, and Wilhelm sat awkwardly in the small chair, balancing cup and saucer and plate and fork on his knees, linen napkin tucked into his celluloid collar. Mrs. Heinze was an older version of the daughter, thicker at the waist and with streaks of gray in her hair. But you could see the pretty girl she had once been.

And she was a gracious hostess who soon put him at ease. "Tell us about America, Mr. Schaller. My own mother's cousins emigrated years ago to a place called Nebraska. I understand they are doing very well there."

He managed to drink the coffee and eat the cake and speak of America and the challenge of transporting delicate vine cuttings all at the same time without spilling a drop or a crumb. And when, in the course of conversation, as he tried not to look at Clara too much, he told them he was Lutheran and learned that they, too, were Lutheran, Mrs. Heinze invited Wilhelm to join them for church services next Sunday.

He readily accepted and spent the next three days with his mind more on Clara than on God or grapes.

After church, they returned to the apartment above the chemist's shop for midday dinner, at which her mother served a generous and welcoming bratwurst with sautéed potatoes and sauerkraut, hot bread rolls spread with butter, followed by apple cake. Clara's father, a plump, jovial man, wanted to hear all about California and Wilhelm's father's plans for a new vineyard. Helmut Heinze himself had known a few men who had taken their families to America to settle in German communities in places called Pennsylvania and New York. Wilhelm had a much less difficult time talking with the man of the house, and Clara watched in amazement as he opened up to her father in a way that he had so far been unable to do with her.

"The land my father purchased in California," he explained to the Heinzes, who were fascinated, "an abandoned vineyard—had originally belonged to a Spaniard who had been granted the land—a 'rancho'—by the Spanish crown as a reward for dedicated military service protecting the Franciscan missions. The Franciscans had gone out to California in the late 1700s, you see," he said, warming to his subject because his audience was so attentive, "to build missions and convert the Indians to Christianity. In 1833, when California became an extension of Mexico and the missions were secularized, the lands were given as rewards to men who had served Spain well. Such was Don Francisco Diego, who planted a vineyard on the land and founded his own winery using the original grapes that had been brought from Spain in 1769. They are called Mission grapes and are the common black grape."

Wilhelm cleared his throat self-consciously, sipped at his coffee, and got nods of encouragement from his hosts to please continue. "But a series of setbacks and misfortunes had driven Diego to sell his property to an American who tried to make the farm and winery prosper. But drought and root disease had led him to also give up and move away. The property had been for sale by the State of California for the past twenty years, which was why my father had been able to purchase it at a low price. He went out there a year ago, and he had written to my brother and me that, when he looked at the weedy, neglected, and overgrown acres, over five hundred of them, he did not see failure, he saw revival and success."

"Amazing," said Helmut Heinze, who wondered if he himself would have had such foresight.

As Clara listened to Wilhelm speak of California in such glowing, sweeping terms, her mind filled with wonderful visions. Going to California, with place names such as Dos Lagos ("Two Lakes"), Los Angeles ("The Angels"), and Palos Verdes ("Green Sticks"), sounded like going to Spain and Mexico as well. Three exotic countries in one! It moved her to feel deeply for the man who spoke of it. She was in awe of him. How was it that he was able to describe her own dream of seeing the world so perfectly?

She wondered if this was what falling in love felt like. She had no one to talk to about it. It wasn't something you could just bring up at a coffee group, or ask your mother about. Her two sisters had fallen in love, gotten married, and moved away. She wished she could talk to them now and ask them what it was like so she could compare her experience to theirs. As the town chemist, her father had a telephone, and her sisters had telephones. But they would shriek at the expense of such phone calls simply to discuss so outlandish a subject as Clara falling in love! No, she would have to work this out on her own.

She needed to spend more time with Wilhelm Schaller.

When she asked her mother permission to show him around the town, Mrs. Heinze had to give it some thought. After all, the Heinzes were one of the town's prominent families. It wouldn't do to have their daughter engaged in any improprieties such as stepping out with a young man whom no one knew. Still, it was a kindness to show hospitality to a stranger, especially a young man separated from his family, and he *had* attended church with them, so it was arranged that Gerda, the maid, would accompany them.

And so, under Gerda's discreet but watchful eye, Clara took him up the village clock tower for the amazing view. They watched a puppet show, and the oompah-pah band. Clara pointed out ancient Roman ruins and told him the history of the fourteenth-century castle that loomed over the town. Of course, Wilhelm's own village would be very similar, with its own Roman ruins, medieval castle, clock tower, narrow streets, and outdoor cafés. But that wasn't the point. She was showing him her home as a way of showing him herself. The three stopped at an open-air café and lunched on bread and sausages until Gerda finally declared it was time to go home. Wilhelm thanked Clara for a wonderful day and struck off for the home of his cousins, the tailor and the seamstress.

Clara hadn't wanted the day to end, and as she watched him stride up the cobbled street, she tried to think of a way to see him again.

"*Riding bicycles*?" her mother said that night as they sat by the fire, mending socks and shirts.

"I think Wilhelm would enjoy going for a bike ride in the woods," Clara said eagerly. "He works hard, you know. He's going around to all the vineyards, looking for the best cuttings to take to America. Even Papa takes a day off and closes the shop."

She saw that her mother, though skeptical, was warming to the idea. But now came the tricky part. "Without Gerda."

Eva Heinze snapped her head up. "Without a chaperone?"

"Mama, please. We'll stay on the public trails, there will be lots of people about. And . . . and . . . he's leaving soon."

Eva Heinze laid down her darning egg. She had always been very watchful over her girls, and Clara was the last one. The baby. Eva was worried. She could see that her daughter was smitten with the young man. Was it wise to let this infatuation continue when the boy was only temporarily here? He would go away and Clara's heart would be broken.

Maybe she shouldn't have allowed things to progress as far as they had. Maybe she should have nipped it in the bud and not invited him up for coffee and cake. But Mrs. Heinze knew from personal experience that there was no telling a human heart whom it could and could not be attracted to. Hadn't she herself pleaded with her parents to be allowed to marry Helmut Heinze, a penniless pharmacy student who planned to someday own his own shop? Her father had insisted that she marry someone who was already established. But she had stamped her foot and cried and sworn to run away if she couldn't marry Helmut. And now here she was, thirty years later, finding herself in a re-enactment of a similar dilemma. If she said no, would there be endless drama in the house?

And anyway, Wilhelm Schaller seemed a decent and honorable young man, and all he talked about was America and making wine. So she gave permission, but with rules and assurances from Clara that they would stay at all times on popular bike trails and not go astray.

Her father gave her the day off from the shop, and there was a sunny break in the spring weather. They invited Siegfried and Dagmar to join them, but the young couple were too bent on earning as much money as they could before leaving for America. So Clara and Wilhelm rented two bicycles and went up into the hills on their own.

Finding a sunny spot not far from the village where they could look out over the river, Wilhelm and Clara enjoyed the rare moment of freedom. While awaiting word from his father, and for his brother to finish his university studies in Cologne, Wilhelm was not idle during his stay here. He visited local vineyards noted for their excellent Rieslings, talked to the vintners, tasted the wines, and arranged for the purchase of cuttings when the time came to leave. It was important that he carefully select one-year-old vines, as they were known to have a higher success rate for surviving transplanting than two- or three-year-olds. Their transport and care during the long voyage was discussed and arranged at length—it was crucial that the roots not dry out.

But when Clara said she had gotten permission to spend the day with him, he had decided to take time off from his work to be with her. Not accustomed to analyzing his feelings, he had no way of fathoming them right now. He was attracted to her, but he had no idea how she felt about him. Their talk was always about California and his plans with his father and brother. But if he could gauge her feelings toward him, he thought, maybe he could sort his own feelings out.

"I envy you going to California," Clara said now as she removed her hat and lifted her face to the sun. The ground was damp from the spring rain, and the breeze hinted of more wet weather to come. But, for now, they had the sun. "I like to read novels about strong, courageous heroines who step outside their comfortable lives to tackle all sorts of challenges and adventures. I wish I could prove to others how courageous *I* could be." She looked at him. "Does that sound silly?"

He thought her hair was very glossy in the sunshine. "Not at all."

"I want to prove it to myself. It doesn't take much bravery to ring up purchases behind a shop counter. But when am I ever going to get that chance? I have never been twenty miles from my village. Maybe, someday, I thought that my husband and I would take a holiday to some place exotic, like Greece. But I would need to marry first. . . ."

She wanted to tell him other things about herself, too, but she had a hard time putting it all into words. Her sense of being different from other girls. Wanting to go to faraway places. Wanting adventure. And being Lutheran in a Catholic region added to her sense of "otherness." And here was this young man who had walked into her life, on his way to exotic California, and he was also Lutheran! It was almost as if fate or destiny or whatever were hard at work here.

"I shouldn't complain," she said quickly, wondering if she sounded too forward, perhaps too pushy. Men didn't like girls who whined. "You learn an awful lot about life while working in a pharmacy; it's an adventure in itself," she told him as they watched ferries trail rippling wakes across the Rhine. "More so than, say, working in a bookstore or a yarn shop. People don't sugarcoat their troubles when they come in for medicines for their pains and ailments. They come into the shop for tablets and salves and lotions and powders; and while telling the chemist, my father, about their aches and pains, they also let slip about a lazy brother-in-law, an ungrateful son, a headstrong daughter, a faithless husband. It is as if once you expose weaknesses of the flesh, there is no holding *anything* back."

She suddenly clipped her words short, thinking she sounded too knowledgeable, and knowing things that perhaps a girl of her age shouldn't know. Oh, why was it so easy to talk to some boys and so difficult with others? She desperately wished she knew what he thought of her.

"Yes," he said awkwardly, not knowing how to respond to what she had just said. Wilhelm was not used to girls like Clara. He had only known country girls, like the four sisters on the neighboring farm. Tall, big-boned girls who milked cows and churned butter. He had imagined he would someday marry one of them, or a girl like them. Clara Heinze was a town girl, delicate, educated, very ladylike. Back in his own village, he rarely dealt with female shop clerks. His business was always conducted with men.

Wilhelm had never been good at talking to girls in the first place. They were a mystery to him. He was always afraid of saying the wrong thing and ending up either offending them or making them think he had intentions toward them when he hadn't. With women, Wilhelm found, you either had to be literal and straightforward, or talk in sugary, poetic ways; and since he never knew which, he remained silent.

But he wanted to say something now, something big and import-ant. He suddenly wanted to give her something—he wanted to give her the adventure she craved, the opportunity to show her inner courage. *He wanted to give her California.*

Sitting at his side, Clara sensed that he wanted to respond but didn't know how. From almost the beginning, she had guessed his shyness with girls. But he wasn't very good with words. It was hard for him to say what he felt. Clara knew this about him by now. So she said: "I'm such a talk-ative one, aren't I? I don't seem to give others a chance to get a word in. I'll be good and listen now, and let you do the talking. And if you can't think of anything to say, well, the important thing is to say something, *anything.* Otherwise," she hinted gently, "your silence can be misconstrued in many ways."

She waited, giving him an encouraging smile while people rode merrily by on bicycles or walked dogs both great and small and everyone enjoyed the sunshine. Finally, Wilhelm looked directly at her and said, "You are the most beautiful girl I have ever met."

She stared at him, lips parted.

For a long moment, they looked at each other in astonishment, both startled by his unexpected declaration. And then it was Clara's turn to be speechless.

Suddenly self-conscious, and blushing fiercely, Wilhelm squinted into the westering sun and said, "I think I should take you home now, or your mother will start worrying."

They rode their bicycles home wordlessly and he delivered her safely to the door of the chemist's shop. She smiled and said a demure "Thank you for the day," and he touched the bill of his cap.

They both knew everything was different now.

*   *   *

OVER THE NEXT DAYS, Clara and Wilhelm saw more of each other— in the bits of time they managed to grab: going to church together, Eva Heinze inviting him for Sunday dinner, Wilhelm dropping in at the chemist's shop to buy things for Siegfried and Dagmar in return for their hospitality—shaving cream, scented toilet water, aspirin tablets, tonics, useful items they would need in California. He opened up about himself, telling Clara about his boyhood, how he had missed his mother after she died, how he preferred the outdoors to sitting at a desk, his favorite stories and songs and working with his hands until a clearer, more detailed picture of the young man emerged.

At the same time, he saw the way Clara handled the customers in her father's shop, filling their orders, taking money and making change. And he thought her very capable. When her father was working in the shop, and he told her something to do, the way she said, "Yes, Papa" made Wilhelm think: she is obedient. Clara was also pretty and gentle and kind. She embroidered and crocheted with a delicate hand. She played the piano in a delightful way. She knew how to balance household accounts, and she understood the value of money and how to judge good servants from bad.

But Clara was more than that: She had taught Wilhelm how to talk about himself and his feelings. She had opened up another world for him. And more than anything, she had aroused feelings within himself that he hadn't known were there: feelings of heroism and the fierce desire to protect her. She completed him, and he wanted her for his wife.

Clara was serving a customer when Wilhelm burst into the shop. The cheeks above the beard were flushed and his blue eyes were bright. There was an excitement about him that told her this was going to be a life-changing day. Finishing with the customer and alone with Wilhelm in the shop, she left the counter and went to stand with him in the window that was filled with April sunshine. "A letter came from my father," he said in rare eagerness. "He says that all is ready and we are to join him in California as soon as Johann comes from Cologne." Wilhelm had spoken often of Johann, who was studying the science of agriculture. He always spoke highly and lovingly of his younger brother, and it seemed to her that Wilhelm was now possessed by a special excitement to have his brother joining him at last.

He said, "After that, we will all depart for the north and join others who have placed their trust in my father. We will travel as a group: it is safer that way."

Clara was breathless. She waited for more.

And then *he* waited.

When nothing more came, Wilhelm frowned a little and said, "That is it, Clara. We will depart within the month."

She was confused. Was she part of the "we," or was he referring only to himself and the others? She couldn't just ask him, because she might look the fool. Trying to think of a roundabout way of getting a more specific answer without appearing desperate, she said, "What do I tell my parents?"

His frowned deepened. What about his news had she not understood? It was all very simple. "Tell them that we depart within the month."

Finally she whispered, "I shall miss you." It was all she could say.

The frown remained. "But Clara, you are coming with us!"

"I am?"

"You have said how wonderful California sounds. You have said it would be exciting to start a whole new farm, build a whole new home in a new place. Did you not mean it?"

"Well, yes, but—"

He took her smooth hands and clasped them between his callused ones. "Forgive me, dear Clara, I was never properly schooled in the etiquette of such delicate matters. I am asking you to be my wife. I should have asked. I merely assumed! Tell me I am not wrong! Tell me I have not made a terrible mistake and made a mess of it all by not doing this right!"

His tone was so eager and yet desperate, and he clasped her hands so tightly, that Clara almost thought she was going to swoon. Standing in the window of her father's shop, with people walking by outside and a horse going clip-clop on the cobblestones and sunshine streaming through—all this struck Clara as being the most romantic setting in the whole world. Never had a girl received such a wonderful and passionate proposal of marriage. "Oh," she said, catching her breath. "Yes, Wilhelm, I will marry you."

His face lit up like a sunrise. "Thank you, my beautiful Clara! You have made me the happiest man on earth. You will see. We will be happy in California. And I know you are a practical-minded girl and will understand that our money is best spent in America rather than here. I know you will not miss an engagement ring."

"Of course not," she said, laughing. Why would she want a ring when she was getting Wilhelm and California?

The obstacle came later that evening, when she broke the news to her parents. Their immediate reaction was to frown, both of them, and Clara's heart sank.

"It's a terribly fast courtship, and you're awfully young to be making such a big decision," Eva Heinze said. Her voice shook as she said it. She had feared this moment would come. Something had been allowed to run out of control, and now she had no idea how to stop it.

"You were nineteen when you married Papa," Clara said, determined to keep it all civil. The Heinzes rarely had rows. Unlike her friend Anna's parents, whose only way of communicating seemed to be through shouts and arguments, Clara's mother and father were always reasonable and civil. But the tension was in the air all the same, and her father's frown only deepened. "Yes, your mother was nineteen, but we married after a year-long courtship in which we were chaperoned nearly all the time."

"But Wilhelm and I don't have that luxury, Papa," she said, trying not to sound whiny. They *had* to let her marry Wilhelm. Couldn't they see that this was no ordinary proposal? This was not a traditional union: she wasn't just gaining a husband, but five hundred acres that had once been a Spanish rancho! And she would be the wife of a prosperous vintner. They should be pleased!

"Still, it *is* a fast courtship," her mother said. What might people in the village think? That young Clara Heinze, getting together with a stranger to the town, suddenly had *had* to get married? Would there be a cloud of shame over their marriage? Especially as the young couple would leave Germany before any evidence of premarital activity began to show.

Clara tried reasoning with them. "This isn't the nineteenth century anymore. We live in a fast, new modern age, with speeding trains and automobiles and talking over hundreds of miles by telephone. Long courtships will go out of fashion, you'll see."

"But Clara," Eva Heinze said, already feeling her hold on her daughter slipping away, "you'll be starting a new life, creating a new home, and I won't be there to help you."

"Julia and Brigitte got married here and moved away to start new lives and create new homes and you weren't there to help *them*."

Eva tipped her chin. "They had their mothers-in-law to help. Who would you have?"

"We will all help one another. Siegfried and Dagmar, and the other immigrant families who will be traveling with us. That's how we will do it. And I will learn as I go along, Mama." *I will show everyone how courageous I can be.*

Eva Heinze closed her eyes. This was the very argument she had had with her own parents thirty years ago. And, yes, she would have married Helmut even without their permission and maybe she would never have spoken to them again. *If I say no to this marriage, then my relationship with my precious daughter might be irrevocably damaged forever.*

Clara decided on a different tack. She didn't want tears and a tantrum and threats of running away. She wanted to marry Wilhelm with their blessings. Her father was a rational, educated man who dealt with chemical formulas all day long. And her mother had always prided herself for having a head on her shoulders. Clara would appeal to that side of their natures. "The way I see it," she said as calmly as she could, although she was bunching her skirt in her hands, "two very plain and simple roads lie before me with perfectly clear signposts. One road takes me to Wilhelm and California, the other takes me to another husband and a different destiny entirely. I choose California."

With her eyes still closed, Eva Heinze felt a pang in her heart. Was Clara aware of what she had just said? She chose California. She had not said, "I choose Wilhelm." So that was the way of it, then, what Eva had secretly feared, that her daughter had fallen in love with a man's dream rather than with the man himself. Would she come to realize this in the future and come to hate him for it? Or would the love of his dream bring Clara to eventually love the man himself?

Eva's shoulders slumped. She opened her eyes which were damp with tears. "I've always sensed that I would lose you someday, my darling. Inquisitive even as a toddler, a voracious reader, always wanting to know what lay over the next hill. Whichever road you take, I will lose you. But . . . knowing that a loss is coming still doesn't prepare a mother for the pain of it when it comes. It's always hard to see the last little bird leave the nest." She wiped her eyes with a handkerchief. "All mothers face the day their children leave home. But it's usually just to a husband or to another town. But . . . thousands of miles?" *I shall never see you again.*

*   *   *

STILL THINKING THEY NEEDED a longer courtship, but admitting that circumstances called for a bending of tradition, Helmut Heinze nonetheless insisted that Wilhelm pay him a visit and, man to man, formally ask Mr. Heinze for his daughter's hand in marriage. Wilhelm was happy to comply, proper form was observed, both men were satisfied, and they sealed the agreement with an excellent Chardonnay grown and bottled locally.

Clara then set herself to the task of learning English. It would be a matter of convenience and survival. And Wilhelm's father had written in his letters about the Mexican housekeeper and the Mexican laborers in his fields, so there were a lot of Spanish-speaking people there too, and a lot of cities and counties were named Santa this or San that, so she decided it would be wise to learn a little Spanish as well.

And so, in considering what to take with her to America, Clara started with books. She wanted to please and impress Wilhelm with her new language skills and knowledge of their new home.

While other immigrant women might at that moment be collecting yarns and threads and needles to take along with them on the voyage, and their precious pots and pans, the collections of bread and sausage and gravy recipes, their dressmaking patterns and pins and measuring tapes—while the other immigrant women would be packing embroidery hoops and darning eggs and favorite spatulas and whisks for making hard meringues, Clara Heinze would bring books. She ordered a German-English dictionary, workbooks and pencils, and a map of California upon which she carefully drew outlines in ink of all the counties, meaning to familiarize herself with her new world, memorizing their peculiar names—Humboldt, Mendocino, Napa, Yuba. She found the Schallers' Largo Valley and colored it in with red ink, drawing a black circle around the town of Lynnville, their destination.

But over the next days, as she saw less of Wilhelm because he was so busy with vines and cuttings and contacting the other immigrant families and preparing for Johann's arrival, Clara felt unexpected fears and doubts creep in.

Despite her luminous joy over being a bride and an immigrant facing adventure, Clara was suddenly torn. She woke up one morning and realized how much she loved her home and her village and the nearby fields and dairy farms and vineyards and the great, gray curving river that she had known all her life. Her parents and her friends and neighbors were here. How could she leave them, go thousands of miles away from them, to a country that not long ago had festered with wild savages who tore people's scalps from their heads?

She had grown up on the Rhine. It was her beloved river. She could spend hours watching the ferries and the steam-driven paddleboats and coal barges sail by. When she sang "The Lorelei," she always moved her listeners when she came to the tender phrase "And peacefully flows the Rhine." The dangerous craggy rocks, the melancholy mists, the deep dark river where the ghosts of unfortunate sailors mourned their terrible fate.

How could she leave all this? And yet, how could she let Wilhelm walk out of her life? "I'm frightened, Mama," she lamented as she wept on her mother's lap. It was a gray, rainy day. The sun had not shone its golden face for two days, and some of the damp grayness had settled into Clara's frustrated young heart. "I thought I was being so brave, but instead I am confused! I was so happy, but now I am filled with doubts. Oh, Mama, what can I do? I don't want to leave you and Papa. I don't want to leave my friends. And oh, Mama, I grew up on this river. How can I leave it?"

"My darling daughter, though I love you with all my heart and will miss you terribly, I want you to seize this opportunity that so few are granted—you will discover that there are other rivers, and this is something a great many people never come to know."

She didn't say anything more, the rest she would lock up in her heart and never voice it, that she was committing a mother's most supreme self-sacrifice: letting go of her daughter. Mrs. Heinze had been born in this village. She had never visited a city or even a sizable town. All her life she had wondered what Berlin was like, or Rome or Paris. And America? That shimmering continent never dared enter her dreams. Now she looked back and felt the dark pain of regret. She was getting on in years. She had never seen those places. This was her precious legacy to her only daughter: the freedom to see the world.

*   *   *

A WEEK LATER, JOHANN arrived.

They decided to celebrate the occasion with a picnic. After getting permission from her father to take the day off from the shop, Clara put together a basket filled with hard-boiled eggs, cold sliced ham, soft camembert cheese with a floury rind, and thick, sweetish pumpernickel bread, followed by wedges of Black Forest cake with whipped cream on top and chocolate shavings. The brothers brought bottles of frosty ale packed in straw.

They came to pick her up at her father's shop. The brother, Johann, younger than Wilhelm by two years, resembled his brother but had his own distinctive features as well: neither bearded nor brawny but rather somewhat shorter than his brother with a slender frame, his blond hair clipped short and his blue eyes peering from beneath hooded eyelids—a trait Wilhelm did not have. His clothes were perfectly pressed, he wore a clean celluloid collar, and the crest on the pocket of his blazer identified his school. On his flaxen head, he wore a jaunty Tyrolean hat made of green felt with a corded hatband and a spray of feathers on one side.

They all rented bicycles and as they cycled along the track, riding in and out of sunlight and shadow in the piney scent of the woods, Johann suddenly burst into song: "*Du, Du, liegst mir im Herzen.*" It startled Clara. She watched his legs go up and down, his shoulders and back straight. His voice sailed up to the needled boughs: "*Du, Du, liegst mir im Sinn. Du, du, machst mir viel Schmerzen, weißt nicht wie gut ich dir bin.*" Suddenly, behind her, Wilhelm joined in the chorus with a bellow: "*Ja, ja, ja, ja, weißt nicht wie gut ich dir bin.*"

Both sang off-key, but with such loud exuberance that it made Clara laugh. And then, surprising herself, she joined in with the next stanza, sounding a little better than the brothers, she thought, and together the three sang their way up into the clear air of the woods overlooking the Rhine.

They found a clearing with wildflowers, leaned their bikes against a tree, and spread the blanket on the grass. Through the trees, they could see down to the Rhine and across to the forested mountains. But the spring day had a chill to it, so they did not remove their long overcoats, and they kept an eye on the gray clouds scudding across the sky. They commented on the threat of rain and prayed that the weather would hold.

As they got settled, Clara thought how Johann was not at all what she had expected. Because he was a scholar, she had pictured him as a very studious, and therefore very serious, young man. But his smile went beyond congenial and he had a generous laugh. As they unpacked the basket, Johann said, "Two men were walking across a bridge. One man fell off into the water and the other man was named Fritz."

Clara smiled, and then she laughed.

He winked at her and sat up to open a flask of lager. As he did, his blazer fell open to reveal a chain hanging from the inside pocket. Clara couldn't help noticing, and then her eyebrows rose. "A lucky rabbit's foot?" she said in amusement, thinking that surely a student of science would not believe in luck.

He laughed as he brought out his pocket watch and chain with its white rabbit's foot attached. Giving the paw a quick kiss, he said: "We Germans have a reputation for being rational, efficient, accurate, and punctual. With this type of mentality, you would think we would not have so many superstitions. And yet we do! Germans are more than happy to turn to the supernatural for help. Especially when it comes to taking college exams." He smiled mischievously as he restored watch and chain to his pocket, and Clara thought how unlike his brother he was.

"How did my ugly brother manage to catch the prettiest girl in the Rhine Valley?" Johann cried suddenly, and then punched Wilhelm playfully in the arm. To Clara's further surprise, Wilhelm blushed and laughed at himself. She hadn't actually realized until that moment that Wilhelm didn't laugh much.

Johann, on the other hand, seemed always on the verge of joviality, as his hooded eyes had a slight puffiness to the lower lids that gave the illusion of crinkling in secret amusement. Clara wondered if he had been a prankster at school, the one youth in every classroom who was always up to some shenanigans. She saw him shooting witty quips at his professors and receiving stern remonstrances with suppressed smiles. His teachers would have been annoyed by him, would have sighed over him, but would have loved him for his cleverness. Wilhelm had told her that Johann had graduated at the top of his class.

As Johann spread a slice of dark bread with butter and laid some slices of ham on it, he said, "Have you noticed that everyone wants to go to Heaven but no one wants to die?"

Wilhelm shook his head and smiled as he peeled a hard-boiled egg and dipped it in mustard.

"Wilhelm, did I tell you that I fell off a thirty-foot ladder?"

"My God, brother, were you hurt?"

"No. Luckily, I was on the second rung."

She soon saw that Johann was buoyant of spirit and light of humor. It seemed to her that when the bloodlines were handed down, Wilhelm had received all the Schaller seriousness while Johann saw the comedy in life. They were a good counterbalance for each other. Johann even made fun of Wilhelm's glum face, and this made Wilhelm smile. They were like a stage act, she thought. Two comedians, one smart, one dumb, or one sad, one happy, two men on a stage the exact opposites, and yet each complementing the other to bring about laughter in the audience.

She saw the affection between them, especially when Johann told her about their boyhood and how Wilhelm had always been his protector. Johann clearly looked up to his older brother, and Wilhelm cuffed him affectionately. She loved watching them, listening to them talk about plans for their new home in California. They fed off each other. She had never seen Wilhelm so animated or vocal. Johann literally brought him to life.

And then a strange thought entered her mind. The brothers actually seemed to her to be *competing* against one another, and she had the very flattering feeling that they were competing for her attention.

After they had eaten and they lazily watched white clouds roll across a sky growing gray with rain, Wilhelm stood up and excused himself to go and stretch his legs. As he traipsed through the privacy of the trees, Clara set her face into the wind, smelled the coming rain, and wondered about rain in California. Was it tropical there? Would it be a warm rain there?

And then she felt something creep along the back of her neck, as if the wind had sent out an errant breeze to tickle her and make her shiver and give her a moment of creepiness. She had heard that these woods were haunted. But surely haunts only came out at night, didn't they? Whoever heard of daytime ghosts? Still, the feeling not only lingered, it increased until, despite a rational scorning of her fear inside her mind, she turned to look and she was stunned to see Johann's eyes boring into her. She had heard the saying that one could feel someone's eyes on them, but had always thought it was just a superstition. And yet, just now, she had literally felt Johann's eyes on her.

And he did not turn away. When people are caught staring, it is natural to blush and turn away, or at least it is polite to turn away. Johann did not. He didn't hide the fact that he seemed very interested in his brother's fiancée, and in a very frank and forthright way. It made her vaguely uneasy. She suspected that she must say something, but she had no idea what to say, since his jocularity seemed to have left him. She had never seen such a serious look on a man's face. Her heart jumped. Did he not approve of her? Did he not want her going with them to America? Was he going to interfere with the wedding?

To her surprise—and relief—he said, "My brother is a very lucky man." And he said it with such solemnity that Clara was momentarily taken aback. She broke the spell of seriousness by saying, with a laugh, "*I'm* the lucky one! I'm being carried away on a magic carpet to a paradise called California. And did you know," she added quickly to keep the seriousness from coming back, "that *California* was the name given to a mythical island populated by beautiful Amazon warriors in a popular sixteenth-century Spanish novel? The story describes the Island of California as being east of the Asian mainland. An island ruled by Queen Calafia. And when the Spaniards started exploring the American Pacific coast, they applied this name on their maps to what is now called the Baja California peninsula, which they thought was an island. Once the name was on the maps, it stuck." Clara offered a self-mocking laugh. "I've been doing some reading."

He smiled. "So I see." Johann thought about this enchanting girl whom his brother had managed to win. She was not at all what he had expected, and she certainly seemed not at all what he had thought was Wilhelm's type.

While away at school, Johann had discovered a life quite different from that in the country—and the girls were different, too: very sophisticated and worldly, aware of things beyond the borders of their own little farm. Clara reminded him of those girls who had the brains and courage to attend a large university, to compete with men in the classrooms, to shrug off the prejudice and bias of students and professors who thought women hadn't the brains for higher learning—especially in the sciences! He was interested to discover that Clara, though not having gone on to higher learning, nonetheless still possessed a font of semi-scientific understanding through the private tutelage of her father, a chemist. Fundamental and rudimentary knowledge to be sure, but enough to be able to listen to Johann's ideas and have a grasp of what he was saying.

"It's good to study information about the place you are going to. That way, there will be no unpleasant surprises. In fact," he added with a grin, "we will all be looking to you as our California expert. Wilhelm told me you've even been learning English." He made a mock frown. "An impossible language. I have dabbled in it myself. They put their verbs in all the wrong places."

She laughed. "But you are going to have to learn it well in order to get on there."

"Then I shall expect lessons from my sister-in-law," he said with a smile that was not at all flirtatious. "I tell you, Clara," he said, stretching his arms as if expecting to fly. "I cannot wait to get to California! I thought my course at the university would never end. All those lectures. Professors telling me what to do. Telling me what I must think. I am done with all that. From now on, Johann Schaller is going to be his own man."

She watched him as he sat with his face to the wind, a knowing smile on his face. Johann was very cosmopolitan. Unlike his brother, who was a country boy, educated enough to be a good vintner, Johann had gone to the big city to attend university and had earned a degree in science. She wondered what he thought of her, a small-town girl who had just enough education to read and write and do sums and run a home.

"You know, Clara," he said in a soft voice, speaking as much to the wind and the Rhine as to her, "I am not going to America just to grow grapes and own a big farm. There is a burning within me; it has been there ever since I was a small boy. To make something of myself someday, to be my own man and stamp my mark upon this earth. The future calls to me, America calls to me, and I am filled with visions of what I can do, of the name I can make for myself and my sons. Not to be rich, no, not necessarily that, but to accomplish something, to reach an achievement that will have an impact on people's lives. That is why I am going, Clara, and why I cannot wait to get there."

He stopped then, having spoken in a rush, and then he seemed to remember himself, and even looked a little taken aback by his actions. He hadn't intended to be so open about himself with this girl he had only just met. But she was easy to talk to, a patient listener, and he had a sense that she would understand him.

Clara was glad he had spoken so openly about what was in his heart, and she was suddenly feeling light and joyous again. With his confession, he had infused their adventure with new, electric spirit and drive, and she felt it invade her body as though she had been struck by lightning. Johann's lightning. Oh, it was going to be wonderful in California! The Schaller brothers and their father starting their own winery, starting families. Johann would find a wife and there would be many children, their homes would be filled with brothers and sisters, who in turn would be a crowd of cousins. She could see it—a large, gathered, devoted family all staying in one place, unlike her own scattered siblings and her parents left on their own. Clara was determined to found such a family and see it grow.

Coming back through the trees, and seeing Clara and Johann quietly talking, Wilhelm felt himself fill with pride and accomplishment. He knew how people saw the Schaller boys: Johann was the clever brother who won honors and got more praise in school than Wilhelm did, no matter how hard he tried to compete with him. It had given Wilhelm deep satisfaction to see the look on Johann's face when he had first met Clara. A look of astonishment and envy, and Wilhelm saying "This is my fiancée," with all the pride of a man who has won the most coveted trophy in the world, and to feel that, for once, he had bested his younger brother.

*   *   *

THE DAY CAME WHEN the letter from California arrived. It was many pages long and filled with details and instructions about vine cuttings and their transport, warnings and advice about the ocean voyage and the rail journey, but it all boiled down to a one-word message: "Come."

At last they were to depart for Bremerhaven, where a magnificent four-funnel Kaiser-class ocean liner awaited to take them into the future.

The wedding ceremony took place in the Lutheran church with all the Heinzes' friends attending. Clara wore a white gown that Dagmar had made by adding lace and pearls to a garden party dress. Helmut Heinze walked her proudly down the aisle, while her mother smiled and cried in the front pew. Wilhelm wore a borrowed suit and top hat, his face beaming with joy, Johann standing at his side. The ceremony was followed by a celebratory luncheon at a restaurant that Clara's father had reserved for the afternoon. It was an emotional event, filled with joy for the newlyweds and sadness to see them leaving, but happiness and hope for a bright future as well. Clara's father gave her money for California, and her mother gave her a tight hug, with a murmured "You take my heart with you."

The new Mrs. Clara Heinze Schaller, excited, scared, buoyant, and frightened, said good-bye to her parents, her friends, and her beloved Rhine River and headed north by train with her new husband and new brother-in-law.

*   *   *

JAKOB SCHALLER WRUNG HIS hands as he paced the length of the station platform, back and forth, worried and anxious as other people also kept an eye up the track, waiting for the train from Los Angeles to Santa Barbara.

It had been a year since the birth of his dream when, a widower with two strapping sons, he had looked out over his small vineyard and had thought: It isn't enough. And then he had seen the pamphlets circulating around Europe, urging immigrants to come to America. Pamphlets advertising vast acres of cheap, fertile land beneath balmy skies and beneficent sunlight. The ads had described cattle ranches in Montana, horse farms in Wyoming, golden cornfields in Nebraska. And then his eye had fallen upon "California—perfect for wine-making, where already over 300 varieties of grapes are grown." And Jakob Schaller had known at once that there was where his family's future lay. After that came the letters back and forth with a land broker in California, and then his own ocean voyage and train journey across the continent.

He had written home, urging friends and relatives to take advantage of this opportunity. Jakob had assured them that there were already Italians in the valley, as well as Frenchmen, a Swiss, a Dutch family, and even a Portuguese wine-maker. There would be a little bit of Europe in the California valley. A few had rallied to the cry, those for whom there had been no room in their villages back home. One woman was a skilled designer and maker of ladies' hats, and in her Rhine village her mother and two sisters were also ladies' hatmakers. The blacksmith. The tailor. The cobbler. Their fathers had taught them well, but the sons didn't want to steal custom from their fathers and so they must branch out on their own. They would build little houses and set up storefronts and ply their trades for the Americans.

Jakob had seen to everything. They had given him their money and he had handled all purchases, contracts, deeds. They trusted Jakob Schaller.

Jakob was big in stature. He had burly shoulders like two haystacks, and his bushy beard, like straw, was in need of a good combing. His pants, held up by suspenders, needed patching in places, and his jacket was threadbare. Jakob gave no thought to appearances. He was a man of means and property, and that was all that mattered. He thought only of his new vineyard and his sons working at his side.

Jakob had not been idle. He had found the property overgrown with very old grapevines (a hundred and thirty years old) that produced thick leaves in the summer but were too woody and crowded with weeds, and the grapes weren't edible. His main task was clearing the slopes and pruning the vines as far back as he could, cutting them right down to the ground in many cases, to start afresh. It had been a year, but the new vines were now tall and supported on trellises so that Jakob and his sons could expect a good grape harvest next season and could begin the wine-making process.

What they would do now, with the boys arriving with new vines, was to plant the imported Rieslings in fields that Jakob had spent the past months preparing, with the help of Mexican migrant labor. In the old ruined winery, he had found three wine presses and even stills for making brandy. He and his sons would get to work restoring the derelict Spanish winery, improving the presses and vats, and building better barrel rooms using local brick and adobe.

He had hoped the boys could join him sooner, but there wouldn't be a grape harvest until two years after he'd first arrived here anyway, and he wanted Johann to finish at the university. It also gave Wilhelm one more season with their vineyard back on the Rhine to bring in the additional revenue they would need for the second phase of rebuilding the winery. Wilhelm had handled the sale of their vineyard quickly and efficiently. He would be bringing much-needed cash, as Jakob's savings were dwindling rapidly. He thanked God that labor was so cheap in California, with migrants coming up from Mexico looking for any kind of work at any wage.

"I don't see why you have to go," Jakob's seventy-year-old father had groused.

But Jakob had explained that it wasn't for himself, it was for his sons. He told everyone that in California, Wilhelm and Johann could become men of distinction, where there was not only room for large vineyards, but room for their sons and grandsons and great-grandsons to have vineyards of their own. A place where, Jakob had been told, there were Frenchmen and Italians growing French grapes and Italian grapes and bottling French wines and Italian wines—but there were no Germans, no one to thrill the people of California with wines from the Rhine and Mosel. Jakob had painted a fabulous, broad canvas of the new wine-growing region and how the name of Schaller was going to shine brighter than the sun.

This was what he had told everyone. But the dark truth, his *real* reasons for coming here, he kept to himself.

Jakob would never forget the impact this new place had had on him upon his arrival. He had seen it all with a sweep of his eyes. This was how a new land was won. First came the men, rough and ready, to claim the land and start to build. They lived ruggedly, with barely any rules or manners. When a home of sorts had been accomplished, then came the women with their soap and Bibles and manners and civilizing ways. It had felt strange to Jakob to be in a country that hadn't been conquered and re-conquered over thousands of years. If any battles were fought here, they were recent and fought with rifles. Before that, he could only imagine how Indians had waged war—with toma-hawks and bows and arrows. California Indians, he had learned, were not a horse culture but a peaceful agrarian race, who had been assimilated into the Spaniards and then the Mexicans until little trace of them was left.

Now the Americans were here, and the European immigrants, with their dreams and visions.

It was going to be a new and wonderful life. He would think only of the lush acres that they would plant. He would give no further thought to the small patch of cursed ground he had found on the western border of his newly purchased land.

These twenty miserable acres abutted a foothill called Colina Sagrada. The land agent had said that it was Spanish for Sacred Hill or Holy Hill. Jakob wondered why it had been named that. Was there an Indian burial ground on its crest? Or had the owner of the rancho named it that after he buried a loved one or loved ones up there, evidence of their graves long since erased?

Jakob had squinted with hard eyes at the blighted patch of land that looked as if God had cursed it. It was thin, flinty soil, harsh and dry, with a paltry crust of topsoil that couldn't even support the hardy sagebrush. There was no underground water so no wells could be drilled, and because of the elevation it would be difficult to deliver water to it. The soil was poor, eroded. And western exposure to the afternoon sun, with no treebreaks or protection, made growing impossible in the peak of the summer. It had been recommended to Jakob that he install a line of tall eucalyptus trees as a windbreak and for protection against the sun, but Jakob had sniffed the soil, sifted it through his fingers, thought of Largo Creek so far away and the effort and engineering it would take to bring water to this barren spot, and he deemed this forsaken corner of his land unredeemable and decided that it should be left just as God had made it.

He thought of Colina Sagrada now and wondered if his distaste for that blighted patch of ground was because it reminded him so much of himself. It reminded him of his real reasons for leaving Germany, reasons which not even his sons knew.

Jakob Schaller had come to California because of a promise he had made to the only woman he had ever loved, or ever would love.

Waiting impatiently on the train-station platform, Wilhelm pulled out his pocket watch and snapped it open—not to check the time, but to look at the photograph fitted inside the hinged lid. It was of a woman's face, young and pretty, with luxuriant hair piled on top of her head. Taken over twenty years before, it had faded only a little. With a tear in his eye, Jakob whispered: "It is almost here, Kätzchen, the fulfillment of the promise I made to you long ago. Although you left me, I never forgot that promise. My love for you is strong still and will endure until the day I die . . . and, through God's grace, beyond.

"I couldn't have done it without you, Kätzchen. The loneliness of this past year might have defeated me—never mind coyotes carrying off my chickens and half the vines too rotted to be revived and the weeks of desperately searching for a well, and building the cabin. . . . But you were always there when I reached my lowest point. I miss you so, my dearest Kätzchen, even though you have been gone all these years. Love doesn't diminish with time. Especially when I look at your sweet face every day and talk to you. I know you can hear me. And now the year of loneliness and hardship is up. Our sons will be here and I can begin to fulfill my promise to you." With a smile he snapped the watch shut and said to himself: Blessed is the man who has known the love of a good woman.

The rest—the dark shadow that had trailed him from Germany and continued to haunt him—he would put from his mind on this joyous day.

A whistle sounded, and the train pulled into the station at last with a great noise of brakes and steam. Jakob watched his people disembark, watched how they shielded their eyes from the sun and gaped at the palm trees in wonder. It amused him to see their reaction to the sunlight here—his own had been the same, a year before. It had to do with the latitude: Santa Barbara lay only thirty-four degrees north of the Equator, whereas his home in Germany was at fifty-one degrees north—a difference of a thousand miles! They were in a different climate too—sunnier, warmer, like Italy.

Jakob greeted the young immigrants with enthusiasm. It felt good to speak German again. He had been forced to learn English and Spanish. And as he looked at the round, fresh faces of the brides, he almost smacked his lips at the thought of good German cooking again.

The young men wore dark jackets over white shirts and dark pants, with country tweed caps on their heads. The young women were dressed in white blouses tucked into long black skirts, with smart little jackets. They wore modest felt or straw bonnets pinned to their upswept hair. On their feet, high buttoned boots, practical country wear. They carried baskets and carpetbags and umbrellas and valises. As he exuberantly greeted each one by name, assuring them that their little shops in town, with living quarters, were ready to be moved into, that he had seen to everything, Jakob anxiously looked for his sons. They had yet to disembark. And then—he stared as the conductor and a porter lifted a young woman down from the train in a chair. Under Johann's guidance, they brought the young lady directly to Jakob. He embraced his younger son with tears in his eyes. It was a long embrace, filled with love and emotion. Jakob hadn't realized until this moment just how desperately he had missed his boys. "Where is Wilhelm?" he said, holding Johann at arm's length, filling his eyes with the sight of him. It had been a long year indeed.

"He has gone to see to the cuttings, Father."

Jakob cast a puzzled look at the young lady, who quickly said, "Please do not be alarmed, Father Jakob. I had a bout of the flu but am over it and will regain my strength in a few days." Jakob had the same flaxen hair as his sons, she noticed, although shot with gray.

"'Father'?" he said.

"I am Clara, your daughter-in-law."

Jakob's eyebrows shot up. "Daughter-in-law!" He looked fiercely at Johann.

"She is Wilhelm's wife," Johann said with some embarrassed discomfort. Hadn't his brother written to their father about the marriage?

Jakob murmured a slightly flustered "Welcome" and strode away to help Wilhelm with the offloading of the precious cuttings that had traveled thousands of miles in trunks lined with waterproof oil cloth, leaving Johann and Clara to watch him go.

Clara wished she could have met the father on her own two feet. Perhaps it was her debilitated state that had confused him. When influenza had broken out during the ocean crossing, Clara had been the only one well enough to take care of the others, and then, belatedly, had come down with the flu when the rest had recovered. It had made for a miserable journey across the continent in the rocking train car, with transfers from different rail lines, and then arriving in a very weakened condition at the depot in Santa Barbara.

But it hadn't just been the influenza. The trek had been long and arduous. First, the journey north to Bremerhaven, where the group had met up with the other three young couples bound for California. After that, the stormy voyage across the Atlantic during which Clara and the others, traveling third-class in order to save their money, had moaned and vomited in their berths and wished they had never left home. And then the sighting of the Statue of Liberty. The wearisome funneling through the lines at Ellis Island, the inoculations and questions and forms to sign, all the while wondering if their precious possessions—sewing machines, ceramic chamber pots, darning needles, quilts, pans for Gugelhupf cakes, books, tools, and everything else needed to start a new life in a new world—had arrived safe and unbroken. A sleepless night in an inexpensive New York hotel with Wilhelm snoring at her side—hardly what one would call a honeymoon—and then a frantic gathering of their goods, an accounting of everything, and overseeing the chaotic loading of everything onto the proper train bound for the proper destination, with much examining and re-examining of tickets and passports and trying to explain in the few words of English the group shared among themselves before they finally boarded the train that was pointed westward toward the Pacific Ocean, a frightening three thousand miles away.

Clara had been glad that they hadn't traveled in cattle cars, as some dirt-poor immigrants did. But they also didn't waste a penny on first- or even second-class transport when the third-class part of the train arrived in California at exactly the same moment as the other two classes did. But the train car had been cramped and crowded, and Clara and Wilhelm and

Johann had slept on the floor or across the bench seating, everyone trying to accommodate everyone else as best they could, but they were young and laughed about what an adventure it all was and wasn't it too bad they wouldn't see any buffalo or Indians, as they had all been tamed years ago?

But they were here now. The journey was at an end. Clara had reached her new home.

After the clamorous offloading of their trunks and cases and boxes from the baggage car and onto the enormous sixteen-mule wagon Jakob had hired, Clara was helped into a car and felt her excitement grow as they went through the San Marcos pass to follow a winding, hilly route from the coastal town of Santa Barbara. Around each gentle curve she saw something new: a magical forest, golden pastureland, hillsides covered in wildflowers, cows and horses grazing in rich grass, hawks and falcons riding the winds and currents, and a glorious lake appearing from out of nowhere to steal the breath away.

Finally the cars coughed and stuttered and banged to a halt and, at the rear, the muleskinner called his team to a halt. Clara watched as her fellow travelers alighted from their vehicles and strode and plodded and ached their way up the hill to the top of the ridge where the road's climb ended and would start its descent. Johann lifted his weary sister-in-law from the car so that she, too, could look out over their new home.

There it was, stretching breathlessly before them, their new valley, Largo—Spanish for "long." The afternoon wind blew clean and fresh against Clara's face as Johann held her in his arms. She saw a lush green expanse dotted with white farmhouses and giant oaks and a wondrous patchwork quilt of geometric crops set out in straight lines and perfect squares and rectangles. In the distance was a collection of buildings dominated by a white church spire, and she took this to be the town of Lynnville.

Clara and Johann and their friends were silent in their awe and reverence. After months of planning and dreaming and anticipating and fearing and worrying and throwing up and doubting and almost turning back, they were here at last.

Wilhelm stood ahead of the group, at the edge of the hill, his beard golden in the sun. There was so much room! Not like the small farm cooperatives back home, limited by government regulation and restrictions. Here, the land spread so far away, it almost defied imagination. His father had been right. Here, they could carry on the traditions that had been in the Schaller family for generations, bringing the Rhineland to the heart of California. He couldn't wait to dig his hands into the soil and start planting his young vines brought from home, continuing with the same fine Rieslings the Schallers had been producing for centuries.

Behind him, his brother Johann, with the weary Clara in his arms, was also taking in the sweeping vista and thinking of the grapes they would grow here and the wines they would produce. But his thoughts marched along a different track. He thought not in terms of traditions and ancestors, but of experimenting and discovering and improving. Johann's watchwords were *innovation* and *change*. He had brought with him not only a fine university education in agricultural science, but the tools of the laboratory as well. He looked forward to finding ways of improving grapes, of producing newer and finer wines. Yes, he thought now in excitement. We are in a new land: we should produce new wine.

As their father Jakob pointed toward the distance, identifying landmarks and property lines, saying "That line of trees is where our vineyard begins," and as the others murmured about the town and how like a little jewel it was among all the green, Clara held on to Johann as he carried her in his strong, safe arms, and she looked out over the trees and farms and white houses and saw, meandering its way through the greenery, a thin silver ribbon of a river—the Largo—and she recalled her mother's words from weeks ago: "You will discover that there are other rivers."

"Yes," she said now to Johann who was not her husband, "we will be happy here."

Jakob felt the wind in his beard, he felt also a cold breeze suddenly whisper through his old jacket, and the shadow of an enormous black cloud rolled over the green landscape like a Biblical monster devouring the land. He shivered. Never a man to believe in omens, nonetheless he could not help but think that the cold wind and dark shadow were some sort of sign.

He scanned the peaceful valley, lifted his face to the blue sky and the beneficent sun, and then he looked at the eager young immigrants. Everything looked as it should be. Perhaps it was his imagination. Perhaps it stemmed from the secret motivation for coming here. Jakob Schaller had come to this valley not so much to grow grapes and make wine as to seek redemption.

Finally it was time for the party of adventurers who had been together for so long to split up. They were eager to reach their destinations, little shops and houses, already built and waiting to be moved into. Tears were shed among tight embraces, and promises made: "We will see you in town." "We will come to visit your farm." And then they went their separate ways.

The Schallers followed a dirt road past farms and pastures where horses and cows grazed, past orchards and green spring crops as far as the eye could see. It was a peaceful, bucolic valley; Clara had never seen such a flat expanse of land! It was a valley, yes, but such a *wide* valley. She had thought it would be like the Rhine Valley, narrow in the embrace of towering, menacing mountains, with the Largo River flowing like an artery along the bottom. But this valley was flat, with gentle hills rising around it like a loving bowl. And the river was just a meandering ribbon with flat banks on either side. It was going to take some getting used to, seeing such flat, far distances.

They passed a sign by the road that said BALLERINI FARMS & WINERY and Clara saw, at the end of a long dirt road, a large two-story farmhouse set in the middle of emerald pastures. Three miles down the road they came upon a smaller sign, modestly hand-lettered: SCHALLER FARM. The hired driver turned the car off the main road, and they bumped their way down a rutted track toward a wooden farmhouse, mud-brown and rustic. It was small, more like a cabin really, but Clara didn't mind. It was *theirs,* and she was going to be its mistress.

Wilhelm got out of the car as soon as it stopped, saying to his father, "Which of those old buildings is the winery? I would like to look at the presses."

But Jakob laid a hand on his son's arm and said, quietly, "Tend to your wife first."

Wilhelm blinked, then looked back at the car where Johann was opening Clara's door. Wilhelm reached her in three strides and put a strong arm around her waist.

They were met on the porch by Rosita, a plump woman in her forties who, it turned out, had picked up a smattering of German during her employment with Jakob. She immediately brought the two inside, directing Wilhelm to the other side of the one-room cabin where, in front of a large brick fireplace, three wood-framed canvas cots had been neatly made with sheets, pillows, and blankets.

Laying Clara on one of the cots, Wilhelm told her he had to go out and join his father and brother, and Clara assured him that she would be fine, she was on the mend and would soon be out-walking all of them. The small house, she noticed, was filled with the delicious aroma of beans and tomatoes and onions, and she realized that, for the first time in days, she had an appetite. But as she tried to sit up, the solicitous Rosita made her lie back down and returned a few minutes later with two cups, one filled with fresh cold water, the other with bracing red wine. Clara drank them down and fell into a deep sleep.

When she was awakened from her nap by Rosita, Clara heard the stamp of boots on the floorboards and realized that the men had returned from their inspection of the farm. She joined them at the kitchen table for a hearty meal of enchiladas, rice, beans, tortillas, and beer. The issue of sleeping arrangements came up. Jakob had not been prepared for a daughter-in-law and so he had not designed their rustic living quarters with a woman in mind and her need for privacy. "We will clear space in the loft and let it be her bedroom."

The house, she discovered, was comprised of one large room, really, with a wooden stairway dividing it, leading to a half-story loft above. On the left side of the downstairs was the enormous kitchen with its large black cast-iron stove and a blocky kitchen table with four ladderback chairs. On the right side was what Clara assumed was some sort of living area, dominated by the fireplace. But there was no sofa, no easy chairs, just three canvas cots where the men would sleep.

After dinner, while she did what she could to help Rosita in the kitchen, the men moved one of the cots up to the loft and brought up also her steamer trunk. She would share the loft with other trunks and boxes that Jakob had brought out, and Wilhelm's and Johann's boxes as well. They brought up a washstand, while Rosita provided a white enamel jug filled with water, and a wash basin.

Rosita then wrapped a colorful shawl over her head and shoulders, picked up her basket, said a cheerful "Adiós," and went out into the night.

Clara joined Jakob and his sons at the kitchen table, where Jakob and Wilhelm both brought out tobacco and packed their pipes for a leisurely smoke. She wondered if the great fireplace on the other side of the house was ever used. Perhaps not. She imagined Jakob, thinking of German winters, building this cabin around that big brick fireplace and then discovering that California never got cold enough for a roaring fire when the kitchen stove kept the place warm and cozy enough. Life in this cabin, she imagined, would take place here in the kitchen. Besides, the other side of the cabin was apparently to be the men's bedroom.

She glanced across the table at her husband, brother-in-law, and now new father-in-law. She saw the family resemblance in the flaxen coloring and strong noses, and the differences as well—Wilhelm's beard was soft and yellow and brushed, while Jakob's beard was gray and unkempt and spread down to his chest like that of a Biblical patriarch. And only Johann possessed the fetching hooded eyes.

Clara felt herself overcome with unnamed emotions, feelings she had never experienced before. She felt an intense bond with these men, one of whom was a total stranger, yet from now on she would call him Papa Jakob. It was just the four of them, she thought, in this small cabin, on this wild farm, in the middle of a foreign land. The bond grew. The four of them. . . . Yes. All named Schaller. And with the new bond came a special affection, a kind of love she had never known before. She was happy just to be sitting there and savoring the moment.

Jakob looked content, puffing on his pipe. Wilhelm had produced two bottles of ale, one for himself and one for Johann, brewed and bottled in San Francisco, shipped down by train and sold in one of Lynnville's shops. He had offered one to Clara, but she had declined. She liked watching them sip and relax and withdraw into their thoughts. She assumed those thoughts were much like her own at that moment—the wonder and awe of being here at last, thousands of miles from home, and after weeks of dreaming, hoping, praying, doubting, and planning. Here, on their very own farm, about to produce their very own grapes and wine.

An important threshold, Clara thought.

For herself, the journeying over: she was in her own home, mistress of her own house, and ready to be a proper wife to Wilhelm.

The idea was staggering. Her amazement was spiced with homesickness and a little bit of fear. What if things went wrong? What if her parents needed her? What if the farm wasn't successful? What if Wilhelm was killed in a freak accident?

The crazy ramblings of an insecure, travel-weary mind, she scolded herself. And then her eyes met Johann's. He had been staring at her, an enigmatic expression on his face. She looked away. Papa Jakob was deep into his Bible now. Wilhelm had brought out a notebook and was writing something down. The heat of the kitchen enveloped her, made her go soft and cozy. She looked at Johann again, still watching her.

And then, with tremendous weariness stealing over her, Clara rose from the table, bid the men good night, and modestly retired to the loft. The men remained at the kitchen table, making plans for planting the dormant, bare-root grapevines that Wilhelm had brought from Germany. It had to be done as soon as possible, as late spring was already upon them. They discussed posts and stakes and cordon wires for the new trellises, and hiring more migrant laborers to help—boring talk that soon had Clara drifting off to sleep, but not without first wondering if tonight was going to be her wedding night at last, if Wilhelm was going to take advantage of the privacy—of which they had had none on the ship and the train—and visit her bed.

He did not.

*　　*　　*

SHE AWOKE TO A BRIGHT dawn with a rooster crowing and sounds of industry downstairs. She stretched on the rickety canvas cot and blinked at the plain wooden ceiling slanting close to her head. She didn't mind. It had felt good to sleep in a bed that didn't move. Making use of the chamber pot and washing at the washstand, she brushed her hair and pinned it up—no more girlish ringlets, now that she was married; she then dressed in yesterday's outfit, making a mental note to unpack her trunk and hang up fresh clothes as soon as possible.

Downstairs in the kitchen, she found a cheerful Rosita at the stove. By the plates and cups on the table, Clara deduced that the men had already eaten. Breakfast, it appeared from the remnants, had consisted of tortillas and beans and coffee. Clara noticed an empty tin can by the kitchen sink; sticking up out of it was an artificial flower, a faded pink peony. No doubt put there by Rosita. And she thought: No matter how hard their lives, women always try to make things prettier.

Rosita, Clara had learned, left every night and returned each morning. She lived with her family in the Mexican camp Clara had seen the day before, about half a mile from the Schaller property—a collection of tents and small shacks with open campfires and dogs and children running about, laundry strung on lines. These were the workers on the nearby farms, itinerant laborers who followed the crops and the seasons. The women worked in nearby farmhouses, took in laundry, and had small gardens where they raised vegetables to sell at the roadside. Mostly they were from Mexico, but from Guatemala, Honduras, and El Salvador as well—illegal immigrants who sneaked across the southern border of the United States for a better life.

Clara stepped outside where she saw in the morning sunlight what she had not, in her weariness, seen the day before—a farmyard with chickens, a horse trough, a pump for well water. There was a small barn and stable and a corral for a few horses. And an outhouse with a crescent moon carved into the door. Clara assumed this was the outdoor toilet, built over a pit. Beyond the fence, standing in a field of gnarly old vines and tall dense weeds, were old stone buildings, roofless and tumbling down. She looked around. The car that had brought them from Santa Barbara was gone.

It had been a new experience, riding in an automobile. Clara had only ever traveled anywhere by foot or bicycle or, for special occasions, by carriage. Only last year, the first motorcar had come through her village, loud and stinking, but everyone had gathered round to admire Dr. Zimmerman's new machine. Clara had now *ridden* in one, and she must write home about it.

She paused for a moment beneath the California sun that was supposed to be like Italy's sun, and she wished in that moment for a glimpse into the future. Nothing grand or full-blown, not all the future spread before her, because Clara wasn't greedy. No, just a quick look to see what this farm was going to be like a few years from now. Wilhelm had said it would be so famous that people would come from miles around just to taste their wine. But Clara wasn't concerned with fame. She wanted to see if there were children in that quick glimpse into the future. She wanted to see herself and Wilhelm, for just a moment, surrounded by adult children and small grandchildren, a whole clan of them, the Schallers of Rhineland-Palatinate, Germany, in all their fruitfulness and glory.

She turned and looked back at the cabin. There was only the one door, apparently, with a long and deep shaded porch with chairs. The windows were screened, and there was a screen door over the heavier wooden one. Rustic, possibly even crude, but that was okay, they were just starting out. The money needed to go into the farm, into the vines and grapes and eventually the wine production. Once they got their footing and started making a profit, they could build a proper house. Clara understood this. She had heard all about it from Wilhelm, but had heard also from her parents how they had started out poor, her father still at university, her mother struggling to cook good dinners on a paltry allowance. And then his years of apprenticeship with an established pharmacist as her mother started having babies and continued to find ways to make ends meet. It was the way all young couples got their start in life. Especially here, in a new world, where there were no ancestral lands to inherit, no generations who preceded them and paved the way for them. Pioneers, starting out new and from scratch.

Clara liked the adventure of it, liked the idea of being the *first* in this place, taking part in designing a new homestead, being the one to decide where the vegetable garden would go and even, when Jakob started building the real house, which rooms were to go for what purpose. The original house on this land, built and lived in by a Spaniard named Don Francisco Diego, had been constructed of stone and adobe; but all that was left were tumbled-down ruins in a weedy field next to the cabin. The Schaller home, when it was finally built, was going to be constructed of solid lumber and would be two stories tall with many fine rooms and furnishings. Clara could see it, and it filled her eyes and mind with a shining vision.

She brought herself out of her dream when she saw Jakob and his sons hitching horses to a wagon. She called "Good morning" to them, and when Johann saw her, he strode over to her. "How are you feeling, Clara?" he asked, the concern obvious in his eyes.

"Still a little weak, but I had great sleep. Are we going somewhere?"

"Father and Wilhelm and I are going into Lynnville for supplies."

"Lynnville! I would love to come." Yesterday, driving through the valley, she had been struck by the isolation of the farmhouses. Neighbors were so far apart. She saw how one could quickly become lonely for the sound of a human voice, and suddenly she wanted to take a look at the town that was to become her lifeline to the world.

He hesitated, and when Wilhelm came up, he too paused; and then Jakob said, "No, she is not strong enough."

That was all Clara needed to hear. His first impression of her had been that of an invalid being lifted down from a train and then carried from a car. She needed to correct that at once. "I really am up to it, and I must send word to my parents that we have arrived safely."

Jakob thought a letter would do just as well, but he understood her urgency. A letter would take weeks to reach her family. Normally not one to spend on extravagances, Jakob allowed that this was a necessity. And it was only fair to the people at the other end. He knew how anxious his own sons had been when he left Bremerhaven one year prior. He, too, had sent a cablegram with one word: Arrived.

Jakob held out a hand. "I will go to the telegraph office and send the cablegram for you."

"But . . . there are things in town that I need to buy."

Her eyes met his, he thought about it, then he shrugged and said, "You are welcome to come along if you want to."

They went in a wagon and a buggy, the only conveyances at the Schaller farm, and as Wilhelm guided the buggy down rutted trails, Clara got a better look at her new home.

The old vineyard was not as dilapidated as she had imagined. Certainly, the long rows of trellised vines were not lush and heavy with fruit, but neither were they withered stalks. She had heard how Jakob had labored to bring the old vines back, and that he had certainly done. Acres and acres, as far as she could see, showed thick, gnarly vines sprouting green growth—the miracle of revival.

And not just the old Spanish vineyard, but there were flowers as well— the countryside was brilliant with wild columbine, iris, germanium, and rose, growing out of ditches or climbing over boulders and grassy knolls, while overhead white puff-clouds sailed ahead of an east–west wind. She saw a hawk, high up, riding the currents, wings majestically outspread.

Clara thought about the man at her side, Wilhelm, wordlessly guiding the horse. She couldn't wait for their wedding night. Was he thinking about it, too? But where would they find the privacy?

The nearby town of Lynnville had been founded thirty years earlier by men from New York and Boston, recognizing a fertile valley that would one day be one of this country's biggest crop producers—with California sunshine and fertile soil and Mediterranean climate, anything could grow here. The Americans bought land near the river, platted the town in a grid of numbered streets, and named it after Seamus Lynn, who held the most shares in the new town and became its first mayor. Then they advertised in newspapers and magazines Back East, offering lots for sale at reasonable prices. They also put together delightful pamphlets to be sent to Europe to attract immigrant farmers hankering after land of their own on sizeable acreage—immigrants who came from an Old World with a history of aristocratic privilege, peasantry, and serfdom where for centuries a man couldn't hope for himself or his sons to rise above the station they had been born into.

There was no electricity in Lynnville, but there was talk of it coming. Riding down the dusty street, Clara felt strange and alienated. This was not like home. Here, there were no cobblestones paving the street, no whitewashed brick buildings that had stood for centuries. These store-fronts were wooden and plain and had been built only thirty years ago, or even less. She saw strangers in the street, whose culture and language were not hers. What sort of holidays did Americans celebrate? What customs must she be careful to uphold? What new traditions was she going to embrace?

Their buggy trotted past a storefront with a sign that said, in bright gold lettering, JOSEF DECKER, EXPERT SHOE AND BOOT MAKER. And Clara gave a cry of delight. Josef and Hilde were part of the immigrant group. They had traveled the thousands of miles together and had parted ways where the road from Santa Barbara crested a ridge. Now here they were, thanks to Jakob ordering the painted sign ahead of time, ready to start business. In the window, Clara saw a smaller hand-lettered sign: PIANO LESSONS OFFERED.

It filled her soul with joy and gladness to know that friends were right here, friends from her village on the Rhine, friends who shared *her* customs and traditions and language, and she made a promise to herself that she would come back very soon, visit their new shop and see how they were getting on. Perhaps, she thought in excitement, in a week or two, after everyone was settled, she and Wilhelm should hold a party out at the farm, a reunion of the little immigrant group as a way of reminding themselves that, although it might seem as though they were all alone in a strange land, they were not.

Jakob brought the wagon to a halt in front of the "feed & seed" store, and Wilhelm pulled the buggy up next to it. As they all climbed down, they discussed their needs. Clara's father had given her money to send them a telegram by trans-Atlantic cable. But it was Reichsmarks. When she explained this to Jakob, he took the money and gave her a dollar for the cable.

"Might I have more money, please?"

"What for?" Jakob said.

"I need to buy a few things."

"Things?"

She paused. She had heard Mama ask Papa for money many times, and he had always gladly handed it over, no questions asked. Nonplussed, Clara said, "We need a few things. I will buy them. But I have no money." She hated sounding like a beggar. And she did, in a way, already have money. But Wilhelm had immediately taken it after the wedding and had held onto it since.

Jakob lowered his blond, bushy brows. "What things? *We* can buy whatever you need."

What things? Well, she didn't exactly know. She needed to look, didn't she? Find out what sort of shops there were in this small town, what was offered, what struck her fancy. How could she know ahead of time? But as the three men stood there staring at her, Clara looked up and down the street and saw a small shop just a few doors down. O'BRIENS' HABERDASH-ERY. She did not understand the sign, but she saw in the window that they were a seller of notions: scissors, sewing needles, threads, buttons, pins, collar stays, ribbons, pincushions, lace. Clara smiled. Here was familiar territory. Some things were universal. Whether one was in America or Germany or China, a needle and thread were a needle and thread.

She would start mending clothing that had gotten torn and frayed during the journey.

"There," she said, pointing, and the three turned. "Oh," Jakob said. He reached into his pocket and counted out some coins.

"We will meet back here," Jakob said, and he and his sons strode off toward the bigger stores where bigger merchandise was sold—feed and grain sacks, pitchforks, horse collars, tools, and farm equipment,

The interior of the haberdashery was quiet, with a few customers browsing among the shelves and tables displaying everything from tailor's chalk to the very latest in modern treadle sewing machines. Clara walked among the displays, enjoying the freedom of browsing, inspecting, comparing, without really knowing what she wanted or if she really wanted anything. After weeks of travel and sickness, of being always worried about making connections or losing one's luggage, of having no time alone and being always filled with anxiety, it was such luxury to walk around a quiet shop and peruse their selections.

A woman behind the counter spoke out, and, after she repeated herself, Clara turned and realized the woman was talking to her. "I'm sorry," Clara said, "I don't speak English."

The woman—in her thirties and very full-figured in a black bombazine dress that made her look a little severe—pursed her lips and said something again, very slowly, Clara realized, as if that would make the English that much easier to understand. Although Clara had been familiarizing herself with the language, learning words and trying to teach herself from a workbook, she had a long way to go before she would speak or understand it.

"She wants you to buy something."

Clara turned to find a portly gentleman in a bowler hat and a prodigious handlebar moustache grinning at her. He had spoken German, but with a difficult accent. He was nicely dressed, with a checkered waistcoat under his black coat, and she saw graying hair beneath the hat. He had an olive complexion and she thought he looked Italian. "Arturo Ballerini," he said with a slight bow. "Did I see you ride in with Jakob Schaller?"

"Yes," she said with a smile. She wondered if this was the Italian vintner Jakob had written about in his letters. "I am his daughter-in-law and I believe you own the farm next to ours." Then she said: "So, I am supposed to buy something? Is that what the woman is saying? I can't just look?"

He lowered his voice, even though the lady behind the counter didn't speak German. "Mrs. O'Brien is an impatient woman. She does not like browsers. Once you buy something, you can look all you want."

"It seems backward."

"Indeed it does."

Clara approached the counter where all manner of sewing materials, magazines, and dress patterns were laid out. She examined the goods under the glass and decided upon thread, two spools of white, two of black, and a packet of needles. She had to point them out and Mrs. O'Brien removed them and set them on the counter. When she stated the price, Clara shook her head and said, "I'm sorry, I don't understand." So she held out her hand to show Mrs. O'Brien the coins, as had occurred many times in her father's chemist's shop when a foreigner stopped in. Clara always picked out the precise amount, leaving the rest. To her surprise, Mrs. O'Brien took all the coins and rang them into the cash register. Then she wrapped the items in a square of paper and handed them to a startled Clara.

Surely four spools of thread and a packet of needles didn't cost all that much?

Before she could think what to say or do next, Mr. Ballerini stepped up and said, "I believe there has been a mistake."

To Mrs. O'Brien he said something in English, and she instantly took offense. Clara watched as an argument ensued, which she could not follow, but the gist of which she could gather from the way he was pointing to the goods under the glass counter and the numbers that showed on the register. And then he said something that made Mrs. O'Brien pause, purse her lips, grunt "Huh!" and open the register to retrieve some coins. She slapped them down on the counter and walked away.

"Here is your change, Mrs. Schaller," he said, handing the coins to Clara. "She was trying to cheat you."

"Clearly she was denying it. What persuaded her to change her mind?"

He shrugged and said, with a dimpled smile, "I merely pointed out that it would not do her establishment any good should it get out that the O'Briens will cheat foreigners in their store. There are a lot of foreigners in this valley. And more come each day." He leaned forward and she smelled garlic on his breath. "So you are from Germany?"

"I am from a small village in the state of Rhineland-Palatinate."

"And we are from the village of Bignasco in the district of Vallemaggia in Switzerland."

That explained the accent. Mr. Ballerini was Swiss–Italian, from an area that bordered on the German-speaking region of that country.

"You must come and visit our farm," he said. "My daughter is about your age. She speaks German. You could become great friends."

She thanked him for both the invitation and for catching the "mistake" with the change. She was sure Mrs. O'Brien hadn't done it on purpose. As Clara left the shop, she felt suddenly happy. Being surrounded by people who spoke a language she didn't understand (two, if you added in the Spanish) and who did not understand German, it was nice to know that at least *someone* in the valley could bridge the communication gap. And a girl her own age!

At the end of the day, after an evening dinner of chicken enchiladas, rice and beans, and cornbread, ensconced in her own cot in the converted storage room, listening to the men talk in low tones, Clara closed her eyes and drifted off to sleep. She was satisfied with the day's events, and she decided she would dedicate tomorrow to being useful. Mending clothes would be a pleasant occupation, and she imagined herself sitting on the porch off the kitchen, where red and orange bougainvillea grew in riotous profusion over the posts and roof. After that, she would see to putting up curtains on their bare windows.

And then, of course, she would find out what Rosita's duties were and how she herself was going to go about running the house.

* * *

CLARA AWOKE FEELING BETTER. She was nearly fully recovered from the influenza that had drained her so. She lay for a moment on her cot, listening to the rooster crowing, enjoying the aroma of Rosita's fried tortillas and beans, rich coffee percolating on the stove. Then she leisurely rose from the bed, stretched, visited the washbasin, got dressed, and went down the creaking stairs and into the kitchen. The men, she noticed, were gone, their cots empty.

"Good morning," she said to the Mexican lady who took such good and capable care of them.

"Good morning, Señora," Rosita replied in an arch tone.

It took Clara a moment to realize what she was looking at. The plump woman with the long braids was not in her usual apron, and was packing a basket on the bare kitchen table—a table that was normally cluttered with Rosita's cooking tools and ingredients. Clara looked around. Where were Rosita's usual signs of culinary industry? Potatoes waiting to be peeled, pots in readiness on the stove, flour and rolling pins. Then she saw the dishes in the sink, all that was left of the early tortillas-and-beans breakfast.

"*Lo siento, Señora,*" Rosita said as she angrily snapped a shawl from the basket and draped it over her shoulders, her gestures quick and abrupt. Through her smattering of German and a pantomime of gestures, Rosita managed to convey that Señor Schaller had told her she was no longer needed.

"You're *leaving*?"

Rosita paused, her lips set in an angry line, then she let forth a torrent of rapid-fire Spanish, none of which Clara understood. But there are certain tones of voice, gestures, and facial expressions that are universal, so that Clara quickly understood that Rosita was not happy to be dismissed after a year of hard work and being faithful to Señor Jakob, who apparently was an ungrateful man to dismiss her without warning or compensatory pay. Clara gathered that Rosita had many mouths to feed and that her family had been relying on her weekly wage.

Rosita turned vigorously and left.

Clara followed her out into the yard, but there was no bringing the woman back. When she saw Jakob coming out of the barn, she went up to him. She noticed he was picking his teeth, which meant he and his sons had breakfasted, leaving none for her. "Papa Jakob, why is Rosita leaving?"

"You were strong enough to ride into town yesterday, so you are strong enough to run the house from now on. We no longer have need of Rosita."

Clara watched him walk off, a gardening hoe resting against his shoulder as he headed in the direction of the nearest rows of vines where already Mexican workers were battling weeds. Wilhelm and Johann were nowhere to be seen.

She went back into the kitchen and stood with her hands on her hips. So the cooking and running of the house was now entirely up to her with no help from a housekeeper or maid. Very well. Clara never turned away from a challenge.

She went back upstairs to open her trunk and bring out the bib apron her mother had given her as a wedding present, tying the waist strings behind her back. The first thing, she decided, was to take inventory.

There was a small pantry off the kitchen. It had been built on the north side of the house, where it received the least sun, and it had a small screened window to allow free circulation of air without allowing flies to enter. The walls, Clara guessed, were extra-thick, keeping the supplies cool. Hanging from hooks in the ceiling were sausages of various kinds, and cuts of meat, smoked and salted. Onions and garlic on strings. In a wooden tub, russet potatoes, only a few sprouted. A barrel of salt pork, and a smaller barrel filled with hard crackers and biscuits. Cans of sardines and salmon. Jars of pickles and pork in brine. Bags of beans, rice, flour, sugar. Canisters containing ground coffee, tea, powdered cocoa. Cans of peaches, soup, carrots, peas. She found nothing fresh—no bread, butter, milk, or cream. There was no ice box in the kitchen, like the one at home in Germany. But then, where would the ice come from?

Looking at all this food made Clara's stomach rumble. As Rosita had left her no breakfast, she had to settle for the scraps that had been left on the men's plates in the sink—remnants of corn tortillas, spoonfuls of beans, cold coffee in the percolator. Then she carried a wooden bucket out to the pump in the yard, filled it, and brought it back inside. But it was cold water. She would need to boil some on the stove for proper washing.

She rued the dismissal of Rosita, but Clara thought that perhaps Papa Jakob was right. Tortillas weren't the same as bread, and beans were no substitute for potatoes and sauerkraut. The ground beef or shredded pork that filled tacos and enchiladas couldn't hold a candle to sauerbraten and wiener schnitzel. So Clara understood that the three men were counting on her to cheer up their dinner table. And after all, they worked hard in the fields, breaking their backs digging holes and stringing up trellises and carefully planting bare-root cuttings in faithful rows. They deserved a good meal that tasted of home.

The stove was a large square cast-iron monster with a belly for burning wood, an oven for baking, and, on top, four burners and a square griddle. The stovepipe went up through a hole in the ceiling to vent the smoke. Opening the firebox, she saw some embers. Next to the stove was a hod filled with firewood, and a basket filled with sticks for kindling. She would have this going in no time, and soon have hot water for washing the dishes and cleaning up the kitchen.

She then scrubbed the kitchen table, collected chamber pots to empty and clean, filled washbasins and pitchers with fresh water from the pump, swept the floor with a broom, straightened the sheets and blankets and pillows on the cots, hung up the men's clothes, and opened windows for airing out the room; then she gave thought to dinner. Because Jakob had determined it was time wasted to return to the house during the day for the noon dinner, as they would have back home in Germany, he had decided they would adopt the American meal plan: a hearty breakfast, a cold lunch out in the fields, with the main hot meal in the evenings. In Germany, dinner was at noon. In California, it was at six. It would take some adjusting to.

Clara decided on grilled sausage, fried potatoes, and canned peas.

At sundown, the men came into the yard, washing first at the water pump and then stamping dirt off their boots as they climbed the porch steps. They were laughing, even Jakob. "Smells good!" Johann declared when they came into the kitchen.

But as they scraped their chairs back and took seats at the table and Clara served them, Jakob frowned darkly. "Sausages?"

"After all the beans and rice you've been eating, I thought—" Clara began.

"Sausages are for Sunday only. They are too costly for every night."

"I didn't know. I shall remember next time." She glanced at Wilhelm and received a wink in return.

All day long she had thought about him, about the coming night. Would he find a way for them to have some privacy? The cabin was so small, you couldn't think loud thoughts without the others hearing them.

She sent him a secretive smile and joined them at the table for grace.

They spent the evening with Jakob smoking his pipe and reading his Bible, Wilhelm jotting notes as usual with a bottle of ale, and Johann deep into one of his university texts. Clara scrubbed dishes and pots in hot soapy water, pleased with herself on her first day on the farm.

She looked wistfully at her husband, his flaxen head bent over his page of notes.

She wanted to sleep with Wilhelm, to have him introduce her to the physical love of husband and wife, but how were they to do it in this half-house with an open loft?

* * *

CLARA WAS STARTLED OUT of her morning languor by a sudden banging on her floor. She heard Johann's voice saying "Father, she is still weak from the illness and the traveling."

"She must be made to understand," Jakob shouted. "We cannot go out to the fields with no breakfast."

Clara staggered out of bed in her nightgown. "I'm sorry!" she said to the men below. "I am up now and will see to breakfast."

But by the time she had washed and dressed, she came down to find the men gone.

She looked around the kitchen. The stove had not been lit. There was no coffee in the pot. What had they eaten? And what had they taken with them for their noon lunch? She felt ashamed. They worked hard. They deserved proper meals.

She went into the other side of the cabin and found a rat's nest. Wilhelm's and Johann's suitcases and valises were open and had been picked through. The two cots were rumpled with bedclothes, and a pile of blankets on the floor indicated that one of them had slept there. In shock, she realized that someone had given up his own cot so that Clara could sleep in it.

Which one, she wondered? Who had given up the comfort of a bed for Clara's sake?

Going up to the loft to her steamer trunk, she lifted out a thick quilt, given to her by her mother, and took it back downstairs, where she set about straightening the cots and making a more comfortable bed on the floor using the soft quilt. Then she emptied the chamber pots, rinsed them out at the yard pump, and left them to air and dry in the sun. Likewise with the washbasins, cleaning them, drying them, and restoring them to their stands, with pitchers of fresh water.

It was another day of lighting the stove, hauling water from the pump in the yard, boiling it on the stove, emptying it into the sink, scrubbing the dishes, dumping the greasy water outside. Then, filling a pot at the pump, putting it on the stove and getting water hot for the evening dinner, which this time would be canned beans with salt pork stirred in as they simmered, and boiled potatoes, which called for more water.

Much of her time, Clara discovered, consisted of fetching and disposing of water, and keeping the wood burning in the stove and the fire going.

Although he had left for the fields, Jakob suddenly came into the kitchen, startling her. "The chickens tore into the sack of feed and scattered it!" he said. "Now we shall have to buy more."

"Why did they do it, do you suppose?"

"They were hungry. You are supposed to *feed* them!"

"*I* am?"

"Do you see anyone else around here taking care of the chickens? And where are the eggs?"

"I have no idea. Where *are* they?"

"In the hen house. You are to collect them every morning."

"I'm sorry. I didn't know that."

As he turned to stalk out, Clara said, impulsively, "Papa Jakob, do you think I could have some help?"

He turned at the door. "Help?"

She saw by his blank expression that he hadn't a clue what she was talking about. "Perhaps Rosita could come back."

"You'll manage all right," he said. Then he softened a little and said, "You'll learn. Don't worry."

After dinner, as she scrubbed the stove clean and emptied the ashes and made sure embers were still warm and could be re-kindled in the morning, and as she hauled water in from the pump and boiled it and washed the dishes and dumped the water outside, she looked at Jakob puffing away on his pipe and reading the Bible, Wilhelm scribbling notes to himself, Johann with his head over chemistry calculations. She thought of how it had been at home in Germany: after a light supper, they would spend the evenings with Clara's mother playing the piano while Clara and her father engaged in a game of chess by the fire. They would hear the sounds of people and horses and wagons in the street below. A lively scene. Not dead and quiet like this place.

She realized that there was a lot about this new life that would need getting used to. She had not expected things to be *quite* so different. But she was determined to make a go of it, keep her spirits up and show herself and others what she was capable of. She had been taught cooking and sewing and taking care of a house. But it had been a house in a town with indoor running water, and a housekeeper who also cooked, and a maid of all work. She had had help—or, rather, Clara was the one who had done the helping. And she had certainly never had to feed chickens! Rural life came as a shock after growing up in a village where neighbors were cheek by jowl. Here, the nearest neighbor was miles away. She had

always been surrounded by people—her mother, father, servants, customers in the shop, her friends. And now there was the language barrier and
trying to figure out the money. Somehow, the adventurous heroines in
her novels seemed never to have these troubles, or a handsome stranger
intervened at just the right moment.

All right, then, she thought now, stubbornly, ready to tackle anything.
I know enough of human history to know that mankind faced one crisis
after another, and all were met, faced, and solved. The Schaller farm will
be no less than all of humanity.

*   *   *

IT WAS NOW TEN days since their arrival in the valley, and Clara was
frustrated with placing sardines and crackers on the dinner table, with
limp asparagus from a can, seasoned with salt pork. At least the coffee was
sweetened with canned milk and sugar.

Clara wanted to offer her hard-working men more variety. She
wished she could smarten up evening dinners with cold milk and sharp
cheese. A wagon came by every day from a nearby dairy farm, but Jakob
had told Clara they were no longer buying from them. Sadly, she had to
explain through gestures that they had no need of dairy products, and
watch the wagon move on. The Schallers would have to make do with the
canned milk in the pantry, and no cheese at all.

There was a Guatemalan named Torrez who came by every few days in
his wagon with freshly caught rabbits and ducks for sale. But Clara had no
idea how to skin and cook wild game. He also sold tortillas made by his
wife, and corn cakes, and bell peppers stuffed with rice and tomato sauce.
He offered winter and spring crops: sugar snap peas, red cabbage, cauliflower, artichokes, and apricots. Clara would have loved to take some of
the big earth-covered carrots. But she had no money.

Clara, who thought herself no clever cook in the first place, was to
make do with what was in the Schaller larder.

When Sunday came along, Clara had hoped they would put on their
best clothes and ride into town to attend a church service. Perhaps have
a few conversations with the other young wives who had traveled from
Germany with them—Frieda, Hilda, Truda, and Dagmar—and gain some
helpful cooking advice from them. But Jakob had said there would be no
use in it, as the church service was in English and a collection plate was
passed around with all eyes calculating who gave and how much. Besides,
he said, the good Lord knew where the Schallers were and would hear

their prayers whether they were in church or at their farm. He read aloud from the Bible, and then he led them in prayer.

Jakob firmly obeyed the injunction to keep the Sabbath holy—no working in the fields, no business transactions, no engaging in commerce. However, he also didn't believe in idleness, as this was what brought a man to Satan's attention. The compromise was to engage in "restful" pursuits, stay at the homestead and do small things that needed to be done but didn't take a man's mind off the Lord. Jakob didn't think God would fault a man for wanting to repair harnesses and leather belts and shoes while respecting the day on which the Lord Himself rested (although Jakob secretly doubted that God ever really rested, there was so much to be vigilant about).

Clara didn't understand her father-in-law, who was so stern most of the time. She had seen moments of softness and kindness, but he drove his sons and daughter-in-law with a determined rule. And he drove himself even harder. She wondered why he was so hard on himself. She had glimpsed, on occasion when he didn't know she was watching, the way Jakob would take out his pocket watch, click it open, and stare at it for a long time—too long to merely be checking the hour of the day. She thought she saw a photograph on the inside of the hinged cover. His late wife, perhaps?

But she didn't want to dwell on whatever it was in Jakob Schaller's heart that drove him so. She stared now into the larder at the shelves of cans and packets and canisters of the same things she had been warming up and serving every night—trying to make the table look nice with cloth napkins and polished silverware and wildflowers in a vase, hoping that presentation would somehow make the food seem better. She desperately wanted to please Wilhelm. He did smile at her and peck her on the cheek when he left for the fields in the morning, and thank her for dinner at night. But he had yet to visit her bed, or to make any indication that he even wished to do so.

Last night, she had warmed tomato soup from cans with hard biscuits soaking in it, and salt pork for flavor, and onions that she fried on the griddle. She couldn't serve it two nights in a row. So what for tonight?

She looked at the barrels of crackers and hard biscuits that needed soup or gravy or sauce to be edible. A few days ago, she had asked Papa Jakob if they could go into town and buy some bread, but Jakob had said, "Too costly." He had pointed at the pantry and said, "There is flour in there."

True, but there was no yeast for leavening.

But she wanted to bake something fresh, instead of serving crackers from the barrel. That would please Wilhelm. And Jakob, and Johann too. Johann, who always took a moment to thank her and praise her and tell her how quickly she was adapting to farm life.

In a mixing bowl, she whisked together measures of flour, sugar, and salt, then added water and olive oil, stirring the mixture until she had a sticky dough. Using the rolling pin, and dusting the table with flour, Clara rolled the dough flat. As she did so, with the oven heating the kitchen, and the baking trays ready and dusted with flour, it brought back memories of home and days when she and her mother baked in the kitchen. She missed her mother terribly and wondered if it was too soon to expect mail from home. It had only been ten days since she sent the cablegram. Her mother would have received it and sat down to write a letter. Was it too soon to start checking at the post office for mail?

The dough was ready. Cutting it into cracker shapes, she used a spatula to transfer them to the baking sheets, piercing them with a fork to prevent them from becoming too puffy. She lightly brushed them with olive oil and sprinkled some of the squares with chili powder, others with ground herbs, the rest with light salt, making a variety; then she set the sheets in the oven to bake. The kitchen was soon filled with a wonderful aroma; and when, fifteen minutes later, she saw that the crackers had turned a fetching golden brown, she brought the sheets out to cool.

She tried one. It was very tasty. Not like the stale crackers in the barrel that needed assistance to be palatable. Clara couldn't wait to see the men's reaction.

That evening they came in from the fields, washing first at the well pump, and sitting down to canned beans, canned peas, and salt pork. Three pairs of golden eyebrows rose at the sight of the new crackers. At the last minute, Clara had warmed them in the oven and given them a light brushing with olive oil. Jakob took one and ate it plain. His face lit up. Then Johann and Wilhelm helped themselves, digging into the hot beans with the new crackers and expressing their delight to Clara.

As she stood at the sink later, while the three men debated the pros and cons of trying a new kind of fertilizer (Jakob and Wilhelm firmly supporting old-fashioned cow manure, while Johann promoted factory-produced chemicals), Clara smiled to herself and was pleased with the outcome of the day. It gave her an inner glow to know that she had fed her men a treat that was of her own making. Maybe tomorrow, if she could spare enough butter and sugar, she would try for a cake.

Drying her hands, she left the hot kitchen and went to stand on the porch where the evening breeze had grown chilly. She rubbed her arms and looked up at the stars. To her surprise, she heard music, faintly, from a distance, ebbing and flowing on the night wind—an unexpected mix of guitars, trumpets, violins. And people singing! When the wind shifted, she heard men shouting gleefully, "Yeehaw!" and it sounded like a party. But like nothing she had ever heard in Germany. A different sound, but merry all the same; and she realized it was coming from the direction of the migrant workers' camp. Mexicans and Guatemalans, rising above their poverty and back-breaking labor to celebrate life with music and song.

Clara braved the chilly air and watched the stars and listened to the distant music, while inside the cabin, where Jakob and Wilhelm were remaining firm on the side of cow manure for fertilizer, Johann paused in his argument to allow his eyes to drift to the window where he saw his sister-in-law standing alone, a mysterious smile on her face.

It was the most beautiful smile he had ever seen.

*   *   *

CLARA WAS WOKEN OUT of a deep, dreamless sleep by a sudden movement of her cot. Startled, she wondered if an animal had gotten into the cabin. She was about to call out for help when she realized that it was Wilhelm.

He was wearing only his long-john underwear, his arms, shoulders, and torso bare, and he stood over her for a long, speechless moment as Clara looked up at him, heard the heaviness of his breath, heard also the snores of his father and brother below.

He knelt beside the cot and laid his hand on her face. The light was dim, but Clara saw tenderness in his eyes. She reached out and touched him. She smiled. She had wondered. . . .

When she had thought he would bend to kiss her, he instead startled her by climbing onto the cot, making it groan with shocking loudness in the night silence.

There was little room on the cot, and she feared for a moment that it would break, splinter and collapse in a great thundering sound that would wake the others. "Wait," she murmured.

But Wilhelm's eyes were closed. He was fumbling with the buttons of his long johns.

"Please," she whispered.

And then his face was buried in her neck as his hand dragged her nightgown up and slid under to glide up her bare thigh.

"No," she said in a tight voice. "I'm not—"

He rose up, drawing back so that his face was inches from hers. He was smiling. And then his smile fell. In the pale moonlight streaming through a window, he saw distress on her face. When she had said, "Please," he had thought she was encouraging him. But now he realized she was begging him to stop.

"But Clara," he whispered, and he saw tears spring to her eyes. When he shifted his weight and the cot creaked again, he realized that the snoring had stopped down below.

Then he realized the look on her face had turned to shame. He remembered in shock the proximity to them of his father and brother. Wilhelm had been driven by his carnal need; he hadn't been thinking of Clara's delicate modesty. He backed away, whispering apologies, praying she wouldn't cry. He wanted her, but not like this.

In the morning he avoided her altogether, forgoing eggs and coffee to march straight out into the early dawn and head for the fields with his tools. He plunged himself into his work but was unable to get her face out of his mind. He had wanted only to make love to her, not to have her cringe in horror. He had been mortified. It made him sick to his stomach.

With the determination of a soldier in wartime, he marched down the rows of trellised vines, inspecting the budding flowers for signs of fungus. The merchant at the feed-and-seed store had recommended a special spray to keep the fungus away. But the flowers were looking healthy, for now.

Clara. He couldn't get the look on her face out of his mind. But what was he supposed to do? His sexual desire for her was almost overwhelming. He knew he was clumsy when it came to women. Not like Johann, who was handsome and easy-going and made the girls laugh and flirt. Wilhelm knew he could be a bit of a quiet, methodical man, not unlike his father. But he was honest and faithful and was determined to do right by Clara.

Something would have to be done. He couldn't visit her bed and see a look of fear and shame on her face. And he would never force her. He was not that kind of man.

On the other side of Largo Creek, where the Schaller property had not yet been turned into land for cultivation but was still wild with a thick oak forest, Wilhelm's brother Johann was on his knees digging into the soil. Like his brother, Johann could not concentrate on his work, and it was for the same reason.

During the night, he had heard the creak of the stairs, had seen Wilhelm's hulking shape creeping up to the loft. Had heard the groaning of the cot and some heavy breathing and a kind of long, low moan. A few seconds later, Wilhelm had come back down the stairs.

What had happened? Had Clara said no? Had she not woken up? What was Wilhelm to do? This was no way to live.

But, try as he might to feel sympathy for his brother, Johann could not. His concern was for Clara. How shocking it must be to her maidenly modesty to have to endure the sex act when she knew all the house was listening!

Worse . . . and this was something Johann could barely admit to himself, for it made him hate himself. He couldn't stand the thought of Wilhelm touching Clara, even though they were man and wife. Johann wanted to be the one to touch her, yet she was beyond his reach forever. No, he could *not* be falling in love with his brother's wife. It was immoral, unethical, ungentlemanly, and unsporting—all the virtues he had learned at university. To fall in love with Clara was contemptible and unthinkable. But he did have feelings for her, and was concerned for her safety and comfort.

He had lain awake for the rest of the night. Wilhelm was already deeply asleep, but Johann had been unable to sleep. He had heard soft weeping in the loft above. It was all he could do to keep himself from flying up those stairs and gathering her into his arms, to tell her everything was going to be all right, that someday she was going to have a proper home and servants and a life of ease and comfort, and many friends and no more loneliness—yes, he was keenly aware of her loneliness—but these were things Wilhelm was supposed to say to her. It was not Johann's place. If anything, he must keep these thoughts and urges to himself because they were wrong and sinful.

But there could be nothing wrong or sinful about loving Clara, he argued with himself, with her sweet heart-shaped face and widow's-peak hairline that made her look almost unearthly. An angel from another sphere of heavenly existence. He fell asleep at last, but it was a fitful sleep disturbed by unwanted dreams.

And now, on his knees collecting soil samples to see if these acres could be planted with Riesling cuttings, Johann was troubled by another worry, and it too involved Clara.

He hated watching her at the sink, scrubbing away at pots and pans. The hot water gave her face a feverish glow as she pushed strands of hair from her flushed face. He wished they hadn't had to let Rosita go. Clara could do with help. But they'd had no choice.

What a shock it had been to both himself and Wilhelm to arrive here and be met by bad news: the farm was in trouble. In the past year, disaster had struck their father, and now it was up to Johann and Wilhelm to figure out a way to save it all.

That was their big fear right now. If the bank took the farm, where would they go?

He thought Clara should be told, but he was outvoted. "She's just a girl," his father had said. "She'll get hysterical, and we need level heads."

"I don't want to worry her," Wilhelm had said.

Johann thought his brother underestimated Clara's strength. Still, Johann had to go along with them. And so Clara was not to know that worse things than no privacy and scalding dishwater lay before her.

While his sons were embroiled in their individual labors and singular thoughts, Jakob Schaller allowed his mind to drift as he went about the repetitive task of securing vines onto trellises. He was in the far eastern acres on the other side of Largo Creek, working with Mexican laborers. He paused to put his hands to his lower back and stretch. He looked up and down the rows of young green vines. It had been nearly two weeks since he met the immigrants at the train depot. In the days since, he and his sons had done good work reviving the old Spanish vines. Although some had been beyond help, the majority looked as if they were going to produce a good, sweet harvest.

But he wasn't as joyous as he should have been. There was the problem with the bank, for one thing, and their serious financial situation. And there was Wilhelm and the new wife. He had heard them last night. It was not a decent situation. But Jakob had too much on his mind to have to worry about the problems of newlyweds.

And this was why his thoughts drifted as he tended his vines, the problem of love and the sweet agony it brought to a man. He was thinking of his darling Kätzchen, the love of his life who had died in his arms years ago, and the pain was as sharp as if it had happened only yesterday.

I still miss you, my love, after all these years, his soul cried silently up to the blue California sky. I wish you could see the boys. Wilhelm is a born farmer, but you really should see Johann—he is so smart, such a student! A scientist. You would be proud of him, my Kätzchen. I am building this farm not for myself but for my sons—*our* sons. This is what I promised you when the Good Lord took you from me, and no bank, *nothing*, will divert me from this path. I promise you, Kätzchen, that I will fight for that dream until my dying day—no matter what it takes.

And then perhaps, by the grace of God, my dearest Kätzchen, my soul can find peace at last.

* * *

CLARA WAS DOWN TO her last clean blouse. Stockings and underthings as well. Towels and kitchen linens, aprons—all soiled. On the men's side of the cabin, dirty clothes had been heaped in a corner.

It was time to tackle the laundry.

This was one household task Clara had never been taught, as Eva Heinze believed that the wife of the town chemist should not have to redden her hands or break her back over such menial labor. Once a week, a boy had come to pick up the washing and take it to a laundress in the village. Three days later, everything was returned clean, ironed, and folded. But there was no laundress here. Just Clara. She tried not to see this new task as an obstacle but as a challenge, something to be figured out and conquered.

Clara had seen the big washtubs at the back of the house, the clotheslines stretched between poles. She recalled seeing clean laundry hanging there the day they had arrived. So Rosita must have done the washing.

"Papa Jakob," she asked before he left for the fields. "May I please have help with the laundry? I'm not sure I can do this all myself. Just for one day, please."

He fixed stern eyes on her. Clara tried to be understanding. Jakob had not been expecting one of his sons to bring a wife. And now that she was here, he had every right to expect her to be a useful housewife. His stern eyes continued to skewer her, but then she saw a softening, a relenting, as if he too were working this ridiculous situation over in the mind. She knew that he had big responsibilities himself, just as her own father had with his chemicals and medicines and the need to dispense just the right formula at just the right dosage. Jakob had every right to expect his home to be run smoothly and without his assistance. She also understood his need to be frugal with expenses. But she kept humility foremost on her face until finally he said, "I will send for Rosita. But just for wash day."

Clara was surprised, but also pleased, to see Rosita arrive with two women eager to get to work. Clara was further surprised at the amount of work that went into laundering. In the chicken yard of the Schaller farm, the three Mexican women labored over large tubs that required great amounts of hot water, which Clara kept hauling from the pump and boiling on the stove. The clothes and bed linens were soaked and then scrubbed with strong soap: heavy water-soaked sheets and men's work clothes and Clara's dresses all required rubbing and pounding and stirring and wringing, first the whites and then the darks, an endless labor of soaking, vigorously washing, rinsing, and wringing, and finally hanging on the line.

They were blessed with a warm spring breeze that soon dried the washing. As they took everything down just before sunset, folding everything neatly, Clara marveled that back in the Rhine Valley the day would be gray and damp, while here only golden rays came down from the California sky.

When Jakob and his sons got home at sundown, Clara watched the men at the pump as they stripped to the waist and splashed cold water on their skin, sticking their heads under the tap and shaking like dogs. She thought to take fresh clean towels out to them, and clean shirts, proud of her day's accomplishment, trying not to stare at knotted muscles and clearly defined sinews. Even Jakob, who was old—fifty, at least—was remarkably fit.

Rosita, anxious to get to the migrant camp, held out her hand for the day's pay. To Clara's surprise, Jakob was furious to find he must pay for two extra women instead of just Rosita as he had planned. He informed Rosita that next time it must just be herself, for that was all he could afford. It was a curiously international dispute, Clara thought, conducted in English, Spanish, and German.

Rosita and the women left, and the men came in starving for dinner, to wolf down pickled pork from a jar and canned sauerkraut, along with potatoes Clara had managed to boil and slice and fry while also helping with the laundry. As she watched them—thinking about Wilhelm's disastrous visit to her cot and wondering if he would try it again, afraid that he might and yet praying that he would, torn for her desire to be with Wilhelm but dreading the thought of the other two downstairs, listening in the darkness to something they had no right to hear, wishing Johann had not been witness to her acute embarrassment—she thought about Papa Jakob. What had happened in his past to make him so stingy with money? Thrift was a virtue, but no one admired cheapness.

After dinner, while Clara was washing up, the three men went to their usual seats at the table. Using Clara's German-English dictionary, Jakob read the farm reports in the Lynnville newspaper and studied the almanac for the coming week. Wilhelm smoked a pipe and gazed contentedly at nothing, while Johann wrote letters to school friends back home. After the dishes were done and put away, Clara joined them with her sewing box, to sit and mend the torn pocket of her apron by the light of the lantern.

Johann paused in his letter-writing to look at her for a long moment. Then he said, "Clara, did Wilhelm ever tell you about the time he was invited by the school choirmaster to join the choir?"

She looked up from her sewing. "No," she said, and saw that Wilhelm was grinning. "Brother, not that story again," he said.

"It's true," Johann said, and now they had Jakob's attention too. "Wilhelm was fourteen and he hadn't even tried out for the choir. The choirmaster himself, who was a very important man, had approached him in the classroom and said that Wilhelm was needed in the choir. Well, that was a rare distinction, you know, to be—"

"Sought out and invited by the choir master himself," Wilhelm interjected.

"Well, Father here was so proud that he bragged about it to all his friends, his talented son who had been recruited into the choir by the master himself."

Jakob nodded vigorously. "Indeed I was proud. It was an honor!"

"And then one day Father asked Wilhelm how choir practice was going, what were they singing and so on—"

"And I told him," Wilhelm interjected again, "that I wasn't to sing but just to mouth the words. Turns out they needed a boy of my height to even out a row."

All three Schallers threw back their heads in roaring laughter, and it reminded Clara of the picnic she and Wilhelm and Johann had shared in the glade overlooking the Rhine, with Johann bringing his quiet brother to life until they were finishing each other's sentences, like entertainers on a stage. She smiled and resumed her mending, telling herself: It will be like this always.

*　　*　　*

CLARA HAD FINALLY ADJUSTED to the rhythm of a farm day, waking up as the first pale light came through the windows, jumping out of bed as the rooster crowed, using the chamber pot and washstand, getting dressed, and hurrying down the stairs.

By the time Jakob was up, hoisting his suspenders over his enormous haystack shoulders and scratching his rump, Clara had the coffee percolating in the pot on the stove and eggs and potatoes sizzling on the griddle.

She sent the three men off to the fields with lunchboxes packed with buttered flat bread, thermoses of soup, jars of pickles, and locally grown olives. One such day, Clara was scrubbing the dishes when she saw a wagon pull into the yard.

She recognized the visitor as the gentleman who had rescued her from being overcharged at the O'Briens' haberdashery, Mr. Ballerini from the next farm over. She had learned that in the past year Jakob had done business with the Swiss grower. When Jakob had first arrived, taking over the abandoned Spanish rancho, Mr. Ballerini had been very helpful in discussing the local soil, making recommendations for fertilizer, telling him which merchants to trust in Lynnville, generally helping out a fellow immigrant.

"Good day to you, Mrs. Schaller!" he called robustly as he secured the reins and climbed down from the wagon. He was dressed in a white jacket and white trousers, with a red waistcoat underneath. On his head, a bowler hat was set at an angle. A bright smile appeared beneath his prodigious handlebar moustache.

She came down the steps wiping her hands on her apron. "Good morning, Mr. Ballerini."

He doffed his hat and his thick, longish hair retained a bowler shape, with the sides sticking out like handles by which he could be picked up. He looked around. "I have been remiss in paying my new neighbors a visit. But here I am! I was hoping to meet Jakob's sons."

"They're working in the vineyards."

He reached into the back of the wagon, not an easy feat as he was short and rather portly. "I have brought you a proper welcome gift." It was a bottle of wine—Chianti, in a fat bottle in a straw basket with the Ballerini winery label on it. "I have also brought your mail."

"Our mail!" Her heart leapt.

"It is what we do out here so far from town. When one of us goes into Lynnville, we collect our mail and that of our neighbors as well. We help each other in this way." She greedily accepted the bundle and although she wanted to madly go through the offerings—they seemed to be magazines of some sort—Clara restrained herself and politely asked after Mr. Ballerini's wife and daughter.

He crossed himself in the Catholic manner. "My dear wife has gone to her reward, may she rest. But my daughter Feliciana is well, thank you. For the moment, she is up in Monterey visiting her sister."

"I look forward to meeting her."

"And I look forward to you meeting her. The two of you have a lot in common."

"When will she be back?" Clara asked, eager to meet a young woman of her own age who spoke German and who shared something in common.

Mr. Ballerini looked away just then, and Clara thought she saw a strange expression on his face. And when he said, "Ah . . . her sister is not well at the moment. I do not know when Feliciana will come home. . . ," she thought his tone evasive. And then she decided it was her imagination.

She changed the subject as she suddenly realized she was starved for news—of the outer world, of her friends in Lynnville. She had been so focused on overcoming challenges and making herself fit into this farm life that she had not realized how isolated she had become.

"Yes, yes," he said upon her query about the others. "The photographer has opened his studio. The baker is doing well with his breads and pastries. The piano teacher has two pupils."

Clara grinned with joy to know that they were all settling in and doing well.

But as she watched him guide the wagon out of the yard, Clara thought it odd that he referred to his other daughter as Feliciana's sister without once mentioning her name. And then she chalked it up to the man's German dialect, which Clara was going to have to accustom herself to.

He left her mind as soon as she opened her hands to savor the arrival of mail. The magazines turned out to be mail-order catalogs, and there was a letter from someone named Schaller back in Frankfurt.

It was a thick envelope. Clara had learned that her father-in-law was a voracious newspaper reader. There were hundreds of German-language newspapers in America, but he couldn't afford a subscription from one of the many publications coming out of New York, Pennsylvania, Ohio, or Indiana. He had a cousin send a Frankfurt newspaper by mail, and although the news was weeks late, nonetheless it was a vital link with home.

She laid it all out on the kitchen table for Papa Jakob. But as she returned to the potatoes that needed peeling, she was drawn back to the catalogs. She knew that Jakob never ordered from them: they would be too expensive. But he used them in the outhouse. Clara had never really looked at the book that hung from a string next to the toilet, simply tearing off a page as she needed it. It was too dark in the privy to see what was on the page, and then it went down the hole.

But now she looked, flipping the pages in the light of day, scanning the seductive offerings from retailers called Sears and Roebuck, Montgomery Ward, and Bloomingdale's in New York. And as she scanned the illustrations of clothing, accessories, and housewares, each picture accompanied by a description of the item, it occurred to her that this would be a good aid to learning English. A drawing of gloves said, "Gloves" underneath. Shoes said, "Shoes." A set of what was clearly tools for a small garden said, "Garden tools" underneath. Although she was not sure of the pronunciation, she worked through each one as best she could.

Keeping the Bloomingdale's catalog and leaving the rest for the outhouse, Clara decided she must learn five new words a day, starting with Page One: Ladies' Cashmere Coats and Jackets.

That evening, when the men came home and she set their dinner before them, Clara told them about Mr. Ballerini's visit, adding that she was looking forward to meeting Feliciana.

"Who?" said Jakob as he spooned buttered peas into his mouth.

"Mr. Ballerini's daughter." She knew that Papa Jakob had visited the Ballerini farm several times in the year that he had been here. Surely he had encountered the girl.

He shook his head. "Never even heard of her."

Clara paused in ladling the soup. Maybe she was away a lot, if the sister was sick a lot. And anyway, when men got together to discuss business, the subject of a daughter wouldn't come up often, would it?

Still . . . Clara sensed a mystery surrounding the daughter of the congenial Swiss vintner, and her eagerness to meet Feliciana grew.

*   *   *

CLARA TOOK STOCK OF the larder and found they were low on everything, from canned peas and sardines, to flour and sugar. The canned butter was gone, as it didn't last long without an ice box. She had enough salt pork, crackers, canned soup, and strawberry preserves to last two more days. So she informed Jakob. He absorbed the news somberly, the way he had absorbed the news from the paper his cousin had sent from Frankfurt. After a moment, he nodded and said, "We shall go into town and buy new supplies."

Clara could barely sleep from the excitement. She would pay visits to Hans and Frieda, Josef and Hilde, Fritz and Truda, and Siegfried and

Dagmar, and see how the bakery was doing, and the shoemaking trade, and the tailoring and dressmaking. It was going to be so good to see them again. It seemed far longer than just three weeks since they had stood on the ridge overlooking the valley and said good-bye. Now she would walk into the shops and see the breads and pastries, and talk to Truda about her piano students, and see what photographs Fritz had taken, and she would tell them about life on the farm (glamorizing it a little, of course).

The next morning, Jakob and his sons set off in the wagon, which was loaded with posts, wires, and trellises for new vines. At sundown, Johann and Wilhelm returned on foot, stopping at the pump as they always did, to wash away the dust and sweat of the day. Clara came out with towels. "Where is Papa Jakob?"

"He went into town for supplies," Wilhelm said, pausing to brush a strand of hair from her forehead. He hadn't stopped thinking about her all day, as he had put his mind to the design and construction of a room addition to the cabin. *Their* room.

"He *what*?" she said in astonishment.

And at that moment, as if summoned, the wagon appeared on the rutted lane coming up to the house, and Clara watched with burning cheeks as Jakob smiled and waved and brought the wagon into the yard, loaded with sacks of flour, sugar, and corn meal, and packets of coffee and tea, and barrels of salt pork, crackers, and hard biscuits, and baskets of potatoes and onions and a gunny sack filled with cans of soup, sardines, shrimp, peas, and carrots. Clara kept her fury and disappointment bottled up as she helped them carry everything into the house. How dare he deprive her of a visit to the town! To her friends! Surely he must have known how dearly she would have loved to go, she thought bitterly as she noticed that there was no milk, no cheese, no fresh meat or fruit or vegetables to alleviate the monotony of their coming meals. Purchases *she* would have made had she been allowed to go along.

Surely, she thought with a dark mind and a heart suddenly as hard as a brick, the man wasn't that blind!

*　　*　　*

IT WAS SUNDAY, AND Clara awoke to find the world blanketed in white. She had read about coastal fogs that rolled into the inland valleys during spring and fall. As she stood looking out a window, she felt as if the farm were swathed in cotton wool. It made her feel as if she was moving through an unreal world. She had awakened to find tears on her pillow. She had been dreaming of Germany and crying in her sleep.

And now she felt trapped, without even the hope of a ride into town to look forward to.

Clara's people welcomed celebrations and jumped at any chance to have a party, to sing and dance: Carnival marking the beginning of Lent, then Easter, Midsummer Night, the autumn wine festivals, St. Martin's feast in November, right up to Christmas. Weddings, births, and even funerals were celebrated with costumes, ceremony, and colorful tradition—any occasion to wear masks and drink wine. Clara missed that. She had never felt so lost. What was she doing here? *Mama, I made a mistake. I want to go home.*

But she didn't want to be a failure. She didn't want to let Wilhelm and his father and brother down. More, she didn't want to let herself down. Everyone back home—her parents, friends, neighbors, customers in her father's shop—had said how brave and courageous she was to be embracing such an undertaking. She had blushed and accepted the praise with self-effacing modesty, secretly thinking *Yes, I am rather brave, aren't I?* And that had been her dream all her life, to be courageous like the heroines in her novels.

But now she was a mess of confused emotions again, thinking she would never fit in, she would never properly be Wilhelm's wife. Not as long as their bed was in a loft without privacy. And there was the promise of Mr. Ballerini's daughter, but a girl who was shrouded in mystery.

Thinking about Feliciana and how desperately she wanted to meet her, and thinking of the sharp disappointment of Jakob going into town without taking her along, it suddenly came to Clara what was ailing her.

People. This was what was missing from her life. Aside from the one or two Mexican farmhands who spoke no German, she saw not another human being. With a sigh, she turned away from the window, wondering if homesickness had a cure and how one went about finding it.

Out in the foggy yard, Johann was deep in thought as he sharpened tools, a chore his father deemed suitable for the Sabbath. Jakob and Wilhelm had ridden to the Ballerini farm to pay a neighborly visit, as one did on the holy day of rest (although the visit was actually to barter for some bottles of wine). Johann saw Clara come out to stand in the yard and gaze into the white mist that was already dissipating. He wondered what she was thinking. She had been quiet for the past few days. Filled with a kind of melancholy. He knew she was lonely. This was an isolated life. He wished there was something he could do for her.

Laying aside his tools, he went to her side. "Tell me what you are thinking," he said quietly.

She looked up into his eyes. "I was thinking of my village, built on a slope, the narrow streets terraced like vineyards so that one always has a view of the Rhine. I miss my family and friends, the people of the village whom I encountered every day. But most of all, I miss my river, Johann. I find within myself a need to be near a body of flowing water. Does that sound silly?"

He smiled. "Not at all. We have a river here, you know. The Largo." Days ago, he had taken a horse and ridden out to visit their new river and had found it to be a pleasant haven. It reminded him of the Mosel, a tributary of the Rhine. Unlike that larger river, with its air of melancholy and even, at times, menace, the Mosel was nothing but light and cheer, a carefree winding valley with a countryside gentler and less dramatic than that of the Rhine. He suspected the Largo would be the perfect medicine for Clara's ailing spirit.

"How far is it?" she asked.

"Ten miles. Would you like me to take you there?"

She looked at him, gratitude shining nakedly in her eyes.

They went in the buggy, and they talked about light subjects, nothing deep or penetrating—vines and chickens, and how benign the weather was. As they drew near, on a rutted dirt road, Clara leaned forward, eager, thirsty. The fog was completely gone now, revealing a green countryside. Johann reined in the horse, tethered it to a tree, and helped his sister-in-law down. She walked ahead of him, tramping through tall green spring-time grass, and went to stand on the lip of a steep bank.

Unlike the Rhine, cold and dark, tumbling from the Swiss Alps to travel north 760 miles to empty in the North Sea, the Largo was a warm, gentle river that meandered without hurry a mere ninety miles from the Largo Mountains in the east toward an ocean in the west named for its peaceful nature.

The Largo was also wide and flat, with gentle grassy banks. Where were the towering rocks where a siren maiden could sing and lure sailors to watery deaths? No rugged mountains dotted with castles and monasteries. No hiding places for pirates to lurk. You stood on one side of the Rhine and saw towering mountain peaks opposite. But you stand on the Largo and you see flat farmland and gently rolling hills on the other side.

The Rhine was embraced by dense alpine forests. But along the banks of the wide, flat, meandering Largo sycamores grew, and willows and cottonwoods, their reflections seen on the river's placid surface. Tall grasses grew at the water's edge, and marshy areas where cattails rose up in profusion, their brown spikes bursting open with white fluff in the springtime breeze. The scene was painted in the colors of spring wildflowers: yellow lilies, white asters, purple clover, orange poppies, in God's generous profusion. Clara saw ducks, brown ones, green ones, gray ones; and tall white herons strolling majestically, one long stick-leg at a time, through the water. She saw familiar fish swarming in the shallows, rainbow-colored trout, long brown pike, and striped perch with red fins often seen in the buckets of hardy Rhine fishermen.

She closed her eyes to the warm wind. At that moment, in Germany, the days were gray and rainy, and noses were bitten with cold. But a benevolent sun shone over the Largo, and the breezes were warm.

As he watched her, Johann thought: There is a sadness within her. She is lonely here. She looks at the river and she thinks: It is not the Rhine.

He felt the same. He was homesick too. But at least he had his work, his dedication, and the dream he shared with his father and brother. What did Clara have? What satisfaction was there in cooking and washing? Johann had never really given women's work any thought. Since their mother died when he was eight years old, Papa had hired women to come take care of them. He paid them. They did a job. Johann had never thought what must it be like for wives and mothers to drudge all day to keep their men fed and clean and happy. They did it for love, he assumed. That the contentment of their husbands and children were reward enough.

What was there for Clara here?

He thought of her many trips to the water pump and thought that surely there must be a way to send a pump down to the water table directly from the kitchen. That way, she would have running water in the sink. But it would be too expensive, and they hadn't the money. Clara had come from a comfortable, middle-class life, her father a respected professional, with a cook and a housemaid. She had come all these miles to live in near-poverty, for that was surely what they had come to. And should the grape harvest fail and the bank take the property, then they would be impoverished indeed, and homeless, with nowhere to go and no money to buy passage back home.

It chilled him to think that Clara faced such a future—although she didn't know it—and he wondered at the wisdom of keeping this bad news from her. Was it better to tell her the truth, or to keep her in a world of fantasy? Either way, the skin on her hands was growing red and raw, and it killed him.

He was glad he had brought her to the river. He knew it would be balm for her spiritual sickness. And he would bring her again and again, whenever she asked.

*   *   *

FINALLY, A LETTER FROM her sister. "I'm sorry I wasn't able to come to the wedding," Julia had written. "Mother said you were a beautiful bride. You already know how I feel about the institution of marriage, so I shan't lecture you here, especially now that you have gone ahead and entered into it. I just want to remind you of your independent status as a human being. Keep always in mind that marriage is a contract between equals. Do not let him lord it over you. Certainly my own Max agrees with me. He and I are equals, but so many of my friends live in unbalanced marriages. I have enclosed an article I clipped from a newspaper. I believe it will help to open your mind, should you need to. You can be too nice, Clara. You have always had a giving and gentle heart, always eager to please and to do favors. Now do a favor for your older sister: do not let your husband become your master.

"Please do not forgot us in Germany who love you. And please send me a bottle from your first vintage. You know I love a good glass of wine."

Unfolding the enclosed article, Clara read it through tears. When she was done, she smiled, then she laughed out loud. Only Julia would send something like this to a new bride.

I will write to her at once. . . .

But Jakob explained, the next morning, that stamps were costly and that letters to Germany must wait.

She knew where Jakob kept their money, in a tin box under the wooden floorboards. Jakob Schaller did not believe in banks. But *her* money was in there as well, and all she wanted was the price of postage, she told herself as she knelt and lifted the box out. As she had expected, important papers were in there—birth certificates, passports, her and Wilhelm's marriage certificate, and. . . . She frowned. Some sort of bank papers. But they were in English.

Something was missing. She couldn't think what. And then it came to her. Where was the deed to the farm? Surely that should be in here with the other important papers.

Settling back on her heels, she stared at the box. There was no money in there. Where was the bulk of the cash? A few one-dollar coins, but no real money. She looked at the bank papers again. A contract of some kind, with figures—dollar amounts—and signatures. Was it a loan agreement of some kind? Had they borrowed from the bank in Santa Barbara, using the farm as collateral, and now the bank held the deed?

She thought back. The first few nights here . . . Jakob and Wilhelm filling their pipes with tobacco after supper. The three men enjoying a glass of beer bought in Lynnville, or a glass of local red wine. Not much in the way of luxuries, she thought now, but still, something of a reward after a day's work. When was the last time they had filled their pipes? When was the last time they had enjoyed a glass of beer or wine? It struck her now that it had been at least two weeks since she had seen them relax by the fire. She had been so embroiled in her own work that she had been unaware that Jakob and his sons were suddenly going without their treats.

Were they broke? Was the money—her own money—all gone? And they weren't telling her?

She shot to her feet. It wasn't fair, treated like a child. She decided she wasn't even going to wait for them to come home for dinner. Julia's letter had suddenly imbued her with feminine pride. A woman had to stand up to certain things.

Hanging up her apron and abandoning her stove, she left the cabin. It was her first time out on the farm, away from the yard and walking between rows of trellised vines that were blooming with spring flowers. Bees buzzed in the warm air, butterflies flashed their colors as she followed the meandering Largo Creek, a tributary of the Largo River ten miles away. She encountered occasional workers with their hoes and baskets with weeds on their backs. They offered humble smiles, touched the brims of their straw hats, and said, "*Buenos dias, Señora.*" It was a tranquil atmosphere, carefree and refreshing. But she would not be lulled into a state of sweet complacency. She was angry and she would not forget it. When she found Jakob, she was going to put her foot down.

Soon, the peace and quiet was disturbed by ripples of noise, heard distantly at first, but growing louder as Clara neared a hill neatly laid with blossoming grapevines. Lifting her skirt, she plodded up the hill and could now hear men's shouts, and the hacking of farm tools, and great crashing noises as heavy things fell to the ground.

Clara crested the hill and came to a jarring halt as her eyes widened at an impossible scene. Spread before her was flat valley. No gentle slopes here garlanded with picturesque vines. This was the westward acreage of the Schaller property. To her right, the Largo Creek divided the Schaller property into hilly vineyards on one side, a parkland of oaks on the other. What met her astonished eyes now was a scene of vast industry and clamor and dust and energy as men busily chopped down wide-spreading oak trees, hauled the trunks and branches away in wagons, and pulled up deeply rooted stumps from the soil. She had never seen such a united effort of men working together, sawing, chopping, pulling. She watched as men sawed through massive tree trunks and then ran shouting, running for safety as the trees fell with great thundering crashes. Other men running in at once to chop up the trees and haul them away. Swarms of men on the stumps, using shovels and axes, mules and creaking harnesses.

It made her think of a strange battlefield—man against nature. She wondered that the defenseless trees didn't scream at the ignominy of their fate. She saw rabbits and squirrels darting through the grass and knew that not all would survive the onslaught. For onslaught it was—or more an invasion, Clara thought in fascination. This peaceful valley, unsullied for perhaps centuries, now beset by the machine called progress. It wasn't enough that Nature had planted oaks to produce acorns and shade and wood. Now Man came along to change it all, saying that this would now be grape-producing land. But in order to bring that about, he must ravage the land, bend it to his will, put himself in the role of God.

And then she saw the Schaller men—not standing idly by and barking commands as she had imagined, but down in the earth themselves, digging with spades, hacking away at ancient roots, heaving for breath, pausing only to wipe their arms across their sweating brows. Johann and Wilhelm had removed their shirts so that their naked torsos glistened in the sun. Clara saw rippling muscles and sinews. Their faces were streaked with dirt. Jakob was trying to handle a team of mules, as he pulled on their bits and collars, urging them on with shouts, while Mexicans worked behind, cracking whips over the mule's haunches as the animals strained against their harnesses to haul the stubborn tree stump, attached to the leather harness, from the ground.

The mules struggled, their hindquarters quivering, their eyes rolling, their front hooves rising up and down, struggling to find foothold in the air. She watched Jakob, fearless, holding on, shouting commands, "Come on! Come on! Pull now!" while the Mexicans' whips made gunshot sounds in the air.

Clara was spellbound at the sight of it all, the power of man's will over nature, and then her heart rose to her throat when she realized the danger of it all. Those massive trees crashing to earth, with the men never really knowing which way they would fall. Jakob's body so close to the mules' rearing hooves. And the stump, slowly groaning its way up from the soil—Clara held her breath. If it should suddenly come up, come flying out of the ground, the mules would bolt forward and trample Jakob Schaller.

And then—

She gave a cry. Jakob slipped on the loose earth and down he went, arms and legs flailing as he landed with a thud on his back and the mules backed up, stamped nervously, and tossed their heads.

Jakob lay stunned and motionless as the mules spooked and started to jump nervously. Seeing their hooves flailing perilously close to him, she began to run down the hill, but when she saw Mexican workers run to his aid and pull Jakob to his feet, and she saw him wave his arms and restore his hat and make reassuring motions with his hands, she stopped, her hand to her throat. Jakob was quickly back at the mules' heads, seizing their bits and collars, getting them under control as the men at the rear resumed cracking their whips as the giant tree stump started to give way.

Pressing her hands to her breast, overcome with awe and emotion, seeing that Jakob was okay, stubborn and determined, while Johann and Wilhelm worked nearly as naked as Adam had been in Eden, placing themselves in hazardous situations, Clara suddenly felt humbled and put to shame.

She had had no idea! She felt childish and stupid, fretting about money for a stamp when they were losing the farm and Jakob and his sons were risking their necks at a dangerous endeavor. Why hadn't they told her?

She turned and, picking up her skirts, ran back to the house.

As she entered the yard, a shadow swept across the ground, startling the chickens, causing them to squawk and run about. It made Clara stop and look up. Was it a chicken hawk? She had had an impression of great outspread wings.

She looked this way and that and finally saw, up on the roof of the house, a giant white bird. He had come to roost there, calm and unfluttered.

Clara stared. He was a barn owl, with a pale heart-shaped face and black eyes that looked like a flat mask with oversized, oblique black eye slits, the ridge of feathers above the bill somewhat resembling a nose. The face was bright white, as were his underparts and legs.

Clara stood in awe at such a rare sight. You're beautiful, she said silently to him, amazed to see this nocturnal bird in the sunshine. And he wasn't on his way from anywhere to anywhere, but seemed quite at ease to rest his sleek body on the peaked roof of her cabin, eyes closed, feathers unruffled, as if this were where he always slept his days away.

She couldn't take her eyes off him. The day seemed to grow distant, memory of the great oak-felling scene receding. The moment stretched, time became something else, another dimension, and the blue sky encompassed the entire earth. Clara was gripped with the feeling that he had come here on purpose.

She heard his message: *Be calm.*

"But how can I be calm?" she said out loud, aware that she was standing in the middle of a farmyard talking to a sleeping owl. "I have so much to do! Finish cooking the dinner, feed the chickens and find the eggs, and boil water and keep the oven going while my men are risking their lives to expand the farm and save it!"

Be calm was the reply. Engage in a task that will clear your mind, organize your thoughts. Leave the crackers to bake in the oven, because that was what fire and dough and ovens were for. And leave the water to boil on the stove and let the potatoes cook. These things take care of themselves, once they are started. Because until your own inner house is in order, the owl said, then how can your outer house be in order?

Clara tried to think. She pressed her fingers to her temples to clear her mind. Was she hallucinating? Whose voice was she hearing? Her own?

She gazed up at the placid bird. To see a white owl during the day was a good omen: it meant you were being watched over and guided by someone in the spirit world. But that was in Germany. Were there fairy folk in America? *Or do we bring them with us?* Perhaps the local Indians had their own invisible magical beings who brought signs and portents and messages from the spirit world. Would the Indians have thought the owl was a sign of good luck? *Some things are universal. . . .*

Yes, Clara knew she had to calm down. She would be no help to the others if she was panicked and hysterical.

She went into the cabin and looked around. So far, the oven was doing what it was supposed to do, baking the crackers and boiling the potatoes. So what should Clara do? What would straighten out her mind to let her think?

Straighten something else out, she told herself. Tidy something physical. Her mother had always held that straightening the house straightened the mind.

She went up to the loft. Her clothes were hung neatly on pegs and the bedding on the cot was made up. The bowl in the washstand was clean and there was fresh water in the pitcher. And then she saw her steamer trunk. She had ignored it for a month, removing only things on top, a few clothes, her toiletries, personal effects. Everything else slipped so far down on the priority list as to have been forgotten.

She knelt and lifted the lid, recalling that her mother had helped her pack it. Hadn't there been a few last-minute wedding gifts? Would she have put them in here, under the books, the extra tablecloths, the embroidered dinner napkins from Frau Hoff? As she lifted things out, Clara felt her hopes rise. The courtship with Wilhelm, the romance, the whirl and swirl of the wedding—she had completely forgotten about wedding presents. Was it possible that someone had given the young couple something as valuable as silver candlesticks? *I can give them to Papa Jakob to help pay some of his debt and save the farm.* It was the least she could do.

The mules, the oak trees. . . .

As she lifted out spare nightgowns she had forgotten, and a heavy winter coat that she knew she would not be needing here, Clara thought of Jakob, the horse's hooves flying dangerously close to his head, her heart rising in fear, and she realized now that he must have gone into town for supplies on his own, without her, out of pride. He must be running up debts with the merchants in Lynnville. Who knew what promises he had made in order to put food on his family's table? And he would not have wanted his daughter-in-law to witness his humiliation.

There were no silver candlesticks, no heirloom jewelry to help with the farm debt. When the trunk was completely unpacked, all Clara found at the very bottom was an old battered book, a familiar one, which she had seen in her mother's kitchen all her life. It was titled *The Housewife's Companion*, and it had been published many years ago.

There was a note inside: "Welcome, dearest daughter, to your new home. My mother gave this book to me when I entered my new house as a bride, and now I pass it along to you."

Oh, Mama, Clara thought in a wave of engulfing sadness. You

thought I would have found this on my first day here. You pictured me walking into my new house and straightaway unpacking this trunk and hanging out my clothes, possibly with the aid of a servant. You heard Wilhelm speak of Rosita; you would have imagined a lady's maid perhaps. But because I have been in a struggle of confusion and loneliness, because I have been frightened and lost, I ignored the trunk and took from it only what I needed. You are expecting a letter by now. You are watching for the mailman, anticipating a letter that I have not even begun to write!

She flipped through the book—a compendium of cooking recipes, housekeeping tips, and feminine wisdom. Many times Clara had seen her mother refer to it during the concocting of a meal. She opened it. A chapter on "How To Prepare and Cook the Best Spaetzle." In the margin, someone had scribbled in ink: "Rule of thumb, use one more egg than the number of people who are going to eat the spaetzle." Clara smiled through her tears and felt a budding excitement within her. Stuffed between the pages were slips of paper, bits of notes, a card or two, all with something written on them. "Nothing is insurmountable. As long as you are alive, you can do something about your problems."

She turned to another chapter and a small envelope fell out. This was not old and yellowed like all the others, but new, and part of her mother's personal stationery. "For Clara," it said on the front. She opened it and found a small fortune in Reichsmarks.

Her mother had given her bridal money, something with which to start her own housekeeping account.

A book of help and wisdom, Clara thought, clasping it to her breast. Containing a loving bundle of cash, and appearing just at the moment she needed it. How long would this rescue-book have lain in the trunk before she found it? Perhaps months, years.

Her smile grew. This was no coincidence: the owl had been sent to tell her about the book. She hurried outside to thank him.

The owl was gone.

*　　*　　*

WHEN THEY CAME HOME, she wordlessly served them. There was a lump in her throat for these prideful men. Her having seem them at their desperate labor, breaking their backs to cut trees in the hope of saving the farm, made her feel closer to them. The feeling was almost one of intimacy, as if she had spied on them doing some secret thing.

Wilhelm—she had seen him shirtless beneath the sun, laboring with the grand physique and muscles of a hero-warrior. Clara was in awe of him again.

But in awe of Johann too, and even Jakob.

She couldn't tell them about it, that she had watched them slaving away clearing oak trees. She didn't know if men liked being observed at their labors. Dispensing pills in a white coat was one thing: a chemist was clean and genteel. But sweating without a shirt on? Dirty and grimy, grunting with axes and saws like Egyptian slaves building the pyramids? She wanted to tell them there was majesty in what she had seen, a kind of nobility. But she didn't know how they would react, and so she kept silent.

They were silent, too, she noticed, as they cleaned their plates and prepared to settle into a short evening of newspaper, books, notes. For once, instead of boiling water for the dishes, Clara joined them at the table, taking a seat, folding her hands in front of her. They looked at her, startled and expectant.

"I have learned that we are out of money."

Wilhelm gave her a surprised look. "How—?"

She held up a hand and said, "Please tell me: Are we in danger of losing the farm?"

Wilhelm cleared his throat. "We are short on money."

"I should have been told."

"You do not need to be told anything," Jakob cut in defensively. "Your job is to cook and clean and make sure we have fresh clothes to wear, that the chickens are fed and that we have a vegetable garden. I do not see any garden, do you? And why should we tell you anything? What could you do in this situation? How would *you* keep the workers here?"

"Where did the money go?" she asked calmly. "Why did you need to take a bank loan?"

Jakob Schaller, a widower for years, was unused to explaining himself to a woman, let alone a newcomer who was less than half his age. A man's financial affairs were a personal thing, not something for an uppity girl to stick her nose into.

"Papa Jakob, I have a right to know," she said respectfully. "I work hard in this house. And I truly do wish to please. But how can I, if I do not know everything that is going on with this farm? If we cannot afford Rosita and other help, then tell me and I will work around that." She paused, then added, more gently, "Shouting at me does not help."

Johann cleared his throat. "There was a root blight last fall. Nearly half the vines were lost."

Clara looked at the three faces and suddenly understood what lay at the bottom of all the secrecy: pride. For a man who had believed himself to be one of the finest vintners in the Rhine Valley, it would be a shameful blow to lose half his vineyard to a plant disease.

She knew that butting heads with Jakob was a useless endeavor. He was intractable in his thinking. However, she did know one way she could get through to him.

Reaching into her skirt pocket, she drew out the printed article Julia had enclosed in her letter, which Clara had found amusing but which she now found to be wise and sage. It had also come, she realized in amazement, at the perfect time, as if her sister had somehow known Clara would need it—and at this moment.

She showed it to each of them, pointing to the name of the author of the article. "You see that he is a Lutheran minister. I assume you trust the word of such a man?"

Jakob nodded and scowled at the same time.

"I will read it to you," she said, drawing the kerosene lamp closer and holding the paper near the light.

"One of the most frequently misunderstood terms in the Bible," Clara read, "is the term 'helpmeet' in the book of Genesis. In Genesis 2:18, it says *'And the Lord God said, It is not good that the man should be alone; I will make him an helpmeet for him.'* The common way in which the term 'helpmeet' is interpreted is to mean that Eve was to be Adam's helper or companion on the earth."

Clara paused to look at the three faces before her, their attention fixed, their eyes filled with curiosity. Clearing her throat, she continued: "But the term in its original Hebrew means something much more profound and powerful than just a helper, and when we understand what God was saying to Adam, we come to see Eve's role and the role of women on this earth in a much different light."

Clara paused again, expecting Jakob to voice a loud protest, perhaps even to leave the table. Yet she had his attention. Perhaps it was because she was reading words written by a man of the cloth.

"In Hebrew," she continued to read, "the two words that 'helpmeet' are derived from are the word *ezer* and the word *k'enegdo. Ezer* is commonly translated as 'help' but is really a rich word with a much deeper meaning. The noun *ezer* occurs twenty-one times in the Hebrew Bible. In eight of these instances, the word means 'savior.' These examples are easy to identify because they are associated with other expressions of deliverance or saving. Elsewhere in the Bible, the root *ezer* means strength . . . the word is most frequently used to describe how God is an *ezer* to man. And the root *ezer* is the same word that God used to describe to Adam who Eve was. She was not intended to be just his helper or his companion; rather, she was intended to be his savior, his deliverer."

Clara paused again, expecting an outburst, or at least a dismissal of what she was reading. But she saw only interest on the three faces and saw that they wanted to hear more. What better way, she thought, to get through to the Schaller men than by way of the Bible?

"The other part of the term 'helpmeet'," she continued, "which is commonly translated as 'fit for,' is the word *k'enegdo*, which means 'in front of' or 'opposite,' like when you look at yourself in a mirror. Eve was not designed to be exactly like Adam. She was designed to be his mirror opposite, possessing the other half of the qualities, responsibilities, and attributes which he lacked. Just like Adam and Eve's sexual organs were physically mirror opposites (one being internal and the other external), so were their divine stewardships designed to be opposite but fit together perfectly to create life. Eve was Adam's complete spiritual equal, endowed with an essential saving power that was opposite from his."

She paused, both for dramatic effect and to strengthen her voice: "And so the passage in Genesis should read: 'It is not good that man should be alone. *I will make him a companion of strength and power who has a saving power and is equal with him.*'"

She set the paper down and looked at the three men. "Can you argue with that?" she asked Jakob.

Frankly, he couldn't, and he was amazed that she had gone to the Bible to support her argument. It showed astute thinking.

"I am part of this family," Clara said. "I need to be told when we are having difficulties. We are all in this together. I can find ways to save money, perhaps even to earn money. After all, we do have a lot of chickens."

Now was the moment of decision. Perhaps the biggest decision in her entire life. The money her mother had sent her could pay for her passage back to Germany. She might take some shame from abandoning her husband, but at least she would be free of this drudgery and Jakob's tyranny and the loneliness that she suspected would never go away.

But then she looked at Wilhelm and Johann, two brothers, each handsome in his own way, one a worker of the land, the other a scientist, but both sharing a love of viticulture and a determination to build something in this new land. She thought of the love she had for Wilhelm, which was starting to change, to mature out of a dream and into a more realistic view which she had yet to understand. And a new affection for Johann, who had taken her to a new river. Finally, she pictured the three as she had seen them on the west acres, sweating and laboring to turn the land into their dream.

And her decision was made.

She reached again into her pocket. "When my mother helped me pack my trunk, she laid a gift at the bottom of it and I only just found it today."

She respectfully handed the cash to a stunned Jakob who was thinking that another woman might have kept the money a secret, spending it only on herself. "I make only one stipulation," Clara said. "That out of this money you buy me a proper bed." Her eyes flicked to Wilhelm. "I know that one of you is sleeping on the floor. Or perhaps you are taking turns. I cannot have that. You work too hard, and need your rest. Take my cot back and buy me a bed—nothing fancy, and it can have the plainest mattress. After that, the money goes to the farm as you see fit."

Johann took the cash out of his father's hands and handed it back to her. "It's yours, Clara," he said with a smile. "You need your own money."

"But the farm—" she began as he pressed the bills into her hand and curled her fingers over them.

"Clara, the farm will be fine. We decided to clear the west acres and cut down a lot of oak trees."

Yes, I know. I saw.

"We have sold the wood to a lumber company. The money will be enough to pay the bank and get our property deed back."

Her eyebrows rose. "It will?"

His smile widened. "It is a lot of wood, Clara, to go into building houses and making furniture, and even wine barrels. What is left over will be sold for firewood. Keep your money. It's yours."

As Wilhelm watched them, he was speechless with emotion and he looked at his wife with new respect. His love for her deepened: *I will build a room onto this house and will install a proper bed for two people, and give Clara the nice things in life that she deserves.*

He tried to ignore the smoldering resentment in the pit of his stomach. The selling of the oak timber to save the farm had been *his* idea. He had pushed for it, and his father had only acquiesced when Johann had spoken up, saying he thought it a good idea, and it had saved the farm!

But no thanks or praise came from his father. It was Johann, with his education and city sophistication, who had negotiated the deal with the lumber company and secured a cash loan from the bank to pay the Mexicans who labored to clear the oaks, and so it was Johann who got the praise and thanks for saving the farm.

Wilhelm tried not to let it gnaw away at him. He had always worked at suppressing resentment when, at times, it had seemed that Jakob favored Johann. He tried to tell himself that maybe that was the way it was in families—the youngest being the favorite. He told himself it shouldn't bother him. Like the time when it came to discussing advanced education. Only Johann was considered for the university. Jakob hadn't even asked Wilhelm if *he* wanted to go. As it turned out, Wilhelm hadn't wanted to, but his father could at least have asked. And all those other times when family decisions had to be made, and Johann got the larger say-so than his older brother. Was that the way it was going to be here in California too?

Ah, well, he thought, reaching for the ale he had treated himself to. Nothing to think about now. It was all in the past. The fact was that their farm had been saved. What did it matter who got the credit?

Papa Jakob smiled and thought that Wilhelm had done a good thing in marrying Clara, and decided to take her into town the next time he went and take her around to the shops and establishments her friends operated. And maybe one Sunday they should go into town for church service and thank God for the bounty brought to the Schallers by the destruction of a beautiful oak grove.

It had been a difficult decision to make, destroying that forest. Some things in nature should be left as God created them. He thought of Colina Sagrada, the twenty acres of blighted land on his property. It was thin, flinty soil that couldn't support a crop, and so he had decided it should be left just as God had made it. Jakob had loved the forty acres of oaks the first time he had set eyes on them and had decided they wouldn't be cleared for a vineyard, as a reminder of God's majesty. But Johann had been right. Those oaks saved the Schallers from bankruptcy and humiliation. Maybe that had been God's intention all along.

Besides, he had made a promise to a dying woman. I told you, my sweet Kätzchen, that I would give our sons a brilliant and esteemed future. I was not going to let the bank rob me of fulfilling that promise. And now we will do well, and we will prosper, and someday I hope to find some peace from the guilt that still eats away at my soul, even after all these years. It is the least I can do for you, my dear Kätzchen, to repay you for keeping our secret. You protected my honor and my name when you could have done so much worse. You are truly one of God's angels.

Only Johann was troubled by mixed feelings.

The way Clara had offered up her bridal money to save the farm. It had moved him beyond words. He had wanted to weep. She was right: they should have told her the farm was in trouble, and then they should have told her they had saved it by selling their oak trees. She wanted to share in their ups and downs, not be protected. It seemed that every day since leaving Germany, Johann had discovered something new and wonderful about Clara—her inner strength, her cheeriness of spirit, her generosity. And the way she had so sincerely thanked him for taking her to the river. It was just a river. Yet she had looked at him as if he had handed her a king's ransom in jewels.

And just now, holding her hands between his, in the warmth of the kitchen and in the glow of the lantern. . . . She wore her chestnut hair up in a loose knot at the back of her head. A few stray curls had fallen and lay upon her white neck. He wanted to reach out and touch them.

His feelings alarmed him. He was proud of her and admired and respected her, but what had started out as brotherly affection was coming dangerously close to forbidden feelings. She was his brother's wife. He must never think of Clara as anything else.

In the close cabin, with warm shadows in the corners created by the inviting glow of the lantern, Clara felt a new bonding with these men that went beyond the giddiness of courtship and the hopeful earnestness of marriage vows. This was intense, almost physical, even though none of them touched. It was in the air, in their souls, the way they looked at one another. A strange and pivotal moment had been reached, each of them knew. *Family* had been created in a way that no vows or signed and witnessed certificates could.

She looked at the three men, strong and self-sufficient men who drew giant oaks out of the stubborn soil. And yet they were vulnerable too, capable of falling victim to root rot and heartless financial institutions. A wave of tenderness came over her. Strong men, yes, but needy too—in need of her taking care of them.

Clara felt as if a spell were being cast over her. She felt close to the Schaller men who had saved the farm, as she too had wanted to save it. She realized in that moment that although she loved her village back home and the Rhine River, she had never felt as connected to her father's chemist's shop and the apartment over it as she did to this humble cabin and the earth beneath it.

That was it, she knew now, it was the land itself casting the spell. And then, miracle of miracles, she felt a little of the homesickness slip away.

That night, as she climbed into the cot that she hoped was soon going to be replaced, Clara closed her eyes and smiled, picturing the green valley that was now her home, and its peaceful river that she hoped some-day to grow to love, and the men who were now her family. She thought of the white owl, and finding the *Housewife's Companion,* and knew that she wouldn't be lonely ever again because as long as she had her mother's book, she had her mother.

She truly felt the mistress of her own house now. She was going to teach herself things, and learn whatever she could and do the Schaller men proud. And prove to herself at last that, yes, she *could* be brave and courageous.

*   *   *

NOW THAT THE OAK trees were gone, Jakob decided they might as well put the land to good use. So he and his sons, along with a dozen hired Mexican workers, were using pickaxes and shovels to break up rocks and prepare the soil for planting. Stubborn tree stumps that couldn't be dug up or hauled out of the earth were set on fire and closely monitored; like-wise, brush and shrubbery and wild grasses were raked up into giant piles and set on fire. It was a warm day filled with smoke and good-natured industry, the workers wearing wide-brimmed straw hats and bandannas around their sweating necks.

While the removal of the great oak forest would bring in enough reve-nue to buy the farm back from the bank, there was still a question of this land's suitability for grape-growing. Jakob and his sons had gotten locked in a debate that revolved around such factors as alkalinity versus acidity, pH levels, trace minerals, percentages of clay, silt, and sand. Jakob had walked the newly cleared acres, dug his fingers into the soil, sniffed the dirt, sifted it through his fingers; had turned his face to the sun and wind; had gauged the gradual slope; and had drawn upon his basic instincts as an old-fash-ioned grape grower—and had discovered doubts about the cultivation of the land. Wilhelm, always anxious to please his father, agreed with him. But Johann, with his litmus papers and chemistry books and knowledge of the latest manufactured agricultural chemicals, was certain that those acres would produce the best grapes this valley had ever seen.

Johann had tried to make light of the controversy, laughing and saying, "Then why did you send me to university, Father, if not to make use of my education?" But there was annoyance in his tone, an impatience to get to work on these acres and start preparing the soil for new cuttings, while Jakob—with Wilhelm seconding him—said they should wait for the harvest of the western acres before pouring more money into dirt that might prove useless. "We do not know that that soil can produce anything other than oak trees," Jakob had said, Wilhelm nodding in agreement. And Johann had shot back, "How will we know if we don't *try*?"

So Jakob had given in, and now here they were, hard at work preparing the ground for vines. But Wilhelm, for reasons Jakob couldn't understand, wasn't pleased with his father's acquiescence. Instead of being willing to put these acres to the test, he had grumbled something about no one ever listening to him. And now working out in the fields with axes and shovels and hoes and rakes, the two boys were arguing again. It gave Jakob an ache in his heart. He had thought that coming to California and working five hundred acres would put an end to the boys' rivalry. Back home, the Schaller holding had been small and he had feared that it would not be big enough when the brothers inherited it—especially as Wilhelm and Johann approached viticulture from opposite disciplines. While Jakob himself tended to side with Wilhelm on that issue, there was nonetheless a part of him that admired Johann's education and knowledge of science, that thought he should have a chance to put his theories to the test.

Tired of the arguing, he paused in his labor, wiped his brow, and said, "Wilhelm, it wouldn't hurt to let Johann see what he can do with his modern ideas. If he fails, he fails and we try something else. Many of the vintners in this valley raise other crops too."

"It's a waste of time," Wilhelm said with a frown, making his father wonder at his refusal to budge.

Jakob felt his impatience rise. "Johann," he said, "why don't you take over these acres yourself and work them as you see fit, while Wilhelm and I run the other vineyards in our own tried-and-true ways?"

Wilhelm gave his father a frankly dumbfounded look. "You're *giving* Johann this acreage? To run all by himself?"

"Son, why can't we wait and see—"

Wilhelm threw down his shovel in disgust. "Why do you always side with Johann?" And, to Jakob's surprise, he strode away.

Jakob heaved a discontented sigh. His hope that coming to California and working so many acres—enough to satisfy both sons—would put an end to the bickering hadn't panned out after all. In fact, Jakob thought now as he watched Johann run after Wilhelm to placate him, the rivalry only seemed to have gotten worse.

Did I cause this? he asked himself as he watched his sons argue and make angry gestures. Have I not treated them equally and fairly and shown no favoritism? Kätzchen, if only you were here to advise me, to tell me what I am doing wrong—*if* I am doing something wrong.

And then an unthinkable thought skated across his mind: What if they know the secret I have carefully guarded all these years and have followed me to California despite my attempt to run away from it?

No! An unthinkable thought indeed! Retrieving his pickaxe, Jakob raised it high and brought it down hard on the rocks to drive the frightening thought from his mind. Brothers fight. It was a fact of life.

* * *

IT WAS SUNDAY, AND Clara was checking on her apricot cake in the oven when she heard a horse-drawn vehicle pull into the yard, disturbing the ever-roaming chickens. She looked out and saw an astonishing sight—a handsome four-passenger surrey with a hard top decorated all around in a fringe, drawn by two matching prancing bays. What caught Clara's eye was the color: the body of the carriage was painted bright red. The second was the driver—a young woman with raven hair, wearing a lemon-yellow dress with a matching yellow bonnet that sported a billowing white plume. She reined in the horses and climbed down, saying "Hello!" while she opened a yellow parasol and propped it over her head.

Clara was momentarily speechless. She had never seen such a beautiful girl. *Woman*, really, with her voluptuous curves and generous bosom. And she was a few years older than Clara, around twenty-five. Who on earth was she?

"Feliciana Ballerini," the visitor said gaily, holding out her gloved hand and dazzling Clara with her smile. "I have been away in Monterey, and my father informed me we had new neighbors. I have come to introduce myself."

It took Clara a moment to gather what she had said. Like her father, Feliciana spoke a dialect of German that Clara was unfamiliar with, but she knew that in a short time her ear would become accustomed to it.

She couldn't help but stare. Mr. Ballerini had referred to her as his "unmarried" daughter. Why wasn't she married? Clara would have imagined that in this valley populated with so many bachelor farmers, she would have been spoken for long ago.

"I am very pleased to meet you," Clara said, and she was indeed thrilled to finally meet her neighbor. "Will you stay for coffee and cake?"

"I would be delighted."

Clara saw how Feliciana kept looking around the yard, at the barn and henhouse and beyond the fence, and finally at the rustic cabin, curiosity shining from her eyes. "The cake will be done soon," Clara said, feeling plain and drab next to the colorful woman. "May I show you around?"

Feliciana's smile indicated that there was nothing in the world she would like better than a tour of what Clara was certain must be the humblest homestead in the whole valley. "There isn't much to show," she said as she led her visitor away from the tethered surrey. "But it is home. . . ."

She was glad Miss Ballerini had chosen today for her surprise visit, as the Schallers had just gotten back from attending church service in town and so Clara was wearing her best dress and her hair was done up nicely.

And oh, God, it was so wonderful to finally meet a true neighbor. Clara was suddenly flooded with relief.

After she had witnessed the dangerous tree-felling and she realized that Jakob and his sons did more than just spend their days tying vines to trellises, new emotions had flooded her. Namely, fear. She watched the three men leave each morning and watched until the vineyards swallowed them up and they literally *vanished*. All day, she had no idea where they were, or if they would come back. What if one of them got injured? Or all three of them. Neighbors were miles away, and she didn't really know them. Who would she go to for help?

The worst part of the day was late afternoon and the approach of sundown. She would feel her anxiety rise. A nervousness would catch her in a grip as she made frequent trips to the door to look out for them, to listen for their voices. She especially hated it when they took the wagon in the morning, because that meant they were working farther out. So she listened for the creaking of harnesses and horses' hooves. She would look out and look out, until the anxiety took over altogether and no matter what needed seeing to in the kitchen, Clara would stand on the porch, anxiously wringing her apron as her eyes searched the long shadows and dusk for the men. Sometimes there was a moment when the sun was gone and they weren't home yet and her heart was in her throat. She would hold her breath and listen to the world, to hear for any evidence that

Jakob and his sons were still alive. And then she would hear it, a peal of laughter, Wilhelm's booming voice, horses' hooves, wagon wheels creaking. And then she would see them, and she would send silent thanks to God for bringing them safely home.

This had gone on for a few days, until Clara had decided she must end this isolation, that she needed to create some sort of security for herself. She needed someone to turn to in times of trouble. The immigrants in town, the people she had traveled from Germany with—they were the place to start.

And so, just this morning, Sunday, Clara had requested to be taken to church in town. Just as Jakob had not been able to argue with a Lutheran minister who defined the term "helpmeet" in Genesis, neither could he deny his daughter-in-law's request to attend church. So the Schallers had put on their best clothes and ridden into Lynnville for the church service. They would have preferred it to be Lutheran, but it was a non-denominational church that accommodated all Christians, except for the Catholics who made the long trip to Santa Barbara and the Mission chapel there.

The Lynnville church, with neat pews and a white steeple, was under the care of an American named Reverend Brown. He was delighted with the addition of new parishioners, even though he knew they were fresh from Germany and didn't understand his sermon. Regardless, it was good to see his flock increase.

Afterward, the Schallers had gotten together with the others for an impromptu reunion feast at the photographer's house, where they ate bratwurst and sauerkraut and good solid German bread with butter. It was wonderful to be with the others again, to get caught up, to hear how the other girls were getting along, and even Clara bragged a little about the adventures of farm life. Jakob, Wilhelm, and Johann enjoyed themselves as well, German immigrants getting together to re-unite and sing familiar songs and drink beer and eat wursts and share news and talk of home. And when they left, with hugs and kisses, Clara knew they would be doing this again next Sunday, and all the Sundays after that.

She had friends in town, and now she had met a nearby neighbor.

As she escorted the dazzling Feliciana around the modest homestead, the two communicated through Feliciana's Swiss German, what little she recalled from childhood—although the more she spoke it, the more came back—and through the little bit of English Clara had taught herself these past weeks, with gestures and pantomime filling in the rest. "We're building an addition," Clara explained when they reached the back of the cabin.

The lumber had arrived a few days ago and then the Mexican laborers, and soon Wilhelm was pacing out the floorplan for the new room that was going to be built onto the cabin—his and Clara's bedroom. It would be slow going, as Wilhelm and the workers were needed in the fields to cut away the new sucker vines and to position new tendrils on the trellises for optimum sun exposure. But Clara could be patient, now that she saw a promise coming true—that she and her husband would have privacy at last. And each time Wilhelm came by to inspect a newly framed wall, to instruct them to make the window larger, or to reposition the placement of the door, he sent her a smile and a wink and she felt like a bride again.

Clara was happy, especially now that they could afford stamps and she had written letters to her family, knowing that in a few weeks she could look forward to receiving replies and news from home.

Their short and uneventful tour at an end, Clara invited Feliciana inside the cabin, where Clara immediately set the percolator on the stove, stoked the fire, and brought a cake out of the oven to set it to cool. She was delighted to entertain her very first guest in her new home. Feliciana was like a breath of spring. She was so beautiful and lively and colorful. It was a relief from the new tension that had started sprouting, like a young vine, among the Schallers. Nothing she could name or point to, just an intangible tension in the air between the two brothers. And it was growing.

But now, on this lovely sunny Sunday afternoon, Feliciana Ballerini's presence brushed all such gloomy thoughts from Clara's mind as she poured the reheated coffee into china mugs brought from Germany, set out bowls of sugar and canned milk, and finally sliced the cake, which was still warm and filled with sweet apricot preserves and topped with crumbled, buttery streusel. With the help of the *Housewife's Companion* and her mother's and grandmother's added notes, Clara had busied herself, with great success, in mastering the art of cooking fish, rabbit, and duck, and she had even managed to create a spaetzle that had Papa Jakob's eyes rolling in their sockets.

They sat down and took forkfuls of cake as if they were the oldest of friends. Clara tried to use as much English as she could, while Feliciana thought back to her childhood to fetch back as much German as she could recall.

"We came here eleven years ago. I was fourteen. My mother died in Switzerland, and my father wanted to start a new life."

She spooned up some cake and rolled it around on her tongue. "Mmm, this is delicious. You must give me the recipe. Papa will love it. I've learned English and some Spanish. It is strange, when you think. We come to America, to California, and it feels like we have been dropped into the middle of Spain. The Mexicans celebrate very lively fiestas, you know. I love to watch their colorful dances."

Feliciana was stunningly beautiful, distracting even, and not just to men: Clara found herself being very aware of the young woman's perfect features, the creamy olive skin, the thick black lashes, and the light in her eyes. Not only that, but her personality sparkled, yet she seemed unaware of her charm and allure. She made fun of herself and laughed at her clumsiness while Clara found her to be amazingly graceful and without fault. The two ended up laughing, and Clara just knew they were going to be wonderful friends.

Yet she could not help asking herself once again, Why wasn't Feliciana married? Was it possible that her father drove suitors away?

Clara had learned that the Ballerinis were very prosperous. Not only was their winery doing well, but Ballerini planted hundreds of acres of crops that were in demand in a region where the population was rapidly growing.

Feliciana finally rose, extended a gloved hand, and said: "Now I really must go. I have yet to pay other visits to friends who will have heard that I have returned from Monterey and wonder why I haven't called. Let me invite you to our home next Sunday. We always have friends for dinner. I will introduce you around."

*   *   *

ON THE PORCH, BENEATH a full moon, Clara shelled snap peas into a bowl. Wilhelm and Johann were inside the cabin, continuing their argument over the management of the new vineyards, while their father had joined Clara on the porch to smoke his pipe in peace.

Jakob shook his head. "Even as boys, they were always competitive. I would tell them that brothers are supposed to love one another. I don't know." He shook his head again.

Suddenly, the screen door flew open and Johann stormed out. Wilhelm was close on his heels, saying, "No, you do not walk away from me. I am telling you that we cannot till potassium into the soil. It will kill anything that tries to grow there."

Johann spun around. The two had descended the steps from the porch to the front yard, near the water pump. "And I am telling you that I have seen with my own eyes the proof that there is already potassium in soil—it is *natural*, Wilhelm, and where there is insufficiency, then it is up to the farmer to supplement that which is already there."

"You with your classrooms and laboratories!" Wilhelm shouted, and it startled both Jakob and Clara.

Setting aside the snap peas and bowl, Clara watched the brothers. The new tension was in their stance, there was a startling edge to their voices. She should have seen it before, in earlier conversations, even back in Germany at that first picnic when Wilhelm had jokingly made fun of his brother the scholar. But now she saw clearly: There had only been enough money for one son to go to higher education. The younger son, for some reason, had been chosen. And now it festered in Wilhelm, who had no answers to Johann's scientific recommendations for the vineyards. Compared to his well-read brother, Wilhelm must feel a dunce.

And then Papa Jakob giving Johann autonomy over the acres where the oaks had been cleared. Yes, even she saw the unfairness of it.

"Listen," Johann said, facing his brother with his hands outspread, a man trying to reason with an unreasonable man, "potassium deficiency is common on very sandy soils, which is what we have where we intend to plant the bare-root cuttings. Such soils must be periodically replenished. You yourself have seen deficiency symptoms in the grape leaves. The leaf edges are losing their green color and even dying, and it is not yet summer."

Wilhelm's hands curled into fists. "Don't speak to me as if I were a child!"

"My God," Jakob said, rising from the rocking chair.

"Even a child would listen," Johann said, losing patience.

"I said don't speak to me that way!" Wilhelm shouted, and his fist shot out so quickly that Johann didn't see it coming. The blow sent him staggering backward.

Clara cried out and jumped to her feet while Jakob bounded down the steps. "Boys! Stop it! Stop it now!"

But Wilhelm's fists curled again; he planted his feet apart and threw another punch. Johann reeled, cupping his jaw in disbelief. As Wilhelm advanced on him, Jakob reached them and planted himself between his sons. "I said stop this!"

Wilhelm tried to push forward, but Jakob restrained him with his hands on his son's shoulders. They struggled for a moment, and then Jakob's boots slipped in the mud that was always around the water pump. "Now stop this," he said again, holding Wilhelm back. And then his feet flew out from under him altogether and down he went, the back of his head cracking on the iron pump.

"Papa Jakob!" Clara screamed.

The sons were immediately on their knees, saying "Papa! Papa!"

But Jakob was unconscious. He didn't even moan.

"Quickly, inside!" Clara said, and she ran ahead as Wilhelm and Johann lifted their father by armpits and ankles and hurried him into the cabin. Laying him on a cot, they brought a lamp close and saw blood streaming from a gash in his scalp.

Clara quickly came with a bowl of warm water, soap, and towels. "Is there a doctor in Lynnville?" she asked. She looked up at two pale and stricken faces. Johann's jaw was already turning purple. "Is there a doctor?" she said sharply.

"Santa Barbara," Wilhelm said in a faint voice.

It was too far. Forty miles each way on winding, hilly roads at night.

She cleaned the wound and packed it with lint she found in the medical kit from the pantry. She then applied a few drops of tincture of ethyl alcohol for antisepsis. The medical kit had been a gift from her father and she knew how to use everything in it. Once the bleeding stopped, she applied a dressing and then wound a bandage around Jakob's head to hold it in place.

She sat back and looked at him. His face had gone shockingly pale. "That is all we can do for now," she said.

Jakob remained unconscious through the night, so the next morning Johann saddled his horse and set off on the forty miles to Santa Barbara. By the time he returned that evening, to report that the only doctor in town had taken the train to Los Angeles, Jakob still had not regained consciousness. Wilhelm rode into Lynnville to ask Reverend Brown to pray for Jakob Schaller.

There was nothing they could do but keep vigil at the bedside, and watch the wound for complications.

Over the next few days, he was in and out of consciousness, able to take some sips of water, drink some soup or broth, mutter incoherently and say that his head hurt terribly. Clara stayed at his side, leaving only to cook and to keep the fire in the stove going.

Then the fever appeared. "He is burning up," Clara said, her hand on Jakob's forehead. "We must get the fever down. Cold water from the well, *now*."

The sons both ran out while Clara took care to remove Jakob's shirt and trousers. She looked at the bandage. There was a little seepage through the gauze, but nothing alarming. She gnawed her lip. Should she change the dressing, add more antiseptic? She didn't know what to do.

When Wilhelm and Johann came back with cold water freshly pumped from the underground well, Clara began sponging Jakob down with wet cloths. He moaned as she did so. Was this a good sign, she wondered?

Johann took his horse and rode again to Santa Barbara, and this time he came back with the doctor, who followed him in his motorcar. The man checked Jakob's wound, which was oozing with green pus. He drenched it with carbolic acid, trimmed away necrotic tissue, and did what suturing he could. Then he said, "Aspirin every four hours," leaving Clara with a bottle of white pills and instructions to crush them in water and make him drink.

The fever grew worse. Jakob tossed and groaned, sweating copiously so that he drenched the bedding. Reverend Brown came and prayed over him. Rosita came wearing her shawl and tucked a saint's medal under Jakob's pillow. She prayed out loud so that God was now being beseeched in Spanish, English, and German.

On the seventh night, while a small crowd had gathered out in the yard, Mexican and Guatemalan migrant workers holding candles and praying to the Virgin Mary, Jakob Schaller lay burning in delirium. His eyes were open, sunken into their sockets. They darted this way and that as his parched lips worked over voiceless words. The doctor had come one more time and said there was nothing that could be done. Once a wound infection found its way inside the body, prayer was the only cure.

Clara sat stoically at his side, holding a hot, dry hand. She struggled not to cry. Wilhelm and Johann were so bereft that she thought her own tears would send them over the edge. They paced in the room, unable to sit still, perhaps in an effort to keep the angel of death from entering the room.

At midnight, Jakob's eyes suddenly focused. His mouth stopped twitching. He looked directly at Clara. "Ilse?" he said. "Is that you?"

It startled her. Wilhelm and Johann rushed to the side of the cot. "What did you say, Papa?"

But Jakob seemed unaware of them. His gaze was fixed on Clara. "Ilse?"

Clara looked up at the two brothers. "Ilse was our mother," Johann said. Ilse Schaller, who had died twelve years ago.

"No, Papa Jakob," she said gently. "I'm Clara, your daughter-in-law."

He smiled and gave her hand a squeeze. "Oh, Ilse, it is so good to see you. I am dying, you know. God is calling to me."

"No," she said. "Please don't go."

"What a good woman you are, Ilse. So full of goodness and generosity. You will understand what I must tell you. I cannot go to God with sin in my heart. My dear Ilse, I have to tell you something, I have to confess my terrible sin to you."

Clara swallowed with a tight throat. She glanced at the brothers and knew they were thinking the same thing: they did not want to hear this terrible confession.

Jakob's voice crackled. He wheezed in breath and heaved it out. His eyes now blazed with fever and fire. Clara felt his hand tighten around hers with startling strength. "Ilse, do you remember when your sister Hannah came to us and told us she was with child? When she came tearfully and repentant to us, your unmarried sister with a bastard in her womb? She came to us because your parents had thrown her out of the house. . . . She came to us, begging us to take her in, and you begged me to let us take your sister in."

Clara, Wilhelm, and Johann, their faces pale in the glow of kerosene lamps, sat like statues as dread filled them—dread for what was coming.

Jakob sucked in air and exhaled in a barrage of words. "And so I agreed and we kept Hannah hidden, and we made up a story about her being married to a sea captain whose ship had gone down in a storm. And she gave birth to her bastard son in our house, and she died soon after from complications. . . . We said we would keep him. In her dying hour, we promised her we would raise Johann as our own and love him. And we did, didn't we? We loved Johann as our own."

Jakob's eyelids fluttered closed and he labored for breath, while those gathered around the bed stood frozen with shock. Wilhelm lifted his eyes and looked at his brother in confusion. Silence filled the small cabin. Outside, the migrants had stopped their chanting and were drifting back to their shantytown camp, as if they instinctively knew the final hour had come. The rest was now in God's hands.

Clara opened her mouth but couldn't speak. She kept looking from one to the other—Johann, stunned; Wilhelm, confused. Could they have heard wrong? Were they simply the words of a man raving in delirium? Was there any truth in what he had said?

Johann went back in his mind, back to when their mother was alive, trying to remember what he had always been told about Aunt Hannah. She had died when Wilhelm was two and Johann was just a baby, their mother had said. Hannah had died of scarlet fever. This was what Johann recalled.

He turned and walked away with leaden feet, to go nowhere, just around the cabin, to stop here and there and listen to the night. It couldn't be true. Jakob and Ilse Schaller weren't his real mother and father? Wilhelm wasn't his brother?

Suddenly, he spun around and stared at Clara and Wilhelm with wide, uncomprehending eyes. Am I a bastard? he wanted to shout.

"Dear God," Wilhelm said, sinking into a chair while Clara continued to sit in shock and Jakob's chest rose and fell in labored breathing, his lungs crackling and gurgling with effort.

Johann wrung his hands. What did this mean? What did this mean?

All his life, he had loved Jakob and was proud to be a Schaller. But now . . . he was another man's son? A man he knew nothing about, not even a name?

He suddenly felt sick. And betrayed—he was not sure by whom, Jakob or the unknown father? Or Ilse, not his mother after all? Which one of them had misled him and let him down? I am the bastard son of Aunt Hannah, who supposedly died of scarlet fever years ago but in truth died giving birth to me.

It tortured Clara to watch Johann. She wanted to go to him, put her arms around him, tell him that it didn't matter, that Jakob and Ilse had loved him and raised him as their own.

Other, stranger thoughts flew through Wilhelm's mind now, like unwanted crows devastating a newly planted field. The word cousin, over and over. Not my brother. Not a Schaller. We don't even know Johann's real name! Wilhelm felt as if the world were spinning out of balance. How could God have allowed this to happen? And what did it mean . . . from now on? For the future? This was Schaller Farm. Who was this younger cousin working by his side? What should he call him? Should he even own part of the farm?

At that moment, Jakob's eyes snapped open, he sucked in a great heaving, noisy breath, and he blurted, "I have lived with a terrible secret all these years, dear wife. Adultery is immoral and a sin against God's law. It is also a crime in man's law."

Clara exchanged a puzzled look with the brothers.

"I worry about Hannah's soul," he wheezed on. "I should have been strong. Leviticus, Chapter 18, verse 18 states very clearly . . . that a man must not have sexual relations with his wife's sister while his wife is still alive. And then Hannah died. Was it God's punishment for a sin that I had led her into?" His eyes flew open, feverish, unfocused, as he spoke to the ceiling. "I was weak! I should have stopped it before we went too far. Hannah was innocent. And I do not blame Johann, an innocent baby, for Hannah's death. I blame only myself. I haven't been able to forgive myself since. But by fulfilling my promise to her— by seeing to it that Johann be given a successful and brilliant life—I can hope for absolution."

Jakob ran a dry tongue over cracked lips while three ghostly faces stared down at him. "Even if the absolution doesn't come from God, I hope that I can finally forgive myself and find some peace and redemption in California. That is why I must go there, Ilse. It is the only way—I must leave Germany for a better life for Johann and to bring peace to Hannah's soul. Hannah, my beloved Kätzchen. . . ."

He looked directly at Clara again, his fiery eyes blazing like a madman's. "My dear Ilse, when you questioned your sister about the father of the child, she would not name the man. She died with his name locked in her heart. Listen to me now, before I go to God!" Jakob roared with the sudden, final tapping of strength known to happen in one's final moments on earth. "God forgive me! Ilse, *I* was that man!" His powerful, final voice filled the cabin, filled the night, rose up to the stars to fill the cosmos. "*I* fathered Johann, and Hannah—my sweet Kätzchen—she never told! That is why I took him in and why I loved him with all my heart, why I loved him more than I could love Wilhelm. . . ."

The world shifted just then in the rustic Schaller cabin. An evil, dangerous shift that was teetering toward a frightening edge.

Jakob said, in a croaking voice, "A father isn't supposed to favor one son over the other, but I love Johann with all my heart. Wilhelm was conceived out of marital duty, but Johann sprang from my love for my Kätzchen, pure and holy and with the deepest passion I have ever known. He is all I have of her, and of that love. So I must hide my favoritism. Forgive me, Ilse, I loved your sister more than I could ever love you! *Forgive me!*" he shouted, his lead lifting off the pillow. And then he fell back, his eyes wide and staring, and then his chest closed down on itself, collapsing as the lungs within collapsed and Jakob Schaller drew not another breath.

The heaviest silence in the world descended upon the scene in that moment as three people stood or sat in frozen shock.

And then suddenly, with a strangled cry, Wilhelm bolted from the cabin and out into the yard, where he stumbled against a tree. Suddenly feverish, he supported himself against the trunk, clutched his stomach, and started retching violently. Clara came out a moment later, stunned to see her towering husband bent over, covered in sweat, vomiting with wretched sounds. It froze her to the spot. Something terrible had just happened: for one brother to hear his own father declare, with his dying breath, that he loved the other brother more. . . .

Her heart went out to Wilhelm. She ran to his side; but when she reached for him, he shoved her away. "Leave me alone!" he bellowed, his golden beard streaked with bile and vomit. "Get away from me, woman!"

Clara slowly retreated; and when she reached the kitchen steps, she saw Johann standing there, white-faced in the moonlight, in such a state of shock that she wondered if any of them would ever again have the gift of speech.

*   *   *

WILHELM RODE THE EIGHT miles to Lynnville, where he informed the sheriff of what had happened. He then went to the undertaker, who came out to the farm to collect the body and measure it for a coffin. The sheriff then informed, by way of telegraph, the County Coroner of Jakob Schaller's death, which was ruled accidental. Jakob was buried in Reverend Brown's non-denominational Christian churchyard with a minimum of fanfare. All the young immigrants paid their respects to the man who had given them the vision and the courage to come to America, who had enabled them to undertake the great adventure. They cried and embraced Wilhelm and Johann and Clara, and told them what a tragedy it was that Jakob had not lived long enough to see his dream of a great vineyard come true.

These were wooden, dreamlike days in which the three at the farm moved like automatons, unable to believe that their driving force was gone. Unable to believe the final things he had said. None of them spoke. Clara wanted desperately to comfort both men, but Wilhelm would not have it and Johann had distanced himself from the human race. She had no idea what either was thinking or feeling; she could only guess.

They had been burned by a double lightning strike—not just Papa Jakob dying—that was bad enough—but then to hear his terrible confession. Clara could not imagine it. She could only place their tragedy against the backdrop of her own experience, trying to imagine being at her father's bedside when he breathed his last. Not a natural old-age death, but one brought on by a freak accident—caused by his sons! Surely one thing on Wilhelm's and Johann's minds was: If only we hadn't been fighting.

So they carried the grief of a freakish and untimely death, plus the guilt of their own part in it. But on top of that . . . Jakob's confession. She tried to imagine her own father, the educated and respected chemist, blurting out a story of adultery and illegitimate birth. Clara's mother had a sister, Aunt Sonja. Clara tried to picture her father, dying, declaring that he loved Sonja more than his own wife, and that Clara was the fruit of that adulterous union and that Julia, his older daughter, had only been the product of marital duty.

Clara shook her head and attacked her pastry with a vengeful rolling pin. It was unimaginable! It was all so impossible to believe. Perhaps Jakob had been raving and it might not be true.

She paused to push a stray hair from her face. But it had to be believed. The pious and moral Jakob Schaller had confessed before God on his deathbed. It was the truth. Wilhelm and Johann were half-brothers, with Wilhelm the result of duty, Johann the favored love-child.

She looked through the kitchen window at the rows of vines nearest the homestead. She had no idea where Wilhelm and Johann were working that day. The brothers hadn't spoken to each other since the funeral. She had no idea what poisons festered in their hearts as they chopped down sucker vines and pulled up weeds and dug new postholes and strung new trellises.

What was the future going to be like from now on? It frightened her, what the days ahead held for the Schallers of Largo Valley.

*　　*　　*

WILHELM ATTACKED THE SUCKER vines with a machete as if to lay waste to all the vineyards of the world.

He was weeding and pruning a section of acres far from where Johann was working. Wilhelm could not stand to be near his brother, could not stand to look at him. In the days since the funeral, Wilhelm's festering pain had found a twisted outlet in a new hatred for his brother.

All his life, he had looked up to his father, worshipped him. The senior Schaller had been a staunchly moral man, and Wilhelm had tried hard to live up to his example. But now that hero had fallen, and the disillusionment was so great—that his father had known his wife's sister sexually—that Wilhelm's anger was directed at Johann, who was the breathing, physical reminder of Jakob's fall from grace. It was almost as if the child were the cause of the father's sins, which of course was backward. Wilhelm looked at Johann and saw him as the reason for Jakob's seduction—for that must be what had happened. Jakob, a moral and righteous man, would never have done what he had if he had not been seduced by a wicked woman. That wickedness would be in Johann now, and Wilhelm could not tolerate his half-brother's presence.

*   *   *

JOHANN CAME HOME AT sundown.

He had worked another section of the vineyard, as far away from his brother as he could, laboring alongside the Mexicans until his hands were raw with blisters. His mind was a wasteland, his soul a barren desert where cold winds blew. Words swirled through his tormented mind: bastard, adultery, half-brother. It didn't matter that he had been Jakob's favorite. In fact, that made the situation worse. He didn't want to be favored. He wanted only to be equal with the brother he loved and had always looked up to.

Everything was wrong. The world was wrong. He felt as if he had fallen into a deep pit and couldn't claw his way out. Dangerous and unwanted emotions brooded in his heart. Never a man to hate, Johann now hated his father for committing adultery, for confessing to it, for being a martyr and then dying with a clear conscience without having to serve any punishment. He hated Wilhelm for being the legitimate brother and the only son of the mother Johann had loved. But most of all, Johann hated himself, simply for being himself.

Clara was on the kitchen porch, lighting the lanterns for the evening. Johann paused when he saw her—willowy and slender as she reached up to slip a burning match into a globe. His heart rose to his throat. In everything that had happened, he hadn't thought of *her* feelings, what Clara must be going through. It had to be terrible for her to see her husband so cast down, and she so powerless to comfort him.

Clara blew out the match and happened to glance in Johann's

direction. She paused. They stared at each other across the darkening yard. Soon Clara stood in a golden glow, and it filled Johann with a jumble of unfair, forbidden emotions. She was so beautiful, and so untouchable. He waited. She didn't turn to go inside. Her lips were parted. She looked like a timid deer, wondering which way to flee. Johann took the steps in one bound and pulled her into his arms. He didn't kiss her. He buried his face in her sweet-scented neck and unleashed a burst of pent-up sobs. Her arms went around him. She held him tight as he wept into her hair.

Finally he drew back and looked down at her. "I love you, Clara," he said.

"No," she said, placing a fingertip on his lips. "Don't say it. You are grieving. You don't mean it. You need comforting and solace and someone to soothe your damaged soul. Do not mistake these things for love."

He took the hand that was held to his mouth and kissed the palm.

At the end of the tree-lined lane that led to the western acres of the Schaller farm, Wilhelm had come to a sudden halt. He stood with gardening hoe and rake propped against his beefy shoulder, like a soldier's rifle. He had seen Johann come into the yard, Clara light the lantern and blow out the match, and the two of them stare across the yard at each other. He had seen his brother take the steps and reach her in one bound, drawing her into his arms. And now he saw how Johann kissed the palm of her hand, how pliant her body was against his, how they delved into each other's eyes and were held by a mutual passion.

Strangely, no fury or rage burst within Wilhelm in the moment. Instead, a very calm and reasonable voice, like a ghostly whisper from another world, spoke between his ears: It isn't fair. First Johann steals Papa's love, and now he steals Clara's.

And *then* the explosion came.

Here it was at last, the target of days of anger and hatred. The dark, evil emotions that had been bubbling and festering within him since his father's death now finally coalesced, like parts of an arrow floating in the air—shaft, arrowhead, fletchings—coming together and pointing directly to where Wilhelm's venom must go. To his brother. Johann was the cause of all pain and emptiness in the world. He had to be punished.

He waited for them to go inside and then, a moment later, he joined them. They were in the kitchen, not speaking, going about mundane tasks as if nothing terrible and world-changing had just happened. Dinner was eaten in a strained silence. Only the sounds of forks on plates disturbed the night. Clara could have screamed with the tension. She felt as if they had become trapped in a queer sort of stage play—a one-act play with only three characters, the theme of which was struggle and loss and the futility of believing in anything at all. If you find out that people aren't who you thought they were, including yourself, then what in the whole world was there to trust? Maybe, she thought absurdly, you couldn't trust a butterfly to be a butterfly, life was that astounding. It made for acute insecurity, and she desperately wished the author of this stage play would hurry up and write the ending.

Finally, the potatoes and onions and salt pork all gone, the buttered flat bread and San Francisco ale all gone, Wilhelm pulled the napkin out of his collar and said, "Johann, we have to talk."

"What about?"

"Things. You know. Legal matters. Family stuff. Now that Papa's gone. . . ."

Johann nodded. "Yes," he said. "I see." The inheritance. The farm. Now that the hierarchy had changed, things needed to be worked out.

"Let's walk," Wilhelm said, rising. "It's a good night out. We can clear our heads."

In the moonlight they walked solemnly, Johann with his hands in his pockets, unable to put Clara from his mind, the feel of her body against his, the taste of her neck as he had wept there, the scent of her hair, the tremendous sexual desire that had rocked his body. How was he going to live with her from now on?

He was so embroiled in his quandary that it took him a moment to realize that Wilhelm had strode on ahead and then had stopped and turned and planted himself in Johann's path. "Now listen," Wilhelm said in a growl Johann had never heard before. "*I* am the real son," he said. "Do you understand that?"

Johann didn't know what to say. There was a queer look in his brother's eyes, and his face was set in a strange cast. He was almost unrecognizable. Johann glanced back over his shoulder and saw the lights in the cabin. They had walked quite a distance. They were at the front edge of the property, where the driveway met the road and all was in darkness. "*I'm* the legitimate Schaller," Wilhelm growled in a voice that made Johann's blood run cold. "*I* inherit this land, not you! You are the bastard son of a whore! You don't belong here any more."

"Wilhelm," Johann began, disbelief choking his throat. He could say no more, and so tears sprang to his eyes, as if his throat had squeezed them out. The hatred in his brother's eyes—this brother whom he worshipped and who had always been his protector. Do not turn on me, brother! We have lost Papa, do not let me now lose you!

The first strike caught Johann square in the chest, knocking the breath out of him. Wilhelm steadied his stance and struck out with his second fist before Johann could raise a defense. The blow caught him directly on the side of his head. He felt pain as he had never felt before, and stars exploded behind his eyes. He stumbled back. Johann raised his hands to protect his face. The next blow landed in his stomach. His arms dropped down.

Wilhelm kept his fists coming, the neck, the shoulders; then he kicked and used his knee to the groin. Johann tried to fight back, but uselessly due to shock and being winded. He flailed his arms until they landed on Wilhelm's shoulders. Johann drew his brother to him, as he had drawn Clara to him, and held on to him, sobbing, begging Wilhelm to stop. "I love you, my brother," Johann gasped. "Please don't do this." But the assault raged on, knuckles pummeling him in all the tender places until Johann's knees gave way. He slumped to the ground, dizzy, out of air, sick to his stomach. While he was down, Wilhelm laid boots on him, slamming his feet against his brother's back and buttocks and thighs, feeling within himself a rocket burst of anger and joy, the deliciousness of revenge, the bitterness of assailing the boy he had always protected.

He wished it was Jakob he was beating up. The father who had fallen from grace. Who had chosen Wilhelm to be second best. And Clara was somewhere in those skyrocketing emotions as well, the woman who had betrayed him, who had been found comforting the wrong brother, the *preferred* brother.

Wilhelm finally stopped. His chest heaved. Sweat dripped from his face. He was spent. He reached down and, grasping Johann by the wrists, dragged him on his back, grunting and puffing, hauling his helpless brother over the dirt and grass, lacerating him further until, after a long and strenuous trek, he dumped him down and said, "There. This is the edge of Schaller land. This is the boundary of Schaller property. Get away from here and don't come back."

He stood over him as Johann struggled to get on his hands and knees. Wilhelm booted him mercilessly, sending him sprawling onto the ground. "Get up!" he cried. "And get away! Don't make me kill you!"

Johann managed to lift himself up and stagger away with widespread legs. As the darkness of the night swallowed him and he was one tall candle of pain, he heard his brother's voice bellow behind him: "If you set foot on my property, or if you come near my wife again, *I will kill you!*"

As Johann disappeared into the night and Wilhelm walked slowly back to the house, his father's words tolled like a bell in his mind: I love Johann more because I loved your sister more. . . .

As he entered the cabin, he hid his bruised hands and said to Clara: "Johann is gone. He won't be coming home. We had an argument. He says he wants no part of our father's legacy. He wants no part of Schaller farms. He's gone to find work elsewhere, and he said he will never set foot here again."

He turned sad eyes on Clara, a false sadness that hid his feelings of victory and triumph, and of sadness and horror as well. "My brother has left us, and we will never see him again."

"Wilhelm! No!"

The lie came so easily that it frightened him, but not as much as the next thought in his mind frightened him: that yes, if Johann came back and set foot on Schaller land or touched Clara again, Wilhelm would without a doubt kill him. "I pleaded with him to stay. I told him we are still brothers. And we are! But he called himself a bastard and said he can never forgive our father for the lie."

"I don't believe it," she whispered. "Johann wouldn't."

"These were his exact words, Clara," Wilhelm said, forcing tears of sadness into his hard eyes. "'*You* are the real son,' he said to me. '*You* are the legitimate Schaller. *You* inherited this land, not I. I am the bastard son of a whore. I do not belong here any more.' His exact words, Clara."

"No, no!" she cried, clutching her stomach. Johann . . . *gone.*

Wilhelm watched her as something broke inside himself. It was as if he had suddenly split in half. The shock and anger at his father's confession, to see the great righteous Jakob Schaller tumble down from his godly pedestal . . . it was too much to bear. But now this was too much to bear. He saw it nakedly on her face, the thing he had been blind to—that Clara was in love with Johann.

And it gave him no pleasure to see her pain. He wanted to take it all back. Confess his lies. Go after Johann and bring him home. But he knew that would never happen. How was he going to live now? How could he go on, having lost all the love he had ever felt sure of—his father's, his bastard brother's, and, most of all, Clara's? He thought of the village overlooking the Rhine and the pretty girl behind the counter who had called him brave and courageous and how she had made him feel like a hero. He felt like none of those things now and doubted he ever would again.

He turned away from her. They hadn't come to California after all: they had come to the deepest pit of Hell.

Out on the road, staggering in the darkness, sick at heart and woebegone, bleeding, his body screaming with pain, Johann paused and turned, swaying, to look back with pounding head and double vision. He could barely make out the trees that marked the edge of the Schaller farm. He didn't understand what had just happened. But through the fog of his misery and the searing pain in his body, one thought came through chillingly clear: Wilhelm is right. I am no longer a Schaller. I do not belong here. For I am Johann Neumann, son of Hannah Neumann. That is who I am. And from this day forward, for as long as I draw breath, no Neumann will ever set foot on Schaller land.

In his sickness and waves of great pain, feeling blood trickle down the insides of his sleeves and pants, and his entire body throbbing, part of Johann's tortured mind found a kind of ironic justice in the name Neumann, as it meant "new man." And that was what he was, a new man. Completely re-created, like Adam in Eden, with no father or mother.

And as for Clara . . . yes, he had fallen in love with her, he could admit that now, from this distance. . . .

He would never see *her* again either.

He swayed some more, then turned and ploddingly set one foot in front of the other and, having no idea where he was going or what he was going to do, shambled off, hurting and alone, into the night.

The Present Day

The first to arrive at the Schaller farm were two uniformed cops in a black-and-white cruiser, stepping out into the morning sunlight, settling their official hats on their heads and adjusting the nightsticks on their belts. The radio in their squad car kept up a constant squawking of distant voices. Nicole went forward to meet them. "It's this way, officers," she said, diverting them from the parking lot, around the main building of the winery, to the area out back where workers' trucks and equipment stood about, along with half a dozen dazed Mexicans who looked as if they'd seen a ghost.

"It's in there," she said, pointing to the open doorway to the barrel room. "I don't know—" The skeleton looked very old and decomposed. It must have been in that wall for *years*. Nicole shuddered to think of all the times when, as a child, she had played hide-and-seek in the barrel room. Children's squeals of delight falling upon dead, decaying ears. She could see the local headline: HAUNTED WINERY. Who was the victim? What had he or she done to deserve such a fate? And who had pulled the trigger and masterminded the devious burial?

Biggest question of all: Why had neither she nor anyone ever heard a thing about it?

"Wait here, please, ma'am," one of the cops said as he drew out his long flashlight.

For some reason, Nicole held her breath, as if breathing might upset the delicate balance of the universe. Anxious, she pressed her hand to her stomach. What was she hoping for? That these official men with badges would come out and say with a laugh that there was nothing in there at all. Just a trick of shadow and light. And because they were official men with badges, that meant it was true and everything was all right after all, just one of those unexplainable blips in the cosmos.

They were only in there for a minute, sweeping their beams over the gaping hole in the wall, the icky thing lodged inside. One of them got on a cell phone, presumably to headquarters. Nicole caught words: "Decomposed human remains. . . . Suspicious circumstances. . . ." And her stomach sank. So it was really true. There was a corpse in the wall of her barrel room where exquisite Rieslings slumbered in oak casks—wines grown from grapes brought over from Germany over a hundred years ago. It didn't seem right. Something sacrilegious was going on in there.

They came out as Nicole and the Mexicans and the nice Canadian couple waited for some sort of pronouncement, an answer perhaps to what had been found in the wall. One of the cops said, "Homicide detectives are on their way. Don't let anyone inside." They then proceeded to stretch yellow tape across the doorway that blurted CRIME SCENE DO NOT CROSS.

Nicole's heart did a somersault up to her throat and down to her stomach. Crime scene? Her home had gone from being a quaint boutique winery of historical interest to a *crime scene*? She looked over at the nice Canadians, named Macintosh, and wondered how horrified, repulsed, and scared out of their minds they must be. They were smiling. They looked as if they were on a holiday.

The officer took out his notepad and wrote Nicole's name on it. "Do you have any idea who that might be in there? How they ended up in the wall?"

She mutely shook her head.

He waited expectantly, as if hoping she would suddenly remember a hushed-up murder in her family and spill all the details so he could have the case wrapped up before the detectives got there and made him the cop of the hour.

"No," she said.

More police cruisers arrived. A lot of milling around by men in uniforms, a few unnecessary questions because even though it *was* a crime scene, it was a very old one and Nicole couldn't possibly say that she had seen any suspicious people hanging around or heard any gunshots.

She heard a motor coming down the driveway and turned to see a pickup truck pull up. To her shock, the words NEWMAN FARMS were stenciled on the driver's door.

THE FAR RIVER / 101

Nicole was further startled to see the driver get out. It was Lucas Newman. She couldn't believe it! No Newman had set foot on Schaller land in over a hundred years. They weren't welcome here, any more than Schallers were welcome on Newman land. It stunned her to see him. She didn't know what to say. And she felt a rare indignation rise within her as she thought: How dare he?

Their families were enemies, but Nicole knew Lucas very well. They had, in a way, grown up together, at least attending the same schools, although Lucas was always three grades ahead because he was three years older. They went to the same local sports events and holiday celebrations in town. But other than both families being wealthy farmers, they had little in common. Schaller wines had been a large and famous enterprise, bottling a wide array of vintages from cheap jug wine to expensive champagne, while Newman winery had remained small and exclusive, putting out award-winning, estate-bottled quality wines.

He came to a halt and squinted at the police cars, the men prowling inside with flashlights. "I just heard," he said without preamble, without even a hello, as though he showed up here every day, "and had to come and see for myself if it's true."

As she bristled—he had no right to be here, he hadn't been invited—she saw the tension in his own body, as if he didn't want to be here himself. He was restless, impatient, agitated. She wondered if old Melvyn, his father, knew that he was here. He had come out of necessity rather than curiosity, she suspected.

She noticed he made no mention of the issue that had stood between them these past few weeks, communicating as they had through lawyers and real estate agents. When Nicole had put her property on the market, the Newmans made an offer. But it had been specified in Big Jack Schaller's will that should his heirs decide to or need to sell Schaller winery, under no circumstances were they to sell to Newman Farms. So Nicole couldn't sell to them, no matter how desperate she was. The feud between the Schallers and the Newmans was legendary in the valley, although folks didn't know why. It had had its beginnings over a century before, the reasons for the bitter feud lost to memory.

She folded her arms and rested on one hip, a gesture she hoped looked more defiant than defensive. "Why do you care about a skeleton in our wall?" she asked bluntly.

He finally shifted his gaze to her, and it unsettled her. Lucas Newman had sexy, hooded eyes with a slight puffiness to the lower lids that gave the illusion of amusement. Even though she knew he wasn't here for a pleasant social visit—in fact, he looked aggressive and angry—his eyes had a mischievous cast to them, reminding her that Lucas Newman had been known, in the schools they had both attended, for being a class clown. He had been notorious for warming the bench in the principal's office more than most boys. He had also been the football team's star quarterback and class valedictorian at graduation.

"We had a relative go missing some years back," he said. "Never found him. I want to know who got killed here and who's buried in that wall." It sounded like a command, and Nicole suddenly got her hackles up.

Nicole knew what was in his mind, and she resented it. Lucas suspected foul play that had been some part of the ridiculous family feud, maybe payback or revenge. "You think one of us had something to do with it," she said.

His look turned hard. "My men said something about a bullet to the skull."

Lucas was tall and too good-looking. She recalled seeing his picture in a wine connoisseur magazine when he won a gold medal at the recent San Francisco International Wine Competition. His winery's Sauvignon Blanc had taken the top sweepstakes spot. His Merlot took Best of Class, and the double gold went to Newman's Petite Sirah. The Newmans always won competitions. No Schaller had ever congratulated them, and Nicole wasn't about to start now.

She felt like walking away, to show him what she thought of his veiled accusation. But she stood her ground. "The policemen only said it *looks* like it might be a homicide. It could be suicide."

"Then how did the victim bury himself in the wall?"

She shrugged. She didn't like having to explain herself to Lucas Newman. This was Schaller property and a Schaller private affair. He had no business being here, missing relative or not. "It might have been covered up. But I don't know who it could be. No one in *my* family has ever gone missing," Nicole added with an accusatory tone, as if the Newmans had a sloppy habit of losing family members.

Lucas let it fly past him. "But someone in *my* family did go missing. I came to see if it could be him."

Her eyes bored into his. "And you think," she said in a hard voice, "that if he was murdered and buried on Schaller land, then a Schaller must have done it."

"Your words, not mine." And then he insolently pushed past her, as if Newmans walked on Schaller soil every day, and called "Hello?" through the open doorway.

She couldn't help staring. Even though they had almost nothing to do with each other, she saw a lot of Lucas Newman, if only to pass on the sidewalk in Lynnville. They knew each other from a kind of snarling distance, each having been raised to hate the other family. He had the lean, muscled physique of a man who worked in the fields. She had heard that Lucas Newman was no "desk vintner": he picked grapes and got his hands dirty.

He came striding back. "The cops don't know anything. They're waiting for the detectives and the crime-scene guys." He stood with his hands on his hips, impatiently, as though the discovery of a skeleton on Schaller property were greatly inconveniencing him.

Lucas had a cowboy look about him—with his blue jeans and high-heeled boots and Western-style shirt and tan-colored straw cattleman's hat. Well, he *was* a California farmer where the cowboy look had been a long tradition. Nicole just wished he wasn't so damn good-looking.

A van arrived at that moment with CRIME SCENE UNIT stenciled on the side. Four men in dark blue uniforms and windbreakers, carrying kits, stepped out and ducked under the yellow tape to disappear inside. Amazingly, the Canadian Macintoshes had their phones out and were taking pictures. A couple of the Mexicans, too.

Was this about to hit the Internet?

Nicole closed her eyes. Her father Big Jack, if he'd still been alive, would have ranted about the skeleton, and then he would have ordered the men to seal the hole and plaster it over and not say a word to anyone or there would be hell to pay. He'd make sure the wall looked as good as new and the thing inside never mentioned again. Big Jack didn't believe in calling the police.

Her father. . . .

Nicole rubbed her arms, waiting for the CSI guys to come out. Nicole hadn't been able to make her father, Big Jack, understand her need to make her own way in the world. She had brought it up just once and it had ended so badly that she never mentioned it again. When she had come home with her MBA from Santa Barbara, Jack had grumbled about "fat lot of good that's going to do you here when the operation is already going smooth as glass." He had conveniently overlooked the fact that he had lost heavily in Las Vegas and certain "collectors" were pressuring him to pay what he owed. And he was heavily into the whiskey by then and selling off parcels of Schaller land. Yes, Nicole might be able to save the farm, as Big Jack implied. But that was *his* responsibility. "I want to create my own path in the world, Daddy. I want pride in myself," she had said, irritated with him, but feeling sorry for him and loving him all at the same time.

"*Pride!*" he had boomed and the veins at his neck had bulged. "Are you telling me, little girl, that you have no pride in what the Schallers have built?" He had thrown out his meaty arms to encompass the big house, the vineyards, the winery. "What my grandfather and father built up here, *you have no pride in?*" He hadn't waited for an answer. "By God, you're an ungrateful snip when every other son and daughter in this valley would give anything to have a roaring big family business simply handed to them!"

She had said nothing more, seeing the red face, watching him pour another glass. He wouldn't understand, not then, not ever, so that she had begun worrying if she was ever going to be her own person or just another Schaller in a long line of Schallers.

And this was no impulsive decision. In high school she had fantasized about getting away, going to a town where no one knew the scandalous Schaller story, where she could start anew and build her own thriving business. Besides, she *had* to sell the farm. Big Jack had left her with debts. It wasn't just his gambling and unwise investments, it was his big-hearted generosity as well, buying drinks for everyone in the casino when he had a big win and then unable to cover the tab because after the big win he had suffered an even bigger loss. He was just a poor money manager, Big Jack.

Nicole massaged her forehead. The day had gone wrong. She had gotten up that morning ready to show her home to potential buyers, her stomach fluttery at the thought of putting on the best front. She had planned an interesting tour of the main buildings and the house, followed by a trek out into the vineyards where workers were conducting a pre-harvest test to establish grape maturity. After that, treat the buyers to dinner in the restaurant off the wine-tasting room—specialty of the house: roast beef with gravy, mashed potatoes, and Yorkshire pudding, accompanied of course by a bottle of Schaller's best full-bodied red wine.

She looked down the long drive that led to the main highway and saw a police car, lights flashing, and two cops diverting traffic. A limousine had pulled up, bringing wine-tasters. They were told to move on. Schaller Winery was one of the stops on a very popular wine-tasting tour in the valley. Nicole realized with a sinking heart that customers were going to be turned away all day long. Word was going to quickly spread that something weird and official was going on at Schaller's.

In the meantime, Lucas was giving Nicole a long, searching look. He had arrived defensive, chip-on-shoulder, prepared to insist he had a right to be there. He had thought she was going to shout at him and have him thrown off her property. Instead, she seemed derailed and at a loss. She looked worried and vulnerable, and he didn't know what to make of it. He had assumed she was a ball-breaker, like all the Schaller women, going straight back to the supreme Lady Boss herself, Clara, whose name was never to be mentioned in Newman presence. A family of wimpy men and castrating women was how Lucas's father had always described the Schallers. Okay, perhaps the vitriol was a bit overboard, but old Melvyn himself had been raised by an equally vitriolic father who had poured poison into his son's ear, just as Melvyn had poured it into Lucas's. It was a solid Newman tradition to despise anyone named Schaller.

But Lucas suddenly found himself feeling sorry for Nicole. Certainly it hadn't been her golden dream to find a skeleton in one of her walls, especially a skeleton with a bullet in its skull. And now all these police and crime-scene techs and detectives coming. This wasn't her fault. And he sort of grudgingly sympathized with her.

Nicole wasn't bad-looking, he thought. She had inherited the attractive widow's peak through her father, who had borne a vague resemblance to Leonardo DiCaprio and had had the same V-shaped hairline. Usually, when Lucas saw her in town, she wore jeans and work shirts, her brown hair drawn back in a ponytail. She was stylish this morning, dressed to impress. He glanced at the middle-aged couple who looked very out of place in this bizarre setting. Potential buyers?

Nicole looked back at the barrel room, the strangers stomping around with their fingerprint dust and brushes or whatever they were doing—she pictured scenes from TV shows—and felt her impatience rise. Where were the detectives? Let's get this show on the road. Clean up that mess in the barrel room and resume her selling tour of the property. For some reason, she suddenly blamed this whole thing on Lucas Newman.

She gave him a long look and wondered what he knew about the fight, long ago. She hadn't thought about it in a long time, the cause of the feud between the Schallers and the Newmans. She wondered if Lucas knew what had happened. He would no doubt slant it, say the Schallers were to blame when Nicole had heard all her life that it was the Newmans who had started it.

Lucas took off his hat to expose longish, tousled blond hair. Motes floated in the sunshine, the buzzing of bees filled the air. She wanted him gone. "The police said the medical examiner will determine age and gender, and maybe identity," she said. "I'll let you know as soon as they tell me anything." She hoped he would take the hint and leave.

But Lucas scanned the scene with a wrinkled nose while Nicole bristled at his audacity.

A car horn sounded. Nicole turned to see a dusty black convertible sports car come racing down the drive from the main road and grind to a halt on the gravel parking lot, sending up a cloud of sand and grit. The driver jumped out with shouts of "Holy Christmas, what the heck is going on here?"

Nicole's best friend since grade school, Michelle. She had been Nicole's second call, after the police.

Michelle was wearing a traditional German folk dress called a dirndl, which consisted of a bodice, a white peasant blouse, and a full skirt, forest green, with a lighter green apron over it—the costume she wore when working at the family bakery in Germantown. The tourists expected it. She must have dropped everything and come straight over without changing.

Her curly henna-red hair stood out in all directions. "Those cute cops back at the road almost wouldn't let me in, but I told them I was your sister and flashed them a little thigh. God, am I hallucinating?" she said, gawking at Lucas.

"Hi, Michelle," he said blandly.

She looked aghast at Nicole. "It spoke! God, he's real. Girlfriend, what on earth?"

"Lucas thinks the body in the wall might be a missing relative."

Michelle's eyebrows shot up. "This is *too* juicy!"

Lucas gave her a look of disgust and turned away.

She watched him wide-eyed, as if he were Godzilla trampling Tokyo. Michelle made no bones about staring. A Newman and a Schaller standing together and no blood was flying. As this year's head of the Oktoberfest committee, it was Michelle's job to see to it that the Schaller and Newman wine-tasting booths were at opposite ends of the festival grounds.

She put her hands on her hips and stared at the bizarre scene: the cops, the CSI van, the Canadian couple she knew were interested in buying the place, the Mexicans, and, in the midst of it all—Lucas Newman standing right there in front of the Schaller winery as if he were just anybody and had a right to be there!

Michelle had never liked Lucas Newman. He walked with a bit of a swagger, like he was the only bag of chips in town. She imagined him practicing his walk in front of a mirror, adjusting his cattleman's hat, making sure he got the cowboy vibe just right. She allowed that he *was* good-looking, if you went for that sort of thing. And yes, when he smiled (she had seen him goof off around the school campus) he did kind of light up the day. And she had heard that he was kind to animals and old ladies. But still.

Standing there in the bright sunshine as if they were actors awaiting their cues, Michelle thought how strange it was that these two enemies, Nicole and Lucas, were related. Their great-grandfathers had been brothers or something, and then there had been a falling-out and they had gone their separate ways. From the scuttlebutt in the valley, the falling-out had been over everything from money to a land dispute to a fight over a woman. No one knew for sure.

"I never heard about a Newman going missing," she said to Nicole.

Nicole shrugged. "One of those family secrets, I suppose."

"My God," Michelle said in a tone that sounded almost like delight, "a genuine skeleton in the closet!"

Nicole didn't think it was funny. She felt sorry for the poor man or woman who had met such an undignified fate and who was now receiving undignified attention. She was also worried about what this scandal was going to do to the Schaller name, and to any potential sales of the winery.

Michelle said, "I'm sorry," and touched Nicole's arm. She knew how important the sale of the winery was. "You know me. It's just my way of dealing with the incomprehensible." What Michelle didn't clarify was that the incomprehensible was not so much the grisly find in the barrel room, but her friend's determination to leave the valley.

Michelle loved this place, the tidy small towns, neat little farms, patchwork-quilt vineyards, white church steeples, the peaceful Largo River, the close-knit community of friends. Still, she understood why Nicole would want to run away from this, especially since she had been *born* into it, unlike Michelle whose parents had moved to California when she was five.

Nicole had confessed to her that she needed to make her own way in the world. It was what most of the girls in their circle had done, moved away for careers and marriage in glamorous places, maintaining the girl-friend circle through Internet media. Her own parents had pulled up their roots in Wisconsin and re-planted them here in this sunny valley. Michelle had married into one of the oldest families in the valley, the Eberhardts, who had come out here a century before. She liked the idea of being both an outsider and an insider. She thought it gave her some color to be foreign and yet a member of local royalty at the same time. She had grown up hearing about the Schaller–Newman feud and, like everyone else, wondered what it was all about. Nicole herself didn't know, and she was a Schaller!

Michelle wished Nicole wouldn't leave. She was practically a celebrity here. And the valley was interesting now, not just a lazy small-town place. It had become a haven for free spirits, New Agers, people going back to the land to grow organic food and free-range poultry, artists and free thinkers, writers and people who made jewelry and pottery. Michelle had begged her to stay, not to sell the winery, but Nicole had to go.

Michelle knew it had to do with Big Jack, Nicole's overbearing father, and what he had done to the company, the mess he had bequeathed to his daughter. After Jack Schaller's death, Nicole had gone through the company's books with the accountants and lawyers and had discovered that the winery was nearly bankrupt. Big Jack hadn't paid a bill in months, and they were barely able to meet their payroll. Her father had inherited a fortune and burned through it. Big Jack had invested heavily in get-rich-quick schemes that went belly-up. He had had to sell a lot of Schaller holdings, but still never got out of debt. Every penny Nicole was going to make on the sale of the estate would go to creditors. But at least she could walk away from it debt-free and start over.

Still . . . was she going to be happy in her new life? Michelle suspected not. She suspected that her best friend had no idea how tied to this valley she was, how in tune with its rhythms and moods. Nicole had always seemed to instinctively understand this place, could sniff the wind on a sunny day and tell you that rain was coming. Was Nicole aware that she was of two conflicting minds and that only one could end up being happy?

Just then the medical examiner's van arrived. Two men unloaded a gurney with a black body bag folded neatly on it. A third man, wearing rubber gloves with a badge clipped to his windbreaker, led them inside the barrel room.

Michelle saw the Canadian couple snapping pictures on their phones and madly texting. This crime scene, and their peripheral participation in it, was no doubt going to be the biggest thing to shake up Moose Butt, Canada—or wherever they were from. A town, Michelle imagined, where they wore plaid lumber jackets and hats with ear flaps, and went around saying "Eh?"

And *these* were going to be the new owners of Schaller's Winery?

Despite the debts and the bankruptcy, Michelle had tried to talk her friend out of leaving. But Nicole wanted her own career, wanted to get away from rural and small-town life. She'd love to live in New York and work in a career that was electric and moved fast. The wine business moved at the speed of grapes ripening in the sun, a passive industry impelled by nature's own good time rather than the speed of man. There was no rushing a ripening, no hurrying fermentation. Nicole said she felt as if she had been born to run, but was living where the facts of life required a person to *wait*.

A dusty blue Chevrolet arrived and a portly man stepped out, wearing an obviously cheap suit, narrow tie, and scuffed loafers. He was bareheaded, an orange comb-over barely covering the scalp, and a detective's badge was clipped to the pocket of his suit jacket. He went first to confer with the uniformed officer in charge, who pointed to Nicole and Lucas, then he came over and introduced himself as Sergeant Quinn. He smelled of chili and cigars. "Are you the owners?"

"I am," Nicole said.

He looked questioningly at Lucas, who said, "I'm a concerned party, Lucas Newman. Is there just one of you?" he said, glancing back at the dusty car.

"My partner's off with the flu," the detective said vaguely, as if, wasn't it obvious that a case like this didn't warrant two detectives? He continued: "Would you mind waiting here? I have a few questions I'd like to ask." And then he ducked under the yellow tape and joined the others inside the barrel room.

The wait was interminable. Nicole glanced at the Macintoshes, who were still there. They seemed titillated. They had earlier tried to pry family scandals out of her, and now they were getting it in spades. She had tried to find a way to remove them from the scene, distract them from this sordid happening. She had given them the map of the property and suggested they drive out and take a look at Colina Sagrada, the supposed Sacred Hill that actually looked cursed. She had hinted that there might be Indian arrowheads to be found in the barren, desert-like soil, but the Macintoshes wouldn't bite. Homicides beat cursed hills any day.

When Quinn came back out of the barrel room, he said: "The ME's guys say they can't determine the age of the skeleton or its sex. That's for the autopsy to determine. But it's very old. Decades, the crime unit guys estimate. They'll get cement and soil samples back to the lab, see if forensics can pinpoint a more accurate date at time of death." He held out a clear plastic bag. "Does this mean anything to either of you?"

There was an object inside. A silver ID bracelet with words engraved on it. *"Amour de ma vie."* Nicole and Lucas examined it, shaking their heads. Michelle leaned in for a look too.

"Do your employment records go back very far?" Quinn asked.

"I'll have to look," Nicole said. "My father took care of all that. He died recently. A lot of the old records went to our lawyer for safe storage. Why?"

"The skeleton might have been an employee here, or just someone passing through. I doubt the victim is Mexican. This inscription looks French."

He then asked routine questions: Did Nicole have any idea who the victim might be? Was she aware of anyone missing in her family? Did she have any idea at all what might have happened here and when?

"We can probably pinpoint the date of the murder to when this wall was last renovated," he said airily, as if he were discussing a feeble poker hand. Homicide always seemed so exotic and romantic on TV. Nicole decided that in real life, it must be very routine.

She realized he was looking at her expectantly, his eyes a bit bulgy, like his stomach. "Oh," she said. "You want to know when this wall was last worked on?"

"That's the plan," he said. "The crime-unit techs went over this opening with magnifying glasses. This wall wasn't broken open to hide a body and then plastered over. At some point it was being renovated maybe and before it was finished, someone took advantage and hid a body in here. Then it was covered over and no one was the wiser." He paused, all expectant again.

"Yes," she said, wondering if he thought she was a scatterbrain. He couldn't know that this murder business had upset her. With a grisly reputation now, how was the winery to find buyers? Well, it might attract lookie-loos and people who got a thrill out of crime scenes, but it wouldn't attract serious wine lovers. And she had the Job of the Century waiting for her in New York.

"I'll have to go through the records," she said, trying to think back and not recalling any renovating in her own lifetime. And she had never picked up any rumor or hint of scandal or something being hushed up under her own roof. Her parents had never acted as if a body was concealed on their property. So it would have happened three decades ago or more. And that would call for searching through records and papers that were stored away in archive boxes. "I'll call you when I've found something."

He sucked a tooth and said, "Okay," as if she were purposely making his job harder. "In the meantime," he said, "my office will go through files and see if anyone was reported missing. We might have to go back quite a few years."

Lucas spoke up. "Detective Quinn, a member of my family vanished years ago. We searched, never found him."

"When was the disappearance?"

"Around 1997, I think. My father would know for certain."

"Did you report him missing?"

"I don't know. We probably did."

"And this ID bracelet and inscription means nothing to you?"

"No."

"We'll need all the pertinent information on your missing relative."

"What are the chances of your people finding the culprit?"

Quinn shrugged. "A twenty- or thirty-year-old murder? The chances of finding witnesses, suspects, evidence, motive?" He did a flipping gesture with his stubby hand.

He turned to Nicole. "I understand your father passed away last year?"

The non sequitur caught her off guard. "I beg your pardon?"

"How old was he?" His pen was poised over his official detective's notepad.

Nicole bristled. What kind of questioning was this? Where was he going with it? Big Jack had been a notorious gambler and famous for his temper—but enough to kill someone? "He was fifty-eight," she said, seeing the wheels of math turning in the detective's head. Yes, her father would have been around at the time of the murder. Now she saw another headline: BIG JACK SCHALLER IMPLICATED IN LOCAL HOMICIDE.

Nicole felt her emotions bubbling up dangerously. She wanted to shout and scream and rant at this plodding detective, at the uniformed cops who milled about uselessly like stage props, at the crime-scene techs all full of science and self importance, at the medical examiner's team who were taking their own sweet time removing the monstrosity from her barrel room, at Michelle, even, who seemed excited by the whole thing. Most of all, she wanted to scream at Lucas Newman for showing up with his silent accusation of murder, acting as if *he* were the injured party here and laying undeserved guilt on her.

But she wouldn't. Nicole would stay calm and in control because ranting and shouting was what Big Jack would do, and she was not Big Jack.

The detective turned to Michelle. "And you are?"

"A friend of the family. Michelle Eberhardt."

"Eberhardt? As in the bakeries?" He grinned, giving her a once-over, pausing to appreciate the way the tightly laced bodice of her costume emphasized her bosom. "My wife swears by your glazed crullers. Buys 'em every chance she gets."

One of the medical examiner's men came out and murmured something to the detective, who nodded and said, "Thanks. Get it over to ballistics, will you?"

He took a moment to survey the three standing before him: one impatient, one anxious, the third with cheeks red with excitement—the bakery lady with the big crullers. Normally he would put their names on the suspect list, but they wouldn't have even been born at the time of the murder.

"The bullet was still in the skull," he said.

"Oh, my!" Michelle blurted, as if this detail added a splash of color to the drama.

"The medical examiner has determined that the victim was shot from several feet away; a very close-range shot would have gone through the back of the skull. So we can rule out suicide."

The detective saw an older couple standing a few yards away. Outsiders. He didn't suppose they would offer any useful information. He also didn't think they would suddenly produce the gun the bullet had been fired from.

Normally he would see this case going nowhere had it not involved two of the most famous wineries in California. Every Christmas, gift bottles of Schaller and Newman wines were exchanged among his family and friends. He and his wife had recently celebrated their twenty-fifth anniversary at Newman's upscale wine-tasting room, where they served the best T-bone steak this side of Texas.

So, fame and wealth. Soon there would be news vans and tabloid reporters. "It was a nine-millimeter bullet," he added, watching their faces.

Suddenly, Nicole felt a frisson of alarm. She didn't know why. Perhaps she was on edge simply because of all these people with guns and badges. But something cold and threatening had just shot into her heart. The day was going from warm to hot, typical of California in September. Flies now bothered them, and the drone of bees grew louder. Dust filled her nostrils. She watched Lucas as he tipped his cattleman's hat back on his head, and Michelle's gold-loop earrings flashed in the sun.

And then it came to her, just like that, a long-forgotten memory from her childhood. Outside her father's office, she recalled hearing him talking to a visitor, saying, "Isn't she a beaut? There's nothing more elegant than a well-oiled nine-millimeter Beretta."

Now, remembering, a terrible chill swept over her. Dear God, don't let it be so. That her father Big Jack, grandson of the revered Wilhelm and Clara Schaller, had killed someone and buried him in a wall. And please God, don't let the victim turn out to be a Newman.

Nicole wondered if the gun was still among her father's things. And if she found it, should she turn it over to the police?

The detective turned to her. "I'm afraid you're going to have to halt work on the renovation, Miss Schaller. There might be evidence buried with the victim. Everything has to be left intact."

She dreaded the delay. Stringing it out would only spotlight the scandal, get tongues wagging and newspapers running gossipy stories. Would the cosmetics firm in New York hold the position for her? Her contract with them had stipulated that she start her employment on November first.

Quinn watched the Schaller woman carefully. Quinn considered himself an expert on body language, and she clearly didn't like the Newman fellow. Why was that? Were they in cahoots, the two of them covering something up, and she resented it? Quinn suspected everyone he met of harboring dark secrets. No one was above his personal suspicions. He reckoned it was what came of being in a profession that required a man to be an inquisitor and to trust no one.

Quinn was also naturally nosy. He enjoyed prying into people's lives. It was why he had become a detective in the first place. He had been with the Chicago Police Department until Quinn's mother had moved in with him and his family. The winters got to be too much for her, so he packed up his family and moved them to Arizona—where it was too hot. And then a holiday driving trip through the California wine country had introduced them to the Largo Valley, which was "just right." So they moved here and had stayed ever since. That had been twenty years ago. His mother was still alive and healthy and called Lynnville the "Goldilocks place."

The crime rate wasn't high, with just enough robberies and homicides to satisfy Quinn without overwhelming him, the way Chicago had. But this was his first genuine murder, an actual cold case, and it set his imagination on fire. This was one case he was determined to get to the bottom of, no matter how stubborn these two mortal enemies were going to be about it.

"So tell me about your families, the Schallers and the Newmans."

Both of them got defensive over this. "Why?" snapped Lucas.

"It's been my experience that family feuds are always a good place to start when looking for motives behind foul play." He paused. He saw a reluctance to talk about their families, and he had already picked up on their hostility toward each other. "I would sincerely like to put the words 'full cooperation' in my report. You know what I mean? So, you two are related? I'm not sure how. Your grandfathers or something were brothers, but your last names are different." He left his words hanging in the air, allowing them the option to give "full cooperation."

Nicole looked at Lucas, his handsome face darkened in shadow. "It's true, Detective," she said. "Our two families descended from two brothers and yet we have different last names." She pictured Clara Schaller in the portrait over the fireplace, elegant and poised, the wife of one of the Schaller brothers. Why then weren't the Newmans also Schallers? Had the other male line died out, leaving only daughters who had to marry outside the family and take on a new name?

She frowned. But no . . . didn't it say on their wine labels that Newman Winery had been founded in the early nineteen hundreds?

Quinn said now to Lucas, "Do *you* know why you have different last names?"

Lucas got agitated over this. "Detective Quinn, I can trace myself through my father, Melvyn, and him through *his* father, straight back to Johann Newman, who came out from Germany. No one had to marry outside *our* family."

"Then how. . . ?"

"The notion that Wilhelm and Johann were brothers is erroneous," he said as he flicked an impatient glance at Nicole. "Despite what some people think, our great-grandfathers were cousins, possibly only distant cousins, or possibly even just friends."

"No, no," Nicole interjected. "They were brothers. Everyone in my family always said so."

He shook his head. "They were definitely cousins. The idea of our great-grandfathers being brothers makes no sense. How do brothers live side by side on neighboring farms and not speak to each other for years?"

Quinn thought cynically: Brothers not speaking and yet being neighbors? Oh yeah, very possible.

For the first time in her life, Nicole was suddenly interested in the history of their two families, the rift that had made them rivals, and now the mystery of what Wilhelm and Johann really had been to each other. And had that rift somehow filtered down through the years to end in a brutal murder?

PART TWO
1914–1918

"HAVE YOU NOTICED?" HILDE the shoemaker's wife said as she held a bottle to her infant's mouth. "Women want everything from just one man, while men want just one thing from a lot of women."

"Men say it's in their nature," Truda chirped.

"Men are pigs," Anna, the widow, said.

"No need to insult pigs."

They burst out in peals of laughter.

It was a hot August day. The women at Eberhardt's bakery, gathered for their weekly kaffeeklatsch, wore the latest fashion—lacy shirtwaist dresses with long, narrow skirts that fell to the top of the foot. The married women wore their hair drawn back in the popular Grecian knot, while Mrs. Mueller's young daughter wore her hair in long ringlets.

There were eight ladies in the weekly kaffeeklatsch: Clara Schaller; her friend Frieda Eberhardt, whose husband owned the bakery; Hilde, the shoemaker's wife who also taught piano; Truda, assistant to her photographer husband; and Dagmar, a seamstress whose husband was a tailor. These were the original immigrants who had come out to California with visionary Jakob Schaller.

Three newcomers were Mrs. Elke Mueller, whose husband had opened a new hotel in Lynnville, her sixteen-year-old daughter Mathilda, and Anna, Elke's widowed sister. Young Mathilda did not join in with the women's ribald laughter and scorn of men: Mathilda loved men and thought they were God's greatest invention. She had her eye on Klaus, the bachelor who had come out with them two years before. He was a blacksmith, now becoming an auto mechanic, and while she dreamed of him night and day and hoped to run into him at the occasional barn dance, Mathilda's mother disapproved, wanting more for her daughter than a blacksmith.

Clara thought Mrs. Mueller a bit of a snob but didn't let it bother her. She suspected that people who were snobbish and pretentious were that way to make up for failings and inadequacies in their private lives. Mrs. Mueller's daughter had a very nice singing voice and entertained everyone with folk ballads and the popular songs of the day, but Mrs. Mueller would lift her nose and say, "I would prefer that my daughter sang opera." But folks liked the husband, who ran the hotel, as he had a great sense of humor. Above the reception desk was a sign that said SLEEP FAST, WE NEED THE BEDS.

You never knew what went on in people's lives, Clara thought forgivingly. Like the wife of the mayor of Lynnville, a self-important little woman whose husband, it was whispered about, preferred boys. And Clara's own hidden life, kept secret behind glowing smiles. She had a feeling that these ladies would love to know what had happened to cause the rift between two brothers who had, two years ago, seemed so close and full of plans together. These women did not know the brothers' secret pain any more than Clara knew these women's secret pains. She decided that most people lived their lives behind façades.

However, she had discovered that intimate settings, especially with just women, along with a relaxing of the rules, were often conducive to confessions and admissions. In the months that the ladies had been meeting for their weekly klatsch, Clara had heard a few unexpected revelations. And this afternoon's setting was the perfect atmosphere for soul-baring. The Eberhardts' shop was just like bakeries back home, warm and inviting, filled with delicious smells and offerings that delighted the eye. Only by looking out the window did you realize you weren't in Germany, with shop signs in English and a few Ford automobiles chugging down a street that was made of hardpacked dirt instead of fifteenth-century cobblestones. Clara knew that the view from that street would be one of a vast, wide valley of farmlands with the nearest mountains being far away, the river even farther.

"I miss Bierfest," Hilde said as she set the empty baby bottle aside and laid her infant against her shoulder to gently burp him.

"Americans don't celebrate the harvest the way we do in Europe," Truda said all-knowingly.

"We did in Pennsylvania," said Mrs. Mueller, surreptitiously eyeing Dagmar's swollen belly beneath a billowing dress, and looking forward to the day of welcoming her own first grandchild. But *not* sired by Klaus the blacksmith, not if Elke Mueller had anything to say about it. "There are many Germans living there. They celebrate Bierfest every year."

"Perhaps we should start the tradition here," Clara said, suddenly liking the idea. Wilhelm had bottled his first vintage. It wasn't the imported Rieslings. They wouldn't be ready until this October, and then the pressing and fermenting process must begin. This was wine from the original Mission grapes, planted by the Spaniards over a hundred years ago—the vines Jakob had found abandoned and derelict three years ago but which he had lovingly revived and brought back to lush fruitfulness. There was as yet only a small market for Schaller wine, as they were newcomers to the valley and had yet to be discovered by wine lovers, and so they were struggling financially. However, Wilhelm was optimistic. He was spending all his days out among the vines, inspecting the plants for insects and fungus, thinning the leaves for better sun exposure, positioning tendrils on the trellis for better sunlight. He treated his vines, Clara thought, as if they were his children. She prayed they weren't to be his only children.

The others jumped at Clara's suggestion to arrange a Bierfest celebration. A nice harvest festival would be wonderful, a reminder of home and a distraction to take their minds off the one topic they avoided bringing up: the clouds of war that were supposedly gathering over their homeland. In Clara's mother's last letter, she had said, "We fear that war is coming. Your father and I are very worried about Julia's husband. He enlisted in the Army and we have no idea where he will be sent." Clara shared her parents' worries. Ever since letters had started to come from Germany, two years ago, Clara had savored the news—her sister Julia getting married! Her other sister having her third child. And news of the village, stories about her father's customers. But lately, the tone of the letters had turned dark and threatening.

Ever since the assassination of the heir to the throne of the Austria-Hungarian Empire, Germans in America had been anxiously following the news. Since that time, only four weeks ago, Emperor Franz Josef had declared war on Serbia, Russia had announced full mobilization of its armed forces as an ally of Serbia, and the German Empire had mobilized its armed forces and declared war on Russia.

But although they did not speak of this prominent news of the day, there was no lacking in topics for these ladies. Conversation at the klatsch consisted of gossip, stories, reminiscences, observations. And opinions. There were always plenty of opinions. Mrs. Mueller, in her forties, didn't like the way the world was changing. Women weren't ladies any more, and men certainly were no longer gentlemen. Her widowed sister Anna, in her thirties, feared that these new motion pictures were going to do away with books and reading. Those in their twenties speculated on a world where women might be able to vote, and rising hemlines, and a lot of shocking talk in Europe about birth control.

But ultimately the subjects always came back to men. "Have you seen the new lawyer in town? Mr. Gilette? Very handsome. I'm told he handles all kinds of cases, including property management and wills. He is going to do very well for himself."

"I wonder if he's married."

"He checked in alone at the hotel. He didn't say he was expecting anyone to join him."

"Mavis Pruitt said he wants a room in her boarding house as soon as one becomes available."

They all smiled like self-satisfied police detectives who had solved the crime of the century. So—the new man in town was a bachelor. And a great competition was born right there and then, between Mrs. Mueller's sister, who was tired of being a widow, and Mrs. Mueller, who wanted the lawyer for her daughter.

Although German would have been easier, the ladies were speaking English. This was their permanent home now, and as loyal as they were to their homeland, and as determined as they were to hold on to German traditions, they knew they must adjust to American ways. Mrs. Mueller and her widowed sister had an advantage, as they had lived for a while in Pennsylvania. Mathilda especially spoke excellent English, having emigrated from Germany when she was only five. She spoke like an American and enjoyed an easy grasp of the ever-changing slang and idioms.

The Muellers weren't the only recent newcomers. Lynnville was growing. Two spinster sisters had come out from Boston in search of husbands and had started a laundry business that was doing so well, they had already expanded their premises and now employed four Mexican women. The sisters had contracted with the Muellers to handle all hotel linens, and had an arrangement with Dagmar the seamstress and her tailor husband to send all mending and alterations their way in exchange for ironing jobs. There was now a doctor and his wife, a nurse. A new grocery store had opened, and a bank as well. A widow from Montana had opened a "good food" restaurant at the edge of town where she did an excellent trade with hungry farmers coming to town to buy seed and equipment. The schoolhouse had added a new room and the town had hired a second teacher—that was how you knew Lynnville was coming up in the world. The Largo Valley was a place where anyone with vision, fortitude, and determination could make a new and better life for themselves. Clara had heard that, under Johann's college-educated guidance, Arturo Ballerini's farm, where Johann had worked these past two years, was producing five times what it had before, especially in bean crops that he sold to food-manufacturing plants in San Francisco and Los Angeles at healthy profits.

Along with learning English and taking up American customs, one major thing they all had to adjust to was the seeming lack of seasons here. The snow came, but it was up in the mountains. The immigrants had to look east toward the Los Padres Forest, where the highest peaks were white with snow. Winter here was not like the white wonderland and picturesque snow-laden trees of Germany, silent and pure and mysterious. California winters delivered torrential and punishing rains off the Pacific Ocean, giving lie to its name, "peaceful." The Largo would overflow its banks, mudslides would block roads and lanes, leaks would sprout in every ceiling, creating a run on buckets at the general store. But no one complained, because the grazing fields and farmlands would get such a good soaking that abundant grass and crops were guaranteed for the rest of the year.

And today, August, though hot, was tempered with breezes from the nearby Pacific Ocean. The climate in Central California, Clara thought, was merely a series of variants on spring. Yes, the summer was hot and it rained at Christmas. But there was no discernible autumn, just weeks when leaves fell and yet the weather was mild, and then weeks when flowers came back into bloom and the weather was mild. They had all brought fur coats, heavy gloves and mittens, boots made for snow. But they rarely had cause to bring them out.

The climate was a pleasant adjustment, as they had soon found they could obtain food all year round that had never been available in Germany during the winter, such as oranges and pears, lettuce and cauliflower. No going without fresh vegetables and fruits for months in this Eden.

"Oof!" Dagmar said suddenly, putting her hand on her abdomen. "He is kicking."

"How do you know it's a boy?" Mathilda asked, unschooled in the mysterious world of sex and babies, wondering if pregnancy came with a built-in gift for prophecy.

Frieda, who was busy tatting—handcrafting durable lace from a series of knots and loops that would go onto doilies, collars, and other decorative accessories—glanced at Dagmar and Truda, both pregnant, and said, "I've heard that dry hands and cold feet are signs of a boy."

Mrs. Mueller said, "Craving sweets means you're going to have a girl. Salty and sour cravings indicate a boy."

To those young wives not yet blessed, the lucky ones offered, sagely, "Don't let your husband take hot baths. This damages his seed. Cool baths only."

"Eat a lot of broccoli and you'll get pregnant."

"Mix a drink of sauerkraut juice, raw egg, and hot sauce. Drink it every day for a week before you have sex with your husband. Guaranteed you will get pregnant."

"Make love during the full moon. That's how I conceived Mathilda."

Clara took it all with a grain of salt and refused to bring up her intimate marital life. For her, sex with Wilhelm wasn't spectacular. It wasn't even particularly satisfying. When they had finally been able to enjoy their wedding night, it had been a disappointment for Clara. But she did enjoy the feel of her husband afterward, Wilhelm's powerful masculine body overwhelming hers, protecting her in the night. She liked that part and waited for the babies to come. Still, she listened to their advice and thought it couldn't hurt to try some of it.

The klatsch had evolved over the past two years. In the beginning, they had noticed a natural separation during Sunday fellowship after the church service, with the women gravitating to one side of a house or garden, the men to another. They wanted to discuss private, gender-specific issues, as it was the only time in the week when they could all get together and be free of the demands of their Monday-through-Saturday labors. Stores were closed. Sunday was a day of rest and visiting. So the women gathered, and the men gathered, but not as a mixed group. The women talked about children and the problems of breastfeeding or menstruation, while the men discussed farm equipment and crop blights and politics. Wilhelm continued to receive a newspaper from Frankfurt, and several of the other men subscribed to German-language American newspapers. They brought these to their Sunday gatherings to pass around and share, and to express concerns about the news back home, but also to be free to smoke cigarettes and cigars and pipes away from the delicate lungs of their wives.

The women's klatsch was held in a different home each Sunday, with the hostess providing the cake and coffee. Since Clara could never hold a klatsch at her farm—the ladies agreed it wasn't feasible for them all to pack up after the church service and ride out to the Schaller farm—she never came empty-handed, always bringing something freshly baked from her own kitchen. But when the klatsch was being held in a bakery, as today's was, Clara brought two dozen eggs that she gathered only that morning. A gift for Frieda.

While the ladies were gathered in the bakery, their menfolk were socializing at Mueller's hotel. Mr. Mueller offered coffee and cake to his new friends, served in the comfortable lobby of his establishment, and the less pious among them were not opposed to accepting a friendly mug of ale or lager. If a man couldn't enjoy an innocent beer on a Sunday afternoon, then what exactly had God meant about the Sabbath being a day of rest? Nothing was more restful than beer, the congenial Mueller said.

As Clara relaxed and listened to feminine chatter, she thought of Feliciana Ballerini. What had happened to the potentially marvelous friendship that was supposed to blossom between her and Feliciana? Clara had thought Miss Ballerini would come around again as she had done that one time. But she never came back. Clara had thought of paying Feliciana a visit herself, taking the buggy to the farm next door and paying a friendly call. But by then Clara had heard that Johann had taken a job there working for Mr. Ballerini, and she couldn't bear the thought of running into him.

Later, when she encountered either Mr. Ballerini or his daughter in town, Clara was met with politeness and distance, and she wondered what had happened to dissolve a friendship that had had such potential. What had Johann told them? Clara had had no contact with him since the night he left the Schaller farm. When Wilhelm had told her that he and Johann had had a fight, that his brother had left and was never coming back, she hadn't really thought it would be so permanent.

And yet here they were, two years later, and not a word. It hurt her deeply.

She put Johann from her mind, as she always must, and brought herself back to the bakery with its gossip and advice and high, tinkling laughter. Clara smiled to herself. It was good to have friends. People to talk to, share confidences with, not like the lonely days when they'd first come to the valley and she hadn't had even Rosita's companionship. She especially liked Frieda Eberhardt.

Clara thought it interesting how one gravitated toward some people and away from others without even really knowing why. She had gotten to know Frieda Eberhardt a little on the ocean voyage and then the long train journey across America's vast expanses, but Clara had been too sick with influenza to make any real friends. It was only after the Sunday lunches got started, evolving into the kaffeeklatsch, that Clara realized how much she liked Frieda, how she looked forward to their weekly get-togethers. Frieda was the same age as Clara, twenty-one, with blond curly hair, blue eyes, and pale skin. She laughed freely and was as generous with compliments as she was with her peach and apple strudels.

And it was clear that Frieda felt the same toward Clara. This was how friendships were formed, Clara thought. You might find little things in common and you agreed on so many issues and you tended to laugh more with that person—but that was just the surface. You could have things in common and agree on issues and laugh a lot with other people too, but this was more social than deep friendship. So there was something else, an unidentifiable ingredient that was needed for a true bond to form.

Clara also liked Frieda's husband, Hans, a very likeable, jovial fellow. Who wouldn't be, surrounded by sweets and the heavenly aromas of baking bread all day? He was always handing out free samples to everyone who came into the shop, some of whom, Frieda noticed, never bought anything but were here every morning to taste the latest bagel or donut.

As Hilde gently laid her sleeping infant in his cradle, she said, "I was in the O'Briens' the other day and saw a big bruise on Mrs. O'Brien's face. Oh, she tried to cover it with powder, but it's as plain as day. He's hitting her, you know."

Frieda nodded as she concentrated on her lace-making, guiding the small, oval-shaped shuttle through loops to make knots. Without losing a beat of her rapidly moving fingers, she said, "Mrs. O'Brien claims she walks into doors. She tells me she's terribly clumsy."

"He hits her, that husband of hers," Dagmar said. As a seamstress, she visited the O'Brien establishment at least once a week for fabrics and sewing supplies and considered herself an expert on the Irish couple.

Clara stirred her coffee and looked out at the street. She thought of Kathleen O'Brien, who co-owned the notions shop and who had tried to cheat Clara the first time she shopped there. In the two years since, Clara had discovered that Kathleen was a miserable woman, always complaining. Clara wondered about people like that, why they did that to themselves. Maybe they complained all through life so that when they died they wouldn't mind it so much.

Or perhaps Kathleen had good reason to complain. Maybe her husband did hit her. Clara didn't like Sean O'Brien. He spent too much time at Gilhooley's Saloon and was known to have an eye for the ladies. If he was in the shop when Clara went there to buy sewing supplies, he would shamble over and stand too close, brush his arm against hers, and ask with whiskey breath if he could help her find something.

Thinking of the notions shop made her think of Mr. Ballerini, who had corrected Mrs. O'Brien's "error" at the cash register. And, of course, thoughts of Mr. Ballerini led to thoughts of Johann.

Clara knew that the ladies of the klatsch were curious about the Schaller brothers' split-up but were too polite to ask. All anyone knew was that a week after their father's funeral, Wilhelm and Johann had had a falling-out. Wilhelm inherited the farm, while Johann went to work for Arturo Ballerini. They saw Johann in town occasionally, sometimes with Mr. Ballerini and his stunning daughter. Johann never attended Sunday services at Reverend Brown's church, and although the immigrants took care always to invite Johann to dinner and celebrations and festivities, he never came. What could have happened, everyone wondered, to have caused him to isolate himself so?

Clara's secret agony was that Johann had never said good-bye to her. A few days after Jakob's death, he had simply left the farm without a word. Wilhelm had said the two of them had had an argument and that Johann had said he wanted nothing more to do with the Schallers. He had found work at the Ballerini farms and was now the top foreman there. Clara had heard through town gossip that Johann had changed his name to Neumann, forsaking his father's name and embracing his mother's.

For a while, Clara had kept expecting Johann to come back, or Wilhelm to go to the Ballerini farm and extend an olive branch. She had thought that there would be a reconciliation—the shock of their father's shameful confession fading, followed by acceptance of the brothers' true relationship to each other, a return of brotherly love. But nothing of the sort had happened. In fact, rancor seemed to have supplanted affection. Wilhelm would not even allow Johann's name to be mentioned. Clara had wondered if she should try to intervene, be a mediator, help them to find their way back and take up their father's dream once again. But she didn't know how. And as days and weeks and months passed, and Johann hadn't sent word to her, a note or a letter, a request that they meet—*nothing*—she wondered if her interference would make matters worse. So she had let it go.

The ladies were startled by the sudden and premature arrival of their husbands in the bakery shop, with Hans coming through the door leading the group of worried-looking men. "What's wrong?" Clara asked in alarm when Wilhelm came over to her, a hard and grim expression on his face.

"We need to talk, all of us," he said as the men retrieved more chairs and joined the women. Hans Eberhardt, Clara noticed, was holding a newspaper, the Sunday afternoon special edition. She cried out when she saw the headline: GERMANY DECLARES WAR ON FRANCE.

Everyone fell silent. There was no longer any hiding from it. Europe was about to become embroiled in a bloody conflict. Suddenly, the small group of immigrants were frightened, thinking of loved ones back home. Never had they felt so isolated and helpless as they did in that moment.

Clara looked through the window of the bakery and was startled to see Johann across the street, buying a newspaper. He stood on the sidewalk, staring in shock at the front page. He looked up, as if sensing her watching him. Their eyes met. Clara wanted to run to him, because she was suddenly filled with a great presentiment. Something terrible awaited on the horizon, and their lives were once again going to undergo an unthinkable upheaval.

*   *   *

HE HAD GALLOPED ALL the way from town, the headline news burning in his pocket. Europe at war! This would affect the Ballerinis as well: they still had family back in Switzerland. He had to let Arturo know.

He couldn't get the image of Clara out of his mind. He had gone into town for the weekly newspaper, and he had seen her in the window of Eberhardt's bakery, sitting in a halo of sunlight. She had looked straight across at him and he had felt her eyes touch his.

He hadn't stopped loving her since the night his brother beat him nearly to death and kicked him off their farm. If anything, his love for Clara had grown as he had wrestled in torment over what to do with his life. Try to make amends with Wilhelm? Try to forget the terrible secret they had learned that night? Try to put from his mind that the father he had so worshipped and admired had slept with his wife's sister and produced a bastard son?

It made his heart turn to lead. No, there was no going back, no handshake of peace between him and Wilhelm. The wall that their father had thrown up between them was too high and too thick to be scaled. And he was a Neumann now. That night, his body a column of pain and despair, tears and blood streaming down his face, barely able to stand on his feet, Johann had vowed to heaven that he was no longer a Schaller.

But it also meant there would be no going back to Clara. She was out of his life forever, and it killed him to know she was only on the next farm, and went to church on Sundays, and was frequently in town.

Johann's secret agony was that Clara must have known that Wilhelm had thrown him off the farm, forbidding him to return, and yet she had made no attempt to come and see him. He had enacted the imagined scene so many times in his head that he had come to believe it as the truth: Wilhelm returning to the house after nearly beating his brother to death, grimly saying to Clara, "I have banished him from this family. He is never allowed to come back." But surely she could have found a way to get word to him, to meet with him. Surely she hadn't given up on him just like that, without even saying good-bye or wishing him well? But apparently that was what had happened. Wilhelm had said Johann was gone and she had accepted it.

As he neared the two-story home that Arturo Ballerini had built for himself and his daughter, Johann reined his horse in and stayed in the saddle, deep in thought.

What did it mean for them now, this war in Europe?

His heart was heavy. He wished he could join the other immigrants in the valley in this time of sorrow and fear, but he could not. Pride kept him from coming into any kind of contact with Wilhelm, even through other people. It was best that he keep to himself. For a long time Johann had been consumed by a devouring sorrow. He had lost not only father and brother in one night, but his mother as well. Ilse Schaller, for whom he had wept when she had died of tonsillitis when he was a boy of ten, turned out not to be his mother at all but his aunt, while Hannah Neumann (his father's Kätzchen), the aunt who had died when he was born, turned out to be the mother he never knew.

The mother who had died *while bringing him into the world.*

For a long time it was all too much, and the only way he could get through the days was by toiling for Mr. Ballerini, supervising fieldhands, overseeing planting, weeding, pruning, harvesting—not only of grapes for the prestigious Ballerini label but of a new crop he had so much to learn about—*Phaseolus vulgaris*, the common bean. Ballerini's was a diversified farm, with a vineyard for table grapes and wine, orchards that produced peaches and apricots, and vast acres that grew artichokes—a vegetable not native to the United States but which had been introduced to California by the Spaniards and had been a favorite food ever since.

And Johann was now the senior foreman over it all.

When he had recovered from his injuries and Arturo Ballerini had invited him to stay on with no questions asked, Johann accepted the offer in exchange for work. Upon hearing Johann's impressive university credentials, his expertise in the latest in agricultural science, Ballerini hired him on as an inspector and consultant with the aim of improving farm production and output. Johann had borrowed a horse and ridden the property from boundary to boundary, stopping to kneel on the ground and dig up the soil to let it crumble through his fingers. Huge live oaks stood majestically here and there. He leaned in their shade and patted their rough trunks as if to introduce himself because, after only a few days, Johann knew that this was where he was going to stay and live for a while—work another man's land before finding his own place in the world. There was no thought of moving on or running away from his pain. He had to stay here, close to Clara.

Besides, he had grown to love every inch of these thousand acres. It had been the old Vasquez land grant, a gift from the Spanish Crown for loyalty and service to Spain, back around 1800. Like the land Johann's father had purchased, the Vasquez "rancho" had been a major producer of Mission grapes and, like Jakob Schaller, Arturo Ballerini had come out from Switzerland with his daughter to start a new life beneath sunny skies, growing grapes and making wine. There were old ruins on the property—the remnants of adobe buildings. One would have been the main house, the hacienda, built in a square around a central atrium open to the sky. On days when spiritual and emotional pain threatened to overwhelm him, Johann liked to walk among the ruins and engage in silent dialogue with old Vasquez, long since gone to his reward. He imagined that contented Spaniard strumming a guitar and singing romantic songs from home. Perhaps drinking a cup of his own vintage, content with his days. He would have been called Pedro or Carlos or Esteban. Was he a happy man? Had he produced an abundance of children? Was he sorry that Mexico had lost the war to the Yankees, who took over California and annexed it to the United States? That was over a hundred years ago, and yet Spain was still here, in the place names, in the plants that had been brought over from the Old Country.

Besides being drawn to the Spanish ruins, Johann returned frequently to the roadside ditch where the Mexicans had found him that night two years ago. He didn't know what drew him there week after week; perhaps it was a kind of homage to the hour that his old life ended and his new one began. The Mexicans who found him had been new to the valley, streaming northward in search of work and a better life for their bedraggled families who had known only poverty and hunger in Mexico. Therefore, they had not known the identity of the unconscious man they had at first thought dead. They hadn't known he was one of the German Schaller brothers on a farm just a quarter of a mile ahead. Instead, they had grabbed him up in a panic and run toward lights they saw at the end of a long road, a two-story farmhouse with windows glowing with lamps. He must live here, they thought, their minds filled with hopes of a monetary reward for rescuing the husband or son of the house.

Johann had no memory of this. No memory of the days that followed while he was in Feliciana's gentle and vigilant care. The doctor in Santa Barbara had been called, a man who fixed Johann's broken bones and stitched his wounds and applied antiseptic and dosed him with morphine and who later kept his mouth shut, leaving the sheriff and the authorities out of it at the request of Mr. Ballerini, a wealthy and influential man in the valley who said he would take care of everything. Mr. Ballerini paid the doctor handsomely, and the doctor kept the whole incident to himself. Especially after he heard that the young man had eventually recovered and was restored to full health. No sense in stirring up old trouble.

Johann now turned his face westward, into the hot wind. These were the dry months in California when rain rarely fell, between the end of May and the beginning of November—and sometimes even longer. But two centuries of studying the land, taming it, bending it to man's will had produced a clever network of canals and ditches and irrigation furrows from the Largo River, all watched over by Mexican workers who bent their backs in the sun to make sure the flow of water never stopped. As a result, these thousand acres were robed in tall, golden wheat and squares of green alfalfa. Ballerini grew corn, too, and strawberries. He hired a lot of migrant laborers, and they respected him. They felt a kind of bond with a patron whose native tongue was so similar to their own. English and German were a trial to the peasants of Central America. But Mr. Ballerini said, "Si" and "Signor" just like they did, and "Grazie" was close enough to "Gracias" that he had their loyalty.

Johann also oversaw the small hillside vineyard from which Mr. Ballerini produced an exquisite wine. They were Mission grapes, growing on the original vines brought out from Spain a hundred and thirty years ago, now under the loving husbandry of an Italian from Switzerland and his foreman, a Rhinelander. It made the world seem very cosmopolitan, and very small.

The bean crop, covering acres as far as the eye could see, looked healthy and promising. When Johann had first inspected the land, he had determined that Ballerini's soil was acidic and suggested that he add lime before planting. He had also recommended mulching early, to prevent weeds. Mr. Ballerini had followed his new foreman's advice and now looked forward to another profitable harvest. He had even been contacted by two new food-processing plants, eager to buy his beans so that they could be cooked, seasoned, sealed in cans, and distributed all over the United States. Apparently, canned pork and beans was rapidly becoming a favorite staple in American kitchens.

In appreciation for improving his crop output, Arturo Ballerini had given Johann a small hillside vineyard of his own. In October, he would be harvesting his first grapes, pressing and fermenting them in Ballerini's winery and bottling the wine under his own label: Neumann.

Across the fields covered in lush crops, he could see a curious phenomenon called Colina Sagrada—Sacred Hill, although it looked more cursed than sacred. It was part of the Schaller property but was utterly useless for farming. A freak combination of western exposure, convergence of winds, soil erosion, and poor makeup of the soil itself had created a miniature desert in the middle of fertile farmland. His father had briefly considered, and then dismissed, the idea of trying to irrigate and improve those twenty acres. It would cost too much for very little yield and would require too much manpower to maintain.

Johann shifted his gaze to the other boundary of Schaller land, where the farmhouse stood hidden behind trees. His heart felt a tug. Not for his brother, but for his brother's wife. He and Wilhelm were strangers now. Although they shared the same father, they were no longer womb-brothers. Only Wilhelm had the privilege of loving the mother they *both* once had loved. Merely half-brothers now, with half the love and admiration and loyalty. But of course, there wasn't even that. Not after feeling the impact of Wilhelm's boot against his ribs. Where had the fury come from? Johann had never thought his brother capable of kicking a man while he was down. And yet he had done just that. And to his brother.

Johann had never been able to sort out his emotions, nor did he think he ever would be able to. Disillusionment, disappointment, feelings of betrayal and abandonment. Sharp, ugly emotions that ran too deep to be sorted and categorized and tucked away. He and Wilhelm were more than strangers, he knew: they were enemies. Was this how wars began?

He closed his eyes to the wind and thought of the winds of war sweeping across Europe. How long would it last? Would his cousins be fighting in it? Would they die?

It seemed so remote and dreamlike as to be unreal. Some of the Germans in the valley were talking about going home, to fight. Johann would not go back to fight; he could only pray that the conflict would be swift, would come to a speedy conclusion. He hated war and thought that men of reason should come to agreements and compromises without shedding blood.

He spurred his horse and soon arrived at the house where he saw Feliciana in the bright August sun, tending her garden.

Johann knew that Feliciana had figured into his decision to stay here, live here, and run Ballerini's farm for him. Johann wasn't in love with her, but he would never forget her tireless and tender nursing care when he had lain in such pain that he wanted to die. After a while, he rejected the morphine and asked only for her cool hand on his forehead. She was beautiful, given to laughter and gaiety, but she could be solemn and quiet, too, in the presence of a man's pain.

She had spoon-fed him and bathed him and shaved his face and changed his bed linens and slipped the bedpan under him. Intimate acts. But he hadn't fallen in love with her. There was room in his heart for only one woman, and that woman would always occupy it.

However, for Feliciana he would always feel gratitude, admiration, and even fondness. And there was a strange vulnerability about her that made him wonder what would become of her should anything happen to her father. The Ballerinis had no family in America. So Johann took it upon himself to be a brotherly protector should she ever need one.

She was tending her garden packed with brilliant summer flowers, which she had planted back in late May. He had watched her out there every day, the familiar parasol over her shoulder while with the other hand, encased in a protective glove, she trimmed and pruned and mulched and picked off bugs and breathed loving life into scarlet zinnias, bright orange French marigolds, snow-white shasta daisies, blushing pink dahlias, all grown in pots or beds, from seeds or cuttings. Feliciana knelt among them now, a flower herself, in a gauzy lavender dress that molded itself to her slender, goddess-like figure, her black hair caught back in a matching lavender scarf with tendrils escaping in the summer wind.

Johann could not fathom this enigmatic beauty. Every family had its secrets and mysteries—weren't the Schallers a prime example? And the Ballerinis were no exception. But the big mystery there was: Why wasn't Feliciana married? After all, he had heard she was twenty-seven. Oh, suitors had come, awkward young men presenting themselves with sweet chocolates and nervous invitations. But as soon as Feliciana showed any interest, Arturo intercepted bulldog-like and let it be known that it was a father's duty to be protective. And the nervous suitors got the hint, leaving without coming back. Why did Arturo seem so determined that his daughter remain unmarried? Maybe it was because she had no mother, or she was his only offspring. He was forever clucking over her like a hen, watching her, asking after her health, had she slept well, how did she feel? At times, Johann sensed a curious anxiousness in Ballerini when Feliciana entered a room.

But then there *were* the occasional trips to Monterey where her sister lived with a husband and five children. Was there a man up there? Johann wondered. Someone who filled Feliciana's needs and who was perhaps the real reason she visited her sister so often? Did Arturo know about this? Would that staunch Catholic condone such behavior?

Johann had seen her working tirelessly in her garden. Where did she get the energy from? An early riser, Feliciana was always seen just after dawn among her blooms, inspecting them, inhaling the various perfumes. Whenever Johann happened by, she would call out to him, vigorous and full of life. She took endless walks and was often seen on horseback around the farm, or on her way to town in her bright red surrey. Always smiling and waving, asking wasn't it a *beautiful* day when everyone else was sweltering in the heat. Johann enjoyed Sunday dinners with them, with Feliciana insisting on serving herself despite having a cook and two maids. She would chatter pleasantly, asking questions, sharing gossip.

Unaware that she was being watched, Feliciana reveled among the colors and fragrances of her riotous flower garden. She could not recall ever having been so happy. Ecstasy bubbled in her blood. Her skin was tight and electric with joy. She wanted to jump off a mountain and fly to San Francisco.

It was because she was in love, love, love. It made her deliriously happy. And Feliciana loved happiness. It intoxicated her like wine. Before Johann, she had had her spells of joy. She would wake up already giddy, perhaps from a wonderful dream, now forgotten. But, since Johann, she could pinpoint the source of her happiness.

Oh, but it had begun so darkly. Finding Johann in a ditch, near death, savagely beaten. Her father had sent an urgent message to the Schaller farm that their brother needed help, but there had been no response. And then, when Johann started to recover, he confessed to Feliciana that it was his brother who had done the beating. That explained why no one had come to see to him. How could Clara turn her back on her brother-in-law like that? There had not even been any inquiries into his well-being! They had thrown him out and no longer cared. Well, if that was what the Schallers were like, Clara included, then Feliciana wanted nothing to do with them.

Hearing the jingle of harness, she looked up and shaded her eyes with her hand. Johann!

She called to him. "Come and take a look!" Whenever she was with Johann, they spoke English. Her own command of the language was perfect, but Johann needed the practice.

He dismounted and she freely took his hand, leading him. "This is *it*, Johann!" she cried with childish delight. "I have found my true calling!"

He smiled. She had said the same thing last year when she took piano lessons from Hilde Decker, who came out three times a week to teach her. And the year before that, a sudden passion for watercolors, carting her easel and stool and paints all over the farm to capture "rural heaven." What would it be next year? Her interests changed seasonally, and she entered into each wholeheartedly.

When she had returned from Monterey a few months ago, after a long visit with her sister, Feliciana had arrived with stacks of books on gardening, horticulture, flowers, botany. She had learned all the scientific terms. He had seen her poring over the books, drawing layouts for the flowerbeds. Late at night, he had seen light glowing in her bedroom window.

He found it delightful as she led him from shrub to shrub, color pot to color pot as the Latin names tripped off her tongue. *Vinca roea. Thymophylla tenuiloba*. She had told him that she loved to surround herself with beauty. That was why, she said, she and her father didn't attend Reverend Brown's church in Lynnville but went instead into Santa Barbara, forty miles away, to the old Mission there. Catholicism was beautiful, she said. She felt sorry for Protestants, whose churches were so plain. What was a church service without statues and incense and bells and Latin?

She plucked a blossom and held it to Johann's nose. "*Gardenia augusta*," she murmured, and he inhaled the heady perfume. She observed him from under long black lashes—a look that might have appeared coy or seductive in another woman. But Feliciana, for all her beauty and exotic coloring, retained a curious innocence that slightly unbalanced him.

Suddenly remembering the newspaper rolled into his pocket with its headline of war, the delight of the moment darkened and he said, "I must speak to your father. Do you know where he is?"

She gave a little shrug and a sly smile as if they were playing a game.

"Miss Feliciana," he said politely, touching the brim of his hat. He remounted and rode off.

She watched him go, tall and handsome in the saddle, the most beautiful young man on God's earth. She was glad he had accepted a job working for her father. And now he was operating his own small vineyard. She knew he harbored grand plans for his wine someday. So he had ambition, education, and intelligence. And her father trusted him. Her father was very watchful of young men who came around, who might express any interest in his only daughter. And she didn't blame him. Men can't be trusted, her father always said, and him a man himself! But then she supposed only a man could really be an expert on what men thought.

She suddenly wanted to run and dance and fling her arms into the air and act in the most unladylike way possible. Run barefoot! Fling away her bonnet! Hike her skirt up to her waist! She impulsively plucked random flowers, a ragged bouquet of willy-nilly petals and colors, and hugged them to her bosom.

Watching from a window on the second floor of the house, Arturo Ballerini watched his daughter in worry. She was doing *that* again. And how long would it last this time? Dropping the curtain, he turned away and looked at his desk, strewn with papers, ledgers, and responsibilities. But the most pressing responsibility right now was his daughter. Perhaps the time had come to make the decision he had been dreading to make.

And in the next instant he knew—it was definitely time. He would leave for Santa Barbara at once.

*　　*　　*

ALTHOUGH THERE WAS NOW a lawyer in Lynnville, a very capable man educated at one of the Eastern colleges, Arturo Ballerini preferred to go the forty miles to keep his problem a secret, especially as the man was willing to open his office on a Sunday. As his new Ford automobile took the twisting turns in the hills, heading home now, he honked his horn—*aa-oo-gah!*—to warn any animals that might be around the bend. Going twenty-five miles per hour, Arturo didn't think he could stop in time. Besides, he loved the sound of the horn. *Aa-oo-gah!* He sounded it at every opportunity.

He had planned to enjoy a pleasant dinner with the lawyer after their business was concluded, at a seaside restaurant that offered scampi on rice, mussels in wine, lobster in cream sauce. But then he had seen the shocking news headlines, made his apologies, and headed straight home. Arturo was suddenly worried sick. A war in Europe could ruin everything. What if the Germans left this valley? What if they decided to go back to their homeland and fight with their kin? He couldn't lose Johann. Not after all his hard and careful planning. Arturo had hoped to have a little more time to plan his approach to the young man, but now he decided that the time was now to put his new plan into action.

He had to think of Feliciana. Suppose he dropped dead of a bad heart and she was left all alone to run that big farm? His poor daughter would be at the mercy of every scoundrel and rogue in the valley wanting her money. No, he needed to ensure her safety and continued care, and to see that the Ballerini farm continued to grow and thrive, and possibly to be inherited by the children Johann Neumann would give her.

Parking his car near the stables, he saw Johann's chestnut gelding tethered to the hitching post at the side of the house. And then he saw his foreman talking to one of the Mexican farmhands. Their eyes met, and each saw in the gravity of the other's face that they had both heard the news from Europe. "It is a sad and frightful thing indeed," Mr. Ballerini said as he looked at Johann's newspaper. "How long will it last, I wonder," he murmured.

Arturo, a man in his fifties with only a little gray at the temples and none in his prodigious black moustache, and whose paunch added a notch to his belt every year, reached out and touched Johann's arm. He said, "Walk with me," three words carrying heavy meaning.

As the sun dipped behind distant mountains and shadows began their relentless crawl across pastures, meadows, farmlands, and river, the twilight exploded with the beginning of nighttime's natural orchestra:

cicadas, crickets, frogs all filled the air with their bluster and noise and determination to find mates.

Ballerini produced a cigar, bit off one end and spat it out, then struck a wooden match on the sole of his shoe—the slow and deliberate movements of a man putting his thoughts in order. Johann sensed that something more meaningful than fertilizer or a new mechanical harvester was to be tonight's topic.

The older man spoke with caution. He thought he knew Johann very well, but still it wouldn't do to frighten the boy off right from the start. After all, what he was about to offer wasn't something nasty and unpleasant. In fact, Arturo would guess that many a man in the valley would jump at his proposition.

"I'm not a young man any more, son," he said companionably, puffing and picking a bit of tobacco off his tongue. "And not getting younger. And I have this big spread with all these crops and a winery that's got an established name. But I have no heirs, you see. No one to leave all this to in case . . . in case. . . ."

Johann smiled and planted his hands in his pockets, to put Arturo at ease. "Sir, is this about Feliciana? I mean, she isn't married. I am not married. And I have become practically part of the family."

Arturo chuckled. "Astute as well as educated." So now that the door was open, he stated it plainly: "Yes, young man, I need my daughter to be married. I need someone to pass my estate on to. I need heirs. But I cannot trust just any man who shows an interest in Feliciana, surely you understand this. But you I trust, Johann. I can be blunt and honest with you."

"You want me to ask Feliciana to marry me," Johann said. The dusk was deepening, the night noise growing incessant, and some of the day's heat was finally waning.

"Not just that. I'm not just asking you to marry her. I offer you an incentive, something in return."

This did catch Johann off guard. What sort of incentive did Ballerini think he would need? Feliciana was beautiful, charming, and a delight to be around. She knew how to run a house and how to be a witty companion. What man in this valley would need an added incentive to take her to his bed? He was curious. "What are you offering?"

"My farm."

Johann snapped his hands out of his pockets. "Your farm!"

"All of it. To be put in your name, if you will marry my daughter."

Johann wanted to say, What's the catch? Because surely there must be one, something he didn't know, was unaware of. Feliciana was prize enough herself, the man didn't need to throw in his prosperous farm.

"I want my daughter well taken care of. That's all there is to it. With the farm in your name, in her husband's name, then I am guaranteed of the marriage being firm."

Ah, Johann thought, so that's it. He doesn't want me running off with another woman should the notion catch me.

"I will rest easy, you see, knowing that my estate is in such capable hands and will continue to be so after I'm gone." Arturo brought the cigar to his lips and a little red glow flared in the deepening dusk. "I have all the papers drawn up already. You have only to sign. Financial and legal arrangements are in order. I think you will find it all satisfactory. You need not be in love with her, although I suspect she is quite besotted with you. Love will come after time, Johann. Isn't it that way with most marriages?"

Johann was not surprised by Arturo's proposition and was in fact relieved. He wondered if being married would make him dwell less on Clara. Not *love* her less—that would never happen. But wedlock would force him to pay thought to his wife. Johann believed in duty and a man upholding his responsibilities.

It was a simple, practical arrangement between two men: marry my daughter and I'll give you my farm. Still, Johann needed to think. While Arturo went into the house to sit down to a dinner of sausage and potatoes, Johann remained outside in the balmy, perfumed night and looked up at the summer stars, at blue Venus and red Mars and the moon round and ivory. He felt he had reached a turning point in his life, a moment in which he was going to be saying both hello and good-bye. In fact, there really was no thinking to do, no deciding to be done.

He invited her to go for a walk along the Largo River. The day was not too hot, breezy enough, the mosquitoes holding off their savage business as if aware of the delicacy of the situation. Johann was not nervous, as he had always thought he would be when the day came to propose marriage. He supposed now it was because he wasn't in love with Feliciana, that his heart wasn't on the line. It felt, in fact, more like the legal arrangement he had entered into with Arturo to be his foreman. Johann felt quite matter-of-factly about the whole thing. But he was sensitive to Feliciana's feelings, as he knew this was a big moment in any girl's life.

They came to a shady willow tree. He stopped and faced her, took her free hand into his and said, "I believe you know why I have brought you out here, among all this privacy?"

She smiled and looked at him from beneath long lashes. Johann thought she was going to say "Yes" before he even set the question to her, but she waited.

He had prepared a long speech, filled with words like "affection, respect, loyalty, protection. . ." but carefully avoiding the word *love*. He suspected that Feliciana might fill that word in herself, that in the years to come she would look back on this sunny afternoon and tell herself that, yes, Johann had indeed said he loved her.

He watched her, Feliciana's eyes bright with expectation. He sensed that she brimmed with excitement and was bottling it up. He had to take the final step. "Will you do me the honor of being my wife?"

"Oh, yes," she said. "I will marry you, Johann dearest!" And now it all came out. She dropped the parasol and threw her arms around his neck. "I will marry marry marry you!" she cried. He laughed, took her into his arms and twirled her around. And then they kissed, and it was hard and electric and could almost extinguish the pang of guilt that Johann felt because he was wishing, in just the smallest way, that it was Clara in his arms and kissing.

Arturo wanted the wedding as soon as possible. Because they were Catholic, they got married in the chapel of Santa Barbara's old Spanish mission on a warm October day. Most of those invited made the forty-mile trip to attend the wedding. Wilhelm and Clara Schaller did not go. But then, they hadn't been invited.

*　　*　　*

THE RAIN WOKE HIM.

Johann lay in bed for a long moment, staring up into the darkness. It was January, just two weeks into the new year of 1915. He listened to the torrents come down on the roof and pelt the windows. It gave him a cozy feeling. He also thought, as farmers do, of the good soaking the acres would receive. If the rain kept up like this for more two months, they would have another banner year in crops. And Ballerini would find himself a wealthier man.

Well, Johann too. Technically, at least, as his name was on the deed to the house and property and winery. But that was just a legality. In reality, this was Ballerini's land.

Johann felt happier than he had in a long time. As he lay cozy in the bed, thinking of the beautiful woman lying at his side, he thought back over these past three months that had made him think he had died and gone to heaven. After the wedding, Ballerini had given the newly-weds an astounding gift: a brand-new automobile which Johann quickly learned to drive so that he and his bride could go on a week-long motoring honeymoon. He had thought she would want to go north and visit her sister, but Feliciana had laughed and said, "All those kids? They would drive us crazy. I want to be alone with you." So they had headed south along the California coast to sight-see, visit other wineries, all the way down into the desert where it was sandy and rocky and dry—a landscape that had reminded Johann of Colina Sagrada. They had returned in time for the fall harvest, always a big and busy time in the Largo Valley, with hordes of illegal immigrants swarming up from Mexico and Guatemala to help with the picking and threshing and winnowing and sorting and packing and shipping of the many crops California sent out to America and the rest of the world. And then the Christmas season was upon them. It had made Johann sad, as there was no word, no greeting from his brother or Clara, nor had there been upon his marriage to Feliciana.

But he would not be the first to communicate. That was Wilhelm's responsibility. If the two never spoke again, it would be on Wilhelm's head.

He reached for Feliciana, wondering if he should wake her. On their wedding night, he had been astounded at her sexual appetite. She had been insatiable in bed, at the various hotels and inns during their motor trip. She hungered for it more than once a day, often drawing Johann away from their lunch to pay a visit to their room. He supposed it was her Italian blood, and he didn't complain one bit.

He was glad now that he had accepted Ballerini's arrangement. Could a man be happier? Especially after the news that Feliciana had delivered four days ago—that she was expecting their first child. He or she would be a summer baby. Johann's heart raced with excitement at the thought of it. When they had told Arturo, he had startled them by erupting into song. And then he had danced his daughter around the living room, but delicately, mindful of her condition. They had already started picking out names. But they couldn't decide: Italian or German? Or perhaps American, since he or she would be an American citizen, the first American in the family.

He reached for her, deciding he would wake her after all, and he knew she would welcome his embrace because she always did. But he found only empty space on the other side of the bed. He rolled over. She wasn't there. Then he sat up and looked around the spacious bedroom. When his gaze reached the window, where rain streaked down the panes, he thought he could make out a shape sitting in a chair. "Feliciana?" he said.

There was no reply, no movement.

Striking a match, he lit the lamp on his nightstand and took it over to her, to place it on the small window table and sit opposite her. There was a strange look in her eye. "Fee? What's wrong?" She had been unusually quiet for the past few days. He had thought it was the gray, wet weather. Or perhaps she missed her sister. It had been eight months since she last visited Monterey. Or perhaps it was the maternity state. She hadn't slept well the last few nights, and had only picked at her dinner. Maybe that happened in pregnancy. Johann wouldn't know.

It was a long time before she spoke. "You don't love me," she said in a dull voice.

He stared at her in surprise. "What?" he said. "Fee, what are you talking about?"

She looked at him with glassy eyes, slightly unfocused. "You love Clara. Schaller. Don't hide it."

He was taken aback. In their more than two years together, he could not recall Feliciana ever speaking Clara's name. What on earth had brought it up now? "No, that's not true," he said, hoping he'd kept the tone of a lie out of his voice.

"You love her, the wife of the monster who tried to kill you." Her eyes shifted beneath heavy lids. They came to rest on his face, and this time they focused with astonishing clarity. "Don't deny it, Johann. We both know it." No bitter accusation in her voice, just a startling sadness. "When I was nursing you back to health, when I was taking care of your wounds and feeding you and taking away your pain, you called out to her. You did not call out for me, but her."

Johann frowned. He remembered little of those days when he had lain in this very room, on that bed, so consumed with pain—both physical and emotional. But he had no doubt that he had called out for Clara. He had loved her then, as he loved her still.

"Feliciana," he said gently, taking her hands. "That was then, and I was out of my mind with pain and morphine. I married *you*, Feliciana." He knew what he needed to say, what she needed to hear, but his throat closed over it. He had always despised lies and people who lied. But, for

the first time in his life, the moral and ethical mind of university-edu-
cated Johann Neumann saw the gray areas in life that didn't sit well with
his science orientation. Not everything was black and white. Not everything fell into right or wrong. One had to think of consequences, positive and negative.

He looked into her sad, empty eyes, felt the cold hand lying limply in
his, the way her body looked as if it had given up. It was more important
to rescue her from this puzzling unhappy state than to hold to his own
morals. So he would lie. "I love you, Feliciana."

There was not even a flicker in her eyes. It startled him. He was
certain those would be the magic words to snap her out of whatever this
bizarre state was.

"No, you don't," she said dully. "And I don't want to live with that
thought."

His mind searched for other miracles. What had caused this? How to
snap her out of it? "Listen to the rain, Feliciana. Think of the garden you
will grow in the spring."

She didn't need to listen to the rain. It had invaded the room and her
skull and was now raining inside her head, over her brain and down her
throat. She was cold and wet inside. Her heart was a lump of sand in the
Largo River. Her blood was the color of India ink. "Garden," she said.
She pulled a face, it made her strangely ugly. "I had no business trying to
grow a garden. Gardens die." She absently stroked her abdomen. "Everything dies," she said and it alarmed him.

She looked at him. "I just want to go to sleep and never wake up."

He took her by the shoulders. "Don't say that. You have so much to
live for. The baby—"

"Baby! Baby!" she screamed suddenly, shocking him, making his
hands fall away so that he fell back in the chair. It was as if this wasn't even
Feliciana but some horrific impostor who wasn't quite getting it right.
Her hair was dull, he noticed now, and wondered if she hadn't bathed in
a few days. Now that he looked back, Feliciana had been more than quiet
over this past week: she had been listless, disinterested, saying she was
tired all the time. Only yesterday morning, she had had difficulty getting
out of bed. But once again, he had blamed it on the pregnancy.

She jumped up suddenly and ran to the desk on the other side of the
room, snatching up the sharp letter opener. "Feliciana!" he cried.

"I don't want to live!"

He ran over and seized the upraised hand. "Stop it!" he shouted. She struggled. She was amazingly strong. She pushed against him, the silver letter opener, like a sharp, dangerous dagger, glinting in the lamplight. They wrestled against the wall. Feliciana slipped back, grappled for the fireplace mantle, knocking a ceramic vase off to send it crashing to the floor.

"Let me die!" she cried. "I don't want to live!"

As he held her to keep her from harming herself, wondering what the hell was happening, the bedroom door swung open and Arturo Ballerini rushed in, his hair standing on end, a plaid bathrobe flapping about his legs. There was something in his hand.

"Papa!" she cried. "I don't want to live! He doesn't love me!"

"Hold her," he commanded as he took her wrist and pushed the sleeve of her nightgown up her arm. With one hand he pinched the flesh just below her shoulder, with the other he jabbed the hypodermic needle he'd been holding in and slowly pressed the plunger with the expertise of a medical man, or a man who had done this many times. He massaged the arm, drew the sleeve down, and said, "There, there, my sweet thing. You'll be all right. Papa's here now."

She dropped her head on his shoulder and wept bitterly. Over the mass of dark hair, Arturo met Johann's eyes. "I suspected it was coming."

Johann suddenly felt like lead. "*It*?" he said.

"The depression. The first signs are silence. She stops speaking and loses her vitality. Then she loses her appetite and becomes listless."

Johann stared at him disbelief. "She's done this *before*?"

Arturo spoke over the top of his daughter's head as he stroked her hair and rocked her like a baby. Tears streamed down his cheeks. "It's called manic depression and she has suffered from it for most of her life. There is no known cause, no cure."

Johann turned to stone. "You *knew* this was going to happen?" He could barely contain his outrage.

"Forgive me," Arturo whispered.

Distant thunder rumbled. The room went dark and cold. Johann tried to conjure up his vivacious and sunny Feliciana, her arms laden with flowers. He tried to recall her high laughter. The way she came to his embrace in bed. But that Feliciana was nowhere to be found.

The girl went limp in her father's arms. Johann gathered her up and carried her to the bed, pulling the covers up to her chin and stroking her hair.

"She'll sleep now," Ballerini said wearily and went to sit in one of the chairs by the window.

Johann joined him, sensing tension and caution in the air, a sense that something had been revealed at last and something more was about to be disclosed. Manic depression. Remembering what Arturo had said at the wedding, about his other daughter having to deal with five children and a husband who worked too much, the fact that they couldn't get away for the wedding, Johann had thought it strange at the time, but only fleetingly. Families were like that. Priorities were never unanimous.

"What is really in Monterey?" he asked, already knowing, feeling his stomach knot in anticipation of the response.

"A mental hospital."

Johann felt such a sinking in his gut that he thought he might go right through the chair. The rain kept coming down, Feliciana slept in the bed, Arturo sat there with wild hair and an empty hypodermic syringe. It was like something out of a bad stage play.

The two men sat in a much-needed silence, each sorting out his thoughts, picking his way through questions and admissions. Johann thought back to the evening when Arturo had offered him the farm. "All of it. To be put in your name, if you will marry my daughter." Johann had wanted to say, What's the catch? Because surely there must be one: Feliciana was prize enough herself.

Now he knew the catch.

Arturo finally found his voice. He knew that deep apologies must come, a sincere begging of forgiveness, an explanation of his reasons for the duplicity, but he needed to pave the way with calmness and reason. "You have seen how enthusiastic she is when she takes up a new interest. Piano lessons last year, watercolor paintings the year before. Then it was the garden. You may have noticed that the interest fades when she goes to Monterey and then is renewed when she returns. That is a symptom of her illness. I could show you the unfinished needlepoint tapestries, pottery never fired. She got into candle-making once and nearly burned the house down. One year she announced she was going to write a novel. She worked at it feverishly day and night, scribbling page after page. One day, as she slept in exhaustion, I took a look at those pages. It was all gibberish."

"That is the mania," Johann said woodenly, realizing that he had only ever seen one side of the woman he had married. "And now we have the depression."

Arturo nodded.

"How long will this last?" Johann was trying to keep a level head, to keep himself from screaming.

The Swiss shrugged. "Weeks. Sometimes months. They give her medicines. They shock her brain with electricity. You see what a problem this has been for me. Why I needed my daughter to be married, but not to just any of those young fellows who came around. I had to be careful in selecting a son-in-law. The man had to be of good character, strong, reliable, and devoted to Feliciana. But it was so difficult, trying to get to know the bachelors in the valley. People always present their best front. How could I tell which would end up being a drunk or a wife-beater or an adulterer? But I had two years to observe you, Johann, to get to know you and your character, and I knew I couldn't find a better man for Feliciana."

He paused to watch the rain streak down the windows. In the glass he saw the reflection of two unhappy men sitting with a lamp between them.

"But there was something more in my choosing you," Arturo said. "Her spells used to be much worse and closer together. And then you came to stay with us and I saw her change. She improved. Her doctors said it was a miracle. She had fewer depressed episodes and longer happy ones. I knew it was because of you. From the night she washed the blood from your face, and during all the days and nights she sat with you, I saw a calmness come over her, I saw the gentling of her troubled soul. I held a hope that, with you around and the influence you had on her, Feliciana might even live a normal life. These past two years—even though she had to have four hospital stays—have been blessed. Her times in the hospital were shorter, and the doctors said she was nowhere near as bad as she had been before. It was as if the act of looking forward to coming home to *you* helped her out of the depression. There certainly has been no talk of suicide since you came to stay with us."

"Until tonight," Johann said, noticing that the letter opener still lay on the carpet. "You should have told me."

Arturo nodded guiltily. "It was dishonorable of me, I know. But I had Feliciana's interests in my heart. I had to think of her, first and foremost. Even if it meant luring you into a marriage and not being completely honest with you."

"What do we do now?" Johann asked. "After she wakes up. . . ?"

"In the morning, I will take her to Monterey."

"Why can't we just keep her here, bring in a nurse?"

"She needs to be watched night and day. There have been suicide attempts. . . ." Arturo massaged his face. "I always accompany her by train and see that she is safely checked in."

"I'll go with her this time," Johann said firmly.

Arturo shook his head. "It is best that I go. I can gauge her moods, I can sense if she is about to have an outburst. And I can control it. And I need you here to run the farm. Son, I wouldn't blame you for being furious with me right now. You have every right to hate me."

Furious? Hate? No, those weren't the words Johann would use. He wasn't sure there were words to cover how he felt. Dazed and stupid would be a start. Was he really so naïve and gullible? First betrayed by his brother, and now by his father-in-law? Was he a natural victim? Did he draw deceit and treachery to himself like a magnet? I take people on their face value, he thought as he watched the man in the plaid bathrobe grow small before him. I believed my brother would always love me and protect me. I thought Arturo to be a man of honor.

His thoughts went out over the miles, over the soaking fields and pastures to another farmhouse, where Clara slept. She was the only person in the world he could trust. And she was the only person he could never be with. A man needed someone he could rely on. Johann realized in this cold, staggering moment that he had no such person, not in all the world. A father who had kept his son's true maternity a secret. A brother who had nearly killed him. A father-in-law who had drawn up legal papers to lure him into a nightmare. A wife who needed a mental hospital.

Never in his life had Johann felt so suddenly and sharply alone.

"I don't hate you," he said at last, feeling life and energy drain out of him. He felt a hundred years old. The rain came down, punishingly, and thunder rumbled in the distance. The farm was going to bring in stupendous profits this year. The grapes would be full and sweet. But he drew no joy from this. "And I am not furious with you, Arturo. You did what you had to do. I understand that."

"I know I lied. I kept a terrible truth from you. But would you have married Feliciana had you known?"

Johann stared at him, Arturo's olive coloring gone pale, his thick moustache drooping. A man with a paunch, shoulders stooped beneath too much weight. "I honestly couldn't say," Johann admitted, and in that instant he forgave the man for his duplicity. He'd had his daughter's welfare first and foremost in his heart and mind. A man who would do anything to protect his child.

Just as Jakob had protected *me* from the truth.

And in that moment, Johann forgave them both.

"What will you do?" Arturo said in the voice of a very old man. "I would not blame you for seeking a divorce. No judge would deny you, given the details."

But Johann shook his head, wearily, the weight of the world upon it. This was all his fault; he could only blame himself. If he hadn't pressed Wilhelm on the issue of adding potassium to the soil, holding his university education up to his older brother's eyes as a kind of mocking superiority, and triggered a struggle that their father had intervened to stop, ending up cracking his head on the pump handle, leading to infection and delirium and confessions and an even worse fight between two brothers and a painful staggering off into the dark night to fall into a ditch and lie there, wishing for death until Mexicans found him. . . .

He looked at the sleeping Feliciana, this poor girl who had sat by his own sickbed night and day, nursing him back to health. It was his turn now, and he would not turn his back on her. "I will stay married to her and take care of her, Arturo. I will take care of them both. Feliciana and the baby."

They fell silent, and then Johann asked: "This illness. Can it be inherited?"

Arturo looked at him in horror as the same thought occurred to both men in that moment. The child to be born in the summer. . . .

*   *   *

AS CLARA PACKED A basket lunch of thick sliced ham and mustard on rye, hard-boiled eggs, pickles, early cherry tomatoes, a wedge of apple cake, and a thermos of hot sweet coffee, she looked at the April sunshine slanting through the kitchen window and felt her happiness soar. Wilhelm was leaving today for a long business trip, and he was most optimistic that it would be a great success.

It was going to be his first absence from the farm, and Clara already found herself missing him. A few weeks ago, they had privately celebrated their fifth wedding anniversary. And then last week, in town with their friends, they had celebrated the immigrants' arrival in California five years ago, April 1912. A few weeks from now, they would solemnly mark Jakob's death and Johann's departure from the farm.

She brushed back a lock of hair. Following the latest trend, she had had her chestnut hair cut short, just below her ears in what was called a "China Doll" cut, parted in the middle and clipped back on either side. Clara Schaller was twenty-four years old, confidently and competently running a farmhouse and its adjacent yard with chickens and vegetable patch. And now she hugged a warm, sweet secret to herself. She had a very strong feeling that last night's lovemaking with Wilhelm was going to result in a baby. Call it women's intuition.

There had been such a . . . *closeness* to it. When Wilhelm had taken her into his arms, it had been with more tenderness than usual; she had felt a special affection and need. Perhaps it was because he was going away today. There had been almost a desperation in the way he had made love to her, the extra deep penetration, as if he had wanted to crawl inside her, all of him, all the way in, and stay there permanently. Was he afraid of this trip? Afraid that, after all the expense and investment into the vineyard, he wouldn't find enough clients and enough orders to cover their debt? Or had he known that he was going to miss her so terribly that he had conveyed it with his body, rather than words? Whatever the reasons, Clara had happily complied, as she always did. And afterward, as he slept, Clara had lain there in bed, her hand on her abdomen, and she had almost magically felt the miracle starting already.

This was what she must focus on, she told herself now. Not her newest fears.

Since the sinking of the SS *Lusitania* two years ago by a German U-boat, anti-German sentiment had crept into the valley, like a crop blight. Nothing overt, no signs in store windows saying WE DON'T CATER TO GERMANS like they had back East in New York and other big cities where even Americans of German descent were being ostracized for something that was happening thousands of miles across the ocean and out of everybody's hands. But now the ill feeling had made its way to the West Coast. Just in small ways—a suspicious glance from a stranger in the street, the sheriff reminding Wilhelm and the others that all German males over the age of eighteen were required to register at their local post office, to carry their registration card at all times, and to report any change of address or employment. The way, sometimes, people would fall silent when she walked into a shop, as if they had been discussing government secrets and Clara Schaller might be a spy for the Kaiser.

The Bierfest celebration, suggested during the kaffeeklatsch three years ago, never came about. With their spirits down about the war back home, the immigrants were in no mood for planning such an event. And they weren't sure how it would go over in an American town where a few citizens were not too shy to voice harsh opinions about the war.

Clara feared the atmosphere of distrust and suspicion would grow a lot worse should America enter the war, no matter how much President Wilson promised the nation that that would never happen. She didn't relish being alone on this farm for the next few weeks, and considered asking Wilhelm if she could have Rosita live in while he was gone. But she bit her tongue. She didn't want to worry Wilhelm and distract him from the purpose of this business trip—to secure wider distribution of Schaller wines.

Pressing these fears down—why spoil such a beautiful spring morning?— she went outside to place the picnic basket in their new Ford motor car.

It was good to see Wilhelm so cheerful. For a long time after Jakob's death and Johann's departure, he had sunk into a morose state. He had said their dream was shattered, and Clara had tried to make him see that he could create a new dream. That was the blessing of this country. A man didn't have to follow his father's dream but could make one of his own. After a while, Wilhelm had plunged into working the vineyards until soon, beneath the warm sun, the taste of sweet grapes on his tongue, the first crushing and pressing, the first wine dispensed from an oak cask—he had discovered himself and had told her that she was right. Just because Jakob had died and Johann was gone didn't mean Wilhelm couldn't carry on the ages-old Schaller wine-making tradition.

They were prospering. The house was bigger. Three rooms had been added. There was now a nursery, ready for when babies came, and a formal parlor with a proper front door that opened upon a flower garden. The kitchen was now considered "in the back," and the loft was used for storage. The other side, where the men had slept on cots, was now furnished with a sofa and chairs arranged around the big fireplace. And best of all, Rosita was now back as their housekeeper and cook, coming every morning and leaving every night.

California wines were now in big demand because of the war in Europe. Business in general had picked up and prices had begun to rise. British purchasing agents roved about the country, buying food and cloth and metals and chemicals. The agricultural industry was benefiting particularly from the war.

But the world was changing in other ways having nothing to do with the European conflict. Electricity had come to Lynnville, and the tele- phone too. Everyone thought it very convenient. Of course, with speed- ier communications came swifter news of the war, which everyone had hoped would end after only a few months but which now had dragged on for almost three agonizing years. America was not officially in the war, but millions of young men around the country were already training, in case. Clara and the others in the kaffeeklatsch rolled bandages for the Red Cross and were knitting caps for soldiers to keep their tin helmets from freezing to their scalps.

What she missed most were the letters from back home. They came sporadically now, if at all, and were filled with bad news about long lines and food shortages, and the names of those who had perished in the trenches. Clara feared that soon all communications with Europe would stop and she and her small community of expatriates would be cut off from the homeland altogether.

She wished Wilhelm and Johann had not had their falling-out. They could have been a family now. Three years ago, Johann had married Arturo Ballerini's daughter, Feliciana, who was now Clara's sister-in-law. And they had a son, Adam. They should all be a family now, but the rift remained and the two families had nothing to do with each other.

Up in the bedroom, Wilhelm whistled a merry tune as he packed his suitcases. His spirits were high. It was a beautiful April morning, last year's bountiful grape harvest had been crushed, pressed, and fermented and was now undergoing the second aging process and would soon be ready for bottling—and he was about to embark on what he expected to be a very successful business trip. He was filled with optimism and enthusiasm. Wilhelm hoped to line up many customers up and down the coast of California.

He had brought improvements to the vineyards. Because grapes begin to deteriorate the minute they are picked, it is essential that they be rushed to the vats on the crushing pad as quickly as possible, or spoilage will ruin the wine. Wilhelm had borrowed money to purchase trucks to replace wagons. As a result, at harvest time the grapes were hauled quickly to the crushing vats, the trucks racing off down the rows of vines to collect more. It was quicker, more efficient production, resulting in a better quality of wine.

And now, because of the war, with wine no longer coming out of Europe, the demand for California wine was high. Wilhelm was going to go up and down the state, seeking contracts with distributors who had the farthest-reaching delivery networks. Once the people of America tasted Schaller Rieslings, he knew they would clamor for more. He saw himself and Clara standing on the first rung of a great, golden stairway that was going to carry them up to wealth and success. Worldwide recognition of California wine was imminent.

As he opened a drawer to bring out fresh shirt collars and cufflinks, he found a small white object that made his heart hit a double-beat.

The morning after his brutal beating of his brother, Wilhelm had gone out at first light to the place where he had assaulted Johann. He didn't know why he had gone there. To find his brother, perhaps? To find answers and reasons for why he had done what he did? Of course, Johann was nowhere to be found, but his blood was on the ground. Stark, boiling proof of Wilhelm's heinous crime.

On the bloody ground, Wilhelm had seen a strange object. He picked it up. It was the rabbit's foot that had always hung from Johann's watch fob. It had come off during the beating. He fingered it, the fur stiff with his brother's blood. And then he had put it in his pocket and dragged himself back to the house. He had no idea where Johann had gone, or even if he had lived through the night, but he wasn't going to search for him.

The days that followed the terrible night had been dreamlike for Wilhelm, as his body had gone through the motions of chores and ritual tasks, but his mind had been caught in a maelstrom of fear and worry. And then a note had come from Ballerini on the next farm saying that Johann had been brought injured to their house and was being seen by a doctor. Wilhelm had burned the note, sent no reply, and mentioned nothing of it to Clara. His brother was alive. That was enough. The incident could now be forgotten.

Johann had done well for himself since, Wilhelm thought grudgingly as he snapped his case shut. Marrying the daughter of a prosperous farmer. Wilhelm had heard about men from the government Food Administration coming around and offering contracts for crops to be exported to France and Britain. Arturo and Johann had entered into a lucrative arrangement with the British Purchasing Agency to provide canned beans for their forces fighting in France. Should America enter the war, Wilhelm knew that there would be such a demand to feed the troops that Ballerini and other valley farmers were going to be pushed to the limit meeting demand. And getting rich off it.

"I'm ready," he said to Clara, who stood in the doorway, ready to go with him to the train station. Clara had learned to drive. She would accompany Wilhelm to the depot and then bring the car back to the farm. He settled his broad-rimmed hat on his closely cropped flaxen hair (although the fiery beard was still full and commanding) and picked up his two suitcases. Wilhelm was going to be away for at least six weeks. He paused to look at her, still the same pretty girl he had fallen in love with back in Germany when she had made him feel like a hero. "I will miss you," he said softly.

"And I you."

Half an hour later, Wilhelm boarded the train, a porter helping him with suitcases and lunch basket. Not a believer in public displays of affection, Wilhelm took Clara by the shoulders and pecked her cheek. But she saw the glow in his eyes. Even though he was nearly thirty, he looked curiously boyish in his new suit and stiff white collar. She knew he was nervous, excited, hopeful, and filled with visions of the future. She wished she could add to his happiness by divulging her own possible good news. But she held back, just in case.

She waited until the train pulled out, Wilhelm waving out the window and Clara waving back. She felt confident that everything was going to be wonderful and bright, that she was indeed pregnant, and that Wilhelm was going to come back with his order book filled with fine numbers and figures and that Schaller wines were about to become nationally famous.

She turned away from the track and headed across the platform just as a man in overalls was delivering a stack of newspapers to the newsstand. As he cut the string binding the papers, Clara saw the headline on the front page: AMERICA DECLARES WAR ON THE GERMAN EMPIRE.

*   *   *

"MY SISTER BACK IN Boston," one of the men in Gilhooley's Saloon was saying, "her two boys enlisted in the army. They'll be shipped to the Front. She's worried sick. She said her hair is falling out."

"We have no business being in that war," another patron groused into his beer. "It's between them, not us."

Other men, elbows on the polished bar, one foot hoisted on the brass rail, all agreed, all with something disparaging to say about Woodrow Wilson, the Kaiser, and warfare in general.

Sean O'Brien, who owned the haberdashery shop in partnership with his wife, Kathleen, had no particular beef with Germans. He didn't give a damn about the war in Europe. Sean O'Brien thought only of himself—disappointment in himself and disillusionment about how his life had turned out.

He and Kathleen had come to America with enough money for a modest farm to run some sheep. But during their brief stay in New York,

Sean had fallen for a scam that was being run on new immigrants. They were introduced to a man who said he could double their money almost overnight in an investment venture that only a select few knew about. Sean O'Brien should consider himself lucky to be one of the last ones included. Sean and Kathleen waited for over a week. The man never came back, they never found him. Sean had lost nearly all their money. Kathleen had screamed at him what an idiot he was. That was the first time he had hit her. It came easier after that.

By the time they came to Lynnville, they had only enough to rent a store and stock it. Sure, they got back on their feet and did good business, but Sean O'Brien was not meant to be a shopkeeper! He wanted to be a man of the land. Run his own animals. Make money from wool, lanolin, and meat. A spread where he could walk his acres with his head held high. But standing behind a counter, ringing a cash register, telling a fat old matron where the sewing-machine bobbins were? That was no life for a real man!

Back in Ireland, he had mucked out a rich man's stables; and when he had scraped together enough money to come to America, he had arrived with big dreams and a swagger. The dreams were gone, but the swagger was still there. He was short, with a chest like a bantam cock's— and he crowed the same way, too. He was angry—hadn't someone back home told him that America's streets were paved with gold?—but he didn't know where to direct his anger. He could only knock his wife around so much, the way his father had done to his mother, before the local doctor and the sheriff and Reverend Brown would try to put an end to it. Besides, there were the three kids now and Kathleen with the baby at her breast.

Sean had ginger hair and a scrappy nature, but he could be pleasant and even generous when drunk. Which was why he always gathered a small knot of men about him at Gilhooley's Saloon. The subject tonight, as it had been since August 1914, was the war in Europe, which had come to a stalemated standstill with both sides stuck in trenches and fighting a hopeless fight. And now America had been dragged in!

The piano player launched into a maudlin song of love and loss, and it made Sean remember when he had fallen in love with Kathleen, back before the frustrations, before he'd started hitting her, back in County Mayo when he had gotten down on one knee, hat in hand, and begged her to marry him, to make him the happiest man on earth. They had been so giddily in love that they had actually laughed at the altar.

Where had it all gone? The euphoria, the dreams, the promises? He slammed down his empty glass and called to Gilhooley. "Boyo, a man could die of thirst in this place!" And Gilhooley cheerfully refilled it with Irish whiskey.

"*Usquebaugh*, the water of life!" Sean said with a nod and a wink to his neighbor, a corn farmer who ordered great mugs of beer while secretly adding shots of bourbon from his own flask. The farmer said, "They're sending a hundred thousand troops to France. My sister's boys are among them. They'll get killed, you'll see. Cannon fodder, and only nineteen years old."

The man to his left, hoisting his sixth shot of gin, muttered: "Woodrow Wilson should be sent to the trenches. See how *he* likes it."

Sean O'Brien, downing his whiskey, felt their disgruntlement somehow mingle with his own dissatisfaction. All up and down the bar and at the card tables, men were airing their grievances with the state of politics, the economy, the ignorance of army generals and heads of state. As Sean refilled his drink, losing track now of how many whiskeys he had had, and his legs feeling wobbly and his hand unsteady, it seemed to him that the atmosphere of acrimony swirling in all that acrid smoke and alcohol fumes was bonding very well with his own entrenched anger. And it fueled his bitterness all the more.

He was mad, and he wanted to take it out on someone.

He didn't want to go home, which was filled with the stink of dirty diapers and wailing kids. Especially as his wife wouldn't give him what was rightfully his.

Gilhooley's catered mainly to a hard-working, beer-and-whiskey clientele, but he kept a few specialty items behind the bar, just in case. Sean now fixed his bleary eyes on one of those unopened bottles—he could just make out the label: *Schaller Vineyards.*

In his muddled mind that was by now an unstable mix of whiskey, anger, and the political disgruntlement of men who resented the war overseas, Sean thought of the prospering Schallers who had done so well when he hadn't, and it occurred to him that yes, the war in Europe *was* all wrong and American soldiers were going to be killed—and someone had to pay for it.

Recalling that the big German wine-maker had gone on a long train trip, leaving his pretty little wife alone at the farm, Sean grinned sloppily through his whiskey haze. She wasn't Kathleen, but she would do. Besides, she had it coming, with all her high-and-mighty airs whenever she came into their store. No one would blame him, and somebody might even reward him with a medal.

*   *   *

CLARA HUMMED PLEASANTLY TO herself as she warmed a pan of milk on the stove. She was in her nightgown and the hour was late, but she hadn't been sleeping well while her husband was away and she found that warm milk helped. It wasn't just Wilhelm's absence that kept her awake. The hoped-for pregnancy had not materialized. Two weeks after Wilhelm's departure for Southern California, her period arrived, dashing her hopes. But she would try again and again. She was only twenty-four. She was healthy. And Wilhelm certainly was robust. When he came back. . . .

As she lifted the pan from the stove, she was unaware of a car rolling to a silent halt down the road from the house, unaware that a man came on silent feet in the darkness to peer into her windows, to go from one to the next, seeking a helpless target. Unaware, as her back was to the window, that Sean O'Brien now was watching her through the glass panes, a man in violent heat, driven by a burning lust that was fueled as much by anger and self-hatred as the need to punish someone for his disappointing life.

The back door swung noiselessly on well-oiled hinges and he was across the room before Clara realized she was no longer alone. He grabbed her from behind, reaching for her hair, seizing nothing, cursing because she had one of those new-fangled haircuts that women were crazy for these days. He liked pulling a woman's hair when he was having his way with her. If Kathleen ever cut off her long red Irish hair, by God, he would knock her clear into next week.

Clamping his hand over her mouth before she could scream, he swung her around and bent her over the kitchen table, pulling her arms back and holding them by the wrists as if they were a horse's reins. He pushed her nightgown up and plunged himself into her.

Clara struggled and fought to free herself, but he held her down. She closed her eyes as he savagely violated her, pushing at her so that her cheek was pressed against the table, banging her face on the rough wood. She tried to scream, but he was knocking the breath out of her, making her gasp for air.

Sean didn't speak, but when he was finished he bent close to her ear and whispered, "That was for the Kaiser."

He left quickly into the night, to drive away in his car while she stayed there shaking and in shock until she collapsed to the floor. Her face hurt. Her wrists throbbed. And her lip was split and bleeding where she had bit it. But the worst pain was between her legs, where she had felt a painful tearing. And then she passed out.

It was morning when Rosita let herself in as usual, dropping her basket when she saw the Señora sprawled on the floor. Rousing her, the Mexican woman helped Clara to the bedroom, where she cleaned her up and asked if she should send for a doctor or a priest or someone from town. But Clara rolled her head from side to side and then lay in bed for a whole day and night, in a daze, wrapped in fog, barely aware of Rosita fluttering around her like a kindly brown moth. Clara didn't want to relive the experience, wanted to forget it as totally as she could, but she needed to know who had done this to her and the only way to find that out was to go over the whole terrible thing step by sickening step. She couldn't identify her attacker, because he had come at her from behind. Nor could she identify him by his voice. She had heard only grunts and moans, and the few words he *had* spoken had come out in angry, vicious tones, not the normal "Good day, how are you?" voice that she knew the town men by. And if he had spoken with an accent, her English wasn't good enough to detect it. All English sounded the same to her, whether spoken with a Spanish or Italian or any other kind of accent.

No, she had no idea at all who had done this to her.

What was she to do? The attack had been swift and brutal. There was no evidence that anyone had been there. It was only her word. What would she say, who would she tell? She doubted the sheriff would care. She had heard an anti-German word or two out of his mouth. She suspected he wouldn't rush to her aid.

Her assailant was going to get away with it.

As the shame built up inside her until she thought she would die of it, thoughts of death did enter her mind, real death, an escape from this nightmare. One night, as she lay in bed, in the darkest night and all alone, she reached her lowest, most despairing moment, and she found herself thinking of the pesticide that was stored in the barn. Yes, her mind whispered. A teaspoon stirred into a cup of tea. . . .

She was startled by a sudden crashing sound in the parlor.

Her attacker had come back! She pulled the covers up to her chin, shaking with terror, trying to think, wondering how she could escape, fight back. But she lay in the darkness and no footsteps came into the bedroom. The house was silent. After a few minutes, Clara crept out of bed and, picking up the ceramic pitcher that stood on the washstand, grasping it like a weapon, she went softly into the hall and then into each room and finally into the parlor where, by the moonlight that streamed through the window, she saw a broken picture frame and shattered glass on the floor.

Puzzled, she bent down. It was a photograph of her mother. She straightened and examined the nail in the wall. It was still there, intact, firmly embedded. She picked up the frame and looked at the back of it. The hook from which it had hung was also intact. Why had it slipped off the nail?

Removing her mother's picture from the frame, she brought it into the moonlight to look at the smiling face of Eva Heinze. "I miss you so much," Clara whispered as tears filled her eyes. "I need you, Mama. I'm alone and sad and in pain. I wish you were here." And suddenly, as if night had burst into day, a memory flooded Clara's mind. She was eight years old and had suffered a bout of scarlet fever. A nurse had come to the apartment above the chemist's shop and had shaved Clara's head in order to reduce the fever. When she recovered, her mother tied a color- ful scarf around Clara's shaven head and sent her off to school. But Clara had come home crying, saying the children had pulled her scarf off and made fun of her bald head. She had cried and cried, saying she didn't want to go back to school until her hair had grown back. Her mother had sat her down for a stern talk. "There will always be cruel people in the world, Clara," she had said. "We cannot hide from them. If we do, if we deny ourselves a full life, then they have won. If you stay home until your hair grows back, weeks will have gone by and you will have missed lessons. Those children will be ahead of you in sums and grammar, while you will be held back to learn what you missed. In this way you will let them win. Is that what you want? To let the bullies run the world?"

So Clara had gone back to school and had removed her scarf in the classroom to expose her bald head and the children never made fun of her again.

As she looked at her mother's picture and heard her mother's voice and the wise words, Clara looked through the window and saw the moon, ivory and gibbous, sitting contentedly among the stars, and she marveled once again at the workings of the cosmos. Just as a white owl, never seen during the day, had perched on her roof to tell her to be calm, and that calmness had led Clara to open the steamer trunk and find desperately needed money inside, this was another such message. She felt her mother's presence at her side. That picture had not fallen of its own accord. Things happened for a reason. Clara believed this most sincerely. And although feelings of despair and shame and humiliation did not immediately vanish—Clara knew that she would need time to come to terms with what had been done to her, if she ever really would—she nonetheless began to feel a calmness settle over her, and a fresh way of looking at things. No, Mama, she thought. The bullies will not win.

In the days that followed, Clara felt a new determination enter her soul, and a strengthening of spirit. Her mind cleared and thoughts became more rational. Instead of thinking about poisoned tea, she examined her situation, her life, and one clear thought came through: she was glad Wilhelm hadn't been here. If he had, if he knew now, he would go on such a rampage that the war in Europe would be brought right here to the Largo Valley. Wilhelm must *never* know. Nor must anyone ever know. Clara did not want to be the woman in town known as the one who had been raped. It would paint a red letter on her—not the "A" of adultery but a worse one—a woman who had invited the wrath and rapacious lust of men upon herself.

Clara told Rosita that no one was to be told of this, especially Señor Wilhelm. Rosita understood. In her world of impoverished migrant labor camps, violence against women was a fact of life.

Clara looked at her bruised and swollen face in the mirror, the scabbed lip that looked bee-stung. She looked at the dark marks on her wrists, humiliating proof of what he had done to her, and she thought: No, I will not accept this. I will not be a victim. The shame is his, not mine.

And she suddenly knew what she had to do. But she had to act quickly, before the marks of violence had faded.

*   *   *

CLARA WAS SCARED.

She hadn't wanted to leave her house, where all doors were now safely locked with Rosita resolutely stationed on a chair in the kitchen with peas or potatoes in a bowl on her lap—squat, staunch, loyal, her Latina chin thrust forward as if to dare any man to invade this woman's world. The walk from the house to the car had taken every ounce of Clara's strength, and it had taken her some minutes before she got up the courage to start the motor. The drive to town had been terrifying: danger lurked everywhere.

Clara parked the Ford at the edge of a dusty field where other cars and wagons and buggies were parked and a few horses were tethered to posts. She had arrived late on purpose, wanting to make her entrance when the Sunday service was already underway. She turned off the motor and sat there shaking. Could she do this? Was she strong enough? Brave enough? If you do not do this, she told herself, then he has won and you will be his victim forever. But what if she found him, sitting there in the church? What if she could tell by his face, his guilt-ridden look, the way he squirmed, that he was the one? What would she do then? Clara had no idea.

She got out of the car in the May sunshine, trembling, bruised, in pain. She wore a cream-colored skirt that fluttered daintily about her calves, and a white silk blouse with a modest cameo brooch. On her short chestnut hair, a close-fitting hat with no brim to hide the obscene bruises, swellings, and cuts on her face and mouth.

She pulled open the church door and stepped in to hear the organist playing "Rock of Ages." Clasping her prayer book over her bosom, so that everyone could see her purple wrists, she made a slow procession down the center aisle, bride-like. Heads swiveled, voices whispered and murmured. She felt all eyes on her as the organ fell silent and the hymn died. Where *his* eyes on her as well? If he was a member of this community, she was counting on his guilty conscience sending him to church. A few people in the back stood up to watch the slow, stately walk down the center aisle. Something had been done to her, they saw.

Clara let this conclusion swim in their heads for a minute. It couldn't have been Wilhelm, they would be thinking, he's been gone a month. A Mexican farmhand? They wouldn't dare. And then she saw light dawn in their eyes, the slight parting of lips as a horrible conclusion was arrived at. Clara Schaller, German. Anger among many of the citizens, and fear as well, that their husbands and sons might be drafted into the army and sent to fight.

When she reached the pulpit she murmured "Reverend," who opened his mouth but was too derailed to speak. She turned and faced the congregation. While she gave them time to come to obvious and shameful conclusions, Clara pointedly looked at each and every man sitting in the pews, meeting them square in the eye. Not the immigrants, of course, not

Hans or Josef or Fritz or Siegfried or Klaus. She also dismissed young or elderly males. Her attacker had been a man of robust form. She saw pity, worry, embarrassment in the men's faces. A few looked at each other, or at their wives. What was going on here? She even saw a little annoyance as some undoubtedly wondered who she thought she was, usurping Reverend Brown's service when few of them wanted to be there in the first place.

Even though, after five years, Clara had gained a good command of the English language, she wanted to make sure she was understood here today, and so she had spent the previous evening going over what she wanted to say, and she had looked up words in her German–English dictionary. Her accent wasn't thick, as Wilhelm's was. She knew the congregation would understand her message.

She would not tell these people what had happened, would accuse no one. Let them see the evidence and draw the obvious conclusion. Perhaps her attacker had bragged to friends so they could look at her and make the connection. She hoped he was a local man and not a vagrant who was a hundred miles away by now.

She had to choose her words carefully. Tongues wagged, towns talked. She had to make sure that whatever reached Johann, whatever got back to Wilhelm would sound noble and innocent and non-accusing. She also had to speak carefully for these people's own sake. If she spoke the truth, she could literally set Lynnville on fire. Her words, accusations, would inflame feelings and passions and set neighbor against neighbor. Start a local war that the town and nearby farms might never recover from.

She spoke calmly but was heard all the way to those in the back. "I did not start the war in Europe. I did not send your sons over there. Your President Wilson did that. We are only simple country people who wish to be allowed to live in peace."

She paused and saw lights dawn on faces. So, it had been a crime driven by anger and prejudice.

"My family and I have done nothing to hurt yours. No man or woman in this congregation is responsible for the war in Europe; we are not responsible for the decisions made by governments. The war is not our doing. We all know one another. We are all peaceful people here."

She paused again to scan the faces, pausing at each man who could have been her assailant—flies droned in the air and people coughed or shifted in their seats, but no one interrupted her. She came to the face of Sean O'Brien who met her gaze and sent her a self-satisfied smirk. It shocked her, rooted her to the spot. When he pursed his lips and sent her a kiss, she knew she had found him.

Suddenly, she was sick. Her knees threatened to give way. She clasped her prayer book tightly, as if it could hold her up. The memory of the attack washed over her in all its horror and terror—the atrocity that had been committed upon her. She felt herself sway. The church seemed to do a spin and perspiration trickled between her shoulder blades. His eyes locked with hers. She saw amusement there. He wasn't going to turn away in guilt and shame.

Realizing that the silence had gone on too long and people were starting to look at her with suspicion, she drew in a breath and said in a stronger voice, "Perhaps there is something you do not know. The word 'German' is a very old word. It comes from the Celtic language and it means 'neighbor.' We Schallers are your neighbors."

She thanked them and walked toward one of the front pews where men and women quickly scuttled over to make room. She took a seat, her head held high.

Reverend Brown's sermon, once he got over his shock and resumed the service, was about tolerance. It was not a rehearsed speech. It sounded as if he were making it up as he went along, speaking from the heart.

After the service, out among the cars, as her German friends clustered around her in concern, the sheriff came up. "Is there something you wish to report, Mrs. Schaller?"

"I fell," was all she said.

She joined the kaffeeklatsch afterward and although the ladies talked about the weather and fashion and anything but war, Clara knew they were all waiting for her to warn them, as surely she must, of the predator in their midst—name him so that they could protect themselves. They waited respectfully and Clara knew what they wanted, what she could never give them. But Frieda understood. She reached across the table where cake and coffee went untouched and laid her hand over Clara's. No questions, no prying, no advice. Just the comfort of unconditional friendship. And the consolation that Frieda *knew*. It was a relief, knowing that Frieda knew. It was a secret too heavy to bear alone. To the others, Clara said, "Stay close to your husbands until this war is over."

Now she had sympathy for Kathleen O'Brien, who "walked into

doors" and never reported her husband's abuse of her. One would rather be seen as clumsy than as a victim.

* * *

CLARA KEPT A CALENDAR on the wall in her kitchen, compliments of the new bank in town. Every month she made a discreet mark on the day her period was due. She counted the days now, tapping each little square with a quivering fingertip.

There was no doubt about it. She was five days overdue.

Wilhelm wasn't coming home quickly enough. "One more week," his last telegram had said, sent from San Francisco. Clara was a nervous wreck. She had expected signs of remorse and a guilty conscience in her attacker. She had not expected him to smile and send her a pantomimed kiss. She couldn't sleep. She was having terrible nightmares, waking up screaming. What did Sean O'Brien's wink and kiss mean? That he was coming back to do it again? Every night she went around checking and re-checking the windows and doors to make sure they were locked. Rosita had taken it upon herself to sleep on the couch in the fireplace room and she had two of her strapping sons camp out in the yard overnight, armed with machetes and pitchforks.

On the day of Wilhelm's scheduled return, Clara was at the depot two hours early, nervous and anxious. When the train pulled in, she wrung her hands. When she saw Wilhelm descend to the platform, she ran to him and nearly knocked him over with her embrace.

He laughed with embarrassment. "Hey, hey," he said, delighted.

"I missed you so," she said against his barrel chest.

He stepped back and took her face in his hands. His eyes brimmed with tears and happiness. Clara thanked God that her injuries had healed and cleared up, leaving no sign that anything had happened in her life other than feeding chickens and keeping the vegetable patch going. Should anyone mention her bizarre performance at the church to him, she was prepared to laugh it off, say "I fell," and that she had wanted to remind everyone that their German neighbors were friends.

Wilhelm would understand. He had encountered prejudice and hateful looks and comments during his weeks of traveling, as news of American fatalities at the Western Front were being posted in newspapers.

"I have good news!" he boomed as they went to the car. "I have more orders for our wine than we can fill. I will expand the winery, Clara. Hire more help. Plant more acres. We are going to see our farm grow!"

When they arrived at home, she put on an act of great celebration, telling him that they were to have his favorite dinner of bratwurst and sauerkraut with potatoes, followed by Black Forest cake. While it had been an ordeal to walk into the church and search for her attacker and to act normally since then, now came the real trial: keeping Wilhelm from even suspecting that a brutish horror had taken place in this cheery kitchen.

Even harder was that Clara knew they must make love at once to convince him that the baby was his. But she couldn't bear to be touched, and she knew that when he entered her, it would bring the nightmare back in all its sickening textures. But she *had* to do this. She had to give Wilhelm this child. He had suffered two great losses—his father and his brother: she could not hurt him further by letting him know that his wife had been made pregnant by another man. It didn't matter that the man had forced himself on her. A terrible shame would descend upon this house that could never be lifted. And so, with a racing heart, skin that cringed at his touch, a mouth dry with fear, she took him into her arms, pulled him to her breast, and stroked him and told him she loved him. At least not everything about the act was a lie.

She waited three weeks. Wilhelm knew of the kitchen calendar, knew what the cryptic symbols meant. She saw him coming across the yard to come in for dinner. She positioned herself in front of the calendar, hoping it didn't look too stagy, a thoughtful look on her face. "Oh," she said in feigned surprise. "I didn't hear you come in."

He looked from her to the calendar and back to her. A questioning look dawned on his face, and Clara offered a coy, secretive smile.

"Is it so?" he said in a disbelief so filled with hope that it broke her heart.

"Yes, Wilhelm. The night you came home from the trip. . . ."

He suddenly pulled her to him and lifted her up and swung her around. She clung to him and silently vowed to protect him from the truth no matter what. "Give me a boy, dearest wife," he murmured into her neck. "Please God, give me a boy."

Clara had always wanted a girl, a sweet little daughter of her own. But now, smothered in Wilhelm's desperate, hopeful bear-like embrace, she prayed to God with all her might that the baby was a boy.

They attended church every Sunday, Wilhelm having no idea that as he entered a pew with a heart bursting with pride, that his wife was being met each time by a humiliating smirk and a wink from Sean O'Brien.

The winter of 1917–1918 was a strange and confusing time for Clara Schaller. On the one hand, she was pleased to see Wilhelm so happy, and pleased too to see Schaller wine being bought up in almost a frenzy, bringing more money to the farm than she had ever thought possible. But at the same time, it was a dark time for the world. The Germans continued their push against the Western Front, while Clara and her friends worried about loved ones in Europe. Letters from home were scant and far between, and they arrived unpredictably. It was a time of mutual woe, and mutual comfort.

It was a frightening time for Clara for another reason: she felt nothing for the child she was carrying—no love, no hatred either. It was a limbo feeling, a waiting without eager anticipation. But as her due time came nearer, she began to be afraid, and then she was terrified— that she would hate the spawn of Sean O'Brien, who still smirked at her every Sunday.

On a cold February day, Clara's pains began while she was feeding the chickens—a month early if anyone was reckoning, but no one was. Rosita, peeling potatoes in the kitchen, looked out and saw what was happening and knew what to do. With herbs and incense and special amulets and prayers, she helped Clara bring her child into the world while Wilhelm paced in the outer room, nearly wearing the floorboards through. Friends had come from Lynnville to support him, Fritz and Siegfried and Hans, who had themselves gone through the agony of waiting for a baby to come.

Finally, he heard the tiny wails. Rosita popped her head out and said, "*Todo esta bien*," then disappeared back into the bedroom. Wilhelm waited several agonizing moments longer.

When Rosita had cleaned up both mother and child and told Señor Wilhelm he could come in, Clara dreaded receiving the baby. Rosita presented him to his father first and then brought him to Clara, who was terrified she would turn away. But when the kindly and all-wise Rosita gently encouraged the Señora to take the newborn to her breast, a miracle took place.

Clara felt the warm bundle in her arm, saw the little face, all round and pink and perfect, and every bit of anger and vengeance and fear left her. "He's so small," she murmured as Wilhelm knelt at her side, tears streaming into his beard. Clara touched the soft tiny face and knew in that instant, with love flooding her heart, that this was not Sean O'Brien's child but hers and Wilhelm's.

Wilhelm was overcome with gratitude as he knelt at Clara's side and cried big tears, thanking her over and over. It did not occur to Wilhelm that the child had come a month early. Wilhelm was a man who governed his year by seasons rather than months. They had made love in the spring and so it was a winter baby.

On naming the child, Wilhelm wanted Wilhelm Junior. But Clara had learned something about names. Many were universal in any country, any language. She had heard Arturo Ballerini addressed as "Arthur." And Guiseppi Franchimoni was called "Joe." Wilhelm was William in America, and Johann was John, as Jakob was Jacob. But there were names also that had no counterpart in English, and there was one man in Lynnville who must never be allowed to forget that he had fathered a German child— one man whom she counted on to be aware that this baby's birth came nine months after his assault on Clara. "He will be called Helmut," she said firmly. "After my father." Wilhelm was so deliriously happy that she had given him a son, he would have granted her anything. He would have reached up and pulled down the moon for her. "Helmut he is."

When Clara had recovered and was able to travel, she and Wilhelm brought the baby to Reverend Brown's church to be christened. Everyone in the congregation made a great fuss over the Schallers' first-born, wishing them many more.

On the church steps she walked up to Sean O'Brien and looked him directly in the eye. "My son's name is Helmut, after his grandfather. It is a noble *German* name. And he will be raised to love the land of his ancestors."

And Sean O'Brien, who *had* counted the months and knew the truth, looked at the infant and the smirk finally fell from his face.

*   *   *

SHE HAD BUNDLED HELMUT into the car and driven to the Largo River, where she needed to think.

It was an autumn morning. The date was November 11, 1918, a day in which newspaper headlines around the world proclaimed the end of the Great War and church bells pealed in thousands of steeples. Back in May, when everyone had thought the war would go on forever, American troops had carried out a major offensive that turned the tide of the war.

The attack had been a complete success, as two powerful German coun-
terattacks were repulsed. Now, five months later, the bloody conflict was
at an end. Newspapers were reporting that military and civilian casualties
amounted to thirty-eight million dead or wounded, and the first World
War was being called the deadliest conflict in human history. President
Wilson hailed it as the "war to end all wars," and people held out hope
that this was true.

A ground fog swirled over the water and among the reeds and cattails.
Overhead, a red-tailed hawk rode the currents. Clara looked at her son,
safe and secure in his little basket. She could laugh now to think how she
had feared that she would hate him. How ridiculous. As soon as he had
been placed at her breast, Clara had known she would love and cherish
her precious son for the rest of her life. He did not remind her of Sean
O'Brien or a night of rape. All she saw when she looked at Helmut was
her baby, a gift from God.

Nineteen-eighteen, she thought. Six and a half years since a group of
young immigrants had arrived scared and hopeful at this valley, wondering what the future had in store for them. So much had happened since
then. Marriages and births and deaths. Frieda Eberhardt had given birth
to two babies, a boy and a girl. Mrs. Mueller's daughter Mathilda, now
nineteen, had married Klaus the auto mechanic who, because of the
increasing popularity of motor cars, was plying a busy trade in fixing
engines, repairing tires, and selling gasoline. And when Frieda's sister
came out from Germany, she had been snatched up by Mr. Gilette,
the handsome new lawyer in town. They all had children now—the next
generation, all American citizens, had been born.

Clara looked at her baby in the basket, now nine months old. Already
he was sprouting a pretty little head of reddish-blond hair. She thanked
God that Sean and her husband shared this one important trait. While
Wilhelm's scalp hair was blond, his beard was a reddish-gold, not unlike
Sean O'Brien's head of hair, which was a little more gingery.

Hearing a horse's hooves, she turned to see a rider coming toward
her. She widened her eyes, caught her breath, and felt her heart do a
queer flip-flop. It was Johann! With a little boy riding in front of him on
the saddle, Johann's arms around him.

Clara sat frozen, and a rush of emotions swept over her as he
came closer.

It was a beautiful morning, and Johann hadn't been able to resist
taking his son for a horseback ride. When the newborn had been placed

in his arms, Johann had been rocked with new emotions. Intense love and even more intense feelings of protectiveness. This boy was going to have a good life, the *best* life. Suddenly, the baby's name rose in staggering importance. He and Feliciana had already decided on Mary if a girl, Robert if a boy. The child was American, the first in the family, and so he should have an American name. But then, as Johann had looked down at the little pink scrunched face and seen the tiny fists waving in the air, Johann recalled that his son's last name was Neumann, which literally meant "new man." And so his Christian name should reflect the same characteristic. And then it had come to him. Adam. The *first* man. Adam Neumann.

No, Johann had realized in the next instant. Not *Neumann*. Newman. We are Americans now. My boy will grow up American and speaking English. He will be Adam Newman. A name meaning fresh starts, hopeful beginnings, a future filled with possibilities. My son will be anything he wants to be. He will leave his mark on this earth.

He brought the horse to a sudden halt. A familiar figure was sitting beneath a willow tree. Were his eyes playing tricks? It looked like Clara. And in the next instant he realized it *was* Clara, sitting in the very same spot he had brought her to six years ago, when he had sensed a sadness in her and had brought her to the Largo.

His first impulse was to turn and ride away. They had not exchanged a word in over five years. What on earth would they say to each other now? But a stronger desire to see her kept him going.

As he slowly rode toward her, she woodenly rose to her feet. He was so handsome in the morning sunlight. Words bubbled up in her throat, as there were suddenly a hundred things she wanted to blurt. *I can understand how badly your feelings were hurt that night when you and Wilhelm argued, how it must have caused a terrible break between you and your brother, and why you no longer wanted to live there. But your argument was with Wilhelm, not with me. You never said good-bye to me. And in the six years since, no letter, not even a note, not a word from the Ballerini farm. Everything I know about you since you left, I had to learn from hearsay. You hurt me, Johann.*

As he neared her, Johann's thoughts and emotions were a confusion. He had loved her secretly. He loved her still, secretly, but in a different way now—a love tucked away and not thought about out of respect for his wife, whom he also loved.

There was pain in loving Clara. *I don't know what Wilhelm told you, probably not the truth, but you never sought me out to ask me my side of what happened. Arturo*

told me he had sent you a note informing you of my condition, how badly injured I was,
how close I was to dying, and there was never a reply.

Clara clasped her hands tightly as he drew near, dismounted, and brought the boy down with him. Her heart raced. She had seen him in town, encountered him in Eberhardt's bakery, but these were brief wordless encounters filled with wondering and mystery. What did he think about her? Did he think about her at all? She had thought about him every day, and now she didn't know what to say to him.

"Johann," she said, holding out her hand. "It is good to see you."

He took her hand and held it. He smiled down at her. "And it is good to see you too, Clara."

Their eyes met and held as the autumn breeze swirled around them. Keeping her tone light, Clara said, "I heard that you legally changed your last name to Newman, English spelling. Wilhelm and I are not quite so Americanized. We will probably always be Germans raising American children." There was so much she wanted to say to him, so much she wanted to keep from him. She realized to her shock, in this close proximity, that there seemed an aura of sadness about him. She recalled the day she had met him, back in Germany, the bike ride, the picnic in the woods. His humor. How quick he had been to laugh, to say witty things, how funny he was. That seemed to be all gone now.

"It is not a bad thing," he said quietly, standing close, his eyes boring into hers, "to be from two worlds."

The locked gaze went on too long. He released her hand and squinted up at the blue sky to see wild ducks flying over the Largo Valley, a giant wedge of them heading south. It heralded the approach of winter—or at least as far as it was winter in California, not like in Germany where, right now, the days were cold and gray and rainy, and maybe even with snow.

"He has your eyes," Clara said, referring to the hooded lids and the little pouching out of the lower lids indicating a private amusement.

"I heard," he said, looking down at her baby. "Congratulations."

"He is your nephew."

Half-nephew, he wanted to say but didn't. There was so much Johann wanted to say, but he kept silent on it all. "And this is Adam, *your* nephew."

"How do you do?" Clara said to the grinning little toddler in a perfect little sailor suit. To Johann, she asked, "How is your wife?"

"She's fine," he said without blinking. "She is up in Monterey visiting her sister." He watched Clara's face. If she had any inkling of the truth, if she had heard rumors or gossip, she gave no indication. Instead, she said, "I would have thought she would have taken the child with her."

"Apparently one of the nieces has mumps. Feliciana didn't want to expose Adam to it. So he's being watched by a nanny." It amazed Johann how easily lies now tripped from his tongue. He understood his own father now more than ever. How Jakob had lived with the lie of Johann being Wilhelm's full brother rather than the result of adultery with his sister-in-law.

They looked at each other for a long, silent time, while orange dragonflies skimmed the river. They both knew there were things to be said. Clara thought, If Johann takes the first step, then I shall take a step, too. Johann thought, If Clara says the first word, then I shall have words, too. But neither moved nor spoke, and both ended up waiting until each came to the same silent conclusion: that the past was in the past, today was a different day, a different world. They were married now, each with a firstborn, each with a fresh new future before them. Each wishing the other well, each concealing a terrible truth that would never be spoken.

And in that moment, Clara felt something change in the world around them, or perhaps it was only within herself. She couldn't explain it. She loved Wilhelm and always would. But the deep feelings she was starting to develop for Johann were different, and she couldn't say how. Perhaps someday she would figure it out. Or perhaps she might never figure it out at all. Only the future would tell.

In fact, between them, they both sensed the budding of love and the start of a new yearning. A desire and yearning that they both realized now had actually begun during a picnic in the woods overlooking the Rhine River and which they had unknowingly brought with them and now felt being breathed into life on the bank of this river so far from home.

Suddenly, questions were forgotten—Why didn't you say good-bye when you left? Why did you never ask after my wellbeing at the Ballerini farm?—as these were no longer important. It was 1918, the war in Europe was over, and it was an autumn of new beginnings.

Without speaking of it, Clara and Johann knew that, somehow, they would meet again in this new future.

The Present Day

NICOLE COULDN'T DRIVE FAST enough. She *had* to get away.

This time, the urgency wasn't to get away from Lynnville and the valley and rural life: she just had to get out of the house. Cops were swarming all over her property, searching for the murder weapon, poking in all the buildings and yards, hunting for abandoned wells where the gun might have been tossed years ago. It was a long shot, since it was surmised that the murder had taken place perhaps as much as thirty years ago, but they had to explore every possible avenue if they were going to get any kind of handle on this cold case.

Amazingly, the Macintoshes, the Canadian couple interested in buying the property, were still interested—probably more so with all the grisly notoriety the case was attracting. They had even taken Nicole's advice and had driven out, map in hand, to Colina Sagrada, the barren patch of ground on Nicole's property where nothing would grow, and they were not only still interested, but Mrs. Macintosh had pronounced Sacred Hill as "very romantic." They had extended their stay at Mueller's Hotel, saying they found it quaint and historical. They should: a sign at the front entrance said ESTABLISHED 1913.

News stations and papers caught wind of the macabre find at Schaller Vineyards and were now hovering like vultures with their microphones and cameras and recorders. Since there wouldn't be any visitors for tasting or buying wine or ordering in the restaurant, Nicole had called her best friend Michelle to see if she was free for an hour or two and had then jumped in her car and raced off.

Instead of taking the highway, which was a straight shot into town, Nicole took back roads that brought her to the picturesque route along the Largo River. It was a busy place, a popular tourist spot and a favorite among the locals. There were boats and pleasure craft out on the water, fishermen lining the banks with their rods and reels, families picnicking on the grass, Frisbees flying, dogs chasing and barking. She tried to imagine what this place had been like over a hundred years before, when Lynnville was a small pioneer town. Had Great-Grandmother Clara liked to come here to the river? Was it peaceful and quiet back then? There would have been no bait shops, no boat-launching ramps, no noisy outboard motors.

It reminded Nicole of a term used in the art world—*pentimento*—the revealing of a painting that has been covered over by a later painting. If you scraped away this bustling modern scene, what would you find underneath? The picture of a more genteel age? Ladies in long white dresses? Gentlemen with waistcoats and moustaches? A serene, peaceful scene, perhaps, with the rare swan or two on the water.

She pulled over and parked in the shade of a weeping willow tree, needing to sort out her thoughts.

The lead detective on the case had called that morning. "In instances where a firearm has not been recovered for comparison with the bullet," Quinn had explained, "examiners look at bullets for general rifling characteristics, and these can often determine, with the help of the FBI database, what brands of firearms the bullet may have been fired from. In this case, Ms. Schaller, forensics has established that the gun was a nine-millimeter Beretta. So, if we can find the gun and establish ownership. . . ." He let her fill in the rest. Did he already know? Was that what she should be reading in his implication? She knew her father had owned a nine-millimeter Beretta. Had he registered it with the police years ago and this man already *knew,* hoping to trap her or catch her in a lie? Did the man honestly think she had known about the ghoulish remains in the wall of her barrel room all these years?

She sighed. Detective Quinn was just doing his job.

What she should do was look for her father's gun. It was most likely in his den. But she needed to get up the courage to go into that room, untouched since his death. She was afraid to enter. Why? What was she really afraid of finding in her father's sanctum sanctorum—a place she had always feared to enter?

His tyranny had begun when Nicole was twelve and her mother died of leukemia and her father changed overnight into the dictator of Nicole's life. Without Lucy Schaller around to give him the son he had desperately wanted, Nicole was now the sole heir to the Schaller property and fortune. It was up to her to carry on the family business. And it wasn't what she had wanted at all. Not that anyone asked her what she wanted. Daddy became a full-blown despot, ordering Nicole around, forcing an education of viticulture into her that she did not want. Suddenly, a heavy burden was placed on her shoulders and a prison was constructed around her. She was never to leave the farm or this valley. Everything rested on her to carry on the name and business—never mind that Jack was losing the family money right and left to drunken weekends of gambling and women. A fine role model he was, Nicole often bitterly thought.

And yet. . . .

She gazed through the windshield to watch a man on water skis being pulled at top speed along the river.

And yet . . . she had loved Big Jack, too, despite their fights and her determination to get away. She had loved most their walks among the vines, quietly discussing this and that, pausing to inspect leaves, to taste a grape. There had been a connection during such moments, a spiritual bond almost, between father, daughter, and the miracle of nature all around them.

She sighed. Why couldn't things be simple? Why did people always have battles going on inside themselves?

She thought about Lucas Newman. What a shock to see him drive onto her property yesterday, coming up to her aggressively, insisting on his right to be there because the skeleton that had just been found might have been a relative of his—a Newman possibly killed by a Schaller. And the curious issue of the brothers-versus-cousins story. Nicole made a mental note to ask her lawyer if there was any way of determining if Wilhelm and Johann had been related, and in what way. She didn't know why, but it suddenly seemed very important.

Starting her car and pulling out of the shade, she continued along the road that presently brought her to a scenic village that looked as if it had been plucked by a giant hand right out of the Rhine Valley and gently set down here in the middle of California.

A sign on a corner lamppost said, "WELCOME TO LITTLE GERMANY. FOUNDED IN 1953." Thanks to its unique half-timbered architecture, cobbled streets, gas lighting, and Old World atmosphere, Germantown had become a major California tourist attraction, with over a million visitors every year. The popularity had started in 1954, when a feature article in the *Saturday Evening Post* about the town had attracted visitors in flocks. After that, word of mouth expanded the community's reputation. Tourists came for the authentic German beer halls, the statues of the Brothers Grimm, the medieval houses, and the rural Lutheran church, as well as German music and folk dancing. In addition, several restaurants and pastry shops served German specialties. A replica of a nineteenth-century horse-drawn streetcar took visitors on sightseeing tours around downtown Germantown, where there were high-end boutiques, art galleries, and wine-tasting rooms.

Nicole looked at the tourists strolling down the sidewalks wearing shorts and tank tops because the September day was so warm. A few employees from nearby shops were taking a sunshine break wearing colorful lederhosen and dirndls. There was a banner across the street announcing the annual Oktoberfest, coming up in a couple of weeks.

Waiting at the only red traffic light in town, Nicole looked in the window of the antiques store. The proprietor was Jim Decker, a lifelong resident. His grandparents had been among the first group of German immigrants to arrive in Largo Valley, he liked to boast. A young couple—a shoemaker and his piano-teacher wife—had arrived with the Schallers. When Nicole's father died, Jim had offered to sell the estate on consignment—all those family heirlooms on display in the big house. But Nicole had explained that they were part of the property sale. The violin and meerschaum pipes went along with the vineyards and the wine bottles.

Nicole loved Germantown and was especially proud to know that her family had had a large hand in founding and constructing it. She would have liked to park and walk about, see what new paintings and sculptures were being offered, perhaps buy some warm apple strudel with vanilla ice cream and sit in the sunshine in the main square. But she was not peaceful in her mind and heart, and she felt the tug of friendship. She needed the company of her best friend. So she continued on until she left the Grimm Brothers' fairytale town behind and soon arrived at Lynnville, a very American town where she found street parking near Eberhardt's Bakery.

As she entered the shop, embracing its Old World ambience, it occurred to her that it might be nice to take a trip to Germany. She had never been there, had never really felt the urge. But she did now, wondering if she could locate the village her great-grandparents had come from, see if there were any Schallers still living there. They would be distant relatives, to be sure, but relatives all the same.

And perhaps someone there could settle the mystery of Wilhelm and Johann—which was it, brothers or cousins?

Eberhardt's was a delight to the human senses. The rich brewing coffee smelled like no coffee you smelled at home, and the air was filled with the comfort of fresh-from-the-oven breads and cakes. The eyes danced at the sight of icings and almond slivers and cherries-on-top. And the taste buds, well, the taste buds told it all.

"Girlfriend!" Michelle was wearing the Bavarian dirndl she always wore in the shop. Even though this wasn't the Germantown store, tourists still stopped in at the original Lynnville bakery—loving the idea that it had been in operation for over a hundred years. Michelle was what was called "full-figured," and the dirndl didn't help disguise that at all. She wore her long, henna-red hair in corkscrew curls that made you think you could open wine bottles with them.

Michelle had married into the local aristocracy. The Eberhardts had owned the local bakery since its founding in 1912. Now they had five outlets in the valley with ovens on the premises, the most popular and famous one being in Germantown, where tourists grabbed up the fresh German ryes, pumpernickels, big soft pretzels, dark kommissbrot, buns and rolls and mini-breads dressed in sunflower seeds, onions, nuts, and oatmeal—after all, Germany was affectionately called "Bread Country," producing more varieties of bread than any other country in the world. Folks came from all over to taste famous Eberhardt caraway rolls, sweet coffee cakes, apple muffins, and spicy gingerbread.

There were two girls working the counter, and Michelle's husband was in the back, overseeing his baking staff and the ovens. Michelle brought over two plates and two cups—coffee and cake. Michelle always kept a little "reserved" card on the window table, for special customers and friends. This morning she was serving warm pumpkin spice cake with melted peanut butter drizzled on it, accompanied by generous mugs of the day's spotlighted coffee—Sumatra Ika Organic, with hot milk and sugar.

"How are you doing?" Michelle asked as she leaned on folded arms and gave her friend a genuine look of concern.

Nicole aired her worries about the police investigation and what if the skeleton turned out to be a missing Newman and everything pointed to a Schaller committing the murder? It was a tremendous, heavy weight.

And it didn't help that the arrogant Lucas Newman had now insinuated himself into the whole brouhaha.

Michelle stirred her coffee. What a mess. Two snobbish families looking down on each other, somehow defying the law of physics. She could laugh. Her own parents had come out and bought a humble apricot orchard. They had done well, and still were doing so. Michelle had married into valley "aristocracy." Her husband's family had come out over a hundred years ago, with the first Schallers. They were the snooty hoity-toities of the valley, just because they'd been here pretty much longer than everyone else, except for the Indians and the Mexicans— but apparently they didn't count. The turnoff from the freeway to get to Lynnville was Schaller Boulevard, and the main street in town was Newman Avenue. Nicole and Lucas and Michelle and all their friends had attended Clara Schaller Middle School. Clara had been a great force and contributor in the valley. It must have seemed weird to Nicole to attend a school named for her great-grandmother. But then everyone had picnics in Newman Park and took walks along a quaint cobbled street called Ballerini Walk and listened to music being played on Sundays at the Eberhardt Bandstand. Those who never leave are doomed forever to live among their ancestors.

It was good to sit like this with Nicole, despite the circumstances that had brought them together this morning.

Michelle and Nicole were having coffee and cake in the very same window where, a hundred years ago, young immigrant women had held their weekly Sunday kaffeeklatsch and shared secrets, aired worries, offered advice, and engaged in warm sisterhood—a seamstress named Dagmar, a piano teacher named Hilde, photographer's assistant Truda, hotel owner Mrs. Mueller, Frieda Eberhardt, great-grandmother of Michelle's husband, and Clara Schaller, Nicole's great-grandmother. Decades of female history had unfolded in this cozy, sunlit space. The tables and chairs were different, the sidewalks and paved street were different, but the topics of their conversations had been no different from what women talked about today, all over the world.

Here was where Michelle had confessed a secret of her own to Nicole.

Michelle was under pressure by her husband's family to produce kids. "We're trying," she would tell them. "Yes, I got checked out." What no one except Nicole knew was that the fault lay with Michelle's husband. He had occasional erectile dysfunction and was currently seeing a specialist in Santa Paula for treatment. But Michelle loved him and was so protective of him that she hinted that the problem lay with her. "It isn't easy being married into a family whose tradition—their *religion*, in fact—is always thinking of the next generation. They're so proud of the dynasty they started here a hundred years ago that they're eager to welcome in the next bunch and put rolling pins in their hands. Don't get me wrong. I'm fond of my in-laws, but sometimes the looks they give me. . . ."

Nicole suddenly felt the weight of family legacies and responsibilities. On the wall over the cash register hung a picture of honor: it was very old, dated 1912, the portrait of a young couple standing in front of a small shop with a sign that said EBERHARDT BAKERY. The great-grandparents of Michelle's husband. Nicole had a similar photograph in her house, taken by the same photographer, a man whose photography studio still plied a good trade in Lynnville—by his descendants, of course. It seemed that a lot of immigrants who came to this valley persuaded their descendants to stay and carry on the family business. Just as Nicole had. And Lucas Newman did. And Michelle's in-laws. All following in traditions and footsteps they had neither chosen nor had any say-so in. But at least Nicole was leaving, as soon as the problem of the murder was cleared up and the winery was sold.

As Nicole's eye settled on the sepia portrait of the two proud young immigrants, she thought of the similar photograph at home, of Clara Schaller standing with three men greatly resembling one another, two of them bearded. Nicole knew they were Jakob and his two sons, Wilhelm and Johann, two young men she had always thought were brothers. They had had a mysterious falling-out and had gone their separate ways. As a child, Nicole had loved staring at that picture, finding the clothes funny and their manner so stiff and unsmiling. But she thought Clara was very pretty, and the other brother (or cousin), who was clean-shaven, quite good-looking. They were farmers, but they appeared to be in their Sunday best, just like the couple in the picture over the cash register. Maybe the portraits had been taken at the same time, perhaps after going to church. She imagined that those young people so far from home would have gathered together on a regular basis. It made her smile to think that those long-gone people would be extremely pleased to see how their descendants were carrying along the family heritage, that their early labors and dreams had given rise to this prospering farm town and the adjacent Germantown, where tourists came from all over for an authentic taste of Germany.

"What a shock to see Lucas Newman there yesterday," Michelle said.

"Does he really think the corpse is his missing relative?"

Nicole hadn't slept well the night before, and the handsome Lucas Newman had contributed to her sleeplessness. His appearance at her place had unsettled her. He had also haunted her dreams in what sleep she did manage to snatch. It was strange to be discussing him with Michelle when the name Newman hadn't come up in one of their conversations in years, possibly not since high school. It was amazing the doors that opened when a skeleton was found in one's wall.

"He's what? Three years older than us? That makes him thirty. It's weird to think that you and Lucas are cousins in a way. Your great-grand-daddies having been brothers."

"Lucas disagrees." Nicole told her about the curious brothers/cousins theory that had been brought up yesterday. "He thinks Wilhelm and Johann were cousins or maybe not related at all."

"Wishful thinking," Michelle said. "A way to cut the Newmans off from the Schallers altogether. It's childish if you ask me." She tasted her coffee, added cream. "What if the skeleton is his missing relative?"

Nicole prayed it wasn't. It would mean she and Lucas would be dragged into a sordid melodrama, perhaps a sensational investigation and murder trial of some sort. Local gossip would be all over it, everyone saying that they had seen it coming, the famous Schaller–Newman feud finally ending in homicide. But who was dead, and who had done it?

She didn't want to cross paths with Lucas Newman again. Please make the skeleton be a homeless vagrant who got into bad company and got buried in her wall because it was convenient and had nothing to do with her family at all. Just an unfortunate coincidence, that two illegal migrants got into a fight and one knew about the renovation going on at the Schaller barrel room and took advantage of it as a way of hiding his crime.

She sighed. Oh, that's good, Nicole, she thought, chastising herself. Blame it on the helpless Mexicans. Wasn't that the way it always was?

Michelle moved bits of cake around her plate. She was worried about her friend. She thought about the great position with a cosmetics firm in New York that Nicole had sought and won, and Michelle was proud of her for it. But what if Nicole woke up one morning and suddenly realized she should never have left? What if she discovered that she missed the Largo Valley so much that it made her sick? This was what Michelle was worried about. That one day hindsight was going to hit Nicole like a wrecking ball and make a mess of her.

Michelle had tried arguing Nicole out of leaving. "New York City isn't real, you know. They only built it for making movies."

"I crave skyscrapers, Michelle."

"No one craves skyscrapers. And they're just empty movie sets. There really isn't a Radio City Music Hall, you know."

"Like Lynnville is real? Don't-blink-or-you'll-miss-it Lynnville? Nothing happens in Lynnville. It's against the law."

"You're just still mad that Danny asked you to marry him."

That part was true. He had gone and ruined everything by proposing. "I was already tied down by *my* family name. Why would I marry into a family that's been here even longer than the Schallers? There's nothing more suffocating than old Santa Barbara money. It makes me think of those feudal estates in old Europe. All those little kings and dukes joining houses by marrying each other's sisters."

Michelle knew that, deep down, Nicole loved the winery as much as her parents and grandparents had. It was in her blood. She was a Schaller and, according to family legend, the Schallers had cultivated Rieslings in Germany way back into Roman times. Nicole could no more deny her vintner DNA than she could her brown hair. Once the vines get into you, they're there to stay.

Just like the Eberhardts, Michelle thought in sympathy. German wheat and German rye were in their genes as well, and she would guess that the Eberhardts had probably baked loaves for Caesar's legions.

Nicole's cell phone suddenly chimed. She checked it. "Mind if I take this? It's my lawyer. He's searching through records for the police."

"Miss Schaller," came Mr. Gilette's voice over the phone. "Can you come to my office? I have found something you might find of extreme interest."

*   *   *

THE GILETTES HAD BEEN the Schallers' lawyers for decades. In fact, Mr. Gilette was vaguely related to Michelle, his great-grandfather having married Frieda Eberhardt's sister back in the day. Another family line going back over a hundred years, putting roots down in Lynnville and staying put.

It made Nicole feel a little stifled. She had already been wanting to get out of the valley and start fresh in a faraway city; but this morning, for some reason, sitting in Michelle's bakery where so many ghosts from the past continued to hang out, and now sitting in Mr. Gilette's office where photos of prior Gilettes hung on the walls, *really* made Nicole want to rush out, get on the nearest plane, and throw herself into a city that was full of last names she had never heard of.

Mr. Gilette was a balding, fussy little man who cleared his throat a lot. "I have been going through your family's old archived records stored in our basement, Nicole. Some of them are in terrible state. Nothing yet on any renovations to the barrel room to determine when the body might have been placed in the wall. I will alert you and the police as soon as we come upon something. But we did find this. It's a letter that appears to be from your great-grandmother. No postage, no address, so it was never mailed. My associates and I have not opened it."

Nicole looked with interest at the yellowed envelope with a note clipped to it that said, "To be given to my granddaughter after my death."

"I suppose that would be you, Nicole," Gilette said as he handed it over.

Nicole opened it and read it. Signed by great-grandmother Clara and addressed simply to "Dearest Granddaughter." It was dated 1965. "I write this letter as the beginning of a family chronicle in the hopes that you will come back to us someday and find this legacy waiting for you—because you need to know where you came from, what came before you that has gone into making you who you are. You may think you know the whole story of the Schallers, but you don't. For a long time, you didn't even care. When you were young and I tried to tell you things about the past, you would shrug and sigh and roll your eyes as if to say 'Not that old ancient history again!' But perhaps when you return, you will be more mature and with world experience and finally understand that every woman should know her roots, her seeds, her beginnings, because then she will have a better understanding of herself. And when one understands one's self, one can govern one's life with better direction and success.

"But beginnings do not exist in a vacuum. Seeds and roots are not of themselves enough, for they need soil and water and sunlight to sustain them. By this I mean, dear Granddaughter, you came from *me*, but I did not exist totally alone and isolated. I am part of a family, which means people, which means emotions and thoughts and aspirations and disappointments and love and, yes, even hatred. We have not had a smooth road. It has been rocky. And I am sorry to say, there is a great deal of shame in our family. I will not cover it up. You need to know."

Nicole's hand shook as she read the letter. Was it nerves, or fear? Excitement, perhaps, that tremendous discoveries and revelations were about to unfold. And then she read: "You already know about the Schallers, *your* blood, but there are things about your family that you do not know but deserve to. I must also tell you about the Newmans, whom you will say you already know, but the Neumanns back in the old days, long before you were born, were different. In those days when Johann and his brother had a terrible falling-out and Johann changed his name to Neumann, his mother's maiden name. You were taught to mistrust the Newmans, to regard them as our enemy, yet our two families are inter-twined like red and white roses growing on a trellis."

Nicole sat back in shock. So Wilhelm and Johann *were* brothers, not cousins as Lucas Newman believed.

"Mr. Gilette, is there any way of verifying the authenticity of this letter?"

He cleared his throat. "It should be no problem. The local library houses some of Clara Schaller's writings. She became politically active in her later years. Handwriting analysis, the ink and paper. . . ."

She stared in wonder at the delicate, swirling script with nouns capi-talized as they were in German, a habit her great-grandmother had obviously never gotten over after she learned English. But who was this mysterious granddaughter Clara was writing to? As far as Nicole knew, her father never had a sister. Had she fallen from family grace and moved away, never to be spoken of again, to wind up another Big Family Secret?

She resumed reading: "Dear Granddaughter, I will tell you the history of our family. But first I must tell you this: do not hate the Newmans. This ridiculous feud has to end, and you can be the one to end it. I have tried, to no avail. You need to know that Johann Newman, who is your great-uncle, is a good man and always has been. People forget that he was really a Schaller, my brother-in-law, and it was only after a falling-out with his brother, Wilhelm, that he changed his name to Newman. So no matter what you might think you know, or what lies you have been told, the Newmans are really Schallers and your closest kin."

That was the end of the letter. Nicole frowned, then went back to the top of the letter and re-read what her great-grandmother had written: "I write this letter as the beginning of a family chronicle in the hopes that you will come back to us someday and find this legacy waiting for you." She looked at Mr. Gilette. "Was there just the one letter? Clara alludes to this being only the beginning."

"I'm afraid the storage boxes are a mess. The river flooded some time back and a lot of records in the basement got destroyed. The clean-up afterward wasn't done in the tidiest manner, I'm sorry to say. If there are other letters, I imagine we'll find them eventually."

Nicole thanked him and left. She was going to go straight back home, to see if the police had had any success in finding an old gun, but first she had to make a stop along the way. No point in putting it off. No point in waiting for Lucas Newman to make another swaggering entrance onto her property. It was time for Nicole to stage a swaggering entrance of her own.

*   *   *

LUCAS TRIED TO DO some work at his desk, but he couldn't concentrate. He was worried about his father. When news of the skeleton found at the Schaller place had reached the old man yesterday, he had fainted. Lucas had wanted to send for the doctor in Lynnville, but Melvyn had quickly recovered and insisted he was fine. But Lucas had seen how his father shook, how pale he had gone. He knew what was going through his mind—that the homicide victim must be the cousin who had come to stay fifteen years ago. Jason, who was the son of Lucas's father's sister, Aunt Sofie, who had married a San Francisco businessman and moved away. Jason had come one summer to experience farm life. He had vanished one day; and when he hadn't shown up at his Bay Area home, his parents had reported him missing to the police and had hired private detectives. With no success.

And now this terrible possibility that Melvyn would be forced to make a phone call to his sister that was going to devastate her.

Lucas wished he could somehow soften the blow for Melvyn. Ever since Lucas's mother left them, ten years ago, it had just been the two of them, father and son looking out for each other, worrying for each other. His dad had always been there for him, teaching Lucas how to fish, showing up at all of Lucas's ball games. They played chess in the evenings, talked about the vineyards and wine, and politics. Lucas suspected that sometimes the old man got lonely. Lucas had known his parents' marriage wasn't the greatest and that his mother had stayed mainly for her son. But still, Melvyn had felt her absence sharply and Lucas liked being there for him.

Lucas got up from the desk, stretched his tall frame, and went to stand at the window to watch gardeners mowing the emerald lawns that surrounded the three-story house he had been born in and where he would always live. That was the way it was in farming country—the boys always stayed while the girls left. He hadn't been surprised when he had heard that Nicole Schaller was selling the property her father, Big Jack, had left to her. It also hadn't surprised him that she had turned down his own offer to buy her place. Probably a stipulation in Big Jack's will, as Big Jack's hatred of the Newmans was as strong as Lucas's father's hatred toward the Schallers. It was something Lucas couldn't understand. Why carry on a feud that had started over a hundred years ago and had nothing to do with the present? Especially when no one even really knew what had started the feud in the first place? A pair of cousins, or friends, fighting over a woman, a piece of land, a disputed well? No one knew, and no one cared.

But he really wanted that Schaller land. He *needed* it. But how to get his hands on it?

He wondered if, after the Canadians bought it, he could turn around and buy it from *them* at a reasonable profit. Or would Nicole be crafty enough to have a clause in her sales agreement with them that, should they decide to turn around and sell the farm, it was not to go to the Newmans? Would Nicole be that farsighted, or that narrow-minded and spiteful?

She hadn't seemed spiteful yesterday, just flustered and a trifle woebegone. Well, he supposed people didn't like having decomposing remains found in their walls. It was already in the newspapers. He imagined lookie-loos were doing slow drive-bys of the Schaller property.

It was strange being in such close proximity to Nicole yesterday—so close that he could see a small sexy mole in the hollow of her throat. He had seen her occasionally at the schools they attended, at plays, sports, other events. He saw her around Lynnville and once in a while in Germantown. Until about a year ago, he'd always seen her in the company of a lawyer who had a practice in Santa Barbara. The valley gossip mill spoke of a break-up. Lucas wondered who had done the walking out.

He didn't really want to think about her, but he had no choice. He wanted to purchase her property.

A maid in a gray uniform and white apron knocked on his open door to inform him he had a visitor. It was Miss Schaller. He stared at the young Mexican maid. Nicole? Here? "Show her in." And just at that moment, the phone rang, and he picked it up.

When Nicole was escorted in, she saw him on the phone. He held up a "one minute" finger. He turned his back to her and lowered his voice, but she caught a few angry words: "My manager tells me you still haven't made good on your delivery. You promised last week—hey, we all have problems, but I'm happy to take my business elsewhere."

Nicole tactfully stepped away from the desk and tried not to look like she was eavesdropping. She took a few steps around the room, Lucas's book-lined home office, with leather chairs by the fireplace, diplomas and other framed documents hanging on the wall. While Lucas hissed his displeasure into the phone, he glanced over at her. She wasn't dressed like yesterday, all hostessy as if getting ready for a wine tasting. Now she was in work clothes—jeans and a man's shirt, her long brown hair in a ponytail. She never wore makeup. He didn't think she needed it. He couldn't help noticing her butt. He liked the way the jeans fit.

Trying to feign interest in being there, but anxious to get this unpleasant visit over with and get back home to see if the police had found anything, Nicole went to the window to inspect a handsome stained-glass panel that had been inset between plain glass panes. It was a very colorful scene of a sunset and fields and trees.

After he ended his call, Nicole said, "This is lovely"—only as an icebreaker rather than out of any real interest in the glass.

"It was made by my great-grandmother Feliciana back in the 1920s. She was a very talented artist, I've been told."

"It's beautiful. Are there others?"

"Apparently she made only this one stained-glass window. It seems she dabbled in all kinds of creative interests. If you don't mind, can we get to the point of this visit? I'm rather busy right now."

And rude, too, she wanted to say. "My lawyer found something of interest in his storage vault." She reached into her shoulder bag and brought out the envelope, yellowed with age. "It's a letter written by my great-grandmother." She found it curious that in the space of less than a minute, she and Lucas had both referenced their great-grandmothers.

Without inviting her to sit, Lucas remained standing behind his desk, opened the envelope, and read the letter. While he was reading, Nicole looked around at the collection of photographs on the walls. Apparently Lucas's hobby was salmon fishing. There were several pictures of himself and his father, on rivers, proudly holding up fat, shiny fish. Pictures, too, of himself with friends white-water rafting on the Colorado River.

There were women in the pictures, leggy and laughing. It struck Nicole suddenly that she'd always thought of Lucas as a loner. And yet here he was, with all these friends.

She wondered about girlfriends, what he was looking for in a woman. He was thirty and unmarried. She wondered why. But then, *she* was twenty-seven and unmarried. But Nicole knew why she wasn't married.

Was there something similar in his life, something that came first and precluded deep relationships?

It was strange. Nicole thought back over the years. They had attended the same grade school. She always saw Lucas on the playground. But when she entered the fourth grade, Lucas vanished. You no longer heard his prankish laughter on the ball courts or saw him punch his pals in the cafeteria. He had moved on to the seventh grade and now attended another school. When Nicole entered the seventh grade, he had moved on again, into the tenth grade and high school. When Nicole was in the ninth grade and Lucas was a senior, a lot of kids in her class attended the high school football games where Lucas was the star quarterback. And when she moved into the big brick building, she discovered that Lucas Newman had made a legend of himself there. His picture was in the main-hall trophy case and other kids still talked about him. He was always ahead of her, a legend, a colorful character, and an admired school hero. And now here they were, and Lucas was staying put.

While Lucas concentrated on the letter, his brow knotting in a frown, Nicole saw an antique photo over the fireplace. A wedding photo. She recognized the man from photos in one of her own family albums. It was Johann, Wilhelm's brother. The young woman in the wedding gown was astonishingly beautiful and exotic-looking. She would be Feliciana, the one who had made the stained-glass window. Nicole saw Johann's resemblance to his great-grandson. Just as she herself had inherited Clara Schaller's distinctive hairline, Lucas had inherited Johann's sexy eyes.

Lucas was still frowning when he finished reading. He turned the letter over, then examined the envelope as if Nicole were trying to slip him a clever forgery. "How can we trust this letter?"

Of course he would be suspicious. It had been brought to him by a Schaller and had supposedly been written by a Schaller. "My lawyer says there are ways of verifying authenticity. But on the way over here, it occurred to me that there are a lot of elderly people in this area who would have known Wilhelm and Johann." Even Lucas's father, Melvyn, who was seventy, would have known Wilhelm and his own grandfather, Johann.

She saw that he was uncomfortable with this, and she understood why. He believed what his family had always told him—that Wilhelm and Johann had been distant cousins, that the two families weren't really connected at all. This new information took him out of his comfort zone, made him look at his family's history in a new and unsettling way. Brothers? That took on new, Biblical significance, not to mention the legal quagmire that might arise from this. Who really did own the Schaller and Newman

184 / Barbara Wood

farms now? Had there been an equitable settlement decades ago, or had land been stolen and did someone still owe someone something?

Lucas couldn't stop reading the letter over and over, as if he was missing something vital and it would soon jump out and clear everything up. The news was more than unsettling. If what this letter said was true, why had he been told all his life that Wilhelm and Johann weren't brothers? Why would his father lie about it?

But even more unsettling was how his father would take this news so soon after the discovery of the skeleton in the wall. Melvyn Newman, though robust and still able to work the farm alongside younger men, was nonetheless getting on in years; and he *had* fainted yesterday. What was this letter going to do to him?

Lucas looked at Nicole. "The author of this letter seems to hint that there are more letters. Are there?" Almost an accusatory tone, as if she were holding out on him.

"My lawyer says it's a possibility." She could tell Lucas was unhappy about this turn of events. The brothers/cousins debate, this unexpected letter from Clara Schaller with the possibility of more to come (and how slanted against the Newmans were *they* going to be?), and the possibility of a ghastly scandal blowing up in the valley—if the skeleton *was* his missing relative, then what? There was no statute of limitations on murder. A major investigation would have to be launched, their pasts dug up and scrutinized under a microscope, all sorts of dirty family laundry brought to light. But then Nicole herself wasn't pleased by this unexpected turn of events. She had to be in New York by November first.

"You!" came a shout from the doorway. "Get out of here!"

They turned to see old Melvyn hobbling in on his cane. He had the typical farmer's sunburn contrasting his leonine shock of white hair. He wore dusty jeans, work boots, and a plaid shirt.

"Get out of my house!" he shouted at Nicole.

"Pop—" Lucas began.

"I don't want her here!"

Lucas reached for his father. He had never seen the old man so agitated. Ever since the skeleton in the wall. . . .

Nicole held up her hands and backed away. "I'm sorry, Mr. Newman," she said. "I just wanted to show Lucas something."

"I know what you're up to!" he cried, brandishing the cane. And then, suddenly, his face turned red, then purple. He clutched his chest and collapsed to the floor.

PART THREE
1922–1930

CLARA WAS DRIVING ALONG the river road, in and out of the shade of the weeping willows that lined the banks of the Largo. It was a beautiful October day and for once she was alone. Wilhelm always insisted that she take one of the farmhands with her when she made her rounds, but Wilhelm had gone up to Salinas and wouldn't be back until tomorrow. So she had left four-year-old Helmut in Rosita's watchful care, packed her car with boxes and packages and a basket lunch, and had gone on her rounds. She liked driving alone when she made her deliveries and picked up new orders. She liked the freedom of the road, the silence to think her thoughts.

There was so much to think about. It was 1922, and the world was recovering from a devastating war; a new law had disrupted life in the wine-growing valleys of America; and it had been ten years since she and Wilhelm had gotten married, and so far there was only the one child out of the union—and it wasn't really Wilhelm's.

Her thoughts going thus, round and round in circles with no solutions to various challenges, she turned off the main river road and onto a narrow country lane that skirted the eastern boundary of the Ballerini farm. She often took this long way around on her way home in the hope of glimpsing Johann, who liked to ride the property on horseback. Once in a while, if she was lucky, he would recognize her car, wave, and gallop over for a friendly chat.

Although more automobiles were coming to the valley, many of the rural residents still relied on wagons and carriages, or rode horseback.

She would see Johann ride into town. He sat high in his saddle. He had learned to ride while at the university. Among his academic courses was a required course of physical activity. While most young men chose fencing, Johann had taken an equestrian course, and Clara was glad he had. A man on a horse was bigger than a man on foot, she thought. There was something almost spiritual about a man on horseback. To see Johann on his chestnut gelding made her throat close up and a sweet ache to descend upon her body. He was so elegant, so regal. Never had she seen a man ride a horse so. He rode tall and prim, his back ramrod-straight, shoulders square and chin tucked in, his broad-brimmed hat shadowing his handsome face. Except for the cowboy hat, he looked for all the world like an imperial guardsman on parade. Her heart swelled for this man she loved but could never love, this man with the bearing of Kaiser Wilhelm, and it made her want to weep.

She had heard the gossip about his wife, Feliciana, that she used to go to a mental hospital for lengthy stays but that now she was home with nurses around the clock. Clara didn't know if there was any truth to it, but when the ladies at the weekly kaffeeklatsch tried to bring the subject up, Clara would close it down. They respected her wishes because she was, after all, Johann's sister-in-law and therefore Feliciana's. And everyone knew that *that* relationship was strained and in itself shrouded in mystery.

Clara had also heard that Feliciana had miscarried twice and that a doctor had warned them against another pregnancy. So Adam was to be Johann's only child. Clara wished their two boys could be friends. Adam and Helmut were cousins, after all, but there was a three-year age difference and their families were estranged. The hoped-for reunion between Wilhelm and Johann had never materialized and clearly was never going to. Stubborn brothers, both yearning to be friends again, Clara suspected, yet both determined to hold out until the other apologized. For the past ten years they could have been celebrating Christmases and Easters together, and the big American feast, Thanksgiving. Instead, they barely acknowledged each other in the street. Both were in the wine business, both pretended the other didn't exist—or, at least, they recognized each other as a competitor to be outdone.

To bridge that gap—and it was a very tenuous bridge—and to make up for a chasm that shouldn't be there, Clara and Johann had started to meet occasionally in places where they wouldn't be seen. They felt the draw, the need to talk, but both knew what town gossips would say, and that Wilhelm would be furious if he ever found out. And so they met secretly in isolated places—Colina Sagrada, the Spanish ruins—but there was nothing improper about their rendezvous. Nothing adulterous, everything above-board. Just two friends sitting in companionable silence to watch the clouds and the birds and to sense the air around them becoming charged with emotion. They both suspected they were falling in love, but it was never voiced.

It was interesting to Clara how, in talking to other residents in the valley, one learned about oneself. At the weekly kaffeeklatsch, and sitting in farmhouse kitchens or on front porches, discussing jams and jellies and raisins, sharing recipes and insights about life, Clara had learned in the past ten years not only the secret dreams that held individuals together and gave them courage and awareness, but about herself as well. People are mirrors, she had discovered. Look hard at another human being, and you see yourself. And what Clara had discovered in these years of starting her own business and traveling the roads and lanes of Largo Valley was that love was transmutable. Like an ocean tide, it never stayed the same.

*   *   *

AS SHE HAD BEEN learning about herself, she had started to see Wilhelm in a different light. And the love she had once felt for him was different, too. She often wondered lately, if he had been a local vintner back home, if he had lived near her village with no plans ever to leave Germany, would she have gone all starry-eyed over him? Or would he have simply been one of many grape growers who came into the village for supplies?

It was Johann's absence from the Schaller farm that had started her on these ruminations. She had not realized what a big part of her life he had been, from the moment she had met him, all through the journey over here and starting the farm. Making breakfast for the three men in the morning, sending them off with their lunches, having dinner ready for them in the evenings. Johann had been a big part of that, with his humor, his wit, his interesting tales to tell. During their short courtship, Clara had had to coax Wilhelm out of himself, she had even once told him that he must say something, anything, so that his silence wouldn't be misconstrued. And then Johann had arrived, and she had seen animation in Wilhelm, confirming her understanding that yes, she loved him.

And in the weeks and months after their arrival, Johann had brought mirth and entertainment to their table after dinner, drawing Wilhelm into reminiscences of their boyhood, with Jakob interjecting his own jolly memories. Those evenings had been warm and convivial, and Clara had thought they would go on forever.

Looking back, Clara saw how Johann would change the mood in the cabin when he came in. Jakob and Wilhelm might come home early, to pore over seed catalogues or balance the books or debate the merits of a new piece of equipment—two quiet, pensive, and serious men. Clara would feel the weight of their solemnity like a heavy shawl on her shoulders as she grilled the sausages and steamed the sauerkraut, her ears crying out for merriment. And then Johann would come in, bringing sunshine even though it was night out, and laughter, and Clara would feel everyone's spirits lift. Clara realized now that she hadn't really seen Wilhelm as he naturally was, only through the golden glow of the word "America" or as he acted around his lively brother. Clara hadn't had time to get to know the real Wilhelm.

Her mother was right: the courtship had been too short.

And now, with Johann living on another farm, Wilhelm had gone back to being quiet, and it was exhausting to draw words out of him. This was simply his nature, she knew now. She had married a silent man. The loquacious one, the brother with wit and things to say, had walked out on them, leaving a void for Clara to fill with her own bewildered thoughts. She wondered now if she had fallen in love with Wilhelm not with her heart but through her imagination. He had said one word: America. And it had swept her away.

But she was here now, in America, living her adventure, finding courage and ingenuity within herself, reservoirs and bravery she had never known were there. But in seeing these, she saw her situation and Wilhelm more clearly. She had thought she loved him at the time, but now she wondered if she had loved the *idea* of him, and his dream. But now the dream had been fulfilled and the idea of Wilhelm was fading, to be replaced by a quiet man whose needs were simple and few. She loved him, yes, but in a different way now. A quiet, simple way, while a new love was budding within her that was forbidden and dangerous.

As the car bumped along the road, she heard the song of glass clinking against glass in the back seat. Deliveries she had yet to make.

Ironically, it was the prohibition of one major industry in the United States that had sent Clara Schaller into an entirely new, unexpected, and very exciting industry of her own. Her enterprise had started small, in her kitchen with a few sterilized jars and pots bubbling on the stove. Using her mother's *Housewife's Companion*, Clara had learned how to make jams and jellies from grapes, since the making of wine was now illegal. That had been three years ago. Now she plied a thriving little business.

Her friend Frieda Eberhardt had been the first to offer Schaller products in her bakery, displaying the jars in the window. Frieda's husband, Hans, had switched from purchasing fruit fillings from a San Francisco supplier to using Clara's grape products in his cakes, pies, and strudels. Word of mouth among his customers led to such a demand for Schaller jams, jellies, grape butter, marmalade, sweet vinegars, and raisins that Clara had moved her operation from the kitchen to one of the winery buildings that was no longer in use because of Prohibition. She hired Mexican workers and oversaw a smoothly run cottage industry that was starting to see very nice profits.

She knew she could hire a man to drive around the countryside delivering special orders and taking new orders, but she liked to do it herself. It gave her some freedom away from the farm, and it was an opportunity to chat with distant neighbors and make new friends. After three years of this, Clara Schaller had become a regular sight around the valley, and a welcome visitor to farms and homes.

She couldn't thank Frieda enough for helping her get started. Their friendship had become precious to Clara. She had read in the *Housewife's Companion* on the "Wit, Wisdom, and Advice" page that one's appreciation of something doubled if one actually counted oneself lucky to have it. "If we had golden blazing sunsets every night," the author had written, "then we would stop marveling at them." Clara marveled at Frieda and loved her all the more.

Frieda was the one person in the kaffeeklatsch who didn't harp on Clara's having only the one child. No one was rude enough to come out and say "When is the next one coming?" But you could tell it was on their minds, those women with their five and six and seven children. Frieda never asked or insinuated. She accepted your life the way you lived it and never presumed to know how to conduct your life better than you knew. She wasn't like nosy Elke Mueller and her sister Anna, who would say out of the blue "You know what you should do?"—and you hadn't even asked.

As for her lack of bearing another child, Clara couldn't voice her suspicion that the fault must lie with Wilhelm, because no one knew that Helmut was another man's child and that therefore *Clara* was working properly. The truth was, Clara desperately wanted another child. She was twenty-nine and prayed she would get pregnant before she turned thirty. But three years of trying, every Saturday night like clockwork, had produced no results.

And then she had come into some startling information that now weighed heavily on her heart. There was a new member in the klatsch, the wife of a doctor, who had told Clara about something called a "tipped uterus" and that often the position used during sex was important for conception. When this information had settled into Clara's mind, it had appalled her—the significance of it. When she and Wilhelm had sex, it was always face to face, with him on top. Once in a while, he woke up in the early morning with an erection. She would be lying on her side with Wilhelm behind her, molding his body to hers, and she would feel the hardness. She knew he wanted to enter her that way—but that was how Sean O'Brien had done it and she could not relive his terrible assault. She would immediately turn over and take Wilhelm into her arms.

But now she knew . . . Sean O'Brien's position in the attack had resulted in little Helmut.

She thought about what the doctor's wife said, focused on it, dwelled on it, became obsessed with thinking about it; and each time, she broke out in a cold sweat and started to shake. No, she could never submit to Wilhelm that way, the way Sean had assaulted her. They had to keep trying the other way. Surely, at some point, one of their efforts would result in a child.

It was the least she could do for Wilhelm, who had suffered too many blows in his life.

For as long as she lived, Clara would never forget the sight she had come upon the day after the sheriff had come by with the devastating news that the winery had to be closed down because of the new Prohibition law. On January 16, 1919, a law ushered in the beginning of the prohibition of alcohol in the United States. Vineyards had been ordered to be uprooted and cellars were to be destroyed. Clara recalled that dinner was ready that day, baby Helmut was asleep in his cradle, and Wilhelm had yet to come in from the fields. She had gone looking for him and found him in the press room, his face in his hands, his shoulders shuddering as he wept. She had never heard a man sob so. It had rooted her to the spot. And then she had run to him and thrown her arms around him. He was seeing his dream being crushed before his eyes. How can you tell a vintner that he can no longer make wine?

And that was when, like an epiphany, solutions had flooded Clara's mind. She had no idea where they came from. Perhaps this was the sort of thing that made people turn religious. "Wilhelm, Wilhelm," she had said, stroking his broad back. "It is not all over. We are not finished. We will simply change. We will adapt. We will not destroy this winery, and no law or police on earth can make us do so. It is a foolish law and will not last. Everyone says so. But in the meantime, we will do as the Americans say: if life gives you lemons, you make lemonade. Wilhelm, you will make grape juice. You will continue to grow your grapes and bring them to the presses and bottle the juice for people to drink. You will simply skip the fermentation step."

It had sounded too simple, and yet simple it had turned out to be. Once the idea was planted in his head, it had taken hold and germinated, and Wilhelm Schaller the vintner had his dream restored. He had ordered a new line of bottles from a fruit-juice plant in San Francisco, had new labels printed up, and continued to keep his winery in full operation by simply skipping a few steps. The Schallers now produced quality grape juice and distributed their fine product throughout the state. They doubled their grape crops because, by a strange irony, the demand for table grapes had gone up sharply. People were buying them up like mad in the markets, and the suspected reason was that folks had taken to making their own wine in bathtubs.

Wilhelm did continue to produce *some* wine, as the law allowed two hundred gallons per year per family for personal use; and if Wilhelm happened to go over the limit by a few gallons, who could blame him for sharing them with friends and neighbors? Besides, there weren't enough federal inspectors to poke into every winery, brewery, and distillery in the country. Many small operations continued to produce whiskeys and vodkas and clarets and Bordeaux to keep companies afloat until the ridiculous law was repealed, which everyone said was bound to happen. The majority of the population was very unhappy with the temperance law. As Wilhelm often bellowed, "Jesus drank wine! It's in the Bible, for God's sake!"

One of the unforeseen consequences of the new Prohibition law was the thousands of deaths caused by drinking alcohol purchased from disreputable sources, and further deaths and injuries resulting from home distilleries exploding. Lynnville's own experience with this was when Sean O'Brien blew himself up while distilling alcohol in a shed behind his store. He had been making and selling illegal hooch—"White Lightning." Not enough for Federal agents to come sniffing around. But operating a still can be tricky business, especially if one is drunk while doing it. Kathleen and her children had mourned a respectful amount of time, and then she took up with another man who put cash into her haberdashery, they expanded the store and increased the stock, and were now doing very well.

For Clara, it was the closing of an ugly chapter in her life. Although O'Brien was never again cocky or smirking when he was around her, his presence at church and in his store was still a reminder of something she would rather forget.

While she was thinking all these thoughts, she didn't see a dark shape suddenly dart from the bushes along the side of the road, right in front of her. She slammed on the brakes and felt the car jolt. Thinking she had hit the animal, she got out and looked around. No, she had only bumped into a pothole. As she started to get back in, she heard a high, keening sound and wondered if she had hit the animal after all.

She walked slowly through the small woods that stood at the side of the road, holding her breath, following the sound. An injured animal? She came to a small clearing where she found a hastily made lean-to shelter constructed of branches and brush with an old blanket thrown on top. Whimpering was coming from inside. Clara bent and looked in. She saw what looked like a mound of clothes under a filthy quilt.

Something moved under the quilt. Drawing it down, Clara found a curly-headed little girl cuddled against a man who appeared to be asleep.

"Hello," Clara said gently. "Who are you?"

"Da-Da won't wake up," she said and Clara was captured by two big guileless eyes.

Clara reached out and touched the man's neck. There was no pulse, and his skin was cold. She started to pull the ragged quilt over his face, then stopped. Thinking of the little girl, Clara arranged the dead man to look as if he were in a peaceful sleep.

Drawing the child out into the daylight, Clara knelt before her and said, "What's your name?" She was about two or three years old, Clara reckoned, but it was hard to tell, as she appeared to be malnourished and the dirty dress was too big for her. She had a delicate oval face and large, lost eyes. "What's your name?" Clara asked again. She could see serious thinking going on behind the dark irises. Finally the child said, "Little girl."

Clara was puzzled for a moment, then she realized this must be what the father had called her. A term of endearment. She went through the poor man's pockets, hoping to find letters, photographs with names written on the back. But she found nothing to tell her the child's name. Clara pictured the father saying "Come on, little girl, eat your porridge," while lovingly stroking her dark curly hair.

Reaching for the child, Clara picked her up. She couldn't just leave her here. She'd take her to the sheriff in Lynnville. After all, the sheriff had to be notified anyway and send some men out to see to the burial. Maybe the sheriff could learn the man's identity, or knew a family who could take the child in.

The girl went with Clara compliantly, as if being taken away by strangers was a common occurrence in her life, her little arms trustingly around Clara's neck. She rode silently in the car, big dark eyes looking straight ahead.

When she got home, Clara entered the kitchen, where Rosita was cooking and Helmut was playing on the floor with a Tinker Toys construction kit. Using wooden rods and spools and caps and couplings and joining them all together, Helmut spent hours creating structures that no one understood but that he seemed pleased with. He jumped up and ran to her. "Mama!" And then he stopped short when he saw the little girl in her arms.

"Aii, poor little thing," Rosita said, wrinkling her nose at the filthy dress and matted hair.

"I'm going to give her a bath and then we'll give her something to eat." To her son, Clara said: "She's a little girl who will stay with us tonight, and I'll take her to town tomorrow to find her family."

"She's lost her family?" he said in disbelief, his four-year-old mind trying to imagine how you'd lose a whole family.

In the bathroom, Clara removed the tattered dress to find a shockingly skinny body underneath, one that hadn't seen a bath in ages. After sponging her down with warm, soapy water and toweling her off, Clara draped one of Wilhelm's clean shirts over her, buttoning it up to the collar and rolling up the cuffs to free her hands. The child didn't resist or question. She just watched Clara with big, solemn eyes.

They ate dinner in the kitchen, the girl eating with amazing daintiness, nibbling the crispy edges of Rosita's tortillas, sipping the cold milk, using her napkin properly. Helmut just stared, and the girl said nothing. Afterward, Rosita cleaned up and retired to her small room off the main house, built when Helmut was born so she could live in and help take care of the baby. Clara put Helmut to bed and said his nightly prayers with him, in German and English. Then she installed the little girl on the sofa in the fireplace room, lots of nice pillows and blankets holding her in protectively. Clara went to bed exhausted. It had been a long day, and an emotionally draining one.

She couldn't sleep. She usually didn't sleep well when Wilhelm was on a business trip. But also she was thinking: What if the sheriff couldn't find out the girl's identity, or a family to take her in? What if she was ultimately sent to a horrible orphanage, where she would be ignored?

Clara got out of bed, wrapped a shawl around her shoulders, and walked barefoot into the fireplace room where, ten years ago, Jakob and his sons had slept on cots. She found the little girl sitting up, staring into the darkness. "Da-Da?" she said. "Where is Da-Da?"

Clara lit a lamp and lifted the child into her arms. Taking a seat in the rocking chair, she held the girl in a loving embrace and rocked back and forth. She thought of the poor dead man. He had looked young. And terribly poor. Signs of a hard life. He had starved to death in a valley bursting with fruits and vegetables. She had looked at his shoes. The soles were worn through and the insides lined with newspapers. The child was curled up against him, not leaving his side. Her skin was translucent, her eyes glowing. Clara knew it was the final stages of starvation that created such an ethereal look.

As she sat in the rocking chair and the child molded herself to the contours of Clara's body, warm and yielding, Clara began to sing her favorite song, "The Lorelei." *"Ich weiß nicht, was soll es bedeuten, daß ich so traurig bin,"* she sang, and she felt love, like sweet wine, flood her being. She held the child close and sang the haunting song of seduction and death, and felt the little body against hers as they rocked together, slowly back and forth, the little trusting creature in her arms, like a kitten or a baby bird, and she knew in that moment that when she called the sheriff in the morning, she was going to tell him about the man she had found in the woods, but she would not tell him about the girl. Clara was going to keep this God-sent angel and she was going to name her Lorelei.

A sweet peace descended over Clara as she thought: God gives us children in the most mysterious and unexpected ways. Sean O'Brien gave me my beloved son out of his hatred for an enemy he knew nothing about. And today I went to sell jams and jellies to neighbors and came home with a daughter.

"Mama?"

She opened her eyes to see little Helmut standing there in his nightshirt. She smiled and held out her free arm. He crawled onto the rocking chair and snuggled into her side, tucking his head at her shoulder while he stared in curiosity at the little girl in the other arm. Closing her eyes, Clara resumed rocking, a child in each arm, both soon sleeping while she sang "The Lorelei." Her two babies—one a foundling, one the result of violence. And she loved them both.

* * *

THE MUELLERS, WHO OWNED the hotel in town, had started a taxi service—at first, to collect out-of-towners arriving by train and bring them to the hotel. And then they had added two more cars to carry people to outlying farms and homesteads. There was always a Mueller taxi at the train station, waiting to catch a fare. Wilhelm thought it a fine service, as it saved Clara having to come and fetch him, sometimes waiting for hours if a train was delayed. He was glad it wasn't one of the chatty drivers who always felt it necessary to fill the returning resident in on all he had missed while he was away. Wilhelm's driver today was a taciturn young man who didn't see much future in driving yokels around in a taxi someone else owned, so he stewed in his thoughts while Wilhelm was embroiled in his own.

Wilhelm couldn't wait to get home and give Clara the good news that his business trip had been a success. More contracts with fresh-produce distributors for Schaller table grapes, another bottling company for his grape juice. Wilhelm refused to feel less of a man just because he had been reduced to growing table grapes, making out of them jams, jellies, and raisins. He was still a proud vintner. And he was proud of his wife. Clara's jams and jellies were a big success, with the Eberhardts using them in their pastries and also selling the jars in their shop. Mrs. Mueller also sold them in her hotel, and the owner of the Lynnville grocery store stocked them as well, prominently displaying the jars.

Wilhelm would abide by the law, since it was there, and keep wine production to a limit; but he would be damned if he would destroy his precious vines, and those that had been planted by the Spaniards. This vineyard was *their* legacy as well. He was a grape-man through and through, and would continue to cultivate them until the foolish law was erased from the books.

The German community on the whole was prospering and, indeed, growing. As happened with expatriate communities, newcomers gravitated to their own kind, and thus the Poles went to Wisconsin and the Swedes to Massachusetts and the Italians and Jews to New York and the Irish to Boston. Germans who had settled near Lynnville wrote to friends and relatives back home, and those who liked what they read in the letters—of golden sunshine and balmy winds and blue-blue skies—saved their money, sold their homes, packed their treasures, and immigrated to the Largo Valley—thrifty, honest, hard-working men and women, proud of their new home.

Wilhelm felt he had done well for himself in these ten years and that his father would have been pleased with his son's success. Johann, too, was doing well. Wilhelm gave him that, although grudgingly. A man doesn't quickly forget that his bastard half-brother was their father's favorite.

But Wilhelm's biggest pride and achievement was his son, Helmut. Now he knew how Jakob had felt about his two sons, how everything he had done was for them. But one son wasn't enough. Wilhelm wanted more boys. But it had been four years since Helmut was born, and still no second baby. It was not for lack of trying. Wilhelm kept a diligent calendar, just as he did with his crops, as any farmer would. Every Saturday night without fail he literally discharged his husbandly duty. And every month, disappointment. It troubled him. All around the valley and in Lynnville, families were growing. Some had as many as ten children. Having just the one was starting to become an embarrassment. Of course, Johann had only the one also, but people seemed to forgive him that as his wife was unwell and it was rumored that she had suffered a miscarriage or two. Maybe they were just cursed, the two of them. Or maybe it was God's punishment for what Wilhelm had done to Johann.

He wished he could go back to that night and stop himself. But jealousy and grief are powerful stimulants to drive a man temporarily out of his mind. Because that was what it had been—a brief spell of insanity. He wished he and Johann could be friends, but he knew his brother would never forgive him.

When the taxi drove past Colina Sagrada and the abutting twenty acres where nothing could grow, Wilhelm frowned. That barren patch of ground was a sore point for him. It was as if that soil were challenging him to do something about it. Over the past decade he had come out here to stand with his feet apart and hands on hips to survey the scrubby patch of stubborn earth, a man determined to bend nature to his will. But he had come up with no solution. The soil was poor and it would be too costly to bring in fertilizer, fresh dirt, and nutrients. And even if he could, then there was the problem of water. Altogether, the land wasn't worth the effort. And so it remained a stain on his proud success as a farmer.

The taxi dropped him off at his house and Wilhelm was rewarded with the appearance of a little guy bursting from the back door to run down the steps shouting "Papa! Papa!"

Wilhelm scooped Helmut up into a big bear hug, held him high, and then brought him to his chest to squeeze the breath out of him. "Have you been a good boy?"

"Yes, Papa."

Clara came out, wiping her hands on her apron. Wilhelm filled his eyes with the sight of her. The short chestnut hair, escaping its clips in the afternoon breeze. A dusting of white flour on her cheek. He couldn't wait to make love to her.

She kissed him and welcomed him home. Then Clara sent the boy off with Rosita and said to Wilhelm, "I have something to tell you."

They went inside where he found a solemn little girl, a tiny thing, sitting silently at the kitchen table. He stared at her as Clara poured him coffee sweetened with milk and sugar, and set a slice of warm apple cake before him. As he ate, Wilhelm listened to a remarkable tale of how his wife had found the little girl, summing it up with the even more remarkable announcement that she intended to keep the child. "I telephoned the sheriff and told him about the man I found in the woods. He and his deputies took care of it. But I made no mention of the child."

Wilhelm sat back in astonishment. He looked at the pale girl with the big eyes, who so far had said nothing, which he found amazing since Helmut had not stopped speaking since he learned his first words. And then, when the significance of it all sank in, Wilhelm said, "It is indeed a heartbreaking story, but she is not ours to keep, Clara. We must tell the authorities." Wilhelm Schaller was a law-abiding man, and wasn't there proof in the fact that while other vintners in the valley had turned to making secret, illegal alcohol, Wilhelm stuck to the letter of the law?

"What about the girl's mother? What if she's frantically searching for her?" he asked.

"Believe me, if you could have seen the state of the father and the state this child was in, you would know there was no mother on the scene. Whatever happened to her, that poor young man and this girl were homeless and itinerant. I doubt there are even grandparents looking for her."

Clara leaned forward and said, "I believe I was meant to find her, Wilhelm." She held up her hand. "Please hear me out. Something ran across the road. I thought it was an animal, but I found no evidence of one, no tracks in the dirt, no disturbed vegetation. Something made me stop my car and get out. Otherwise I would have driven right on by and that little girl would have stayed with her dead father until she, too, was dead."

He gave her a soft smile. "Clara, Clara, these superstitions of yours. . . ."

She tipped her chin. "If I were to say the Bible was full of superstitions, you would be angry and offended. What makes your beliefs any more valid than mine?" Clara did not believe in coincidences. Everything happened for a reason. But she would not debate this with Wilhelm who believed that God spoke to mankind through Jesus, prophets, and angels. But there was no reason He could not just as well send messages through white owls and photos that fell from their hooks for no reason. Therefore Clara knew in the deepest part of her soul that a phantom animal had run across the road so that she would find this child. And so she was not going to let Lorelei go.

But Wilhelm, rising from the table, said, "I stand firm on this, Clara. The child must go back to her own family or be taken by the authorities. I will not have us being accused of kidnapping or child-stealing."

Clara thought about this, saw the stubborn set of his lips. "Then please, before we inform the sheriff, let me inquire around first. I have many friends among our neighbors, and customers in outlying farms. Perhaps someone knows something of the child. Give me a bit of time before we have to give her up. She might get put in an orphanage, and that would be terrible."

Wilhelm looked down at the child's large, swimming eyes, the translucent skin, the skinny arms and legs, and felt his heart soften. "Very well," he relented. "You may ask around first. But if we do not find out who she belongs to, then it is out of our hands and it is up to the authorities to deal with her."

As he went to unpack his cases and wash up for dinner, Clara remained seated with her arm around Lorelei's thin shoulders, and she remembered what the doctor's wife had said about "tipped" wombs and sex positions for conceiving. Clara had sworn that nothing on earth could get her to relive the night of Sean O'Brien's attack. But now another thought came to her: memories of how Wilhelm had treated her during her pregnancy with Helmut. There was nothing he could refuse her. Wilhelm would have given her the moon, had she asked him.

And so she knew now what she must do in order to keep Lorelei. She must face up to her fears and prepare to endure the unthinkable.

The next early morning that Wilhelm awoke with an erection, Clara scooted back to him, lifted her nightdress and snuggled her buttocks into his groin. He gave a moan of delight and took advantage of her recep- tive mood. She pressed her face into the pillow so Wilhelm couldn't see that she was crying. It made her sick. She wanted to scream. It didn't matter that it was her loving husband doing it—it was Sean O'Brien all over again, and she had to resist the urge to turn around and scratch him to ribbons. But it was the only way her tipped uterus could conceive, and so she screwed her eyes tightly shut and endured the "attack." When it was over, and Wilhelm slept, Clara lay very still and prayed.

She vowed that she would continue the torture until she was pregnant, but it turned out not to be necessary. A month later, she was rewarded. And as she had predicted, Wilhelm was so elated that he knelt before her and said, "We shall keep the little girl."

*   *   *

ADAM NEWMAN RACED HIS bike along the muddy lane as fast as he could, streaming past April wildflowers and startling cottontails from his path. He had such *wonderful* news for his mother. He couldn't wait to tell her! He had actually heard the news that morning, when he first got to school, and then he had had to sit for an *entire day* in a classroom, watch- ing the clock, itching to get home and tell his mother. Not an easy feat for a fifteen-year-old boy with the energy of an entire baseball team. And in fact, he was the star pitcher for the local youth baseball team. He was the fastest thrower and fastest runner, and now he couldn't make his bicycle go the lightning-fast that he wanted.
Mom was going to be so pleased!

You couldn't tell by looking at him—seeing that wild mop of tawny hair, the exuberance beaming out of his young face, imagining that here was a boy who was on top of the world—you wouldn't know it, but Adam Newman was a lonely boy. A handsome, popular, well-liked boy, yes, but utterly and devastatingly *lonely*.

It was because of his mother's mental illness, a shameful secret that was no longer a secret. Adam saw pitying looks cast his way. Kids teased him at school. The school principal had had him interviewed by a psychologist as they were clearly worried that he might go like his mother. So he compensated for this stigma by making himself popular and excel- ling at everything he did. He had all the friends he could want, but that was like trying to sate a Thanksgiving hunger with lettuce. Friends weren't solid like blood. They came and went. They were unreliable. And they weren't always forgiving. They patted him on the back, but he suspected they thought he might be crazy. And he knew a lot of the boys liked him because he was so good at sports. They gravitated toward him but weren't part of him. Not like genuine brothers.

He knew the story of how his father and uncle had split up. That they had had an argument over how to run the farm, and Johann had picked up and left, deciding it would be better to run his own farm and vineyard. Apparently, Wilhelm had taken it badly and now they weren't speaking. But if Adam had a brother, he wouldn't let that happen to them. He'd be loyal and stick by him no matter what. He wouldn't be false like his friends, cheering for him when he hit a home run but talking about him and his crazy mother behind his back. The whole time Adam was growing up, he prayed for a little brother to come along, but none did, not even a sister.

He did have cousins, though, Helmut who was twelve and Lorelei who was ten and little Billy who was eight. He envied them. They led a normal life. Not like him and his father. Sometimes it seemed like it was just them in the house, because Adam's mother stayed in her room all the time. And now Grandfather Arturo was gone. One morning he hadn't come down for breakfast. The doctor said it was a heart attack during the night. It made Feliciana's spells of depression worse, and longer-lasting. Sometimes her mood shifts were sudden and startling, with no warning. Because of this, there were few visitors at Adam's house. Certainly no parties or merry festivities. He heard of Christmas gatherings at the Schaller farm, and birthday parties for Helmut and his brother and sister. But none for Adam Newman. Yet he wouldn't voice this out loud. He loved his father with a fierceness. He would not be disloyal to him by complaining or pointing out how others had things better. No, he told his father he was happy being alone, not having friends over to the house. What a bother all that was, anyway.

But Adam yearned for a normal life, to live as other boys did. Everywhere he looked, there were big families. His school friends all had mobs of brothers and sisters. The Schallers, although a small family by local standards, nonetheless consisted of a normal father, a normal mother, and two boys and a girl, the kind of family you read about in books. He would have liked to be included in their celebrations, to address them as Uncle Wilhelm and Aunt Clara, and proudly introduce Helmut, Lorelei, and little Billy as his cousins—to show the world what a normal family he was part of. But he knew his father and uncle had had a bad falling-out long ago and that it was a sore point between them. Adam knew it was all Uncle Wilhelm's fault, whatever had happened, but he adored his father: Johann Newman could do no wrong.

He neared his farm and pedaled faster. His friends had wanted him to join them in town to see a new Marx Brothers film. Now that movies were all "talkies," they were a bigger rage than ever. But he had to tell his mother about this new essay contest that he was going to enter. He was doing it for her, because he knew that winning the essay contest and shaking hands with the governor of California would cheer her right up and she'd never be depressed again.

Reaching the main house, he jumped off his bike, burst through the front doors, and dashed up the stairs. He gave a polite knock at his mother's door, as he had been taught to always do, and then went in when there was no response because there never was. "Mom!" he said, seeing her in her usual chair by the window. The nurse set aside her book and tactfully retreated to give them privacy. "I brought you some nice flowers, Mom. Here, aren't they pretty? I'll put them in this vase and throw these old ones out. Wait'll you hear about this contest. Imagine having lunch with the governor of California! That's the prize." It was a statewide school competition with one winner from each school district. They would each get a trophy and a bus trip to Sacramento and a visit to the state capitol where they were to have a big sit-down lunch with the governor. Adam blotted out the negative things he had heard grown-ups saying, things about the contest being a blatant ploy to take people's minds off the recent stock-market crash and the sudden nationwide panic over the economy. That this contest was meant to bolster people's confidence in America and had nothing at all to do with encouraging young people to learn.

He moved a magazine out of the way to set the vase of flowers closer to his mother so she could smell them. It was the latest issue of the *Saturday Evening Post*, dated April 10, 1930, and it hadn't been touched. Every week, his father brought her the magazine but she never looked at it.

Adam fussed around the room as he always did when he visited her, straightening things that didn't need straightening, filling her water pitcher in the bathroom, re-arranging the pillows on the bed, all the while telling her about his day at school, his friends, his baseball game, and now this new contest that he was determined to win.

Every so often he would glance her way to see if there was a glimmer of recognition in her flat eyes. But there never was. Feliciana hadn't spoken a word since the morning her father had been found dead.

It killed Adam, to see her this way. As a child, he had been smothered with love from his mother. This was what he remembered: being held in her perfumed arms and rocked back and forth while she stroked his hair and read him stories and fed him chocolates and called him her baby, her angel, her sweetest little thing. He remembered her as a glittering fairy, all beauty and color, as she wove tapestries one frenetic summer, and made lace another hot summer when the baker's wife, Frieda Eberhardt, had come to the house to teach her how to use the hooks and the threads and create intricate patterns, and one year she had decided to make her own soap for herself, her household, and all her friends by melting fats and oils and fragrant herbs on the stove, a big production in her kitchen that made the cook cover her eyes, and had the whole house smelling of almonds, lavender, and beet roots, until the lye burned the skin on her hands and she had to give it up. His mother was like that, finding new interests, throwing herself wholeheartedly into them with passion and verve. She would never stick with one. After a while, she would grow tired and bored and, in the early days when Adam was very little, she would decide to visit her sister in Monterey. As he grew older and as his father decided there would be no more visits to Monterey, Adam learned that there was no sister in that town, that it was a mental hospital, and that his mother's hobbies were a manifestation of an illness that swung between extremely high, vivacious moods and spells of gloom and suicidal silence.

But, as years went by and she stayed in her room with two nurses, Adam saw that his mother's energetic spells grew shorter and less frequent, with the depressions lasting longer and longer until, with this last episode, she didn't come out of it. That had been a year ago. Thirteen months, to be precise, when her latest spell was triggered by Grandpa Arturo's unexpected passing. After the funeral, Adam's mother had retreated to this bedroom, and she hadn't taken a step outside since.

He missed his mother of the old days, when she had held him and sung to him and rushed through the house with yarns and oils and glass-cutters and Japanese folding paper with all the enthusiasm of a sports fanatic. In Adam's memory, she was incandescent, like a comet. Now she was a burned-out candle. He wanted that other mother back. And he was determined to find a way.

"I'll go now," he said after a while of one-sided dialogue, all about the essay contest and how he was going to win it for her. "Let you get some rest." He lovingly straightened the blanket over her knees.

To his surprise, her pale hand slowly reached out and touched his sleeve. He looked down. And then looked at her face. The eyes were focused. There was a brightness in them he hadn't seen in a long time. He thought—or imagined—he saw a smile play at the corners of her mouth. He dropped to his knees. "I miss you, Mama," the great big fifteen-year-old boy whispered.

There was indeed a smile at her lips. Her fingers touched his shirt, he felt them on his arm. "Adam," she said in a dry voice. "My baby."

He burst into tears and dropped his head in her lap. He cried and cried, broken boyish sobs, and vowed to bring her that trophy, no matter what.

*   *   *

"You might think there's no big deal to blending wines, son," Johann said to Adam as they sat at the workbench in the winery's laboratory. "Well, the blending part *is* a simple task. You take one wine and stir it with another, and the result is a wine that tastes a little like both. But the truth is, there is much more to blending than simply stirring something into something." Three evenings a week, right after dinner, Johann brought Adam to his lab and tutored him in the science of wine-making. The boy was good about it, attentive, and sometimes even asked intelligent questions. But Johann sensed that tonight Adam's mind was elsewhere.

He suspected it was about the essay he was writing.

They were seated before flasks and test tubes and beakers and graduated cylinders, reagent bottles, Bunsen burners, test papers, microscope—a great construction of glassware of all sizes and shapes joined together for the scientific measuring and analyzing and producing of Cabernets, Syrahs, Zinfandels, Chardonnays.

While most of the other wineries in the valley had been forced out of business eleven years ago by the new Prohibition law, Johann had had the luck to be the son-in-law of Arturo Ballerini, a very active and prominent member of the Catholic Church (having three times been named Catholic Layman of the Year). As a consequence, Ballerini had managed to contract with the archdiocese of Los Angeles, which included Santa Barbara and Ventura counties—serving over two hundred parishes—to provide sacramental wine for their churches. Although the Prohibition law made the production of wine illegal, wine for religious use was exempted, and so a legal and very profitable wine production continued at Ballerini vineyards. This had allowed Johann to keep up with his experimental blendings against the day when the law was repealed and wineries would be in full production again. Johann intended to be ahead of the game with a new line of exciting varieties.

He saw that Adam wasn't paying attention. His thoughts were all on winning that essay contest. Johann was proud to see his boy so determined to make his mother well again. Adam was certain that winning the contest would snap her out of her depression.

Johann loved his handsome boy. He knew the girls at school were all in love with the fifteen-year-old. But he suspected Adam was too filled with pain and loneliness and confusion to notice the girls. It was because of Feliciana's deteriorating mental state—and Johann wished he could take away his boy's misery.

"That's enough for tonight, son," he said, ruffling Adam's blond hair. "I know you're anxious to get back to work on your essay."

As he watched his son dash away toward the house, Johann thought of Clara. They had met secretly the day before, by a prearrangement to meet at the Spanish ruins, and she had told him that her son, Helmut, had also entered the essay competition.

What a remarkable woman she was. Taking in an orphaned child eight years ago and a year later giving birth to her second son, but still overseeing the busy production of jams, jellies, and raisins in huge stone-and-mason processing sheds that had been specially built. She still drove around the countryside in a truck, taking her sweet concoctions to customers and friends. She attended all her children's school functions, and she took them to Adam's baseball games. And of course he saw her every Sunday at the new Lutheran church on the outskirts of town. They would look at each other and remember the affection they secretly shared but could never express, their mutual desire to keep the families somehow connected. And he so desperately wanted to take their love to another level. But now more than ever, Johann must keep his longing for Clara a deeply buried dream. His wife needed him. Feliciana was drifting away more and more each day, and so he must be a diligent and devoted husband. But he could not help his straying heart. Nor his yearning thoughts.

As Johann resumed work on testing a new blend of Cabernet with a Merlot, he thought about Feliciana. Living with a shell of a woman. . . . It was Johann's own brand of loneliness. In this regard, father and son were alike. Johann knew that Adam wanted to win the essay contest as a means of bringing his mother out of her depression. In his naïve and youthful optimism, the boy thought her sort of sadness could be "jollied" out of a person. But then, hadn't Johann thought the same thing when he had taken her out of the mental hospital for good, to bring her home where he could care for her himself with the help of nurses? He had been so sure the hospital wasn't working, that the treatments and psycho-therapy were possibly making her worse. Surely, being at home in famil-iar surroundings and among people who loved her would be a better medicine.

But it had not turned out that way. Now he understood what the doctors had been trying to tell him. That Feliciana's mental state had nothing to do with normal people's emotional ups and downs. Hers was an illness that needed special attention. Still, he couldn't return her to the hospital. He had promised Arturo he would always take care of her, and now he was doing his best. But it was very lonely business.

But the farm kept him too busy to dwell on his loneliness. His bean crops were doing better than ever. Now that the country was entering what appeared to be an economic depression, people were cutting back on expensive foods, denying themselves steaks and fish and choosing cans of beans instead. Once more, the plight of others lined Johann Newman's pockets.

That was why, at harvest time, when the well-oiled threshing machines moved through the acres of ripe bean crop, leaving behind great piles of bean chaff, Johann allowed the women and children of the field work-ers to rush in with blankets, pile the chaff onto them, and toss them into the air to let the wind finish the job the threshers hadn't. Because the threshers weren't as thorough as their manufacturers would have farmers believe, old fashioned winnowing of the chaff with blankets often, in an afternoon, resulted in twenty or thirty pounds of beans per worker. Over several days, poor Mexican families could count on carting out maybe three hundred pounds of beans to go into their campfire pots. While other farmers might swoop in and claim those beans as part of the private crop, Johann always let the hard-working women and children cart their prizes away. Times were hard enough as it was.

Returning to his beakers and flasks and his Cabernet and Merlot, Johann wondered if next time he might try blending a little peach wine with some Riesling.

*   *   *

IN THE DINING ROOM, at the large mahogany table that seated twelve but these days saw only Johann and his son, Adam sat hunched over a pad of lined paper with books opened out on the table, a chewed pencil in his mouth.

The subject of the essay was "What It Means to Be American," and the entries were going to be judged on originality, cleverness, research, accuracy, and of course the usual spelling, grammar, and neatness. Adam was using big words and long sentences. He went on and on, to please and to impress, using more pages than the rules stipulated, and with a great many misspellings. He quoted from patriotic songs and wrote about "purple mountains' majesty" and what it said at the base of the Statue of Liberty about "huddled masses yearning to be free." As his pencil raced across the page, Adam tried to push doubts and insecurities away. So many other boys were entering the contest—kids who were better at lessons than he was, who made good marks and were always being praised by the teachers. Adam, although a good athlete, was not the best of pupils. Which made him work all the harder at the essay that was for his mother.

He would clear a space over her fireplace for the trophy so she could look at it every day and never be sad again.

*   *   *

CLARA BROUGHT HELMUT A plate of freshly baked cookies with coconut and chocolate chips in them, and a glass of cold milk. She paused to lay her hand on his head, like a benediction. Her angel, with Sean O'Brien's coloring and eyes, but which only she could see because no one else would look for it. The child she had once thought she would hate because he would be a reminder. But she could never hate this sweet boy. And now she had a daughter and another son. She felt blessed.

The house was nicer now, too, with new floors and all the rooms wallpapered and lovely electric lighting fixtures, even a modest chandelier glowing in the parlor. There was no sign of the rustic cabin it once had been. But even so, Wilhelm was talking of building a bigger house, a "proper" house, as he called it, with two stories and tall windows and a balcony all around. She suspected it was to compete with the Newman house, originally built by Arturo Ballerini. Certainly the Ballerini house was grander, but Clara was happy with *this* home. Still, if Wilhelm insisted on building something on a more imposing level, she would not stand in his way.

Especially once the prohibition on wine-making was lifted, as surely it would be. Everyone was saying that day was coming, and when it did, the Schallers were going to be proper vintners again—but on a bigger scale than anyone had ever seen. When Prohibition put smaller vintners out of business—good and honest, hard-working Frenchmen, Italians, and Spaniards—Wilhelm had bought their properties at fair prices. His most recent purchase was twenty acres of Zinfandel and Gamay. While land was power, Wilhelm knew that *more* land was more power. The Schaller holdings were now twice the acreage they had been when his father had bought the first property. And Clara was proud of him for it.

She thought of Johann, who was also prospering, and marveled at the power of stubborn pride. She saw him on a weekly basis now, every Sunday. Five years ago, a Lutheran minister had come to Lynnville to visit relatives and had fallen in love with the valley and decided to stay. So the immigrant community had pooled together resources to build a modest church on the outskirts of town, painted white with stained-glass windows and a steeple that tolled a bell. The service was in both German and English and Clara had taught her children to say their nightly prayers in German. Johann and his son attended Sunday service, sitting across the aisle from the Schallers. It was just him and Adam; Feliciana did not accompany them. The public excuse was that Feliciana was Catholic, but the whole town was in on the secret. Clara would glance across the aisle and meet Johann's eye in silent communication and love. But the brothers exchanged not a nod or a word . . . not even after eighteen years.

As she watched Helmut labor over his essay, "What It Means to Be American," carefully writing a sentence, she thought of Johann's son, who had also entered the contest. Adam Newman. A handsome American boy with an American name. Tawny-haired and athletic, with his father's irresistible eyes. She had taken Helmut and Lorelei and little Wilhelm Junior to see Adam's baseball games, a sport she didn't understand and which seemed to consist of a lot of standing around and waiting. But Adam did throw a strong ball and received more cheers from the crowd than any other player. She had seen him, after a winning game, being carried on the shoulders of his teammates, and she had seen Johann beam with pride. She was happy for him, considering the darkness that awaited him at home.

Her own son, twelve-year-old Helmut, showed no interest in sports or physical activities. He was scholarly, and she imagined that he would grow up to be a doctor or a lawyer, or a chemist like his grandfather. Clara had paid Hilde Decker to give him piano lessons, but he showed no aptitude for music. Perhaps he would turn out to be a poet, another Friedrich Schiller or a Johann Wolfgang von Goethe. Or maybe a scientist like Max Planck or Albert Einstein. There were so many possibilities. But before Helmut could know where he was going, he needed to know where he had come from. And Clara wanted her children to be proud of their German heritage. When the limestone bust of a beautiful Egyptian queen named Nefertiti was discovered in ruins along the Nile by a German archaeologist named Ludwig Borchardt, Clara had followed the story very carefully and had read it out loud to her children every day from the newspaper. She wanted to take Helmut, Lorelei, and Wilhelm Junior to the Egyptian Museum in Berlin to see the bust and take pride in their countryman who had found it.

Clara and Wilhelm often spoke of going back to Germany for a visit, to show the children their roots, but it was always "next year." Wilhelm was forty-two, Clara herself was thirty-seven, and her parents were getting on in years. "Next year" must come soon.

Ten-year-old Lorelei was also at the table doing schoolwork. Clara knew that Helmut adored little Lorelei, who was only two years younger, but she was small because she had been in so malnourished a state when Clara had brought her home. They didn't know her real birthday, so Clara had decided that the day she had found her was her birthday. And every year, Helmut treated Lorelei like a princess and gave her the biggest share of the cake. She followed him around like a puppy, but Helmut didn't mind because he liked being a hero. He had told Clara that. And then there was seven-year-old Billy. His real name was Wilhelm, like their father. But because he had started school the year before, everyone just called him Billy.

Helmut said he liked having a brother and a sister. He was their leader and he got to tell them what to do. He also looked out for them at school and made sure none of the other kids picked on them. He had been picked on himself, by the American kids who made fun of his name. Clara had offered to let him choose an American name if he wanted. Even the sons of the other German immigrants had American names, but Helmut declared he wasn't going to let the kids bully him into being a Joe or a Tom. Being "Helmut" made him special.

On the other side of the table, seven-year-old Billy was struggling with big printed letters on lined paper.

In the warmth of the kitchen, with Wilhelm at the winery overseeing the packing and shipping of five hundred cases of grape juice, and with a late spring rain whispering in the night, Clara thought that she had never known such contentment. She wished Johann could find some of the same happiness in his own life. At least he had Adam, and Clara knew he was proud of the boy. Johann spoke little of his wife, who never left her room and rarely spoke. Clara wished she could fill that sad void for him. But what woman could be a wife to two men? What woman would even want to?

Sending a silent prayer to God to bring Johann some measure of happiness, she went to sit next to Wilhelm Junior, her miracle baby, and helped him with his big, awkward letters.

*   *   *

IT WAS A BREEZY, SUNNY Sunday afternoon and the boys were walking down to Largo Creek with their bamboo fishing poles, hooks, and cork bobbers. It was a great time and place to be twelve years old, with the freedom to run and get dirty and dig up worms and catch brook trout. Most of all, it was the perfect time to complain about how adults were always telling them what to do, when to go to bed, criticizing. "Old people like our parents don't remember what it was like to be young," Steven said.

"Maybe they were never young," quipped a thirteen-year-old named John. These were not their real names but the names they went by at school and among friends.

Helmut wasn't listening as the knot of restless boys headed for the cattails and tall reeds along the creek's banks. He was preoccupied with the essay competition. He had finished his own essay, and all entries were to be turned in at school tomorrow. He just *had* to win. It was because he was small and needed to prove himself somehow. Kids called him "runt" and "pipsqueak"; he never got picked for teams. Helmut always sat on the bench. He needed to show everyone that he could excel at something. He envied his cousin, Adam Newman, who was practically an athletic hero. People cheered for boys who ran fast, threw hard, and hit far. Helmut did none of those. He was small and weak and had thought that by the time he was twelve, he would start to grow and fill out, but here he was twelve and he still felt stunted and left behind.

It didn't help that his name was Helmut. There was no American equivalent. One of his friends was Bart, but Bart's real name was Bartolmeu because his parents, who owned a large artichoke farm, came from Portugal. Another friend was Giovanni because his grandparents were from Italy, but he called himself John. And Sven was from Sweden, but he added two letters to his name and called himself Steven. And there was Helmut's own little brother, who was named Wilhelm Junior when he was born, but everyone called him Billy. But there was nothing you could do about "Helmut." It was something you were stuck with.

They reached the water and saw that the creek was running cold and fast and clear. This afternoon's catch was going to be good for sure, and the boys would run home with their prizes to get smiles from moms and dads. Laying aside their rods, they dropped to their knees and dug into the muddy soil for night crawlers and angleworms, the best bait for catching brook trout.

As Helmut stuck a wriggler on his hook, he wondered if he had prayed hard enough to win the contest. He knew that grown-ups were always striking bargains with God. They did it a lot in the Bible. But did God make deals with someone as insignificant and puny as a twelve-year-old? A short one, at that? Helmut didn't think he was a terribly big sinner, certainly not compared to the sins people committed in the Bible, and that was a *holy* book. Just a bit of cheating off Sven Einarsson's math exam, and snatching the occasional pack of bubble gum from Spengler's candy store, and telling his mother he had washed his hands when he hadn't. He had offered all kinds of good deals to God, promising never to lie or steal or cheat again and to always wash his hands, even behind his ears, if God would just let him win the contest.

The problem was, how did you know if the contract had been sealed? There was no paper to sign, no handshake, and you didn't hear God's booming voice saying "We have a deal!"

"Hey, Hell Mutt!"

The boys looked up to see some bigger boys on bikes come riding up. Their leader was Adam Newman. "Hell Mutt!" he shouted again. It was his nickname for his cousin, and it always made the other kids laugh. Adam straddled his bike as he said sneeringly, "*I'm* going to win the contest. *I'm* going to have lunch with the governor."

Helmut thrust out his chin. It wasn't fair. Adam was three years older. That always gave a kid an advantage. "*I'll* win," Helmut said with no confidence at all. "You'll see."

Adam laughed and his voice broke. "Newmans are better than Schallers. Everyone knows that. You shouldn't even bother writing an essay. I've already got pages and pages. I'll say hi to the governor for you." And he and his laughing friends pedaled off.

Helmut burned with fury. As he watched his cousin ride away, he curled his hands into fists, and tears of shame stung his eyes. He had struggled mightily with his essay, having no idea what it meant to be American. He had finally managed three pages about freedom and voting and having rights that couldn't be taken away from you, basically parroting what teachers had lectured to him without knowing what the words really meant.

The boys caught trout and ran home with their catches, and everyone had fish for dinner, but Helmut sulked and seethed the whole time. During the night, while his family slept, Helmut stole from his bed. He was mad at the world. His friends hadn't even stood up for him—Bartolmeu and Giovanni and Sven. They had just let Adam ridicule him. Reaching into his school satchel, Helmut pulled out the finished essay and ripped it to shreds. By the light of a candle, he took a fresh sheet of paper and wrote something else entirely. He didn't care how the judges were going to take it. He had spoken his mind, and he felt better for it.

But on the day of the awards assembly, as parents and families and students sat on folded chairs on the school lawn, the Newmans sitting as far away from the Schallers as they could, Helmut had terrible misgivings. He belatedly wished he had turned in his original essay. He scanned the faces of the judges on the dais and wondered if they were planning to single Helmut Schaller out of the crowd and point him out for the sore loser he was.

He wished he had never been born.

And then the school principal, after a long and boring speech about patriotism, called out in a ringing voice, "And the grand winner, for originality and brevity and boldness, is Helmut Schaller!" Everyone applauded, and his brother and sister cheered, and Helmut sat in stunned silence. Apparently God *did* strike bargains with twelve-year-olds.

As he woodenly went up for his trophy and handshake and to have his photograph taken with the judges, as he felt the envious eyes of the other students on him and especially the appalled, stricken eyes of Adam Newman, Helmut heard the principal say very quietly to him, "The judges called your essay bold. I call it having chutzpah."

Helmut stared at the man in shock. In answer to what it means to be American, Helmut had thought of his friends who hadn't stood up for him, those boys with changed names, and he had angrily written just one sentence: "It means your family came from some place else."

*   *   *

FELICIANA WAS DREAMING OF her father. Oh, it was Papa, all right, with his magnificent black moustache and his generous Italian smile. It was so good to see him again. "I miss you!" she cried as she ran to his open arms. She had never known such happiness. She was bursting with it. And when her eyes snapped open and she saw the midnight darkness of her bedroom, the happiness did not die. It stayed with her, beating in her heart. She lay there smiling and full of joy.

Papa had come to her in her sleep. He had come to tell her that he was happy where he was and that even though he was dead, he was never going to leave her, that he would always watch over her and make sure she was happy.

And happy she was! Feliciana sat up in bed and hugged herself. She looked around the shadowed room. Her night nurse would be napping in the small adjoining dressing room, ready to be on hand should Feliciana call out for help. But Feliciana didn't need help, and she never would again. She was cured! She knew beyond a doubt that all the sadness and despair that had weighed her down these past months were gone—and for good. She would never have a "blue" spell again for as long as she lived.

She jumped out of bed and tried to decide what to do next. Wake Johann up? Make love with him? Go downstairs and cook a special breakfast for him and Adam? Crispy bacon fried with tomatoes and sunny-side-up eggs. Pancakes and waffles with plenty of butter and syrup. And those spicy fried potatoes Adam so loves. Adam loves fried chicken too. It's so American. They always serve fried chicken and hot dogs at his baseball games. Is it okay to serve fried chicken and hot dogs with mustard at breakfast?

There was no question of going back to sleep. Feliciana decided she might not sleep ever again. She had never felt so suddenly alive, so full of joy and optimism. She felt as if she had just awakened from a long sleep. Yes, that was what it had been. Sleep. In which people had visited her in strange, distorted scenarios, their faces deformed, their speech muffled. Adam, her precious son, bringing her flowers and tears and talking about a contest, a trophy, and the governor of California. Had it been real? She must make it up to him. What a sad, lonely boy he must be to have so silent and unresponsive a mother. She had loved him when he visited her, but she had been trapped inside a shell and unable to show him that love.

But not any more!

Feliciana sprinted quietly around the four-poster bed so as not to wake the nurse, and slipped into the adjoining bathroom, a spacious chamber of marble and gold fixtures with a sunken tub that would do a Roman empress proud. Turning on the lights, she closed the door and looked at the woman in the mirror.

Dear God, who was that pale creature with shadows under her eyes, long black hair streaked with gray and streaming over her shoulders? That drab exterior in the long granny gown did not reflect the shimmering glow she felt inside. How was anyone going to believe how happy she was if they saw sallow skin and sunken cheeks and that awful dull hair? Feliciana remembered that she was forty-three years old, yet she looked sixty. But inside, she felt like a girl of sixteen! The first thing she had to do was fix her looks—make the outside reflect the inside.

She started rummaging madly through drawers. She had worn a little makeup once, surely she still had some powder, rouge, pencils? Oh, the plans she had! She was going to be a good wife to Johann from now on. And a doting mother to Adam. She was going to open up this dreary house that had turned into something out of a gothic Victorian novel and have visitors again, gay parties, outdoor fêtes.

Where had the nurses stowed her cosmetics? Where were her hairbrushes and combs?

A birthday party for Adam. They would invite all his school friends. Everyone in the valley was to come. I have been so neglectful of him. . . .

She opened drawer after drawer of towels and sponges and washcloths and soap. Awful-smelling creams for a bedridden patient. Liniments and aspirin and bandages. Good God, even a bedpan! When had this stopped being a lady's private bath and turned into a nurse's supply closet?

And Johann! Surely Feliciana wasn't too old for them to try for another child? She had been so neglectful of her wifely duties. She couldn't recall the last time they had made love. Tonight, it must be tonight. But she couldn't go to him like this, streaky hair and an old cotton nightgown.

At last, in the bottom drawer, a box of sweet-smelling bath salts. A bottle of rose-scented oil. A tin of perfumed dusting powder. This was more like it, and all relegated to the bottom-most drawer as if stored away for when the lady of this elegant bathroom would return.

With delight, Feliciana removed each item one by one, deciding that she would have a hot, soapy bath first, change into something made of silk, and tiptoe down the hall to Johann's bedroom.

Her fingers met something cold, hard, and metallic at the back of the drawer. Drawing the object out, she found long, sharp scissors in her hand. She gave a cry of delight. Yes! She would cut this awful harridan's hair. Give herself a youthful, modern trim.

As she brought the scissors up and seized a hank of hair, Feliciana's thoughts raced. We will have parties again. I will be the belle of this valley. Johann and I will be *the* society couple and will be the envy of all our friends and neighbors. Oh, Johann and Adam, the precious men in my life. I love you both so much. And I have so much time and neglect to make up for.

This was why Papa had come to her in a dream. To wake her up and remind her of everything she still had to live for.

What day was it? What month? It might be spring. A big outdoor party. I'll order honeyed hams and baked ribs from the butcher in Lynn-ville, and German sausages and sweet Italian sausages and garlicky salami and every kind of bread you can think of. And cheeses—cheddar, gouda, Swiss. We'll order special cakes and strudels and pies from Eberhardt's bakery. We'll have croquet and lawn tennis, and we'll hire musicians and have a dance floor. I will insist that Johann invite his brother Wilhelm and his wife Clara and their children. It was time to end this bitter feud and all be a family again. Yes, it was terrible, the beating Wilhelm had given to Johann. But they had been young hotheads back then. Now they were mature vintners, prosperous businessmen who were respected in the community. It was time for Johann to forgive his brother. *I* will extend the olive branch, *I* will be the peacemaker. And that's what we'll call it—the Reunion Party and everyone in the valley will witness Johann and Wilhelm embracing for the first time in eighteen years.

As she started to cut off the first hank of hair, Feliciana saw a reflection of the bathtub in the mirror. She should be running a hot bath while trimming her hair. In a quick, impulsive move, she spun away from the mirror and took a step toward the tub. But her foot caught on the little fluffy rug that protected bare feet from cold tile. Before she could reach out and catch herself, down she went, face first.

She felt a sharp pain and cried out. It wasn't her head she had hurt, but she *was* momentarily disoriented. Rolling onto her side, she looked down at where the sharp pain was coming from and saw the scissors imbedded deeply into her abdomen, her fingers still curled around the handle. When she saw how quickly the blood trickled out, pooling on the floor, a red stain spreading across the white nightgown, she whispered "Oh, no. Please, God, no. . . ."

As an unearthly weakness spread through her muscles and bones and robbed her of breath to call out for help and coldness stole over her and darkness closed in, Feliciana sobbed bitterly.

Now she knew the *real* reason her father had come to her in a dream. He was waiting for her to join him.

* * *

WHEN CLARA SAW JOHANN'S car pull up, she rose from the log she had been sitting on, under a weeping willow on the bank of Largo Creek, far from homesteads and roads and passersby, where they could be alone beneath the broad blue sky, and went to greet him. She had sent him a note. Discreetly. It was how they met these days.

Johann had lost weight. He was pale. She slipped into his arms as easily as she slipped into her husband's. In a way, in her heart, Johann was her husband too, but in a different capacity. They had never been intimate. They hadn't even kissed. But the love was there still, and growing.

"I am so sorry," she murmured against his shoulder. He knew how she felt. Clara had come alone to Feliciana's funeral and had expressed her sorrow with glistening eyes. He held her tightly to him now. He was a widower. He was free. But Clara was not. When their embrace went on too long, he stepped back and said, "It's good to see you, Clara."

"How is Adam doing?" She had seen him at the funeral and a more dejected boy, pasty and hollow-eyed, you would never see.

Johann bent to pluck a long blade of grass. He squinted out over the flat green fields where cows grazed. "I don't know that he will ever recover from this. I know it haunts him, as it does me, to think how dark and despairing her final hours must have been. I can't stop thinking about the terrible thoughts that must have been going through her mind to drive herself to commit such a horrific act. To take a pair of scissors—" His voice broke.

Clara's heart sorrowed for him. So much tragedy in his life. She wished she could console him. At least Feliciana was at peace now. If only he could take some comfort from that. But these were thin, empty words and not something one said to a grieving widower.

"To kill herself in such a painful and violent way. Don't women usually choose gas or pills?" He sighed raggedly. He spoke with the voice of an old man. "I shouldn't have moved to a separate bedroom. But it was so difficult sleeping with her . . . well, being the way she was. Or maybe I should have kept her in the hospital in Monterey. But she didn't like it there and didn't seem to be getting better. But if I had kept her there, she would still be alive and Adam would at least still have a mother."

"You did everything you could."

"The night nurse blames herself, but I don't blame her. A person can't be expected to sit for eight hours through the night and watch someone sleep. If only Feliciana had known that she could come to me. I was only two doors down. She could have come into my room and asked me to help her."

He stepped back and, thrusting his hands in his pockets, paced back and forth over the grass. "I'm worried about Adam. He has started acting rebellious. He thought that winning the essay contest was going to snap Feliciana out of her depression. I tried to explain to him that the doctors had said there was nothing we could do. But he went into a rage when we found her body. He was screaming that the trophy was to have been for Feliciana, to cure her. If Adam had won, he said it would have saved her. And now he is so full of hate and rage. . . ."

Johann rubbed his hands over his face. "I'm afraid I've handled it all very poorly, Clara. I allowed my anger at Wilhelm to taint Adam's feelings toward you and your family. I should have been man enough to try to reconcile with my brother, but pride held me back. Our boys could have had a happy childhood together. Instead, the stubborn pride of their two fathers kept them apart and taught them to look upon their cousins with suspicion. I wish I could do it over again. Now, Adam is so consumed with anger that I can't talk to him. I've tried. I've tried to tell him about his aunt and uncle and cousin and that we should all get together. . . . He shuts me out. And now he is blaming Helmut for Feliciana's death. I don't know what to make of it."

"Don't blame yourself, Johann. Adam had noble intentions, as every son does toward his mother. They were just far-fetched and unreasonable. But he's too immature to understand that. And as far as our two estranged families goes, Wilhelm has done the same with Helmut and Billy. He will not allow your name to be spoken in our house and so my children know nothing about the Newmans. Only that we are all somehow related. I tried asking Wilhelm to consider extending the olive branch, but he won't hear of it. Johann, one of you has to apologize for the argument you had, but I doubt that's going to happen."

Johann had long suspected that Clara didn't know the truth about what had happened that night when Johann left the Schaller farm forever. An argument. Was that what she thought it was all about? Silence all these years over *words*? But it wasn't his place to tell her about her husband's senseless brutality against his brother.

Clara thought about Adam. Children mimic their elders. They see two brothers—neighbors, in fact—who aren't speaking to each other, and so the behavior is picked up by sons who turn into rival cousins who don't speak to each other without having any understanding *whatsoever* of what the original contention had been about! It was sad and tragic.

Johann slumped down on the old log and watched trout flutter in the creek's shallows. He had never felt so alone. Eighteen years ago he had lost his father and brother. And Clara too, although she had never really been his. Now he had lost Feliciana, and felt Adam pulling away. He had always thought that being alone and being lonely were two different conditions. But now, in this moment, he saw that they were the same. Even with Clara at his side. Or *especially* with Clara at his side, because he knew her companionship was only temporary and she must soon return to her family, who were her priority.

Adam . . . Johann had lost others in his life. He wasn't going to lose his son as well. He was going to fight to keep Adam, to set him on the right path and be the best possible father a man on his own could be.

Clara laid her hand on his arm and said, gently, "In a way I wish Adam had won the contest instead of Helmut. I love my son and I'm happy he's going to meet the governor. But isn't this just one more stoking of an old fire? Adam hates Helmut now. The bad blood that began with you and Wilhelm has spilled over into the next generation. I keep praying for a reconciliation of the two families, but now. . . ." She spread her hands and didn't voice the rest. That she feared too much damage had been done. That the families were doomed to be enemies forever.

And then, she didn't care about the families at all. She cared only about Johann. In life, Feliciana had made him sad. In death, she had made him sadder. But Johann would survive. Clara knew this, that he would not lead the mourning life. And she would do whatever she could to help him, to fill voids, to bolster him when she saw he needed it—but within limits, as she was not a free woman.

Clara thought about Papa Jakob. Recognizing her own secret shame in his shocking confession—to suddenly discover that the righteous and moral and God-fearing Jakob Schaller had committed the same sin in his heart that she had in hers: to marry one, but to love another. How difficult it must have been for Jakob to pretend all those years to be raising another man's son. But surely his wife would have seen the resemblance between the boys and Jakob? Had she suspected? Had she, too, lived with a burden too terrible to speak of?

People are not always who they seem, Clara thought now as she watched the slump of Johann's shoulders. It doesn't do to judge them on the surface; we can never know what prickles a man's heart, the night-mares that fill his sleep, the demons that dog his steps. Poor Jakob had married one woman but loved her sister. The only difference was, he had acted upon his urge and had slept with his sister-in-law. Would that have been incest? Clara wondered. Was she herself guilty of incest, if only in her heart, yearning for her brother-in-law? Clara drew comfort from the thought that she knew she would never cross that line. No matter how much Johann filled her thoughts and made her yearn for him and made her heart jump every time she saw him, she would never take him into her arms and know him intimately. Never.

*   *   *

ADAM TAPPED POLITELY AT his mother's door, as he had been taught to always do, and then went in when there was no response because there never was. And never would be again. He hesitated in the darkness, then he moved forward, as if afraid of disturbing the spirits of this cold room. "I brought you the latest *Saturday Evening Post*," he said to the ghosts. "Just the way you like it, Mom, fresh from the drugstore." He laid the maga-zine down on the small round table that stood next to Feliciana's empty chair. Her lap blanket was folded neatly in readiness, although she was never coming back.

Dropping to his knees, Adam crossed his arms over the blanket and buried his face in it, as he had several times before buried his face in his mother's unresponsive lap. And then he let the tears come, in great weep-ing waves and the broken sobs of a fifteen-year-old whose voice was trying to find its way to manhood.

Adam thought he, too, would break. Into a million pieces. She was gone, that bright comet from his younger days, his fey and fairylike mother he had so worshipped. He wished he hadn't told her about the essay contest. He wished he hadn't promised her he would win it. Because he had let her down. In the final hours of Feliciana Newman's life, she had known her son had been a failure.

As he gulped for air and bawled like a lamb, soaking the lap blanket, the hurting boy could see only two things in his agonized mind. That he shouldn't have bragged. And that he hated Helmut Schaller beyond all possible words. He also made two vows as he cried into what he thought was his mother's lap: that he would never brag or be boastful again—that he would keep his wishes and feelings secret. And that he would never, ever forgive Helmut Schaller for winning the contest.

The Present Day

.

"DOES THIS COLOR SUIT me?" Michelle Eberhardt turned this way and that as she looked at her reflection in the bakery-store window. The bodice and skirt of the traditional dirndl were bright marigold orange, while the apron was white. "I was afraid the color would clash with my hair."

"It goes great with your hair *and* your complexion," Nicole said with a smile. She knew Michelle liked the whole costume thing and didn't mind having to dress up in the bakery. Her husband, Joe Eberhardt, though a third-generation American, was really into Bavarian tradition and heritage. His great-grandparents had experienced Oktoberfest in Munich and had wanted to recreate it here outside of Lynnville. He belonged to a yodeling club, and on weekends they donned lederhosen and green Tyrolean hats with feathers and yodeled in Germantown for the tourists.

Michelle said, "I like *your* dress."

Nicole looked down at herself, as if she had forgotten she was wearing clothes. "It's too warm for long pants," she said, liking the feel of the floaty sundress with spaghetti straps, made of canary-yellow cotton.

"I wish I could wear something that sleek and skimpy. But my girls need a home," Michelle said with a laugh as she cupped her hands around her generous breasts.

"How's Mr. Newman doing, poor old thing?" she asked as she brought over coffee and authentic *pflaumenkuchen*—plum cake. They sat at their usual window table.

"I telephoned Lucas last night to ask about his father. He said Melvyn refused to go to a hospital, despite what his doctor advised. Lucas said he was going to hire a home nurse to take care of him. So I assume the old man is still at home. I feel so bad about what happened. I shouldn't have gone over there. I could just as well have met Lucas on neutral ground."

The whole valley was already talking about the mild heart attack Melvyn Newman had suffered yesterday while Nicole Schaller was paying an unexpected visit to their home. In fact, the whole valley was talking about the fact of a Schaller visiting the Newman farm. Tongues were also wagging about the skeleton found in one of the Schaller barrel rooms and the investigation into a possible homicide. The local newspaper carried a headline that shouted GRISLY MURDER LINKED TO BITTER FAMILY FEUD. Nothing like a scandalous homicide to wake up a sleepy farming valley.

"God," Nicole said when she saw the folded newspaper beside the bakery's cash register. "They're already pointing fingers at *us*."

"Well, the victim *was* found in your wall, and Lucas's family *is* missing a cousin. It's a reasonable leap."

The Internet and tabloids had already jumped on the Big Jack angle, digging up pictures of Nicole's late father that had been snapped by paparazzi in Vegas when Jack had "dated" starlets and socialites. His name was linked with underworld characters. Nothing specific, of course, everything only hinted at. His enormous gambling debts. Chopping up the Schaller wine empire to pay them off. Hints of paying off husbands and abortionists as well. So who knew *who* the poor bastard was that had gotten himself killed and walled up in a Schaller barrel room?

Life was crazy weird, Nicole thought now, marveling at the sudden turns that could come up. Lucas Newman, for one. Nicole had rarely given thought to the Newmans. But now Lucas was dominating her thoughts. She had suddenly become curious about him. Nicole knew all about his mother, Karen, who had left ten years ago and now lived in Hawaii. Nicole had been seventeen at the time, and the whole town had talked about it. She got the facts from Michelle, who got them from Thelma Peeples who owned the town's most popular hair salon and who came into Eberhardt's every day for a blueberry muffin and Jamaican coffee in exchange for gossip. She told everyone that Karen Newman realized she shouldn't have married a man nineteen years older than herself and that she had only stayed in the marriage to be with her son and raise him properly. But Lucas had turned twenty and gone off to school and Karen wanted a new life. Everyone had always known that she had never adjusted to farm life. She had always remained an outsider, not even joining the Lynnville Women's Service Club even though, as a Newman, she was inherently guaranteed membership.

As a teenager, Nicole had seen Karen Newman occasionally—around town, at public holiday celebrations, in the Newman wine-tasting booth during Oktoberfest, and at school events to support her son—a tall, willowy woman with good taste in clothes. But an outsider all the same.

"Are you holding up okay?" Michelle asked, searching for and finding signs of stress on her friend's face.

"I don't have time for this. I have a lot to do before I pick up and go to New York. Time was already tight, and now everything's on hold thanks to the police investigation. Can they go any slower?"

"It's only been two days, and it *is* a very cold case."

"I need to have the sale of my property wrapped up and finalized soon. The company won't hold that job open indefinitely." She looked at her watch. Again. Mr. Gilette hadn't been able to see her right away, as he had morning appointments.

"Are you really that interested in your great-grandmother's letters?" Michelle asked.

"I honestly don't know. What I'm hoping is that there is something in them that will help the police solve the case and get me on my way to New York."

"'Dear granddaughter,'" Michelle said in a falsetto voice and an exaggerated German accent. "'The spring rains promise a bountiful harvest this year and, oh, by the way, a murder was committed in the winery and I helped hide the body in a wall.'"

"You're no help, Michelle," Nicole said, but she said it with a smile to hide her annoyance. She didn't want her best friend to think she was annoyed with *her*. It was the whole situation that had Nicole on edge, making her check her watch every five minutes. "I promised the company I would be there, at my desk and working by November first for the start of the big holiday shopping season. Even if the winery wasn't sold, I told them I would be there anyway, that nothing would stop me. I gave them my word, Michelle, I *promised*. But now I'm stopped and it's driving me crazy."

Two things Michelle loved about her best friend was that Nicole always stood by her word—when she promised to do something for you, by God, the hounds of Hell couldn't stop her. And she was driven. When she put her mind to something, she stayed with it until it was done. How many times had Michelle heard the screaming matches between Nicole and Big

Jack over the issue of Nicole's going away to university to study business? "I've damn well taught you all the business you need to know to run a vineyard and a winery!" Big Jack would bellow. And Nicole would dig in her heels and say, "Well, I intend to learn *more* than just how to run a vineyard and winery!" Nicole won in the end, going off to the University of California at Santa Barbara. And then Big Jack had gone to the graduation and thrown a huge party for his daughter, the proudest man on earth.

As she stirred sweetener in her coffee—Nicole had no appetite for the dessert—she absently settled her gaze on a display in the glass case beneath the cash register: Schaller's popular line of jams, jellies, raisins, and syrups that were sold in supermarkets all over the country and seen on restaurant tables everywhere. One very popular fast-food chain offered baked turnovers filled with "genuine Schaller grape jam." But Nicole saw not a penny of profit from it. Big Jack had sold that very lucrative arm of the business when he had lost heavily at the race track, and he owed money as well to some thug-types in Las Vegas.

"By the way," Michelle said, "the Canadian couple were in here this morning for coffee and muffins. They're very excited about buying your farm. I heard them discussing plans to turn the barrel room into something called the Mystery Room, and it will be part of a tour of the winery."

Nicole groaned. She didn't like this strange new reputation that was attaching itself to her family home. She looked at her watch again. Besides being anxious to hear from Mr. Gilette, she was also waiting to hear the report on the medical examiner's findings. Hopefully, the age and sex of the skeleton, and something with which to make a positive identification. She prayed it wasn't Lucas's missing cousin.

At the same time, Mr. Gilette was searching through storage archives for her property's original blueprints to see if they could cast any light on when the barrel room had been worked on. He had called that morning to say he had come across a cache of more letters written by Clara Schaller to her unnamed granddaughter.

More letters . . . disclosing what? Nicole wondered. Were other misconceptions about the two families going to be blasted out of the water? She debated sharing them with Lucas. Mightn't the letters only exacerbate the already bitter rivalry between the two families?

Sometimes things were best left hidden.

Her father's gun also weighed on her. The police had stopped searching the property for the murder weapon, possibly disposed of there twenty or thirty years ago. Now it was up to Nicole. She knew she had to tell the police that her father had owned a nine-millimeter Beretta, the same type of gun that was the supposed murder weapon. But going into his den wasn't as easy as one might think. She hadn't set foot inside that room since his death.

Michelle reached over and touched her best friend's hand. "You don't have to sell, you know," she said quietly. "You don't have to run from Big Jack any more. He's no longer there."

"Yes, I do, I have to sell," Nicole said with a ragged sigh. She had gotten very little sleep in the two nights since the grisly discovery in one of the winery walls. "My father *is* still there. He'll always be there. It's crazy, I know, but I still talk to him, I still argue with him. Michelle, I'm all alone in that big house, and yet I still shout at my father. He will never give me my freedom. I have to *take* it."

She leaned forward, as if about to divulge the world's greatest secret. "Michelle, I am honestly excited about this New York job."

"I know you are. And I am happy for you."

"I'm full of ideas. I will have creative and innovative license. It's going to be great fun and a great challenge."

Michelle thought, but didn't say: You could apply that same creativity and innovative license to your winery. Your father let the company get run down. It's become third-rate. You could turn Schaller vineyards around and restore the company to its former glory.

But she knew that Nicole was adamant about going. She had to find herself, she said, find out who she was besides being a Schaller.

"I'm going to miss you," Michelle said, pulling a sad face just as some customers entered the shop, chatting about cherry strudel and the "best coffee in California."

As Nicole got up to leave, she said, in a low voice, "Oh, sweetie, in all this mess I forgot to ask you about the appointment with the specialist yesterday. How did it go?"

Michelle glanced over her shoulder. The customers were being waited on by the girls behind the counter. She said, quietly, "We have a choice. Since Joe can't give a specimen the usual way, they'll use surgical aspiration. It's when the sperm is removed directly from the male reproductive tract. Or vibratory or electric stimulation, when the male cannot ejaculate in the usual way. You can imagine how mortifying this is for Joe. Absolutely no one in our family can know. He would be too humiliated." Nicole knew that Michelle was taking the blame on herself for their childless state, telling her mother-in-law and Joe's sisters that *she* was seeing a fertility specialist in Santa Barbara. "It just seems more dignified somehow, to say that the fault is mine and not that Joe can't . . . well, you know. It would kill him if his brothers-in-law found out he couldn't get it up."

Nicole envied such a marriage, for a woman to so love her husband that she took the blame for a fault that wasn't hers, just to spare him the humiliation. Nicole wished she could find a relationship like that. She had come close, with Danny the lawyer from old Santa Barbara money. Nicole herself couldn't even say why she hadn't married Danny when he proposed. She told Michelle it was because she didn't want to be tied down by yet another old and venerable family. But was that really it? They had been together for three years. But she had kept waiting for the spark. Maybe she had grown up on too many romance novels and chick flicks, but she honestly believed in a love that was like a wrecking ball, where the spark is so intense that you think you'll literally burst into flames at his touch. A love so deep and passionate that you think you'll die if you can't be with him.

It never happened with Danny. She had grown comfortable with him. But wasn't that for old age, after the kids had grown up and moved out? But the day it really occurred to her that it wasn't true love was when she was sitting with Michelle in the window of the bakery, over coffee and apple strudel, and Michelle had made Nicole list Danny's qualities, and after Nicole had enumerated honesty, loyalty, affection, protectiveness, and devotion, Michelle had cried "My God, you're describing a Golden Retriever." That was when Nicole knew Danny wasn't her Forever Man.

She looked at her watch. Time to see Mr. Gilette and letters from Great-Grandmother.

*   *   *

LUCAS CAME QUIETLY INTO the bedroom to peek in on his father.

Melvyn was sitting up in bed, with sunshine slanting across the blue bedspread, reading the latest issue of *Wine Spectator*. Lucas was pleased to see him looking so much better. Seventy years old with the rugged face of an outdoorsman, white hair contrasting the ruddy complexion, this was the man who had raised Lucas with love and a firm hand, teaching him through word and deed what was right and what was wrong, to be respectful of women, to be kind to animals, and to be honest and fair when dealing with other men. Melvyn had been Lucas's role model. Ever since

Karen had left, ten years ago, it had been just the two of them, relying on each other, taking care of each other. Lucas couldn't bear the thought of losing his dad.

He came all the way in and sat on the edge of the bed. "Don't scare me like that, Pop. I don't want to lose you."

Melvyn laid the magazine down and removed his reading glasses. "You're not losing me, son."

"Why'd you shout at Nicole like that?"

"She's a Schaller."

"She's never done us any harm. Besides, she's leaving the valley." Lucas paused. "I can tell you're frightened, Pop. You're worried it's Cousin Jason that was in that wall and you'll have to give Aunt Sofie the bad news. Let's not worry about that just yet. The police are still gathering evidence."

Unfortunately, sending for Jason's dental records wouldn't help. When the workman's sledgehammer caused the wall to cave in, too much damage had been done to the skeleton's teeth.

Melvyn looked at his son and smiled. "Don't worry about me, Lucas. I get irrational sometimes. It's a privilege of old age." He patted the hand that lay on the bedspread. Now it was his turn to do the worrying. "Sorry I gave you a scare. I'll be fine by this afternoon. Got to prepare for the first crush. Are the Chardonnays ready?"

Lucas smiled with relief. "They sure are, Pop." Melvyn was right. It had only been a scare. Still, it was something that should be looked into. "Pop, are you sure you don't want to see a specialist—"

"Specialists!" Melvyn barked. "These days, doctors know more and more about less and less." But he smiled. "I know you mean well, son. But I'm made of tough stuff. Don't worry about me. I'll be fine. And we have a chess game to finish."

"That we do," Lucas said with a smile and got to his feet. "I'm going to get over to the lab and make sure everyone's working."

"You know they are, son. Never seen a staff so loyal to their boss."

As Lucas left the bedroom, he was pleased that his father was looking better. Still, he couldn't shake the feeling that something else was going on with the old man. Something that Melvyn was hiding.

Melvyn watched him go, a tall, handsome young man who lived a life of integrity. But Melvyn was worried about him. It was all work and no play with Lucas. A thirty-year-old man ought to be married by now and starting a family. Melvyn knew this because he himself had put off getting married until he was thirty-nine, and to a girl nineteen years his junior who had been able to give him only one son and then had left when Lucas reached twenty and he was at college. Karen had announced one day that she was forty-one, still young and deserving of a second chance at a happy life. Melvyn hadn't been able to argue with that—they had not really had anything in common except for Lucas, and she had never adjusted to farm life. He hadn't blamed her for leaving him. They weren't compatible. In fact, he gave her kudos for staying in a life she didn't really like in order to raise her son. Because of her self-sacrifice, Lucas had a normal upbringing.

Melvyn was amazed, looking back, that Karen could put on such a good face. He knew that *she* knew he hadn't really loved her. Karen had probably suspected that there was a love somewhere in Melvyn's life that he was either stuck on or had let him down. Actually, it was both. A girl he had loved and lost, yet still loved. He and Karen hadn't been in love when they got married. She had been infatuated with a rich, mature man who was the boss of so many people. And as for Melvyn himself, what man at almost forty wasn't flattered when a pretty girl gushed over him? It hadn't been anywhere near the love he had suffered from years ago when he had so loved a girl it had been at the *cellular* level. And when he lost her, he knew he would never love like that again.

Maybe that was what Lucas was looking for. He had certainly had his share of relationships. Had gotten close to a few. But no walk down the aisle yet. Lucas needed to think of heirs and keeping the family name going, and this was a sore point that greatly worried Melvyn.

*   *   *

A secretary escorted Nicole into the attorney's office and said that Mr. Gilette would be with her momentarily. She took a seat. The September day was warm. The windows were open, admitting breezes and sounds from the street, shouts from the nearby Largo River where the last of the summer vacationers were barbecuing, fishing, rowing their boats. A reminder that the upcoming Oktoberfest was going to be the first one in decades in which Schaller Vineyards would not have a tasting pavilion. It suddenly made Nicole sad, and she wanted to apologize to her forebears for letting them down.

Mr. Gilette came in, a balding, fussy little man who cleared his throat a lot. While searching for records of when restoration and renovation had been done at the Schaller winery, hoping to pinpoint a date when a murder victim had been placed in an unfinished wall, Nicole had suggested he look for the original blueprints of the buildings on the property. They hadn't all been built at the same time. The property had been expanded and added to over the years.

In his search for blueprints in the mishmash that was the storage archives downstairs, Mr. Gilette had found more letters written by Great-Grandmother Clara Schaller. And it occurred to Nicole now that maybe the answer to the murder mystery was in those letters. Clara had said in her first letter that she was going to divulge family secrets. Had she maybe known the victim or had an idea who might have done the shooting? But wouldn't she have told the police?

When Gilette handed her the small stack of letters, Nicole noticed the indentation where a paper clip had once held them all together. So the letter he had given her yesterday had been part of this bunch and they had somehow slipped out of the paper clip. She looked at them greedily, overwhelmed with a need to tear them open and devour them on the spot. But she would force herself to wait, read them at home, alone and in privacy.

As she got up to leave, she said: "Mr. Gilette, the police told me that the bullet found in the murder victim came from a nine-millimeter Beretta. My father once owned such a gun. I don't know what he did with it, or even whether he kept it. Would you have any knowledge of it?"

He shook his head.

"It might be in his den. . . ." Nicole said doubtfully.

"You need to tell the police, Nicole," he said, understanding her reluctance. He too had seen the news headlines. Word of the gun was going to bring Big Jack into even bigger prominence in the homicide. They would blow everything out of proportion and convict him before the evidence was even examined. "Do you want me to look for it for you?"

She gave him a grateful smile. "I have to face going through his things anyway. I know you took care of the legal aspects of his estate, but there are personal items in my father's den that I still have to clear out. I'll let you know what I find."

She tucked the letters into her shoulder bag and left.

But, once in her car, Nicole found herself unable to turn the key and start the engine. No, she couldn't wait until she got home. She had to open at least one letter.

As she sat with warm autumn sunshine streaming through the windshield and a man in a Chevrolet waited for her parking space and then made a rude gesture and drove off, Nicole read the opening lines on the first page of the letter. They so startled her that she sat staring ahead at the street for a moment, digesting this new information. In the next minute, she knew that this must be shared with Lucas. It was as much his story as hers.

She chewed her lip. She had hoped not to have to deal with him again, although it was starting to look as if their paths were destined to cross in the next few days. There was no avoiding him, especially while a murder possibly involving both their families was being investigated. She called him on her cell and he answered right away. She told him about the letters.

He was silent, then he said, "Look, I really don't like you coming here. If my father should see you—"

"Then can we meet somewhere?"

"I can't interrupt my work right now."

Nicole decided she could dish rudeness just as well. "Fine. Whatever. But this *is* about your family, too, you know."

"I'm in my lab at the greenhouse," he finally said. "It's behind the winery."

*　　*　　*

LUCAS AWAITED NICOLE'S ARRIVAL with impatience. He had work to do, and this interruption was the last thing he needed. Especially as Nicole's presence on the farm was greatly upsetting to his father.

But she had more letters, she had said on the phone, and insisted that they would be of importance to him. Lucas wasn't so sure. He was a man who looked to the future—who *lived* for the future, wanted to change it, making it better for everyone. He couldn't see the value of dredging up a musty old past that his family had gone to a lot of trouble to keep buried.

But there *was* the skeleton and the matter of his missing cousin. It was possible that something in those old letters could solve the murder mystery. And he did feel obligated to Jason and his family in San Francisco to see this through. But once this whole business was cleared up and all bodies and ghosts laid to rest, Lucas Newman was packing his bags and heading off for a remote patch of Arizona desert where no one had heard of the Schaller-Newman feud.

*　　*　　*

NICOLE TURNED OFF THE main highway and took the paved road to the Newman winery. Out of curiosity, she had visited the Newman website. She had never set foot in their tasting room or restaurant, but there were nice images on the website. There were also photos of the winery's many awards. Her own winery had won just a few, and those were local, given mostly out of loyalty to the memory of Wilhelm Schaller.

In the Newman parking lot she saw a few cars, some limousines, and a tour bus. She parked her car and followed a stone path that went around the winery, a Spanish-style building with arches and columns and colonnades. It could have been a Catholic mission with a church and bells. It was a very romantic atmosphere. From the tasting room she heard murmured talk and gentle music. Around the back she had a view of more vineyards stretching away to the hills, and, a hundred yards up ahead, a long, glassy greenhouse shining in the sun.

Lucas emerged as she drew near. To her surprise, he wore a white lab coat over his blue chambray shirt, denim jeans, and snakeskin cowboy boots. It struck her that something was wrong with that picture. The white coat lent him an air of dignity and authority that she found vaguely unsettling. He was frowning and had the same agitated air about him that he had had two days ago, when he had heard about the discovery of a skeleton and had come to her place at once.

"Lucas," she said. They didn't bother with handshakes or formalities. Neither welcomed this meeting.

He walked toward her, thinking she looked kind of dressed-up in a sundress and sandals, and he wondered why. He wasn't used to seeing her in clothes that exposed her back and shoulders and almost cleavage. He thought the bright yellow suited her. And she was wearing her hair down and loose so that it danced in the breeze. He said, "I hope this is as important as you said on the phone. Something about a letter?"

Nicole didn't know what to say. Was he really going to keep her standing out here?

"Dr. Newman?"

A young woman stood in the doorway of the greenhouse, also wearing a white lab coat and looking, to Nicole, like a college student. "You have a phone call."

He turned and went in. Without being invited, Nicole followed him inside, and while he took the call at a messy desk, she looked around. She found herself in an impressive state-of-the-art laboratory with trained technicians working at various stations, no doubt concocting, Nicole thought, yet another award-winning wine. On the other side of the glass partition that separated the lab and office from the growing and cultivating end of research, long trestle tables were covered in flat beds of plants in various stages of growth, people moving among them, nurturing, inspecting, testing. The lab itself was expensively supplied, Nicole thought. Beyond the usual flasks, test tubes, and glass piping, there were calibrated pressure gauges and electronic scales, tools for moisture-testing in soil, augers and cone penetrometers, Shelby tubes, soil-core sampling kits for field work, and tools for testing for soil nitrates and macronutrients. Soil-color charts, pH charts. Nicole was familiar with these things, as any good vineyardist tests his or her soil on a regular basis. What intrigued her was the wide range of testing that seemed to be going on here, and what appeared to be for purposes and conditions other than those that existed in the Largo Valley.

The female staff member had called Lucas "Dr. Newman." Nicole remembered that he had studied at the Department of Viticulture and Enology at the University of California at Davis, from which he had graduated with a PhD. But all she had thought he was using that education for was making yet more award-winning wines. She hadn't expected this.

A poster hung on one of the walls—Earth, as seen from space. It said: "We only have one mother. Treat her with respect." Nicole recalled that Lucas had been an activist in college, concerned about climate change and global warming, chaining himself to heavy moving equipment, getting arrested, and organizing rallies against big oil interests, especially those in oil-shale mining.

On Lucas's cluttered desk, she saw printed matter from various environmental organizations, letters from concerned groups, articles clipped from newspapers. Among it all was a framed photograph of a smiling blonde, tall and willowy in an elegant Hawaiian muumuu. She knew it was Lucas's mother, who had left ten years ago. Nicole didn't remember much of her own mother, Lucy, who had been taken by leukemia when Nicole was twelve. She remembered Lucy as a gentle woman with a soft voice and thin bones. It seemed to Nicole that that was when Big Jack had taken a wrong turn in his life. It was as if Lucy had been the glue that held him together, and he flew apart after her death.

As Lucas hung up the phone, Nicole said, "Very impressive," waving her arms toward the rows of tables on the other side of the partition.

He sighed. "Overwhelming is more like it. I sometimes wonder if it's a bit too ambitious. I occasionally have my doubts. But. . . ." His face took on a faraway look, as if forgetting for the moment where he was or who he was with. "For a long time, I have wanted to do something that was entirely my own. I have had a feeling of unfulfillment. This farm, these vineyards, and this winery were handed to me. No man wants something just handed to him. When I'm a hundred years old and lying on my deathbed, I don't want to die knowing I hadn't done anything that came strictly from Lucas Newman."

Nicole stared at him. That was exactly how *she* felt. It was why she needed to leave. She had inherited the family business, and that was all she was known for: being the Schaller heiress.

"So!" he said, suddenly remembering himself, and seeming a little embarrassed to have unwittingly bared his soul. "Can we get to the point of your visit, please? I really can't spare the time."

Rude again. "Lucas," she said, "tell me honestly. Have I done something personally to offend you? Or are you just following a family tradition of rudeness?"

He gave her a steely look, then he ran his fingers through his hair and made an exasperated sound. "It's not you. I'm sorry. That detective came around this morning to ask a bunch of questions about my missing cousin. He really needs to talk to my father, I was only a kid at the time of Jason's disappearance. But my father can't be disturbed."

"I'm sorry," Nicole said, meaning it. "I hope he hasn't had another attack?"

"He's just resting." When he saw the interest in her eyes as she looked around the lab, Lucas invited Nicole to take a seat on one of the tall stools at the workbench, seated himself on another, and said, "We're experimenting with rootstocks that can grow in arid, salinated soil with the aim to breeding salinity-tolerant grapes."

Her eyebrows arched. "Really? I hadn't known that."

"As you are aware, an estimated four and a half million acres of agricultural land in California contains saline soil, including major grape-growing regions. Our goal is breeding grape rootstocks tolerant to salt stress, and to develop molecular markers for the alleles that confer this tolerance. To date, no such markers have been defined in the scientific literature for grapevines."

"What rootstocks are you working with?"

"*Riparia Gloire,* one of the first rootstocks used after the phylloxera crisis in Europe. It roots and grafts well and has strong phylloxera resistance, but is susceptible to some strains of root-knot nematodes. Additionally, Ramsey, Thompson Seedless, and French Colombard. Each of these genotypes is being tested both on their own roots and with additional plants grafted with a common scion of Pinot Noir.

"We have to face it," Lucas continued, "the California drought has hit the industry hard and shows no sign of letting up. With climate change and global warming, we have to find ways to adapt. We need to develop a hardy strain of grape that can grow in warmer summers with less water. Last year was California's warmest year on record, and we had the lowest amount of rainfall in fifty years. Some people think there is no such thing as global warming. They might be right, but climate change is a fact: we already see evidence of it worldwide. As I know you've heard, French wine grapes are maturing earlier. The whole industry is going to have to adapt."

"This is all very commendable," Nicole said, a bit overwhelmed. She had not been aware of this side of Lucas Newman's life.

He paused, then folded his arms. "Look, I'm sorry that we got off to a bad start. I have a lot of work on my hands and very little time to do it in. And this police investigation has thrown a wrench into my timetable."

"I thought you were annoyed with me because I wouldn't accept your offer on my property."

"I can understand why you wouldn't sell to me. It's probably stipulated in Big Jack's will."

"As a matter of fact," she said, "it was. But . . . to sell to *you*? I thought the offer came from your father."

"My dad has no interest in owning your land."

"I just assumed. . . ."

"That we would take it over and put the Newman name on it, putting Schaller out of business altogether?" He shook his head. "No, I'm not interested in the vineyard or winery, actually. I want the acreage that abuts Colina Sagrada."

She frowned, and then her eyebrows shot up. "You want to buy *No-Man's-Land*?"

"Is that what it's called?"

"Well, it's what I've always privately called it since I was a kid. No one could possibly want that miserable plot of land. It is absolutely unworkable."

He grinned. "And that is precisely why I wish to buy it."

She thought for a moment, and then said, "High-salinity soil."

He smiled. "You have to admit that the curious climate and soil conditions at Colina Sagrada are like a miniature desert. At Colina

Sagrada I can carry out some very specific experiments that I can't conduct here."

"I wish you had just come to me about it. I'm sure we could have worked out an arrangement."

"With *our* family history? The idea of a civilized sit-down talk with you never even entered my head."

They fell silent then as technicians worked wordlessly and machines clicked and chimed. The moment held and the world, the cosmos, underwent a subtle shift.

Nicole suddenly found the atmosphere in the greenhouse strangely alluring and seductive. Warm, sultry, and filled with the loamy smells of propagation and fertility. Also, curiously romantic. It occurred to Nicole for the first time that romantic settings weren't always ocean sunsets or heart-shaped beds with pink sheets. And it startled her. Where on earth had the notion of romance come from? She was here to share her great-grandmother's letters with Lucas Newman because he had a right to know their contents. That was all. No romance. Period.

"Do you have time for a short drive?" he asked suddenly, standing up and shedding his lab coat

"A drive? Well, I . . ." she looked at her watch. "I only came out here to show you the letters."

"We can look at them out there."

"Out *there*?"

They went in Lucas's Jeep Wrangler with the top removed so the sun beat down on their bare heads and the wind blew their hair about.

They drove past fields of ripening pumpkins glowing orange in the sun. There was one spread, called Farmer Joe's, that would soon open its gates to the public for children to swarm over to pick out their own pumpkin to be carved into a Halloween jack-o'-lantern. There would be scarecrows and a challenging maze constructed of stacked hay bales, and a costume parade and contest for little witches and goblins and Star Wars troopers and ballerinas and Ninja Turtles. It was an exciting time of the year for the residents of the valley, with the big fall harvest that everyone took part in, and then the very merry Oktoberfest with Halloween close on its heels, followed by the big feast day of Thanksgiving and the beginning of the countdown to Christmas. One could feel the crisp excitement in the air.

Lucas glanced at Nicole, noticing reddish highlights in her wind-whipped hair. "I hear you got a job with a cosmetics firm back East."

"They want my ideas. They think I'll be good for them." Nicole looked at him. "You think working in cosmetics is frivolous, don't you?"

He gave her a surprised look. "I was thinking no such thing."

God, she thought in sudden contrition. What brought *that* on? How can I accuse him of thinking something he never even voiced? *Unless I was thinking it first.*

There's nothing frivolous about working in the cosmetics industry, she wanted to say. It's a perfectly honest and respectable career. A woman with a bit of lipstick and eyebrow pencil walks taller and has more self-confidence.

They sped past Schaller vineyards, where vines as tall as a man were heavy with ripe fruit and fieldhands were getting ready for the harvest. The Jeep took dusty narrow roads, sailed over gentle hills to see yet more rows of vines, as far as the eye could see, with loading trucks being positioned for the pickers to empty their baskets into. The word was already out—it was going to be a good harvest.

"Here we are," Lucas said unnecessarily: the grassy hill and its curious adjacent wasteland were a familiar landmark to Nicole. Lucas turned off the engine, and he and Nicole looked out over the hardscrabble ground where only the thinnest of grasses and weeds grew after heavy winter rains and then quickly died off under the sun.

This strange, blighted patch of land was thin, flinty soil, harsh and dry with a paltry crust of topsoil that couldn't even support the hardy sagebrush. Looking out at Colina Sagrada, Nicole recalled that Great-Grandfather Wilhelm had called this place cursed, as had her grandfather and her father, each parroting the others. But what Nicole saw now, independently of what others had said, was a place of *beauty*. Stark, yes, barren and bleak. But so was the moon, and no one ever called the moon cursed or ugly. Long ago, Spaniards had named this place "sacred." They must have had a good reason.

Nicole understood now why Lucas wanted to buy it. "My father told me that over the years my family tried to do something with this patch. He said it really got to his grandfather, Wilhelm, how he cultivated lush acres of grapevines and yet could not master this one spot. I think my grandfather tried once or twice to do something with this ground but finally gave up."

Lucas gave her a serious look. "Are the Canadians still interested in buying your farm?"

"They're more interested than ever."

"Do you think maybe they'd sell this parcel to me? Or let me rent this spot? It's of no use to them."

"I have my doubts. Mrs. Macintosh said she thinks this place is romantic and wants to make it part of her winery tour. Besides, I don't know how she'd feel about having an agricultural experimental station on her land."

She felt his keen disappointment. And her own, too. Suddenly, things were not as clear-cut or black-and-white as they had been a few days ago. Nicole realized that her perception of Lucas was changing. He was no longer one of the greedy, selfish Newmans Big Jack had taught her to despise. He was a scientist with ambition—a new image that was going to take some getting used to.

Listening to the wind whistle through nearby trees, and the distant cry of a red-tailed hawk, Nicole closed her eyes and felt centuries slip away. There was something about this blot on an otherwise perfect landscape that, for some unexplainable reason, deserved respect. It was almost as if God had set this plot of ground aside just for His own personal amusement. Didn't those old Bible prophets—and she pictured God as being one—enjoy wandering around bitter wastelands?

As they listened to the lonesome wind, Nicole realized she was feeling envious toward Lucas for some reason, but she couldn't pinpoint why. Something had arrived at the edge of her consciousness without making itself known. It was like something tapping at a window, wanting to come in. But she couldn't see it, couldn't name it. Something about Lucas and this place.

"You wanted to show me some letters."

Lucas's voice brought her back from her mental wanderings. Reaching into her shoulder bag, she drew out the letter that she had opened outside Mr. Gilette's office. "My lawyer found nine more," she said, handing it to Lucas. "I have only read this one so far."

Lucas opened it and read silently. Nicole discreetly watched his profile. He was good-looking, fit and confident. If they had met as strangers, if they had met two days ago for the first time in their lives and knew nothing of each other's background, Nicole knew she would have been attracted to him and would want to know more about him. In fact, she realized she was struggling with her attitude toward Lucas Newman, realized that she was *trying* to dislike him and to keep the family friction going. But it wasn't easy. She had discovered nice, and even honorable, things about him. And there was no escaping the fact that there was a bond between them—they *were* distantly related: they shared a hundred-year-old legacy.

It suddenly struck her how similar their lives were. She was an only child, as was Lucas. Nicole's mother had died fifteen years ago; Lucas's mother had divorced Melvyn ten years ago and gone to live in Hawaii. So just as it had been only Nicole and Big Jack in the Schaller home, it was just Lucas and his father in the Newman home.

"Listen to this," Lucas said, struggling to keep the sheet of stationery still in his hand as the wind kept trying to tug it away. "'You confided your secrets in me, dear granddaughter, it is only right that I reciprocate. You should know that secrets were kept from you—even during our visits together in which you told me your heart's pain and asked for my advice. Even then, I withheld things that I now think you should know. These are turbulent times and I fear that the battle that is waging has distorted everyone's views and emotions. We are not thinking clearly and logically, we Schallers and the Newmans. The war must end.'"

Lucas looked up from the letter. "What war is she talking about? The rivalry between our families?"

"The letter is dated 1965. I was thinking, the Vietnam war? She says the word 'battle' and says that it's distorting everyone's views."

Lucas withdrew into thought; then he said, "The sixties was also the time of the labor strikes here in the valley. Some of it got quite bloody."

"What I know of that power struggle, between the growers and the laborers, I've only read in books. My grandfather and grandmother were caught in the middle of that bloody strike, but they never spoke of it. And my father, Big Jack, was only a kid at the time. He does remember fights at picket lines."

"I seem to recall that my grandfather, Adam Newman, was a key figure during those strikes. And I imagine my father was, too, but to this day he won't talk about what happened here in the sixties. It's something shameful, I would guess."

They fell silent, staring out at the curious wasteland in the middle of so much lush greenery. Colina Sagrada. A blight on Schaller land that no one had been able to make fruitful. Could Lucas really grow a new breed of grape here? Nicole wondered. She felt a small rush of hope and excitement and suddenly understood what drove Lucas Newman. She had heard it in his voice back at the greenhouse, had seen it flash in his eyes as he had described his dream.

Now she understood something. When he had first made an offer on her property and she had turned him down, Lucas had come back, through his agent, with a request to purchase just part of the property. She had shut him down at once without hearing him out. Her father had done enough whittling and slicing up of Schaller acres that she sure as heck wasn't going to let a Newman shave off even more!

She wondered now if she *could* sell just this part of the property to Lucas.

"I have to get back," Nicole said, looking at her watch.

"As do I." Lucas handed the letter back to her.

"I'll read the rest when I have time, and if there's anything pertinent to your family, or to the murder investigation, I will let you know. In the meantime, I've been putting off an unpleasant task, and I have to face it. Finding my father's gun . . . I'm dreading it. I hate guns. They scare me. What scares me even more is that it might be the murder weapon."

Lucas gave her a long steady look, grasping the dreadful significance of what she was saying—pointing an accusatory finger at her father. He also thought of the possibility of the skeleton being that of his missing cousin, and he realized he couldn't leave Nicole alone in this. "Do you want me to help you search for it?"

She gave him a look of astonishment and was surprised to find herself experiencing a rush of relief, and of gratitude. "Thanks," she said. "If you don't mind, I would very much appreciate your help."

They went back to the greenhouse, where Nicole picked up her car and Lucas followed her home in his Jeep.

The sun was setting as they entered the front door. "It's this way," Nicole said, and they went down the hall to a closed door on the left.

The way she hesitated, drew in a breath, and held it, Lucas understood that this was a monumental step for her. With a moist palm, Nicole turned the knob and, as the door swung open, the odor of mustiness and stale air and year-old cigar smoke washed over her. She had been prepared for this, knowing the room hadn't been aired out since Big Jack's death. But then the memories slammed into her and nearly made her fall back, strong and heavy memories as if they had been bunched up behind the door waiting to be let out.

"Are you all right?" Lucas said, standing close, touching her arm.

She caught her breath—birthdays flashed before her, breakfasts in a sunny kitchen, running home with a straight-A report card, her father cheering her on during a footrace, cupping his mouth and shouting "You can do it, sweetheart!" "Yes, I'm fine," she said, and she stepped inside.

It was just a room, she told herself. Four walls, a window, a fireplace. A big mahogany desk with a blotter, pen set, telephone, framed photographs. Bookshelves. Leather sofa and matching chairs. Burgundy rug on the floor. Artwork on the walls.

Just a room. Nothing to be afraid of.

She could never fathom why her father was always so angry. He had railed against life and its unfairness. She knew he had wanted sons. She once snapped at him: "It's not my fault I'm an only child! Wasn't that *your* job?" The truth was, Nicole had no idea why she was their only child, why others hadn't come along. Just the one daughter, and then his wife had died of leukemia twelve years later. But that didn't give Big Jack the right to be angry all the time, did it?

She went to his desk to start her search there. Surely he wouldn't have left the gun in just any drawer, would he? She saw a photograph in a silver frame. She didn't recognize who it was, but by the clothes it appeared to have been taken around 1930. A young boy shaking hands with an important-looking man. Nicole picked it up to read the inscription on the back: "Helmut meets California Governor Young."

It felt strange, going through his things—pens, stationery, even picking up the stapler seemed an invasion of his privacy. She cautiously opened drawers as if they might be full of snakes. She felt guilty, as if she were betraying her father, turning him over to the police. A snitch. But didn't the victim in the barrel room wall deserve justice?

"Did Big Jack have a wall safe?" Lucas asked when a search of the desk and other cabinets and shelves turned up nothing. They had switched on lights. It was getting dark out.

"Yes, it's behind that painting."

Lucas swung the bucolic vineyard landscape aside and they both stared at the safe embedded in the wall. It had a combination lock. Nicole tried the obvious ones—Big Jack's birthdate, his wife's, their anniversary.

"Try *your* birthdate," Lucas said.

"Mine!" But she tried it, and it worked. She swung the door open to expose letters, papers, a small antique coin collection, and—Nicole's heart sank like a stone—in a wooden box lined with velvet, a nine-millimeter Beretta.

Nicole gingerly placed the box on the desk so that the lamp shone on the pistol. This was a big moment, and she and Lucas both realized it. Was this the murder weapon? Had Nicole's father, for some reason, killed Lucas's cousin? *Was a terrible event in their past about to blow up in their faces?*

For the first time, Nicole wasn't thinking about her new sweet job in New York and Lucas wasn't thinking about new breeds of grapes. Both were thinking: What on earth had happened in the barrel room that had led one man to take the life of another?

Also crossing their minds simultaneously was the heavy question: Should we just put this back and let sleeping dogs lie?

But Lucas finally said, solemnly, "I'll take this to the police station, if you'd like."

She looked up at him, at his handsome face cast in shadow and light, at his hooded eyes that would melt a movie audience. "I'll take it in," she whispered. "It's only right that I do it."

The desk phone rang, startling them. It was Detective Quinn, calling with the autopsy results. Nicole put the phone on speaker so that Lucas could hear. "The victim is female, Ms. Schaller," Quinn said. "A *young* female, possibly in her early twenties." And Nicole saw naked relief wash over Lucas's face. She knew what he was thinking. The skeleton wasn't his missing cousin after all. The Newmans were most likely not involved in the murder. Lucas's elderly father could now rest easily and not worry about another heart attack.

"There's something more," Quinn added. "There is evidence in the pelvic cavity that she had been pregnant at the time of her death."

PART FOUR
1943

"THESE SANDWICHES ARE MARVELOUS, Mrs. Schaller," young Fay said to Clara as she nibbled daintily on white bread spread with butter and laid with slices of tomato and ham. "You have a knack."

As she spoke, twenty-year-old Fay Reed eyed Bill Schaller across the dance floor, tall and handsome in his Army uniform, and decided that tonight she would make her move to seduce him.

"Thank you," Clara said politely, knowing full well that the girl didn't come to these dances for the sandwiches.

It was a lively, happy, hopeful scene, with boys in uniform socializing with well-dressed young women, dancing to a live band, enjoying free food and drinks, and everyone leaving the war outside. The summer night was hot, all windows and doors were open, and ceiling fans stirred the air. But the temperature didn't stop the high-kicking young people from dancing and jiving the night away. They danced the foxtrot and jitterbug to popular songs like "Chattanooga Choo Choo" and "I'll Never Smile Again."

The evening was being held at the public recreation center in the town of Lompoc, near Camp Cooke, an Army base. The citizens had voted to convert the center, which was normally used for wedding receptions, awards banquets, and political rallies, into a place for American soldiers on leave to go where there were dances and social events, movies and music, a quiet place to talk or write a letter home, or a free cup of coffee and a sandwich. The hostesses were female volunteers whose aim was to cheer and comfort the soldiers and boost their morale.

Clara and her best friend Frieda Eberhardt were chaperones tonight, as were all the ladies of the Lynnville kaffeeklatsch—Dagmar, Hilde, Truda, Anna, and others. After all these years, they still got together every Sunday to sit at the tables in the window of Eberhardt's bakery over coffee and cake for news, gossip, advice, and sisterhood. The membership had changed. The original ladies were matrons now in their late forties and early fifties—Clara herself was forty-nine, soon to turn fifty—to watch over the younger generation and guide them. Mrs. Mueller had passed away, but her daughter Mathilda still came every Sunday. And she was here tonight, with the others, donating time and sympathy to the boys in uniform.

Also donating time and comfort were the local girls in their late teens and twenties, "hostesses" who were chaste and wholesome and of good reputation. Frieda Eberhardt's two daughters were hostesses, and they always brought boxes of donuts and other assorted pastries donated by Eberhardt's bakery to give the soldiers a "taste of home." The chaperones made sure that nothing untoward went on in the club, that the soldiers behaved like gentlemen and the hostesses behaved like ladies. But the truth was, some of the girls were husband-hunting. Like Fay Reed, who was enjoying Clara Schaller's freshly made ham, tomato, cheese, and cucumber sandwiches on white, whole wheat, and rye bread. Accompanying them were bowls of nuts, pretzels, and home-made potato chips.

As Clara suspected, Fay was indeed man-shopping, and she had specific criteria in mind. She wasn't going to be at the mercy of men who came and went willy-nilly, as her mother had been, bringing home losers and wondering why they left. Fay was going to give herself a rock-solid life with plenty of security. Love didn't enter into the plan. Falling in love only led to disappointment. So as she shopped, socializing with as many soldiers as she could, those just coming back from a deployment, those about to be shipped out, she rejected them one by one for being poor with no prospects, or for being too driven and ambitious, as she didn't want a man with a mind and a will of his own. She didn't want an officer, because those were career military men. No, she didn't want her life dictated by the Army. She wanted a man who fit her parameters. And she had decided that that man was Bill Schaller Junior.

Being a recent newcomer to the area, Fay had done some discreet homework and had found out a lot about him. That his real name was Wilhelm, Junior but he preferred the American version. That he was the son of German immigrants. That he had a sister named Lorelei and an older brother named Helmut, who was currently stationed in the South Pacific, fighting the Japanese. But what she knew best was that Bill was one of the heirs to a very prosperous vineyard and winery, and that when the war was over, he and his brother had big plans for expanding the family business with an aim to making Schaller Wines a household name in California.

Fay had borrowed a bicycle and had pedaled around the valley to see the Schaller spread for herself. Her eyes had bugged out at the sight of so many vineyards stretching as far as she could see. She saw the bottles in the local stores and the prices on them. She had seen the trucks bringing crates of Schaller wine to the train depot, from where they were shipped throughout the state of California. A wealthy wine family. With lots of acres, lots of workers, a nice whitewashed farmhouse, and a shy son who blushed fiercely every time she smiled at him.

She had actually narrowed her choices down to two candidates: the wine-maker's son, and Tom Gilette, son of the town lawyer and himself going to law school. But Tom proved to have too strong a personality, a mind of his own. Fay wanted a man who was a little more easy to control. And she had the perfect fail-safe plan. Bill wouldn't see it coming; he would be a fish on a hook, and all she had to do was reel him in. Now that she had made her selection, she saw no reason to put it off. Tonight her perfect plan would be put into motion.

"Your hair is interesting, Mrs. Schaller," Fay said as she sipped her warm Coke. "How do you get it to frizz up like that?"

Clara gave her an uncertain smile. The girl's compliments had a way of coming off as insults. At last week's dance, Clara had worn a green dress and Fay, eating three cheese sandwiches, had quipped: "Green is such a difficult color, isn't it?" And she had followed it up with, "You know, Mrs. Schaller, I admire women who don't trouble themselves to keep up with current fashions."

Clara suspected that Fay was one of those girls who felt themselves extremely modern and fashionably on the edge. Over the weeks that she had been hostessing these evenings, Fay had bragged that her mother owned an upscale hair salon in Santa Maria, that all the right ladies went there, and that her appointments were booked months in advance. Clara highly doubted it. Everything about Fay seemed false and inflated.

The truth was that Fay had grown up in towns even smaller than Lynnville and had decided long ago that she was going to find a way out and not end up like her hairdresser mother, who could never make ends

244 / Barbara Wood

meet, had never gotten married, and had suffered a string of disappointing boyfriends. When war broke out and a new army base was suddenly under construction near Santa Maria, Fay had decided that that would be her ticket out. And Fay was determined to marry rich. Fay had witnessed enough about men, through her mother's boyfriends, to know they were good for only one thing: security. You married a man to have a place to live and food on the table. Fay wanted more than that. She wanted real money, status, and security. Children, too, if they should happen along. But more than anything, Fay thought with passion, she wanted to be accepted in a group, to be invited to join the right clubs and associations, and to be embraced as an equal to the elite. This she wanted more than anything in life.

Fay knew that lessons learned from parents can be just as much about what *not* to do as what *to* do. Even as a child, Fay recognized her mother's mistakes and how bad the consequences would be. The small-eyed man with the box of chocolates and bottle of awful-smelling perfume. Little Fay would have refused his gifts. Not her mother. She took them, went goo-goo over him for a while, and cried real tears when he left one day without a word. After witnessing a few of those god-awful predictable melodramas, Fay vowed that that would not be the pattern of her own life. She would choose wisely, not be the victim, not get fooled by cheap gifts, and then make sure he could never leave.

Fay didn't blame *everything* in her hard childhood on her mother. She knew that harsh economic times drove people to commit foolish mistakes. And how many times had her mother cried when all she could put on the dinner table was canned beans heated on the stove, accompanied by stale sliced bread and margarine? Fay never had new clothes. They bought everything from church thrift shops. They often ate at charity soup kitchens. Fay knew her mother couldn't help it when people's money shrank because of the Depression, that luxuries were the first to go, especially appointments with a hairdresser when a woman could just as easily shampoo her own hair and put in curlers at home. But did her mother have to bring men home just for a bit more food on the table? Did she know how many times Fay had had to wedge a chair against her bedroom door at night?

The problem was that to her mother, a man was a man, and any man would do. She wasn't picky or choosy and had no standards. Fay had never known who her father was, and she had learned at an early age the word people had for children like her—bastard. Her mother didn't know the

father either, as she had had more than one boyfriend at the time Fay was
conceived.

It had infuriated Fay at twelve, thirteen, fourteen. Even a kid that
young knew that first of all, you don't bring a transient man into your
one-room apartment and pray that he would stick around and take care
of you. You choose a man who is tied to something—a family, a good job,
the land. Then you make sure he has a sense of honor. But most of all, he
had to be like clay—to shape and mold.

More than anything, Fay wanted to stay put.

She and her mother had moved around a lot. Fay understood that
Ruth had had to leave places because she was dodging creditors, land-
lords, abusive men. These were facts that children could quickly grasp.
But there also seemed to be in Ruth Reed a compulsion to be on the
move, to drift from place to place. They'd get to a small town in their old
car, her mother would find them a place—always furnished, usually shab-
bily so that other people had already sat on those old sofas and chairs, and
slept on those stained mattresses. She'd get a job in a hair salon, or serving in a diner, or working in a laundry; she'd promise Fay that they would
stay here, it was the last place, they would settle down. Fay would get her
hopes up, make friends with other girls, and then the strange men would
start coming to stay until her mother announced one day, just when Fay
had friends and was comfortable in the town, that the two of them were
moving on.

It was almost as if her mother had a gypsy soul, a need within her to
keep moving, even when she had a steady job and the rent was paid and
there was food in the pantry. Something seemed to beckon to her. And it
was something Fay never wanted to know or understand. If it was in her
mother, then it could be in *her*, and that frightened her most of all.

She was seventeen when she had seen the true path her life was to take.
His name was Roddy, and he had a way of making people laugh. Generous, boyish (even though he was near thirty), with rough good looks. All
the girls in Victorville had been in love with him, but he had singled out
Fay Reed, driving her around in his car, taking her to soda fountains,
showing her off like she was a hard-won trophy. She hadn't known that
love could be so deep and all-consuming, filling her head with thoughts
of Roddy night and day, thinking she would die without him. And the
happiness? Fay hadn't known the world held such joy, that a human heart
could soar the way hers did when she was with Roddy. She gave herself to
him, her virginity, her body, her soul.

They made plans and promises. They painted a future together. She gave him her babysitting money and a pair of rhinestone earrings her mother cherished. And then he was gone. His landlady said he had skipped out on his rent and had taken some of her silver as well. Fay had cried for a year while her mother took them to another town and tried to comfort her heartbroken daughter, saying there would be other boys and she would get over Roddy.

Those words had frightened Fay. Rather than bring comfort, her mother's advice had only opened Fay's eyes to a terrifying reality: that she had unwittingly fallen into the pattern of her mother's own life—a life of falling in love, followed by heartbreak and finding another man. Fay had seen all too clearly that she must break away and pursue dreams of her own, dreams of security and being rooted.

So when she turned eighteen, she pooled her scant money together with four friends, and they said good-bye to Oakley, California, and moved to Lynnville, where they shared a cramped little house and supported themselves waiting tables, babysitting, laundering other people's dirty clothes. In Fay's case, because of things she had learned from her mother, she got a job at a hair salon shampooing, sweeping the floors, keeping the stock filled and tidy. It was a scrimping, bare-bones existence, but the girls had their eyes on the prize: the boys stationed at Camp Cooke.

And now that Fay had made her choice—a family that owned a huge tract of vineyards and a winery was about as stable and permanent as you could get—she made another vow: once she had hooked wealthy Bill Schaller, she had no intention of letting her mother know. Wouldn't Ruth Reed be the worst embarrassment at the wedding?

"Look at that," Fay said, tipping her head toward the front entrance. "Do you believe the nerve of them?"

Clara turned toward the doors and saw two young women standing there, looking in. They were dressed to the nines in colorful skirts and blouses, hair done up perfectly, careful makeup—beautiful creatures, really, she thought, like butterflies. They hesitated in the doorway, dark eyes scanning the crowd. They looked at each other in silent communication and then backed away and let the doors swing closed.

They looked Hispanic, probably Mexican, Clara thought, and they had seen none of their own kind in here. They would have romantic, lilting names like Alejandra and Guadalupe, and Clara wanted to go out and urge them to come in and enjoy the evening. But she thought that might

come across as condescending and embarrass them, further pointing out
their separateness from this all-white crowd. Sometimes doing a kind-
ness made things worse.

Those pretty girls with their raven hair and olive skin would not be
persuaded to join the dance, Clara knew. They would find a cantina
owned and patronized by their own kind, where they would find young
men named Carlos and Juan, and dance to mariachi music and eat enchiladas and drink Mexican beer.

Maybe that was all prejudice was—the basic human instinct to stick to
the familiar.

If the dark-eyed señoritas had come in, they would have been made
to feel welcome. The soldiers would have competed for them. White boys
consorting with Mexican girls was accepted. There were even white growers with Mexican wives and racially mixed children. But it could never be
the other way around. If Hispanic soldiers came in and tried to dance
with the white girls, it would end up in a brawl, with the sheriff and military police called in.

Us and Them, Clara thought as she handed glazed crullers on a plate
to two grateful servicemen. But it was more than that. It wasn't just racial,
it was cultural and economic divisions. The owners of the big farms, the
"growers," were white, and they had all the money and the power. The
workers in the fields, "the pickers," were mostly Latino and poor, with
no power. Growers' wives did not have Latina friends. There was not a
single Mexican woman in the weekly Sunday kaffeeklatsch at Eberhardt's.
Yet they hired Latina women to work as domestics and nannies in their
big homes.

The señoritas who had looked in at the door, for instance, would
be poor, Clara thought, because that was how it was here in the valley,
and they had spent hard-earned money on one good evening outfit
each. They were the daughters of maids and housekeepers and laun-
dresses and cleaning ladies. Their fathers were poor dirt farmers,
manual laborers, migrant pickers. They lived in a shantytown or, if
they were lucky, a proper clapboard house with maybe electricity and
indoor plumbing. The girls would have left school by the age of twelve
to help support the large family and had little hope of rising out of
their situation.

It didn't make sense to Clara how some people worked hard and
prospered, like the Schallers and the Newmans, and how some worked
even harder but remained poor, like families named Gonzales, Flores,

or Ramos. It seemed a strange imbalance to Clara, considering that the Spaniards and Mexicans had been here first.

Clara knew that the states of California, Arizona, New Mexico, and Texas had all once been part of the country of Mexico, and then there had been a war a hundred years ago the Americans won and they claimed all that land and established a new border between the United States and Mexico. But that didn't make the inhabitants of those regions automatically change. For centuries, borders in Europe were changed, moved, re-shaped so that new governments and new crowns ruled over them. But the people in those regions retained their old cultures, traditions, religions. Borders might change in Europe yet again before this latest war was over.

"They knew better," quipped young Fay, who now had a finger of shortbread to her lips.

"I beg your pardon?" Clara said.

"Those Mexican girls. They knew not to come in here. Thank God."

Clara stared at her and thought of other racial comments she had heard in the valley over the years. Who creates these barriers, anyway? she wondered. There were no signs that said NO MEXICANS ALLOWED. There were no written laws, no spoken rules. People just seemed to do it them-selves. Invisible, mental fences had been somehow erected over the decades, separating Us from Them. Two races living side by side for over a hundred years, sharing the same winter rains and blue summer skies, kept separated by a prejudice that Clara, after thirty years of living here, could still not fathom. She knew that Hispanic soldiers were serving in the U.S. armed forces and were fighting overseas alongside white Amer-icans. Her son Bill had told her about boys of Mexican heritage serv-ing in his own battalion. And yet where were those boys tonight? Clara looked around and saw no one who might be named Gonzales or Flores or Ramos.

It made her sad as she thought of Rosita and all her help and kind-ness when a naïve and inexperienced young German immigrant had first come to this valley. She especially remembered how Rosita had tenderly taken care of her after Sean O'Brien's vicious attack.

The band struck up the lively jitterbug song "Boogie Woogie Bugle Boy of Company B." "I'd better get myself out onto the dance floor," Fay said, "and work off some of that butter you slather a little too heavily on the bread."

As she watched Fay sashay out onto the dance floor, Clara wondered if the girl was aware that her compliments weren't compliments at all. Was she saying these things on purpose, or was she truly oblivious of how her comments came across? There was that other time, a few weeks ago: "I love your hat, Mrs. Schaller. It's not just any older woman who can wear it the way you do."

Clara would have liked to give the girl the benefit of the doubt; but Fay clearly had designs on Bill, and that made Clara wary of her. She couldn't pinpoint why, but all her instincts and intuitions set alarms off in her mind: this girl could not be trusted, she would be bad for Bill. Clara knew what wartime was like for romance and marriage. She prayed that Bill wouldn't fall for false charms and marry too soon and live to regret it.

The rules of this club were that the hostesses weren't to be exclusive with any particular GI, that they were to socialize with all the soldiers and not single any out. But favorites and pairings were inevitable. In the past few months, Clara had seen romance and even true love blossom among some couples. But she knew also that many of the girls who volunteered here were husband-hunting, and the soldiers were incredibly lonely and homesick and therefore vulnerable to feminine wiles. She had learned to spot the hunters in the crowd, and there was no doubt that Fay Reed had her sights set on Bill.

She wasn't a very attractive girl, Clara thought, with a rather bland, broad face and a chunky body. And there was a predatory look in her eye that Clara didn't like. Bill would never see it. He was of such a friendly and easygoing nature that he hadn't a distrustful bone in his body. Gullible, some might say. Clara preferred to think that her son just believed the best about people. She wished he was a little less trusting and a little more suspicious of others. He was the perfect target for con artists and gold-diggers.

Clara sighed as she spread mayonnaise on slices of white bread. All soldiers like the ones here tonight flocked to clubs like this all over the country, all over the world, supported and financed by local citizens wishing to contribute to the war effort. Clara's heart went out to them. And out to her own two sons who were in the Army—Bill here, Helmut in the South Pacific, where she hoped hostesses at a similar club were easing his loneliness and homesickness. When she got letters from Helmut, they were sent from a rest camp in New Zealand, where he went for R&R before being sent back into the fighting. She prayed the girls and the chaperones there were as kind to her son as she and the other volunteers here were to these boys—all sons of mothers somewhere who were missing them.

She looked across the noisy, crowded room at her own son. There had been no more children after Wilhelm Junior, who preferred to go by Bill. Clara had endured the act of childbirth just the once, so that she could keep Lorelei. After that, she and Wilhelm Senior had had normal relations but, as she had known, no conception would result because of the position of her womb. Three were enough, and she loved them with a passion.

Clara kept a particularly watchful eye on her daughter Lorelei tonight. A tall, lithe girl with an ethereal air about her, she had come with her mother to the dance but sat alone in a corner, beside a tall plastic plant that was supposed to be a palm tree. Clara often wondered about Lorelei's birth mother, if the girl had inherited some of her other-worldly airs from that unknown woman. Or had it something to do with lying curled up, starving, next to the cold body of her dead Da-Da? Growing up, Lorelei had been distinctively different from other girls—quiet, introspective, often staring for long spells at nothing. She was strikingly beautiful, thin, graceful. But something about her seemed to warn men away. Rather than being the center of soldierly attention, as one might expect, Lorelei was often by herself, sipping a soda, watching. Oh, the boys looked at her, no doubt about that, with hunger and curiosity, but they stayed away so that Clara wondered if her twenty-three-year-old daughter would ever marry.

Her eye strayed back to Bill, who was leaning against a far wall, arms casually folded. Clara was proud of her younger son. Tall and handsome, the image of his father, Bill Junior had inherited his mother's widow's-peak hairline. Unfortunately, the Army wouldn't allow the beard. She remembered her reaction when Wilhelm had first walked into her father's chemist's shop thirty years ago, and she fell for his heroic looks. She wondered what American girls thought when they first met Bill. Luckily, he and Helmut had the same coloring, so no one doubted they had been fathered by the same man. But then, no one would look for Sean O'Brien when they looked at Helmut.

Frieda came up with a basket of fresh, sugar-dusted donuts. She wiped a stray lock of hair from her forehead with the back of her hand. She had just taken the donuts out of the oven in the kitchen attached to the recreation center. Like Clara, Frieda was also facing her fiftieth birthday, and she had grown quite plump over the years, which she jokingly attributed to owning a bakery. Clara, on the other hand, had retained her slim figure, which she credited to her long solitary walks around the farm. There was something restful about looking at a vineyard, the neat and tidy rows sweeping upward and away in graceful symmetry. A vineyard said that all was right with the world. Now that her children were grown and self-sufficient, and her jam and jelly company moved on its own like a perfect machine—a far cry from the first boiling grapes on her stove and rows of sterilized jars on her kitchen table—Clara rewarded herself with hours spent among the vines.

And once in a while, when she was lucky while out walking, she would espy Johann and wave to him and receive a wave and a smile in return. She told herself it was enough.

"Good crowd tonight!" Frieda declared, red-faced and smiling. Once again, Europe was war-torn, and once again Clara and her immigrant friends were riddled with conflicting emotions. They were worried about loved ones back home, they were worried about some of these American soldiers who might be sent overseas to help France and Britain fight Germany.

Wilhelm didn't talk much about this second war, didn't show the obsessive interest he'd had back during the first World War. His focus now was all on expanding his acres. Just that morning, he had said: "The Biscotti brothers own four hundred acres of prime vineyards with an annual yield of eight hundred tons. I'd like to buy them out."

Twenty years ago, Prohibition had triggered a land hunger in Wilhelm. Hating to see healthy vineyards being abandoned and running to weedy waste, he had bought the properties of men who had given up their dreams and gone elsewhere. Wilhelm had seen it as rescuing vines that had plenty of life in them yet, rescuing premium grapes from withering—and perhaps Wilhelm himself had believed it at the time. But in hindsight, Clara saw now how he hunched over survey and topographical maps with a kind of lust in his eyes that would have done Napoleon proud. He would get in his truck and drive for miles, inspecting his latest acquisitions and looking for new ones. The word "empire" had started to creep into his vocabulary.

There is a fine line between determination and stubbornness, Clara thought as she handed sandwiches and napkins and sodas to soldiers who thanked her gratefully. The determined man is admired, she thought; the stubborn man is reviled. Wilhelm Schaller was a devotedly stubborn man. He had a will like a barnacle. Once he set himself to something, there was no dislodging him. By the time Prohibition had been repealed, ten years ago, only a hundred and forty wineries were still in operation around the nation. Schaller's was the largest in California, and Wilhelm was determined to own the largest, grandest, richest vineyard and winery in the United States.

The only blot in his otherwise shining empire was Colina Sagrada and the barren, unworkable land that surrounded it. The sandy wasteland had become his Moby Dick. He would drive out there and stare at it for hours. Why couldn't he just let it be? Clara wondered. A curious aberration in the middle of lush farming country. Maybe there was a reason for its being like that. Wilhelm had made an attempt, a few years ago, to pipe water to the spot, but it had failed.

As she refilled cups of hot coffee and pointed out the fresh, warm donuts to new arrivals at the food tables, Clara looked around the dance hall at the laughing and smiling people and thought how everyone here was worried about something, although it didn't show. Each and every one of us carries a secret fear. Was there ever a worry-free person on God's earth? She thought about her occasional rendezvous with Johann in isolated places, innocent meetings that must be kept from prying eyes. He was worried about his son, Adam. The angry boy had grown into a silent, introspective young man. Johann said that Adam no longer blamed himself for his mother's death. He had done a lot of reading since Feliciana took her life, went to libraries and read books on mental illness. He had even written to specialists, and had come to the realization that nothing could have been done to save Feliciana. And so Adam had reached a kind of peace with what had happened. And Clara knew that Johann had learned to let Feliciana go because she was never really his in the first place and he had seen how doomed she was, that tragedy was inevitable.

Clara and Johann shared a curious, chaste romance. They couldn't stay away from each other. They liked to meet in the shelter of a low-hanging willow down by Largo Creek, at a remote spot far from roads and houses, always making sure there were no passersby, no one to see them. There was no kissing, no murmured words of endearment, no exploring beneath clothing, as these would have been betrayals of marriage vows. They shared their love in the chastity and innocence of children, a tight embrace in which they exchanged warmth and devotion and allowed their souls to flow into each other. She spoke to him of Wilhelm and the children; he voiced his concerns about Adam, who seemed to have closed his heart to women and romance. They shared hopes and dreams as well, but always there was a wall between them—her husband and his brother, Wilhelm.

Clara assured herself that it was enough—*more* than enough. After thirty years of marriage, she and Wilhelm had become a married couple who did not hug or embrace or kiss outside of the twice-monthly sex, which had become quick these days. They touched by patting on the shoulder, a clasping of a hand. Clara craved a full-bodied embrace, chin to toe. She would slip into Johann's arms and he would hold her there, tightly, for a long time, not speaking, just holding, hearts beating together. Yes, it was enough.

When she saw that the cream jug for the coffee was empty, Clara pulled herself out of her meandering thoughts and went out to the kitchen to fetch more.

Across the dance hall, as the band switched from a jazzy selection to a slow tune, Bill Junior took out a pack of cigarettes, chose one, and lit it, throwing the match to the floor. Nearly everyone was smoking in the club, filling the hot evening air with haze. But nobody minded. Everyone was having a good time. It was a break from the routine of life at Camp Cooke. He considered himself lucky to have been stationed there, just a few miles northwest of the valley, so he was able to take leaves and come home on a regular basis. Assigned to the 5th Armored Division, Bill was trained in the use and maintenance of anti-aircraft artillery, and trained other outfits that passed through on their way to deployment.

He leaned against a wall and surveyed the offerings. A lot of the "hostesses" were pretty and well dressed, but he had his eye out for Doris, a perky redhead who had attended the last few dances and had jitterbugged with him more than was allowed, but there was something between them and he couldn't wait to get her out on the dance floor again.

He saw his mother at the sandwich table, pretending to put snacks together for the boys, but he knew her real job was to make sure no hanky-panky went on. He wondered if she was aware just how much hanky-panky there really *was* going on. Certainly a lot more than met the eye. Horny soldiers let off the base for an evening of feminine company? The atmosphere of this club didn't lead to celibate thoughts. Phone numbers and addresses secretly exchanged. Quick dips outside for some fresh air and a little nookie.

Bill was in the mood for some female company tonight, hot and pliant female company. And Doris was the star of his fantasy. His mom and the other chaperones couldn't keep an eye on everyone every minute, not with the music so loud and the dance numbers so energetic. Still, it was a chaperoned dance and decorum was expected. A lot of his buddies from Camp Cooke found entertainment at highway roadhouses that offered bowling and beer, with aging hookers upstairs. That was not to Bill's taste. Besides, he knew his mother expected him to come here and not some seedy place like Sharkie's on Highway 66.

War was a funny thing, Bill thought as he watched the busy front entrance for Doris's arrival—he was *really* in the mood to hold her in his arms tonight. Yes, war was a funny old thing when you considered how it both divided people and united them at the same time. Japanese and Americans might be trying to annihilate one another, but just look at the merry crowd in this boisterous dance hall—strangers who might never otherwise come together to smoke and dance and play cards and laugh and share life stories. Yet here they were, drawn together because armies were fighting.

While he watched for Doris, he kept an eye on his sister, who was sitting by herself with the expectant air that she seemed always to have about herself. He knew Lorelei wasn't really his sister but an adopted orphan, but he loved her and was very protective of her and would be quick to deliver swift justice to any fellow who disrespected her. Strangely, despite her movie-star good looks, the boys stayed away. Maybe they knew they'd have to face big Bill Schaller if they so much as looked at her.

A pair of cute girls sauntered by just then, winked, and said, "Hi there, soldier."

He smiled back. He knew it was the uniform.

Bill didn't like this army business. He felt like a fraud, an actor in a costume. People looked at him and thought him brave and courageous. But he hadn't volunteered, he had been drafted. He didn't like being in the military, standing at attention, saluting, shouting "Yes, sir!" to men he didn't respect. He wanted to be his own man, out in the vineyards beneath the sun, moving at the pace of ripening grapes. His father didn't order him around. The pair worked side by side and produced sweet crops.

More than anything, he didn't want to get sent into battle. He admired his older brother Helmut, who seemed to have been born with more fight in him than Bill had. Helmut had joined up, and now he was supporting U.S. Marines in the Pacific. Fighting was fine for Helmut: he had chosen it. But Bill's place was at the vineyards and winery. It greatly aggrieved him that Adam Newman, his twenty-eight-year-old cousin, had dodged the draft and avoided military service altogether, leaving him free to pursue his ambition to produce higher-quality wines. Bill was driven by an ambition as well—not so much to bottle better wine, but *more* of it and in a bigger variety.

Here was where he and his father parted ways. While Wilhelm Sr. was amassing land, which was a good thing in Bill's mind, he wasn't interested in increasing production. Bill wanted to expand the winery, introduce new grape varieties, and experiment with blending. Before his draft notice arrived, Bill had uncorked an experimental Cabernet Sauvignon bottled back in 1933. It had a nice finish to it. "And it's amazing what that extra spring rain did for the color. It's like a ruby," he had said to his father, who had only grunted as he was studying the survey map of land for sale.

And there were Johann and Adam Newman working in a scientific lab to expand and improve *their* products while Wilhelm Schaller stubbornly remained stuck in old-fashioned farming ways. Bill vowed that when the war was over, he was going to initiate some big changes at Schaller Vineyards, whether his father liked it or not. Bill wasn't going to let a cowardly draft-dodger like Adam Newman get the better of the Schallers.

"Hi, there, Bill. I've been waiting for you to come over and ask me to dance."

He suppressed a groan. Fay Reed again. She was getting a bit clingy and possessive. He tried to be nice and polite to her, joke about how the chaperones were going to lecture them, maybe ban them from the club. He tried to tell her how much he liked her, which he didn't really, so as not to hurt her feelings. It was Doris he was interested in, but she hadn't arrived yet.

She stood with her hands on her plump hips, her belted shirtwaist dress making her rear end look bigger than it probably was. She wore too much lipstick and too many pearls, and the hibiscus behind her ear was almost laughable. She tilted her head to one side, coquettishly. "You won't get a better offer than me."

Bill figured, why not? He threw down his cigarette, tamped it out with his spit-polished shoe, and said, "Sure, let's dance."

As Bill led her through a slow dance, in the center of a lot of clinging couples, Fay kept her eye on the chaperones at the food tables. All she needed was to lure Bill away from his mother's watchful eyes. Just once, and just long enough.

While they danced slowly, she rubbed her pelvis against him and pressed her breasts into his chest and breathed hotly on his neck, and after a while she felt the inevitable response. She smiled dreamily up at him, and he bent his head almost to kiss her. She knew he was ready. Fay watched the sandwich table where Bill's mother was slicing ham. When Mrs. Schaller turned suddenly and slipped into the kitchen, Fay seized the moment.

She whispered against his ear, "Let's go outside." She didn't have to offer a second time.

They weren't the only hot and eager couple in a clinch in the darkness outside the club. They just needed a wall to prop themselves against, Fay helping him with his zipper while he slipped her underpants down. She had to pretend it was her first time, remembering to squeak out a virginal "Ow," when he penetrated her, but assuring him it was heavenly as he thrust her against the wall a few times and then he was finished. Tears had threatened, as his body against hers had reminded her of Roddy back in Victorville, but she pressed them back and she kissed him and told him over and over how wonderful it had been for her. Then she calculated the days to when she would drop the bombshell.

She dropped it on him six weeks later when they met once again at the recreation center. It was the middle of the week, a light afternoon; no band was playing, no dance going on. Soldiers were there playing chess and checkers, listening to the radio, reading, writing letters home. Fay had called him at the base and said she needed to speak to him as soon as possible on a matter of some urgency. Bill had been able to get a day pass but had to return to the base that evening.

They sat at one of the patio tables beneath the meager shade of an umbrella. The day was hot with little relief from the Pacific Ocean. He nearly fell off the bench when Fay said she was pregnant. And yes, the baby was his. He was the only boy she had been with, and how dare he imply otherwise. And if he didn't do the honorable thing, she was going to his parents. "Your mother saw us plenty at the canteen dances."

And then she burst into tears, the way she had rehearsed it.

It was the worst hour in young Bill's life.

And just then a bit of patriotic music came over a nearby radio, *The Stars and Stripes Forever,* and suddenly Bill Junior remembered the war and that he was a soldier and he had had duty and responsibility and honor so drilled into him that he took all this duty and honor out of the Army and the battlefield and into real life as he thought about what it meant to be a real man. He suddenly felt calm and manly and responsible while the entire world came collapsing around him like a theater set being torn down. He was a soldier facing cannons and tanks and stood as cool as John Wayne in *The Flying Tigers*. For a brief moment, Bill Schaller Junior felt tall and noble, felt that someone should pin a medal on his chest as he said, "Don't cry. We'll do the right thing." He awkwardly patted her hand. He didn't love Fay, didn't even really like her, but she was carrying his baby and he would love that child.

"I know how we can do it," Fay said, sniffing back her tears and composing herself, as if an idea had only just occurred to her. "Tell your parents you've just found out that your orders came through. You're being shipped out and we are so in love we want to get married before you are sent overseas. That'll explain the rush."

"But I won't be shipping out," he said thinly, feeling unreal and almost dead. The rush of patriotism had passed and the bravery had been only skin-deep. His heart raced beyond counting, and he thought he was going to be sick. He couldn't seriously be thinking of marrying this dreadful girl.

"After we're married, tell them your orders were changed and you're staying at Camp Cooke after all." She blinked wet, helpless, teary eyes at him, and he saw no way out.

Clara and Wilhelm told their boy they understood, although Clara had her fearful suspicions which she did not share with her husband. After all, war was a time of quick weddings and skipped honeymoons. It was a modest ceremony at the Lutheran Church. Fay told the Schallers that her mother couldn't attend because of illness. The truth was, she hadn't even told her mother, who might want to horn in on her daughter's windfall.

And then, a month later, she weepingly told Bill she had miscarried. The plan, so perfectly crafted one evening at a dance where lonely soldiers went to socialize with wholesome girls, had been a success. Fay Schaller was now a member of a family who owned a prosperous and *growing* winery.

All she had to do was craft her next plan: to usurp the seniority of Bill's mother, Clara, and claim that throne for herself.

*　　*　　*

ADAM ROUNDED THE CORNER of the house, wiping his hands on a cloth, and came to a sudden halt. Damn, there she was again!

Sitting at an easel on the lawn in front of the main house, painting flowers that grew along the white picket fence that separated the residence from the rest of the farm and winery.

Adam hated running into her. Since she was staying with the Newmans, there was never any knowing when their paths might suddenly cross. Was it too late to dodge her now? Had she seen him? Or could he get away with it? An awkward moment. He stopped to think; and while he did, he couldn't take his eyes off her legs. Like a lot of girls these days, she had taken to wearing a new style of shorts that were white and pleated, and they came down to mid-thigh, exposing much of her creamy golden legs. Her shirt was pink and oversized, the shirttails tied in front at the waist—"calypso style," he thought it was called. It enhanced her bosom, another thing he couldn't take his eyes off of.

He wondered if she had a boyfriend—someone back home in Kansas, or in the Army or Navy, stationed in Britain or fighting the Japanese. In the week that she had been there, he had learned two things about her. First, like himself, Queenie Young had lost her mother. Neither the Professor nor his daughter were forthcoming on the details, but Mrs. Young had died ten years ago and Adam assumed it was of the kind of illness people didn't speak of—much as in the case of his own mother, Feliciana, whose mental illness and death was never mentioned. The second thing he knew about Queenie Young, and on this subject the girl herself had been most outspoken, was that she wasn't attending college to find a husband as so many of her friends were doing. She was pursuing an education to secure an active career, either in botany or in art, and that plans for marriage and family lay in the distant future. She had said it almost defensively, or as a warning. She wanted it known right up front where her priorities lay. So if there was a boyfriend back home or stationed overseas, he was not high on Queenie Young's list.

Adam didn't know why he pondered this or why he should care, because he, too, was not in the market for marital prospects. In fact, bachelorhood suited him just fine. It was the one topic upon which he and his father had frequent debates. Adam's self-imposed isolation and solitary life worried Johann Newman. "Son, a man needs a woman. It's a lonely, loveless life you lead." "Plenty of men live without women, Dad, and are happy and successful." "But it's not just yourself you have to think of, Adam. Who will this land go to if you have no heirs? Have you thought of that?"

Of course he had thought of it. A thousand times, but there were no solutions. He admitted that the property needed an heir. But he couldn't tell his father the truth, as it might come across as accusatory. The truth was, twenty-eight-year-old Adam Newman was terrified of passing his mother's mental illness along to the next generation. But how could he tell his father that? How could he say "You married a mentally ill woman, and now I must live a life of bachelorhood?" Adam had done a lot of reading on the subject, checking books out of the library, writing letters to professors of psychology. He had even taken a few psychology courses at the local college, and his professors had thought he was interested in entering the field. But Adam was interested in only one disorder: manic-depression. And more precisely—was it an inheritable disorder? The consensus seemed to be yes, it was possible the illness could be passed along to descendants. And that was something Adam could not risk.

In the years since Feliciana's suicide, Adam had matured and come to terms with the fact that he could not have saved her—no one could have. So he had stopped blaming himself for her death. But now it was his responsibility to see that no future Newmans were going to suffer his mother's terrible fate.

Anyway, there was Queenie at her easel and Adam had to decide whether to be manly and say hello or cowardly retrace his steps back behind the house. Was there anything lonelier than being attracted to someone but having to deny the pleasure of their company?

The very lively and pretty twenty-year-old girl from Kansas was here because the son of one of the Newmans' neighbors had gotten killed in the Japanese attack on Pearl Harbor; and after that, all the life had gone out of the radish farm that abutted the old Ballerini bean-crop acres. Mr. Simpson had been eager to sell and go live with his family in Texas. Adam's father had paid the asking price, sold the last radish crop, and was now looking to plant something more profitable and in demand.

Newman's Farms was providing beans and corn to the U.S. military and was getting increasingly wealthy. But Johann wanted to try something new, and because he was more of a vintner than a vegetable farmer, he had decided to enlist the help of a professional to survey the new acres, analyze the soil, and bring a body of science to the cultivating of a new crop. He had read an article in an agricultural journal about new crops, written by a Professor Young at the University of Kansas. He had written to the man; letters had been exchanged. The Professor had said he would be delighted to come and help. Johann insisted that the man stay in the main house. But Professor Young had shown up with his daughter. He apologized. He thought he had mentioned it in a letter. He hadn't wanted to leave her alone for the summer. Johann said it was okay. There were two very nice guest rooms on the third floor. They would have privacy. A tidy and convenient arrangement that avoided motels and boarding houses.

The problem was, Queenie didn't *stay* in the guest room. She wasn't involved in her father's work. She had an easel and canvases and paints and was seen all over the property.

Professor Young's area of study was experimental crops, which was what Johann was interested in. The Professor estimated that there were at least twenty thousand species of edible plants on earth, but only a handful of crops fed most of the world's people—wheat, rice, corn, potatoes, barley, tomatoes. He wanted to expand the diversity of plant food in the human diet. Soybeans were a relatively new crop that was starting to gain worldwide acceptance. Originally cultivated in China, soybeans gradually spread throughout Asia and had become a staple food there. High in protein, soybeans were currently grown in the Western world as animal feed. Adam's father didn't see why concerted breeding efforts couldn't result in edible varieties of soybeans for humans, lessening world reliance on other crops.

His father was also having a greenhouse constructed behind the winery, with an attached laboratory, for experimenting with new crop breeds. And every day you saw Johann Newman, tall and straight for a man of his age, fifty-three, which Adam thought was old, striding over the construction site to make sure everything was going according to plan. Professor Young was always at his side, a smaller man with rounded shoulders and owl-like glasses perched on his nose. It amazed Adam that a man who looked like a potato could produce such a striking young woman as Queenie.

Adam himself had no interest in beans or corn or experimental crops. He oversaw the vineyards and ran the winery, his first love. He was especially into blending wines, using lessons learned from his father years ago. Lately, he had experimented with wines that were from different years and had discovered that, in general, this did not work well. Wines blended from different years seemed to pull the older vintage back to a youthful harshness.

Now he was on to a new problem: understanding that a wine's weaknesses were just as important as its strengths, and usually easier to identify. Quite often it was an awkward aftertaste or a lack of roundness in flavor, and that was another reason why, with his mind so preoccupied and with problems to solve and a determination not to pass the Ballerini curse (as he thought of his mother's mental state) along to sons and daughters, Adam could not afford to spend time in idle conversation with Queenie Young—a pretty girl from Kansas who he was becoming attracted to and didn't want to be.

Queenie was interested in both art and botany which, combined, he had to admit made for beautiful paintings of flowers. But, as much as Adam was strangely attracted to her, she also irritated him for some reason—and he had no idea why. She had done nothing wrong, nothing to offend him. She was pleasant and polite, if a bit giggly. She gave the impression of being constantly tickled. Was that it? Or was he inventing the feeling of irritation to make it easier for him to turn away from his attraction to her? He had protected his heart for a long safe time. He couldn't weaken now.

Too late. She had seen him. She waved and he had to go over. "Aren't these irises just too heavenly?" she asked.

There was no denying it, the girl had a gift for capturing detail and transferring it to canvas.

Suddenly he felt sorry for her. There was something lonely about her out here. Was she really going to spend her entire summer this way? Sitting alone in her bedroom, going for walks by herself, sitting at this easel while the world went on about its business without her?

"Have you seen the town yet?" he asked impulsively. "Lynnville?" Adam couldn't believe his own ears. Was he really about to invite her out?

"No, but I would like to."

He looked this way and that, at the vineyards, the winery, the house. She wasn't his responsibility. No one had expected the Professor to bring a daughter. And Adam was getting good at avoiding relationships. But he couldn't stop staring at how her curls captured the sunlight, and the hopeful, expectant look in her eyes, and then he told himself she was leaving at the end of summer anyway and he would never see her again.

"It's Saturday," he said, trying to make the offer sound as casual and non-committal as possible. "And it's going to be a warm evening. There'll be lots of people out. It's cooler by the river."

Her face lit up as if all her birthdays had come at once. "I would love to!" she said.

And Adam instantly regretted it.

He didn't get dressed up, just jeans and a clean shirt, and he gave his jaw a cursory go-over with a razor. He left his hair as it was, with no Brylcream to make him look as if he was making a play for her. And he decided definitely no fancy dinner. He didn't want her getting the wrong idea. This was just a casual outing between two people who had just met and probably weren't destined to become close friends. During the hot summer weather, Eberhardt's added cold sandwiches and salads to their menu, so that was where they went, to sit at one of the little tables that were always commandeered by the ladies' kaffeeklatsch on Sundays.

"I've never been to Kansas," Adam said when their ham-on-ryes arrived. "I hear it's very flat."

She laughed. "It's no place for mountaineers. I don't know anything about wine-making. It seems an exotic occupation. I've seen the grapes fattening on the vines. The colors are beautiful. Your father was kind enough to give me a tour of the winery. You know what I learned?"

Adam found himself captivated, the sandwich forgotten in his hand. "What did you learn?" he asked, genuinely wanting to know.

"I discovered that when the vintner bottles wine, sticks a label on it, and stores it away in the cellar, he has safely saved away a part of that year. And if it was a good year—not for the wine but for yourself, like maybe when you got married or first fell in love—well, years down the road you can go down into the cellar, retrieve the 1930 Chablis Blanc, say, open it, pour it, taste it, and just like that, you have some of your favorite year back, on your tongue, going down your throat, to take you back to that special time. I wonder if perhaps that's why people buy certain vintage years and not others. That it really has nothing to do with the wine itself but with the year."

Adam stared at her. The bakery grew quiet, voices dampened, the sound of the cash register came from far away. He couldn't take his eyes off her as she daintily ate her ham sandwich. He suddenly wondered what year she would choose, if she could find it on a shelf and taste it again. The last time she'd seen her mother? There was a poignant loneliness about Queenie Young, coming here with her father but spending her days alone. Did she make up for the lack of a Mrs. Young? Was the Professor the center of this girl's life as she saw to his needs, provided companionship? He suddenly wanted to know more about her.

But at the same time he didn't. He had no right to involve himself in any girl's life. He had nothing to offer. There was no future for a girl with Adam Newman.

"What about your mother?" he asked.

"I don't like to talk about her." He noticed that Queenie averted her eyes with those words, and a kind of sadness crept into her tone. "I heard that *your* mother died. I'm sorry," she said.

"Yes," was all he said, because there was danger, and shame, in the details.

They left Eberhardt's and took to the sidewalks along with throngs of others, the evening being too warm to sit in houses and listen to radios. There were even some sailors, making people wonder where they had come from, this far inland and so far from a naval base. They walked past the ice cream parlor, where teenagers sat at the soda fountain and bobby-soxers danced to a lively Frank Sinatra song. Adam thought: there's a war going on, but you wouldn't know it in Lynnville on this hot and jumping summer night. Adam and Queenie passed the brightly lit movie theater where *Jane Eyre* was showing and soldiers from Camp Cooke were getting in for free. A stop at Mueller's hotel for a glass of chilled wine, and then a stroll along the Largo River, where they found some relief from the heat, and where other couples and families enjoyed the summer dusk.

Queenie wondered about the handsome young man at her side. He didn't seem to have a girlfriend—otherwise, why was he free on a Saturday night? His work at the winery seemed to be his entire life. She wondered if he was ever lonely. Queenie Young knew about loneliness, was an expert on it.

They paused near a weeping willow to look out over the water where boat lights were reflected on the surface. As he watched pedestrians stroll by, soldiers with girls on their arms, Adam was reminded that people must think of him as a cowardly draft-dodger. Worse was when his cousin Bill Schaller was in town on leave with his Army buddies, the way they strutted, the way girls flirted with them. Even when there were no soldiers in town, there were reminders everywhere: at the movie theater ticket window: FREE ADMISSION FOR MEN IN UNIFORM. The barber shop: FREE HAIRCUTS FOR SOLDIERS. Eberhardt's bakery: FREE COFFEE AND CAKE TO THE MILITARY. It wasn't so much the free stuff the soldiers got, it was the automatic respect from people who didn't even know them. It wasn't fair. Adam had tried to join up, he had *prayed* they would take him—in any capacity! He couldn't be blamed for having a bum heart valve. And most of those GIs reaping all those rewards had been *drafted*. They weren't even wearing the uniform by choice.

He thought about the girl at his side. He didn't know why, but he suddenly felt the need to explain something to her. "I signed up, you know," he said out of the blue.

Queenie looked up at him. Even though she was wearing three-inch heels for the occasion, matching her handbag and contrasting her summer dress, she was still shorter than Adam.

"I tried to enlist," he said quietly, watching the water, the lights winking on the far opposite bank. "But apparently I have a faulty heart valve. It isn't life-threatening. I'll live forever. But it was enough for them to slap me with a IV-F status." He tried to talk matter-of-factly, to keep the rancor out of his voice, when what he wanted to do was shout about the unfairness of it all.

Queenie seemed unconcerned. "My cousin tried to enlist, and he was turned down because of something about his foot arches not being right. *Someone* has to work in the civilian sector. They can't send all our men off to fight. Who would keep the country going? So I'm guessing they had to draw the line at fallen arches and faulty heart valves."

It wasn't so much her words as her tone that he appreciated. There was nothing condescending in it, no patronizingly false sympathy. She might even believe what she said. He didn't, but at least the issue was out in the open, over and done with—the elephant in the room. Or maybe a man's military status wasn't as big a deal to some women as it was to him.

Still, there had been a simple quality to her voice, her manner, an open honesty that touched him.

"It kept me out of baseball as well," he added, feeling the need to explain himself to this girl he did *not* want to get involved with. "During a physical done by a recruiting team, this previously undiagnosed heart murmur had been detected. I had hoped the Army doctor wouldn't detect it, but he did."

"Baseball, huh?" she said, eyes sparking with interest. "I love the game." "You do?"

"Before the war, my father and I would go to Kansas Jayhawks games all the time. Unfortunately, with so many players getting drafted, baseball's mostly been temporarily suspended. What position did you play?"

"I was a pitcher."

Her eyes automatically slid to his muscular arms. "I'll bet you're good," she said, and suddenly Adam thought the evening was becoming a bit too sultry, the river too romantic, the pedestrians too giddy and flirty and happy. Adam decided this evening had been a mistake. What he had intended to simply be a touristy jaunt for an out-of-town guest smacked too much of a date, the beginning of a courtship; so he said, abruptly, "We'd better get back to the house."

As he started the car, he vowed that this would never happen again.

*   *   *

QUEENIE COULDN'T SLEEP. THE night was hot. Mosquitoes whined in the air. And her thoughts would give her no rest.

She couldn't stop thinking about Adam Newman.

She'd been there a month now, living under the same roof, never knowing when she was going to run into him, therefore keeping him always to the front of her mind. There had been no more outings to Lynnville with Adam, but Mr. Newman had taken Queenie and her father there a couple of times for a movie and dinner at Mueller's hotel. Mostly, they stayed on the farm. The four ate meals together, but it was Mr. Newman and her father who did all the talking. All excited about soybeans. Once in a while, Queenie would catch Adam looking at her. Or he would reach for the wine and catch *her* watching *him*. Unspoken questions hung in the air. The fathers were oblivious to the silence of the young people, thinking only of a future filled with edible legumes that would save the world.

The Fourth of July had been a big event here, with the Newmans putting on a huge barbecue for their workers. By hiring Mexican women from the migrant camps, the Newmans had provided the cook and house-keeper with extra help. Local white farmers and their families had come. The Newmans' cousins, the Schallers, had not come, nor did Queenie think they had been invited. It seemed strange to her, cousins or brothers or something, neighbors for thirty years and not speaking. She wondered what the story was. She went into Lynnville once to get her hair trimmed and conditioned, but the gossip she had heard there had been conflict-ing. A land dispute. A romantic triangle. Greed and jealousy were usually what started family rifts.

Adam was the one she was most curious about. She had the strang-est feeling that he was avoiding her. She told herself he was just a hard worker. He didn't like to leave things to his managers but had to over-see all steps to the grape-growing and wine-making processes himself, spending long days out among the vines, and long hours in the fermen-tation and aging rooms, inspecting each new barrel that the wine was to be stored in, inspecting new bottles and labels, and of course forever work-ing in the laboratory where he was engaged in what seemed his passion: blending wine.

She was glad they had come to California, glad her father had accepted the job of consultant to Mr. Newman. Queenie had seen her father go gradually downhill these past ten years. She knew he missed her mother as sharply today as he had the day they had lost her. This job had done wonders for him, as he walked the many acres with Mr. Newman, as they studied schematics and plans and equations and inspected seeds and roots in the new greenhouse. Her father was happiest when growing something. He himself had come from a Kansas corn-farming family, so he had this in common with Mr. Newman. They had become fast friends.

If only the Newman son weren't so standoffish. "Loner" was the word that most came to mind. He was very attractive in a moody, silent way, she thought, but could sometimes be seen to be smiling, especially when he was playing host in the tasting room of the winery. There was talk of putting a restaurant in there as well, but that would be after the war. These days, everything was being put off until after the war.

Queenie prided herself on being a no-nonsense girl "with a head on her shoulders." Not like her dreamy friends who sighed over film stars and thought that going out with boys was what they had been created for. Twenty years old, and this was the first time Queenie had lost sleep because she couldn't get a man out of her mind.

She wondered if a glass of warm milk would help. She slipped out of her bedroom on the third floor wearing just her nightgown—who was she going to encounter at midnight?—and went down a flight of stairs. On the landing, before continuing on down, she glimpsed a light coming from a door in the second-floor hallway. Curious, she walked quietly toward it. The door stood open. She looked in to find Adam sitting at a table by the window, fully dressed, staring out at the night. It was a very feminine room with a frilly four-poster bed, satin counterpane, and fresh flowers in a vase.

The light was coming from the only lamp in the room that was turned on. Sensing her, Adam looked up.

"I'm sorry," she said. "I didn't mean to intrude. I saw the light." She began to back away.

"This was my mother's room," he said simply.

It sounded almost like an invitation, so she stepped inside. She took the other chair and waited and wondered. Somehow, it didn't seem odd to be sitting in a strange woman's bedroom with a fully clothed man she barely knew while she herself was wearing only a gauzy nightgown at midnight. It almost had a movie feel to it: *Rebecca*, and she was Joan Fontaine.

"It's a lovely room," she said, for lack of anything else to say. How strange this was, a grown man sitting all alone in his dead mother's bedroom.

"I've kept it exactly as she left it. The maid comes in once a week."
He paused to look at her, his handsome face half in shadow, half in
the light of the lamp on the table. "What kind of a name is Queenie
anyway?" he said.

She smiled. "My real name is Shirley. When I was six years old, I
made a crown out of paper and wore it on my head everywhere, telling
everyone that I was the Queen of England. My parents had no idea where
I got the notion from, but my father thought it was so cute that he started
calling me Queenie, and the name stuck."

"I like it," Adam said. "Anyone can be called Shirley—and quite a few
are—but it takes someone special to be called Queenie."

His words took her aback and the moment suddenly seemed too intimate. She looked around and said unnecessarily, "So this was your mother's room."

Adam saw how the light picked up blondish tints in her brown hair.
He wondered if the curls were natural, or if she had them done. He was
acutely aware of the nightgown, the bare shoulders, the fact that she had
just come from her bed. It didn't seem right somehow, to have sexual
thoughts in this room. But he couldn't stop them, just as he hadn't been
able to stop thinking about Queenie since their visit to Lynnville. He
shouldn't have done that. The evening had opened up a doorway that
needed to be kept closed.

"I like to come in here. It brings me peace somehow. I like to think
she's still here. I suppose you heard that my mother committed suicide.
She had a mental illness. The doctors said there was nothing that could
be done. I tried to save her, you know. I was just a boy and thought that
she could be jollied out of her depression."

She wanted to get up and put her arms around him. Trying to think
of the wise and tactful thing to say after such an unconventional declaration, Queenie said, "I know why you come in here and keep fresh flowers
here—to keep her alive. It's understandable."

He turned anguished eyes to her, sensing that, for just this moment,
he could open up and share his pain with someone he suspected would
be sympathetic. After all, Queenie had also lost her mother. "There is a
terrible irony here," he said in a rush. "I was so burdened with guilt over
the feeling that I had somehow caused her death, that I had plunged into
research on her condition and found that it wasn't my fault at all, that
nothing can be done with someone suffering from manic-depression.
And so my guilt was lifted."

She waited for more; when it didn't come, she said, "And the irony?"

His eyes filled with pain. "The price I paid for learning that it wasn't my fault was the discovery that the illness might be hereditary."

"Oh," she said softly, and suddenly so much became clear. "Oh," she said again as the full impact hit her. Mental illness. Hereditary. Adam Newman wasn't standoffish or a loner: he was afraid.

And her heart went out to him.

"What about *your* mother?" he asked, wanting to deflect the sympathy he felt coming his way, wanting to take the spotlight from himself. "You don't talk about your mother much. Not at all, in fact." He instantly regretted his words as they sounded like a criticism, which it wasn't meant to be at all. He was genuinely curious about how Queenie felt about her mother's death. Maybe they could find a common ground and commiserate.

When he saw tears prick her eyes, he was genuinely shocked and instantly contrite. "I'm sorry," he said. "I didn't mean it how it sounded."

She shrugged. "It's all right. There's nothing to talk about, really."

"You must have some good memories. Birthdays? Christmas?"

She stood up. "I had no business coming in here and invading your privacy. Good night, Adam."

He watched her go, wondering what had just gone wrong.

Out in the hall, flying down the carpet so that her nightgown billowed ghostlike around her, Queenie couldn't believe how awful she felt. She had never been so angry with herself in all her life. She knew he had misunderstood the tears in her eyes. He thought he had hurt her feelings. He had no idea that it was the other way around, that she felt absolutely sick about how she was treating *him* and that she knew she wouldn't be able to sleep for the rest of the night.

* * *

When is it ever a good time to be honest with someone? Queenie wondered as she wheeled out the bicycle Mr. Newman let her use to get around the farm. Especially after you've already been dishonest with them? How do you come clean without making them mad? After all, when you lie to someone, don't you make them look gullible and foolish? Yes, it's best to be truthful from the start; but it's too late for that now. After the extremely awkward visit with Adam in his mother's bedroom, Queenie had stayed awake the rest of the night wrestling with the dilemma—to come clean, or keep up the falsehood? After all, she and her father were going back to Kansas in a few weeks. She'd probably never see Adam Newman again. But it didn't make her feel less awful about herself.

No, she had to tell him, even if it meant he would think less of her. But she needed the right opening. She couldn't just blurt out "I have a confession to make."

She knew where he was working. She had heard him discussing it with his father at breakfast—taking a crew to thin the leaves in the west vineyard. She pedaled along dusty tracks and paths between rows of fattening grape clusters, and found him working with gloves and a bent back, a boss who didn't just give orders but who labored alongside his crew.

Adam was wearing dusty jeans and the usual cowboy boots, plus a denim shirt with the sleeves rolled up to expose sinewy and tanned forearms. The shirt was open at the throat with the top buttons undone, baring the top of his sweating chest. Add the cattleman's hat to his head, and he was a sexy sight.

"Hi, there! I've been looking for you. I was wondering if I could have a word with you."

Adam looked up, his eyes shaded by the brim of his hat. He was surprised to see Queenie. He hadn't been able to stop thinking about her since their encounter the night before, when things had gone awry. Her hair had been disarrayed and her eyes a little puffy from trying to sleep. The seductive white nightgown, sleek and conforming to her body, the hips and breasts. When the sun finally came up this morning, he almost thought it had been a dream.

"Sure," he said. He glanced at his foreman, a grinning Mexican who nodded in male understanding, and strode over to her.

"There's something I have to tell you," Queenie said as she leaned her bike against a trellis. "Can we go for a short walk?"

He stripped off his gloves, shoved them in his back pocket, and fell in step at her side.

He didn't say anything, as he sensed an anxiousness in her. Was the talk going to be about last night? But she surprised him by asking, "Is all that Newman land out there?" And then he realized she was stalling, building up courage.

He squinted at the vineyards on the other side of a barbed-wire fence. "That's the beginning of Schaller property."

"I heard they were some sort of cousins to you."

"Some sort."

He sensed her curiosity and wondered if she had heard stories in town. The stories would be conflicting of course, as all gossip was. He knew she would be too polite to ask him, to pry, and he wouldn't mind her asking, he just wouldn't know what to say. Helmut had won a contest that he himself had wanted to win; and for that, as a hurting fifteen-year-old, he had vowed to hate Helmut and his whole family for the rest of his life. Adam even recalled vowing revenge, although that had subsided with the years and with maturity. But the hostility toward the Schallers remained. "It's a long story," was all he said.

Sensing an awkward moment, Queenie turned away and said: "Look at these beautiful irises. I just love bulb plants. Amaryllis. Narcissus. Tulips. They're just special somehow."

He watched her, trying not to eye her rear end. There was definitely awkwardness here. She was stalling. And now, for some reason, Adam also wanted to stall. He realized he was a little afraid of the reason why she had asked for this talk. Worried that it might be something uncomfortable or even upsetting: else why would she stall? Had it to do with what he had told her about his mother's manic-depression? He wished now he hadn't been so forthcoming.

And then he wanted her to get on with it, to get to the point. He wanted to get back to work, not stand here looking at her shapely bottom and smooth thighs and calves in those perky shorts. It wasn't fair. They could never be together, could never know intimacy, so why allow himself to be tormented? So he said: "Queenie, why are you happy all the time? Nobody is happy all the time. It isn't natural. What's your secret?" Not in an accusing way, sort of in a teasing manner, to ease the anxiety.

She straightened and gave him a studied look, weighing things behind her sparkling eyes as the wind tousled her curls and lifted the collar of Adam's sweaty shirt. Finally she said, in a surprisingly serious tone that caught him off guard, "I'm happy because I have to be."

"You *have* to be?"

"For my father. He is so sad that I know if he thought I was sad too, he might not be able to function at all. Too much sadness would immobilize him."

"So all this happiness . . . it's all an act? You don't really feel it?"

She tilted her head to the side. "You know, it's a funny thing. At first, yes, it was an act. I faked being happy. It wasn't easy. I fell out of the role many times and I saw my father grow anxious with worry for me. So I worked harder at it and then after a while it started getting easy. It became a role that came naturally to me until. . . ."

He hung on her next words, hoping for admission of a miracle, a divine revelation, the secret to a happy life, a cure for his own cloud of gloom. "Until?" he prompted.

"I realized that I really was starting to feel happy."

"But not all the time," he said with suspicion.

She smiled with dimples. "No, not all the time, because, as you yourself said, it isn't natural."

A breeze stirred around them and between them, hot and summery, and Adam felt a small softening inside himself. "Did the fake happiness help you get over your mother's death?" A topic he wanted to avoid, but realizing it might be helpful to himself now. Did this girl know the secret to getting over a death?

This was the opening Queenie had been looking for. She couldn't put it off any longer. A confession and an apology.

She decided not to be defensive about what she had done. Casual was best. So she lifted her shoulders and said simply, "How do you get over someone's death when they aren't dead?"

His blond brows arched. "Your mother isn't dead? But I thought—"

She gave him honest eyes. "That's my father's fiction. It's his way of coping with the fact that she asked him for a divorce." She watched his face for reactions. "This is what I came to talk to you about. Last night, when I left your mother's bedroom, I had the feeling that you thought you had hurt me somehow. But that wasn't it at all, and I wanted to clear the air. I left so abruptly last night because I realized I had been leading you on with a falsehood, and I felt bad about it and wanted to apologize. My mother isn't dead. You and I don't share that tragedy."

She stopped talking, and silence rushed in between them. She waited while he digested this bombshell. Her heart pounded, and she realized that she cared very much how Adam was going to feel about her after this. Surely he would feel betrayed. That was why he had opened up so freely about his mother's death, thinking he was exposing secret grief to a kindred spirit. And now he was to learn that she belonged in the other camp—the one made up of those who still had mothers. Traitor. That's what he'll think. I'm a fraud and a traitor.

The wind shifted, carrying the distant roar of giant threshing machines harvesting early-season corn. The moment stretched. Queenie braced herself.

To her surprise, she saw him nodding in understanding. "He would rather be seen as a grieving widower than a man who failed to keep his marriage together."

"You aren't mad that I never told you the truth? That I let you believe a lie?"

"Why should I be mad? It's your private business, between you and your father. A lot of people think divorce is worse than a disease. Believe me, all families hide something from the world."

Adam was silent for a moment. Thoughts were whirling through his mind. Is everyone play-acting? Do we see roles being played everywhere we look? Is no one who they seem? Am I really as I think I appear? *We all put on faces and good fronts and hide who we really are.*

It was an eye-opener.

"Do you know where your mother is?"

"She lives in Akron."

He waited for more, then asked, "Are you in touch with her?"

"Not since the day she left. There were cards at Christmas and birthdays, but I threw them out and then they stopped coming."

"That's sad," Adam said, trying to imagine throwing away a birthday card from your mother.

"For a long time I blamed myself for the divorce," Queenie said. "Because I really did try to hold them together." Ten-year-old Queenie begging, hysterically, "Don't go, Mommy. I'll be good, I promise!" Trying to pull blouses and skirts out of Selma Young's half-packed suitcase. "They would fight and I had to be the peacemaker. I tried to be cheerful and I invented nice things that one said about the other. After the divorce, I was plagued by things that I had done, or should have done. I didn't try hard enough. I was too pleasing. I got in the way. I didn't get in the way enough. But you know? I've come to terms with the fact that none of it was my fault, nor was it up to me to fix someone else's marriage."

He shook his head. "You can't really believe you've come to terms with anything. You're mad at her. You won't have anything to do with her. You simply shifted the blame from yourself onto your mother, and now you're so mad at her that you won't speak to her." He tried not to let his rancor show, but the day was hot and his collar was damp and it was dawning on him that this girl had a mother and she had just thrown her away.

"It's natural to be angry. Maybe you're angry at *your* mother as well."

"No," he snapped.

"Adam, I understand. Both our mothers left us—" She reached for his arm.

He backed away. "My mother died of an illness. Yours *chose* to leave. And you still have a chance to fix that." It suddenly made him furious that she didn't see the precious opportunity she was letting slip through her fingers. "You still have a mother. *You* have options," he said heatedly. "*I* don't. Not anymore."

"Adam—"

"You need to find the answers," he said, nearly shouting, feeling a tightness in his chest, ignoring the reality of heart murmurs. Why couldn't she see what she was doing to herself? To her father, her mother? It was in her power to make the world right, and she was throwing it away. "Write to her. Telephone her. Show up on her doorstep and ask her why she left."

The day was so hot, he suddenly longed for night. He looked up at the sun as if to embarrass it into moving along, but the sun dug its heels into the white sky and hung there. "My God, did you ever even ask your mother *her* side of it?" *If I could ask my mother why she chose to take her life instead of staying alive with Dad and me. . . .*

"Why should I?" Queenie said defensively, also feeling the oppressive heat of the day. "You never saw what the divorce did to my poor father. He was devastated."

"There are always two sides to every story. Perhaps your mother was a very unhappy woman. There are always hidden things in a marriage. Things that not even the children pick up on. You should look into it."

Queenie put her hands on her hips, feeling judged by this man when she had really come to apologize to him, and said, "You're so full of advice, how about taking some yourself? Here's what it is. You need to let go of your mother and move on. It isn't healthy bringing her fresh flowers and sitting in her bedroom in the middle of the night."

"Great advice from someone who finds it so easy to throw her own mother away!" he shouted. "What makes you such an advice expert? And another thing, people put fresh flowers on graves all the time. They do it for years. What's unhealthy about that? Come back to me with your advice when you've dealt with your own unhealthy way of dealing with your mother!"

He started to turn away, and then he punched the air with his index finger and shouted: "You have a *living* mother! My God, if I had a living mother I'd go down on my knees and beg her to let me be in her life, no questions asked! I thought you were better than that!"

And then he marched away.

*   *   *

AUGUST STROLLED BY IN a series of hot, lazy days with an awkward silence blanketing the three-story Newman house. Queenie and Adam were civil to each other, polite if a bit arch, but with a hesitancy in their eyes, a reluctance in their manner, both wishing they could turn back the clock and have a re-do of their emotional encounter. But the summer was ending and the new school term was waiting for Queenie back in Kansas. And Adam was facing the fall harvest, the new grape crop, the crush, the fermentation—the whole cycle of vine to bottle starting again.

They each rehashed that day, wondering what had gone wrong, how it could have gone right. Each wishing it didn't dog them night and day, because what did it matter? Queenie's stay here was only meant to be temporary anyway. Sadly, both knew the summer was going to end with regrets.

She looked up from her easel. She was by the side of a deserted road, painting a field of wild purple and pink asters. Adam was suddenly standing there, the sun behind him, a contrite look on his face. She saw the truck and hadn't heard it drive up, she had been concentrating so. "I'm sorry," he said. "You were right. I've been doing a lot of thinking about what you said and you are right. With me, it's just *my* grief. But you have your father to think about and his feelings in this whole thing."

She looked solemnly up at him. "I should be apologizing to *you*. I spoke out of turn. I had no right. I'm a guest here."

He shook his head. "I was being judgmental. I had no right. But . . . you see . . . you have a chance to make peace with your mother. That's the vital part. Peace. For me, what I can't get over is the violence in my mother's death. She didn't just take pills. She—" His voice broke and Queenie knew how hard it was for him to be saying this. Was she perhaps the first person he had told in thirteen years? In all the town gossip, the only word used was "suicide." No one ever said *how*.

He looked directly at her and she saw tears in his eyes as he said, "She stabbed herself with a pair of scissors. That's what I can't get out of my mind. The violence of it. The pain she inflicted on herself."

Queenie was speechless. She sat there frozen and helpless, yet wanting to reach out and comfort him. But she didn't know the proper words, the proper gestures for something so enormous.

He turned away and went to lean against a fence post. He went into deep thought, having unburdened the greatest part of his grief. Then he said: "You know, for a long time after my mother died, I asked over and over why she would prefer to die rather than live with me. And when your mother packed her suitcase and left, you probably asked over and over why she preferred to leave rather than live with you. I was fifteen. You were ten. What did we know?"

"Yes," she whispered.

"When you first came here, Queenie, and I thought your mother had died, I thought you and I had something in common. And then you told me the truth and I thought we didn't have anything in common at all. But now I realize that we do, after all. Loss is loss, and leaving is leaving, no matter the manner of the exit. I'm twenty-eight years old and thought I had no more lessons to learn. But I feel like I'm fifteen again and that a lot of lessons and learning still lie before me."

She parted her lips to say yes, but nothing came out, she was so mesmerized. It was as if he were reading her mind.

"You didn't tell me," he began.

She waited.

"You didn't tell me," he said, "that you had written to your mother. You took my advice."

Her eyes widened in surprise. "How did you know?"

He pushed away from the fencepost and drew an envelope from his back pocket. "This came in this morning's mail."

She stared at it. He handed it over, and she rose from her stool to gingerly take it. The postmark was Akron, Ohio. The return address was for a woman named Selma Young.

"Yes," she said as she stared at the miracle in her hand. "I did write to her. I didn't think she would write back." She looked up at Adam with shining, grateful eyes. "You see, you made me realize that I have been judging her for ten years without hearing her side of things. Ten-year-olds don't see things the way adults do. All I knew was that she walked out on us. Now I know, because of you, that I need to find out why she left us."

He reached out and gently touched her arm. "Just as you made me realize that I had also been judging my mother. How can anyone know why she did what she did?" He pointed at the envelope. "Aren't you going to open it?"

With shaking hands she slit the envelope open and unfolded the single sheet of pink stationery. She blinked with tear-filled eyes as phrases floated off the page: *Missed you. . . . Couldn't believe it was from you. . . . Think about you every day . . . please, let's be friends. Visit. . . .*

She started to cry.

Adam reached for her and drew her to him. He put his arms around her and let her weep on his chest. It felt right. It felt good. This was where Queenie belonged. But did he have the right. . . ?

"I have been so lonely," she said through her tears. "Trying to fill the void in my father's life. I don't want to be lonely anymore."

After a moment, she collected herself and lifted her damp face to look up at him. "You've been lonely too. Not just because of your mother's death, but because you're afraid of the future."

"I can't expect any woman," he said in a tight voice, "to take such a risk. Some experts say the illness is hereditary."

"But *you* don't have it?"

He shook his head.

"Then it's a gamble," she said, "a gamble that any two people take when they get together. No one knows what lies in the future. The point is to not be afraid to live, not be afraid to march into the future and dare to face whatever it brings."

She held up the letter in her hand. "This would never have happened if it weren't for you. I would have gone on for the rest of my life being mad at her. But now I have a chance to hear her side of the story and maybe be friends with her again. You gave me my mother back. I want to do the same for you. I want you to no longer be afraid of what will happen in the future. Your mother's illness should not guide your life."

"You've already done something for me. You gave me advice and I'm going to take it. I'm going to redo my mother's room so that it can be used by guests who come to visit us. I'm going to lay flowers at her grave only. I will be like other people. I will accept what has happened, that things happen in life and that the living must continue on with the job of living. This is what you have given me."

"And as for the future?"

He smiled. "The fear, the worry will always be with me. How will my children turn out? But I suppose every man asks himself that. I have avoided relationships because of that fear. I will not let it paralyze me anymore."

Adam was amazed to find an unexpected inner peace settle within him. He felt armor plating dissolve and drop away from him, making him feel lighter than air. Hooking a finger under her chin, he tilted her face up to his and kissed her slowly and sweetly on the lips. "As soon as this war is over," he said with a smile, "I'm going to take you to a baseball game."

"It's a date," she said, and she lifted herself up on her toes, curled her arms around his neck, and kissed him back, harder and with more passion.

As he pulled her tightly to him and felt excitement and joy surge through his blood and bones, Adam knew that before Queenie left for Kansas he was going to ask her to marry him. And she was going to say yes.

*   *   *

CLARA HAD READ THE LETTER a hundred times; she knew it by heart. But she still liked to actually *read* it, look at Helmut's handwriting, picture the pencil moving across the paper, imagining him pausing to think of the next thing to say. His letters were always upbeat. She could hardly think that war was as pleasant as this. He was doing it for his family's sake, she knew. But this letter, his latest, contained a surprising confession.

"Dear Mom, New Zealand is a beautiful place. Hard to believe there is fighting going on in the world. This R&R camp is good for us. The nurses are pretty and kind. We get plenty of sun. I can see snowcapped mountains from here. As you know, I'm not allowed to tell you exactly where my platoon is, where we've been fighting, where we'll be sent next. But my buddies and I are doing well and in high spirits. Local ladies come by with baked goods and we get lamb for dinner. Sheep are big business in this country. I might like to come back and run a sheep station. That's what they call it. Not a farm or a ranch like at home. A station.

"My buddies and I have become a tight brotherhood, we have each other's backs. It brings home all too sharply how unfortunate it is that Bill, Adam, and I—*cousins*—can't be friends, especially in this trying time. But then, our own two fathers, who are brothers, haven't spoken in years, and still are not speaking, thirty years after arriving in America! I promise I will raise my children differently. I am going to teach them the value of family, of loving one's relations and spending holidays and celebrations with them. This is what war and combat have taught me. Maybe I could even be the one to mend the rift between the Schallers and the Newmans when this war is over. Combined together, we would be the most powerful family in the valley. I wouldn't do it for the power, though: it's all about being part of a big family.

"Thinking about Adam has had me thinking about that essay contest I won when I was twelve. I still feel guilty over winning, because I didn't really earn it. I only turned a paper in because I had already signed up as a contestant and it would have been an embarrassment to the family if I withdrew. Adam boasted about having written pages and pages and that he was certain to win, and when I was unable to come up with anything that could compete with that, I thought of my friends with foreign first names that were Americanized, and I dashed off one angry sentence: Being American means your family came from someplace else. It wasn't clever or bold as the judges said, just the sulky ranting of a boy who felt very ill-done to. For days after submitting the paper, while the judging was going on, I was certain I was going to be punished for turning in something rebellious and disobedient, as if I were thumbing my nose at them. I expected the school officials to show up at our front door with frowns and paddles and harsh words for you and Dad. I had *not* expected a trophy and lunch with the governor of California!"

With tears in her eyes, Clara folded the letter back into its envelope and thought: I carried you in my womb for nine months. I gave birth to you. I nursed you at my breast. I have loved you with all my heart, and I love you now more than words can express.

Sean O'Brien and his vicious attack on her twenty-six years ago was like a distant dream, as if it had never really happened. She prayed to God to keep her son safe and bring him back alive and well when the fighting was over.

Clara then thanked God for allowing her to keep one son at home. She got up from the kitchen table and went to the window to look out at the yard, where her youngest son was helping unload a pickup truck of empty wine barrels. Being stationed at nearby Camp Cooke allowed Bill Junior to come home occasionally and spend time with the family. She just wished she could make him happy. Clara knew that Bill Junior was unhappy with his new wife, Fay. Did he suspect she had tricked him into marrying her? Clara hoped not, as that would only increase his unhappiness and turn the marriage into a miserable mess. What saddened Clara was that Fay had somehow gotten Bill to lie to his parents about needing a hasty marriage because of deployment orders that somehow later got changed. She feared that this might only be the beginning of the girl's manipulation, control, and possible corruption of their son. Bill had brought a viper into their home.

As it was, Clara was having a hard time adjusting to having Fay in the house, not as a guest but as a family member, a daughter-in-law who seemed allergic to household chores and who kept up her habit of compliments that were really insults. "These sausages are wonderful, Mother Clara. I never thought I would enjoy something that contained too much salt."

Clara thought of Johann and his son's marriage to a cheerful girl from Kansas. Two weddings, one in each of their families—Adam's, she suspected was a union of love; her son's was not.

She looked at the letter in her hand. It had arrived back in October. Now it was December and there had been no letters since. Had he been shipped off to some place where sending letters was impossible?

She got worried every time they went to the movies in town and watched newsreels of the fighting in both Europe and the Pacific. It was hard to believe the world was in such a terrible state. The Largo Valley was so serene and enjoying its seasonal cycles as always. Now, the winter wheat and rye had been planted. Schaller grapes were fermenting and aging. And more orders were coming in for their Chardonnays, Cabernets, and Rieslings as, once again, no wine was being exported from Europe.

She started to turn away from the window—she had a braised brisket slow-cooking in the oven—when she saw a car in the drive. Clara went to the back door and stepped out. It was Jim Pope, the postmaster of Lynn-ville. What on earth was he doing here? Jim never delivered mail himself. That was the job of his staff of letter carriers—mostly women and old men these days. His face was solemn as he walked up the path with a single letter in his hand. Clara suddenly backed away from him. She knew of only one reason why the postmaster would deliver something in person. "No, please no," she begged.

Woodenly she tore open the envelope from the War Department. "We regret to inform you. . . ."

The day went dark, her knees gave way, and Clara went down.

*   *   *

THE NOTICE FROM THE War Department informed the Schaller family that on November 23, 1943, Helmut, in the Army's 27th Infan-try Division, had been killed in action on Tarawa Atoll, Gilbert Islands. And he was buried there.

Clara slipped into a deep depression, barely stirring from her bed. Fay helped a bit, but grudgingly. Fay had never met her brother-in-law, was unmoved by his death. Mostly it was their Mexican housekeeper, Maria, who took care of Clara, changing the pillows because Clara cried so much. Clara dreamed and hallucinated and drifted outside her body. *He was only twenty-five years old.* This became her mantra. She fixated on Helmut's age. *What did he do to deserve a premature death?* Her precious boy, the fruit of a racial hatred. *He was conceived because of war, he died because of war.*

People came to visit. Flowers and fruit baskets arrived. Ladies of the kaffeeklatsch took turns coming to the house to bring roasts and hams, cooked sausages and potato salad, loaves of bread, cakes—enough food to feed the family for months. Frieda Eberhardt sat with her for hours on end. Bill Junior, when he came home on leave, sat at her side and held her hand, himself bereft over the loss of his brother. Lorelei was there too, more pale-faced and distant than ever, the child who had found a family because of death. Rains came and went. The vineyards were being pruned, now that the harvest and crush were over, and being prepared for the spring blooming. All of this going on while Clara ebbed in and out of a twilight world of grief and deep sadness.

When she began to come out of it, she saw a gray February sky outside her window. Christmas was a distant memory. Had they even celebrated it? She couldn't recall. The past eight weeks, since receiving the notice, had gone by like a rolling fog. Clara knew she had to pull herself out of it. When she finally left her bed, she discovered that her whole family had been devastated by the loss of Helmut. Lorelei, Bill Junior. His father most of all.

Wilhelm had withdrawn into himself. He came and went, slept in their bed but never touched her, ate silent meals as if he were a lodger. Since Clara firmly believed that the family's happiness was the wife's responsibility, she pulled herself together. She needed to fix her family, bring Wilhelm back from the desolate place he had emotionally exiled himself to, and work on fixing things with her selfish daughter-in-law, try to make friends with her, bring some comfort to her remaining son, Bill Junior.

She started with a few small tasks, tidying up and organizing the things that always need organizing at year's end and which had gone neglected. She helped Maria put the clean laundry away, and in one of Wilhelm's drawers she came across scraps of paper tucked between two folded undershirts.

Lifting them out, she saw that it was a letter, dated in December, and it had been torn into quarters. She pieced them together and read it. To her shock, it was a letter of deep condolences from Johann, saying how sorry he was to have heard about Helmut. The letter went on to ask that Wilhelm and he patch things up between them, that they be brothers again.

It shocked her into cold sobriety. Johann, offering the olive branch! But Wilhelm had torn it up. He most likely had not replied. All this time, Johann would have been waiting and growing increasingly disappointed and saddened with each passing day of silence from Wilhelm.

She pocketed the scraps with firm resolve. The family needed to be fixed. There were too many broken parts to it—Wilhelm and Johann still enemies, Helmut gone, the ungracious Fay making her husband and everyone around her miserable. It was time to start mending things.

Clara telephoned him. "We need to meet. I have something to show you."

It was a crisp blue and green day with a gentle sun in the cloudless February sky. The winter rains mercifully held off their annual assault from the Pacific Ocean. Johann had suggested they meet at the Spanish ruins on his property. She had been there before and found Johann already waiting for her.

The roofless adobe ruins were covered in vines and brambles, with a flooring of thick bed-like grass. Crumbled arches cast romantic shadows here and there, reminders of days both gentle and harsh. The arches spanned centuries as well as doorways. Johann and Clara were back in Old Spain; the modern age, with its death and disappointments, lay far in the future.

She slipped easily into his arms. They embraced. "I was so sorry about Helmut," he said.

Taking Johann's hand, Clara strolled around the ruins that consisted of several tumbledown buildings and bare foundations, parts of tile fountains, now claimed by climbing vines and tall wildflowers, and abandoned birds' nests. They walked for a bit in silence, just thankful to be in each other's presence again after an absence of two months. Johann marveled at how sharply he had missed her. When he'd heard the news about Helmut, back in December, he had wanted to drive over to Clara's house and take her into his arms. Instead, he had written a letter. He wondered if she had even received it. Or would Wilhelm have discarded it? His heart went out to his brother. Johann didn't know what he would do if he lost Adam.

They paused beside a twisted and gnarly old oak, its branches rattling in the cool February wind. Clara fixed her gaze into the distance and said, "My son is buried on a Micronesian atoll that I can't even find on a globe." She turned to face Johann. "He was never meant to be, you know. I think this was God calling him back."

"What are you talking about?"

"Helmut was a mistake. He wasn't Wilhelm's son."

He listened in shocked silence about a rape that had taken place twenty-six years ago. She had kept it a secret all this time. For Helmut's sake, he knew. But now the boy was gone, so Clara could unburden herself.

"My poor darling," he said, laying a hand on her cheek.

"I came to show you something," she said, reaching into her coat pocket. "I debated telling you about it. I didn't know how you would take it."

Johann took the scraps and stared at them. "When I never heard back, I guessed something like this had happened. I couldn't really expect him to want to make a truce, not on the heels of his son's death. But I somehow thought that losing Helmut might make Wilhelm see the need for families to come together and let bygones be bygones."

"But he kept the letter, Johann. He didn't throw it out. That must mean something, right? There has to be hope."

He wordlessly handed the scraps back to her.

She gave a long moment's thought to what she was going to say next. Clara sensed that this was an important, pivotal moment in their lives, one that might never come their way again. "Why did you leave us, Johann? That night, why did you walk out on us? You never even said good-bye." It was important to know in this minute, although she wasn't sure why. It had to do with departure and loss, and losing someone without saying good-bye. Helmut last November, and Johann thirty years ago—they were tied together somehow. She couldn't make sense of her son's death, so she needed to make sense of why Johann had left them. The words tumbled from her lips. "Wilhelm said that he had pleaded with you to stay. He said he told you that you were still brothers. But you called yourself a bastard and said that you could never forgive your father for the lie—that you were the result of his affair with his wife's sister. Wilhelm said that you told him he was the real son, that Wilhelm was the legitimate Schaller. That Wilhelm had inherited the land, not you. Wilhelm said you called yourself the bastard son of a whore and that you did not belong with us any more."

Johann groaned and turned away, running his hands through his longish blond hair. A man who was soon to turn fifty-four, he still had no gray in his hair. He turned to Clara and said, "I had a feeling Wilhelm never told you the truth."

"The truth?"

Because she had revealed her own shameful secret, he was now free to reveal his. And it was her right to know the truth. "Clara, Wilhelm and I haven't been silent all these years just because of an argument. And I . . . I never said those words. I didn't call myself a bastard."

He stopped, and she could see how he wrestled with his thoughts. It was going to be something awful about Wilhelm, she just knew it, perhaps she had always known it, and now he was debating telling her a devastating truth about the man she was married to. "Tell me," she whispered. "*Please.*"

Beneath the blue sky, amid romantic old ruins, Johann told her the story of a terrible night in which a jealous brother so brutally beat his brother that he almost killed him, how Johann had managed to find his way to Ballerini property, where laborers found him and brought him to the house and how Feliciana had nursed him back to health. He spoke with little emotion, as if he were describing something he had read in a book. But Clara knew Johann's eyes, could translate every nuance in those blue irises, the flaring pupils, the hooded lids and slight pouching of the lower lid that always gave him an amused look. He was in pain. And then she was in pain and she had to reach for him. For years, they had both sensed that each was carrying an unbearable secret; and now both secrets were out, and they could share the burdens.

"I am so sorry," she murmured, touching his face, his hair, his lips.

When he impulsively pulled her into his arms, her mind exploded with images and memories: bicycling through the woods along the Rhine and Johann bursting into song: "*Du, du, liegst mir im Sinn. Du, du, machst mir viel Schmerzen, weißt nicht wie gut ich dir bin.*" Finding a clearing, spreading a blanket, Clara and the two Schaller brothers, a bottle of wine with Johann making jokes. A splendid, perfect day in which Clara, nineteen and starry-eyed, had fallen in love with both brothers, but in different ways.

Another beautiful memory as he gripped her arms now and looked down at her with a rare intensity, a memory of twelve young immigrants arriving at the crest of a hill to look down on a verdant valley that was their new home. She had still been weak from influenza and had to be carried from the car. But it was her brother-in-law, not her husband, who had brought her up the hill in his strong arms.

And then another memory, as Johann now bent his face dangerously close to hers, a darker, more painful memory: Clara on the kitchen porch lighting the evening lanterns, Johann in the yard, watching her, the pain and grief of losing Papa Jakob still knife-fresh in their hearts— and the terrible confession that had been groaned out in a delirium. "I love Johann more because I loved his mother more." Johann had walked across the yard to take Clara's hands, to kiss her palms, and to tell her that he loved her. "Don't say it," Clara had whispered. "We can never say it."

But they were saying it now, with their lips, with a kiss that was a long time coming, and then with words as they threw their arms around each other, declaring love, love, love. But they were out in the open, with the eyes of the world on them. Passion and desperation and urgency drove them to seek the shelter of the ruins where Spanish guitars had once thrummed and ruby-red wine had filled golden goblets. There could be no more waiting. There were no rules here, no laws being broken or vows violated. It was the necessary coming together of people in pain and in love.

Clara said, "You make me want to live forever."

He touched her and she felt his love flow from his fingertips and into her bloodstream. There are moments, she realized, which mark your life. Moments when you realize nothing will ever be the same. And time is divided into two parts: before This, and after This.

They spread their coats on the cold grass, but they themselves weren't cold. Even with the winter wind whistling through old arches and around crumbling pillars, they felt only each other's heat as clothing came off and limbs entwined and kisses bruised lips. Clara looked up at the California sky and knew that this was right. This moment with Johann was the most right thing in a very wrong world.

As she lay in his arms afterward, feeling his gentle hand on her hair, Clara made a silent, sacred vow to herself and to Johann—that someday the pain and bitterness of the past was going to be erased and families and brothers would be back together again. If it took her until her dying day, Clara Schaller was going to make the family whole again.

The Present Day

"HAVE YOU EVER HAD sex on top of a washing machine when it's in the spin cycle?" Michelle asked.

"No, but I've done it hanging from a clothesline," Nicole quipped.

They laughed. They were sitting at a little table in the hot kitchen where Joe, Michelle's husband, oversaw the operation of cooking and baking. Michelle was taking a break from the busy trade in the store.

It was noon, and Eberhardt's bakery was hopping. Customers stood two deep at the counter, holding tickets and waiting for their numbers to be called, while all the little tables were filled with lunchers—locals and tourists—and serving girls in Bavarian costumes dodged in and out with trays over their heads, carrying thick pastrami sandwiches and frosty mugs of German beer. Eberhardt's always expanded its menu during tourist season, especially with Oktoberfest coming up and hotels and bed-and-breakfasts all booked in advance.

Michelle was trying to distract her best friend. She knew that Nicole was worried about the pending ballistics report. Handing her father's gun over to the police had thrown Nicole into an emotional turmoil. She felt she was betraying him. A Judas, she had said, turning him in. Suddenly, Nicole was feeling very protective of Big Jack and praying that he wasn't connected to the murder. She was remembering good things about her father now, memories she had suppressed through her anger when he wouldn't let her go to college and follow her own course of study, slamming a fist on his big mahogany desk and insisting that she stay at the farm and oversee the vineyards and run the winery. He had shouted words at her—legacy, loyalty, family. And the more he commanded her to stay, the more she had to get away.

She had won in the end, driving to Santa Barbara, moving in with other students, getting a job as a waitress to pay her own way, earning scholarships so she could be independent of Big Jack's money, graduating with honors and then getting her Master's in business.

Things had been good between them for a while, Jack Schaller so proud of his daughter, bragging how he had encouraged her to go to school and get a business degree. And then she had started dating Danny, the young lawyer from old money, and Big Jack had tried pressuring her into marrying Danny and settling down and running the winery and giving him grandchildren. And then last year—she couldn't recall what the argument had been about—Big Jack's speech had suddenly gone slurry and Nicole had thought he was drunk, and then he stumbled and fell and stopped breathing; and by the time the paramedics got there, he was gone. A stroke, the autopsy revealed. And she had cried bitterly at the funeral, blaming herself, wishing her last words to him hadn't been "I'm sick of you trying to run my life!"

And now she had given the police his gun and was implicating him in a murder and she felt like the worst daughter that had ever walked the planet. Shakespeare haunted her with talk of serpents' teeth and thankless children.

On top of that, she was selling his vineyard and winery. Nicole had gone to the Realtor that morning to sign the papers. The Macintoshes had already qualified for a loan and had come up with a down payment. The sale of the property was now going into escrow.

"You don't seem relieved or excited," Michelle said, stirring coffee that was going cold. It was her sixth cup that morning.

"Oh, I am," Nicole said unconvincingly. She had expected to be very excited about the closing of the sale, but something had intruded into her happiness. It had started the day she and Lucas had driven out to Colina Sagrada, when a startling realization had come to her: that, for some unfathomable reason, she envied Lucas Newman. And there had been something else, too, at the edge of her mind, scratching at the door, wanting to come in. But she was afraid to let it in, afraid of something new intruding into her well-planned life.

"I'm just worried about my father's gun. What if—" Last night, she and Lucas had turned the Beretta in to the police and were now awaiting the results of the ballistics test. Detective Quinn had said he would call as soon as they had a report. It was driving Nicole crazy. She hadn't slept all night.

"It isn't stopping the Canadians from going through with the deal," Michelle observed.

"I think the idea that a murder took place there appeals to Mrs. Macintosh. I just wish Quinn would call. How long does a bullet test take, anyway? They shoot the weapon into a tank of water and then compare the two bullets under a microscope, right?"

Michelle tapped a long, perfectly manicured finger on the table, searching for a way to bring Nicole out of her anxiety. "What's that?" she said, pointing to Nicole's shoulder bag, slouching on a chair. "More great-grandma letters?"

"I stopped by Mr. Gilette's office on the way here. He found ten more."

"Aren't you dying to read them?" Michelle asked, eyes flashing.

"I can see *you're* dying to read them," Nicole said with a laugh as she drew one out and used a butter knife to slit it open.

"What was in the ones you got yesterday?"

"A lot of family and newsy stuff. The Depression, World War One. Clara talks a lot about Joe's great-grandmother Frieda, and about other immigrant women who met every Sunday for coffee and cake."

"Are you learning anything interesting?"

"I'm learning that if you know nothing about your family, if no one speaks of them or tells you anything, then how can you love them and honor them and be proud of them? If you know nothing of their hardships and sacrifices, their successes and trails blazed, how can you feel anything for them? They are just names scrawled on the backs of the impersonal photographs of strangers. But Clara's letters have colored in those impersonal photographs, breathing life into them."

Their table was set next to a wall covered in pictures, mementos, greeting cards, thank-you notes from patrons. Nicole looked at a photograph in a metal frame, black and white, taken many years ago. Great-Grandmother Clara standing with Frieda Eberhardt under a banner that read: DEDICATED TO THOSE WHO SERVE. Best friends Clara and Frieda, in their late forties or early fifties, Nicole judged, were standing with a large group of young men in uniform and lots of pretty girls, all smiling for the camera. One of the dances held for soldiers on leave. Nicole was able to pick out Wilhelm Junior, who had called himself Bill. She remembered Big Jack telling her that during World War II, his father had been stationed at Vandenburg Air Force Base, back when it had been called Camp Cooke.

Before now, it had just been a picture of strangers. But now, after reading a letter about those years and those dances, the picture had been brought to life.

But the letters weren't in chronological order, and Clara herself skipped around in time. Nicole would read about the twelve immigrants standing on a hilltop, looking down into the promising new valley, and in the next about Clara finding Lorelei. Feliciana found dead from self-inflicted stab wounds. Reports of people getting married, babies being born, people being buried. She wondered, Would Clara speak of an unsolved disappearance or murder? Would the next paragraph, the next page, the next letter reveal who had killed whom and hidden her body in a wall?

"Hey," Michelle said, "would it be okay if Joe read the letters that mention the Eberhardts? He would get a hoot out of it, and I know his dad would love reading about his grandparents."

"Sure," Nicole said as she set aside the butter knife and slipped the yellowed stationery out of the envelope. "In fact, the whole town of Lynnville would be interested, as nearly every family is mentioned in them. But there are too many intimate family details for me to share the letters with the whole world. I could let Joe read some that are about his great-grandparents."

She started to read silently: "We met at the Spanish ruins on the old Ballerini property. . . ."

Reading the next few lines, Nicole said, suddenly, "Oh, my God."

Quickly folding the letter back into its envelope and slipping it into her bag, she said, "Sorry, Michelle, I have to go. I have to see Lucas Newman."

Michelle smiled coyly. "Gosh, isn't it just *horrible* how you two are being thrown together?"

Nicole stood up. "Now stop that. All I'm interested in is finalizing the sale of my property and getting my ass to New York. And wipe that smirk off your face."

Michelle stood up, and Nicole gave her a hug. "Thanks for distracting me," she said.

As her friend hurried out, Michelle called after her: "Let me know when you hear the ballistics report. Keeping fingers crossed for you, sweetie."

Nicole called Lucas on her cell. "Sure," he said. "Where do you want to meet?"

She thought, then asked: "Are you familiar with some old Spanish ruins on your property?"

With great irritation, she turned the key in the ignition. She really did not want to do this. She had *plans,* and everything was falling into place so nicely. She was soon to start a new life someplace else and sever ties with this valley and with legends and feuds. And now all of a sudden, destiny was throwing her and Lucas together against their collective will. She had heard his tone over the phone. He didn't want this meeting any more than she did. But it had to be done.

*   *   *

LUCAS NEWMAN *SO* DID not want to see Nicole Schaller again.

He had too much on his mind, too much work to do. The only reason he had agreed to meet with her and take a look at the latest letters was the hope that Clara had said something in them that would shed light on the mystery of the skeleton found in the wall, solve the murder, and send the police packing so he could go back to focusing solely on his experimental grape rootstocks.

On top of that, he was worried about his father. Lucas had thought that news of the skeleton being female would be a relief to the old man, who was still resting from a very mild cardiac event. The homicide victim wasn't cousin Jason after all, and Melvyn didn't have to telephone his sister Sofie with unspeakable news. To Lucas's surprise, the old man's agitation had increased and he had needed to be sedated.

And that was putting a wrench in his plans to visit Arizona, where an ideal patch of desert awaited him and his team of researchers. How could he leave his father when his health was so perilous?

He returned his attention to the client who had recently bought a case of Chateau Blanc 1949 at an estate auction but had grown suspicious of its authenticity and had brought a bottle for Lucas Newman's expert appraisal.

*   *   *

NICOLE ENTERED THE WINE-tasting room where Lucas had asked her to meet him. The décor was very upscale, with subdued lighting, cream-colored walls, and blond wood furniture. A *youthful* ambience, she thought, quite unlike Schaller's wine-tasting room that hadn't been upgraded in years but still had dark wood walls and a slate tile floor and old-fashioned atmosphere. Stodgy, she realized now for the first time, wondering how the Canadian couple were going to refurbish and redecorate it. Something to compete with this trendy tasting room.

In the waiting area, where the hostess's podium and reservation book stood, Nicole saw photographs on the walls, dating way back, a chronicle of the Newman family. At eye level, she saw a color picture of a man and woman grinning happily for the camera. The setting looked Hawaiian. She wore a white muumuu, and he wore white slacks and an aloha shirt. Both wore hibiscus leis. Nicole recognized the man as a much younger Melvyn Newman, Lucas's father. He looked around forty years old in the picture, and his bride was even younger. Nicole knew that Melvyn had been a confirmed bachelor until a holiday in Hawaii had thrown him into the corona of a beautiful tourist who was nineteen years his junior. The courtship had been quick, according to valley gossip, and the result was Lucas Newman. But the May–December marriage had not been a successful one. Karen had stayed only for Lucas, and when he was twenty she had divorced Melvyn. It was said that Melvyn had paid a generous settlement to Karen, who went back to Hawaii to live and was there to this day.

Nicole looked around and saw Lucas at the bar, chatting with a customer. And again Nicole was seeing another side to the Newman heir. Dressed in black pleated slacks, a nicely tailored white long-sleeved shirt, no tie, with the collar casually unbuttoned. Formal, yet relaxed. He kept surprising her in his different guises of hands-on farmer, lab-coated scientist, and trendy, upscale vintner.

He was saying, to a man at the bar, "Do you taste the vanilla? A hint of persimmon? But also a little sucking in of your cheeks . . . an overbalance of tannin in the structure?"

"Yes, I do," the man said. "But, Mr. Newman, that's a two-thousand-dollar bottle of Chateau Blanc, 1949."

Lucas held the wine glass up to the light. "It's not bad, I'll give you that. And it might even be a genuine Chateau Blanc, but it's recent. Definitely not 1949. Probably an eighty-dollar bottle, I would say."

The man looked aghast. "Are you saying my wine could be *fake*?"

"It's easily done, Mr. Keen. You see, the label is legitimate. I can definitely authenticate that for you. The con men get the empty bottles from restaurants or collectors, fill them with cheaper wine, and replace the corks. I'm afraid you got swindled."

"The entire case—*counterfeit*?"

"Counterfeit wine is big business. You have to be very careful who you buy from. I'm sorry, Mr. Keen. You can certainly have someone else analyze your collection. But in my expert opinion, the wine in this bottle does not match the label."

Thanking Lucas and grumbling at the same time, the customer left, leaving his fake Chateau Blanc on the bar.

Lucas looked across the room, and immediately a scowl attached itself to his face.

"I apologize for the interruption," Nicole said as he approached.

"Sorry, I wasn't scowling at you," he said. "I just have a few pressing things on my mind. My father—" he began, then stopped. "You wanted to see the ruins?"

"Is he all right, your father?"

"He'll be fine."

"If you could just give me directions, I can find the ruins myself."

"No, no, I'm happy to take you. Clear my head, maybe. What's so special about the ruins?"

"A very important event in my great-grandmother's life took place there. I'd just like to visit, see what the place is like. I might add that it was a very important event in your great-grandfather's life as well."

"Johann Newman?"

"He confessed something monumental to Clara in those ruins. Something that explains a lot about our two families. But I can just leave the letter with you and you can read it when you have time. Just tell me how to get there."

"It's easier if I just take you there. The ruins are out of the way, and no one goes there. You might miss them altogether."

When they arrived a short while later—and yes, Nicole would never have found the place, it was so remote and overgrown with brush and trees—she gave Lucas the letter and stepped out of the Jeep to give him privacy.

She walked around the ruins, took in the arches and columns, the broken fountains, traces here and there of paved patios, and wondered about those brave Spaniards of long ago who had left their comfortable and familiar homes to make long and perilous journeys to tame an unknown wilderness. They had brought grapes with them—like little babies, Nicole thought tenderly: fragile vines and cuttings—and cleared the new land and planted them. And it wasn't just here. They'd conquered Mexico and South America, spreading their vines and culture and language as they went.

Sitting on a broken wall, she pulled out the next letter, opened it, and read it. She groaned. Another one to share with Lucas. It was about his father as a child. Clara had written: "Melvyn was a precocious little boy. All three of Adam and Queenie's children excelled in school. They had inherited their grandfather Johann's intelligence and their mother Queenie's effervescent personality."

Nicole paused. She felt a gentle but curious pull within her. Clara's words, drawing her back in time, and into a whole new drama with new players on the stage.

She squinted out over the fields and creeks and trees and crops, and she saw how the distant mountains devolved into hills, which in turn gently became foothills that snuggled against meadows and forests and crept down to the banks of running streams—which flowed through grass and flowers and rows of vines to come down to land, where the water seeped under the ground and fed the thirsty vines and softened the grass beneath Nicole's shoes. She looked out at those distant mountains and suddenly felt a direct connection to them.

When had she become alienated from this valley? When had she allowed herself to become separate from it? Had it started with her father's insistence on directing her life, and her natural resistance becoming rebellion? *You will not run my life; therefore, I will run from it.* But this valley was innocent. It had nothing to do with the love/hate battle between Big Jack and his headstrong daughter. The valley, loving and nurturing, like a benevolent and patient grandmother, could only watch and mourn the loss of a respectful granddaughter. It wasn't the valley's fault. After all, Nicole thought in the wonder of sudden revelation, I am part of it. I grew out of this soil, I was fed on this valley's wheat and water, and I grew on the air that blows from the mountains. How can I leave her? How ungrateful can I be?

And yet I must leave. How else am I to know where my family ends and I begin?

Nicole looked at Lucas in the Jeep, reading Clara's letter, and she wondered if the same strange spell was being cast on him. How curious that the mention of Adam's and Queenie's children should trigger such a rush of memory and emotion. This mention of people she had never met, had known nothing about, had for some reason reminded her of how important this valley had always been to her.

Mornings, she would wake up early before the sun had warmed the grapevines and a hush lay over the fields and hills—so early, it made a person whisper. She would go for an early-morning walk and feel the earth full of raw power. Nicole had always respected the land. It was autonomous. This valley didn't need people. If no man ever set foot here, nature would go about its business of growth, death, and regrowth. Nature already knew what to do. Trees grew, vines flourished, flowers blossomed, animals mated. She loved it when, in summer especially, the sun did not just rise in this valley, it positively *overflowed*. A paling darkness one minute, and in the next the valley was like a vast bowl of golden sunlight you could swim in. It made a person wake up believing in life, love, and the future.

How had she forgotten this?

She watched Lucas finally get out of the Jeep, the letter in his hand. She saw a surprising stoop to his shoulders, a slowness in his gait. He was taking it hard, what he had read in the letter. As he came near, she saw that his face was tight with emotion. "So you see? When you thought Wilhelm and Johann were cousins, you weren't really that far off the mark. They turned out to be half-brothers, so I don't think your family lied to you. There was just a confusion."

When he didn't speak, Nicole thought, "No, he isn't upset: he's *angry*." But at what? At whom?

"It's a hell of a thing to take in and digest," he said as he sat on the low wall next to her. "One brother brutalizing another like that. So it wasn't simply a quarrel."

Anger in his voice, but why? Perhaps he felt Melvyn should have told him the truth. Perhaps he hated Wilhelm Schaller all the more now for his violent act. Nicole wished he would voice his emotions, but she wouldn't push him. He could even be angry at *her*, for being the descendant of the brutal Wilhelm.

But Nicole did know one thing. That, as she and Lucas sat in silence amid Spanish ruins, they were both thinking over what they had just read, the description of a brutal beating of one brother by another, a fight over property and a woman, what Wilhelm had done to Johann. She knew he shared her shock, thinking of the two young men, trying to grasp their deep pain, the agony of both, and Johann's brutal physical punishment for being the result of an immoral relationship, a punishment meted out by a brother racked by the pain of disillusionment about a father he had worshipped.

And then Nicole's thoughts shifted from Lucas and the two brothers and back to Clara who, when she realized the rift wasn't voluntary—that Johann had been kicked off the Schaller farm and warned never to return—had vowed to make it her life's work to reunite the two families. But Clara had died before she could carry out her vow.

Nicole said now, quietly, "She mentions revealing a secret of her own to Johann, involving her son Helmut. But she doesn't say what it was."

Lucas's shoulders rose and fell with a ragged sigh. "It was *his* secret, and he was killed in action. I suppose Clara honored his privacy. God, the burdens our forebears carried." He glanced at Nicole's shoulder bag with yellowed envelopes peeking out, and he thought of the burdens contained in them, and that Nicole now carried them. The secrets and woes and agonies and dreams and joys of two infamous families. It was a wonder that she was able to carry the shoulder bag at all.

"All these years," she said, "no one knew the truth. And now we do. You'll want to read this," she said, handing him the second letter, wondering what was happening between them, sensing an inevitable bonding that she neither invited nor wanted and which she suspected Lucas, too, did not welcome. But forces beyond themselves were weaving them together. She had the strongest feeling that she and Lucas were being guided toward a joint goal. But she had no idea what it could be, or the reason for it. Nicole was leaving the valley for a career in New York. Lucas had his own driving ambitions. Why should they be forced along a joint path that could not possibly go anywhere?

He didn't want to read another letter, and yet when she held it up to him he took it and couldn't keep his eyes off the page. An important doorway had been opened. He had to step through.

"My father talked about his childhood a lot," Lucas said quietly as he read the letter. "What a scrapper he was, always getting into trouble. He and his brother Gordon stole chickens, let horses out of corrals, found themselves in all sorts of mischief. And yet here is your great-grandmother, their supposed enemy, saying nothing but nice things about them." There was a tone of wonder in his voice.

While he continued reading the second letter, Nicole opened the third.

Clara spoke now of weddings. Queenie and Adam Newman. Her youngest son Bill Junior and Fay Reed. Names familiar to Nicole: Eberhardt, Gilette, Mueller. Nicole felt herself drawn into family dramas, becoming more familiarized with the past. She knew that when she handed the letter to Lucas to read, he would feel the same thing, and she imagined invisible filaments, like fingers of ground fog, unfurling from each letter and swirling in the air to draw Nicole and Lucas into an invisible net of emotions and revelations and questions and surprises. Luring them into the past, bringing them together.

But the sun was climbing and the September day was growing hot. When Lucas suggested they move to the shade of the ruins, Nicole readily agreed. They settled down on the dry grass and leaned their backs against the two-hundred-year-old adobe-and-stone walls and delivered themselves back into the Schaller–Newman epic.

As she and Lucas read the letters, it occurred to Nicole that there might be mention in here about her father's mother, a woman Big Jack had never wanted to talk about. Nicole knew nothing about Fay Schaller, who had been married to Grandpa Bill. Maybe Clara spoke of her in these letters, maybe some light might suddenly be shed on Big Jack, explaining to Nicole why he had been the way he was. Suddenly, the letters offered more than the possibility of clues to a murder, clues as to why a family had split so harshly in half. Suddenly, Clara's letters became very personal to Nicole.

"I used to be superstitious," Clara had written. "I believed that warnings and messages were sent to us by the cosmos to govern our lives and to prepare us for bad things ahead. But there were no owls, no pictures slipping off wall hooks to warn me that my son was going to be killed in a war. So I became practical and level-headed and decided it was better to rely on common sense and experience than the whims of the cosmos."

Lucas had finished a page and Nicole handed him the one she had just read. She continued with the next. Clara had written: "Johann loved his daughter-in-law, Queenie. He bragged about how well his son had done in choosing a wife. I am happy for him."

"You know," Nicole said thoughtfully, "my great-grandmother talks an awful lot about Johann Newman in her letters. She mentions him way more than she does his brother, her own husband. Do you suppose. . . ."

Lucas looked at her. Their faces were inches apart. Their shoulders touched. Lucas's eyes widened at what Nicole was suggesting. "No. . . ," he said. "It couldn't be." And he suddenly felt uncomfortable at the thought.

"She seems to have a great deal of admiration for him. And people do tend to talk about the objects of their heart's desire a lot. Look here, on the first letter, as she was writing about the night of the brutal beating. . . ." Nicole unfolded the paper. "These look like water stains."

"Tears?"

"I think she was crying as she wrote about what had happened to Johann."

And then she thought how sad it would be if it were true about Clara and Johann, being secretly in love and having to sneak around and live in fear of getting caught. And how shocking a scandal it would have been— members of two rival families carrying on a secret romance.

She looked at Lucas for a moment, then she looked away. It chilled her. No, no. This could never happen again.

While she read about the christening of Hans and Frieda's first grandchild and the laying to rest of Hilde Decker the piano teacher, Nicole tried not to think about Clara and Johann. It would be too sad, too tragic.

Had they been lovers, Lucas's great-grandfather and Nicole's great-grandmother? And had these ruins been their secret meeting place? It was a profound thought, a staggering one, after years of feuding and rivalry, to think that a forbidden romance might have once, in a strange way, bound the families together.

His thoughts moving along a similar track, wondering at the strangeness of family secrets and the strange magic of being bound to someone else and not even knowing it, Lucas was suddenly very curious about Nicole, wanted to know more about her. He had been surprised when he heard she was leaving the valley. A lot of Lynnville girls left, thinking that life was more glamorous elsewhere. It took a certain breed to love farming country. But he had thought Nicole was different from the others, that grape-growing was as in her blood as it was in his. He wanted to know why she was leaving, but he didn't want to open doors.

And yet, hadn't *he* done just that when she visited him in the greenhouse, a very private and tight-lipped Lucas Newman suddenly baring his secret needs to her? Why had he done that, confessed his feelings of unfulfillment, told her about his desire to accomplish something that was entirely his own? Something about Nicole made him want to tell her things—just as, right now, something about her made him want to *ask* her things.

He couldn't stop thinking about the tiny black mole in the hollow of her throat—a "beauty mark." He wanted to touch it. Nothing aggressive. Just lay a fingertip on it, nothing more.

Nicole felt Lucas's eyes on her, searching, taking in her hair, her face, her throat. She felt his eyes linger particularly at her throat, and it was an intimate sensation, like a touchless caress. When he turned away, she looked at *him*, the curl of his blond hair on his shirt collar, the wonderful straightness of his nose, those sexy hooded eyes.

How could she have resented this man for so many years, felt such antipathy toward him, when she hadn't even known him? Nicole felt that their present was changing because their past was changing, and it alarmed her. How much more of her life were Clara's letters going to alter?

She tried to march her thoughts along a practical track: the ballistics report she was anxiously waiting for. The victim had been a young, pregnant female. Big Jack had been a notorious womanizer. Was this some Vegas showgirl who had presented herself on his doorstep to announce that she was carrying his baby? If the murder had happened twenty years ago, as was being speculated, then Nicole would have been seven at the time, her mother still alive. Big Jack would have had a lot at stake if his girlfriend exposed their secret affair.

"This is a lot to take in," Lucas murmured, his head bent over the letter. "To read about Grandpa Adam and Grandma Queenie getting married in the summer of 1943."

"I think that's when *my* grandparents got married. Grandpa Bill was in the Army, stationed at Vandenberg Air Force Base before there *was* an Air Force. He and Grandma Fay met at a dance. It must have been all very romantic, with the war on and everything."

"Where do you think the Baby Boom came from?" Lucas asked with a smile. "All those horny GIs returning home."

Their eyes met, and they sat so close. Nicole felt a warm, swimmy feeling in her abdomen, and she fought it back. No, she couldn't possibly fall for Lucas Newman.

"Must have been interesting times," she said, trying to dispel the suddenly romantic atmosphere that had crept into the moment. "Imagine what it had been like, those years." Just as she often wondered what it had been like to live during the sixties, the hippie years. She suddenly had a sense of having missed out. She herself had been part of no great movement or homecoming or nationwide celebration. There had been the September Eleventh attacks on the World Trade Center, and these had brought the nation together in shared grief and shock. But nothing like soldiers returning from a terrible war and young people dressing like Jesus to protest wars and racial inequality. College campuses were so peaceful these days, and you didn't see people dancing naked in waterfalls.

Passion was sexy, she thought. Not romantic passion, because that was something else. But to be passionate about a cause, an ideal, a dream, like Lucas and his determination to find a way to grow grapes in a deteriorating climate—now, that was very attractive.

Her cell phone saved her from her startling thoughts. As soon as Detective Quinn identified himself, Nicole shot to her feet. "Yes? You have news about the gun?"

While she listened, Lucas also rose to his feet, finding himself just as anxious for the report.

"Oh, thank you!" Nicole cried. "God bless you and thank you!" She ended the call and turned to Lucas.

"Well?" he said.

"Detective Quinn said the bullet isn't a match to my father's gun! Big Jack didn't do it! Isn't it wonderful?" And she threw her arms around Lucas's neck and kissed him very hard on the mouth.

PART FIVE
1953–1958

"I'M WORRIED ABOUT WILHELM," Clara said as she and Johann strolled alongside Largo Creek, where they were the only two people on Earth. "Every day he withdraws deeper into himself."

The air was filled with the delightful fragrance of the many flowering peony bushes along the roadsides, creeks, and rivers, and their blooms delighted the eye with dazzling whites, bright reds, and sizzling pinks.

"I don't know what to do. I've tried different ways to reach him. I try talking to him. He'll discuss wine and the crop and his granddaughter Deborah and politics, but when I try to draw his emotions out of him he throws up a wall of silence. He's brooding about Helmut; and while I once thought time would ease his grief, it seems to have only gotten worse."

Johann gave this some thought as he watched a dragonfly skim the creek water in a delightful flash of oranges and reds. Finally he said, "I don't think my brother is brooding about his son. I think he's brooding about *himself*."

Clara stopped and turned to look up at him, shading her eyes because the sun was behind him. "Himself!"

"Clara, I think that when you got the notice that Helmut had been killed in action, I think Wilhelm discovered an unpleasant truth about himself, and I think that as the years pass it festers in him and he finds it harder and harder to live with."

She squinted. "What truth?"

"That he favored one son over the other."

Her lips parted in surprise. Her eyes turned inward as she sorted through memories. Wilhelm with the boys as they were growing up, helping them with their homework, teaching them about grape-growing. *Did* he pay more attention to Helmut? *Had* he spent more time with him? In hindsight, perhaps. "Favoring one son. . . ." she murmured.

"Just as our father confessed to favoring me over Wilhelm."

Clara remembered that terrible, terrible night of forty years ago.

"The confession," Johann said, "that drove my brother to savagely beat me."

"And now he thinks he's found that trait in himself?" she asked in surprise.

"You have told me more than once that things haven't been the same since Helmut died. That sometimes feelings are strained between Wilhelm and Bill Junior."

"I just thought that all fathers and sons argue from time to time. Plus, Bill's wife, Fay, puts a strain on us. She's hard to take sometimes."

"I think my brother has now found in himself what he hated his own father for forty years ago. When Helmut died, Wilhelm most likely found himself thinking, Why Helmut? If I had to lose a son in the war, why couldn't it have been Bill? Parents aren't supposed to favor children, but I think we're all guilty of it."

Again, Clara searched within herself. *Had* she loved Lorelei more than her sons? How was a mother to know? Love came in different shades, in different intensities, and in different guises. Daughters were different from sons. And wasn't there a special tenderness for a poor little orphaned foundling?

Clara reached out and touched his arm, grateful for the insights into a husband who had become a stranger. Clara had spent many a sleepless night trying to figure out how to reach Wilhelm, how to heal him. It made sense now. Papa Jakob's deathbed confession had been so shocking and disillusioning for young Wilhelm that he had never, in all the years since, forgiven the old man for committing adultery with his wife's sister—and then to prefer the son of that immoral union over his legitimate son. And now he had found the same failing in himself.

The irony was, Wilhelm didn't even know that Helmut wasn't his, but the result of rape. The son that he had preferred over his real son.

Maybe if he could be reunited with his own brother again, Clara thought as she and Johann fell into step and began strolling again, digesting revelations and looking for solutions. Maybe if there could be forgiveness all around, Wilhelm could find a way out of his own personal darkness.

Was this perhaps the opportunity Clara had been waiting for? Ten years ago, she had vowed to find a way to bring the two families back together, but the time, the mood, the circumstances had never been right. But now, for Wilhelm's sake, it was time to *create* an opportunity rather than wait for one. What better way to heal her husband's soul than to bring him back into the fold of brotherly love?

Yes! she thought in sudden excitement. Forty years had passed since the night of the savage beating. It was time to lay the past to rest and for Wilhelm and Johann to be brothers again, and for cousins to acknowledge one another. Clara didn't want her granddaughter, Debbie, to miss out on family togetherness. She and Queenie's little Sofie should be playing together. Her granddaughter was an only child (and by the looks of it, was going to stay that way). Clara fondly remembered playing with her own cousins when she was little, back in Germany. All children should grow up with such good memories.

The question was, how? Johann was willing to take steps. Hadn't he written a letter to Wilhelm when he heard of Helmut's death, suggesting a reconciliation? The letter that Clara had found torn into pieces. Clara had kept it, but there had been no reunion of the brothers. But now she felt hope blossoming in her breast.

I turn sixty this year, she thought, yet I still feel like a girl of nineteen. Being in love keeps a person young. The happy and loving heart is a youthful heart. Johann certainly was youthful and didn't even look his age, sixty-three. There were lines and wrinkles on his face, for sure, but only from working beneath the California sun. He looked rugged rather than aged. There was barely any white or gray in his blond hair, and of course those marvelous hooded eyes would never be marred by age.

She still ached for him, yearned for his embrace, but they had only known the one time, ten years ago, one magical day in the Spanish ruins when he had comforted her and she had comforted him. She had a husband, and Johann was still her brother-in-law. Clara and Johann believed in abiding by laws and morality. But it didn't stop the love, never that. They continued to meet, as dear friends, and they embraced and held hands and touched each other's tears. The occasional kiss to refresh their special bond. But never more than that. Their words and their eyes said it all.

She had asked him once why he had never remarried, and he had said, quietly, "I think you know the answer to that, my darling Clara."

And now they were bound together by a new and special goal: to reunite their families. She didn't know how they were going to do it, but Clara was determined to find a way to bring them back together.

* * *

BE CAREFUL WHAT YOU wish for, Fay Schaller thought. Because it might come true.

She and Bill had the house to themselves now. When they first got married Fay had moved in with Bill's family, and it wasn't easy, living with German immigrants who still held to foreign ways. For Bill's sake, Fay had learned a bit of cooking, but once Father Wilhelm had built the new main house after the war, and he and Mother Clara moved into it, Fay and Bill had inherited the older house, the one his grandfather Jakob had built back in 1911. Fay had insisted on top-to-bottom refurbishing, modernizing, and decorating for the times. She was proud of her house and hoped *The Valley* magazine would send someone around to take pictures and interview her. She also saw to it that she had a cook now, and a housekeeper and maids, relieving herself of those duties. But when her daughter Deborah came along, Fay would not have a nanny. The baby was her responsibility alone, and she saw to the feeding, the diapers, the baths, the naptimes and playtimes all by herself. Even now that Deborah was of school age, Fay couldn't bear to leave the child with babysitters or even with the grandparents, Clara and Wilhelm. As a result, she and Bill rarely went out together. Her one concession was when the movie *High Noon* was screened at the theater in Lynnville and Bill insisted that they go. Fay had thought the movie tedious and kept looking at her watch and hoping that Mother Clara was keeping an eye on Deborah.

Fay had not known that motherhood could be so wonderful. Before Deborah was born, she had seen women with children hanging on their skirts, and she had felt sorry for them. But having a daughter was the most heavenly experience on earth! And now she began to understand a little more about her own mother, Ruth Reed, how doting she too had been, making sure little Fay had had enough to eat, warm clothing, shoes without holes in them, a roof over her head. All those menial jobs and long hours her mother had worked at had all been for her daughter. She wished Deborah could experience the closeness Fay had known with her mother. They hadn't had money, they hadn't had a big house with servants, but they'd had each other.

Mother and daughter, what a magical institution! Every Saturday, Fay drove little Deborah into Santa Barbara, where they went to the best shops and she bought perfect little dresses and shoes and even miniature handbags for her. And once every two weeks, Debbie was treated to an appointment at the best hair salon in Lynnville, sitting in the big grown-ups' chair to have her hair trimmed and shampooed and get fussed over by the hairdressers and other patrons. And once a week, Fay treated her six-year-old daughter to tea at either Eberhardt's or Mueller's Hotel, where they sat like proper ladies and Fay treated Debbie as if she were a true grown-up. There weren't enough toys in the world to fill Debbie's bedroom. There weren't enough books to read to her at night. And once a week, Fay met with Debbie's first-grade teacher and the school principal to make sure her daughter was getting the best attention and education.

Because Debbie received all of Fay's love and affection, a singular devotion that left room for no one else in Fay's life, Fay didn't want another child—certainly no boys, but not another daughter either, because Ruth Reed had had only the one girl and that would do fine for Fay—so she got some advice from somewhere and started secretly using a sponge soaked in an old herbal remedy against conception—a concoction of pennyroyal, salvia, and willow tea. She had used it ever since Deborah was born. And because it was undetectable by the husband, and because Bill was very predictable in his sex urges, Fay always knew when to insert the sponge beforehand.

Such were Fay's thoughts as she went fussily through the house straightening things, checking for dust, looking under furniture to make sure the maids had done a thorough job. She was wrestling with a difficult decision, and it made her antsy and restless. She desperately needed advice on an important issue, and she didn't know who to turn to. It involved the Lynnville Women's Service Club and gaining membership into its elite ranks.

Fay was active in the school's PTA. They couldn't keep her out: she had a child going to that school. And next year, when Deborah turned seven, Fay was going to sign her up for the local Girl Scouts Brownies chapter, and Fay intended to be very involved in that. But what she really wanted was to join the Lynnville Women's Service Club. She had been trying for membership for five years, but kept getting turned down.

The club had been formed shortly after the war by younger women who had done so much for the war effort and the Red Cross that they'd wanted to keep their good work going. So they chartered an organization and at first had held fundraisers for widows and orphans of servicemen who had died overseas. In the years since, they had taken on greater charitable causes, gotten themselves a bit of local fame, and were seen as an elite group in the valley. They didn't let just anyone join; they were very selective in their membership. The club was made up of the wealthiest socialite wives in the valley, wives of men who owned big establishments in town, large farms, and expensive property. They were an influential group who got things done, like getting the funds for the new children's wing in the Lynnville Hospital.

Last year, during the national election campaign, when presidential candidate General Eisenhower had come through Lynnville on a whistle-stop visit, where he had given a political speech from the rear platform of his train, Eisenhower had been hosted at a lunch at the Grower's Club while his wife, Mamie, had been the guest of honor at a luncheon put on by the Lynnville Women's Service Club at Mueller's Hotel, in their very fine banquet room. All members had attended, of course, and even a few non-members had been invited to meet the woman who they hoped would be the next First Lady of the United States. Fay Schaller had not been invited, and she still smarted from that. Especially as Eisenhower had won the election and Mamie now lived in the White House.

She knew it was Queenie Newman who was keeping her out, as Queenie was the club's president. Fay hated Queenie because she was popular. Always leading charity drives for polio, the humane society, and so forth, with her name and picture always in the paper. The pricy, glossy magazine *The Valley* had done a five-page photo spread on her and her home.

It wasn't fair. Fay was just as rich, had married into an important and wealthy family. So why couldn't she get in with the right people? She wondered why her mother-in-law didn't use her own considerable influence to get her daughter-in-law into the proper circles.

Fay pushed the swinging door into the large kitchen, extremely modernized with the latest appliances, and stopped short when she saw Juanita, the Mexican cook, wiping knives on her apron and putting them back in the drawer. She had just used them to cut strip loin steaks and tenderloins from T-bones.

"Don't do that," Fay said in exasperation, snatching the knives from the woman and throwing them into the sink. "I have told you before, you must wash them in hot soapy water."

The problem with this post-war modern age was that white women didn't want to work as maids and housekeepers any more. How often had her own mother cleaned other people's homes and done their laundry so she and Fay could pay their rent? Today, all that was available was Mexican women from the migrant camps, and their standards of cleanliness were nowhere near as high as Fay's. The one redeeming factor in hiring Mexicans was that they worked for very low wages, and they worked hard because they knew they could easily be replaced. So Fay took advantage of this and had the women working long hours and charged them for any food she gave them. Fay didn't like having "wetbacks"—as she called them—in her house, thinking them all thieves. But what could you do?

She paused to look at the food being prepared on the wide kitchen counter. Expensive cuts of meat, lobster imported from Maine, smoked salmon from Nova Scotia, truffles from France, imported cheeses, asparagus out of season—expensive luxury food. As a teenager, she had dreamed of eating like this, had promised herself that some day she would. But now she found herself remembering beans on toast, cheap corned-beef hash with an egg on top. Poor people's food. But nostalgic food, sentimental, a reminder of simpler times. And she found her mouth watering at the thought of it.

Be careful what you wish for, she thought again. Because when you get it, sometimes it isn't as satisfying or rewarding as you had thought it would be. Sometimes, grand wishes come with high prices. And terrible pressures.

She struggled with herself, stood in the kitchen and wrestled with a strong urge that was coming over her. They had started recently, these urges to grab her car keys, hit the road, and just keep on going. She couldn't give in, of course: she had too many responsibilities. But the fantasy was there. She would be putting Debbie's clothes away and find herself daydreaming about speeding down a highway, destination unknown. She even had nocturnal dreams while she slept, about speeding along a country lane, just herself, with no goal or aim, just to be moving.

She knew what the dreams and fantasies meant. They were a form of escape. Fay knew that her life wasn't working out the way she had planned. Yes, she had money, security, and a faithful husband, but she wasn't fitting in. And the more she fought to be accepted socially, the stronger the urges to run away. What was the solution? Give up trying to get accepted in certain circles and just live with it? But that meant living as a failure and settling for a less-than-acceptable life.

It was hard work, keeping up appearances, meeting everyone's expectations, watching every word she said. And she resented how the upper-class women of this valley made her feel inferior. Oh, it wasn't overt; it probably wasn't even intentional. But by never accepting her into their circle, they sent a clear message. How easy it would be to just be out on the road, running away from it all. . . .

She thought about her Cadillac convertible and how much she loved to drive it. The suspension was so heavenly, it was like steering a boat on a placid lake. The perfect atmosphere for clearing the mind and solving one's problems.

She left the kitchen to return to the dilemma she had been wrestling with. The matter of gaining membership into the women's club.

Fay honestly didn't understand why she had no friends. Wasn't she nice to everyone? Wasn't she always handing out compliments, telling ladies how well they could wear orange when it was wasted on the rest of us? Commenting on hats that never went out of style? And then one day she was in O'Brien's notions shop and had heard two women talking a couple of aisles over; and to her shock, she realized they were talking about *her*. "No, I say we don't give her membership to the club. That Fay Schaller never has a nice thing to say to anyone. Always snide. Thoughtless and rude." It had nailed her to the floor. Handing out all those compliments, and this was what she got for it? *Thoughtless and rude*?

Fay had to weigh how badly she wanted to join the club against how much she feared further rejection. If only she could make friends with the members! She finally came to a decision. There was no other avenue. She was going to have to swallow her pride and seek advice from her mother-in-law.

*   *   *

CLARA WAS SITTING ON the front porch of her big two-story house, reading a letter that had just come from Lorelei—she missed her daughter but was pleased she was happy with her husband and children.

When Lorelei had been old enough, Clara had sat her down and told her the whole story of how she had come to be found and brought into the Schaller family. Lorelei had listened solemnly but accepted it all. On Lorelei's wedding day, Clara had asked, "Do you wish your mother could have been here?"

"My mother *is* here." And they had hugged with tears in their eyes.

It was with both sadness and joy that Clara had seen her beautiful daughter drive off with a handsome young man who worked for a major insurance company in Seattle and who was offering his bride a wonderful life up in Washington. *I was privileged to have Lorelei for twenty years, to raise her and love her, but just as the time came for me to marry and leave my mother's house, so it was Lorelei's time to leave my house. She isn't far. She'll come back for Christmas, or Wilhelm and I can go up there. Families are meant to branch out and spread. Perhaps that's why they are called trees.*

When she finished reading the letter, Clara paused to listen to the silence of the big house Wilhelm had built for them so Bill Junior and Fay could have the original house to themselves. Clara had thought she would be surrounded by grandchildren by now, but there was only the one, Deborah, born four years into Bill and Fay's marriage. She was happy for Johann, who had Adam and Queenie living with him, along with *their* three children. That was the way families should grow.

She thought about her own family, the Heinzes, whom she had chosen to leave so long ago. There was no more talk of going back to Germany for a visit. Why was that? After years of saying they would go, why had they really put it off? Although she and Wilhelm had never voiced it, Clara thought she knew the real reason. They didn't want to see how much their homeland had changed. In their minds, the Rhineland was still like it had been in 1912, postcard-perfect. They were afraid to see it now, postwar, places that had been bombed, rebuilding, changing the face of a good memory. Better to keep their village and the beloved river preserved in their minds and their hearts just as it had been forty years ago.

Besides, the children were grown. They were American; they had their own culture to admire. Clara's parents were deceased. Stiff letters from her sisters. News about nieces and nephews she had never met. A family held together by postage-stamp glue. And there was no one left on Wilhelm's side at all. Germany seemed a distant dream. And yet it was all around her as well, in the Rieslings that grew fat on the vines, at Eberhardt's bakery and Mueller's hotel, in the immigrants she had first arrived with and who were growing older with her.

Also, the Oktoberfest festival that someone had suggested years ago— but which had been held off because of two world wars, prohibition on alcohol, and the Great Depression—was now an annual event.

Perhaps this was how Germantown got its start. An unconscious desire to bring the homeland *here*—those who, even after all these years, still missed Detmold and Frankfurt and Munich. After the war, someone had bought a parcel of land opposite the Lutheran church on the outskirts of Lynnville. The idea was to put a restaurant and a gas station there, to cash in on folks leaving Sunday services and attending other church activities and events. The developer was of German ancestry, and so he designed his establishment to look like a Bavarian or alpine inn/ tavern with a quaint name like Stag's Head or Running Boar. Soon, not only local families visited the place, but tourists passing through began to stop. Hans and Frieda Eberhardt's sons and grandsons thought it a grand idea to open a bakery next to the restaurant. And then other merchants joined, opening quaint shops of the same Rhineland–Tudor–alpine-village look.

At that time, Clara had joined the effort to raise funds to expand the local hospital, and she had hit upon the idea of an antique store, a little shop that resembled her father's chemist's shop back home, added to the growing Old World village. She had gone around to the immigrant families and asked them to donate items from their closets, garages, and barns that they no longer had need of; and with all the wonderful treasures people so generously donated, she had opened an antique store to raise funds for charity. Tourists who stopped in at the popular Schaller Antiques knew their money was going to such good causes as polio research, animal rescue, and soup kitchens for the homeless.

Thinking about families and those who were homeless, Clara thought again about her plan to reunite the Schallers and the Newmans, to mend the rift that had driven them apart forty years ago. She hoped that she would soon have the perfect plan and would be able to write all about it to Lorelei.

Hearing a motor, Clara looked up so see a familiar car coming up the paved drive: Fay's turquoise Cadillac convertible, a long, sleek car that was all chrome and flash and dash. She was driving with the top down, her ponytail streaming out behind her head. "Hello, Mother Clara!" she called as she brought the car to a halt and stepped out. Fay was wearing one of those fashionable new wide skirts made of felt. It was pink with a black poodle dog appliquéd to it. On top, a white boatneck blouse with a pink scarf tied around her neck. Her sunglasses were also the very latest style, and Clara believed they were called "batwing cat-eye" frames. They gave Fay a rather startled look.

"Hello, Mother Clara," Fay said again with all the warmth she could muster. "I've come to ask you for some advice. Is this a good time?"

"Certainly. Please come in. I have a fresh pot of coffee on."

They went into the kitchen, where the Schallers' Mexican cook was preparing stuffed pork chops for the evening dinner, skewering the chops shut with toothpicks and laying them on a tray to be placed in the refrigerator and taken out later for pan-frying. To Fay's annoyance, Clara did not ask the cook to serve them in the dining room, instead pouring two cups of coffee herself, setting up a tray with cream and sugar, and bringing along a plate of Linzer biscuits. What were hired help for, if not to serve?

She followed her mother-in-law into the dining room, where they sat at one end of the bulky mahogany table that seated twelve. Clara set the coffee and tray down, and the plate of biscuits. Then she took a seat opposite her daughter-in-law and gave her an expectant smile. Clara really wanted to help Fay and was glad she had finally come for advice. Although their relationship was stilted and Clara would not normally have sought Fay out as a friend, Clara had to admit that Fay was a wonderful mother and doted on little Debbie, Clara's granddaughter.

When Fay seemed to hesitate on how to begin, Clara poured cream into her coffee and cheerfully said she had gotten a letter from Lorelei, who had sent news of her husband's promotion at the insurance company. Fay made a noncommittal sound. She knew how she must appear to her mother-in-law. Clara gushed over every little success of other people, whether it was Susan Eberhardt winning a national pie contest or Siegfried and Dagmar welcoming another grandchild into the world. Fay wished she could be happy for other people, she truly did. Because she suspected that if she could be genuinely happy for others, she could be happy for herself. But she was happy neither for other people's good fortune nor for her own, and she didn't know how to fix it—just like she didn't know how to make friends, how to get herself into an exclusive women's club, and get invited to the best parties in the valley.

Fay looked around the stuffy, cluttered dining room. When her father-in-law built this big house, Mother Clara had decorated it with the ambience of where she had come from, and Fay didn't like the old-fashioned decor.

And then she felt a little stab of guilt over her uncharitable thoughts. She wished she could warm to her mother-in-law. She had honestly tried, but it always seemed a betrayal of her own mother, whom Fay had run out on when she turned eighteen. At the time, she had been glad to be away from her mother's nomadic and nearly penniless lifestyle; but as the years went by, Fay had been stabbed with feelings of guilt for having left her. What must it have been like for Ruth Reed to wake up and find her teenage daughter gone? Had she cried? Worried? Told the police? Had she searched for Fay? Or had she just packed her battered suitcase as she had always done and moved on to the next town?

That was why Fay couldn't just call her mother-in-law "Mother," because she already had a mother somewhere. So she needed to call her Mother Clara, to distinguish between the in-law mother and the *real* mother. And with all these guilty feelings, how could Fay bring daughterly devotion to this woman? She wished she could. Clara Schaller was one of those women you could tell your troubles to.

Fay had seen many of her mother-in-law's friends come through this house to air grievances and seek advice. Once in a while, the kaffeeklatsch was held here if the bakery was too busy, and the ladies would all come with their cakes and pies and gossip and news. Fay was always invited, but she always felt left out. These were immigrant women who came from a different background from hers and spoke with accents and wore their hair in old-fashioned styles. They often slipped into their native tongue when they got extra happy or excited, and Fay would quietly leave. It was one of the reasons she so badly wanted to join the Lynnville Women's Service Club. It was a younger group, and they were Americans or second-generation Germans, Italians, Danes, Portuguese, and French born in America. She had a lot in common with them and felt she could contribute greatly to the club. If only they would give her a chance.

Anyway, she thought as she helped herself to a third sweet biscuit, Mother Clara had the patience and wisdom that old people often had, and Clara was indeed old—almost sixty!

"You might have noticed that I don't have many friends," Fay finally admitted.

Clara wanted to say that Fay didn't have *any* friends, but she kept her silence.

"I think it's because of my upbringing. My mother was a very restless woman, and we moved from town to town, never staying in any one place for long. I never learned the proper way to make friends. But I try, Mother Clara, I really put forth an effort. I praise people whenever I can, and I give useful advice."

Clara stared at her. She had often wondered if Fay was aware of how scathing her so-called compliments were. That she often offended more than she flattered. Did the woman really not know how her comments came across? "Fay, dear," she said now as tactfully as she could, "people don't really want advice if they don't ask for it. They don't like someone to say to them 'Do you know what you should do to look better?' Or 'I know how you can lose ten pounds.'"

"But I'm just trying to be helpful."

Clara sighed. Did she really believe that? "The other day, in Eber-hardt's when we were buying bread, there was a customer at the counter, a woman we had never met, and you tapped her on the shoulder and commented on her hair. Do you remember that?"

"Yes."

"Do you remember what you said?"

"I told her that her hair was very dry and that I knew of a good condi-tioner that would take care of it. What was wrong with that?"

Clara closed her eyes. "Fay, you can't just walk up to a total stranger—or even a friend or a relative—and say something negative about them. It's insulting."

Fay blinked, trying to understand. "I was just trying to be helpful," she said again. "Isn't that what friends do, help one another? Isn't that how you make friends in the first place?" She leaned forward earnestly. "You seem to always know the right thing to say. How do you do that?"

Clara shook her head. "I don't always know the right thing to say. I honestly don't. Sometimes I just say what I think the other person wants to hear."

Clara doubted she was getting through. For a long time, she had thought Fay was simply mean-spirited. But now she thought that her son's wife was just clueless. Socially, anyway. One of those people who were inept when it came to ordinary human relations. And there was no way of making her see that.

Fay stared at the half-eaten jammy biscuit in her fingers and decided this visit had been a waste. Mother Clara was one of those women to whom friendship just came naturally. She had obviously never had to work at it. And she had absolutely no useful advice to offer. So, once again, Fay Reed Schaller was on her own.

As she got in the driver's seat of the Cadillac and started the engine, feeling it rumble and hearing it hum, she gripped the wheel and thought that there was no rush for her to get home just now. It was a beautiful day, and a nice drive through the country could be just the thing to clear her mind.

* * *

"MOMMY, I WANT TO be a mermaid when I grow up."

Queenie paused in stirring the cake batter to give her daugh-ter a surprised look. One never knew what was going to come out of the creative eight-year-old's mouth. "Sofie, why on earth would you want that?"

Like her mother, Sofie had a mop of brown, natural curls on her head and big wide eyes that took in all the curiosities of the world. An eager learner, she was a child full of questions. "Because then I could swim in the ocean whenever I wanted to!" Sofie said with excited delight.

"But then you wouldn't be able to walk on land whenever you wanted to."

While Sofie frowned over this, Queenie poured the batter into a cake pan and lined it up with others to go into the oven.

They were in the big sunny kitchen of the Newman house, making cakes and pies for a PTA bake sale to raise money for uniforms for the school marching band. Besides being active in her children's school, Queenie was also the current chairwoman of the New Projects Committee of the Lynnville Women's Service Club, and one of those projects was the plan to make improvements along the riverfront between Lynnville and the village of Germantown—a challenge she was very much looking forward to.

Queenie couldn't imagine what her life would be like now if she hadn't come out to California with her father. Because of Adam, Queenie had three wonderful children: Gordon and Sofie, the eight-year-old twins, and Melvyn, their younger brother who was six years old. Queenie read to her children every night and when she tucked them in bed, she would kiss her right thumb and then tenderly trace a cross with it on each of their foreheads. Right now, it was summer break and the boys were at a day camp that had lots of activities for rambunctious boys who were full of spirit and mischief.

And without Adam's gentle persuasion, some time back, that she make an effort to reconcile with her mother, Queenie would not now enjoy a wonderful relationship with her.

The reunion hadn't been a smooth bed of roses at first, as there were thorns. It had been a day of shocking revelations. Queenie had always lived under the assumption that her mother had left them and divorced her father. She didn't know now where that notion had come from. Perhaps it had just been something her ten-year-old mind had concocted to make her mother's absence more bearable and logical. But Selma had told a different story. "Your father threw me out, did you know that? I didn't want to leave. He had a real temper then. A short fuse, you might say."

"He did?" Queenie had said, trying to find a short fuse on the quiet botany professor who spent silent hours over microscopes and plant cells.

"I suppose he's mellowed," Selma had said with a sigh. "We all do, eventually. We never should have gotten married. I was young and very immature, and your father had no business being married. Some men are never meant to be husbands. We had terrible screaming matches. I wanted to go out, to restaurants, the movies. He just wanted his meatloaf and mashed potatoes and a quiet evening beside the radio. We were just not suited at all. And then one day, in a fit, I called him some awful names and he snapped. He said I was to get out and I couldn't take you with me because I was going to be a bad influence on you. I couldn't believe it. He said he was going to get a divorce. He was going to blame it all on me and call me an unfit wife and mother. All he wanted was his quiet life and his little girl. That's what he said."

She had sighed again. "Ah, well, it's all in the past. I didn't have the money to fight the divorce or his allegations. I wanted you, Queenie, but my mother was sick and needed me, and I couldn't bring a child into that. You were much better off with him. He could give you a good home and a good life. I spent the next few years taking care of my bedridden mother, and now I'm dating a wonderful man. I tried contacting you, several times. But I suppose your father threw the letters away."

It was Queenie who had thrown them away, in anger, without opening them. But she couldn't bring that up then. It was a topic for another, calmer and less emotional time.

But now, ten years later, all truths were known, she and her mother were fast friends, and they saw each other on holidays. Queenie had never discussed the subject with her father. He was a quiet man, devoted to his various projects, and did not need to become the villain in a very old drama. He and Queenie's father-in-law, Johann Newman, were still very much in touch and kept each other up to date on the latest in agricultural progress. No need to go rocking any boats.

Which was why Queenie so desperately wanted to help Adam now, to do something for him in return, and because she loved him so much.

Queenie knew that her husband lived a life of frustration. Thirty-eight years old, and he saw himself as just Johann Newman's son. He yearned to do something on his own, not just to keep the family farm going, not just to be a link in the Newman chain, inheriting a legacy from his father and passing it along to his sons, like a member of a bucket brigade. He wanted to leave his own mark in this valley. Grandpa Ballerini had started this farm. Johann had made it grow. But what had Adam done? True, he had full control over the vineyards and winery now, but little had changed since his father had turned the running of them over to him. It just killed him to hear how his cousin Bill's farm was doing, the number of vineyards, the expanding variety of wines with the Schaller name crossing the continent, while Newman wine, although award-winning and of finer quality, continued to have limited distribution.

Adam had told her about his last meeting with the wine distributor for the region, what a dismal report it had been. "I'm sorry, Mr. Newman," the distributor had said last week, "but the Los Angeles market is saturated with Burgundys and Bordeaux right now. I can't get retailers to place orders for your products. And as high quality as your wines are, I'm afraid people are looking for cheaper. The Newman label is limited. For instance, we can't place your product in supermarkets. People go there for the cheap stuff."

Adam had told Queenie he suspected the man was hinting at a kickback scheme. "He wants me to pay him under the table to push my wines at the expense of my competitors. He won't try to get LaPlagia or Chateau Blanc or Franchimoni wines on the shelves if I pay him to place ours there. I won't do it, Queenie. Sure, they're my competitors, but it's unethical business practice."

The problem was, Newman's was a small winery. It was difficult to compete with the larger operations, like the Schallers whose wine found its way on shelves all over the country. Adam had approached his father about it many times, but Johann was adamant about keeping the Newman winery small and exclusive.

She wished her father-in-law could be more open-minded about Adam's needs. After all, hadn't Johann himself left home in his early twenties to start a new life in a new country? Adam wasn't asking for all that much. He just wanted to expand the winery and add some labels. Something he could look back on some day and say with pride, "*I* did that."

The problem for Queenie was, how could she help him?

As Sofie collected messy spatulas and helpfully carried them to the kitchen sink, she said, "Miss Jones said that Debbie Schaller and I are cousins. That's not true, is it?"

Queenie had known this day must inevitably come. The girls went to the same school, were sometimes involved in the same activities, even though they were two years apart. Now a teacher had said something and the truth had come out. How to explain something like this to a child? She wondered what Fay Schaller told her daughter, if they spoke about the

Newmans at all. "Yes, you are, in a way," she said vaguely, trying not to sound interested as she stirred cake batter. "Distant cousins," she added, and in a tone meant to close the subject.

"We're neighbors, though, aren't we? The school bus drives right by the Schaller farm before dropping me off here."

Queenie gave her a curious look. "Does Debbie Schaller ride the bus with you?"

"Uh-uh," Sofie said as she stuck her finger in the batter and licked it off. "Her Mommy picks her up every day in that big turquoise car."

Sofie then took a peanut butter cookie, still warm from the oven, and bit into it. She chewed thoughtfully and then said, "Your cakes and pies and cookies are the best, Mommy. You could sell them *for real*."

Queenie laughed. "And how would I sell them for real?"

"You could ask Mrs. Eberhardt to sell them at their shops."

"Oh, no, sweetie. The Eberhardts make all their own products. There's no room in their shops for anyone else's baked goods."

Sofie shrugged. "Then open your own bakery."

Queenie stared at her for a moment, marveling at the mouths of babes. Then she quickly untied her apron, said, "I have to go see Daddy for a minute," and hurried out.

*   *   *

ADAM WAS WITH HIS father in the racking room, where rows of red-brown barrels were stacked up to the ceiling with tubing and siphons trailing like snakes from their taps into stainless-steel vats lined along the opposite wall, but at a lower level to allow gravity to draw the wine down. Adam was trying to convince Johann that a new and modern way of racking wine was the direction for Newman Vineyards to go.

Johann pursed his lips. "We never remove Chardonnay from the oak before bottling. It preserves maximum character."

"It's an experiment, Dad. I think that by racking into the stainless-steel vats first, we get a crisper, fruitier wine. You'll see," Adam said with a wink.

"But you expose the wine to needless risks of infection and oxidation."

Adam swallowed back a retort. He could see he was getting nowhere with his father who, for all his science and university education and personal laboratory for progressive research, was hopelessly old-fashioned in some areas.

Johann Newman's interests lay in the vast agricultural farm he oversaw. He was still proud of their small, quality winery, but he saw no future in trying for increased profits there. Although Arturo Ballerini had had an agreement with the Catholic Church to supply sacramental wine, after the repeal of Prohibition the various Catholic parishes had turned to local distributors for their wine, and so the Newmans had lost that lucrative arm of their wine business. But this did not bother Johann, since his soybean crops were doing spectacularly.

His son Adam, on the other hand, was the most frustrated man on the planet.

He had long ago accepted the fact that he would never be a war hero. Never be a baseball star. Never win essay-writing contests. But he still wanted to make his life count. He had never forgotten what his baseball coach in college had said: "Never let your best be in the past." In fact, of late, it had become a kind of mantra that ran through his mind every day. But that was what he was starting to fear, that his best was in his past. The days of being carried on the shoulders of his teammates had been twenty-three years ago! He refused to accept that. His best *had* to still lie before him.

He couldn't make his father see this. Only Queenie understood, even though, for a woman, a mother, her best was always around her: their three children were Queenie's crowning achievement. They would never be relegated to the past, because they were here now, and they represented the future. Yes, Queenie had tried to convince him that they were his achievement as well, and Adam adored his boys, playing catch with them, giving them their own mitts, gloves, and bats and taking them and their mother to baseball games as he had promised Queenie years ago. But you can't really convince a man—especially a man who was born a competitive athlete—that his kids are the best he is ever going to do. A man needed something separate from himself. Why else did bridges and skyscrapers get built? A man needed a monument to himself. Perhaps not literally, but symbolically, yes. An achievement that stood out from other men. That was what Adam Newman yearned for.

Queenie understood this, listened with a good ear as he complained late into the night about how he was being blocked at every avenue. "He won't let me plant more acres or build a larger docking press. I want to expand the fermentation room and dig additional cellars. Do you know what my father says? He says why do all that when our wines aren't making it to the shelves? Do you see what a vicious cycle that is? I need to produce more wine so we can get retail shelf space, and he won't let me make more wine because we aren't getting shelf space!"

Adam knew that Queenie supported him and wanted to help. What Queenie *didn't* know, and would protest if she knew, was that she herself was part of his motivation to achieve something of his own. He wanted to be ten feet tall in her eyes, and he knew she would protest by saying he was already *twenty* feet tall in her eyes.

Adam hadn't thought it possible for a man to love a woman as much as he did his wife. He had been head over heels for her when they got married, and he hadn't known that that love was going to grow and deepen so that now, ten years later, she was his breath and soul and reason for living. Queenie was the most accommodating wife in the world, always anxious for Adam's happiness and welfare. Was there any other woman so willing to praise the good in life, to rejoice in cheerful things, to forget the painful and the bad? How could a man be frustrated and miserable around a woman like that?

Also, he wanted it for his two sons, Gordon and Melvyn, aged eight and six. He wanted them to grow up and someday be very proud of what their father had accomplished. But no matter how much he chewed on it and stewed on it and racked his brain over it, he couldn't come up with an idea that would be a monument to his achievements and something for his wife and sons to be proud of.

*　　*　　*

After a quick search around the winery, Queenie found them in the stacking room. She paused to watch them, father and son. Mostly they got along fine. It was only of late that Adam chafed at his father's stubbornness about keeping the winery small.

She thought her father-in-law was still good-looking and robust at sixty-three. He was tall and straight, with the posture of a hard-working man. She wondered why he hadn't remarried since Feliciana's death. Twenty-three years was a long time for a man to be alone. It wasn't for lack of eligible women. At social gatherings, Queenie noticed that Johann Newman caught the eye of every widow and spinster in the valley, and a few of the married ones as well. He had a warm personality and a great sense of humor. His grandchildren adored him and enjoyed crawling in his lap, although at eight the twins were getting a bit big for that.

"There you are!" she called out.

Johann and Adam turned to see Queenie standing in the doorway, looking flustered and excited and with smudges of flour on her face. "Adam, can I have a word with you?"

Johann said, "I think we're done here, son." And Adam knew they were.

He joined her in the late-spring sunshine.

"Darling," she said as she linked her arm through his and walked with him, "you know I've been thinking and thinking of ways to help you expand and improve the winery, and it occurred to me, why not set up your own wine distributorship? That way, *you* have control over where your wines end up. You yourself will see to it that the bottles get shelf space. You won't have to pay kickbacks to get it done."

He laughed. "How on earth did you come up with an idea like that?"

"From Sofie, believe it or not, just now. Well? Would it work?"

He thought about it. Adam knew that a distributor did more than just deliver bottles of wine to stores and restaurants. Before even getting to that point, the distributor had to plow through daunting research. What markets were a good match for the wine, its style, price range, and varietals? Was the market already saturated with similar wines? Was there a market that was underserved? How much wine could the winery produce and yet maintain its high standards for quality? Distributors wanted to be sure that if they found a market for a wine, the winery would be able to continue to deliver. A distributor then merchandised and marketed the wine, distributing brochures, fact sheets, and advertisements, and setting up end-of-aisle displays in wine shops and grocery stores. The distributor could even get involved in training and arranging tastings for retailers' sales staffs. The distributor provided daily sales data to his clients (both the retailer and the winery), and competitive market information, and looked for changing market trends.

And that was only the beginning. Adam said, "I already thought of that, Queenie. But setting up and then operating a distributorship would be way too complex and demanding of my time. I would have to be on the road almost all of the year, meet with people, keep up with trends. In effect, I'd be a salesman. No, as much as the idea of owning a distributorship appeals to me, I can't spread myself that thin. You and the kids need me. The vineyards and winery need me."

She gave this some thought, then said, "All right, then why not look for an existing distributorship, one that is already established, has customers and connections, and offer to buy it?" She became animated. "I mean, you have to agree that controlling your own distribution company would guarantee that our wine would make it to the shelves, right?"

Yes, he had to agree, which was why he had already briefly looked into the idea. "But I haven't heard of any for sale. Believe me, I would know if one was coming available."

"Well then shake the tree and see what falls out! Adam, make some discreet inquiries, talk to men, put some feelers out. Who knows, there might be a man out there right now who is thinking of retiring and wondering what to do with his company. You'll never know if you don't ask. You can maybe plant an idea in a distributor's head that he'd be making a good deal for himself, a wise business move, especially if you make him an irresistible offer."

* * *

BILL SCHALLER JUNIOR WAS a troubled man. His thoughts were topsy-turvy as he stomped into the kitchen from the vineyards and proceeded to mercilessly scrub his hands and arms at the sink, mindless of the cook and a maid preparing dinner.

Bill hadn't been a happy man for some time—actually, not since his brother Helmut had been martyred in the South Pacific, becoming an obsession with their father, Wilhelm, who had mourned every single day in the ten years since. Bill might as well not exist. Bill's parents had gone into such deep mourning over the loss of Helmut, and had practically made a shrine of his bedroom, and still asked for a public prayer for him in church on Sundays, that Bill had felt, over the years, like an afterthought. How many times, when the subject over the dinner table segued to Helmut and what a bright boy he had been, winning that essay contest and having lunch with the governor of California—how many times had Bill wanted to shout "Hey, *I'm* here! I'm your son, too, and I'm still alive!"

He was tired of living in the shadow of a dead war hero. He wanted some of the spotlight for himself.

But there was even more than that on his mind this evening, as a maid set the table in the dining room and Fay's shrill voice could be heard ordering the girl to move the flower arrangement.

Ever since going to the Club last night, Bill had been in a stormy mood.

The Valley Growers' Club was an exclusive men's association in Lynn-ville, where white farm owners retreated to enjoy whiskey and cigars, games of cards and agricultural talk, news, gossip, sometimes heated political debates. The Club had its own building with a man at the front desk, a tasteful dining room with tablecloths, and a large parlor/library for quiet reading and conversation. Women were not allowed, and the members were required to wear suits and ties. Wilhelm Schaller Sr. was a member in good standing, as was his brother Johann, but both had managed an arrangement whereby they were never there at the same time, with the exception of two times a year: at the yearly Christmas ball, where women *were* allowed—and they arrived in dazzling evening gowns—and the annual Growers' Awards banquet, a glamorous event where once again women were invited. At each of these occasions, the Newmans and the Schallers made sure they were at opposite ends of the ballroom.

Bill Junior was a member and had gone there the night before to meet with a man about importing Müller-Thurgau grapes from Germany to start a new line of a cheap, sweet, low-quality mass-pro-duced wine called Liebfraumilch. Although produced in Germany since the eighteenth century, Liebfraumilch was suddenly all the rage in Europe and rapidly gaining popularity in the United States. Both Bill and his father believed it good business sense to jump on this rising trend and offer domestically produced Liebfraumilch to compete with that exported from Germany.

Last night, talk at the Growers' Club had been mostly about the alarming problem in the valley of the increasing numbers of illegals crossing the border from Mexico. They worked for very low wages, which meant that white men looking for work on farms couldn't find any. The Mexican migrant workers didn't have permanent communities or villages but lived in tents and shanties because they were always on the move, picking peas and lettuce in the winter, cherries and beans in the spring, corn in the summer, grapes and cotton in the fall. Illiteracy in the camps was high, infant mortality was shocking, and the average lifespan barely reached fifty years. But there didn't seem to be anything that could be done about their situation, because they were in California illegally and therefore were not protected by minimum-wage laws, had no right to attend public schools, and had no access to health care. It was becoming a problem, and no one seemed to have a solution.

But this was not the focus of Bill's thoughts as he scrubbed his arms and hands for dinner.

While meeting with the man about importing Müller-Thurgau grapes, Bill had been dished a very startling rumor—that his cousin Adam, said to be having trouble getting his exclusive wines on retail shelves, had quietly searched for an established wine distributor willing to sell his company. And he had found one! A man named Callahan, owner of one of the biggest wine-distributing companies in California. As the story went, the man hadn't been thinking of selling his operation, but when Adam Newman had presented the idea, Callahan had warmed to it. He had no heirs, having lost his only son in the war. Who would he leave the business to? And it *was* a lot of work, and he *was* getting on in years. Apparently the more Callahan thought of it, the more he liked the idea of an early retirement. He'd always wanted to see Australia. And Newman was making a mighty generous offer. Word was, they had sealed the deal with a handshake, and the next time Callahan was in town they would meet with a lawyer and make it all legal and the purchase final.

It was such a smart idea, Bill wished he had thought of it. Maybe *that* would have gotten his father's notice and made him a little less focused on the martyred Helmut.

But it wasn't just the feeling of being a lesser son. Bill Schaller was disappointed with himself in general. He hadn't married spectacularly, hadn't distinguished himself in the war. Although they would never voice it, he was certain his parents were disappointed in him as well. He knew they felt he had married beneath himself by marrying Fay. They were too polite to ever say anything, and too mindful of his feelings, but he suspected that was how they saw it. They hadn't come all these thousands of miles and worked hard and sacrificed and risen to a fine degree of prominence and respectability in this valley to be dragged down by their son—because that was surely what he had done.

Fay's lack of higher education was obvious, as her literary tastes never went beyond movie magazines and scandal sheets. She had no hobbies or interests beyond their daughter, Deborah. Bill and Fay had little to say to each other, and their sex life, such as it was, was mechanical and uninspired. A man had needs, but apparently a woman didn't. He had one good thing to say about Fay, however: she was a perfect mother. She doted on Deborah.

He wished he could give Deborah a brother or sister, but none seemed to be coming, and it wasn't for lack of trying. He envied his cousin Adam with his vivacious Queenie and three lively children. Two sons! What Bill wouldn't give to have a son.

And what he wouldn't give to have come up with a clever idea like buying a wine distributorship. It could make Schaller Wines the biggest producer in the country. Now, *that* would make his father notice him.

* * *

No, Fay said silently to the plump woman in the mirror: you can't possibly want that life again. Sixth grade, Salinas, California. Fay had gone to school wearing a sweater and skirt set her mother had bought for her at the Salvation Army, and one of her classmates had pointed at her and said, loudly, "Hey! That's my old skirt and sweater set that my mother gave away to the Salvation Army." The kids had laughed, and Fay had burned with shame and never wore the outfit again.

No, she could not possibly want that life again. Then why was she looking back on those awful days so nostalgically? No, it wasn't the seediness or poverty of that life that she had become so sentimental about; it was the absence of responsibility, the absence of needing to impress and please others. Yes, it had been a hand-to-mouth existence, but Fay remembered her mother laughing a lot, and remembered how they had enjoyed life on the road.

She was confused. Hadn't she purposely gone after a dream—Bill Schaller and his miles of vineyards and the big house they now lived in? And hadn't she achieved it? Especially with their little princess, Deborah. So why was she daydreaming about the old days of going from town to town with her restless mother? Why had she started taking secret drives in her Cadillac, just hitting the road and letting the hood ornament take her somewhere? Oh, the freedom of that life! And how refreshed Fay felt each time she came back from a drive. Refreshed and ready once again to take up battle for membership in the Lynnville Women's Service Club.

No one knew about her drives. She managed them when Bill was busy with the grapes and Debbie was in school. She would tell the housekeeper she was going to visit someone and then just drive. She told herself that these excursions into the countryside were simply peaceful spells in which to clear her mind and figure out solutions to her social dilemmas. But a dark little voice at the back of her mind told her that these drives were practice runs and that one day she would hit the road, keep on going, and never look back.

The thought of it terrified her. She had heard of women who abandoned their families. Surely she could not be one of them! But she had become addicted to these "freedom rides," as she thought of them, in which it was just herself and the road and the farmland all around her.

And it worried her that she was staying out longer and longer each time, and the allure of the road was growing stronger.

She stared at herself in the bedroom mirror and recognized the face of Ruth Reed there. Fay wondered if every woman reached a time in her life when she wished she could ask her mother why things had been the way they were when she was a child. Fay had suspected long ago that her mother had possessed a gypsy soul, that the need to wander, to see what was in the next town, to always search, was in her blood. And if so, had the daughter inherited that restlessness? Because the compulsion was growing in her day by day.

She had started asking herself where she belonged. Rooted, tied down, and smothered by family rules? Or on the move? Had Fay been born with a pilgrim soul?

Nature versus desire. What if we wish our life to go in one direction, and yet we are born with a propensity to go in another?

The expression on the face in the mirror darkened. And if I am at last accepted into the Women's Club, will my urges to escape on the road go away, or will I find myself suddenly, terribly conflicted? Fay Schaller, what is it you really want? She closed her eyes and decided to be exceptionally honest with herself. *I want to stop feeling inadequate, clumsy, a failure. On the road, with trees whizzing by, I feel none of these. I feel as free as a beautiful bird, and that is what I want.*

She went downstairs, where she and Bill sat down to roast beef, baked potatoes, and buttered carrots. Fay always insisted on a fully-laid-out table, with a white cloth, china and silver, and crystal and flowers, even though it was only the two of them. Debbie had had her dinner an hour ago and was upstairs in her room.

They politely filled each other in on their day—Bill making his daily inspection of the vines, Fay having gone to Eberhardt's to order loads of cakes and pies for the PTA's bake sale to raise funds to buy uniforms for the school's marching band. Fay had heard that Queenie Newman was actually baking all her own goods to donate. So Fay had topped Queenie by ordering twice as much from Eberhardt's and having it delivered to the school for Saturday's sale. She would sit at one table to take money, and Queenie would be at another. They would not acknowledge each other.

"That cousin of mine," Bill grumbled over his pink and juicy roast beef. "Adam Newman gets all the breaks."

"What are you talking about?" Fay asked, always interested in what the Newmans were up to, always wanting to make sure they hadn't topped anything the Schallers had done.

After he told her about the deal with Callahan, the wine distributor, Fay said, "How much richer will this deal make the Newmans?" God, could Queenie rise any higher in this blasted valley?

"A lot," Bill said, spearing a buttery carrot with an angry stab. "But it's not just the money. It's the power. Callahan's has a wide and influential distributorship. Newman will be able to manipulate the wine market, which means every grape grower in this valley will be kissing his ass."

Fay's wine glass paused at her lips as she found this new bit of information fascinating. She thought: and maybe a few wives kissing Adam's wife's as well, if it will help their husbands. She smiled. Men who will suck up to the biggest wine distributor in California will have wives who will suck up to the *wife* of that wine distributor. And then she could settle down, become part of the smart crowd and push thoughts of long drives and a deprived childhood from her mind.

"Is the deal final?" she asked.

"Not yet. Why?"

"Then you should go to the man himself and make him a better offer."

He stared at her in shock. "I can't do that. They already have a handshake on the deal." He didn't like his cousin and wasn't particularly happy for Adam's success, but Bill was also a basically decent guy who couldn't abide underhanded business dealings. "A man's handshake is his word. I can't go behind Newman's back."

"Why should you treat him so honorably? He's your cousin, and yet he doesn't invite you in on such a lucrative deal, keeping it all to himself. Besides, what have they ever done for us? Why should we worry about their feelings? And what's a handshake? It certainly isn't a signature on paper."

But he kept shaking his head, and she saw it wasn't going to work. She refilled her wine glass, took a sip, did some thinking, and then said: "You're right, of course. It would be unethical and underhanded. What was I thinking? But you must admit it is a brilliant idea. A winery owning their own distributorship. Especially a large one like Callahan's. I imagine Johann is very proud of Adam."

Bill looked up from his dinner, lines etched in his forehead. "What?"

"Oh," she said airily, as if the topic was winding down and losing her interest. "People will be talking about the Callahan deal for a long time. The Newman name will shine, all because of Adam. So imagine how Johann feels about his son's clever accomplishment."

She watched him carefully as cogs and wheels turned in her husband's head. And then she saw a light dawn in his eyes. One thing she knew about Bill: he resented the way a dead brother had been elevated above a living one.

"You know," Bill said slowly, saying exactly what she had maneuvered him into saying, "you might have something there. I have no love of the Newmans. Why should I worry about their feelings? If Callahan is open to selling his distributorship, then what's to say other men can't have a bite from that apple? Yes," he said, brightening for the first time in years. "Yes indeed, my dear Fay, I believe you've come up with a good idea. I will discuss it with my father first thing in the morning. He's more receptive to radical ideas when he's having his coffee."

*   *   *

THEY WERE IN THE OFFICE of the manager of the Lynnville bank, where Bill Junior and Mr. Callahan were signing contracts and money was changing hands. Mr. Gilette, the Schallers' lawyer, was there, as well as Mr. Callahan's own attorney. Clara and Wilhelm were also in attendance, and Fay, looking on with extreme pleasure over the outcome of her small scheme.

When his son had approached him with the startling proposition of buying a wine distributorship, Wilhelm Sr. had instantly taken to the idea. And after hearing the details, he had approved the funds and then gave his son unrestricted authority in handling the transaction, and even praised Bill for such a clever strategy. Imagine Bill having the ingenuity to come up with the notion of searching for a distributor who might be persuaded to sell, and then taking the initiative and finding such a man! Callahan, no less! Bill explained that Callahan had been reluctant at first, but when Bill had thrown in a contract clause guaranteeing Callahan an annual percentage of the profits, the man had jumped at it. Wilhelm was thrilled. Here he was, sixty-five years old, a time when many men retire, and suddenly the world had opened up to him.

As he sat in the plush leather chair watching the two men sign papers, and witnesses cosigning, Wilhelm lit a rich fat cigar and puffed on it with supreme satisfaction. Soon people in New York City would be decanting Schaller Merlots and Chardonnays and Rieslings. Maybe even folks in London and Paris would be requesting Schaller wine. What a thought! Here he was, forty years after coming to America with his little vines and cuttings, cradled like babies during the whole arduous voyage, and the fruits of that long-ago dream were finding themselves in taverns and restaurants all the way back to the Rhineland! Wilhelm would finally have the wine empire he had long dreamed of.

And it proved to him that the ridiculous fear that had been born in him ten years ago when Helmut was killed, the fear that he discovered he had favored one son over the other, just like his own adulterous father had done—this proved that it was a ridiculous fear with no basis whatsoever. Look what he was giving Bill permission to do. Overseeing an enormous transaction involving great sums of money, giving him complete autonomy and trust: Were those the actions of a father who favored one son over another?

Bill Junior was feeling particularly pleased with himself as he signed the papers. He knew his father was a stickler for honesty in business, so when he had presented the idea to him, Bill had carefully omitted a few details—such as that the idea had really been Adam Newman's and that there was a gentleman's agreement on the table. Luckily, Callahan himself wasn't such a stickler for business ethics. A few dollar signs had easily persuaded him to conveniently forget the handshake with Adam Newman.

Beyond the closed office doors, they barely heard a commotion that had arisen out in the bank, where customers were lined up at teller windows and people stood at tables quietly filling out deposit and withdrawal forms. They didn't hear footsteps pounding across the marble floor, or hear the bank security guard shout "Stop!" They barely registered a man's voice bellowing something as the heavy footfall drew closer, and it sounded like the man was calling out Bill Schaller's name. But then the office doors burst open, and they saw a violently red-faced Adam Newman fly into the room, the security guard running after him, and, in the bank, people standing with shocked expressions.

The manager said, "What—" half rising from his chair, while Adam went straight at Bill, growling, "You bastard! You thieving bastard! You knew this deal was mine! You went behind my back, you cheating son of a bitch!"

He hauled a startled Bill out of his chair by the lapels of his jacket, drew back an arm, and punched him hard in the face with his fist, sending Bill toppling backward and onto the floor. While the security guard tried without success to get ahold of Adam, and Wilhelm had risen to his feet, and the lawyers and the bank manager rushed around to grab him, Adam picked Bill up and threw him against the desk, sending pens and paperweights and a stapler flying. Hands reached for Adam, seizing his jacket, his collar, his sleeves. But he was fast and angry and like a wolf on a sheep. Stunned and dazed, his nose streaming with blood, Bill couldn't fight back. Adam got one more hold on him, flinging him hard against the wall, and then the other men had him—Wilhelm, the guard, the two lawyers, restraining him as he struggled in their hold; and Mr. Callahan, white-faced, stood back, his mouth and eyes wide open.

"I'll get you for this!" Adam cried in a strangled voice, spittle flying from his lips. "By God, Schaller, you are going to pay!"

Wilhelm looked in confusion from one cousin to the other, while Clara and Fay stood frozen, their hands to their mouths, and a guilty look spread over Bill's bloody face and Mr. Callahan hung his head sheepishly; and suddenly something became apparent, a double-cross, a betrayal, a stab in the back.

Clara, her heart racing, looked at Wilhelm, who stood in frozen shock, and she thought: the punches that were thrown forty years ago are still being thrown.

Someone in the bank had had the presence of mind to telephone the police, who came to break up the fight, take the report, and sort things out and see if an arrest would be involved here. As the sergeant tried to restore order and take statements, Wilhelm sat immobilized in his chair, unable to take in what had just happened, unable to digest the revelation about his son's underhanded dealing—his son, whom he now looked upon in shock and horror. At his side, Clara, her face white with anguish in the realization of what her son had done, stood motionless, sick at heart and crushed with disappointment.

As Callahan gave his statement, he looked no one in the eye but could only hang his head in shame. When it came Adam's turn, he ignored the sergeant's questions but instead cried, "I'll sue you for every penny you've got, Schaller! I'll have your farm for this!" Bill Junior, feeling no shame but instead turning defensively aggressive, shouted, "Just try it, Newman. No court in the land will hear your feeble case! But give it your best shot!"

And Fay, wringing her hands, confused and worried, wondered if the Newmans truly could sue them, bankrupt them even. What would it mean for their futures? For her daughter's future? And suddenly a homeless life filled her eyes, a vagabond life on the road for mother and daughter.

*   *   *

FAY SCHALLER GRIPPED THE steering wheel until her knuckles were white.

The whole valley was still talking about what happened at the bank—four years later! Despite the heated anger and violent emotions, no charges had been pressed. Neither Bill Schaller nor the bank manager had wanted the police to arrest Adam Newman. But it had been a dirty story in the newspapers and local radio stations, a stain on both families, with the bigger stain on the Schallers once word got out about Bill Junior not honoring a gentleman's handshake. And then the attempted lawsuit that had fallen through—the handshake wasn't legally binding. So the Schallers kept their farm and the distributorship, and they were wealthier than ever.

But they weren't as well liked and respected as they had once been.

Fay's compulsion to go on drives had increased, and the drives were longer. She invented plausible excuses, and anyway, Wilhelm and Bill were so busy with the vineyards and winery, and with not speaking to each other, and Mother Clara with her charities and involvement in local issues, and Debbie at school, no one noticed that Fay wasn't around much.

She had become invisible. She didn't exist, except when she was racing down the tarmac, passing farms and corrals and billboards and feeling her soul soar up to the sky. She wished she could bring Debbie along on these drives—yes, share the adventure, as Fay's mother had once shared it with her. But Debbie needed to be in school, and anyway Fay didn't want her excursions to be found out. What would Bill say, his wife gone all day to unknown places?

And how would she explain it, the need? On the road, Fay would feel her nerves settle and a wonderful, heady serenity enter her soul. She would forget that the ladies of the valley now totally rejected her, because of Bill, and instead would feel a delicious calm settle over her. She would come home hours later, humming and happy, ready to fetch Debbie from school, ready to greet Bill from the fields and sit down to a relaxed family dinner.

The problem was, the urges were coming closer together, the compulsion was stronger, and the lengths of her drives were becoming longer. But she needed it—the long roads cleaving green farms and threading their way under orchards. She would pack sandwiches and fruit and a flask of cold tea and head out, sometimes going as far as a hundred miles, through fields and meadows and beneath endless blue skies. She would wonder what little town was going to pop up next, what little pocket of timelessness would greet her, and she would fantasize about finding a boarding house and renting a room for a while and wading in the ocean, free from responsibility and care and tongues that wagged with gossip.

She thought about her mother, wondered if she was still in California. Fay would sit in her Cadillac on a hill or a cliff, overlooking the ocean or farmland, and she would travel back to the days of her childhood when money was so tight they couldn't afford to buy Schaller-brand jam and jelly but had to settle for a cheaper, less tasty brand. And now here she was, carrying the Schaller name! And she and her mother would eat cans of Newman's pork and beans because that was all they could afford, and little Fay resented it, and now here she was, neighbors with the Newmans, and cousins to boot!

She knew that no one must find out about these day drives—at least, her need for them. Bill sort of knew she went to Lynnville or Santa Barbara for shopping or getting her hair done. If you tell a little of the truth, she had discovered, it's easy to keep all the rest secret. But he wouldn't understand what made her take these long drives to nowhere, visiting towns that almost had no names, stopping to eat at roadside hamburger stands, feeling the vastness and promise of California all around her. And if he found out, he might also find out about her growing fear that one day she wasn't going to turn around and come home. She was just going to keep on going. . . .

She began to wonder where her mother was, if she was still gypsying about, if she was still alive even. Ruth Reed would be fifty-five years old now and possibly in poor health and needing a daughter's help.

Fay thought: as we get older, we start to understand our parents, why they were the way they were and did what they did. We start to regret our unfair judgments of them, but they die before we can apologize. Fay didn't want that to happen. She wanted to find her mother and apologize.

Two hours of hypnotic driving later, she arrived at a small town that she had never visited before. It was very much like Lynnville, but it *wasn't* Lynnville, and as she drove up and down and saw ROOM TO LET signs and PART TIME HELP WANTED, with a car dealership at one end of the main street and a movie theater at the other, and a residential section with gravel roads and shady elm trees, she remembered her mother driving up and down the main street of a new town with little Fay on the seat next to her, and Mom saying, "Look, that house has a nice lawn, and did you see that the stationery store wanted to hire?"

Parking, she got out and leaned against the Cadillac, folded her arms,

330 / Barbara Wood

and looked at the peaceful houses with golden leaves dropping on their roofs. No gigantic dreams were dreamed in these little houses, no preposterous goals were set, no outrageous schemes were spun. Just ordinary people hoping to get by, hoping to make their rent or mortgage payment with maybe enough left over to afford a three-day trip to Lake Tahoe. Modest ambitions, she thought, and it made her smile. Her mother had never dreamed big, because Ruth Reed wasn't greedy. She dreamed of having enough to eat and decent clothes to wear and a warm room in the winter and the occasional outing to a movie or a treat at a soda fountain.

As she stood there and thought these sentimental thoughts, Fay felt a great serenity descend over her. All the tension of the past fourteen years, from the night she had schemed to snare Bill Schaller at a servicemen's dance where his mother served sandwiches and kept an eye on the young people—all the wanting and yearning and trying to make friends and thinking that getting into an exclusive women's club would somehow be the happiest day of her life—none of it seemed to matter anymore.

Maybe you can never escape the way you were brought up, she thought now; maybe it calls you back. Was that the real meaning behind these long, meandering drives?

The guilt of feeling responsible for her husband's disgrace (it had been her idea that he go to Callahan and offer a secret deal, after all), her alienation among the women in the valley, and the nomadic soul she had inherited from her mother made a powerful combination. She felt herself arriving at an inevitable decision that had been a long time in the making. She was going to leave Bill Schaller and the Largo Valley once and for all, and she was going to take her daughter with her.

And it made her suddenly very happy.

*   *   *

WOULD SHE MISS BILL? Possibly. Would she ever fall in love again? Doubtful. Fay had but one focus now—to give Deborah a life of love, security, and adventure.

She must plan carefully. Oktoberfest would be the best time—a big celebration and a tourist draw in Germantown. Everyone would be busy.

Fay decided she would slowly hoard money, pack bags, and hide them under the bed. Show no indication of leaving. Watch what she said and be sure to say things like "tomorrow" and "next week" to indicate permanence. Volunteer to decorate the hospital for Christmas. And then choose a night. . . .

But on the morning of the chosen night, Fay woke up nauseated and barely made it to the bathroom in time to throw up. The flu? No one else had it. No word of influenza in the valley. She had no fever, no aches or pains. Then she looked at her calendar. Dear God, how could she have forgotten?

She went back in her mind. It must have been the night she got home from the leafy, sleepy town where she had made the decision to run away. Bill had reached for her in bed, and she had been so wonderfully preoccupied with her plans that she'd forgotten all about the sponge.

So she would have to put off her plan for a year, and then she would take Debbie *and* the baby with her.

*   *   *

SUNDAY DINNER, ALWAYS AT precisely three o'clock, a heavy meal served by Mother Clara herself with Wilhelm Sr. carving the roast in a great weekly ritual, preceded by a long prayer of thanks to God, and attended by Wilhelm and Mother Clara, Bill Junior, Fay, and Deborah and, once in a while, a favored guest or two. This afternoon, it was the Schallers' senior foreman, an American from Washington State who oversaw all the crews and vineyards. Clara served up bowls of corn on the cob, mashed potatoes, peas, and Brussels sprouts, while Wilhelm took a carving knife to the tender roast beef. There was red wine on the table, and dessert would be peach ice cream.

Fay managed to take mechanical bites of food, chew, swallow. She was in the ninth month of her pregnancy and felt as big as a house. The news of the baby had been received with great rejoicing. The black pall that had hung over the family since the Callahan scandal lifted and flew away—even Wilhelm and Bill Junior were speaking again. All was sunshine and light, with Bill thrilled at the prospect of another child and Wilhelm and Clara excited to be welcoming another grandchild. In the ensuing months, Fay had felt no attachment to the child growing within her and, with the Schallers so excited, she had come to the realization that she could not, in good conscience, take the baby with her. He or she belonged here. The road beckoned only to Fay and her daughter, Debbie.

She had wondered, early on, if this unexpected child might dispel her craving to run away and perhaps anchor her to this place. But the opposite had occurred. The drives had to cease, of course, as everyone became watchful and attentive to Fay. But when the drives stopped, the cravings had increased. With each day that she could not get behind the wheel of a car, Fay thought she was going to scream. Roads and lanes and high-ways filled her daytime fantasies, and at night she dreamed of small towns populated with strangers who made no demands on her.

She had never felt so caged, so stifled. Today was only an example of how smothered she felt on this farm. Every Sunday, at three o'clock sharp, the table was set, the food brought out, the long grace recited, and then the ritual of eating. Conversation was about crops, valley news, Deborah's school work, Clara's latest projects, and general mundane topics. Fay was always on the edge of hysteria. Couldn't we just once, she wanted to say, have Sunday dinner at *two* o'clock? Or eat outside? Or go to Mueller's hotel? Couldn't we alter the routine just once?

But there were family rules. Routine was what kept everything going. The Schallers were not impulsive people. Perhaps they had been long ago, Fay thought as she swallowed a scream with her buttered peas. Perhaps when Clara and Wilhelm were young, they had acted on impulse. But now the Schallers were set in their ways, as was the farm. It was all run like clockwork, with schedules and routines. She listened to them talk—predictable talk!—and felt a scream bubble at her throat.

Excusing herself, she got up from her chair and hurried to the bath-room, where she locked the door and quickly stuffed a towel into her mouth to stifle the scream.

She looked out the window and saw her car parked under the pepper tree. It was all she could do to keep from climbing through the window and driving off in it. But of course she couldn't. Just as she hadn't been able to drive these past months, the getaways would be forbidden to her once the baby was born. Everyone agreed that Fay was going to be a wonderful doting mother to the new child, as she had been with Deborah. At least until the child started full-time school, there would be no more escape drives for Fay Schaller.

The thought filled her with horror.

Someday, I *will* scream, and I will never stop.

* * *

THE LABOR WENT QUICKLY. She willed the child out of her and paid scant interest when he was placed at her breast. She nursed him for three faithful months, then switched him to bottles and formula. Once she and Debbie were gone, Mother Clara would take over the care of her grandson, whom they named Jack.

Because they were rich, they had three 1958 Cadillacs parked on the paved driveway, one of them a powder-blue convertible—big cars with rocket-ship fins, all three shiny and still with the new-car smell. She would take the blue one that Bill had put in her name as a birthday gift.

She was going to show Deborah what it had been like when *she'd* been a little girl, riding along in the passenger seat beside her mother, together pointing out sights that they passed. They would play the license-plate game, as Fay had done with her mother, and call out every time they spotted an out-of-state car. Mostly they were travelers from Oregon, Nevada, and Arizona. If you spotted a New York plate, you got an extra ten bonus points.

It was going to be fun, the good life. Fay had plenty of money and all the furs and jewelry Bill had given her over the years. They would find a nice place to stay, and Fay might get a job doing something clean and respectable—she was good at keeping household accounts and she knew how to type—and they would have pigs in blankets for dinner. And they were going to be unbelievably happy.

It was time. The house was quiet, the family asleep. Fay's luggage was in the car. She tiptoed into Debbie's bedroom to quietly awaken the child. She sat on the edge of the bed, reaching out. Then she paused and, instead of shaking her awake, stroked the girl's hair. Debbie was a heavy sleeper. She also always slept with a night light on because she was afraid of the dark. Fay trembled with love and emotion. Eleven was such a wonderful age. Soon this child would be leaving her dolls behind and wondering why boys suddenly weren't the snotty creatures she had always thought.

The girl would wonder at first why her mother had taken them away from Daddy and this farm. But, in time, Fay was certain she could make Debbie see that she had done it for her own good, to save her from a stifling life, away from gossip and scandal and shame, and mostly away from the unhealthy atmosphere of a festering family feud. I am doing this to protect you, Fay thought.

Fay studied her daughter's fine features. She had inherited the widow's-peak hairline from her father, who had inherited it from Clara, so that Debbie resembled the Schallers more than she resembled her own mother.

Who do *I* look like? Fay wondered. She reached into her purse and brought out her wallet. It contained an old black-and-white photograph that she had carried with her all these years. On the night she ran away from home, back in 1941 when she was eighteen years old, she had paused to take a picture out of a frame. She had rarely looked at it since, but she looked at it now. It was a scene of a woman and a little girl, standing in front of a shabby car at an old-fashioned gasoline station in the middle of nowhere. Ruth Reed and her daughter Fay. They stood side by side with Ruth's hand on the girl's shoulder. They wore skirts and blouses and big grins on their faces. Who had taken the picture? Perhaps one of her mother's temporary boyfriends—and Ruth had been happy. But now Fay saw something new in the picture, and she felt her heart get pulled this way and that.

And she thought: *this* is whom I resemble. Because the girl in the photo definitely belonged to the woman, their features the same.

She sat back in wonder. She had come into this room to waken Deborah and spirit her off to points unknown. But now she paused to reflect.

She thought: I was two years old when my mother started her gypsy life. I had known six towns and six schools by the time I was Deborah's age. But she has only known one place. Stability. Security. Living with a daddy and grandparents. Her life is so different from what mine had been. The Schallers had been one of the first families in the valley to have a television set. And now we are the first ones to have a *color* TV. My little girl has only ever known a good and easy life, with her own bedroom and lots of dolls and toys, attending the same school for the past five years with a network of friends and clubs that she belonged to.

A world of difference from the childhood Fay Reed had known. I *hated* that life when I was eleven, and waited seven years to run away from it. That's what Deborah will do. She will hate that life even more than I did, because she wouldn't be used to it and will have been uprooted from life on this farm, and when she's eighteen she'll come running back here and I'll lose her forever.

Even worse, the life I want to take her to would be a nomadic life. Debbie would become like me, like my mother. She would become a rootless vagabond, impelled by a gypsy soul, and Fay wanted better for her than that. She wanted her daughter to have the security and stability that Ruth and Fay Reed never had.

Realizations now filled Fay's head, notions that she had not explored before. It occurred to her for the first time that the only reason for taking Deborah with her was a selfish one. It had nothing to do with the child and everything to do with Fay. She loved the little girl, wanted her company, wanted to show her an adventurous childhood. But it wasn't for

Deborah, Fay understood now. She had been thinking only of herself, not her daughter.

And Deborah had a little brother now. Something Fay had never had. She couldn't deprive her daughter of the experience of having a sibling.

And then another, more startling thought came to her. After she and Debbie left, the family would be certain to search for them, calling the police and the sheriff. It would be a life on the run, a fugitive life. Not fun and casual and conducted at their leisure, but a furtive life, moving at night, using fake names, always looking over their shoulders. She couldn't do that to Debbie. Fay suspected Wilhelm wouldn't launch a search just for *her*. He might even think good riddance. But for his daughter? He would hunt to the ends of the earth.

Fay rubbed her forehead. My God, what was I thinking?

Now she understood the cold truth of her situation. That she couldn't take Debbie with her. That she hadn't the right to do it, that it would be cruel and unfair to everyone. Fay was on her own. She knew that now. She couldn't stay here, and she couldn't stay away from the road. She had to find those small towns. She had to find her mother.

Fay knew she would suffer terrible anguish over leaving her little girl behind. But what kind of a mother will I be if I stay? I will be caged, become bitter and resentful. A spiteful, hateful woman and I will come to blame those who were the reason I stayed.

"I'm sorry," she whispered. "But I have to go. For my own self-preservation, I must go."

With great pain in her heart and tears streaming down her cheeks, she left a note with a single line: "Don't search for me."

Then she kissed the sleeping Deborah, and little Jack, and managed to drive off in her Cadillac until her tail lights vanished in the night.

*   *   *

JOHANN LOOKED AS IF he hadn't slept, the look of a man wrestling with moral demons, life-and-death decisions. And it alarmed Clara as they walked along deserted Largo Creek with the day to themselves.

Yes, their friendship had come under a strain these past five years. Their talks had been superficial and almost play-acted, each afraid to air the emotions and secrets they had once shared. But today there was a new tension in the air, and it worried her.

It was because of Johann's son, Adam, who had gone into a dark, angry world, and Johann blamed his brother Wilhelm. "I thought Adam would be over it by now," Johann said as they walked in the October sunshine that had a hint of winter in the air. "But his anger and depression are getting worse, and I blame my brother for that. Wilhelm should never have supported Bill in an underhanded business scheme like that."

"You don't know Wilhelm," Clara said defensively. "He's a man of honor. He would never have allowed Bill to go behind Adam's back if he had known about the handshake, the agreement. Once he learned the truth, he tried to cancel Bill's agreement with Callahan, but Mr. Callahan had made a lot of money out of the deal and insisted it was all legal."

Clara knew that Wilhelm was sick at heart about his son being involved in unscrupulous business practices. *Lying* to his father. Saying he had heard that Callahan wanted to sell, and so Bill wanted to make him an offer. Leaving out the important part about the idea being Adam's and that Adam had approached Mr. Callahan about purchasing his company, persuading Callahan to sell so that, yes, it really was Adam's deal and that what Bill did was dishonest. Wilhelm had raised him better than that. Now the two were barely speaking. So Clara now had *two* reconciliations she was hoping to miraculously bring about. But she held little hope. The gap between the Newmans and the Schallers was wider than ever. And now her husband and son were strangers under one roof.

Clara's world had been turned upside down. She hadn't been fond of Fay, but the woman had been a perfect mother. What a shock that she should leave in the night, abandoning the daughter she so cherished and her newborn son. Should they have the sheriff searching for her? But Fay's suitcases were gone, her clothes, jewelry, personal mementos—all evidence that she had ever lived at Schaller Farm, gone. It was a deliberate departure. She didn't want to be found. And her note had confirmed that.

Would she ever come back? And what was Clara to tell Debbie, or little Jack when he grew up asking where his mommy was?

"It's not so much that Bill stole the distributorship," Johann said, "It goes deeper than that. The business deal had been Queenie's idea. And you know how devoted Adam is to her. So his anger at Bill is over the fact that Bill stole from Queenie. What Bill did is an affront to Adam's wife."

"I understand," Clara said. And, sadly, she did. It wasn't merely business, it was personal. One man disrespecting another man's wife. And the bitter roots of such outrage ran deep. But the continued, and possibly growing, vindictiveness in Adam Newman's heart frightened her. It was history repeating itself. Cain and Abel. Wilhelm and Johann. And now Adam and Bill, and she was terrified for her son's safety.

Johann stopped suddenly and turned to face her. "I have to be honest with you, Clara: I am mad as hell over the whole thing. *Everyone* knew about Adam's business deal with Callahan, the handshake! It was a gentleman's agreement. A handshake seals the deal; the signing of papers is a mere formality. There wasn't a single other grower in this valley who would have approached Callahan with a counter-offer. Only Wilhelm and his son!"

Clara gasped in shock. "But I told you that Wilhelm disapproved of Bill's underhanded action. Why do you accuse Wilhelm? Unless," she said, her bottom lip trembling, "you do not believe me and you think that I was saying it out of loyalty to Wilhelm. Johann, are you saying that I am lying to you?"

"I don't know what to think! Wilhelm hasn't changed since the night he nearly beat me to death and left me bleeding on the road. He's a rotten bastard through and through, with no ethics and no scruples, and his son is no better!"

His sudden outburst so shocked her that she started to cry. She didn't want to, but she couldn't help herself.

Grimly, Johann said, "We can't go on meeting any more, Clara."

Her hands flew to her mouth. "*No!*"

"I've tried these past five years, but everything has changed. It's as if the very air were poisoned. I'll always love you, Clara, but my brother and his son are vile men and I can't be part of their lives, and that means never seeing you again."

"Johann, I couldn't bear never seeing you again!" she sobbed, reaching for him.

"Your son did irreparable harm to *my* son."

Clara was taken aback by the vehemence in his voice. She could almost hear him say "It was *your* son, so I blame *you*." And eyes that had always looked at her tenderly or with amusement and love now seemed to be filled with disgust. She felt a great coldness rush into her soul.

Johann went on. "Just as Wilhelm tried to destroy my life forty-five years ago, Bill has done the same to Adam. My son has changed. His life is dark and angry. He barely speaks to his wife, he barely looks at his children. He is consumed with fury and thoughts of revenge. I can never forgive Wilhelm and Bill, and that is why you and I can never be together again, because it is only natural that you must defend them. And," he added more gently, to ease their pain, "I don't blame you for that. They are your family and you are staunchly loyal to them. It is one of the things I love about you."

He turned and walked stiffly away. She called after him. "Johann, Johann, I love you! Please don't make me choose between my husband and son, and you."

He stopped, turned. "I'm not asking you to."

"How can you just walk away from me like this?"

"Do you think this is easy for me?" he shouted, eyes flashing with tears. He could barely speak, he was so choked with emotion. There she stood, the woman he had loved for four decades, and he *had* to turn his back on her. There was no choice: it was time. He had had his chance and missed it long ago, before she and Wilhelm took their marriage vows. Johann knew that his love for Clara had been doomed from the start, and it was killing him to finally admit it.

"Your life is with *them*, Clara, not with me," he said in a strangled voice. "My life is with Adam and Queenie and my three grandchildren. My duty is, as the head of the Newman family, to try to restore peace and harmony, and to help my son to heal. I swore forty-five years ago that I would never again have anything to do with the Schallers, and I renew that vow today before God. Good-bye, my dearest Clara. I will do what I can, I promise, to keep Adam from doing something rash, but his anger is beyond any man's control. I cannot predict what will happen."

She stared in disbelief as he walked away, a man having difficulty walking, as if he had just been savagely beaten.

She couldn't be losing him! A love like theirs transcended the vicissitudes of life, didn't it? Theirs wasn't an ordinary love. Oh, God, what was she going to do without him?

Clara sank to the ground, buried her face in her hands, and wept.

The Present Day

"SO THAT WAS THE real start of the feud," Lucas said as he finished reading Clara's letter. "The *real* beginning of this bitter rivalry between our families."

He and Nicole had been sitting in the shade of the Spanish ruins on the old Ballerini property, reading more letters from Mr. Gilette the lawyer. But it was early evening now. Lucas had gone to the Jeep for a camping lantern so they could finish reading the letters by its pale glow. The one they had just read had been very disturbing, about despicable business practices and vows of bloody revenge. Nicole was too choked with emotion to speak. Johann walking away from Clara like that.

Now Nicole knew where the very profitable wine distributorship had come from. Of course, by the time Nicole inherited the estate, that branch of the business had been long gone. Big Jack had sold it to keep some Vegas thugs from coming after him to collect gambling debts.

Big Jack—her father. She was trying to digest the remarkable insights she was receiving about him, felt his image shifting and changing in her mind. Yes, a womanizer and a gambler, but also abandoned by his mother as an infant. That could go a long way to explain his extravagant and irresponsible behavior.

She thought how negative memories were like selfish, unruly children. They insisted on being the center of attention and, because they were loud and trantrum-ish, they pushed the gentler memories away. Now that Nicole was seeing another Big Jack emerge, she was recalling her own sweet memories of a much more tender and loving father—carrying her on his big shoulders, bragging about prizes she'd won at school, letting her stand on his feet as they waltzed around the ballroom at the Growers' Club Christmas ball, teaching her when to double down in blackjack, saying, "There's my clever girl."

In one of her letters, Clara had written: "Poor little Jack. He was always asking why he didn't have a mommy like other kids did. As he grew older, he would ask endless questions. Why did she go away? Where did she go? Where was she now? And the biggest question of all: Why didn't she come back?"

Nicole was enthralled by her great-grandmother's letters as she spoke of little Jack growing up to be Big Jack. It was mesmerizing to read about the life that had shaped him because, after all, hadn't Nicole's father shaped *her*? So in a way, she was reading about the seeds that had eventually shaped her own life and the mindset she held today. Nicole's need for having—and determination to have—independence had come from the early years of a bewildered little boy who wondered why he didn't have a mommy like other kids.

Nicole saw a small window open into her father's psyche. All those arguments and fights she had had with Big Jack—she had simply thought he was a tyrannical control freak. But now she caught a glimmer of cause and effect. Nicole had wanted to go away to school. Not far. Fifty miles. But to live in a dorm or an off-campus apartment. But the operative word was "away." That was what had scared him. His mother had gone away one night and never come back. His hippie sister had run away. And now his daughter wanted to go away.

Her father had needed her, she realized now. He had been scared to see her go. Was he afraid of his own weaknesses? Gambling, giving money away, letting the farm go to ruin? Had he been relying on Nicole to save the family business? To save *him*?

She felt something dart at the edge of her mind. It was the same feeling she had had when she and Lucas had first visited Colina Sagrada and she had sensed something wanting to be heard. It was when she had realized that she was feeling envious of Lucas, and yet she couldn't say why. She had tried several times to give that phantom a voice, but she had been unsuccessful. Now, sitting next to Lucas, her mind filled with the startling revelations of their families' histories and new insights into her own father, Nicole felt the elusive new idea come into sharper focus.

It had to do with revelations about her father and her envy of Lucas. How were they connected?

And then it came to her. Lucas was needed. He was needed here in this valley; he was needed by a world facing climate change and global warming. And she had envied him for that, because she herself had never felt needed. But now she realized that her father had needed her. He just hadn't been able to articulate his need. Instead, he had shouted and pounded his fists, like a frustrated little boy. But she knew now that he had needed her to stay with him.

Look at Michelle, she thought in amazement. *She* was needed—by her doting Joe, who couldn't pick out the day's socks without his wife's help. And all those in-laws looking hopefully to her for the next generation of Eberhardts.

But who needed Nicole Newman? And she realized that this was a large void in her life, her yearning to be needed, by someone or something—and she hadn't even been aware of it.

She felt Lucas shift at her side, heard heaviness in his sigh as he stared into the night. Remembering that this was his journey, too, she laid a hand on his bare arm—the shirtsleeves were rolled up, as the day had been warm—and said, "What are you thinking about?" She felt hard muscle beneath the warm skin, reminding her that this was a man who handled machetes and tractors as well as test tubes and pipettes.

He gave a small laugh. "A million things."

The laugh didn't fool her: Lucas was hurting, too. This was what they shared now.

Which was why Nicole could never read the letters without him. Over the past two weeks, it had become their personal and private ritual, their special trip down their own memory lane. Last week, when Mr. Gilette had found five more letters and Nicole had telephoned Lucas, he had apologized and said something had come up and that he needed to make a quick trip to Phoenix. While he was gone, she had been sorely tempted to read the letters, but she had waited until he came back. And when he did, she had given her housekeeper the night off and had cooked lamb chops for Lucas and herself, and then, over glasses of an excellent Bordeaux, they had read more of Clara's story, the stories of the Newmans and Schallers, the stories of everyone in the valley.

The letters were also planting strange new ideas in her head. Nicole had always known of her Great-Aunt Lorelei's existence and her huge family in Seattle, but she didn't know much about that branch of the family. Clara's letters had shed so much light on Lorelei that Nicole found a growing curiosity within herself to search for those people. And now she understood the current popularity of genealogy and creating family trees.

At her side, in his own kind of silence, Lucas was thinking how this letter went a long way to explain his father's bitter hatred of the Schallers and why he had pounded that hatred into Lucas his whole life—because Adam would have drilled that hatred into his sons Melvyn and Gordon. *And I inherited an unhealthy prejudice that was not at all of my own doing.*

It wasn't fair. He and Nicole had been raised to be enemies, trained from birth to hate each other. But shouldn't people be allowed to make their own enemies, to form their own prejudices and rivalries? If it's all laid out for us before we're even born, then what's left for us to form on our own? The letters struck him as being neutral territory, sort of a little Switzerland in the middle of the Schaller—Newman war zone. The letters were a meeting ground for him and Nicole to get together as impartial parties, to learn the truth about the past and form judgments of their own.

He thought: no wonder we are both seeking a way to pave our own paths, to be masters of our own lives. Because our lives have been based on the past. We each come with a hundred years of baggage. We each don't know where our families end and we begin. We both want to escape from our pasts, but neither of us should have to leave this valley to do that.

And yet that was what was going to happen, with Nicole going to New York and Lucas to Arizona.

He looked at her, sitting so close to him that their shoulders touched. He had grown up hating this woman, and now he couldn't fathom it. She wasn't the Nicole Schaller he had seen in school who he had thought silly and giggly and the daughter of an evil family. And what must *she* be thinking? Discovering that her grandfather had been a dishonest businessman. But that happened in the corporate world all the time. It suddenly seemed a shame to Lucas that an underhanded business deal should lead to such grief and heartbreak, tearing apart two families who could have been together all these years.

And now causing disruption in the present. When Melvyn learned of the letters, he forbade Lucas to have any more involvement with the murder case, Nicole, or Clara's letters. But Lucas couldn't obey. He was finding answers in these letters that no amount of probing his father had ever provided. And his curiosity was growing about who this victim of foul play might be. But most of all was his growing attraction to Nicole. They had something huge in common that was far greater than any differences they might ever have had.

I don't want to hate this woman any more. . . .

But his change in attitude was causing discord between himself and his father, upsetting their normally affable relationship and forcing Lucas to do things behind Melvyn's back. He and Nicole had been meeting secretly every day, sharing the shade of the Spanish ruins and Clara's letters—the detailed lives of their two families, with surprises, insights, even some humor. Since Nicole's impulsive kiss two weeks ago, when Detective Quinn had called to say that the bullet hadn't come from her father's gun, they had both felt confused, bewildered, and slightly derailed. Neither spoke of the incident. She had broken away from him, embarrassed and flustered, and they had talked about how relieved they both were with the news, as if that were the only topic in the world and that a Schaller kissing a Newman had *not* just happened. And in the two weeks since, it had been business as usual, reading Clara's letters, gaining better insight into their families, waiting for Detective Quinn to solve the murder, waiting for escrow to close on the winery, Nicole packing her bags to go to New York, Lucas making arrangements to set up an experimental agricultural station in Arizona. On the other hand, neither could stop thinking about the kiss either.

"Adam's revenge," Nicole murmured now, feeling overwhelmed with emotion. She looked at Lucas, met his eyes. "Do you think your grandfather's revenge is connected to the murder victim?" The police had come no closer to determining the identity of the skeleton. They said they needed to know when the barrel-room wall had last been repaired, and Mr. Gilette had yet to find any record of it.

After the medical examiner had determined that the victim was female and around twenty years old, Quinn had sent out a bulletin to other police agencies, asking for missing-persons reports. "But it's a long shot," he had told Nicole. "A lot of young women have gone missing, voluntarily or against their will, over the last twenty to thirty years. I'm not expecting to get a good lead, and the pregnancy is no lead either, since she most likely kept it a secret."

It had briefly crossed Nicole's mind to wonder if it could be her aunt Deborah, who was said to have run away a long time ago. What Nicole had always been told about her mysterious Aunt Deborah (and by now Nicole had asked a few of the older residents in the valley) was that she had been a hippie in the sixties and had run off with a rock band; and her father, Grandpa Bill, never forgave her and said he would never take her back. Besides, it was the sixties, and kids were running away all the time. Someone claimed to have seen her at the Woodstock music festival in 1969, but after that she had lost touch with the family. Nicole was reluctant to go around inquiring further. She didn't want to dredge up her family's dirty laundry and didn't want people in the valley to start connecting the runaway Schaller daughter with the shocking skeleton—especially as the victim had been pregnant.

Even if the family story were true, Nicole couldn't help the slowly creeping feeling that Aunt Deborah and the skeleton in the wall were somehow connected. *Had* her father's sister in fact been murdered and had there been a huge cover-up? Or had she really just run away? That was the way it was in these farming communities. The girls tended to marry and move away—as Nicole's Aunt Lorelei had, and Lucas's Aunt Sofie. The sons tended to stay because they inherited the family holdings. So Deborah had simply joined the feminine exodus—as Nicole herself was preparing to do.

The whole case hinged on when that wall had last been worked on. If the last repair had been in the seventies or eighties, then it couldn't be Deborah, and Nicole would have dredged up a lot of Schaller dirt that was best left to rest. With Mr. Gilette and the police coming up with no answers, the last hope rested on Clara's final letters—if there were any more to come.

Lucas rose and stretched his legs. He looked down at Nicole, who seemed small and vulnerable. He reached down and helped her to her feet. She looked up at him in the pale glow of the lantern and said, "Do you think Johann and Clara ever got back together? I couldn't bear it if her story ends with him walking away like that."

"I don't know," he said, his voice heavy with emotion. "Mr. Gilette said the storage basement is nearly all cleared out. He said he doubted he would find any more letters."

She looked up at the star-splashed night. A golden harvest moon dominated the eastern sky. The air was balmy and sweet. "I got a phone call from my new employer in New York yesterday. They said they passed my marketing plan to the parent company in Switzerland, and they were very impressed. They want me to fly to Zurich for an important meeting with them."

His pause was significant. "When do you leave?"

"Day after tomorrow," she said, searching his face for a reaction.

He stood very close to her, but she couldn't read his face. "And when do you come back?"

"I don't know. Michelle is helping me pack up all my personal stuff to put in storage so the Macintoshes can move in as soon as escrow closes. Why?"

"Remember when I went to Arizona last week?"

"Yes."

"Well, I'm going again, probably Monday. The soil there is ideal for my rootstock experiments."

"What about your father? He isn't well, is he? Can he be left alone?"

Lucas was touched that she cared about Melvyn's welfare. Melvyn, who had shouted at her and thrown her out of his house before he collapsed. "Yes, that's a problem. I worry about him, wonder if I should put my project on hold."

Nicole looked up into Lucas's handsome face and suddenly felt guilty. Her grandfather had swindled his grandfather in a terrible way. "I am so sorry," she said softly, thinking that today was a day of revelations and apologies. "For what Grandpa Bill did."

He smiled, and it made her heart jump. "It's not your fault, Nicole. You aren't responsible for the deeds of people who came before you."

But she was reminded of a Bible quote, or perhaps it was Shakespeare. Something about the sins of the fathers, and the sons having to pay for them.

It was yet another tie binding her to this man, an obligation, a need to make restoration for what her grandfather had done. She felt as if she and Lucas were being woven into a tapestry that was not of their own making. And yet they were soon to go their separate ways, leave this valley and most likely never see each other again.

"We are being recruited into a drama we want no part of," she said with a hint of resentment. "So why can't we just walk away from it? If Mr. Gilette calls and says he's found more letters, I should tell him I'm not interested. I've read enough."

His smile deepened and her heart did another jump. "Would you really be able to say that?"

"I have to," Nicole said with renewed intensity. "I have made promises, so many people are counting on me to live up to my word." She had said this before, but there was so much more significance to her promises now. Her grandfather had stooped to lies and deception in order to rise to wealth and power. Keeping her word suddenly seemed the most important thing in Nicole's life. Poor Clara! How disappointed she must have been in her son. The whole valley would have heard about what Bill Junior did to his cousin.

Impulsively, Nicole pressed her face against Lucas's chest, and he put his arms around her as if it were the most natural thing in the world. He looked at the collapsed stone walls that had been put up by a Spaniard two centuries ago, and it occurred to him that he and Nicole had created a world of their own here, a world in which no one else belonged.

Lucas Newman found himself wishing a million things under the million stars as the golden harvest moon rose majestically in the October sky. Feeling Nicole's supple body against his, he felt barriers come tumbling down, like these old stone walls. With a hand under her chin, he lifted her face to his and gently kissed her on the lips.

She responded, curling an arm around his neck, kissing him back, gently at first, but then with urgency.

Lucas groaned. She felt so good in his arms, tasted so good on his tongue. Nothing had ever felt so perfect and right in his life.

But then he suddenly drew back and Nicole looked at him, confused. Then she said, "Is it the letters? Are they doing this to us? Clara and Johann? Casting some sort of spell?"

Battling his desire, he stepped away from her and ran his hands through his hair. He was sure that they were under no spell, but maybe Nicole needed to believe in forces beyond their control. They both knew they couldn't be together. They had no possible future. They had separate career paths that would take them each to faraway places. Both were leaving the valley. Two intelligent people falling under a spell.

"It's getting late," he said, needing suddenly to be alone and to think things out. The world had gone upside down. Falling in love with Nicole Schaller!

He drove her home. It was a silent drive. Each wanted to say something, but each had no idea what it was. When they arrived at her house, she said a small "Good-bye," and he saw in the rearview mirror that she watched him drive off. He knew he wasn't going to get any sleep that night.

* * *

LUCAS COULDN'T STOP THINKING about Nicole. She filled his mind the way a bright summer sun would. When he dropped her off at her house, he had wanted to reach for her, stop her from getting out of the Jeep, start kissing her and never stop. He ached with desire in a way he never had before. This was a feeling he had never experienced: it was wild and unruly, defying reason. And he suddenly felt alive and daring.

Was that what he was feeling for Nicole Schaller? Was it love? Or was it just an intense desire to taste forbidden fruit?

How could he let her go? How could he kiss her like that, and let her kiss him back the way she had, and then let her leave the valley?

Because I have to leave too. Whatever there was between them, it was doomed and should be allowed to fade before things got harder for them. He prayed there were no more Clara letters. It would be easier to make a clean break that way. Nicole would fly to Switzerland, and he would drive to Phoenix.

He turned onto his property and followed the driveway to his house. When he saw his foreman come running toward him, waving his battered straw hat in the beams of the Jeep's headlights, Lucas brought the vehicle to a quick halt and jumped out. "What is it?"

"It's Señor Newman, *jefe*. He's very upset."

"What about?"

The Mexican farmhand shrugged. "He is in the fermenting room."

"Thanks, Rodrigo," Lucas said and headed for the winery buildings.

He strode into the vast, high-ceilinged room stacked with 55-gallon stainless-steel drums wrapped in insulating material, with thermostats registering and controlling the various delicate temperatures needed for the perfect fermentation process. The warehouse-like room had a stone floor, with steel ladders and catwalks connecting the tiers of vats.

He saw his father lumbering down a steel stairway, frowning heavily, his shock of white hair somehow a show of his displeasure. "Where were you today, son?" he boomed, his voice echoing off whitewashed stone walls. "I could have done with your help. I looked everywhere. No one knew where to find you."

When Lucas didn't immediately reply, Melvyn said, "My dear God, you were with *her* again!"

Lucas thrust his hands into the pockets of his jeans. He wasn't going to be drawn into an argument about Nicole. "What did you need me for, Pop?"

A sour look came over Melvyn's face. "I can't tell if there's enough yeast in this Cabernet. According to the logs, it should be fine. It just doesn't look right to me. There's not enough foam."

"I'll take a look."

Lucas started up the ladder to the overhead catwalk, then paused and said, "Pop, we need to talk."

Melvyn turned away.

"You have to face it sooner or later," Lucas called after him.

Melvyn spun around in fury, his cane catching him from falling. "I don't have to face anything! It's *you* who have to face reality. That girl is no good for you. She's warping your mind."

"Pop, 'that girl,' as you call her, is a decent person and not only do I not find anything unlikeable about her, I happen to like her—a lot. Pop, I want to talk about what happened between Bill Schaller and Grandpa Adam."

"It happened a long time ago," Melvyn said. "I was only six years old at the time. Gordon and Sofie were eight. We weren't even aware of what was going on. So I don't want to talk about it."

"But *I* do."

Melvyn turned on him with an anger Lucas had rarely witnessed in his father. "I saw what losing that distributorship did to my father. I saw how the anger and bitterness weakened his heart. I blame the Schallers for his death. To his dying hour, your grandfather never forgave the Schallers and neither will I. And," Melvyn added forcefully, "neither will you."

Not only could Lucas forgive the Schallers, he felt sorry for them—for Wilhelm and Clara, whose son had lied to them and cheated in a business deal. It was a stain on the Schaller name that could never be scrubbed clean. Even though it had happened a long time ago, the stealing of the distributorship and Adam's attack on Bill Junior was still remembered by some of the old-timers and was one of the legends in the valley.

"You should read Clara's letters, Pop. They shed light on so many things. There's no reason for our two families to be enemies. It's not our fight any more. The falling-out was between Johann and Wilhelm, and then Bill and Adam. Why have you insisted on continuing this bitter rivalry for so long? It isn't even your fight. Like you said, you were just six years old when Bill Schaller stole a lucrative business deal from your father."

Melvyn didn't say anything, just leaned on his cane, glaring at his son. And then Lucas asked, in a quieter voice, "Or is it something else? Is there something you haven't told me?" His eyes widened. "Is it something that's been kept a secret and you're afraid it will come out in Clara's letters?"

"I thought you were going to Arizona to find land for your experimental crop. Why are you letting all this Schaller crap get in the way of your dream? You're letting that girl seduce you."

"Stop calling her that! I happen to respect and admire Nicole Schaller. She isn't seducing me from anything. In fact, she's been helping me to understand my family and therefore myself."

"That's a load of bullshit. You don't understand anything. If Nicole Schaller is so great, why doesn't she sell you that blighted patch of land at Colina Sagrada, saving you many unnecessary trips to Arizona? *Tell me that!*"

When Lucas saw a scarlet flush rise from his father's neck, he strode forward, placed a hand on the old man's elbow, and said, more quietly, "Hey, Pop, let's not fight."

"You could supervise your experimental crop from right here, if she would sell to you. But she won't because she's a greedy Schaller." The wind had gone out of him as he let his son guide him to a chair and helped him to sit down.

"The truth is, Pop," Lucas said gently, "Nicole said she would have sold me that land if she had known that was all I wanted. Unfortunately, the property has been sold and is going through escrow right now."

Melvyn looked long and hard into Lucas's eyes, and then there was a slight slumping of his shoulders. "Son," he said softly, "please believe me when I say that I am only thinking of your own best interests. It is a father's duty to protect his children. I am doing my best to protect you right now."

"Protect me from *what*?" Lucas cried.

But when he saw how pale his father had gone, with fear in his eyes, Lucas decided to drop it. There was definitely something here that the old man wasn't telling him. Melvyn Newman's hatred of the Schallers went deeper than just something he had been raised to believe. Adam couldn't have inculcated this much vehemence into his boy. Something must have happened in Melvyn's time, a personal encounter with the Schallers, as there had been with Johann and then Adam. But Lucas wouldn't grill him on it now. The old man needed to rest.

It frustrated Lucas. Melvyn was seventy. He had *known* Clara and Wilhelm and many of the people mentioned in the letters. He could tell stories, he knew things, could shed light, but he refused. But Lucas understood. Melvyn had loved his father, had grown up idolizing him, and now he was very protective of him. Lucas knew a lot about Grandpa Adam, who had died before Lucas was born. There were pictures of him and mementos all over the house: Adam Newman receiving yet another prestigious award for his quality wines, Adam elected five years in a row to the presidency of the Growers' Club, Adam being thanked by a California senator for his philanthropy in the valley and his political support.

But Lucas suspected there were secrets being kept. He hoped one of

Clara's letters would illuminate this particular mystery for him, if there *were* any more letters, as he didn't think Melvyn's confessing the experience, reliving it, would be good for his heart. Lucas found himself trapped in a dilemma. Was his continued involvement in the investigation of the unsolved murder—and further delving into the past through Clara's letters—going to cause his father serious harm? Should he back off, forget about Nicole, and get on with his own life? But how could he, now that his heart was seriously involved? Was the day coming when he was going to have to choose between Nicole and his father?

*   *   *

"KEEP THIS IN MIND, granddaughter. People are alike all over the world. We are no different from one another, no matter race, nationality, religion. We're just human beings, feeling the same things worldwide. When I was young, I thought foreigners were either stronger than us or weaker, smarter than us or stupider, sharper than us or duller, more energized than us or lazier. They were either someone to be feared, or not to be feared at all. They were never the same as us, and that was a big mistake I made back then. I either overestimated or underestimated the foreigner, but never saw them as equal. We have to always keep that equality in mind because it makes us more tolerant and helpful. Above all, making others your equals will teach you a lot about yourself."

Nicole was standing in the morning sunshine that streamed through her living-room windows, looking up at her great-grandmother's portrait over the fireplace. It seemed an appropriate spot to reread one of yesterday's letters.

She had grown up with this woman's eyes staring down at her. For Nicole as a girl, it had just been a picture of a wealthy old lady. But of course, as Nicole got older, the woman in the portrait grew younger. How old are you here? she silently asked, trying to guess but knowing that portraitists tended to flatter their subjects by shaving off a few pounds, a few years. Judging by the hairstyle and fashion of dress, Clara had sat for this painting sometime in the fifties.

And she was no longer a stranger to Nicole, who had rarely given her father's grandmother a thought. But now she *knew* the woman in the painting, could hear her softly spoken voice, her words spiced with an exotic German accent. Now that Nicole knew this woman's dreams and tragedies and secret loves, she saw a gentler figure, a softer face. No longer a stiff, detached, and impersonal stranger, the woman seated so calmly and looking down at Nicole with wise and understanding eyes was a loving grandmother, the origin of Nicole's own being, the bestower of widow's-peak hairlines that only yesterday, with a shy blush, Lucas had said he found very attractive.

"I wish I had known you, Great-Grandmother," Nicole said to the painting. "But I suppose I already do, thanks to your letters. You have given me a past, roots, and for that I am grateful. Tell me Great-Grandmother, did you and Johann ever get together again, or did he walk away from you that terrible day for good?"

Nicole rubbed her neck with a sigh. After last night in the ruins—the letters that sparked intense emotions, the delicious hot clinch with Lucas—Nicole hadn't slept a wink. She couldn't stop thinking about him. The kissing and caresses. God, she wanted more!

She looked at the boxes stacked in the entry hall in preparation for her move to New York. Although a lot of the furnishings and antiques in the house were going to the Macintoshes, things that the Canadians hadn't wanted and Nicole wasn't taking with her were in labeled boxes to be given to charity: bed linens, towels, dishes, kitchen utensils, small appliances. But she wasn't finished, and Michelle was coming by to help her with the rest.

She felt suspended, up in the air. For years she had been dreaming of leaving the valley and creating a life of her own. But was she doing it now for the right reasons? So much had changed. Was she only sticking with her plan because she had committed to the job in New York? She hadn't been aware of how close she felt to the vineyards and the valley and the people in it, until the moment of departure came. Now the doubts were creeping in.

And then there was Lucas. How could she be falling in love with the son of a family that had been her own family's archenemy for a hundred years? She was supposed to hate him. Or at least to not trust him. Certainly not warm to him and start to enjoy his company and then wake up looking forward to getting together with him to read more of Clara's letters. Sitting side by side in the sunshine, their shoulders touching, pressed together even, although they both pretended they weren't aware of it. Occasionally looking at each other, faces inches apart, wordlessly sharing the same experiences, the same emotional reactions. It was almost as intimate as sex.

And now she really did want to have sex with him—hot and frantic—and it made her ache unbearably. They were both leaving in two days. Would she see him before then? They hadn't said anything, made any kind of date or time to get together and say good-bye.

Hearing a car pull up, she looked out and saw Michelle's dusty black convertible sports car come to a halt at the front steps. Michelle was wearing Bermuda shorts with a man's plaid work shirt, and her crazy henna-red curls were caught up in a bandanna, 1940s style. She was here to help Nicole pack up the rest of her things—clothes, books, DVDs, pictures, mementos, and knickknacks—which Michelle was going to keep in storage at her house until Nicole had found a place to live. Her friend came in carrying a picnic basket and some extra cardboard boxes folded under her arm.

Nicole went to help her. The boxes were going to come in handy. "So tell me," Michelle said breathlessly, a flush to her cheeks. "Did you read the last of the letters? Anything new and exciting?"

"A lot of new stuff to tell you—and disturbing as well, unfortunately." It was on Nicole's lips to blurt out about the kiss in the Spanish ruins. She was bursting to tell her best friend, explain that it had been no mere meeting of mouths, a test kiss to see if there was anything there. No, this had been the real thing, a kiss that would have sparked a forest fire.

"We are positively swamped at the bakeries!" Michelle said before Nicole could speak. "What with all the tourists pouring into town for Oktoberfest."

"You don't have to do this, Michelle. I'm capable of packing my own boxes."

But Michelle turned wide, bright, tear-brimmed eyes to her. "I had to come, girlfriend; I have to help you." She hefted the basket and faked a smile. "I brought us a lunch. Cream cheese and ham on rye, roast beef and cheddar on a Kaiser roll, potato salad with Bermuda onion, key lime pie with graham cracker crust."

Michelle turned such a woebegone face to Nicole that Nicole was taken aback.

"What's brought all this on?" she said.

"I'm devastated that you're leaving!"

Nicole blinked. "But you said you were happy for me."

"I've been faking it, being all happy for a friend and all. An act, most of it. Yes, happy that you landed such a great job in New York, and you'll be moving up the corporate ladder. But I'm telling you, this business of 'if you're happy then I'm happy' is way overrated. Even if you *are* happy, Nicole, I'm miserable as hell. What am I going to do without you?" Tears rose in her eyes. "You're *really* leaving, and you'll be thousands of miles away!"

"There's still phones and texting and email and Skype."

"It's not the same!" she wailed dramatically.

A wave of sadness rolled over Nicole. Their friendship went way back and was held together with indestructible mortar. In grade school they'd swapped lunches and clothes and homework. They'd giggled over boys and gossiped about other girls and styled each other's hair and painted each other's nails and mooned over the same movie idols. Especially after Nicole's mother died when she was twelve and Big Jack was away a lot, Nicole spent many sleepovers at Michelle's house. When Nicole started her period, Michelle's mother guided her through it. When the two friends started dating boys, they shared horror stories. And when Michelle married Joe Eberhardt, Nicole had been the maid of honor.

Closer than friends, they were sisters. And now they were feeling the reality of a departure that was going to be an unendurable test of courage and strength.

Michelle started to cry and Nicole tried to diffuse the high emotion. "Have you set a date for the procedure? I wish I could be here to hold your hand."

Michelle ran her hand under her nose. "It's set for two weeks from now. First they take a sample from Joe and then they put it in me. Everyone thinks I'm going in for a routine D&C. You're the only one who knows our secret."

Nicole put her arms around Michelle and said, "I'm going to miss you."

"We never took those yoga classes we always talked about."

The house phone rang. Nicole picked it up in the entry hall. It was Mr. Gilette, the lawyer. "The basement is now all cleared out," he said. "I found a few more blueprints, but I don't think they'll be of any use. Some old contracts and outdated documents. Inspection reports from the Department of Health. Nothing useful, I'm afraid. Oh, and five letters from your grandmother. They were stuck in a box of old bills of lading. I'm afraid that's it, Ms. Schaller. Unless you have any papers or records stored away at your house or in the winery. . . ."

There weren't. Nicole had already done a thorough search of her place with Michelle's help, and they had turned up nothing. Apparently when Bill Junior died and Big Jack inherited the estate, he had turned all important papers over to Gilette's law firm for safekeeping.

Her heart plummeted. She had thought she would be pleased that all this was coming to an end. But instead. . . . Once she and Lucas read the last of the letters, there would be no more secret meetings at the Spanish ruins. But at least it was a reason to see him one more time.

Nicole said to Michelle, "More letters. Definitely the last ones. I have to go get them."

"Wow." Michelle and her husband had also been drawn into Clara Schaller's drama. Nicole had passed along letters that contained interesting information about the Eberhardts and other families in the valley.

"I have to call Lucas."

"Of course you do," Michelle said wryly.

"Don't start that again. There is nothing between us," Nicole said, but her words tasted chalky in her mouth considering what had happened last night in the ruins, considering that Nicole wanted it to happen again.

"I'll come by tomorrow to help with the packing," Michelle said, and she left.

She called him and he answered right away. "I'll swing by in ten minutes and pick you up," he said. "We can go to Gilette's office together, and this way we can get the letters out of the way today."

Get them out of the way. Yes, that was the best way to look at it. And then get on with their separate lives.

*   *   *

THEY DROVE IN AWKWARD silence, both knowing that the same thing was on their minds, neither knowing what to say. Nicole used every bit of her strength not to reach over and touch his knee.

At Gilette's office they were stilted and polite. The lawyer assured Nicole he would keep her apprised of anything that might come up about the estate, and that he would be in communication with Detective Quinn, although he had a feeling, he said, that they had hit a dead end.

Nicole took the last five letters, in their sealed envelopes with "For My Granddaughter" written on the front, and slipped them into her shoulder bag. She was both eager to read them and terrified of reading them.

By unspoken agreement, she and Lucas would open them at the Spanish ruins.

It was with a kind of sadness that she rode at his side down Lynnville's main street. They drove past the Growers' Club, which carried much more significance for Nicole now. The club had changed from her grandfather's day. Women and Hispanics were members now. A few doors down was the building that belonged to the Lynnville Women's Service

Club. Nicole's mother Lucy had been a member right up until the chemo kept her from attending meetings.

Traffic was heavy, the sidewalks crowded. Oktoberfest was about to open and the valley was getting ready for a huge wave of tourists, visitors, and guests. Along the riverfront, Nicole and Lucas saw men wearing tool belts and overalls, hammering and sawing as long trestle tables were assembled on the grass and wooden booths were being constructed for the wine tasting and the sale of beer. Barbecues were being made ready for the beef and pork and chicken and fish that would be cooked for the merry crowd.

This time next week, this park would be packed with families and children and dogs and out-of-towners, and the air would be filled with music and laughter and delicious aromas and a universal feeling of goodwill among strangers.

And Lucas and Nicole would not be part of it.

They rode down the highway in silence. Everything had changed now. Nicole thought. Last night, they had kissed. And she knew it had been real, she had felt Lucas's desire and passion, and he had felt hers. She knew they could have taken it to the next level, but they had had the presence of mind to stop. And now there would never be another chance.

The journey they had shared these past eighteen days was coming to an end.

They had come to think of the Spanish ruins as "their" place. Just as it had once been Clara and Johann's secret place. Nicole couldn't shake the eerie feeling that she and Lucas were reenacting an old drama.

When they arrived, they stepped down onto yellowing grass that was littered with orange and gold leaves. Autumn was in the air. They went to their usual wall, which was chair-high, and, without speaking, Nicole solemnly brought out the first letter and opened it. She was surprised when a photograph slipped out. In color, it was a snapshot of three smiling teenagers. She and Lucas stared.

"This boy looks just like *you*," Nicole said in amazement.

"That's my father, Melvyn. The other boy would be Gordon, his brother, who died in a car accident when he was twenty." He stared at the girl between the two boys. "And she looks like *you*. She has the hairline." The smiling girl, about seventeen or eighteen, wore her long hair straight, parted in the middle and held in place with a hippie headband.

Nicole had never seen a photo of Big Jack's sister. When Deborah ran away from home, Grandpa Bill had been so angry that he had had all traces of her removed from the house.

"She *could* be Deborah," murmured Nicole. Yes, she did bear a resemblance to this girl who might have been Big Jack's sister. "But . . . if this is my aunt, then why was she photographed with the two Newman boys, and why are they smiling?"

Lucas shot to his feet. "Okay," he said resolutely. "It's time for answers. My father will know what this is about."

"I want to go with you, but I don't want to give your father a heart attack."

"I'll ease into it. This photograph has as much to do with you and the Schallers as it does with me and the Newmans."

*   *   *

NICOLE WAITED POLITELY IN the doorway of Melvyn's home office until the old man grudgingly gave her permission to enter. He looked tired and beaten.

Lucas handed the photo to his father. Silence descended as Nicole and Lucas watched for a reaction. After a moment, tears rose in Melvyn's eyes. He reached out and touched the picture with a shaking finger. "That's me," he said in a dusty voice. "And that's my brother, your Uncle Gordon, and that's. . . ." He sighed deeply and raggedly. "That's Deborah Schaller." He looked at Lucas with tear-filled eyes. "Do you know? This photo is deceptive. We weren't the friends that we appear to be here, as if we hung around together. We didn't. Our families would never have stood for it. This picture was snapped after a baseball game which Lynnville High won. Everyone was celebrating. Clara Schaller just happened to grab this shot as we were all running around hugging one another. It's not what it looks like at all. . . ." His voice trailed off.

Lucas leaned forward, placing his hands on the desk. "What happened to Deborah, Pop?" He said it in a tone that meant he wasn't backing down this time.

"She ran away. She became a hippie and hitchhiked with other hippies. She never came home. That's all I know. Son, that's a painful time for me. That was when my brother was killed in a fiery car crash. I witnessed it, and I don't wish to relive it." He rose slowly from the desk and walked out of the room with as much dignity as a limp and a cane would allow.

As Lucas and Nicole stared at the picture, the girl smiling for the camera but the two boys only looking at *her*, Lucas murmured, "Deceiving? I don't think so. I think that what is in this picture is very clear." They were looking at a photograph of a love triangle. Had Lucas's father and uncle been in love with Nicole's aunt?

Lucas had wondered if something had happened in Melvyn's life to re-ignite an old family feud, something that went beyond grudges between fathers and grandfathers. Could this be it?

PART SIX
1965

"WHY DO YOU WEAR your hair like an Indian, Deborah?" Frieda
Eberhardt said as she rapidly tatted a white lace doily in her ample
lap. Despite being seventy-two, Frieda still had quick, nimble fingers
and there was hardly a chair or table in the valley that didn't have one
of her beautiful lace doilies gracing it. She was enjoying a break from
bakery work, visiting her best friend in the Schallers' kitchen where
Clara was preparing pitted cherries to make preserves.

Deborah didn't take offense at her Aunt Frieda's comment. A lot
of older people didn't understand today's styles. Deborah liked her
new hairstyle. It made her feel free and unrestrained. At some of the
bigger college campuses around the country, students were starting to
grow beards and wear their hair long, but not in the Largo Valley, which
was about twenty years behind the times. While students at the Berkeley
campus of the University of California had taken to wearing sandals and
tie-dyed shirts, the students at the Santa Barbara campus were still wearing tasseled loafers and shirts with button-down collars. A few edgy coffee
houses had opened up near the campus, where trendy kids went to listen
to hip poetry and smoke cigarettes, but otherwise life was ordinary and
peaceful. But Deborah wanted to stand out.

"We are no longer slaves to curlers and hairspray, Aunt Frieda,"
the eighteen-year-old said in a superior tone as she sat on the kitchen
counter, swinging her long, slender legs. "The world is changing."

Frieda exchanged a patient, knowing glance with Clara, who said,
"The world is *always* changing, Debbie. You'll discover that someday."

Changing in more ways than you think, Grandmother, Deborah thought, thinking how shocked these two old ladies would be if she told them her secret.

Deborah was desperately in love but couldn't tell anyone. How could love be so wonderful and so heartbreaking at the same time? She suspected that Grandma Clara might understand—Grandma knew all about the heart and feelings and emotions; she was always dispensing wise advice to her friends. But Deborah knew that her father and Grandpa Wilhelm would be furious if they knew she was in love with the enemy. The problem was: How to sneak away to be with him without getting found out? It wasn't fair. They were just two innocent people who had nothing to do with the circumstances that were keeping them apart. So she had to be careful not to accidentally say his name, when that was precisely *all* she wanted to say!

As Clara scooped the cherries into a saucepan, she thought: the world *is* always changing. But then, perhaps it is changing at a faster pace today. Young people are different from the way we were, more headstrong and less obedient. And the racial lines are blurring. Because of the Civil Rights Movement and the protests in the South for racial equality, Negroes were no longer called Negro. They wanted to be called "black," which used to be a derogatory term, which was probably why they embraced it. Clara understood their reasoning. "You call us Negro," they were saying now, "which is simply Spanish for black. Why hide your racism behind a Spanish word? If we are black, then black we are."

And now the Mexican Americans had embraced the term "Chicano," which had also been an insulting term for years in California, Arizona, and Texas. But they now proudly called themselves Chicano and Chicana.

Clara had lived in California for fifty-three years. She had some experience with the Mexican migrant workers. She had seen their camps. While she found the conditions deplorable and she sympathized with the people who had to live in them, Clara was torn. She was also an immigrant. But she had come to this country through legal channels. Papa Jakob had worked hard for a year, dealing with a bureaucratic maze, clerks who didn't care, complex paperwork, providing documents to secure visas for his sons and the other young immigrants. When the American consulate finally granted them their visas, they all came over and got to work. No one sneaked across any borders and squatted in filthy camps.

Clara saw a powder-keg situation coming to the valley. Agitators had already arrived to give public speeches and put on demonstrations, to distribute inflammatory literature. Men from outside the valley, professional union organizers, and Latino activists bent on stirring up the workers and calling them to strike. It was making the growers nervous. With the right men agitating these people, who had nothing to lose, unifying them, things could turn dangerous and volatile. Wilhelm and Bill Jr. had always paid their workers a fair wage for humane hours. Clara knew that the Newmans did too. But other growers in the valley were not so caring about their labor force. Such exploiters saw an endless source of labor that was almost slavery, and they took advantage of it.

News commentators were saying that America was in the middle of a social revolution, that the old ways were going to disappear. Perhaps. Clara's own granddaughter was exhibiting signs of rebellion, wearing her hair in such a radical fashion, sporting unladylike clothes. But Clara thought there was something else different about her granddaughter this summer, not just social rebellion. She was sighing a lot, whispering on the phone with her best friend, visiting Lynnville more often than usual. She was absentminded and moony-eyed. Clara recognized the symptoms: Deborah was in love.

Clara wondered who the boy was. She knew it wasn't going to be easy for the two young people. Deborah's father was going to put every boy his daughter brought home under a microscope. Bill was wary of fortune-hunters, and any boy Deborah fell in love with was going to have to pass a strict test.

Clara wondered why Deborah hadn't confided in her about it yet. Since her mother had left when she was eleven, Deborah had gone to her grandmother with every secret and confidence that girls were prone to. And Clara never judged; Deborah knew that. So why keep him a secret? Clara wondered if it was anyone she knew.

She prayed that it would lead to happiness. Ever since Johann had walked away from her that day years ago, Clara had carried a pool of sadness inside her. Luckily, happy moments came along. Like this morning, making jam in the kitchen with her best friend and her granddaughter. What could be better than this?

Clara was proud of her granddaughter, who had turned out to be surprisingly pretty, considering that her mother, Fay, had been plain and somewhat chunky. Deborah was graceful and lithe, more like her Aunt Lorelei, although there was no blood relation there. A happy free spirit who had always done well at school.

She knew the Newmans were prospering, and she was happy for them too. Like Wilhelm, Johann treated his farmworkers fairly; therefore they were loyal to him. If the threat of an impending strike turned out to be true, she prayed the Schallers and the Newmans would be spared. They had heard frightening news coming from Texas and other agricultural states—of picket lines and bloody riots and fighting.

She wished she could talk to Johann about it, like they used to. But they had stopped secretly meeting seven years ago when he had walked away from her and left her weeping beside Largo Creek. They had met congenially since, at the Growers' Christmas ball, at Oktoberfest and wine festivals, at barbecues hosted by other growers. Always polite, but stilted, with the Callahan wine distributorship standing between them, and the knowledge that Bill Junior had done very well for himself and his family, expanding the distribution of Schaller wines across the country and even to Europe, making them richer than ever. All stolen from Adam Newman.

As she added apple juice, lemon juice, and pectin to the cherries in the saucepan, Clara glanced at her granddaughter perched on the kitchen counter in blue jeans and a gypsy blouse, with her long, straight hair and Indian headband, and thought how interesting it was how familial traits got handed down. Deborah hadn't inherited much from her mother, more from her father; and Bill had inherited Clara's widow's-peak hairline, which was a Heinze trait, not Schaller. She noticed the same thing among the next Newman generation, noticing that Adam's sons, Gordon and Melvyn, had inherited their father's very fetching hooded eyes that always hinted at secret amusement, even when they were dead serious. She supposed that familial traits were reminders that, as John Donne had said, no man is an island.

And then the most unexpected thought jumped into her mind. What if a Schaller were to marry a Newman? Would *both* traits show up in their children? Clara nearly laughed at herself, the notion was so absurd. The sun and stars would burn out before a Schaller and a Newman married!

Clara stirred the sweet cherry mixture on the stove and brought it to a boil. There was something comforting about a kitchen. Clara thought of their first home here, the rustic cabin built by Papa Jakob in 1911. Back then, it was just a kitchen, really, with an adjoining space for a fireplace and room for cots to sleep on. That cabin was gone now except in her memory. Sometimes Clara, at the wise age of seventy-two, yearned for those simple days of sleeping on cots again and living all the phases of their lives at the kitchen table.

Eighteen-year-old Deborah, on the other hand, felt itchy. She hadn't a domestic bone in her body. Kitchens and cookware didn't interest her. She longed to travel, to see the Nile and the Amazon and Mount McKinley and the Great Wall of China. She didn't want to go to college or have a career. She also didn't want a husband or babies. She wanted to fight for a cause.

Deborah looked out the window. Earlier, she had seen her father drive off in his truck. She knew where he had gone: to fetch the mail from their box out on the main road. She knew the trip was going to be fruitless. She knew that at some point she was going to have to tell her family the bad news. In fact, she had two pieces of bad news for them, and she had been putting it off. But the summer was in full swing, and soon fall would be here and she would have to speak up. But how? How could she face her father and grandfather and grandmother and tell them that she was in love with a boy they considered their enemy? How could she tell them that, when Deborah herself didn't know how *he* felt about *her*? That was the problem. That was what was stalling things. There had been smiles between them and knowing looks and innocent dialogue. But had she only imagined that he was returning her feelings? Was she reading something that wasn't there into his smiles and words? What if there was nothing there at all, and she went ahead and told her family and caused World War Three for nothing?

Deborah knew it wasn't going to be easy finding a boy to love, especially with her father being so protective of her. Deborah was an heiress worth millions. She didn't want to be worth millions. She wanted a boy to love her for herself, not for her family's fortune.

In a strange way, she and her father wanted the same thing: to protect her from unscrupulous fortune-hunters. But where they differed was in the kind of man he wanted her to marry. Bill Schaller Junior could not settle for his daughter marrying "beneath" her, as he put it. Deborah's pool to choose from was very small, as she could only marry either an equal—someone who was just as rich—or a professional man who had money and prospects of his own. God forbid Deborah should fall in love with a plumber. Which was why he was insisting she go to college and earn a degree. "Men in high positions don't like to marry uneducated or unpolished women," he had said a million times. "They want their wives to be sophisticated, poised, well spoken, and articulate." But she couldn't go to just any school. He had given her a list, and she couldn't believe it. Barnard, Bryn Mawr, Mount Holyoke, Radcliffe, Smith, Vassar, and Wellesley. All-girl schools! And all of them something like three thousand miles away.

He might as well pack her off to a nunnery! And she bet he would, if he could. And he would positively croak if he knew she wasn't a virgin.

This whole college issue made her grind her teeth. She didn't want to go from one set of rules to another. A song that had come out two years ago kept going through her mind, Lesley Gore singing "You Don't Own Me." About being young and free and wanting to experience life. Deborah wanted freedom. "The world will be my classroom," she would pontificate. "People in the streets and cafés, fishermen and waitresses and flower sellers will be my teachers, and life will be my major." Her father would roll his eyes and tell her to stop being so pretentious.

"You're only eighteen," he would say. "You don't know what you want."

But that was precisely it. Deborah *was* eighteen and she knew *exactly* what she wanted. Old people weren't clued in to today's hip world. They were calling it "the generation gap," and a truer phrase hadn't ever been coined. It was like they were talking two different languages.

She looked at her grandmother and Aunt Frieda, contented women at their domestic chores. But on the kitchen table were newspapers and magazines. News headlines about a war in a country she had never heard of, and a photo on the cover of *Life* magazine of Marine helicopters flying over rice paddies. Another newspaper with a picture of students carrying protest signs. Young people all over the country were standing up for what they believed in, whether it was integration of black students into white schools, or calling for American troops to be withdrawn from Vietnam.

Looking out the window, watching for her father's return from the mailbox, she saw Grandpa Wilhelm leading little Jack around on a pony. Her heart went out to her little brother, only seven years old and confused about things. He had inherited his father's widow's-peak hairline, just like Grandma Schaller's. It gave the boy a roguish, elfin look. He'd been christened Jakob, after his grandfather Jakob Schaller. But Jakob sounded too old-fashioned, and he soon became Jack. He called Grandma Clara "Mama." But he also called Deborah "Mama." He seemed to accept the fact that he didn't have a specific mother, but it was certainly going to have to be explained to him one day. And when he learned that his mother had abandoned him at birth, how was that going to screw him up with women in later life? Plus the big expectations her father was going to have for him. If Bill Schaller was controlling with Deborah, how much more controlling would he be with his son? She already felt sorry for the man Jack was going to be some day.

As Clara stirred sugar into the boiling cherry mixture, she glanced up from the stove and saw where Deborah's eyes were, watching Grandpa Wilhelm leading little Jack around on a pony. Her husband was seventy-seven but had the tall, wiry body of a hard-working farmer. He was in excellent health and figured he still had another good twenty years of working his vineyards.

She knew he was worried about the clouds of labor unrest on the horizon. Grape-growing was an iffy business anyway. Everything depended on the harvest. Late summer and early fall were always a tense and vigilant time. But now with the threat of a workers' strike? Pickers refusing to work, leaving the grapes to rot on the vine? It was enough to keep a man awake at night.

Little Jack came running into the kitchen just then in short pants and a T-shirt. He threw his arms around Deborah's legs. "Mama, can I have a cookie?" He was too big to lift up anymore, so Deborah hopped down and ruffled his shaggy hair. Reaching into a ceramic jar on the counter, she brought out a chewy oatmeal cookie loaded with raisins grown and processed right there on the Schaller property, a cookie so big the boy had to hold it with both hands. "Thank you, Mama," he said and ran out.

It warmed Clara's heart to see the two of them like that. Absent a mother, it was only natural that the boy should be drawn to his older sister. Clara was glad Deborah returned Jack's affection.

Deborah saw her father's truck pull into the yard. When he got out, she saw the handful of mail and catalogs in his hand. A moment later, Bill was striding into the kitchen. "Hello, Bill," Frieda said without missing a stitch.

He gave her a distracted nod.

"Anything?" Clara said as she removed the saucepan from the heat.

"Nothing from any colleges," he said, throwing the mail onto the kitchen table. "How long does an acceptance process take anyway?" He went to the refrigerator and brought out a long-necked bottle of beer, uncapped it, and strode out of the kitchen.

Deborah's heart raced as she heard him plod down the steps and out into the yard. He was going to find out sooner or later. The bad news. That she wasn't going to college, and that she was in love with a boy they considered their enemy. So she must choose: her family's happiness, or her own.

There was no choosing at all. She definitely chose her own happiness. Her grandparents and her father had made their choices and had lived their lives. Deborah was young and still had a future, and she knew beyond a doubt that she wanted to be with the boy who had stolen her heart. There were so many reasons she had fallen in love with him. She loved him for his bravery. He was afraid of nothing. He spoke his mind and wasn't intimidated by authority. A rebel, yes, that was what he was. He fought for what he believed in. Plus he had very sexy eyes. She suspected a lot of girls had crushes on him; but he would want a girl who was equally strong-minded, who also stood up to authority and who was free to go wherever their destinies took them.

I will be that girl.

Yes, best to break both bad pieces of news to the family at the same time, she decided now, squaring her shoulders and taking deep breaths for courage. The outcome was going to be disastrous, no matter how long she stalled. But there was something Deborah had to do first. She had to know exactly where she stood with *him*. She had an idea where he would be tomorrow. She would casually show up, make it look like a chance encounter. Talk to him a little bit. Gauge his reactions to a bit of mild flirting. It made her heart race to picture it, to live the scene ahead of time, to plan what she would say, choreograph her smile, her impulsive laugh. Maybe act impressed by something he said, maybe reach out and touch his arm.

Would she have the courage to finally blurt out how she truly felt about him? And how would he react?, she wondered. After all, she only *suspected* that he held the same feelings for her. She didn't know for sure. And just as much as he was supposed to be her enemy, *she* was supposed to be *his*. Both sides were going to get stirred up like hornets' nests. If it turned out the sentiments were mutual, they would have to find a private place to meet, somewhere secluded where they could express their love for each other. They both risked a great deal if they were seen together.

Yes, she thought now with a little more courage in her bones. This was the best course of action. Before she could stand up to her father and tell him she wasn't going to college, she needed to get this other thing cleared up, so that when the day came, given all the good luck in the world and her wish come true, they would stand together and face her father with the worst news he was ever going to hear.

*   *   *

"I'M TELLING YOU, BRO, it's a sure thing," Gordon Newman said as he and his brother sped down the highway toward Lynnville. "My new custom Mustang is guaranteed to make Deborah Schaller fall in love with me!"

"You're crazy," eighteen-year-old Melvyn muttered as he looked at the passing farms. But Gordon, at twenty and a hoity-toity college student, couldn't see that his crush on Debbie Schaller was going to lead nowhere. First of all, their dad would kill him before allowing him to date a Schaller. And second, Debbie wouldn't give Gordon the time of day. Okay, so she occasionally smiled at him and said, "Hi" when their paths crossed, and maybe he'd bought her a hot dog at a ball game, and okay, she did attend every baseball game that Gordon had pitched, but Melvyn thought his brother's head was in the clouds if he thought a new sports car was going to win her over.

But Gordon knew better. They were soulmates, he and Debbie. But he knew the reality of their situation. Was ever there a bigger obstacle to true love than the hateful rivalry between their two families? Romeo and Juliet had had it easier! He didn't like to think what his father would do if he found out that his son was in love with his enemy's daughter. The whole valley knew that black revenge still lay in Adam Newman's heart, even twelve years after Bill Schaller had cheated him out of the lucrative distributorship deal. Adam hadn't burned the Schaller vineyards or set fire to their house, or done anything really, other than be as competitive as he could in the wine market. But still, Gordon knew he faced his father's wrath should he find out that Gordon longed to be with Deborah.

They would face it together, he and Deborah. He knew that she felt the same way and only kept away from him because of the feud. He knew it was torture for her. He wanted to stand up for her, rescue her, and be her protector.

It's a hell of a thing, Melvyn thought, slouched in the passenger seat. A Newman falling in love with a Schaller. Gordon was playing with fire. It wasn't just about himself and the girl. They had to think of their father, whose dodgy heart had kept him out of professional baseball and then out of the war and that now required a risky operation called "open-heart surgery." The shock of Gordon's pursuit of Deborah Schaller could kill him.

But Melvyn had another, *secret* reason for not wanting his brother to pursue Deborah Schaller. Brothers should never let a girl come between them. It would put an end to them as the Two Musketeers. For as long as he could remember, it had always been him and Gordo. Even though two years separated them in age, they had been inseparable since they were little. "Those Newman boys," the teachers would call them, shaking their heads over what to do about them. Always into mischief, but with the endearing charm of scamps. Star athletes, Gordon and Melvyn were forgiven almost anything. With their sexy eyes and infectious laughter, even their teachers couldn't resist having crushes on them.

It was summer vacation, and Gordon was home from college to help at the winery. Melvyn had just graduated from high school and was planning on following his brother to school. Two handsome youths in baseball caps racing down the highway in one of the farm's pickup trucks, with Gordon at the wheel. Melvyn was along to drive the truck back after Gordon collected his brand-new 1965 cherry red Ford Mustang "fastback" from the car dealer in Lynnville—the hot new car that was all the rage.

Melvyn leaned over and looked at the speedometer. "You're going eighty-five. We're gonna get pulled over."

"Let 'em pull me over. Cops don't scare me." Gordon was known for his reckless driving. *Rebel Without a Cause* was his favorite movie, and the late James Dean was his idol despite, or perhaps because of, getting killed in a race-car crash on a country road. Nothing fazed Gordon. He was twenty, strong, fearless, his daddy was rich, and he was invincible.

"You ever worry about getting drafted?" Melvyn said suddenly. "I mean, we both had to register. What if we get drafted and sent to, what's it called?"

"Vietnam. Then we'll go. We'll fight those commies and show them what Americans are made of."

Melvyn rolled the window down to feel the hot wind on his face. His thoughts bubbled and boiled. He didn't like the way things were changing. It had always been him and Gordo. Their sister, Sofie, had never really been part of their twosome, despite her being Gordon's twin. She was a girl and had her own friends. And now *she* had gone away, in her second year at Harvard and seriously dating a medical student, and had been invited by his family to stay at their summer home. Now Gordon fixated on Deborah Schaller and the possibility of going into the Army when all Melvyn wanted to do was work the winery.

He knew that Gordon chafed at being sent to an agricultural college, and that he didn't really know what he wanted to be in life. Maybe a professional race-car driver. But Melvyn had been "born to the grape." He remembered when he was ten years old and he was out in the vineyard with his father. Adam had squatted next to him and said, "Pick a grape, son. That's it. Now roll it between your thumb and finger, feel its firmness, the texture of the skin. Study the color. Now take a small bite of it, taste the sweetness. You'll come to learn when we're nearly at premium sugar levels. When it won't be long before the grapes reach proper acid–sugar balance.

"Let me tell you, son," Adam Newman had continued, his voice filled with pride, "I learned grape-growing from my father, he learned it from his father, and so on back through many generations in the Rhineland in Germany, a place I am going to take you to some day. These were skills passed down from fathers to sons so that those skills will someday be yours, son. Generations of trial and error, of testing and failing, of discarding things that don't work and embracing things that do. I don't know if you can grasp this just yet, but those were generations of many hands nurturing the vines and the fruit. When you picked that grape just now, it wasn't just your hand picking it; hundreds of hands picked that grape with you." It was something Melvyn had never forgotten.

Gordon, on the other hand, wasn't thinking of grapes. His head was filled with notions of Deborah Schaller. He had known her all his life. Despite the rift between their families, school had thrown them together. He was only two grades ahead of her, so they attended the same schools at the same time. School events, baseball and football games, dances, glimpses in halls and cafeteria and student store. And then one day, when he was a senior and she was a sophomore, she had literally run into him in the hallway, hurrying to class. A collision, dropping books, embarrassment and apologies, and Gordon had fallen in love. Since then, he watched for her everywhere he went, hung on every "Hi," and cherished every smile and glance his way. Deborah had gone to his baseball games, he had seen her watching him, cheering for him when he pitched. They even hung out with their friends at the same Dairy Queen and burger drive-ins.

He liked her long, loose hair. A lot of girls in the valley still teased their hair into lacquered bouffants. He thought her free style was very sexy. She had started wearing torn jeans and T-shirts while other girls were still in skirts and petticoats. He thought she was very worldly and edgy. He had seen her going into the movie theater where avant garde French films were showing. She was also politically outspoken while other girls thought it wasn't ladylike. Deborah Schaller stood out from the crowd, and it excited him.

He had heard she didn't want to go to college like everyone else. She had told her friends she wanted to hitchhike across the country and see America.

Gordon knew very well the trouble he was getting himself into, but nothing was going to deter him from being with Deborah. She was a Schaller and he was a Newman; the valley was just going to have to get used to the idea. Especially their fathers and grandfathers, who had been fighting and carrying grudges since the beginning of time. Gordon Newman and Deborah Schaller were going to be the first to bridge the gap.

Melvyn said suddenly, "Slow down. What's going on over there?"

Gordon pulled the truck onto the shoulder, and they peered through the windshield at the migrant workers' camp squatting on a vacant field about a hundred feet from the highway. There were shiny new cars parked among the shacks and clotheslines. The brothers saw men in white shirts and slacks, boots and cowboy hats talking to the people. The visitors were Hispanic and looked important.

"Labor organizers," Gordon murmured, squinting at the men who he knew had had come from outside California to unify the farmworkers into a union.

"That tall guy, shaking hands with everyone. I saw him speaking to a crowd in Lynnville Park the other day. He's an agitator. Came from Texas. Got a law degree or something."

"Yeah, I heard Granddad talking about him. Alejandro Ortiz, I think his name is. Stirring up trouble for the growers."

Gordon leaned on the steering wheel and pursed his lips. "You don't think there's really going to be a strike, do you?"

"I don't know. But if there is, they won't hit *our* farm. Dad and Granddad have always been fair to the workers. We give them a decent wage and don't take advantage of them like a lot of the growers do. If they strike, it won't be against us. Greedy bastards like Mayfield and Samson, who treat the migrants like slaves, they'll be the ones who'll lose workers."

"*And* their crops," Gordon added significantly.

He pulled the truck back onto the highway and drove on, both boys feeling a bit chilled by what they had just seen, momentarily brought down from their excitement by a glimpse of reality. "Speed it up, Gordo," Melvyn said. "Let's get you that Ford Mustang that's going to make all the girls want you."

"I only want one girl," Gordon said with a laugh, springing back to his previous high with the resilience of youth, Deborah Schaller back in his thoughts, shiny and bright. "And she wants *me!*"

* * *

DEBORAH ARRIVED AT LYNNVILLE Park, where a small crowd was already gathering to hear speakers on the issue of farm labor reform. On the bandstand, which served as a stage for summer concerts and political rallies, several well-dressed men sat on folding chairs while technicians hooked up the cables and wires of the sound system. A microphone was in place, ready for the first speaker.

Large posters had been tacked to the bandstand posts and nearby trees, shouting in large print for equal rights for farmworkers. In front of the bandstand, long tables had been set up and were stacked with leaflets and books and other literature pertaining to the plight of Largo Valley's migrant workers, while smiling Hispanic women invited people to help themselves. The atmosphere was calm and non-threatening beneath a benevolent blue sky.

Deborah looked around and saw Gordon Newman there, at the park's edge, leaning casually against a new car, one of those Ford Mustangs everyone was talking about. He was watching her. She had seen him at one of these rallies before. The growers were becomingly keenly interested in what the union organizers were telling people.

Deborah kept looking around, her heart racing. She tried to calculate her next move. She didn't want to blunder and ruin everything, make him think her a fool.

Just then, a man on the bandstand stepped up to the microphone and called for everyone's attention. The crowd moved in, tightened, trapping Deborah at its center. She glanced back at Gordon Newman, still leaning against his car, arms folded. His eyes were fixed on her, not on the activities in the bandstand.

She stood there listening to the speeches, the rhetoric from educated men, talking about equal rights and labor laws and minimum wage and health reform for farmworkers. But all she could think about was Gordon Newman watching her. Maybe this had been a mistake. She suddenly didn't feel so courageous.

And then the speeches were over and pamphlets were being handed out, and the crowd began to disperse, with people either agreeing with what they had just heard or grumbling about rabble-rousers. Before she could take a step, a young man came up to her, a tall Latino with olive skin and flashing eyes. He wore long white slacks and a short-sleeved Mexican guayabera of white linen. He looked like a waiter in the tropics.

"Hello, Miss Schaller," he said smoothly, and she saw the brown hand extended toward her.

She returned the handshake and said, "Very moving speech, Mr. Ortiz." She wondered if he could feel her pulse in her fingers, or see it throbbing at her throat. She wondered if Gordon Newman, standing spy-like at his Mustang, was watching closely and could see how flustered she was.

This was the moment. It was now or never.

She had first met Alejandro Ortiz in this park five weeks ago, when he and his fellows were giving speeches from the bandstand. Deborah had just graduated from high school and had no idea what to do with her life. She had known only that she didn't want to get shipped off to a women's college. She had gone to the park that day out of idle curiosity, and Alejandro's passionate and fiery speech in a charismatic voice had touched something in her soul. She had felt like an empty vessel waiting to be filled. She'd never thought about the Mexican migrant workers before, never gave a moment's notice to their plight, their hard work, long hours, lack of rights. She had been captured right from the start. Alejandro was such a persuasive speaker, and so handsome! His smile alone could win trophies. Young Mexican women had gone through the crowd handing out leaflets. Deborah accepted one and read the shocking statistics printed there. Alejandro's magnificent voice filled her ears, his smile blinded her eyes, and she was immediately won over to La Causa.

Fall in love with the man, and you fall in love with his cause.

She had since learned that he had been born in Texas, the son of poor migrant workers from Mexico. He had labored in the fields as a child, picking whatever was in season for less than minimum wage, living in ramshackle camps, existing on tortillas and beans. His proud father had sworn a better life for his son, and he had made Alejandro go to school despite the racial prejudice that segregated Hispanics from whites. Inheriting his father's pride and determination, Alejandro had done well at school and then had attended junior college, supporting himself on janitorial jobs and cleaning chicken coops.

From there, a four-year college and a scholarship into law school, from which he had recently graduated. But rather than go into private practice, Alejandro wanted to work for his people, help them fight their way out of the cycle of poverty and early death that they were locked into.

And so he had joined the rising swell of Hispanic pride and the growing voice of a population that was both invisible and silent. His goal was to take his people's cause all the way to Washington and push for reforms in labor and civil rights for exploited farmworkers.

Despite people crowding around him with questions and praise, Alejandro stood there looking down at Deborah as if they were all alone in the park. "I am glad you came," he said softly.

She swallowed for courage and said, "I was wondering . . . I would like to learn more about your cause. I was wondering if we could talk . . . meet. You know." She shrugged nervously.

A smile played about his lips. "Talk? I would be delighted. Where would you like to meet?"

She licked her lips. "I was thinking . . . well," she shrugged again and wondered how childish she looked. "Somewhere private. You know. Me being a grower's daughter and you representing the unions. People might take it wrong."

"You choose the place. I am new to this valley. I will be free this evening."

Her heart jumped and then thudded, and then she could have sworn it broke loose and swam through her veins. "There's a place where no one goes called Colina Sagrada. I can give you directions." She reached into her purse for a pad of notepaper and scribbled a shaky map.

They agreed on eight o'clock, and then Alejandro turned his attention to his supporters and people who wanted to argue and reporters and photographers, and he was carried away.

"Hi."

She spun around. Gordon Newman stood there, grinning. "Talking to the enemy?" he asked, nodding toward Alejandro.

"I intend to know what plans they have for our farm. A strike would be ruinous."

"Can I give you a lift home? I have my car right over there."

She barely glanced at the Mustang. "I came in my own car," she said coolly. "Thanks anyway."

*　　*　　*

THE HOURS CRAWLED BY until eight o'clock came. She had left home earlier, saying she was meeting friends at the movies. Instead, she had driven straight to Colina Sagrada, where the barren desert in the middle of a green valley was turning red and shadowy in the setting sun. The stars were out by the time she saw two headlights coming down the dirt road.

He parked and got out, to cross to her, his shiny boots crunching the sand. Deborah could barely breathe, she was so crippled with desire. Alejandro was the most exotic and fascinating boy she had ever met. No, he *wasn't* a boy. He was a *man*. She gestured with her hands. "Isn't it just the most desolate place?"

He looked at her with intense eyes. "I see only beauty here."

She stood frozen, caught in his dark, intense gaze. "You wanted to know more about our cause," he said in a husky voice, as if challenging her to confess that she had brought him out here under false pretenses.

"Yes," she said breathlessly. "I want to know about La Causa. Why are you part of it? You're a lawyer. You could go anywhere, make good money."

"I will tell you," he said without stepping away from her, as if proximity would drive his story home. He spoke passionately about his childhood of hardship, his little sister dying of malnutrition, his sick grandfather unable to get medical help because he was "illegal." "My father died when he was fifty, and my mother and I buried him on the side of the road as we moved on to the next harvest. Nobody fought for us. Nobody stood up for us. We had to work in the fields beneath the hot sun, children dragging heavy sacks of onions or picking beans until our fingers bled, our stomachs grumbling, our mouths parched with thirst. We were invisible while the wealthy white people ate until they were fat and sat in big houses and drank lemonade. They didn't know our names, we weren't given an education.

"Now that I am in a position to speak up for the invisible people, that is what I am going to do. It was what I was born to do. You understand, Deborah, don't you?"

He paused, a mysterious smile lifting his lips. Then he said, "I want to show you something."

They drove in his truck. The destination wasn't far—a shantytown camp just off the highway, where shacks were lit by lanterns and camp-fires cast golden glows on tarpapered walls. Deborah heard laughter and music, smelled delicious aromas in the air. She hesitated before getting out of the truck. "I don't know," she said. "They won't want me there. They'll resent my presence."

"Not at all. They are my friends. They are good people. They will welcome you."

As he promised, they were warm and welcoming, with no dirty or resentful looks. She walked among the families with Alejandro introducing her in Spanish. She understood the word "amiga." Frying fish sizzled in skillets over open flames, and beans bubbled in pots. She smiled at a man who was juggling brightly painted dried gourds. She saw men crouched outside their shacks, playing dice and cards. An old man was carving toys out of blocks of wood, a woman weaving a blanket at a loom, a potter with his ceramics wheel and oven. Everybody pitching in, either working in the fields or creating something to sell in town or to the tourists. The strike and local politics might as well be on the moon.

Ragged, barefooted children looked at her shyly. The women with their colorful shawls and long braids were polite and friendly, and Deborah suddenly wished she hadn't chosen to wear a Mary Quant miniskirt for her tryst with Alejandro. These women and girls were all modestly dressed in long skirts that either came to the knee or the ankle. At least she had decided to wear harlequin-patterned tights to wear under the skirt. Still, she felt immodest and even vaguely whore-ish.

Men got up to shake Alejandro's hand, treating him with great respect. Women offered him food and something to drink. He moved with ease among them. It was *his* culture, so spicy and hot and alive. But reverent as well, with little candlelit shrines to the Virgin with flowers at her plaster feet. Alejandro spoke with pride about how the Lord's Blessed Mother watched over her children, *his* people. They were poor but generous, and they shared what they had. They offered Deborah beans and corn tortillas; and they shared their sweet wine with her, which she recognized as sangria because her father's winery produced a popular sangria.

Alejandro and Deborah looked at each other across the campfire as men danced around a sombrero on the ground, their hands behind their backs. She had known she had a crush on Alejandro, but now she fell for him hard.

They drove back to Colina Sagrada in silence, and when they got there Deborah was reluctant to return to her car. She turned to him and said, "I am so sorry," apologizing for her father and grandfather and for all the white growers in Largo Valley. She wanted to march at Alejandro's side and make the evil white men see the error of their ways.

He smiled. "What is there to be sorry for, *chiquita*?" When he put his hands on her arms, she thought she would explode in flame. And when he bent his head toward her, Deborah rose up to meet his kiss. He drew her tightly to him and she moaned with pleasure. It was a movie-screen kiss, exactly as she had fantasized it these past weeks. They found a patch of soft scrubby weeds, and Alejandro brought a blanket from his truck. The lovemaking was perfect, more than Deborah had dreamed. The boy she had lost her virginity to had fumbled and said, "Sorry," and Deborah wondered if it was going to take a lot of trial and error before she found her soulmate. But she had found him in this Latino rebel who had plans to turn Largo Valley and its rich white growers upside down.

*   *   *

THE UNION LEADERS HAD tried meeting with the individual white growers, or alternatively with them in groups, all to no avail. The growers refused to even listen to the labor leaders' requests, and so the requests turned into demands. A clash was coming; everyone knew it. Tension was growing in the valley as young Alejandro Ortiz and his unionists went among the migrant camps and spoke emphatically about how it was *they* who kept Americans fed, *they* who kept the country from starving, and yet look how they were treated. The rich white growers treated their dogs better than they treated the pickers!

Because the growers refused to consider any kind of contract with the unions, the labor organizers decided to take their campaign to the public. The rallies became bigger, louder, more demonstrative. Slowly, passions and resentments were rising. Especially beneath the boiling summer sun; and Mexican men began to think about their painful backs as they were bent over lettuce fields and onion fields all day with little relief, and coming home with barely enough money to feed their families. Where was their dignity, Alejandro asked them in his charismatic way. They listened to him because they knew he came from the same poverty, that he and his father and brothers had been pickers. He understood the farmworkers' tribulations. So they listened to him, and anger began to grow.

When the union organizers threatened to call for a public boycott of locally grown produce, the growers agreed to a debate in a public forum so that both sides could be heard. An impartial mediator was agreed upon—Mr. Frank Gilette, prominent and respected Lynnville attorney. The unionists selected Alejandro Ortiz to be their spokesman. For the growers, it had been a choice between Wilhelm Schaller and Johann Newman, both wealthy and influential with deeply vested interests in the issue of unionizing their farmworkers. Johann won the vote by a narrow margin.

Reporters from all over California were there, as well as television news crews. The story would be carried nationwide. Tensions were running high, with anger and resentments on both sides—the migrant laborers wanting fairer wages and working conditions, unemployed white men feeling cheated out of jobs. As it was Sunday, most of Lynnville's citizens were able to attend, and people came from outlying areas to listen to the debate. Opinions were divided. Many believed the growers had a right to hire whoever they pleased and at whatever wage—and the Mexicans were lucky to have jobs. Others sympathized with the workers and thought they deserved better treatment. Some people even believed that the activists' main goal was to take over California and give it back to Mexico.

For the most part, however, the growers were smug and confident. The workers wouldn't dare unionize, or stage "walkouts" as the organizers were threatening. They needed their jobs too badly. They all had wives and kids to feed.

Today's event was promising to be the largest yet, drawing a massive crowd to trample the grass of Lynnville Park, drawing also the eye of the local police who watched from their patrol cars and on horseback. Already, across the country, a few peaceful demonstrations for civil rights and an end to war had turned violent. So the police were ready today.

But Alejandro called for his people to be peaceful and nonviolent. "We wish only to be heard," he told them. "We wish only to be allowed to tell our side of things. When the growers see that we have the sympathy of the public at large, they will sign contracts with us."

"If not?" the humble migrant workers asked.

"If not, then we strike, and America's lettuce will rot in the fields."

While his father was up in the bandstand waiting for the debate to begin, Gordon Newman was seated in the audience with Melvyn and their mother, Queenie, who was fanning herself with one of the paper fans that were being handed out for free. They were a promotional item with HARPER'S FUNERAL HOME printed on them. Gordon saw Deborah there with her family, seated a few rows back. Folding chairs had been placed in rows on the grass, for the families of the growers and the unionists. Everyone else had to stand, and it was a very large, hot crowd.

Gordon was frustrated. He couldn't seem to find a moment to be alone with Deborah. He sensed she was afraid that her family might find out about her feelings for him, so he understood why she stayed away. It was going to be up to him to open the way for them. The problem was, how? He had heard that her father was ultra-protective of her, especially when it came to boys.

The Schallers were like royalty around here. And they had become stinking rich. All thanks to Bill Junior's clever business strategies.

The Baby Boomers were approaching drinking age, and anyway they were already imbibing in college, whether it was legal or not. Bill Schaller studied the demographics and saw that the students were young and hip and didn't want their parents' wine, they wanted their own *novelty* wine, strawberry and green apple-flavored. They didn't care about tannin, bouquet, notes, body. They just wanted to get high, smoke weed, and let their beards grow. So Bill had come up with the idea of cheap flavored jug wine for the new youth masses emerging from overpacked high schools swarming onto college campuses with their peace symbols and arrogance.

"Make the labels youth-friendly," he told his marketing people, "with pretty pictures, something eye-catching instead of staid and stodgy. We should write snappy jingles for television commercials. Show young people drinking wine just for fun and not as part of an elegant meal, which they can't afford anyway. Don't try to bridge the generation gap. Don't try to get hippies interested in old established wine. Widen the gap. Send a message to young people that this isn't their grandfather's wine, it's *theirs*. Come up with a folksier name. Schaller Wines is stuffy, old school. Something more down to earth, like Largo Creek."

It was also Bill's idea to come out with gallon jugs with screw-top caps instead of corks, and to sell them in supermarkets where the hippies shopped. Before they knew it, the Schallers had cornered the youth market in wine.

Gordon's family, on the other hand, although wealthy from their food crops, refused to get on the novelty-wine bandwagon and maintained their eliteness, producing exclusive and expensive estate-bottled wines for sophisticated palates.

The Schallers were respected on other levels as well. The population of Lynnville and the Largo Valley was expanding so rapidly that Clara had purchased a large tract of land outside the town and donated it to the city for a new school. She had even funded the first classrooms, and, when construction was complete, there was going to be a big ceremony to open the new Clara Schaller Middle School.

Unaware that Gordon Newman was staring at her with hungry eyes, Deborah was watching the stage. She couldn't wait for Alejandro to stand up and speak. The way he fired up a crowd excited her tremendously. She was thinking of their secret trysts in stolen moments. It was very hit-and-miss, as he was busy with the farmworkers and other labor organizers, and he had to be visible for press coverage. They tried, when they could, to meet at Colina Sagrada, but there was always the chance of a passing motorist. Fear of being found out, Deborah had discovered, was a powerful aphrodisiac. Each time they came together, their embraces were hot and urgent and passionate, and each time it left her hungering for more.

She was still working up the courage to tell her father about college. And she had almost done it a couple of weeks ago when he had gotten angry and wanted to know why they hadn't heard from any colleges, with the new semester drawing close. It had come to her lips to tell him the truth, and then she had stopped herself. There was too much tension in his life right now, with these union agitators. Weeks ago, she had planned to stand up to him and tell him that she and Alejandro were in love, but she hadn't found the courage. She had put him off by saying, "College terms start at different times, Dad. I'll make some calls and look into it. The registration packets are probably already on the way." And then he had been distracted by the demonstrations and protests. And now this massive rally. When was there *ever* going to be a good time to break the news to him?

The fiery sun rose high and baked the air into stillness. Later, when the sun's power diminished and the day began to cool, the air would come to life as if resuming a journey. But for now, there was no breeze, no relief from the oppressive heat.

Finally, the debate began. Introduced by Frank Gilette, Alejandro got up and stirred the audience with descriptions of the hard life of the workers, which no one could argue with. Every citizen of Lynnville sympathized with them and felt guilty for having turned a blind eye. Yes, they thought collectively, the farmworkers should be allowed to unionize and get better wages and benefits.

And then it was Johann's turn, who made sure that everyone understood that he was not speaking just for himself but for *all* growers. He, too, was a persuasive speaker. "We are not ignoring the problems Mr. Ortiz has outlined. We are not villains. But we have legitimate, economical concerns of our own. If we pay the scale the unionists are demanding, and pay for health insurance and put in for Social Security, then our profits go down. Not just mine—you all know that Newman Farms are a large company. But many growers make just enough profits to get by and feed their own families and pay their mortgages.

"To meet the demands of the union organizers would mean us losing money. We would be forced to sell our crops at higher prices, which then directly affects the average American consumer when he goes to the market and discovers he's suddenly paying three or four times as much for lettuce, grapes, and wine. By keeping our labor costs down, we guarantee lower prices to the American shopper."

This earned him cheers from the crowd, and suddenly the labor fight had been brought to the consumer's wallet. The fight that had been between workers and growers had now become personal to the average Joe. And sympathy shifted from the workers to the growers.

It was plain to everyone that this was no simple issue, nor were there any simple solutions.

Mr. Frank Gilette opened the meeting for questions. One well-known grower shot to his feet and shouted: "Unionize all you want! We just won't hire you. And when word reaches Mexico that there are thousands of jobs available in this valley, there will be a flood of illegals like you've never seen. *We'll* be the only winners here."

A noisy commotion broke out, and then Johann stood up and the crowd fell respectfully silent. He paused at the microphone, thought for a moment, and then addressed Alejandro Ortiz. "I'm afraid Mr. Mayfield is right. Your worthy plan will backfire. While I disagree with Mr. Mayfield's labor practices, I have to agree with him that unionizing our current workers will only make the situation worse. It will be inviting greater runs on California by undocumented workers coming across the border. And that will only lead to more clashes and more bloodshed."

Alejandro rose from his chair and said, in a loud voice that didn't need a microphone, "We are already talking to men in Washington to crack down on our southern border and increase patrol. We'll stem that tide."

"It's like brushing back the ocean with a broom. There's a thousand miles of desert. You can't patrol all of it. People are going to continue to sneak across and come here to steal jobs. As long as life in America, no matter how squalid or impoverished, is better than in Mexico, they will keep coming."

To everyone's surprise, Wilhelm Schaller shot to his feet and, with great dignity, climbed the steps of the bandstand and drew himself up tall and straight at Johann's side. "I agree with Mr. Newman."

The crowd fell silent as every Lynnville citizen recognized the moment for what it was, and they were momentarily stunned. Tears welled in Clara's eyes, and in Adam's and Queenie's and Bill Junior's. For the first time in fifty-three years, the two brothers stood together, united.

And then one of the union organizers seated in the audience stood up, thrust a fist into the air, and cried, "Then you give us no choice! *Huelga, mi amigos!*"

Others rose and, with fists in the air, chanted: "*Huelga! Huelga!*"

The Mexicans at the edge of the crowd, no longer timid, took up the chant, men and women and children, shouting: "*Huelga!*"

The white growers looked grimly on. *Huelga.* They knew what it meant. Strike.

*   *   *

ADAM NEWMAN CAME DOWN the back steps, a mug of steaming coffee in his hands. The September dawn was just breaking over rolling hills covered in rows of lush vines heavy with ripe grape clusters waiting to be harvested.

He frowned at the silence. The trucks should be pulling in by now, to distribute the workers and their baskets among the trellises. But the yards were dark and empty.

Hearing a motor, he turned and saw one of the farm's pickup trucks racing up the dirt track toward the house. It came to a jolting halt and his two sons jumped out. "Where are the workers?" Adam barked. Today was the first day of harvest. The farm should be a beehive of activity by now.

"They're not coming, Pop," Gordon said, flushed and breathless.

"They're out there," Melvyn added, thrusting his arm in the direction of the main road. "They're all lined up holding picket signs and blocking all roads onto the property."

Adam swore under his breath. The back door opened, and his father Johann came down the steps. "What's going on?"

"They've done it, Dad," Adam growled. "They've gone on strike."

Johann was disappointed but not surprised. He had known it was coming. Two weeks ago, at the big meeting in the park, the unionists had called for a general strike of all farms in the valley. But it hadn't happened right away. It had needed planning, strategy, and persuading all the workers to unite. "*All* of them?" he said.

"The winery workers too," Gordon said. "The buildings are all deserted. Even if we find pickers to bring in the grapes, we have no one to crush and process."

Queenie came out of the kitchen then, looking distraught. She had guessed what was happening. Johann and Adam had assured her that

Newman Vineyards would be spared if there was a strike, due to loyalty from their workers. But apparently that was not to be the case. She closed her eyes and steadied herself on the doorjamb. She had lived at this farm for twenty-two years. In all that time, she had learned about the capricious nature of grape-growing, that nothing was guaranteed, that vintners lay at the mercy of so many unpredictable factors. But none of them had ever thought they would be betrayed by the workers who she felt they had always treated fairly.

Johann and Adam took one of the trucks and followed Gordon and Melvyn back out to the main road.

It was an eerie sight. As the sky paled in the east, light fell on a line of men in work clothes and straw hats, standing silently along the fence that marked the eastern border of Newman land. Many held picket signs.

As Johann got out of the truck, an old-timer approached. His name was Rafael Ortega, and he had been a loyal and trusted foreman at the vineyards for years. Respectfully removing his hat to expose gray and white hair, he said, humbly, "Sorry, *jefe*, but I have my family to think of. These union men, they say we can get better wages and even health insurance, and our children can go to proper schools."

Johann looked at the others, mostly familiar faces, and he saw their sorrowful expressions, their apologetic posture. They didn't want to do this, but the labor organizers had made big promises. Now Johann and his son and grandsons were going to have to resort to a tactic they had prayed they would never have to use: bring in scabs.

*   *   *

AT THE SCHALLER FARM a few miles away, a similar scene was playing out, and it killed Deborah to see the men she loved standing on opposite sides of a battlefield: her father and grandfather on one side, Alejandro on the other.

It turned out that the Newmans and the Schallers had been wrong in their belief that their own workers would not strike against them. In fact, Alejandro Ortiz and the organizers were targeting the Schaller and Newman properties particularly. If the two biggest properties in the valley were so crippled that they gave in to the union demands, then the rest of the growers would fall like dominoes.

Wilhelm and Bill looked up and down the line of picketers, and Bill said: "They aren't all here. These men don't nearly account for the number of workers in this valley."

"There will be other picket lines," his white-bearded father said. "At Newman's place. Mayfield's. Samson's."

"I have an idea," Bill said, turning on his heel and climbing back into the truck.

"Where are you going?" his father called out.

"I'll be right back."

A line of eucalyptus trees stood between the winery and the north vineyard, planted years ago as a windbreak to protect the vines. On the other side of it, land had been cleared to make way for an extension of the winery. New buildings were under construction, and, by the time the sky completely lightened, Bill saw the workers arriving. As he had suspected they would. Although there were Mexicans in the group, they were mostly white men who went about the valley doing construction work. They felt themselves above the lowly pickers; and they were certainly better paid, as they were skilled masons and carpenters.

"We're suspending work here for now," Bill told them. "How would you men like to earn extra money? Just climb in the back and I'll take you to it."

When Bill returned to the picket line and the morning was blazing bright, he was leading a convoy of Schaller flatbed trucks, the ones used for collecting the baskets of harvested grape clusters along the rows of vines. But this time, the drivers would be going out into the valley to harvest a crop of a different kind.

As Bill had expected, at the first migrant camp they came to, men were waiting to be taken to the fields—men who, for their various reasons, had not joined the strike, were not going to join the union. Men who just wanted to work and get paid.

They continued around the valley, leaning out the window and waving dollar bills, calling out "*Mucho trabajo!*" to any men walking along the road-side. Soon the flatbeds were full and they returned to the farm.

The trucks came rolling silently in, filled with standing men, illegal workers from Mexico and Guatemala. A white man stood at the back of each truck, guarding the workers with a rifle. As they drove across the picket line, they tried not to meet the angry looks on the faces of the striking workers. The "scabs" looked frightened and apologetic, their shoulders hunched over, their posture saying "We have families to feed too."

Deborah, watching, had never felt such tension. Her father stood there, rifle balanced casually in the crook of his arm; but a look in his eye said he was prepared to shoot. Her lover, Alejandro, equally stood his ground, a look of fierce defiance and determination on his face.

She knew that this scene was being repeated at the Newmans' farm, Mayfield's, Samson's: workers being trucked in to work the fields while the strikers received no pay and their families went hungry. A shiver went down her spine. This was not going to end well.

*   *   *

IT WAS THE SEVENTH day of the strike, and the number of picketers had tripled as they carried signs that read WE FEED AMERICA, WE ARE AMER-ICANS, GOD BLESS FARMWORKERS! Mexican women with their children were bringing baskets of food and jugs of water for the picketers, handing out tortillas stuffed with beans and chilies.

On the main road in front of the Schaller property, where the picket line was thickest and where onlookers sat on their parked cars, hoping for a spectacle, a female television news reporter was talking to the camera: "Due to the unique nature of California agriculture, a crop that for most of the year requires only twenty laborers for maintenance will require two thousand during harvest time. This calls for a large influx of migrant workers during the various harvests, which occur at different times for different crops. The landowners encourage illegal immigration so much that twice as much labor as necessary floods the valley and, this way, with so many competing for jobs, wages are kept low. The question arises: How can the unionized strikers possibly win?"

The reporter interviewed Alejandro, who assured her that the move-ment was going to grow, that the downtrodden farmworkers were going to be heard. And Deborah's heart swelled with love for him and she looked forward to their next secret embrace. The reporter also interviewed Bill Schaller, who said that the growers would not be bullied into changing their business prac-tices and that they were willing to sit down at the negotiating table but their offers had been declined. And Deborah's heart swelled with pride for him, too, and she dreaded facing him on the issue of her going to college.

So far, it was only local news, while the rest of America was follow-ing the civil-rights movement for black people, and students protesting the Vietnam war. But with rising tensions and the expectation of violence and bloodshed, the national spotlight was now coming to the Largo Valley farmworkers' strike. And the call for a boycott of Largo Valley produce was no longer local, but national, as Alejandro Ortiz and his union-ists were asking people in New York City, in Chicago and St. Louis and

Miami, not to purchase California grapes or wine. "There's blood in them grapes!" was the cry.

When the first trucks arrived, the reporter gave her cameraman instructions to follow them with his lens, keeping on them, one after the other, making it a solemn and grim procession. "Try to capture their faces. Make it human interest," she said. And when the women and children of the picketers started throwing eggs and rotten tomatoes at the trucks crossing the line, splattering on windshields and doors, hitting the workers in the back, causing the armed guards to duck and hold their arms up for protection, the reporter muttered, "Oh, this is good!"

Bill Schaller was not so pleased.

Fifteen minutes later, he was in his office in the main house, a large airy den filled with books and trophies and awards and framed photographs of Bill posing with famous people on the walls. He sat behind his enormous mahogany desk with a thunderous expression on his face. Two men stood before him, each in a different uniform, each with a different official hat in his hands.

"This has got to stop! The strike is spreading! We're importing fewer pickers! That Ortiz bastard wins more over to his side every day, while my grapes are going to rot on the vines! This valley can't withstand the economic disaster that this strike threatens to bring on our heads! I want that strike broken up! I want you to send those outside agitators packing and scrambling their sorry asses all the way back to Texas!" He punctuated his tirade with a powerful fist on the desktop that made an inkwell jump.

The two silent men he was lambasting were the Sheriff of Largo County and the Chief of Police of the town of Lynnville. Both owed their top-ranking and top-paying positions of power to Bill Schaller. Both knew he could pull the political rug out from under them. "Mr. Schaller," the sheriff began, "we're doing what we can."

"That's not enough, Shay. I want every man on your force working on this."

"As it is, Mr. Schaller, we're stretched thin. I simply haven't the manpower." Sheriff Shay Hopkins tried to keep his cool. It did not escape his notice that Bill Schaller addressed the local senior law officers by their first names, while they were expected to address Bill as "Mister."

"The same goes for the police. Yours isn't the only farm they're picketing."

Bill fixed a steely eye on the police chief. "That's not my problem, Harry. My problem is getting those grapes to the press. And I can't do it if picketers make it hard to get scabs brought in. Pull some of your men off other farms. Mayfield and Samson. They can fend for themselves. And if that isn't enough, call in reserves!" he barked at both men. "Drum up local volunteers, deputies from other counties!" He poked his finger in the air, right at their faces. "Don't forget that it was me who got you two elected in the first place, and if you want to keep your badges I suggest you end this strike by any means. Start making arrests! Show the bastards whose side you're on. Use dogs, tear gas. Break their spirit! Whatever it takes!"

Shay Hopkins turned his sheriff's hat around and around in his hands. "What about the men we have patrolling the Newmans' picket line?" Johann Newman was just as much a man to reckon with in this valley as Wilhelm and Bill Schaller. Political clout went both ways.

Bill pursed his lips. "Leave your men there. In fact, increase official presence at the Newmans' picket line."

Sheriff Hopkins's bushy eyebrows shot up. "That's mighty generous of you, Mr. Schaller," he said, thinking of the legendary rivalry between the two families.

Bill's face turned stormy. "In this instance, Shay, it's necessary that the Schallers and Newmans lead the fight together. To break the union, we have to present a united front." It was partially the truth. Bill wasn't about to reveal the rest of it—that by helping the Newmans in the fight, it assuaged a little bit of the guilt he had carried around ever since he had stolen the Callahan distributorship from Adam. "But I want you to keep me posted on what's going on at the Newman property. I want hourly reports. Got that?"

"Yes, sir, Mr. Schaller."

Bill waved dismissively. "Then get started."

*   *   *

K-9 UNITS ARRIVED AT the Newman property line, officers in uniform holding on to German shepherds and Dobermans, sleek, strong dogs with alert faces, straining at their leashes. The strikers in the picket line eyed them nervously.

There were more news crews now, from the national networks, and reporters from all over. A crowd of curious onlookers had gathered across the road. It was as if they had caught the scent of blood and come hoping to witness a gory spectacle. Alejandro Ortiz, who was most frequently seen at the Schaller farm picket line, had also shown up this morning as if he sensed that today there would be trouble.

Johann and Adam went out to meet the police chief, who had come to oversee the deployment of the dogs. "Is this really necessary, Chief Turner?" Johann asked.

"I'm afraid so, Mr. Newman," the chief said, a man in his forties who respected the old vintner. Newman might be pushing eighty, but he was sound in body and mind and had always been known as a fair and reasonable man. Plus, he addressed others with respect, not like the arrogant Bill Schaller who called everyone, from the mayor on down, by his first name.

Johann removed his straw hat and ran his hand through his white hair. "It's just that the dogs and increased police presence might actually incite the very thing you're here to prevent. We've had a peaceful demonstration so far. Maybe a few harsh words and dirty looks, but nothing more threatening than that. But those dogs are making the strikers skittish."

Johann had heard from other growers that police and sheriff presence was being reduced at other farms, and for some reason they were focusing on protecting the Schaller and Newman properties. Johann couldn't understand why. *He* certainly hadn't asked for it, and he wasn't sure increased police presence was going to help. But then, it might. Yesterday a fight had broken out at Mayfield's farm, where Mayfield had had his men spray the picketers with pesticide. The strikers had retaliated with clubs and rocks. It had taken the police forever to break it up, and several people had been taken to the hospital.

Johann saw more police cars arriving, and a large black police van, which meant multiple arrests were going to be made. When the officers got out already holding their nightsticks, Johann said, dryly, "I guess this is a good time to rob the bank in Lynnville."

"Now see here, Mr. Newman, I'd have thought you'd be pleased to have us here. But anyway, I aim to break this strike up. It's gone on long enough."

"They have a legal right to voice their protest."

"They're causing a disturbance of the peace. We're prepared to use tear gas to disperse this crowd and show them we mean business."

Johann stared at him. Then he frowned. "Why this sudden aggressive tactic?"

Chief Turner tried his best to return Mr. Newman's accusatory stare. It wouldn't be good for it to get out that not only had Bill Schaller threatened his and the sheriff's political positions if they didn't break the strike, but that as an added incentive he had offered them very generous cash bonuses if they were successful. "And yes, Mr. Newman," he countered forcefully, "the strikers do have a legal right to protest, but only if they themselves are legal." He paused to look up and down the line of men holding signs and trying to block the trucks from getting in, all those brown faces with Mexican and Indian features. "I'm going to have my men inspect the documents of every striker here today. Trust me, Mr. Newman, arrests *will* be made. It will be up to those who are arrested whether they will be taken to jail peacefully or by force." He added significantly: "And I do mean by force—any force necessary."

But Johann took a step closer to him and said, "If you hurt any of those men, you will have to answer to me for it."

"You can't threaten me. *I* have the authority here."

"No, *I* have the authority. There will be no violence on my property. If there is, these reporters with their cameras and nationally syndicated news shows might find a fresh angle in a grower complaining of police brutality against the strikers. It would gain a lot of public sympathy for the strikers and make the Lynnville police department look bad."

Chief Turner shifted on his feet, licked his lips, and swallowed. He thought of the orders he had received from Bill Schaller, plus irresistible bribes, and suddenly he felt like a bone between two angry dogs.

Turner strode away to quietly address a small group of his men. Johann and Adam looked at each other. "I don't like the way this is escalating, Dad," Adam said. "The police are going to *start* something."

Johann thought for a moment, then strode back to the main house, skirting it to head straight to the winery where non-union workers were unloading flatbed trucks filled with freshly harvested grapes and emptying them into the dock press. Pulling a few of them off the job, he instructed them to take rifles from the barn and drive out to the picket line. Grimly, they did so. Many were friends of the picketers, some of them had even walked on the picket line themselves but then had gone over to the Newmans' side simply because they had families to feed.

Johann and Adam felt guilty about trucking in illegal workers. Crossing picket lines manned by honest men who just wanted a fair wage left a bad taste in their mouths. But it wasn't just about the grapes and the wine: once the grapes were brought in and the process of making wine was begun, the migrant workers would then head for other crops ready for harvesting—typically onions, corn, wheat. For the Newmans, it was their vast acres of beans. Food-processing plants in Los Angeles and San

Francisco would be waiting for tons of Newman beans to arrive for cooking and canning and distribution. This strike was not only going to negatively impact the growers, but every step along the line from picking to the American consumer's dinner table. Thousands would feel the economic impact. So Johann and his son had to keep the farm going as it always had, keep the crops harvested, the fields plowed, and new crops planted. As much as Johann admired the union organizers and saw their side of the fight, he had to think of his farm and keep it running.

Inside the main house, Queenie wanted to grab a pitchfork and fight alongside her men. But Adam had insisted she stay inside, where she followed events unfolding on the television news. She was glad her daughter Sofie, who was twenty and high-strung, was away at school Back East. Her twin brother Gordon's college term had started, but he had put off going back in order to help the farm during this crisis. Most of the growers in the valley were faced off in this fight. On the Samson farm, some of the white men had attempted to plow into the picketers with tractors, but police and tear gas had intervened. The picketers had been arrested, the white men hadn't.

She couldn't keep her eyes off the TV, where a dangerous situation was unfolding a hundred yards from her house. Would those angry strikers, carrying signs and shaking their fists, get it into their minds to storm the fence, swarm over the property, and attack her house like it was the Bastille or something?

As she watched the reporter interview a handsome young man named Alejandro, Queenie started to notice the women in the background, with brown skin and shawls over their heads and children clinging to their skirts. For the first time, Queenie wondered what they thought of all this, seeing their husbands and sons and brothers standing up to the wealthy white bosses. What did Mexican women think about, anyway? It was strange: here was a whole other race and culture living cheek by jowl with white people, and yet Queenie didn't really know anything about them. Her own cook and maids were Hispanic, yet Queenie had no idea who they were, if they had families, hopes, dreams, disappointments. She felt vaguely ashamed of herself. They would be like women everywhere. They might wear different clothes or speak a foreign tongue, but they would be susceptible to all the woes and weaknesses—and strengths, judging by those on TV standing with their men—of women everywhere. Have dreams, fall in love, bear children, fight to protect their families.

You didn't see the Mexicans in Lynnville much, despite there being so many living in the valley. They certainly never shopped in the stores that Queenie and her friends patronized. You never saw them in Germantown or Eberhardt's bakery, or Mueller's hotel except as room maids or janitors with brooms. Where did they buy their clothes? she wondered now. Where did they do their grocery shopping? She imagined a small hidden community somewhere that had shops selling . . . well, whatever it was that Mexicans bought. How did those women meet their future husbands? What were their courtship customs? What did they do for entertainment? Her cook and maids came every morning from one of the migrant shantytowns, and went back every night. What did they talk about? What did they think of the rich white folks they worked for?

Queenie didn't like to think about it. There was too much enmity between the two sides for her to try to understand the opposition. She had to stand with *her* men, too, didn't she?

Out on the road, emotions were running high. Alejandro Ortiz was talking to a TV reporter when he saw a truck arrive from the direction of the winery carrying white men holding rifles. As the men climbed down, the police chief ordered his men to spread out along the picket line and start dispersing the strikers. And then someone pushed someone, and someone got shoved back, and then a fist shot out and a rock was thrown, and like a brush fire it spread until a full-on fight had broken out. Johann and Adam and Gordon and Melvyn tried to stop it, but Johann's white workers started firing their rifles, shooting over the heads of the strikers, stoking up anger all the more. Some of the police dogs were unleashed. Men screamed as fangs sank into their arms and legs. Cameras rolled while news reporters, aghast and excited at what they were seeing, informed a shocked TV audience about what they were already seeing with their own eyes.

Queenie, on the edge of her seat, watched with wide eyes and a slack jaw as her father-in-law, husband, and two sons got suddenly trapped in the middle of a violent brawl, with policemen using their batons to subdue and handcuff angry strikers, cops trying to control dogs gone wild, men throwing punches, shouting, yelling, faces distorted.

Queenie watched as Adam tried to pull a Mexican off Johann, when another striker flew up behind him and cracked Adam over the head with the wooden post his protest sign was attached to. Queenie saw Adam go down and get swallowed up by the mob.

*　　*　　*

ALEJANDRO WAS OUT OF JAIL.

He had been arrested at the Newman property and been released only after the union received enough donations to provide the $12,000 bail. Ortiz had not taken part in the physical fight, but had tried to shout at his men to back off. Still, the police had arrested Ortiz—for "violating the air space" of a grower, and they had arrested over forty activists for trespassing and assault. It didn't stop him or slow the strike. If anything, the riot had only strengthened the union's determination to persuade the pickers to unionize. The riot had so inflamed tempers that Alejandro's organization had gained hundreds of new members and the protests grew.

Deborah hadn't seen him since before the Newman riot, but now there was to be another rally in the park, and she would seize the opportunity to get a message to him to meet her, and where.

Today's wasn't a peaceful rally, as the riot had stirred up anger on both sides so much that the speakers could barely be heard. Deborah watched for a good moment and was finally able to get close to him, praying that one of the news photographers wouldn't capture her surreptitiously slipping him a piece of paper. It contained directions to the new place she had found for them to meet. A place that had been abandoned and would provide them with perfect seclusion for their lovemaking. It was a partially constructed barrel room far enough away from the house and the old winery for them not to be caught.

*　　*　　*

GORDON WAS ON HIS way to the hospital to visit his father, who was recovering from a blow to the head during the riot, when a pale blue Corvair passed him on the highway, going the other way. It was Deborah Schaller, and she seemed to be in a hurry. Suddenly excited, he whipped a tire-burning U-turn and followed. This could be the very moment he had been watching for, away from crowds and prying eyes, a chance to declare his feelings for her and to give her the same chance to finally declare her own love for him. They were such a tragic pair, he and Deborah, and he was determined to save her from unrequited love, from interminable yearning and unhappiness. We will show the world that we can overcome the obstacles our two families have thrown in our path. We can show the world that true love *will* be victorious.

When he saw Deborah's car pull off the highway onto a deserted dirt road, he continued to follow, staying far enough back that she wouldn't see the red Mustang. He rounded a curve and saw cleared acres with stone buildings under construction. He had heard that the Schallers were expanding. These would be new winery buildings, only half finished. Clearly, work had come to a halt because of the strike. He slowed his car and watched her park and get out. That was when he noticed an unfamiliar pickup truck parked alongside the roofless building.

He watched as Deborah looked around, as if to be sure she wasn't being seen, and then delivered herself through the doorless doorway into the darkness inside.

Puzzled, Gordon got out of his Mustang and walked on light feet to the construction site that was littered with pallets piled with bricks, bags of cement, tools, sawhorses, a cement mixer—all abandoned because the men were busing in illegal workers and protecting them in the vineyards with rifles. A volatile situation was happening on her farm, and Deborah was paying a mysterious visit to *this* place?

He found an opening for a window that was waiting for glass and peered in. It took a moment for his eyes to adjust. He heard the sounds before he saw who was making them.

It so stunned him that it was moments before his brain registered the scene: two people on the floor, locked in an embrace on a rumpled blanket, arms and legs entwined.

Gordon blinked in shock. Deborah—*his* Deborah. Lying on her side, being kissed and caressed, kissing and caressing back.

The breath stopped in his chest. He felt as if he had been punched with a big heavy fist. He slumped away from the window, trembling, breaking out in a sweat. Deborah was kissing one of the union organizers. A Mexican named Alejandro Ortiz. The enemy of every grower in the valley. One of the son-of-a-bitch Mexicans who had hurt his father and put him in the hospital.

Backing away, he stumbled to his car. He couldn't let this happen. It wasn't right. That man laying hands on his precious Deborah. Gordon somehow fell into his car and gripped the steering wheel until his knuckles were white. Somehow, that Mexican bastard was going to pay.

*   *   *

THE STRIKE WAS WORRYING Clara something awful. It filled her with anxiety and robbed her of sleep. She couldn't stop thinking about the families of the strikers. The men hadn't been paid for a while now. Wages that would have gone to the picketers were now going to the scabs. So how were the strikers' families getting fed?

On top of that, Lorelei had telephoned from Seattle, having seen news footage of the strike and the riots, and wanted to come down and be with the family. But Lorelei was forty-five now and had a family of her own to take care of. Clara prayed she wouldn't get it in her head to fly down here out of worry.

So not only did she have all that on her mind, now *this* had come up, and here she sat with a grim Bill Junior waiting for Deborah to come home, and Clara was sorely dreading it.

Deborah entered the house through the kitchen and was startled to see her father sitting at the kitchen table. It was the middle of the day. Why was he here? And then she saw the furious expression on his face. To her further surprise, Grandmother Clara was with him, also looking unusually grim.

"What's wrong?" Deborah said, suddenly wondering if they had found out about her and Alejandro. Dear God. Her father would kill them both!

"I got to wondering why you hadn't heard from any of the colleges," Bill said, "so I had my secretary get in touch with one of them. The admissions office said they never got your application. So we contacted all the others. You never sent any of the applications in."

Her heart pounded. This was the moment she had put off for so long. Now the truth had to come out. "No."

"You and I sat at this very table and I helped you fill in the forms, and I wrote out checks for the processing fees. We signed them together and sealed them in the envelopes. What happened?"

"I threw them away." Without remorse, but without defiance either. Just statements of fact.

"You deceived me? You sat there and lied to my face?"

"Try to understand, Daddy. I don't want to go to college."

He threw up his hands. "Am I dreaming this? What girl in the world wouldn't want to go to the college of her choice and have it all completely paid for by her father? Do you know how many girls don't even get to go to college? Or they have to compete for scholarships, or work at jobs to put themselves through school?"

"It's not about the money, Daddy. I don't care about money. Being rich isn't everything."

"That is something only a rich brat would say!" he shouted. "I didn't hear you complaining about being rich when I bought that sports car for you, or when I sent you to Paris that summer to study art. And all the expensive clothes you buy. Look at you!" he shouted. "Dressed in jeans and a gypsy shirt. And that Indian headband is ridiculous. Are you trying to look like a beatnik? Is that it?"

"Dad, no one says *beatnik* any more."

"And you *are* going to school. I didn't work hard and make sacrifices so you could throw it all away."

She met his glare with her own glare. They had had this argument so many times, she was sick of it. He was still treating her like a child. After the pressure of the strike and all its attendant worries, and the sneaking around with Alejandro and constant fear of being caught, something snapped inside Deborah and the latent defiance came gushing out.

"Work hard?" she screeched. "How hard was it to steal the Callahan wine distributorship from the Newmans? I don't want your money if that's where it came from. I don't want your expensive clothes and fancy car and Ivy League school."

She thrust her chin out at him, hands on her hips, before she realized a terrible silence had descended over the room. And then she saw the look on her father's face, the kind you see in movies when someone's been shot or stabbed and they're frozen in a moment of surprise before they collapse. Her father just stood there staring at her, and suddenly Grandma Clara was rushing over to him, putting her arm around his shoulders, saying, "She didn't mean it, Bill darling. She doesn't know what she's saying." Clara turned a furious face to her granddaughter. "Apologize to your father right now!"

Deborah realized she had gone too far by throwing the Callahan deal in his face, but she had just as much stubbornness in her as any Schaller and she wasn't going to back down. She didn't want to go to school. She loved Alejandro and wanted to join noble causes with him and carry picket signs and change the world. Only idiots sat in classrooms and parroted what teachers said.

Thinking of Alejandro and how brave he was and how he was leading his people to glory, she felt her heart expand inside her chest, and she said: "Not only will I not apologize, I have something more to say. Daddy, I think you should sign a contract with the farmworkers' union."

His face drained of color. "*What?*"

"Give them what they ask for. Don't keep the pickers down by pressing your foot on their necks. Don't be a capitalist oppressor."

His eyebrows shot up. "What the hell?"

"Deborah!" Clara said sharply.

"You make money off the broken backs of poor working men. You make them live in squalor. You live in a big mansion and drive shiny cars while they can't get medical care for their children."

"Who the hell have you been listening to?" He strode toward her, but she stood her ground. "Who has been feeding you this garbage?"

"I think the union organizers are right! And I'm embarrassed to be a grower's daughter."

His hand shot out so fast she didn't see it coming. The slap landed hard and sharply on her face, and Deborah was spun off her feet. She collapsed to the floor, stunned.

"Bill!" Clara cried, running to her granddaughter.

Deborah scrambled to her feet and fled from the kitchen, to thunder up the stairs to her bedroom where she flung herself on her bed and sobbed.

Clara came in behind her and sat on the bed. "Good God, girl, what made you say those things?"

"Grandma, you don't know how hard it was for me growing up, hearing from other kids what a crook my father is."

"You've hurt him terribly, Debbie."

Deborah turned a boiling red face to her. "How can you defend him?"

"He's my son, child. My first son died in the war, my daughter moved away, and Bill is all I have left. I know he isn't perfect, but no one is. And yes, he disappointed his father and me. But he is still my boy and I love him. Maybe someday you'll know what that's like."

Clara paused, then said, "Deborah, you must apologize to your father. You have hurt him terribly."

But Deborah mutely shook her head.

Clara's heart softened. She knew why Deborah was the way she was, stubborn, with a mind of her own. Clara would do anything to protect her granddaughter.

Deborah suddenly collapsed in tears and sobs, crying in Clara's lap. "Oh, Grandmother, you don't know what it's like! I am in love with a boy who is forbidden to me!"

So that was it. Clara had guessed rightly that her eighteen-year-old granddaughter was suffering the growing pains of young love. Clara stroked the girl's head and said with a bittersweet smile, "Yes, my dear, I do know what it's like."

"It's agony!"

"Yes," Clara said softly.

Deborah lifted her tear-streaked face. "You were able to marry Grandpa Wilhelm. Nothing stood in your way. You fell in love and got married, and it was all so simple for you."

Clara's smile was sad and wistful. So simple? Marrying a man and then falling in love with his brother? "Sweetheart, nothing is ever *so simple*." She wanted to add, You're only eighteen. When you are seventy-two, you will have lived through war and loss and wonder and joy. You will have gained experience and wisdom and you will have learned to accept with serenity the things you have both gained and lost. But you are only eighteen. You have to live your life to learn its lessons. Clara did not voice any of this, because she was remembering when *she* was nineteen and had wept in her mother's lap because she was confused about marrying Wilhelm and leaving her beloved river. Her mother had said there would be other rivers, and she was right. But what else had gone through her mother's mind that day as her daughter wept into her lap? Had she, too, thought: When you are my age you will understand things more? But my telling you now will make no sense. You have to live your life and learns its lessons yourself.

Thus it went through the generations, Clara thought. It was simply the natural order of life.

Clara heard a sound and, turning, to her shock found little Jack standing in the doorway. He had a dirty smudge on his face and he was sucking on three fingers. His eyes were big and confused and frightened. Poor little boy, seven years old and wondering all at the same time if his sister was his Mama or if his Grandma was his Mama, or if he didn't have a Mama at all. Sometimes Clara thought he was going to grow up very confused about women.

She remembered when he had learned to walk and followed Deborah around like a little duck. He had a small wooden dog on wheels that he pulled along on a string everywhere he went. Clara wanted to cry, but it wouldn't be good for the child to see both mothers crying. "It's all right, Jackie," she said. "Mama just doesn't feel well."

Deborah lifted herself up and held out her arms. He ran into them and gave her a hug. "Get better, Mama."

"I will, sweetheart."

After he ran out, Clara said to Deborah, "Now go downstairs and apologize to your father."

But the defiance was still in her. Composed now, Deborah came to a new decision. She had to sever herself from this family. She wanted to be a crusader. Important causes called to her. She and Alejandro would go away together and she would never return to the Schaller farm. "I will not, Grandmother. I only spoke the truth. I have my own life to live and that's that."

With a heavy heart, Clara went back downstairs, where she found her son still sitting at the table. He suddenly looked very old. She knew that many weights burdened him—the strike, the possible loss of the grape harvest, a daughter who refused to fulfill his dream of having a brilliant, successful college-educated daughter. He must feel as if the world had turned on him.

"I'm sorry," she said, laying a hand on his shoulder.

His broad shoulders heaved, he shook his head. "It's all right," he said in a flat voice. "I didn't know—" His voice broke. "I didn't know she hated me so much. I gave her mother everything she asked for, and she ran away. I gave Debbie everything *she* ever asked for, and now she flings it all back in my face."

He stood up and looked at his mother with empty eyes. "She doesn't have to go to school. She can do anything she wants. I won't interfere any more, because I don't want anything thrown back in my face again. And now I have to get to the winery and help with the crush."

*　　*　　*

GORDON KEPT AN EAR out for sounds or voices; he also kept watch out the window as he went through his father's desk looking for the gun, the nine-millimeter Beretta.

But he knew no one would suddenly come home. They were either at the picket line or overseeing the harvesting and loading of the flat-bed trucks. He himself wasn't missed. With the continuing strike and the constant influx of new workers, all the Newmans had to be everywhere at once. He had told his father, who had recovered from the head wound, he was going to supervise the north vineyard, and he had told his grandfather the south vineyard, and told Melvyn he was going to be wherever Melvyn wasn't going to be. He had done this for the past three weeks, ever since the riot and finding Deborah with that Mexican. In the meantime, he had kept an eye on her, secretly stalking her, following her, getting to know the pattern of their trashy affair.

And during all those days, twenty-year-old Gordon Newman had seethed and boiled and gotten eaten up with jealousy and rage and vows of revenge. Long ago, his father had sworn revenge for a wrong done to him but he had never carried it out. Well, this Newman was going to see his vow of revenge through.

He had seen her in the park today, passing a note to Ortiz. So he knew they would be meeting at the unfinished barrel room tonight.

Here it was, in the bottom drawer, the gun his father had bought for protection at the beginning of the strike. Gordon wasn't going to actually kill the Mexican. There was too much risk of getting caught, and his father's heart, needing an operation, could never withstand the scandal of a trial. Gordon was just going to wave it around and scare the bastard off. And who knew? Maybe Deborah would look at Gordon differently. Here was a man who would fight for her. Maybe it would win her heart. Some women loved brave and violent men.

* * *

DEBORAH WAS QUIETLY PACKING a bag up in her room. No one was in the house. No one knew she was running away.

There could be no more secret meetings with Alejandro. They could no longer even stay in the valley. But she was happy and excited. She was certain now that she was pregnant. She and Alejandro would go away together and get married. She didn't care where they went. She would let him choose. She supposed it would be Mexico. And they were going to be so happy!

But she couldn't leave Grandma Clara in the dark. The note was for *her*. Deborah kept it concise. "I told you I was in love with a boy who is forbidden to me, and he is in love with me. Father and Grandpa Wilhelm will never approve, because he is Mexican, so you see why we have to leave. I love you, Grandma." She purposely left out the pregnancy bit. No need to add more worries to her already distressed grandmother.

The moon was silver and high over the unfinished buildings when she arrived with her suitcase. Alejandro was already there, eagerly awaiting her, the blanket spread on the dirt floor of what was someday to be a barrel room. But when he took her into his arms, she held back. "What is it, *mi amor*?" he said.

Her eyes shone as brightly as the moon as she looked up at her tall, handsome hero. "I have news. We're going to have a baby."

He stared at her. Then he frowned. "What are you talking about?"

She laughed. "I'm pregnant! Now we can get married."

The frown deepened. "How is that possible? Didn't you . . . protect yourself?" These days, girls had access to things, he knew. Especially free-spirited girls like Deborah who so freely gave of her body and her love and who talked of peace and freedom. One of the hippie girls you saw on the news. Surely she had gone to a doctor . . . he had just *assumed*.

Her smile fell. She didn't understand the frown. This was not how she imagined this scene would play out. Why wasn't he kissing her and hugging her and telling her how happy she had made him and that they would go down to Mexico and stand before a priest and make an offering to a statue of the Blessed Virgin and go somewhere to dance and drink margaritas and feast on beans and chilies and avocados? Maybe in a small sleepy village where they would raise their child in the sun.

Why was he standing there like a statue?

"Deborah," he began. And it shocked her. After weeks of being "*Cariña*" and "*Mi corazon*" and "*Mi vida*," suddenly she was "Deborah."

And then it hit her, cold and hard. Alejandro was not happy. Not by a long shot. She had just told him the worst news a teenage girl could ever tell her illicit, forbidden lover. And she suddenly knew beyond a doubt what was coming next.

"You must know, Deborah," he said gently and with some confusion in his voice—this man who coalesced armies of farmworkers and inspired uneducated peasants to stand up to their overlords—suddenly at a loss for words or command. "I can't marry you."

"But I'm eighteen."

He shook his head of beautiful thick black hair. "It's not that. Deborah, you and I are from two very different worlds. We can never get married. I thought you understood that."

Now it was her turn to stand in shock. "But . . . the baby."

He heaved a worried sigh. "*That*," he said, summing up their entire situation in one bland word. "That is a problem. I don't know what to tell you. My people come first. I work only for La Causa. You know that. After we have unionized the California laborers, we plan to move on to Arizona. I will always be on the move, Deborah. I will always live in other people's homes and rely on other people's charity. I have no money and I never will. I doubt that I will ever marry. But if I do, I will find a Catholic Mexican girl, that is the only kind of person I can marry. I thought you knew this."

Tears sprang into her eyes. "But what about us? Coming here all these times. Did it mean nothing to you?"

He smiled tenderly, as he would at a child. "We had a summer romance, Deborah. You told me at the beginning that you wanted to see the world, that you didn't want to be tied down or go to school or live by rules. Remember?"

"That was before I fell in love with you. Oh Alejandro, you can't leave me! What will I do?" She had thought he was so noble and filled with honesty and integrity. She had thought he always did the right thing. Where was his honor now?

"You must tell your family about the baby. They will figure something out."

She stepped back from him, aghast. "Are you *serious*? My father would kill me! They'd throw me out, and then where would I be?" Oh God oh God oh God. Her world was collapsing all around her. She thought the room was spinning and there was a roaring in her ears. But it was a car pulling up outside, the pulsing engine of a new Mustang, and the tires screeched to a halt. She and Alejandro turned toward the open doorway at the same time. They heard someone shout, "I know you're in there!"

"Who—?" Alejandro said.

"Oh God," Deborah said.

And then there was a silhouette in the moonlight. A young man. Deborah gasped. "Gordon!"

And then they saw the gun in his hand.

"Oh hey," Alejandro said, holding his arms out. "There is no need for this, my friend."

"I am not your friend!" Gordon screamed as he aimed the gun at him. "You stole my girl!"

"Your girl!" Deborah said. "Gordon, what on earth are you talking about?"

"You and I are meant to be together." His face was red and his eyes were filled with tears. She saw spittle fly from his mouth as he shouted, and she was suddenly very afraid.

"You don't want to do anything rash," she said as calmly as she could. "Lower the gun, Gordon. Put it down and we'll talk."

"There's no need to talk. I'm here to stop this bastard from ever laying hands on you again."

Alejandro stepped in front of Deborah, his hands held up before him. He searched for an exit, a weapon, a way to get out or defend themselves. He kept his eyes on the Beretta. He didn't like the shaky way the boy was waving it around.

"You come to this valley," Gordon said bitterly, "and strut around and stir everyone up, and you get my father a crack over the head that could have killed him and then you steal our women. *Who the fuck do you think you are*?" He straightened his arm and aimed the gun right at Alejandro's face. "You're going to be sorry you ever came here."

"No!" Deborah cried, darting from behind Alejandro to stand in front of him. She reached for the gun. "I can't let you do this!"

"Get out, Deborah," Alejandro said, giving her a push. "Go for help. I can handle this."

"No!" Gordon screamed, the gun shivering in his grasp. "Run, you bastard. I'll give you to the count of three to haul your sorry ass out of here. And then keep running and never come back."

"Gordon!" Deborah cried. "Please don't do this. We can talk. Lower the gun." She grabbed for it. His wrist was sweaty in her hand.

A look of confusion swept over Gordon's face. "Tell the Mexican to get out of here," he said, and in the next instant the gun went off, filling the night with the loudest sound any of the three had ever heard.

Deborah looked at him in surprise, a perfect round black-and-red hole in the center of her forehead. Then she dropped soundlessly to the floor.

Gordon stared in horror at Deborah's body crumpled at his feet. She looked small and doll-like, and in a strange position, like a marionette that had been cut from its strings. He stared at her for a long time, wondering where he was, what had just happened, why the gun had fired. He heard "*Dios mio! Esta muerta!*" And turned to see Alejandro run from the unfinished barrel room and disappear into the night, his boots rapidly crunching rocks and debris, a vehicle starting up and driving off.

Tucking the gun into his belt, Gordon knelt beside Deborah and, with tears rolling down his cheeks, he checked for a pulse but knew there wouldn't be one. His mind was thrown into turmoil. Deborah was dead, she was *really* dead.

He took her lifeless body into his arms. Her head flopped onto his shoulder as he rocked with her and cried into her hair. "I'm so sorry, Debbie. I didn't mean to do it. We belong together. I just had to stop him from touching you. It wasn't your fault, I know that. You were seduced. You were innocent." He wept until her hair was soaked.

And then he grew strangely quiet. He looked around the room, the brick-and-mortar walls, one of them unfinished as the masons had been pulled off the job to pick grapes. Gordon felt himself step out of his body as he stared at the scene in a mixture of awe and interest. Most of his mind went blank, but a small voice in his head told him he had to fix this right away or something terrible was going to happen to his family, to this whole valley.

What should he do? Call the police, tell them Ortiz did it? But then he'd have to explain how he knew. How would he explain his presence here, and witnessing a murder? Would they even believe him? What if Ortiz was going to the police right now, telling them what had just happened?

He should just run away and leave the body here to be discovered by workers.

He felt sick. Dear God, what had he done? No, he couldn't just leave her here. There were coyotes in this valley, and other scavengers. He couldn't bear to see her beauty destroyed by fangs and claws and talons. His beloved soulmate needed to be placed in a safe spot, out of harm's way.

Then he looked at the gaping hole in the unfinished wall.

She would be safe there, unharmed. Just for a while, just while he thought things through. Then he would come back. . . .

He struggled to get the body into the wall, weeping and sobbing the whole time, as it was a tight fit and her arms kept falling out. But he worked at it, gently, as if he were putting a sick baby into his crib. And then he paused to look at his dear, sweet, slumbering Deborah. He would let somebody know where she was. They would come and get her. He just had to work out the details.

He stood up to leave and then paused. The day he had picked up his new custom Mustang, back when he was on top of the world and certain he was going to win Deborah Schaller's heart, he had gone to Faulkner's jewelers and ordered matching his-and-her ID bracelets. They would need something to pledge their love to each other with, and rings seemed somehow corny and premature. The bracelets were sterling silver with a Cuban link chain and lobster clasp fastener. He had worked hard at coming up with the perfect message to engrave on the plate, had spent hours at the library and had decided on *Amour de ma vie* (Love of my life) for both bracelets—French being so much more romantic than English. He had planned on giving it to her during their first ride together in the Mustang, and since that had never happened, he had carried the bracelets in his pocket in case the proper occasion should arise.

Reaching into his jeans, he brought out the one for Deborah, shorter and more delicate than his, and, sobbing, put it around her wrist, his tears falling on the bracelet as he fastened the clasp. Then he stumbled outside, heading toward his car. In the distance he heard the howl of a coyote. They would smell her presence in here. They would drag her out like garbage and feast on her.

No, no. Gordon had vowed to be Deborah's protector. He found the bag of plaster, found a pump for well water, returned inside where bricks had been stacked for weeks, waiting for the workmen to come back and finish the job. Blindly, without thinking, and sobbing his lungs out, he packed the gaping hole tightly with bricks until Deborah was completely hidden, making him think of a ghoulish short story he had read in high school by Edgar Allan Poe or someone, then he plastered over the bricks and silently promised Deborah that he would send someone to fetch her.

He staggered out, tripping and falling, scraping the palms of his hands on construction debris. Mindlessly, he stripped off his plastered shirt and ran his arms and hand under the water pump. Throwing the shirt in some bushes, he jumped into the Mustang and drove the hell out of there.

By the time he arrived at the big Newman house, he was out of his mind. He found Melvyn there, in the kitchen, fixing himself a sandwich. When Melvyn turned and asked Gordon how the harvest in the west vineyard was going, saying that their dad was down at the picket line, talking to the police chief, Melvyn stopped and stared. Gordon was all freaked out and agitated about something, blathering about shooting Deborah and burying her body where no one would find it. "I messed up big time, Mel! I only took the gun to scare him off. I didn't even know it was loaded!"

Melvyn felt his insides turn to water. "Oh God, man. Oh God. Are you sure? What are you talking about? Where's the gun?"

Gordon blinked like a madman. "I . . . I don't know." What *had* he done with it? Had he thrown it from the car on the highway?

"Where is she?" Melvyn said, grabbing his brother by the arms. "Where did you . . . put the body? We have to tell the police." But even as he spoke the words, he knew they would never tell the police. The authorities could not be brought in on this. The arrest, the trial. It would tear the valley apart, not to mention how news of this would devastate his family. And what revenge would it trigger among the Schallers? A Newman murdering a Schaller could only end in bloody violence.

He tried to think. He had to make sure the body would never be found. And then his shoulders slumped and his eyes filled with tears. Only eighteen years old and looking out for his older brother, Melvyn felt the burden of a terrible secret settle into his soul. He knew that this was something he and Gordon were going to share for the rest of their lives. It made him feel sick.

"I can't live with myself!" Gordon suddenly cried, breaking away from his brother. "I can't go on!" he screamed.

Before Melvyn's startled eyes, Gordon ran from the kitchen and his footsteps thundered down the hall. When he heard the front door open, Melvyn took off after him. He reached the front porch in time to see Gordon jump into the driver's seat of his Ford Mustang fastback. "Wait!" he yelled.

"I'm sorry," Gordon shouted back at him. "Tell Mom and Dad and Grandpa that I love them!"

"Jesus—" Melvyn flew down the steps as the Mustang took off in a cloud of burning rubber. He ran after the car as it fishtailed down the paved driveway. "Oh my God! Gordo, *stop*!" Melvyn pumped his arms and legs as hard as he could, but Gordon sped away so that his brother watched in horror as the Mustang veered from the drive and headed straight for the cluster of winery buildings. "*Stop!*" Melvyn screamed. And then the Ford sped up, gaining such speed that Melvyn knew there would be no stopping now, no swerving. The aim for the brick wall was straight and purposeful and deadly. The car that was meant to win Deborah Schaller's love made a sickening sound as metal and glass slammed against the wall, and in the next instant it burst into a ball of flame, lighting up the night.

Melvyn ran toward the fire, but he couldn't get close enough. "Gordo!" he shouted until his voice cracked. "Gordo!" Tears streamed down his face. "Oh God, oh God!" He dropped to his knees and sobbed as he watched helplessly as black smoke rolled up into the sky and farmhands came running and men came out of the building that had just shaken like an earthquake and thunder combined. It was the Newmans' barrel room he had collided with, dying instantly.

Later, a numb and mumbling Melvyn told the police that his brother had been showing off what the Mustang could do. He was driving recklessly in the driveway, talking about how he was going to become a professional racecar driver or maybe a stunt driver for the movies and handle all the car-chase scenes you see in police movies and TV shows. But then, for some reason, Gordon lost control of the car. He tried to correct it but couldn't, and the car simply went into the wall before Gordon could escape. It was just a terrible, terrible accident.

And that was all Melvyn told the police.

*   *   *

"CAN YOU EVER FORGIVE me?" Johann said as they walked along the bank of Largo Creek. They had the world all to themselves.

After Gordon's fatal accident and Deborah running away, Clara had decided it was time to reconcile with Johann and resume their private visits. He had jumped at it. This was something they both needed.

"There's nothing to forgive," she said.

"I let my anger at your son stand in the way of our love. Bill is Bill and Adam is Adam. They have their own lives to live, just as you and I have ours. I have missed you these past years, Clara, I have missed you so desperately. We don't know what the future holds, but I pray that we can face it together." Clara was seventy-two and he was seventy-five, but they had the strong and healthy constitutions of hard-working farmers. They still had years ahead of them.

They paused beneath a wild apple tree. It was old, and no one knew how it had gotten there near the creek. No doubt an apple seed carried on the wind or the feathers of a bird. It reminded Johann of a memory long ago, back in Germany when he and Wilhelm were boys and always getting into trouble. They had trespassed on a farm to climb apple trees and steal the fruit. Johann had snagged his short pants on a branch and called out for help. The farmer had caught them and collared Wilhelm, whose shirt was all lumpy and bumpy with stolen apples, and the farmer had said, "What do you think you are doing with those apples?" And Wilhelm in all wide-eyed innocence had said, "What apples?" That night, Papa Jakob had given them the hiding of their lives. It was a good, warm memory that brought tears to the eyes, and he wondered if Wilhelm ever thought of that day.

"How is the family doing?" she asked as a fresh breeze kissed their faces.

"Adam is coping as best he can. Melvyn has gone into a strange silence. Who can blame him, witnessing a bizarre accident like that?"

"I am so sorry, Johann."

He forced a smile. How strange—he and Clara had both lost grandchildren at the same time.

"Sofie has taken a leave from school to mourn the loss of her twin. Although Gordon had actually been closer to his brother than to his sister, still, a twin is a twin. Sofie had also seen news footage of the strike, saw her father getting injured, and decided home is where she needs to be right now."

He paused to watch a rainbow trout flutter in the clear creek water.

"How was the crush?" he asked after a moment. He had never stopped being interested in his father's vines, planted fifty-four years ago.

"They finished picking around seven last night. The last truckload was crushed around ten."

"What did the chardonnays yield?"

"Between two and three tons an acre."

He nodded. "That's not bad for the age of the vines."

"Not bad, considering what we had to go through to rescue the crop. Do you think this battle will ever end?"

Johann squinted into the distance, as if he could see the future there. Alejandro Ortiz, the main organizer, had gone back to Texas, where he was suddenly needed at the union's headquarters. Another man had been sent in his place to keep the strike going. "I don't know. Both sides have legitimate grounds. I can understand the workers and their demands. Adam and I have been talking about maybe signing a contract with the union. After all, we can afford to absorb the loss. But we're not sure."

Clara sighed. "Wilhelm and Bill have been saying the same thing. We don't want to go through this again. And the workers do have rights. But if Schallers and Newmans hire only union workers from now on, it won't be good for the small growers."

"The union will put pressure on them. I'm afraid a lot of the smaller farms won't survive this fight. So . . . do we all stick together and stand against the union, even though we can see their side of things?"

She smiled sadly. "Standing together. It has a nice sound to it. I remember the day in the park when Wilhelm went to stand at your side. And for a while, during the worst of the strike, we all stood together. It was a good feeling."

He searched her face. "And how are you doing, Clara? With Deborah leaving so suddenly like that. . . ."

"My son is very angry. He said the apple doesn't fall far from the tree. Fay left him without warning, and now Deborah. He figures like mother, like daughter. And he remembered the things Fay had told him about her mother, how Ruth Reed hadn't been able to stay put in any one place for long. Fay had inherited the same weaknesses, as had Deborah apparently. Bill has taken down all her pictures, packed up her room, and won't talk to little Jack about her. I'm worried about my grandson. It isn't a healthy atmosphere for a boy to grow up in."

Little Jack was going to learn a skewed history of his family from his father, she suspected, about faithless women and heartless mothers and ungrateful daughters. There was only so much Clara could do to counter her son's influence on his own son. That was why a mother was so important, to bring balance to a child's formative years. And Deborah, only eighteen, how much of her family history did *she* know? And what about buried truths? For little Jack and Deborah to know their own full story would mean an unveiling of lies and omissions. It also would mean including the Newmans, who were their flesh and blood because they were Schallers, too.

I will write it all down, Clara decided now. I will record a chronicle of our history for future generations. I will put it all down in the form of letters to Deborah, even though I don't know where she is. I will write to her and keep the letters until I hear from her.

"Do you think Deborah will ever come back?"

Clara smiled and nodded. "I know she will. I will never give up hope on two things: that my granddaughter comes home, and that our two families become one family again someday."

The Present Day

NICOLE HAD HAD A dream. It was one of those strange scenarios that are so vivid and realistic and filled with emotion that it follows you around all day. The problem was, as soon as she awoke that morning, the details of the dream dissolved, leaving only intense, tangled emotions that dogged her footsteps as she conducted a last walk-through of her property.

She had the odd feeling that the dream had been trying to tell her something, and was trying to still.

This was the original winery, built back around 1912. The newer buildings, constructed in the sixties, were on the other side of the eucalyptus trees and had been built there to be close to newer vineyards as the Schaller operation had continued to expand. Nicole had spent the morning walking through the various rooms, silently saying good-bye. She was leaving tomorrow for Switzerland, and then New York after that; and who knew when she would pass this way again? Not too long from now, Schaller wines would be under new ownership.

As she stood in the doorway of the fermentation room, she looked at her watch. Lucas was late. He was supposed to have been here an hour ago, but he had called to say he was being held up and that he would be here soon. They were both eager to read Clara's final two letters. They had read three yesterday at the ruins, but had been interrupted when Lucas got a call from their housekeeper saying that Señor Newman wasn't feeling well. They suspected it was because of the photograph they had found of the three smiling teenagers—Deborah standing between Gordon and Melvyn, in what looked like a love triangle. Lucas had wanted to stay with his father, who had been emotionally overcome, but Melvyn had insisted that they leave. But then Melvyn had asked the housekeeper to send for Lucas after all.

The final two letters. . . . And then all this would come to an end, Nicole to get on to her new career, where high-powered people were eagerly awaiting her ideas, and Lucas to get on with the next stage of his experimental crop. But things were not going as smoothly as planned, for herself and for Lucas.

The Macintoshes had dropped a bombshell on her yesterday. "We are going to make our winery more family-oriented," Mrs. Macintosh had said with a big, proud smile. "Kid-friendly, you might say. We're going to create a play area for children like you see at some fast-food restaurants, with crawl-tubes and plastic ball pits and slides. And a video arcade for the older kids. This frees up the parents to spend more time in the wine-tasting room. We'll also offer excursions out to Colina Sagrada for Indian arrowhead hunts, with us discreetly planting the arrowheads ahead of time, of course." It had horrified Nicole.

As for Lucas, his father had finally agreed to a full physical exam, after which the doctor had put Melvyn on medication and had given him strict orders to take it easy, to work less. So Lucas had had to cancel plans to set up an experimental station in Arizona. "I just don't have the right soil around here," he had told Nicole. "So I've decided to approach the work on rootstocks another way, through hydroponics. That way I can work here on the farm and keep an eye on my father."

"But is that as accurate?" Nicole had asked. "You'd just be working with water, not soil."

"No. It's not as accurate and it will take much longer, but it is a legitimate avenue that is currently being used in the search for hardier grape rootstocks."

She was sorry he had to change his plans, sorry she hadn't sold Colina Sagrada to him. After the other night in the ruins—the letters that had sparked intense emotions, the delicious hot clinch with Lucas, Nicole couldn't stop thinking about him. She wanted to have sex with him—hot and frantic—and it made her ache unbearably. But she was leaving. It was best to keep emotions suppressed and not acted upon.

She almost wanted to hold on to these last two letters, tell Lucas she had put them somewhere and now couldn't find them. They'd be insurance, something to keep her tied to Lucas, to give her an excuse to call him from New York and make up some story about having stuck the letters in a book and, guess what, she just found them!

But no, she couldn't hold on to the last two Clara letters, filled with mystery and answers and fresh discoveries. They had to read them now.

Nicole peered down the road that led to the main highway, anxious to see Lucas.

There was a stack of magazines on a bench just inside the door—trade journals, news bulletins published by the wine industry. Nicole had stopped reading them when she had decided to leave, and switched instead to print media devoted to the manufacture and marketing of beauty products, to familiarize herself with trends and her new employer's competition. But she had held on to the wine publications for the new owners.

She glanced now at the one on top of the stack. It had a color photo on the cover of two smiling men in white lab coats lifting tiny glasses of red wine. They were toasting the opening of their new micro-winery in Lausanne, Switzerland. Nicole hadn't read the article but was familiar with a trend toward exploring new fermentation processes, and the various experimental devices were being called "micro-wineries."

And it suddenly came to her—the dream she had had last night that had been dogging her. It had been about a micro-winery, and in the dream Nicole was overseeing its operation. This cover photo must have triggered the dream, or perhaps something she had read, or overheard at the Growers' Club the last time she'd been there. How curious, she thought now, recalling that the dream had been an emotional one—a confusion of melancholy and happiness.

What did it mean?

"Hello?" She looked up and saw Lucas, waving from his Jeep. Her heart jumped. "Your housekeeper told me you were here. Sorry I'm late."

He had had another fight with his father and he was worried about Melvyn's health and the strain the murder investigation and Clara's letters were putting on the old man. Lucas knew that secrets were being kept from him—that his father was holding something back.

"Shall we read the last two letters?" he said. Lucas still didn't know if anything had happened to Melvyn personally to keep such animosity going between the two families. Perhaps Clara was going to reveal yet another injustice from one family against the other.

His smile disguised the turmoil in his soul. Lucas had never felt so divided in all his life, like he was being pulled every which way. He was mad at himself. Why did he have to go and fall in love? And with *her*, of all people?

She felt the same way. He could see it in her eyes, and that made things worse. Secret longing was one thing. A man could live with that. But *shared* longing? That was too scary and shaky. It wouldn't take much—a glance from her, a fingertip on his arm, a cheeky smile—for him to go over the edge.

When she hopped into the Jeep, Nicole realized she suddenly felt stupidly giddy. "You have the letters with you?" he asked as the Jeep rolled down the drive, and she said a breathless "Yes!" as she patted her shoulder bag.

She noticed that Lucas was dressed very upscale today, in a tan Ralph Lauren polo shirt and brown corduroy slacks that looked pricey and new. Had he dressed for *her*? Nicole had certainly devoted thirty minutes to selecting the silk top and tight skirt she was wearing, with a gold chain bracelet and tasteful gold locket necklace. Just to go sit in some old ruins and read old letters? Were they both so obvious?

As they started off down the dusty road, Nicole felt herself suddenly in the grip of an impulse. She didn't want to hide any more, the way Clara and Johann had. She realized she hadn't visited the river in a long time, as if she had started leaving this valley weeks ago. "You know what?" she said. "Let's go to the river. I want to look out over the water. I want to feel the breeze. One last time."

Lucas drove upriver, away from Lynnville and Germantown where the banks of the Largo were crowded with tourists. They found a beautiful spot beneath a weeping willow where they could sit on an old log fallen long ago and watch the trout in the shallows, the boats farther out, dignified white herons, necks stretched long, walking among the tall reeds.

They sat close together, their faces to the wind. Nicole gently slit open the first letter and unfolded the pages, to begin reading silently, as they had been doing, with Nicole passing the page to Lucas to read to himself while she silently read the next. But he said, "No; read it out loud." To savor Clara's final words together at the same time.

Nicole bent her head and read: "When I found your note, Deborah, saying you were going away, it broke my heart. But I understood also. I had a secret and forbidden love of my own. It was too late for me to be with the man I loved, and so I am happy for you, that you have the freedom to go away with him and be with him. I had hoped you would come back and be part of our family again. But I suppose you joined another family. Perhaps, as my own mother said, you found another river.

"For a long time after you left us, Deborah, I kept thinking I would hear from you. I jumped every time the phone rang. I would run out to the mailbox, hoping for a letter or card from you. But, remembering how painful things had been between Johann and Wilhelm after their terrible fight, I was not surprised that you could not forgive your father for the things he said to you. History has a tendency to repeat itself, especially in families.

"The strikes continued for months after you left the valley, and then peaceful accords were agreed upon. But you already know this, dear Deborah, if you've read the news. With the unrest over, we were able to resume expanding the farm. Construction was finally finished on the new buildings that had stood half finished. At last, we had a new fermentation room and a new barrel room.

"Poor little Jack. He was inconsolable after you left. He sat in your room day after day, calling out 'Mama?' Just like you did when you were eleven and Fay left us. It's no wonder he turned wild. He started acting out in school, always being sent to the principal's office. In high school they started calling him Big Jack because he grew so tall. He had a lot of girlfriends but no respect for women. And then the gambling and the arrests for public drunkenness and poor Bill having to bail him out. Jack turned out to be an embarrassment to the family, but who could blame him, losing two mothers and not even a single grave to visit? My big worry is this farm. I don't know if Jack will ever marry and have children. After Wilhelm and I and Bill are gone, how will Jack run the vineyards and winery? He seems to be only interested in carousing and spending money. I fear he will recklessly misuse his inheritance and perhaps even run this farm into the ground. What will become of the wine empire we have built up from that struggling vineyard many years ago when all we had were young cuttings and a dream?"

Nicole had reached the end of the first letter. They sat in thoughtful silence as she slipped it into her shoulder bag and brought out the last letter. As she slit it open, Lucas watched how the autumn wind stirred her long brown hair. She had a delicate profile. It belonged on an ivory cameo brooch. He nearly trembled with desire. The thought of her leaving, never seeing her again—

Nicole licked her lips as she unfolded the pages of the last letter. She noticed that the handwriting had gotten shaky now. And then she began to read.

"In the summer of 1979, two years after my own dear Wilhelm passed away at the age of eighty-nine (and unfortunately without having ever reconciled with his brother), I heard that Johann was sick. He was eighty-nine and they said he had pneumonia. I was very worried. And then I was startled to receive a visit from Adam Newman, who had not set foot on our property in many years, and he offered to drive me back to his home so that I could have a private visit with his father, who was asking for me. I was allowed into the bedroom and left alone with Johann, who was sleeping.

"I sat at his side and spoke softly to him. He awoke briefly and spoke. His last words to me were 'I will wait for you at the river. When you come, look for me and I will be there.' Which river did he mean? Does it matter? I know in my heart of hearts, as surely as I believe in miracles and messages from the cosmos, that Johann and I will be together again, and for all of eternity. He closed his eyes then, but I knew he could hear me. I told him that I have always loved him and will continue to love him when we are together again. I saw him smile at this. But I could be strong no longer. I laid my head on his chest and wept quietly as I listened to the unsteady beating of his heart. He stroked my hair. And then the hand on my hair stopped moving and the heart beneath his breastbone stopped beating. My beloved Johann was gone.

"But not everything is sadness, dear Deborah. Big Jack, your brother, finally got married. She's a nice woman named Lucy. I hope she can tame my grandson. My nurse brings me news that Lucy is pregnant. Just think. I am going to be a great-grandmother and you, Deborah, will be an aunt. I have lived a good and long and blessed life, Deborah. I look back and see the things we accomplished here. I was married to a good man, and was loved by another good man. I gave birth to two fine and handsome sons, was led by God to an angel of a daughter, and was blessed with grandchildren. Can any woman ask for more? I wish the very same for you, dearest granddaughter, wherever you are. I pray that your man loves you and is good to you, and that you accomplish things that you are proud of. I failed at only one thing—to mend the family rift. But perhaps you and your generation can take the first step toward healing. Know that I love you and pray for you every night.

"I will pause for now. My hand grows weary, my eyes grow dim. I wish to sleep a little, and I know I will dream. Vivid, lifelike dreams that will seem real to me. And I know that I will dream of the Rhineland and I will be among the pine forests of that far and distant river where Johann is waiting for me. It will be a nice respite for a while. I am ninety-seven years old, but I feel like a nineteen-year-old girl. My outer shell aged and grew small and wrinkled, but inside I am young and robust and full of hope and love.

"I have been writing to you for twenty-five years, Deborah, always in the hope that someday you would come back to us. I will preserve these letters and leave instructions that they are to be given to you upon your return, or upon the visit of your children and grandchildren, should they ever come from wherever they are, to search into their roots. I pray every day that you have been happy, that you have a good life with many friends and children. Strangely, although you went far away, I have always felt you nearby, as if you had never left at all."

That was the end of it. Nicole dropped the fluttering page in her lap and said, "She would have written this in 1990—the year I was born. She knew I was coming into the world and then she died."

They sat in silence and mutual sadness. Lucas reached for Nicole's hand and squeezed it. He tilted his head back and looked up at the blue sky where a pair of red-tailed hawks soared majestically in ever-widening circles. A mated pair, he decided, male and female, hunting for dinner.

He felt a keen sense of disappointment. There had been no answers in these last letters. No blinding insights or discoveries for him to shout "Aha!" And now it was over.

Was there anything in life worse than disappointment?

But as he watched the hawks circle and he felt Nicole at his side, Lucas began to feel an idea start to circle in his mind. It had come out of nowhere, as if trying to get his attention. It seemed important. What *was* it. . . ?

And then it came to him. "Nicole, hand me the first letter, please."

She heard the sudden excitement in his voice. "Why? What is it?"

"I think Clara *did* tell us something." He unfolded the pages and scanned the first one. "That's it!" Lucas said suddenly, slapping the paper. "It's right here!"

"What is?"

"The reason Mr. Gilette couldn't find any records on when the wall of the barrel room was last worked on. It's because there *aren't* any! It was *never* worked on! Clara says here that after the strike they were able to resume construction on the new winery. A new barrel room! Nicole, the last time that wall was plastered was when it was first built, in 1965!"

She stared at him. "So it *could* be Deborah?" she whispered.

"Suddenly a lot of things make sense."

"What do you mean?"

"Well, my father's strange actions lately, for one. Come on. We're going to get to the bottom of this once and for all."

She hesitated. It scared her.

*   *   *

"HOW DO YOU KNOW he'll be there?" Nicole asked as they sped toward the Lynnville town cemetery.

"Because he's been going there a lot lately. Nearly every day since the skeleton was found, he's gone to visit his brother's grave. I'm telling you, Nicole, my father knows the truth and I'm going to pull it out of him. This has to end."

But at what cost? whispered his conscience.

During the late sixties, as the quality of Californian wine improved, the region started to receive more international attention. A watershed moment for the industry occurred in 1976 when several California wineries were invited to participate in a blind tasting event in Paris. It was to compare the best of California with the best of Bordeaux and Burgundy. The event was called The Judgment of Paris. Johann, who was eighty-six at the time, was unable to attend, but Adam, at sixty-four, and Melvyn, thirty-two, went to represent Newman Wines, and they stunned the world by sweeping the competition in both the red and white wine categories. Perspectives about California wines changed after that. The state's wine industry grew as California emerged to become one of the world's premier wine regions.

Schaller wines might have been bigger and more well known, with their jingles and slogans and screw-cap bottles and strawberry- and apple-flavored wines that were consumed by college kids at beach parties, but Newman Wines grew in prestige and was sold by merchants of fine wines and was offered in five-star hotels and restaurants around the world. Melvyn had worked hard to bring the family company to where it was today. What would news of this murder do to the Newman name and reputation? And if it turned out it was Melvyn who had murdered Deborah Schaller out of jealousy, Newman Wines could be destroyed.

Lucas fought the urge to pull over, kill the engine, and say to Nicole, "I can't go through with this." It would be so easy. Just walk away, forget it all, let the police have an unsolved mystery on their books.

But he couldn't. Somehow, they owed it to Deborah and even to Clara to set the record straight, no matter how painful or distasteful.

Nicole was also in a quandary. Were she and Lucas about to reunite the two families in a way Clara had never dreamed of? Through murder and a scandalous trial that would blacken both names? Have I the right to do that to Clara, to Grandpa Bill and Great-Grandpa Wilhelm? And, farther back, Great-Great-Grandfather Papa Jakob, who came here with a simple dream? He helped all those other young immigrants to come here. Michelle would not now be married to Joe Eberhardt, the love of her life.

Nicole felt she owed so much to her family that she questioned now what the right thing to do was. And what about Deborah? What a sordid story it would be in all the tabloids and scandal sheets—the grisly remains of an heiress to a wine empire found buried in a wall. Was it fair to drag her through the mud like that? After all, she was the victim, if the skeleton was indeed her. And what if it was Melvyn who had done the killing? The stakes suddenly seemed astronomically high. How could she possibly go to New York and start a new life with all this hanging over the valley, over Lucas?

As they neared the cemetery, Nicole said, out of the blue, "I'm sorry."

He looked at her. "What for?"

"I feel responsible for this whole mess. I don't know why. I guess it's because it was *my* barrel room and *I* ordered that wall to be repaired."

He reached out and took her hand. "Hey, we're in this together, okay?"

*　　*　　*

MELVYN STOOD SOLEMNLY AT his brother's grave, his hat in his hand, his shoulders stooped. "I couldn't stop it, Gordon. I tried," he said to the headstone. "But I suppose the truth was bound to come out sooner or later. A truth this big can't be kept secret for long. I'm going to tell them what happened. I have to. I'm getting too old to carry this burden. It's time we cleared the air. Maybe, in a way, this can start the healing between the families. The Schallers did something evil to us when Bill stole the wine distributorship, and the Newmans did something evil to the Schallers when you killed Deborah. So we're kind of even now. It's funny: Lucas has been telling me things he's read in Clara's letters. I tried to block him out, but I learned that our grandfathers were indeed brothers and the bad blood started back in 1912 over a brutal beating. The funny thing is, I want to read those letters now. After all these years, I want to know what really happened."

He looked up and saw two familiar figures crossing over the grass. He had been expecting them.

Lucas came straight to the point, but gently, laying a hand on his father's arm. "We think the victim was Deborah, Pop, and I think you know something about her murder."

Melvyn said, wearily, "I've carried this secret for over fifty years, son, and I'm glad it's out. Yes, I knew Debbie had been murdered. But I didn't know where. For the sake of family name and reputation, and to protect my father who was suffering from a heart condition, I never said a word about the murder and let people think that Debbie had run away."

Nicole and Lucas listened in the peaceful silence of the cemetery as the old man painted a grim picture. "We both had a crush on her, my brother and I. She was forbidden fruit, being a Schaller. But poor Gordon had somehow convinced himself that she felt the same way about him. He saw them as Romeo and Juliet. But she was in love with a Mexican boy. Gordon must have gone searching for the lovers and caught them. He said he didn't plan on shooting the gun, it was just to scare them, but Deborah got shot.

"Gordon didn't tell me what he'd done with the body, so I didn't know all these years. I guess he must have panicked and stuffed her body into the unfinished wall of that barrel room and plastered over it. Because of the strike, the barrel room remained unfinished for months; and by the time work was resumed, they just painted the walls. And of course, by that time, the smell of decomposition would have been gone—" The words were choked off by overwhelming emotion. The skeleton . . . Deborah! She had been buried in that wall all this time, and Gordon had so loved her.

Melvyn started to cry, and Lucas put his arms around him. "I'm so sorry, Pop," he said. "I wish you could have told me instead of carrying it around all these years."

Melvyn wiped his eyes and looked at Nicole. "When I heard about the skeleton being found in the wall of your barrel room—" His voice broke. "I thought everything was going to come crashing down and our family name ruined."

Tears rose in Nicole's eyes, as she felt sorry for the old man. He was just a victim of circumstance, a man trying to hold his family together.

He went on. "When he confessed that he had shot her, he crashed that Mustang on purpose. Gordon drove into that wall to kill himself. I lied to the police. My brother committed suicide."

"Oh, Pop. . . ." Lucas said.

"My mind kind of went blank after that. I saw the car burst into flames. . . . I don't remember much after that. For months, I wasn't myself. I know it worried my father and Grandpa Johann. My mother took to drinking. We were a mess. And then somewhere along the line, I started blaming the Schallers. And then my father died in 1975 from complications of heart surgery. He was only sixty. He should have had another good thirty years of life ahead of him. But what Bill Schaller did to him, stealing that wine distributorship, weakened his heart. We watched him waste away.

"I was only twenty-eight when I sat at his bedside and held his hand as he passed away. I vowed there and then never to forgive the Schallers for what they took from me. It seemed that all the bad things that had ever happened to the Newmans were caused by the Schallers. It's ridiculous to think that now; as I look back, we were just two families struggling like any other family. Always looking to someone to blame, I guess."

"Pop," Lucas said gently, "I want you to read Clara's letters. You need to know about Wilhelm and Johann. You need to know the truth about what happened to your grandfather, *why* the brothers split up all those years ago, what started this whole ridiculous feud."

Melvyn removed his glasses and wiped his eyes again. He nodded. "I want to know the truth, son, I really do. I've been so afraid all these years. I don't want to be angry or afraid any more. I want to be happy in the years I have left."

Nicole dashed the tears from her cheeks. "All that time," she said in a tight voice, "Clara was waiting for her granddaughter to come home, hiring a private detective to search for her, and Deborah was here all along. . . ." Lucas took her into his arms, himself too choked up to speak.

And then Nicole drew back. "I'm all right. It's just a bit overwhelming. Lucas, I'm glad my great-grandmother never found out the truth. I'm glad it was covered up. She died believing Deborah was sitting in a beautiful garden in sunny Mexico, raising fat children, happy and blissfully in love. Sometimes a lie is better than the truth."

Melvyn said, "I knew Clara never gave up hope that her granddaughter would return. There were times when I came close to telling her the truth, but then I thought maybe that was more cruel than letting her keep the fantasy."

"We have to tell Detective Quinn," Lucas said grimly.

But Nicole was thinking of Clara and her dream to unite the two families. If the truth were exposed, that unification would never in a million years take place. And Nicole liked to think that she had been given her great-grandmother's letters for a purpose. She had grown to love her family. She wanted to protect them. And yes, maybe bring about a reconciliation with the Newmans. *Should* she and Lucas tell the police what they had learned? Did they have the right to keep it buried?

She laid a hand on Lucas's arm. "What good would it serve to tell the police? To tell anyone, really? It would cause a terrible scandal and cast a pall over this valley. We can tell Quinn that we know the skeleton in the police morgue is Deborah. We'll invent a story about her death. They'll believe it if it's your father who tells them. And then we can lay her to rest here, with the other Schallers. Deborah has received justice. Gordon killed himself. It's a closed chapter. Let's leave it that way."

Everything is closed chapters, Nicole thought now with a sudden feeling of elation and accomplishment overlaying the sadness. All sorts of new feelings rushed in now, as if floodgates had been opened. Thoughts that she had been suppressing these past weeks—her envy of Lucas because he was so needed here, her growing realization of how truly connected she was to this valley and its people—her mind exploded in a kaleidoscope of realizations and epiphanies.

She thought of the activity going on at the winery's docking press that morning, where men were madly unloading baskets of grapes and dropping them into the large square metal de-stemming and crushing equipment where rollers removed the stems from the grapes and crushed the fruit to release the juice. Nicole never failed to find this stage of wine-making exciting. There was energy in the air, the noise of the machines, the men shouting, the trucks pulling in and racing out, hurry, hurry, hurry so that the grapes stayed cool. This was a critical step. Once harvested, the grapes must not be allowed to deteriorate, as that resulted in inferior quality juice.

Nicole had heard that Manhattan was a city of energy and the pace was fast. But she doubted that any city's energy could compare to this.

Everything took on new significance now, things that had been commonplace to a person who had grown up here and found everything familiar and the same. But now, because of Clara's letters, Nicole was seeing everything through new eyes, even her own past and memories, and she saw them differently.

Now she knew why she had had a dream about a micro-winery and what it signified. It was the fruit of two secret yearnings: one, to stay here in the valley; and two, the need to do something new, to branch out, to experiment as Lucas was—to achieve something that was distinctly hers.

"Lucas," she said suddenly, "what do you know about micro-wineries?"

He looked at her in surprise. "Where did that come from?"

"Believe it or not, it came from a dream while I was sleeping last night. What can you tell me about it?"

"Well, the micro-winery is about controlling the fermentation process. It's a slower operation, but because you have more control over the yeast—sugar interaction, pretty much at the cellular level, you can improve the quality of your wines, have greater control over the outcome, as in flavor, body, and so forth. Your field of experimentation is much broader, too."

He paused and looked at her with interest. "In a way, the idea behind micro-wineries is linked to my own research. Both concepts are based on giving the vintner greater control in a world where climate is becoming more unpredictable and putting the vintner at its mercy."

He smiled. "From a dream, you say?"

"A very nice dream."

He stepped closer to her. "It would mean all new equipment."

"I'm not afraid of new things."

"It would mean staying here," he said, suddenly serious.

"I know now that I can't leave, Lucas. I belong here. My head might have been telling me one thing, but my heart is telling me something else. I am tied to this land just as you are. It wasn't Big Jack keeping me here. He understood that I belong here."

Suddenly all the fights with her father came rushing back, as if they had all taken place yesterday and she remembered them in one running argument. She saw them differently now. She had thought he was holding on to her because he was lonely. After his father Grandpa Bill died in 1986 in a farming accident, and then his grandmother Clara passed away, Nicole was all Big Jack had had. But now, thinking of those arguments, she was like a uninvolved spectator on the sidelines, thinking: He only wants her to stay because he knows she belongs here. Why can't she see that? Why is the girl arguing with the father who loves her and only wants to protect her from making a horrendous mistake? He knows that she will never be happy elsewhere, that she will never fit in with freeways and skyscrapers and empty cocktail parties. She belongs to this soil, to the grapes and the mountains and the nurturing rain. And she belongs with the people here as well, people who understand her and who love her. . . .

"I thought that if I didn't go," she said, "how would I ever know who I am? But I realize now, how does *any* of us know who we are? We just *are*, that's all. We make our way in the world, whether it's using something that was handed to us, or changing things within the world we were born into. I don't need to go away to find myself. I'm right here, with you. *We're here, you and I.*"

She felt as those young immigrants must have felt over a hundred years ago as they looked down into a green valley with its placid, benevolent river—that she was looking into the future, that she was looking at hopes and dreams yet to come true.

Lucas started to speak but she held up a hand. "And you don't need to go to Arizona. I will let you have Colina Sagrada. I'm going to back out of the sale of my winery. The Macintoshes will find another place just as suitable."

She thought of the Canadian couple and their plan to convert the farm and winery into a kind of mini-Disneyland, with play areas for children, and a murder mystery tour in the barrel room, and a place to hunt for Indian arrowheads at Colina Sagrada, and it suddenly felt all wrong. Well-meaning people, but the Macintoshes were going to somehow degrade a proud and noble heritage. And what would it do to the image of the rest of the valley? Might other newcomers buy up small wineries and go in that direction, tarnishing the prestigious reputation of Largo Valley?

This valley needed her. Nicole wanted to give back to the land that had nurtured her.

"I'm going to stay here and bring Schaller Wines back to glory. It is what I was born to do. That was what Clara had been telling me in her letters."

She leaned toward him and he leaned toward her to meet in a kiss. While old Melvyn looked on in disbelief, thinking that at his age he would never again see anything that surprised him, the Schaller girl wrapped an arm around his son's neck and Lucas placed his hand on the back of the Schaller girl's head. The kiss was long and deep and, old Melvyn decided with a softening heart, and with new gladness, that it was just one of many to come.

As Nicole walked back to the Jeep, arm in arm with Lucas, she marveled at the workings of fate. Clara had hoped Deborah would reunite the families, and in a way she had.

The healing had begun.